Mateless
and
Rogue Bound

SATURN PASSION

Mateless and Rogue Bound

© 2023 Saturn Passion

ISBN 978-1-66784-950-8

eBook ISBN 978-1-66784-951-5

Contents

CHAPTER 1:

Strangers

"Keep adventuring, Traveler.

Your home is far, but not gone.

Happiness will find you in ways you would never imagine."

He had been running for so long now. It wasn't from anyone or anything. He just ran. Time had flown by since when he had first started his journey. But never in his life had he felt something like this. There was a pulling sensation that was fueling his legs to go faster and faster. An excitement filled him in a way that he had never felt before. Not since he was very little.

The trees and the rocky terrain were nothing like what he was used to when he was younger. There was no snow on the ground, and hardly any barren landscapes. The trees were a vibrant green, with tall, dark brown trunks, and the sun was scorching. It must be summer in this area. He knew that his snowy coat would not like the heat waves that would come from him going further away from where he was born. He would have to stop to drink more water. He already needed to. Drool was forming in his muzzle, slowly slipping out of his mouth, onto the ground that his paws landed on.

He could smell it, though. Water was nearby. This forest seemed abundant in food as well. It would make great hunting grounds. It seemed like it was close to a pack territory. He could sense the borders of marked land nearby. The markings were easy to smell.

He would ignore the pull that he felt for now. His instincts told him to follow it, for it could only lead to good things, but his body screamed for water at least. There was nothing else he could do other than make a quick stop. He would follow that pull as soon as he was satisfied. He had learned a long time ago how to pace himself in his travels. He never stayed in one place for too long, but he needed to stop and make sure he ate and drank water. He had trained his body to handle times with neither, but that made him appreciate the moments he had them available.

"Well, they're certainly not going to let us join," he heard someone say. His legs stopped pumping and he slowed to a quiet walk. There could always be enemies anywhere. That was one of the first lessons he had learnt.

"We won't know unless we try," a woman said. There were two women and one man. The younger woman looked to be pregnant. She had a smell to her that he had recognized as that. She had long brown hair and matching eyes. Everything about her told him that she was a kind and gentle person. But her scent told him that she was a werewolf as well. And he was still wary of his own kind.

The other woman seemed to be a little older. She wasn't an elder, but there were hints of her age showing. She had short black hair. Her eyes were a bright gold color. Age lines on her face showed him that she had been outside most of her life. Her skin was a caramel color, complimenting her eyes well.

"Look, Herb, Jackie," the older woman argued with the other two. All three of them were werewolves, but it seemed like the older woman was the strongest. "I've been tracking and mapping out areas for fifteen years. No pack makes strong boundary lines like that, and wants visitors."

"But where can we go?" Herb said. "We have nothing but the rags on our backs, Madeline! And Jackie's pregnant! We can't keep running around forever. And starting a family as rogues will only make our baby's life worse when they grow up." He looked similar to the pregnant woman, Jackie. Only his hair was darker and his skin was tanner than hers. He grew a small beard that looked like it hadn't been kept in a while.

"I'm not disagreeing with you on that," Madeline said. "I'm just saying that the Crescent Moon Pack isn't a good option to try and ask for membership."

They were arguing by the creek that he had desperately needed water at. He was lucky that they didn't hear him sneaking over to it. Even if they were weaker than him, he didn't want to get into a fight. Fights were just a waste of energy. Energy that he needed if he was going to find the source of this pull.

What they were saying did interest him, though. It was always a good idea to learn about the surrounding areas. This pack they spoke of didn't seem very friendly. It would be best to stay away from them.

But that's where the pull was leading him to. If what this Madeline had said about the strong boundary lines being from this Crescent Moon Pack, then he would have to face them no matter what. She had motioned the same direction that he had been heading in when they were talking about this pack.

It didn't seem logical. It went against everything he had learned in order to survive. But he had survived by trusting his instincts, for they were the closest thing to the Moon Goddess that had spared his life countless times before. And his instincts were telling him to go to that territory.

"Why?" Jackie asked. She held onto her stomach with care as she soaked a piece of cloth in the creek. "I mean, I know it's because of the territory lines. But you've never been one to say that it's a bad idea just because of something like that."

Madeline gave an exhausted sigh. "You know those rogues that we had to escape from the other day?" she asked them. When they nodded their heads, she continued. "Their scents are everywhere on this side of the border lines. I went up to the border of their territory when you guys had fallen asleep one night. All I found was the smell of blood of those rogues all along their borders."

Even he shuddered at that. If that wasn't a clear indication that they didn't want visitors, then he didn't know what was. He could only imagine just how brutal they were. He had seen and heard plenty of horrible things that packs have done. As much as he had longed to be a part of one again, it was terrifying at the same time.

"But look at what those rogues tried to do to us!" Jackie argued. She truly must be a caring she-wolf, to think so kindly of a group that she had never met before. "Any pack would be aggressive towards those barbarians."

"Why do you think that they won't see us as those barbarians?" Madeline asked.

He had been so concerned with what they were saying that he failed to notice the brush that he had put too much pressure on. The crackle from the leaves got the party's attention. Herb immediately went in front of Jackie, taking on a protective stance. His eyes grew darker and he scanned their surroundings.

He didn't want to fight them. It was obvious that the two of them were a couple. With one of them being pregnant, he didn't want to cause more stress on the small group of rogues.

"Who's there?" Herb said. He guessed it still wasn't easy to see him under all the brush that he had used to sneak past them. The other two were quiet, both scanning the area with Herb.

There was no way he could get through this peacefully. Not in this form. As much as he disliked shifting into his vulnerable counterpart, there was no other option. His shift was silent, without even the sound of breaking bones to be heard.

He walked out of the brush with his hands up. He understood that he was naked, but that wasn't the reason they all looked at him with such surprise. He had always gotten those looks from people. It came with his condition, much more shocking in his human form than the other.

"I just need some water," he spoke to them. It had been a long time since he had heard his human voice. He rarely needed to use it. He had forgotten how low it was compared to most of the other ones that he had heard in his travels.

The man, Herb, kept his stance. His eyes were sharp on him, but they weren't as threatened anymore. They looked curious.

They were always curious.

"Go ahead," Herb said. "But, if you so much as move an inch closer to us, I will rip your head off."

"Herb," Jackie said from behind him. "He's trying to be friendly."

"I understand," he told the man, before the woman could say anything further. "I'll drink and then be on my way."

They stayed quiet. Watching him as he drank. Normally, he would have just left and found another water source. But he had ran too long without any water. His body screamed for it, and the sun had ravaged on him for the past two days. He drank and drank and drank. The water was cool and crisp. It reminded him of the place he was born. He had never had such pure water until this creek.

When he was finished drinking, he used some of the water to wash his face and his neck. He didn't have time to bathe himself, but it would help keep him cool, even if it would be just for a little bit.

He had kept his attention on them the entire time, just in case they decided to attack him at his weakest. Thankfully, they didn't. He stood to look at them one last time before he started his travels again.

"Thank you," he told them. They seemed shocked at his words. They must have sensed that he was stronger than them. He was just glad that they didn't wish to be violent. If this pack was so strict with visitors, then he was going to need all the strength he could.

"Wait!" Madeline raised her voice to stop him from turning around. When he looked back at them, her golden eyes met his. "What's your name, stranger?"

"My name?" Now he was shocked. In his travels, people rarely asked for his name. The caramel skinned woman just nodded. "My name is Alistair," he told them. He didn't consider it a threat to tell someone his name. No one knew of him.

"Alistair," Those golden eyes seemed more curious than ever. "Where are you headed, if I can ask?"

"I…" he paused. He wasn't sure if he should tell them. He never confided in anyone or anything. But his instincts didn't advise him against it. "I don't know," he told them honestly. "I'm just following a feeling."

"A feeling?" Jackie asked. She looked past her lover's shoulder. "What feeling?"

"I don't know," he told her. Herb seemed threatened that he was talking to his mate, so he turned his focus back to Madeline. "I wish you all the best of luck in finding a pack. May the Moon Goddess be with you."

"Do you know anything about the Crescent Moon Pack?" Madeline asked. He was trying to leave again, but the woman was insistent on following him. He shouldn't have told her anything.

"None other than what you were saying."

"So, you were listening in on us?" Herb's voice made him tense.

"Please," he told them. "I was only looking to get some water. I didn't want to cause any issues with your group."

"Stop it Herb!" Jackie slapped her mate's arm. "If he was like the others, he would have attacked us already."

"The others?" He couldn't help but ask. This place seemed dangerous. It may be best to try and get out of these lands as quickly as possible.

"There are other rogues around these parts," Madeline explained. "Since you seem to be a werewolf of peace, then it might be best to avoid them. They are brutal and will use everything they have against you."

"Which direction are you heading, Alistair?" Herb asked. His stance was still protective over his mate, but it looked like he had calmed a bit.

"I'm heading east," he said. For some reason, his instincts were telling him to trust these three. It also told him to not leave these lands. He did not know why when there were plenty of warnings and hints. Danger seemed to be everywhere.

"Where are you from, Alistair?" Jackie asked. "You don't seem like you're from here."

"North," he said. "I'm from the far north."

They were all walking with him at this point. There was some comfort that he got from having more around him. It had been a long time since he had made some friends along his adventures.

"Well, if you go any further east, you're going to get to the Crescent Moon territory," Madeline then pointed towards the south, "The next closest is the Harvest Moon Pack to the south. They might be more willing to let you pass through. But those rogues have a hunting ground in between that space, and they don't take too kindly to strangers," Then she pointed towards the west. "Then there's the Blood Moon Pack towards the west. They're well known for their fighting skills. I would be wary about going near their territory."

"Thank you," he told her. "I will keep that in mind."

"Is this feeling bringing you east?" Jackie asked.

"Yes."

"I don't get it," Herb shook his head. "What is this feeling that you're obsessed with?"

"It's a pull," he explained. It was strange that he was talking this much to these people, but he felt like he couldn't stop. "A pull like I have never felt before."

"A pull?" Madeline said.

"A pull," he repeated. "My instinct tells me to follow it."

"Well, if your instincts are telling you to go east," Jackie said, she seemed more excited than before. "Then maybe you can help us get through the Crescent Moon territory."

"Do you want to get through the territory, or get into the pack?"

"We don't know," Jackie shrugged her shoulders. "Herb and I are just trying to find a safe place to grow our family. I don't know if it will be the Crescent Moon Pack. But, if it isn't, then it would be easier trying to pass through their territory rather than go back and face those rogues again."

"By the look of these trees, it seems like these packs that surround this place are old," Alistair said.

"How do you know that?" Madeline asked.

"The ancient trees always hold ancient people," he answered. "Whether it be humans, or wolves. And these woods have an ancient feeling to them."

"How long have you been travelling like this, Alistair?" The woman continued to question. She seemed so curious about him. Usually, more people were curious about his appearance. Maybe that was why his answers were detailed more so now than what was common for him. Everyone was always so shocked about the fact that he was albino that no one really questioned him about anything else.

"Many years."

"You seem so keen on your wild side," she said. They walked through the thick trees, getting further and further from the creek that he had loved so much. "I take it you don't stay a human for this long?"

"Only when I need to," he told her. "My human form is weaker than my wolf. I only change when I need to talk to someone, or tell them that I mean no harm."

"Like you did with us?"

"Yes."

"Madeline, why are you asking him all of these questions?" Herb asked her. "The man obviously wants to be left alone. Let's be on our way."

"I don't think we should," Madeline told him. "Actually, I think you're right about trying with the Crescent Moon Pack."

"What?!" His dark eyes went wide with shock. "Why are you suddenly agreeing with me?"

"Because a werewolf that is able to connect with the forests around them is a wise one," she told him. Then she looked at Alistair. "If you would like to take Jackie up on her offer, we would be honored to have you join us. We were headed in the same direction that you were."

"I don't want to cause any trouble with you three," he told her. "I haven't been around my own kind in a long time. And the only ones that I had come across weren't friendly."

"We're friendly," Jackie elbowed Herb. "We could help you follow this feeling too! Packs find it easier to trust a small group of werewolves seeking refuge rather than just one anyway."

Maybe they could help him. He wasn't against accepting help when it was offered. He had come across the opportunity plenty of times and accepted it. His instinct was telling him to trust these people, and it had never been wrong before.

He closed his eyes and listened to the forest around him. The mysteries that it held was infinite, and the stories endless. If there was one thing he had always learned from the trees it was the true feeling of the forest around. The wind was not one to talk to, but, if you listened to it, it would tell you everything you need to know. The trees told him that there was fighting and bloodshed. But there was also peace amongst the violence.

"A fight for peace," he whispered to himself.

"A what?" Madeline asked. They had all been curious as to what he was doing when he had stopped.

"I think this pack that you speak of isn't as bad as you think," he told them. "I will help you speak with the Alpha, if you want."

"How are we even going to get in there to speak with the Alpha?" Herb asked. "They might try and kill us before we can even try to tell him our story."

"Now you're getting cold feet?" Madeline rolled her eyes. "Right when I agree on this plan of yours too."

"I don't want any of us to get hurt!"

"There's a way you can speak to the Alpha without going into their territory," he told them. "I will show you when we get there."

He didn't know why these three decided to be friendly with him, or why they followed him. He didn't know why he told them as much as he did, or why he agreed to help them in their endeavor. He had always helped when he could, but he had never been asked for help by his own kind. Other rogues were to themselves; brutal; or untrusting of everyone, much like he was.

But there was a connection that he felt with these three. He hadn't known it until they started following him. He had never been a leader. But he was the strongest out of their small group now, and he felt the urge to protect them.

He didn't know a lot of things. But he had learned that it didn't matter if everything was explained down to even the most miniscule detail, or not.

Life was not meant to be written for you. It was meant for you to write.

CHAPTER 2:

Alpha and Luna

Charlie collapsed onto their fluffy bed.

"Are you okay, Apple?" Max looked at him with slight amusement. The blond hadn't even taken off his suit jacket. Or his shoes for that matter. Max decided to put his jacket up on the hook right by the door at least. He would try and undress his mate and get him comfortable after he got his own stiff clothes off. Suits were nice until you had to wear them all day, every day. It was a good thing they had air conditioning, or they would be much more miserable.

"Please tell me these meetings are over," Charlie mumbled into a pillow. The poor thing was exhausted.

They had been going on with these meetings for months now. The Blood Moon Pack just didn't want to budge on their terms for helping with the rogues. As much as Max admired them for their strength and resilience over the years, they were very stubborn about everything when it came to an agreement.

"I'm sorry, Apple," he sighed. He leaned over the bed to hold him. Even with all the stress of leading about two hundred people, they still always found time for each other. And Charlie was the best stress reliever that he ever had. "There's still more tomorrow."

"This reminds me of a Filibuster," he melted into him. Max easily took off his mate's jacket and was swiftly taking off the rest.

"A Filibuster?"

"It's something they do in the government," Charlie explained. His muscles were so tense when he got his shirt off. Max quickly massaged them to work out the knots. "They will stand at a podium and talk about anything and everything. They will talk about why you should go with their law or plan, and then they will just talk about everything from the moon and back. The goal is that the other politicians won't be able to stand it anymore and they'll come to an agreement."

"That sounds horrible," he kissed the mark that he made on the blond's neck. It had been such a hard week for both of them. The Alpha of the Blood Moon Pack, William, was arguing with Leonard, Alpha of the Harvest Moon Pack, about contributions to the rogue matters. They didn't think that the Harvest Moon Pack was giving all that they could.

On top of that, they were trying to come to an agreement fast, since Alpha Williams son, Owen, was about to take the title as soon as he found his mate. Owen had turned 18 a few months ago, but had failed to find his mate yet. They all hoped that he didn't have to wait as long as Max did to find him. A new mindset might be good for that pack at the moment.

It had taken a while for William to get used to Charlie as a Luna. He was very much stuck in his own ways, but he still treated him with respect. He treated him like any other person in that meeting room. Max was okay with it, but he had a feeling that his preference was why the Alpha was arguing with everything he had to say.

That's why they wouldn't have any meetings at the Blood Moon Pack's territory, or anywhere else for that matter. He wanted to keep Charlie safe from all of those hateful glares. And here was where they could be happy.

They smashed all the last meetings into one week in order to finally make an agreement on something. The rogues were starting to organize and attack more than just their pack. Max loved pointing it out to William that it all could have been resolved already if they had formed an agreement sooner.

They started this in February. It was now May. And the frustration of it all was almost enough to make Max forget about getting anyone's help in this matter and take care of them himself. But it was more complicated than that. Because if they took over that territory, there would be fights; wars. And that was something that Max didn't want to do. His family had finally brought the Crescent Moon Pack to the glory that it had been so long ago. This was supposed to be their golden age. Starting a war would ruin everything that Max had planned.

"That almost describes these meetings perfectly, though," Charlie leaned into him. His skin was hot from the layers of the suit, but they cooled off quickly. "I just wish that Alpha William would stop trying to take so much territory. It makes more sense with it being divided equally."

"He's doing this because he doubts our strength," Max explained. "He thinks that his pack will be doing all of the work, and he thinks he deserves more because of it."

"Maybe he should see just how strong we are before he goes making assumptions," Charlie huffed into the pillow. "This is just ridiculous."

"It is," he pulled him onto the bed more. They were now wearing nothing as Max pulled the sheet over them. "He'll break, though. My father said that he always breaks once he realizes that you aren't going to back down."

"So, this is like Filibustering then," Charlie rested his head on his chest. It had started to heat up quite a lot this spring. Summer was sure to be a hot one. "It's just with more dancing around the subject."

"Yup," he kissed the top of his head. "That's another reason why we're doing the week of meetings." He was sure that the rest of his pack was tired of these meetings as well. Owen was picky when it came to food, and loved to criticize everything that Aldi made. And Ian Cooper was a little on the messy side, especially with his lover around.

Of course, Tyler, Sam and Ed were exhausted too. Leah couldn't come to the meetings due to the newborns she just had. They were twin boys. The look on Sam's face once he realized that he had more sons now was enough to brighten everyone's day.

It would be fun for Max to have something like that. Little kids running around their suite made a good picture in his head. But he wasn't going to try and adopt while all of this was going on. He wanted to make sure that he had time for the child, and that they were in a safe place.

He wanted to take care of the rogues before he did anything like that. And he was sure that Charlie felt the same. The man never mentioned it.

"You know what would be nice," Charlie interrupted his thoughts.

"What?"

"A week just like the first week we got together," he intertwined his fingers into Max's chest hair. He knew just how much Max loved when he did that. "When this is all said and done, even having a day like that would be nice."

"Hmm," he pulled his mate closer. The way that he was combing through his chest hair was enough to make him purr if he could. "I do owe you for that."

"You don't owe me anything," Charlie shook his head. "Besides, when we finally finish these meetings, we're going to have to start our plan on taking care of the rogues. We aren't going to have time for that."

"When this is all said and over," he nuzzled into his love's neck. "And all those rogues are gone. You and I are going to have a month-long honeymoon."

"A honeymoon?" he tried looking at him, but Max stopped him by flipping him onto the bed and kissing his neck and shoulders. "Wouldn't we have to get married first?"

"Mmmhmm," his lips moved to his ear, his hands were already starting to do their magic on his mate's private areas. "Don't think I'm not going to marry you, Charlie Fairchild. That last name is going to be Locke if it's the last thing I do."

Charlie let out a gasp. He wasn't sure if it was about what he had said, or the fact that he was already getting him ready to take him in. He learned his mate's body quickly. It was fun finding all the spots that he loved being rubbed, touched, or kissed. He was addicting to love. And every time Max thought he couldn't love him any more than he already did, Charlie would do something to surprise him.

"We're going to get married," he continued, spreading kisses all down his neck. "And then I'll have a small house built for us far into the woods. Completely private and beautiful. We'll spend a month there, with no interruptions. No one saying they need us."

"But what if they really did need us?" the blond argued, leaning into every one of his kisses.

"They won't. It'll just be you and I, and a nice bed like this one," Max knew that he was winning this fight. His lover was melting into his hands. His hips were starting to move up towards him, demanding more pleasure than what his hands could do. He could say that he tortured the man some and waited to hear what erotic sounds that came out of his lover, but he was just as easy to cave in as Charlie was.

He entered him, just like all those other times. Even after the six months that they had been together, Charlie was still quiet in bed. His whimpers and small noises were still just for him, and he loved it. No matter how many times he would make love to him, he would never get used to it.

"Max," he moaned. His wanting body begged him to go faster. The fact that he felt his mate's feelings only amplified his desires. It was ecstasy.

He obliged to his urges and quickened the pace. Every time he entered him again, his mate would let out a moan. It sent waves of lust through him. One of his hands were holding him down, while the other one slowly went over to help please the other part of him that needed attending too. He matched the pace of his hand with his body and listened to the moans that Charlie gave. Each time they urged him to go faster.

He wanted to take his time sometimes. But there was such a need that they both had, it was too difficult to hold back his desires, especially since he had been waiting for his mate for so long. Three years of waiting, and much longer than that of not having sex at all, and he was an uncontrollable mess in bed.

He buried himself in his mate as he finished. Charlie had finished just about the exact same time. They laid there like that for a little, just trying to catch their breath. Max was the first one to move, much to the blond's dismay. He took the condom off and started kissing him again.

"You are the best stress reliever," Max told him. Charlie just chuckled and pulled him in closer. "I love you."

"I love you too," he smiled at him. His hands were now weaved into Max's hair, combing through it with his fingers. He loved when he did that.

"Come on," he picked him up after staying like that for a while. "We should get cleaned up."

"Do we have anything else planned for today?" Charlie hid his face in Max's neck and sighed in content. He was still tired, but he seemed much more relaxed than when they first got into their suite.

"Nope," Max answered, getting the bath ready. "Tyler and Sam are relaxing with their wives and taking care of their kids. Ray and Desmond are on patrol. And Ed is trying to entertain Owen at the moment."

"I really hope he stops making Aldi so frustrated," he could feel his lover frown. "It just seems disrespectful to yell at him like that."

Max remembered what he was talking about. The brat had yelled at Aldi, probably thinking that he was an omega that he could push around. Although the Harvest Moon Pack and Crescent Moon Pack had both modernized enough to treat their omegas equally, the Blood Moon Pack still used them as servants. It was common with a lot of different packs still, much to his dismay.

If your pack was your family, why would you want to mistreat them in any way?

The look on Owen's face when Aldi straightened his back and glared at him was priceless, Max had to say that. Aldi's delta scent came out and Owen was as confused as a homeless man on house arrest. That was when Aldi gave him the lecture of his life. Owen still tried to act like he was above him, but Max told him that he should listen to their elder's words of advice.

"I don't think he's going to start anymore quarrels with Aldi," he brought them both into the tub. It had become one of their routines for the evening time. A nice warm bath for both of them to try and melt of the day's stresses.

"How are we going to get Alpha William to agree with us?" Charlie asked. Of course, there was always the times where he never wanted to stop working. His brain had loved to keep going on about everything that happened that day, and there was nothing Max could do to stop it.

"I have no clue," Max sighed. There was no point telling him to forget it at the moment. He'd just get lost in thought and wouldn't talk to him about what he was thinking about. Max liked it better when his love was talking to him.

"Well, we could try using his words against him," Charlie said.

"What words?"

"He told us that he demands respect and honor above all else," he explained. "It's one of the Blood Moon mottos; one that their warriors say before heading into battle. If he demands respect and honor above all else, then wouldn't he do the same for the other packs that have been nothing but respectful towards him?"

"It's not as simple as that," Max sighed. Alpha wordplay was always annoying. A lot of it was them saying one thing, and doing another.

"I'm not saying that it's what he actually does," Charlie laid his head on Max's chest. They always sat there for a bit before actually starting to wash themselves. "I'm saying we use his wordplay against him. If we can get him to believe that he's going against something that's been tradition to say and follow in his pack for centuries, like that motto, then we might actually be able to corner him into agreeing with us."

"And just how is that motto going to be turned on them?" As much as he hated that Charlie couldn't wind down some days after these meetings, he admired just how brilliant he was. In just a couple of weeks of studying, he had learned the history of their pack, the packs around them, as well as everything else that a Luna needed to know.

"How can you respect someone, if you think they aren't strong enough to help take care of some rogues?"

"So, you're saying we call out the elephant in the room," Now the gears were starting to turn in Max's head. They worked well together when it came to meetings and making decisions. Charlie always brought up the points that no one else saw. When everyone was caught up in emotions, Charlie was the one to bring up the logic that they all forgot about.

Even the way he argued with Liam made things ten times more interesting. Liam was still in the counsel as the representative of the elders of the pack. The former Alpha and Luna sat in most meetings as advisors. They would give advice from their many years of leading. But Liam still loved to have a target when he was arguing. Instead of arguing against everything that Max said, like before, he focused on Charlie.

And the way that Charlie danced around with his words, and turned things onto Liam, was the most amazing thing Max had ever seen.

"Exactly," Charlie snapped him out of his reverie. "He's in our territory right now. If we say the elephant, then we make him believe that we think he has threatened us or insulted us. He obviously doesn't want a war either, or else he wouldn't be going to all of these meetings. So, I doubt he'll want to keep arguing over territory lines much after that."

"And saying that in front of Leonard might make him believe that both of our packs think he threatened us," Max smiled. This was finally their eureka moment. "Having the only two of your neighboring packs go against you would make even his amazing skills in battle fail in comparison to the warriors of two whole packs."

"Perfect!" Charlie looked up at him. His green eyes sparkled with excitement. "I think we finally have something that'll crack him."

He was so beautiful like this. His eyes had never been this bright before, neither had his smile. Max couldn't get over just how much his mate shined as the Luna of their pack. He really did seem like he was fit for the role.

"I think so too," Max kissed him. "We'll wait for the right moment at tomorrow's meeting to tell him."

"Do it right before the first break," Charlie said. "That way, he has the break to start mulling over it. And if he still wants to argue about the new territory lines, we'll have the rest of the day to come up with Plan B."

"Sounds like a good idea," Max kissed him. "Did I mention you're the best Luna ever?"

"Stop," he blushed. His personality had really started to come out when he started living here. He still cooked with Chef Ryan every so often, but he mainly stayed here to perform his tasks as Luna, or to learn more about how he could keep everyone happy. Max just couldn't get over how much he changed since the first time he saw him. He went from a polite man that hid his life from everyone, to a bubbly brainiac that loved to learn and brainstorm about every single issue in the pack.

Since Lunas deal with the pack's more homely problems, Charlie dealt with requests for moving as well as the ones who break the rules of the manor. If anyone has an issue with someone else, and it's worrisome for the pack, they go to him. Since he's human, he has no issues with dealing with an omega and a beta equally.

It took Liam a while to be able to get to that point when he was Alpha. Max couldn't blame him too much. He was raised completely different from Max, and he was having to deal with both the Alpha and Luna responsibilities once his wife was murdered.

The first five months of their leadership was going well. Even with the rogues still on the loose, the pack was doing better than ever. The warriors were able to keep the rogues at bay. They hadn't been able to get far into their territory since December of last year. Max guessed they had killed so many of them that they were holding off on any attacks until they gathered their strength up a little more.

That's why they needed to get this attack over with. They needed to get them while they were down. If they actually were able to gather their strength, then they might be stronger than they were before.

Max didn't want that. He had made a promise to himself that no one in the Crescent Moon Pack was going to die at the hands of those rogues. This was going to be the golden days of his pack, without any blood to taint it. He was going to make sure of it.

But for now, he could finally calm his thoughts and focus on his mate. They cleaned up and helped dry each other off. Since they had a day full of meetings, Max thought it would be best if the rest of the evening was just the two of them. He asked one of the maids to bring him their food, and planned on a nice dinner for them.

That way Charlie could relax a bit more too. He knew just how much the man missed him when they weren't together. The clinginess that their bond made had not gone away, and neither of them were complaining about it. Until they had to be apart from each other, that was.

But now wasn't the time to whine about being away from his lover. Now was the time to celebrate just having him here in his arms.

"Hey, Max," Ed mind linked with him. Max groaned outwardly, resting his head on Charlie. The blond didn't ask anything this time. He just pet his hair comfortingly.

"What's up?" he tried to sound as least annoyed as possible.

"I hate to interrupt your relaxing time, but you might want to come down to the dining hall."

"Why?"

"Owen found his mate."

CHAPTER 3:

Mates

"So," Nick started. "When do you think these fun little get-togethers of the packs are going to be over?"

"I have no clue!" Katy sighed dramatically. "All I know is that if I have to remake an order one more time, I'm going to lose it!"

"Woah there, tiger," he laughed at his friend. "I don't think the Alpha of the Blood Moon Pack would appreciate it if you tore his son a new one."

They had been working longer shifts for the past month just to try and meet all the demands of the visitors that came over. Usually, it was just for a week or two that visitors would come to the pack and they could take comfort in the fact that it wasn't going to be for long. Having a whole month of nothing but being yelled at and working themselves to the bone was exhausting.

Nick didn't mind, though. His family was one that was always up and moving. His mom told him that in India, you always worked hard for what you wanted. The pack that she came from was all about hard work from everyone. But she did recall that the Alpha of that pack was rather lazy. It was always the person at the top of the food chain that would laze around all day.

Of course, these were just things that she had learned from her experience with packs from India. She had no clue about the humans, since they didn't let her go out that much to talk to them. She did tell him that the festivals were beautiful over there. He always wanted to go and see one of them.

"He hates omegas so much!" Katy said, her hair had turned into a mane again, as she didn't bother brushing it when she took it out of its bun. "I mean, omegas are the foundation of packs. We help keep everything running so that the Alpha doesn't have to. And what does he call us? Worthless pups with no sense of survival!"

"Did he say that to you?" he asked. If he did, he was going to find some way to ring the alpha's neck himself. He hated just how high and mighty some of these alphas were. At least in their pack, they didn't have to deal with that. They were all respected equally.

Like right now, they were all getting paid time and a half for working longer shifts. Nick was planning on saving up for a new car with that money. His old one from his dad was starting to fall apart.

"No," she answered. "I heard one of the maids, Heather, tell someone that he told her that. It was horrible though!"

"I just don't get," he popped a vegetable in his mouth. "Why you would be so disrespectful to a pack that you're visiting." He swallowed. "You'd think that he could reign it in for at least a little while."

They were eating their dinner at the dining hall that evening. It wasn't like anyone else was using it. At least they only worked the morning shift. Them working longer meant that they were usually out of the kitchen at 3 or 4. Nick loved their dinners that they would have. It was a great time to vent and talk about the days gossip.

"I don't know!" Katy groaned. "All I know, is if I see him, it's going to be really difficult to not try and choke him."

"You do that and we'll really have a war on our hands," Nick laughed. "At least we're getting good money for all of this."

"I don't care about money," she pouted. "Max better throw us all a party when they're gone. That's a true reason to celebrate."

"A party sounds nice," he shoveled more food into his mouth. Kitchen work always made him hungry. "But I think everyone would like some vacation time over a party."

"Oh, I heard that Max is already planning on it," she said. "The first person he's going to give a vacation to is Aldi. He's already planning on going to a hotel with his wife to get away for a while."

"I don't blame him," Nick said. "He had to deal with the brunt of the workload. And after Owen yelled at him, he lost it. He was about to yell at Max too if he told him to stop. But you know what Max did?"

"What?"

"He told Owen that he should listen to his elders," Nick laughed. "Basically, he told him nicely to stop being a brat."

"What?!" Katy laughed with him. "Only Max would do that. You know his dad would never say something like that."

"No, his dad would treat Owen like the child he is and talk to his daddy," Nick said. "Do you remember how many times he did that to us?"

"Oh, don't remind me!" Katy hid her face. "He did that right when I turned 18 and got in trouble for trying to sneak up to the third floor. It was so embarrassing."

"Oh yeah!" Nick laughed harder at that. They both had done so many things as kids. "I remember that! Hey, at least you didn't have a mom who could speak another language, though. Whenever he told my mom on me, even when I was an adult, she would go off on me in two languages!"

"I remember hearing one of her rants," Katy giggled. "I didn't know when she was going to switch languages on you. It all sounded like some sort of ancient babble."

"Yeah, when you can understand it, it's much worse," he shook his head. Whenever he got in trouble his mom would always go off on him about how he was supposed to be a good kid. He was her blessing. How he was embarrassing her in front of the Alpha. "I practically know it all by heart."

"Did she ever do that to your brothers and sisters?"

"Oh yeah! I wasn't the only one who felt her wrath." Many werewolves thought that omegas weren't scary. None of them had to deal with the anger of an omega mother. They were the best at discipline, and lecturing you until you felt like your ears were going to fall off. "She did the same thing to my brothers, sisters, my dad. Hell, she even yelled at my grandpa one time."

"What? Why?"

"Because he always gave us what we wanted, even when she told us no," he chuckled at the memory. "My dad learned how to speak her language when they first mated so that he could get her comfortable in her new life. He told me just how many times he regretted it just because of her rants."

"I don't blame him," she shook her head. "She's scary when she's mad."

"I can say the same about you."

"What?!" she looked at him, baffled. "I'm not scary."

"Did you think I would just forget that you yelled at Liam, a former Alpha of our pack?" he cocked an eyebrow at her.

"That was because I was worried about Charlie, though!" she argued. "And he was being an ass!"

"Point proven," he raised a finger. "You're going to be hellfire when you find your mate."

"Like that's ever going to happen," she rolled her eyes and looked down at her food.

He frowned. He didn't want to kill the mood. Usually, she just made a joke and moved on. Now she actually looked sad.

"Hey," he grabbed her hand to comfort her. "Come on, Max found his mate after what seemed like forever. You can find yours."

"Yeah," she sighed, "I guess."

Ah, just as dramatic as ever.

"Okay," He leaned back in his chair and got comfortable. "What's wrong?"

"I don't know what you're talking about," she started picking at her food, keeping her eyes down on the plate.

"Come on, Katy," Nick rolled his eyes this time. "You suck at hiding when you're upset. You can't keep anything from me. I've known you since we were three."

"I don't know," she gave another dramatic sigh. It was fun watching her get this way. She always acted like her life was going to end whenever even the smallest thing was bothering her.

"Spit it out already," he pushed. He knew she was going to talk about it anyway. She never kept a secret from him. They were like brother and sister, but closer. Their parents say that they were joined to the hip as soon as they met.

"I just," she paused again. Dramatic affect. "I just wish I were more like you when it came to finding your mate."

"What do you mean?"

"You never think about finding your mate," she explained. "Even as the years go by you don't really seem to care much about the fact that you haven't found yours."

"I'm not destined to have one," he answered. There was a reason why he didn't care about having one. Nick had his own issues that he had struggled to sort out when he was younger. It was better to just keep this routine that he had of work and enjoying his family and friends than going through a whole emotional roller coaster with someone as his mate. He knew for sure that it wasn't going to end well, either.

"Nick, of course you are," Katy looked at him seriously. "We all are. The Moon Goddess gives all of us mates."

"Then, why are you worried about finding yours?" he avoided the argument about his mate. He accepted a long time ago that he wasn't going to find his. He was okay with being celibate the rest of his life. He still had his family, and his nieces and nephews. His family and friends were all he needed in life.

"Because I'm getting old!" she huffed.

"Pfft," he was glad he wasn't drinking anything when he heard that. "Katy, you're only 21. You barely got to be able to drinking age last year."

"But everyone else finds their mate right when they turn 18," she pointed at him accusingly before he could speak. "And don't tell me that Max had to wait three years to find Charlie. He still found his mate before us."

"You'll find him," he told her. "But you can't just sit around dreaming for Prince Charming to come along and whisk you off to the palace."

"I know," she pouted and leaned back into her chair. "I just get lonely sometimes. And then I worry that he's not going to understand me and there's going to be a huge mess of issues with it."

"So, you'll put him through dog training," Nick smiled. "I'm sure you'll whip him into shape in no time."

"Oh, shut up!" she laughed. "I'm not like your mom. I can't go off on someone like she can."

"No," he agreed. "You're scarier than her. You're a lion in a wolf suit."

"You just say that because of my hair."

"I'm saying that because you are," he said. "When you're pissed, you could light up a cathedral, Katy."

"But I don't want to be pissed," she said. "I want to find love finally."

"And you will," he assured her. "You'll find the love of your life; the other half of your soul, soon. Who knows? Maybe he's somewhere close, just waiting to come into your life. One day, he'll just walk in here and scoop you up and you'll live Happily Ever After."

"Excuse me!" He turned to see an alpha that he had never met before looking at them angrily. It must have been Owen with how much he looked like a brat. He had dark hair and maroon eyes. "I've been trying to look for someone for ages! Can you show me where the-!"

Time stopped for a second or two. Nick couldn't do anything but look confused as Owen and Katy stared into each other's souls. The puzzle pieces didn't come together until he heard the word "Mate" and the two of them collided into each other.

Wait. He didn't mean this fast. He was so confused. Why was this happening? Why *him*? He was going to cause hell for her. He was the exact opposite of her. Why did they both look so happy with each other?

He couldn't do anything but watch in utter shock as his best friend turned all lovey-dovey on the guy that she was threatening to choke just a short while ago. He wanted her to be happy, but he guessed that he was a little selfish in that sense. When he realized what had happened, he felt his heart sink.

No. He never had feelings for Katy. But she was the one person he could always rely on to be there when he was alone. She was the one that he had shared his sweets with in elementary school. She was the one that listened to him through all his problems and ailments. They were joined to the hip, even as adults.

Was it selfish for him to not want that to end?

"Hey," he snapped out of his shock as a hand patted his shoulder. He turned to see Ed next to him. "You okay there?"

"Y-yeah," he shook his head. He was supposed to feel happy right now. A good friend would be happy that they found their other half.

He forced a smile and tried to hide the sadness as Katy finally pulled away from Owen. It seemed like he had found his mate.

"I didn't know you were a cougar," he mind linked with her. Her brown eyes went wide and she scoffed at him.

"Shut it," she looked embarrassed that she just did that in front of them. Owen wasn't keeping his eyes off from her. He was looking at her so lovingly.

Good. That's how he should always be looking at her. If he didn't, that he was going to have a hard time. Nick would make sure of that.

"Glad you could find your mate, Alpha Owen," Ed said. Nick stayed silent. He wanted to say something to the man who was going to be taking away his best friend, but he decided against it. Owen didn't like omegas anyway.

And he was Katy's mate?

"You're going to have a lot of dog training to do," he joked with her. Humor was how he dealt with everything.

"You think?"

"That's Owen, Katy. In the flesh." He almost laughed out loud as he saw the shock in her eyes. *"You didn't hear Ed say his name?"*

"NO!" she shouted through their thoughts. *"This is the guy who hates omegas?"*

"Yup. You got a lot of training to do."

Her face was priceless, until she looked back at the alpha. Then she melted into his gaze. There was some talk going on with Ed and Owen, but he tuned it out. He wasn't going to be able to say anything anyway.

She looked so different when she stared at him. She looked nothing like the woman that he had known his whole life. He could see in her face that she had already fallen head-over-heels for him. She was already ready to go with him and get swept into her own Happily Ever After.

At least Max didn't change when he met Charlie. Nick used that as hope that the alpha wouldn't change his best friend when he brought her to his pack.

Pack.

She wasn't going to be in the Crescent Moon Pack anymore. Nick wasn't going to be able to mind link with her anymore. Even when they were far away, they always had the mind link to talk to each other or tell one another where they were at. Now there wasn't going to be any dramatic, whiny voice that he would hear when he was doing some shopping without her.

What was going to happen when she moved to that pack? Would they treat her differently? Would she start being a snob just like them? She was the mate of the next Alpha of the Blood Moon Pack. Which meant that she was the next Luna to be of that pack. Was she going to help them change, or were they going to change her?

So many thoughts flew through his mind. He couldn't stop thinking about it. Everything else was tuned out as he watched her look at her mate as if he were some sort of super hero.

"What's going on?" he heard Max before he saw him come into the dining room. He wasn't in the suit that he remembered seeing him in earlier that day. He was probably trying to relax with Charlie or something. Ed must have told him to come.

When he saw Katy with Owen, it seemed like he was just as shocked as Nick was. He hid it a little better, but he could see it. Max looked at Nick with a confused expression. He just shrugged his shoulders and made a wide-eyed face to show that he was just as surprised as the Alpha.

"This is my mate," Owen told him. He was smiling like Tyler did when he introduced Isabella as his mate.

"Congratulations," Max smiled back. He looked genuinely happy for them both. "I'm glad that Katy was your mate. She's a good friend of mine, along with Nick."

"Nick?" Owen finally looked at him. Apparently, he hadn't noticed him the entire time. It seemed like something an Alpha from that pack would do.

"Nice to meet you," Nick put his hand out. "I'm her brother." He didn't want to come across as a threat to the man. If he heard that they were just good friends, Nick might never see her again. His jealousy would overtake any argument they had about it.

"Nice to meet you too, then," he shook his hand. "I'll treat her with nothing but love and respect."

"Good," he said. He was sure that everyone could see the sadness in his eyes, but Katy was too focused on her new Prince Charming.

Stop. He needed to be happy for her. Even if she was leaving him behind.

"We'll have to throw a party to celebrate," Max said. "We'll plan it for the last day of your stay, after the agreements have been made."

They started walking away quickly, as Owen seemed excited to bring her to his room. Max talked with them as he escorted them. Nick knew the party was going to be a big one. Everyone knew Katy. They were all going to be sad when she left. He was sure she was going to be sad once she had gotten used to the mate bond a little more.

He was sure of it. But it still hurt that she didn't look back at him. Not once. The one who had been there when she was still in diapers.

"Hey, Nick," he heard Ed say. "You okay?"

"Yeah," he didn't look at him. He kept his eyes on Katy's back. "Why?"

"I don't know," Ed said. "You just look a little lost."

Lost.

He was a little lost.

No.

He was very lost.

CHAPTER 4:

An Official Request

He wasn't sure if this would work. Madeline was right, the smell of foreign blood was heavy along the lines of the Crescent Moon Pack. There must have been countless fights to cause such a violent warning against crossing their lands. If those rogues were as brutal as his newly made friends had said, then it was probably them who caused the pack to act with such violence.

Alistair walked with them all the way to the territory lines. It was the best way to talk with them. They didn't want to shift, as that would make their scents stronger, and they had made enemies with those other rogues. He understood. Enemies were never a good thing to make, but it happened quite a lot, no matter how cautious you were. He had plenty of enemies.

"So," Jackie broke through the silence. "Is the pull getting stronger when you get closer to the territory?"

"Yes," he answered. He wasn't used to talking like a human. He wasn't really used to talking at all. He had been a beast for so long, it felt strange to walk on his two legs, rather than the four that he had always run on. "Thank you for the clothes," he looked at Herb. The man had let him wear a pair of shorts. They were worn but it was better than being naked. "I forgot amidst trying to put them on to thank you."

"Don't worry about it," Herb said. He looked amused for a second. He couldn't figure out why. "I take it you haven't worn clothes in a while."

"It's been a while since I've been a human," he answered. "There's not much of a need when you're running all the time."

"What were you running from?"

"Nothing," he answered. "I was simply running."

"You didn't have a pack or anything you were running from?" he looked suspicious as he questioned.

"My pack had left me a long time ago," he answered. The memory was as fresh as snow after a storm. Yet he did not let it stay. He learned long ago that memories like that one was best in the past, where they belong. He needed to focus on the here and now.

"You didn't do anything to cause them leaving you?"

"I existed," he told the man. It seemed to shock them to hear him say that. But he wasn't telling them it to invoke sympathy out of them. He just answered the questions.

"You existed?" Jackie had a motherly look to her. It reminded him of good days with his own mother. He wished the best for her growing child in this one's stomach. "Why would they leave you just because you existed?"

"I don't know," he shrugged. "That is just what I heard from them."

"Was it because of what you look like?" Madeline asked.

"They never told me," he answered. "I just accepted that I was on my own since then."

"How long ago was that?"

"I don't know."

"You don't really know much, do you?" Herb asked. Even though he still seemed cautious whenever Alistair was talking to his mate, he seemed to be more comfortable around him. That must have been why he was starting to ask so many questions.

"Not really," he looked up at the sky. It was dark, the perfect time to make their request. A request to speak with the Alpha or join a pack is always best done under the Moon Goddess' gaze. As long as you are careful in making sure you didn't come off as a threat to them. His scent was strong and his wolf was large, so many were intimidated by his size and saw him as a threat. But he had been successful in being allowed to pass through territories before with the Alpha's permission.

That pull was getting stronger. He could feel it with every step they took. He didn't know what it was still, but his instincts were telling him to keep walking towards this pack. He would determine whether it was within this pack or not after he met the Alpha. Alphas were magical all on their own, and he admired them for it. To be able to lead and take on all the responsibility that it takes to be there for hundreds of people was a level of strength that Alistair did not have.

It was a clear night, much cooler than the day. With the hot sun coming down on them, it was hard to keep up the pace that he had set. His skin burned with every ray of light that hit his bright skin. He knew the pain would pass, though. It always did. He was one of the lucky ones that healed from this ailment rather quickly. His skin would change from pure white, to red, and back to white. It was a cycle that he used to be fascinated with watching when he was younger. Back then, he didn't see that much of the beautiful sun's rays.

They had been walking for a few days at that point. Since they had wanted to stay in their human forms to keep their scent small, the travel to this part of the woods took much longer. He helped them hunt while he was in his wolf form. There was plenty of good game around these parts, all easy to get as well. He was sure that the surrounding packs made sure that nothing got overhunted just so they could have a lasting food supply.

There were plenty of animals giving birth around this time of year. But he wouldn't go after the infants, or their mothers. It wasn't worth the strife.

They treated him with respect. He wasn't used to that from his own kind. As soon as he came back with food, all of them praised him for it. He didn't know why. He had hunted like that plenty of times before. But he supposed that someone who hadn't been on their own for as long as he had wouldn't be able to hunt as well. He didn't ask for their stories, but they told him them anyway that night.

All three of them were from the Citrus Valley Pack, far away from here. He didn't recognize it. Herb and Jackie were running because the Beta of the pack had taken a liking to Jackie, and wanted her to wife his children rather than the man that she was mated to. The Alpha agreed with his second, even when they begged him to reconsider. When there was nothing else that they could do, they decided to make a run for it.

It was a month later that they realized she was pregnant. They didn't have any doctors to check after their initial bonding, so they hadn't been able to find out until they felt the bump. She almost cried as she told him her fears of what would have happened to her infant if she had stayed in that pack with that Beta.

Madeline went with them when she heard what had happened. She apparently was going to get replaced from her head tracking position with a young delta that had no experience in tracking whatsoever. They wanted her to train the young man and then have him take her place. She left without training him whatsoever.

"I'm only 32!" she told him. "It was absolutely ridiculous! They treated me like I was an old hag, with no fighting abilities whatsoever!"

Some packs were bad, and some were good. He had only heard of the bad packs, but he figured that was only because he was on the outside looking in. His mother always told him to never judge a book by its cover. That was why he was willing to give his instincts a chance. He would leave if it came to that, but he would try if it meant that he could figure out what this pull meant.

"So," Herb broke through the silence. There was little to no sound as they got close to the border. "What exactly is this request ritual thingy that you were talking about?"

"It's a peaceful way of talking to the surrounding pack," he explained. "If you wish to go through their territory, or seek refuge, then it is a sign of respect to call for them and ask before stepping onto their territory."

"Where did you learn about that?" Madeline asked.

"One of the packs north of here," he answered. "They were patrolling their territory heavily one night. I didn't want to start a conflict with them, as I was hungry and thirsty. I just wanted to pass through so that I could hunt when I got away from their territory. So, instead of walking in there and trying to outrun them, I howled."

"You howled?"

"I howled at the moon," he looked up at the bright full moon that was shining on them. "It was my way of asking the Moon Goddess what to do. It wound up catching the pack's attention. When they came to the border that I was at, I showed them that I meant no harm and wished to pass through their land without any violence or mal-intent."

"And they let you that easily?!" Herb asked. His eyebrows were raised after he heard his story.

"I waited an hour as the Alpha discussed it with his council," he told him. "Afterwards, he agreed to let me pass as long as I be escorted through it as quickly as possible. Once I had gotten to the other side of the land, they told me that what I did was the most respectful thing that they had ever seen from a rogue."

"It sounds like a good plan," Madeline said. "At least, if they say no, we don't run the risk of getting hurt just trying to leave their land."

"I don't know why someone didn't think of that before," Jackie said. "You'd think that something like that would be passed down through rogues."

"Rogues aren't the type to do that," Madeline rolled her eyes. "They aren't friendly with anyone."

"I've met a friendly one," Jackie said.

"Alistair doesn't count."

"I thank you for the compliment," he smiled. Showing emotion was more noticeable when you were human than a wolf. It was a blessing and a curse to show emotion well in this hairless body. This form was useful in the fact that it helped him stay cooler, though. His wolf coat wasn't built for such warm temperatures.

"Why are you so nice?" Herb asked. "I don't think I've heard of a rogue that actually helps people like us."

"I've learned a lot through my travels," he told them. "One of them was that a life of kindness and care is more fulfilling than one filled with selfishness and neglect."

The silence engulfed them once more as they continued their journey. They had to slow down due to Jackie getting tired. A pregnant woman, whether werewolf or not, should never have to do endure something like this. That was one of the reasons why he wanted to help her. She needed a pack to keep her and the life that was forming inside her, safe from the dangers that lurk in the wilderness.

As for the other reason: it was simply that they were nice to him. Kindness goes a long way, and it shows the purity of the person's heart. He had met plenty of kind people throughout his journeys. Even if he didn't stay to get to know them too much, he appreciated them.

"We're here," he told them. He had smelt the territory marks from miles away, but it was nothing compared to now. He truly did hope that his instincts were correct about this pack. The more he looked past the invisible walls, the more he longed to go through them.

"Okay," Herb said. They dropped the bags that they had been carrying by their feet. "What now?"

"We need to shift," he told them. "Once you shift, follow my example."

They all nodded their head. Madeline changed out of her clothes right there, but Jackie had gone behind a bush to do it. Herb watched to wait until she had shifted to begin his process.

Since the shorts weren't his, he thought it best to take it off before shifting. He didn't want to tear something that did not belong to him. His shift was easy. It felt like he had been a wolf all his life. He looked towards the bushes to see his new friend trio as their wild selves. Madeline was easy to spot, as her golden eyes glimmered in the clearing that the full moon beamed down on. Her fur was short and sleek. The only way he could tell it was brown was through the moonlight, it was so dark.

Herb had longer fur, with eyes that looked like shadows rather than anything else. His mate looked much gentler than him, and smaller. But she held grace in the way she walked out of the bush. Herb stood beside her protectively.

They looked at him just as much as he did them. He forgot that he had changed into his human form before they had seen him. This must be shocking for them. His fur and eyes were always the same color, no matter what form he was in, but red eyes with white hair was always more intimidating on a large wolf rather than a human.

He could feel the pull stronger now that he was in this form. It tried to fuel his legs to run just like before. But he knew better than to go into a territory unannounced. So, he willed his legs to be still and his heart to calm. He could wait just a little longer to solve this mystery.

He sat down in his wolf form and tilted his head towards the moon. His howl was low, much like his voice. Yet it still managed to echo through the land. He knew that a territory with this strong of markings was guarded well.

Sure enough, it didn't take long before one of them decided to come and investigate. On the other side of the invisible barrier stood a brown wolf. It growled at him in warning. He was small, but strength wasn't always in size. And he doubted that this wolf would be alone for too long.

Only packs could mind link with each other. The only time that a wolf could talk to a wolf outside of their pack was if one was the Alpha.

The three friends backed away a little out of fear. But Alistair didn't. The idea wasn't to show that they feared this pack, it was to show respect.

He laid down on the soft ground, watching the wolf and the many that had now come to help him. They all looked strong and battle worn, but they all stopped their growling when they saw him lay. He put his head low to the ground and turned to his side, exposing his stomach.

He was surrendering to them.

The first one they saw cocked his head to the side. They all seemed confused at what he was doing. He found it quite amusing, however, did not show it. The other three that were with him followed his actions. Jackie seemed to have a little trouble, as her infant had even showed in her wolf form.

The unknown wolves looked at each other. He could only assume it was to discuss what to do. Alistair stayed in his position, not moving an inch. He would only sit back up when they felt unthreatened by him. He could tell that they were still defensive over their land due to their stances. They stayed on their side of the border, legs spread apart on the ground. They were ready to attack at any moment.

A gust of wind helped him smell the Alpha scent that was coming their way. He hoped that he would show mercy on them in the very least. Judging by the pack, the leader must be strong. The forest around them was sturdy. They were the foundation for the pack within them.

He looked at the other wolves until they parted. A wolf much larger than any of the guards came out of the shadows. The moon shined on his red fur the most out of any of the other wolves. The Moon Goddess was proud of this Alpha.

"Stand." He flinched as he heard the Alpha's command in his thoughts. He hadn't talked with an Alpha for many seasons. He did as he was commanded. The other three behind him tried to stand as well, but the large wolf growled at them. Jackie cowered behind Herb and they all sat down again.

The Alpha must only be talking with him then. He must think that he was the leader of this group. It made sense. He was the strongest out of the four of them.

He kept his head low as he looked at the Alpha. This one was stronger than most he had met. His purple eyes bored into Alistair's. It felt like he was looking right at his soul with his gaze.

That's when he realized that the pull was stronger when he got closer to this Alpha. He was supposed to be here. He didn't know why, but there was something about this pack that his instincts told him to trust.

"Why are you here?" the Alpha asked. His eyes were cold, yet warm at the same time. It was a strange sight to see.

"We wish to seek refuge, Alpha," he told him. *"We ask that you consider us as an addition to your family."*

"Why?" the Alpha looked just as confused as the guards now. They all watched in unknowing silence as they spoke.

"Some to raise a child and start a family," he flicked his ear behind him for a second, to motion towards Jackie and Herb. *"Some to find work to dedicate their life to."*

"And you?" he asked him. *"Why do you ask of such a thing?"*

He had to think about that for a second. It was hard to speak what his reasoning was. He just felt like he belonged with them for some reason. The Alpha of the Crescent Moon Pack did not stop looking at him the entire time. His soul was exposed to him, just as it was always shown to the Moon

Goddess. And he could tell that he was powerful. He could tell that the Goddess had sent him to this pack for a reason.

"*I want to stop running,*" he said. "*I have travelled far enough. I wish to finally be at peace.*"

He could tell that the Alpha wasn't expecting his answer. The pack didn't seem like they were used to strangers asking them to adopt them as members. As he looked into the Alpha's eyes, he could see kindness in it. It might have taken a while for him to see past the untrusting gaze that he held him under, but Alistair could see it.

"*I will give you an answer tomorrow,*" the Alpha spoke to him. "*However, be warned. If you step into my territory without my permission, you will all be killed.*"

"*I understand,*" he bowed his head at the leader. "*We will stay in this clearing until you come with an answer. You have my word.*"

"*A rogue's word means nothing.*" The Alpha's tone was dark when he said that. He knew that there was much hatred behind that statement. "*But, since you showed us the respect of asking before entering, we will show you the respect of taking your request seriously.*"

"*Thank you,*" he said.

It didn't take long before the crowd dispersed. He knew that there was still a few that would be watching the borders near them. He understood why the Alpha would hate rogues so much. Every other wolf that he had met had been violent towards him. These three were the only exceptions. He just hoped that the Alpha would see them as the exceptions to his hatred.

He looked up towards the moon again. The Moon Goddess shined brightly through the full moon that beamed down on them. Even the water nearby glittered with her blessings. He sent out a prayer that she would share her blessings with him. His strife was not over yet, he knew, but this might be the beginning to the end of his burdens.

He had a good feeling about this. Feelings were never laws set in stone, but his were right more times than they were wrong. He would tell his friends what the Alpha had told him. Then he would watch the moon as it moved across the night sky. He never slept at night. Not when the beautiful white light was shining as bright as this. Not when the stars twinkled their greetings.

Not when he finally had something to be excited for.

CHAPTER 5:

A Farewell Party

The pack house was lit up that night. Music was blasting and people were dressed up, laughing and dancing. Nick was one of them. This was one of the first times he actually decided to dress up at these silly parties that they always held. They were nice, but he hated the fact that they always required him to put on some kind of suit.

This night was different from all the other parties. This night was the last night he'd see Katy in a long time. They still had each other's phone numbers just in case they couldn't mind link with each other, so they could always use that. But she was already so far into the honeymoon phase that he doubted they were going to talk that much.

That Owen had, of course, been keeping her occupied the entire rest of the week. It was common for those who first mate to do something like that. They already marked each other, and he could tell that they were both still high off that feeling.

He was happy for her. He really was.

But, man, had the last few days been the most boring of his life.

He didn't have many people to talk to. They were all busy working on something. Everyone was still working double time since the visitors had still not left yet. So, he just worked longer. He was going to have to get used to it when he became the Head Chef anyway. He was so proud when Aldi told him that he was planning on making him his apprentice.

Working a little extra took some stress off the old chef anyway. They were all used to working like this. They've had visitors like this before, but it had never been for this long. Not with this many people. A visiting Alpha usually counted as five people in one, just because they demanded so much out of them. This time there were three visiting alphas, counting Owen, and their respective mates.

This party wasn't just a farewell to Katy. It meant that they were finally going to be able to rest and get things back to normal in the pack house. Alpha William, Owen's father, had finally agreed on the territory lines. Which meant that all they needed to do was wait for the other packs to start pushing into the unmarked territory and cornering the rogues that plagued them.

He had heard that it might take a while to do. Maybe even months. The other two packs needed some time to get their warriors ready for attack and ready their defenses. The Harvest Moon Pack had to make sure their cities wouldn't get affected by them moving their defenses further away. And the Blood Moon Pack had to set their plans into action, as they were keen on strategizing to perfection.

But, even with the constant planning ahead, all of this was a good sign that at least some things were moving. Max seemed a little worried about Owen taking leadership of the Blood Moon Pack now that he had found his mate. Nick didn't think it would be that bad. Katy would snap at him if he tried to do anything stupid.

Katy. He already missed her. His heart hurt just thinking about the fact that he wasn't even going to be able to mind link with her anymore. More people had seemed to notice that he was upset, because so many of them would go up to him throughout the day and ask if he was okay. Ed was another member that didn't really have much to do outside the meetings and minor duties he had. His wife, Emily, was doing a bunch of internships now. He was hoping that it would be over soon. He could tell just how much Ed wished his mate were around more. For the meantime, he hung out with Nick a lot.

Nick walked into the main hall that the party was taking place in, feeling a little awkward. The only time he had actually worn a suit like this was at weddings he was forced to attend to. He liked to think it looked good on him. He just didn't like all the layers that suits had. It was so heavy. And the fact that it was the beginning of summer didn't help at all.

It was just a plain black suit, with a bowtie instead of a regular one. And something as simple as that still seemed to make him itch and sweat inside it. He really needed to get a summer suit. Just in case he was forced to wear one again in the heat.

"Wow, Nick," Barry, his brother, was the first to notice him. "I haven't seen you in that suit since my wedding."

"Yeah," he shrugged and smiled at him. "I felt like it would be too important of a day not to put something on like this."

"Yeah," Barry looked a little different from him. While Nick had tanner skin, like his mother, Barry's skin was lighter, with light brown hair. They still had some similarities to them. They both loved to dance. Their father wouldn't hear otherwise.

"Hey baby brother!" George, his other brother came over. "Nice outfit!"

"I like my pleather suit with all the sparkles better," he winked at him. George was on the smaller side of all of them. They were all naturally tall, but George was the shortest of the three of them.

"The throwback from the 70s?" George scrunched up his face, making him laugh. "That thing is one of the worst ones that you own."

"Don't say that!" Barry told him. "You never know what he might have found at a thrift store or something."

"You mean like the Christmas suit that I wore last year?" he gave them a playful look. "There's so many fun suits that you can find at thrift stores."

"Oh, that one was atrocious!" George laughed with him. "Still couldn't get the wife to where that ugly sweater dress to the Christmas party either."

"That would have been so perfect," Barry laughed. "We need to all get together and organize an ugly sweater contest this year's Christmas."

"You know I'm going to win," Nick told them. "I know all the best places to get them from."

"Screw that!" George said. "We might as well just make it ugly sweater themed and leave it at that."

"And then do square dancing in the middle of the city," He told them. It was fun being around his brothers. His family was a big one, possibly the largest in the pack, so it was difficult to bring them all together. Nick was the youngest, though. He was the baby that everyone worried and cooed over when he was growing up.

They laughed a little more as they talked about more random things that they could plan just to throw people off. There was enough of them that they could easily organize a public dance in one of the cities. Granted, some of them were in other packs as they found their mates there, but there was still a decent amount of them that stayed home to build their family.

Nick was the baby of twelve children that his parents had. Sisters, brothers, strong, smart, they were all unique in their own ways. He was just unique in the fact that he was the sickly child and, therefore, he got coddled the most by his mom. The rest of them absolutely hated that he got the most attention. Max actually saved him from the beating of some of his brothers. Max always wound up having to save him from things like that. That was how they became friends. That and he knew how to make Max laugh.

Always befriend the tough one, kids.

All kidding aside, it was nice to see even a couple of his brothers there. He hated being alone, and he loved to talk to just about anyone he could.

"Hey," Barry nudged him. He looked a little concerned this time rather than his usual carefree expression. "Are you going to be okay, Nick?"

"Of course!" He smiled at him. "Why wouldn't I?"

"Well, it's just," he looked sheepish as he put his hand behind his head. "We all know how close you and Katy are. We just wanted to make sure you're okay."

"Do I really have to tell you guys again that she isn't my mate?" he rolled his eyes. His family always thought that they were going to marry. His mom had a whole wedding planned at one point. It was the most ridiculous thing for him to walk into on his eighteenth birthday. Their mom liked to think that she was the best at figuring out who her children's mate was at an early age. She was right about some of his siblings, but not many of them. His father said that it was something that the mother werewolves in India loved to do.

"What Barry's trying to say," George hit him across the head. "Is that we're worried about you, because you hang out with Katy so much."

"I'm not really losing her," he shrugged. "Sure, she'll be obsessed with the twerp for a little while. But she'll still talk to me, even if she's in another pack."

He hoped that was the case. All he could do right now was try and be happy for his best friend. He couldn't be selfish, because that would hurt her more than anything else. And he couldn't hurt her. He couldn't try and make her choose between her best friend and her mate, the other half of her soul.

Also, he was pretty sure he would lose that battle, so there was no way he was going to try that. Besides, Katy was the one who always made a scene about things. He just kind of stayed back and watched.

It was going to be so funny when she snapped at Owen for the first time. He could already see it coming. He didn't know Owen too much, but he knew enough to see that he was stubborn, just like her. It would have been so funny if he could see her go off on him.

Almost as funny as when she was trying to throw a mudpie when they were seven and she accidentally let it drop on herself.

He was lost in a sea of memories when he noticed that Max and Charlie had come into the room. They were always dressed nicely. Although, he could tell that even Max was getting sick of wearing suits all the time. Charlie just wore a dress shirt with a black vest over it, rather than having the jacket to match. Max wore a suit with a blazer.

They were such a perfect couple. As much as they couldn't bear to be away from each other for too long, they still made time to be with other people of the pack, as well as friends. He hoped that Katy would wind up like that.

As if on cue, Katy and Owen walked in, their parents right behind them. Katy was an only child, which made her parents all the more sad that she was leaving to another pack. It wasn't going to be that far, just far enough where it would take a while to get to. He knew that she probably promised to keep in contact with them. They were going to be so worried.

She looked great! She wore the sparkly green dress that he had helped her shop for years ago. They always went looking for party outfits, since the pack had them so much. While Katy always tried to go for elegance, he always went for the goofy ones.

What can he say? He liked making people smile with what he wore.

He saw her scan the room before her eyes landed on him. Her face lit up with a smile, and so did his.

"What?" he mind linked with her. "Did you really think I was going to miss out on your last party?"

"No!" she replied. *"And this isn't my last party! We'll have more together, I promise!"*

"You'll have to train the pup to not be so possessive first," he smirked. He could already see just how tightly he was holding her. He was so happy to have her, but Nick knew that if he didn't give her space there was going to be an issue.

"He's not a pup!" she blushed. Nick laughed at that.

It wasn't long before she was mingling with everyone. Alpha William seemed to like her already, which was good. Max and Charlie looked really sad to see her go. Charlie hugged her a bit. The party had just started, but there were already so many sad faces. The whole pack was going to miss her. Even Aldi was trying to hold back tears.

Then their favorite song came on. It was a Broadway song that they both had practiced the dance too at least a million times.

"Excuse me," he tapped on Owen's shoulder. He turned around to look at him with an annoyed expression on his face. "Might I have this one last dance with my dear sister?" He tried to look as sincere as possible. He could tell that Katy was trying to hold back a giggle behind him.

Owen looked at Katy, who was practically bouncing out of his arms. Nick could tell that he wanted to tell him no. But he caved after Katy gave him her infamous puppy dog eyes.

"You aren't going to regret it," Max said. "They're the best dancers in the pack."

He let her go and she ran straight to the stage. The song was a long one, as it was the main song to a play. But it was the most fun they had when they were trying to learn it. There were so many nights where they both went to bed with sore feet from stepping on each other's toes during the slow part. He smiled at the memory. As much as they bickered during that time, they still kept doing it until they got it right.

"Nick," Katy said. They were at the slow part now, which was more of a waltz, but with intricate footwork. "Are you worried about me leaving?"

"No," he shook his head. "Why?"

"I don't know," She shrunk a little. "Maybe because I'm worried about leaving."

"Don't be," he told her. "We'll all still be here. And it's not even that far. You can come here to visit anytime."

"I know," she sighed. He was going to miss her dramatic sighs. "But it just won't be the same. I'm going to miss you so much."

"I'm going to miss you too," he admitted. He could fake being happy throughout this entire party, but he couldn't lie about that. "It's going to be really weird not waking you up in the morning and seeing your crazy mane."

"Hey!" she slapped his arm. "I wake you up plenty of mornings too!"

"Pfft!" he laughed. "Sure."

The song started to pick up and they changed their dancing to a quick one. Tap dancing, twirling, a little bit of ballet. This song required you to know it all. And they had perfected it. The whole pack always loved to watch them dance. They all cleared the dance floor just to give them space to perform.

"I think your mate is impressed," he mind linked with her half way through the dance. He saw Owen completely transfixed with her. Him and his father watched them in awe as they performed.

That was another reason he loved dancing. It always impressed people whenever they came to see them. It almost made him want to do Broadway. But he just couldn't stand leaving his family. He couldn't stand leaving his friends like Max and Katy.

And now Katy was leaving him.

At the end of the song, they bowed and then Katy ran straight towards Owen to hug him. He twirled her around, whispering to her. He was probably telling her that she was great.

That was the only time he really got to talk to her. Every time he tried, there was someone else that pulled her away to talk. Owen wanted her all to himself, which would be okay if this wasn't a farewell party for her. He could have her when they left.

He let it go. He wasn't going to keep pushing to try and talk to her. That would only make the alpha suspicious of him and his intentions. Nick had a feeling that Owen was an only child; one that didn't have any friends of different genders. If Nick hadn't told him that he was her brother he probably would have thought that he had a crush on her or something. Just like everyone else.

So, he stayed in the background, watching the crowds. Every now and then someone would come up to him and they'd talk a little, or he'd dance with his family. But he mainly just watched the happiness around him. All the workers were relieved that they wouldn't have to do such long shifts anymore. They celebrated that the most.

Katy would look around to see if he was still there from time to time. Every time he noticed her doing this, he would make a funny face to make her laugh. She already looked homesick. But he knew that she was going to be fine. She had her mate; her Happily Ever After, just like she had always wanted. He just hoped that she would still talk to him. She wasn't just mated to anyone. She was mated to an Alpha, which made her the Blood Moon Pack's next Luna. It was going to overwhelm her, he was sure. But he knew that she could do it.

Max had disappeared sometime throughout the party. He wasn't gone for long, but he did look a little stressed when he came back. Nick was sure that they would find out soon enough. He wasn't going to pry right then. There was something else he was focused on.

The party ended just as quickly as it began. And soon, Katy was being brought to the Blood Moon Pack's car. He stood outside, watching her walk towards it. She looked back again to everyone that was waving goodbye. She looked so sad to be leaving.

As soon as she saw him again, she ran from Owen's arms to give him a tight hug.

"You better not forget your phone," she told him, tears in her eyes. "I'm going to be calling you to tell you everything every day."

"I'll be looking forward to it," he smiled. "Now go, before the attack dog comes."

"Oh, he'll be fine," she shook her head. "I'm going to really miss you Nick."

"I'm just a phone call away, Kate," he assured her. "Don't worry about me. Have your happy ending."

She smiled through her tears and walked back to her mate that was waiting for her. He looked a little peeved by her and Nick's scene that they created, but his eyes softened once he saw the tears that had run down her face.

"I'm going to miss her," Charlie stood next to him. They quietly watched the car drive away. Everyone walked back inside, whether it be to get some sleep, or to party some more. But Charlie stayed with him as he watched the last bit of the car leave.

"I don't know what I'm going to do now," he told him. Charlie was always someone that he could talk to. He just had an aura to him that made Nick trust him with anything. "I mean, I still want to cook. I just don't know about when I'm not cooking."

"I'm sure there'll be other people around that'll be bored," Charlie assured. "I'll always be around somewhere, probably in the study. And there's always your family."

"My family all have their own families to worry about," he explained. "And you have Max to take care of. You shouldn't worry about me. I'm just whining."

And having a mid-life crisis at the age of 21.

"You're not whining," the blond said. He put an arm over his shoulders to comfort him. "She's been your friend since you were in diapers. It's okay to feel sad that she's gone."

"You see," he wiped some tears from his eyes. "This is why you're perfect as the Luna."

Charlie hugged him. He didn't cry except for the few tears that escaped him. It felt good to be hugged though. Hugs always made him feel better.

"Well, maybe it's your turn to find your mate then," he told him. "And you'll sweep her off her feet, just like Max said."

"I'm not going to find my mate, Charlie," he told him. "It's not my fate."

"Don't say that," he smiled. "You never know."

"Charlie," he shook his head, laughing through a short sob. "No woman is going to want me. I can't even get it up."

"What?"

"I have an issue with my testosterone," he explained. "There was an incident when I was in my mother's womb. It caused me to be a very sickly child. And, when I was around the age for the testosterone to start kicking in and doing its thing, it didn't want to work for me."

"So, you can't get it up at all?"

"I mean, I take pills to help with the rest of my bodily functions," he answered. "Once in a blue moon it will start to work for me, but it's not that frequent." He paused, not sure of what to say at first. "I thought I'd be okay with being celibate my whole life. I could just have my family and friends, and be the best uncle to my nieces and nephews I could be. But," he had to stop himself from choking up as he looked back at the road. "Now I don't know if I can do that. It feels like everyone else is moving on with life without me."

"We'll always be here for you," Charlie said. "And I don't think that means you aren't destined to find your mate. Maybe the Moon Goddess has more in store for you than you think."

"Maybe."

"Why else would you be here, healthy and happy?" the blond asked. "I mean, I wasn't in the best of positions when you met me, but look what happened? I could have easily died or gotten thrown into something that I can't even imagine. Yet, here I am. I think you're going to find happiness, whether it be a mate or something else."

"Thanks, Charlie," he sniffed. "I hope so."

He stood there a little longer, staring off at the road, then the night sky. It was a full moon out that night. He always loved seeing the full moon. He remembered nights when he was alone, talking to it. His father told him that if he talked to the moon, it would talk back to him…

Charlie had left a while ago, saying that there was something important for him to do. He asked him if he would be okay, but he just yessed him to death and let him go. He would be fine. Life would go on. It would be okay.

"Looks like it's just you and me again, friend," he smiled at the moon.

He hoped the moon smiled back at him.

CHAPTER 6:

The Enemy of My Enemy

"Hey, Apple," Ed bumped into him. "Did you like the party?"

"Yeah," he told him. The party was nice and it was fun to talk to so many people and tell stories, but it hurt to see Katy leave. She already looked homesick and she hadn't even left the pack house. "It was fun."

"It's always kind of sad when someone gets mated to another pack and they have to move away," Ed sighed. They were both walking up to the third floor, where, unfortunately, Max had called an emergency meeting. "I'm more worried about Nick at this point."

"Me too," his heart ached just thinking about his friend. Usually, Nick loved being the spotlight of every party, whether it be telling jokes and stories, or just dancing. But tonight, he just stayed in the background, watching everyone else. And with what he had told Charlie before he had to go, it broke his heart thinking about just how lonely Nick felt now.

"You talked to him just now, right?" Ed's golden eyes looked just as worried as him. "How did he sound?"

"Lost," Charlie told him. "He looked so lost, Ed. I didn't even want to leave him alone." He never thought he'd see Nick like that. He always had a 'go with the flow' notion to him. Everything that happened, he just went

55

with. But now it seemed like he was confused about everything. He left him staring at the moon.

"You should have seen him when Katy first found her mate," Ed shook his head. "He was standing there, staring at the door that she left through. I didn't think he could hear me when I asked him if he was okay."

"We're going to have to see how he's doing when this meeting's done," he told him. There was no way he was going to leave Nick by himself that night. Not when he needed them the most.

Would the Moon Goddess really not give someone like Nick a mate? Just because he had a health issue like that? He didn't know whether Ed knew about it or not, as it seemed like something that Nick was insecure about. So, he wouldn't ask him. He was still new to the Moon Goddess that they all prayed to. He was never a religious man, but he never held it against any of them. Maybe he'd try and send a prayer to her, though, just for Nick. Maybe she'd listen to his request and help him in whatever way that she could.

"I'm so sick of meetings," Sam groaned. He caught up with them just as they got to the door of the third floor. Charlie had grown to like it. It was dead quiet, and the perfect place to get things done when he needed to. He had an office in there, right across from Max's where he could do his work and listen to requests from the pack member's. He caught onto the paperwork quite easily. He was used to dealing with office work from school. Studying to be a lawyer always required a lot of paperwork.

The only thing he hated was the fact that the kitchen was so far from here. He still wanted to bake his pies, but it was getting more difficult as his Luna duties were taking up most of his time. Max told him it wouldn't be as bad as soon as they convinced the other packs to help them with the rogues. These meetings had been the most annoyingly frustrating thing imaginable.

Annoyingly frustrating?

Ugh. His brain was so fried.

"I wonder what it's about," Ed said. "He wouldn't tell me until the meeting."

"He left somewhere during the party," Charlie told them. "I'm guessing it has something to do with that."

"He left?" Sam looked at him, his dirty blond hair was still done up professionally for the celebration. "How did we not notice that he left?"

"Because you were with your twins," he smiled. It was so adorable that they had gotten twins. They were identical too. "And Ed was with Emily. And Tyler was falling asleep on Isabelle's shoulder."

"He was falling asleep?" Ed laughed. "I wish I would have seen that. That would have made a funny picture."

"Already one step ahead of you," Charlie pulled out his phone. "I'll show you when we're done, though."

"Aww!" Ed crossed his arms and pouted. "No fair!"

They stopped their talking when they got into the meeting room. It always held such a serious atmosphere to it. As much as it was nice, Charlie was really hoping that he wouldn't have to see it again for at least a while. They had finally finished up with the territory agreements. They had finally convinced Alpha Williams of the Blood Moon Pack to cooperate with them. They were gone, sadly with Katy in tow, and everyone could finally rest.

And now they have another meeting.

Everyone else piled into the room looking just as tired and disgruntled as he felt. He took his seat next to Max, who immediately grabbed his hand from under the table. From the look in his eyes, Charlie could tell that there was something bothering him. And he knew that Max didn't want to be there either.

Tyler looked the most exhausted. He was sure that Max had woken him up when he made that announcement of the meeting. Other than the main leaders of the pack, the advisors were also in attendance, something that they hadn't had for a while. This meant that the meeting was about an internal issue withing the pack.

Was this going to be about Nick?

His mind was swimming with questions, but he kept his silence as they awaited the last few people to sift in.

"What is the meaning of such a late meeting?!" Liam came in looking as grumpy as could be. Charlie actually liked Liam, much to everyone's surprise. The man always put in good points that the rest wouldn't think of otherwise.

Sure, he was always trying to argue against everything he mentioned. But Charlie just took it as the devil's advocate role to keep the pack safe rather than a personal attack. He loved the mental challenges that Liam always gave him too. He could tell that Liam enjoyed it as well, although he was sure that the man would never mention it to anyone.

"Trust me," Max sighed. "I wouldn't be calling another meeting so soon after the territory meetings if it weren't for something important."

"Mind telling us the situation?" Mr. Locke, Max's father, asked. It was strange seeing him move from the role of Alpha to just an advisor. But the man looked content in giving them advice to help them grow in their leadership roles.

"Desmond and Ray found some rogues just outside of the territory," Max explained. Everyone tensed when he said that.

"Did they get hurt?" Charlie asked. He knew just how much Max wanted to make sure that no one in the pack died from this conflict. He took his father's advice to heart when he had told him to keep the pack safe. So far, he had miraculously kept his promise, which left the pack pleasantly shocked.

"No," Max told him. His eyes showed a bit of confusion and frustration. "The rogues howled to show that they were near. When Desmond tried to threaten them, they went into submissive stances."

"They did this without entering the territory?" Mr. Locke asked. Everyone was awake and curious at this point. A rogue doing something like that wasn't heard of. At least, not for them.

"Yes," Max frowned. "I went over there when Desmond told me about it. When I asked the leader of the group what their purpose of being here was," he paused to let out a tense breath. "They requested to join our pack."

There was a moment of silence as they all tried to take in what Max had said. Charlie hadn't been a part of this pack, or this world, for very long. But he knew that something like this was extremely rare for them. Other packs around the world had gotten requests from rogues all the time. But their pack only dealt with rogues that wanted to destroy them. They reminded him of pirates: always wanting to cause trouble and gain as much as they can.

"They cause all of this violence on us," Sam spoke up, venom in his voice. "And then request to join?"

"These can't be the same ones that have tried to hurt us," Tyler looked at the Delta. "There's no chance that they'd think of something like that."

"It gets stranger," Max told them. When they stopped and looked at him, he continued. "One of them is a winter wolf, probably from up north. And there's another one who's pregnant. All four of them smell nothing like the wolves that we've fought. That was another reason why Desmond asked me about it personally."

"A winter wolf?" Mrs. Locke said, speaking for the first time that meeting. She had helped Charlie learn all the paperwork and Luna roles before fully retiring from her position. "He must have come from Canada then. We're close enough."

"Where he's from doesn't matter," Liam spoke up. "A rogue is a rogue. We haven't accepted those kinds into our pack for five generations. And we shouldn't break that tradition today."

"But that is strange," Tyler furrowed his eyebrows. "Usually, they would still try and come into our territory to ask such a question. You're saying that these four didn't come into our borders at all?"

"No," Max shook his head, he looked just as confused as Tyler. "They're still in that same spot, just outside of the Gila border. I told them to wait until tomorrow for an answer."

"You should have said no right there," Liam growled.

"They made a formal request," Max said. "And they still respected our boundaries while doing so. If it were any other situation, I'd just order Desmond and Ray to tear them apart."

"You said that one of them was pregnant?" Sam's face softened at that.

"Yes," Max answered, running his hands through his hair. "It could easily be that they were trying to get out of a bad situation with their packs."

"There are some nasty ones out there," Mr. Locke said.

"There's another reason that my guards up about all of this, rather than the fact that their rogues," Max told them. "The leader of the group is stronger than most of the rogues we've dealt with."

"How strong?"

"I believe he's a beta," he said. "His scent is strong, and he's big enough to be one. The rest are delta, gamma, and the pregnant one is an omega."

"This is an interesting group," Mr. Locke said. Even his eyebrows were furrowed at this point. "But, usually, the stronger the rogue, the less likely they are to stay with other rogues."

"I feel like we should ask these guys some more questions," Ed said. "We can see just how willing they are to tell the truth, and learn their stories along the way."

"We should just tell them no," Liam said. "No good ever comes from letting a rogue into your pack. They're strangers."

"But if we just send them on their way, then there's a chance that they could attack us," Ed argued.

"Then we kill them."

"We're not killing a pregnant woman," Max shook his head. "I don't care whether she's a rogue or not. That's the same as killing an innocent."

"Then spare her and kill the rest."

"Then you'd leave just the mother and an unborn child," Mrs. Locke argued. "Is her mate a part of this group?"

"I think so," Max said. "Judging on how guarded the gamma seemed to be around her. But he could also be a family member of hers. I don't know for sure."

"I have an idea," Charlie spoke up. He liked listening to everyone's thoughts on the matter before telling his own opinion. "Why don't we test them?"

"How?" Sam frowned. "By sending them to deal with the other rogues themselves? That would be the same as killing them off."

"And they could fake it," Liam noted. "It would be as easy as finding one of them that was already injured or dead and using that as evidence that they passed the test."

"I don't mean sending them out on a mission," he told them.

"What's your plan, then?" Max asked, he looked confused. It was kind of cute when he was confused. Charlie didn't see that expression on him often.

"Well," he started. "We have plenty of safe houses scattered along our territory. I know at least one of them is close to our border just in case the warriors need somewhere to rest in case of emergencies. What if we allowed the rogues to stay in one of the outer safe houses and let them prove themselves through working as extra guard?"

"That sounds ridiculous!" Liam shouted. His purple eyes were furious. "That puts our whole pack at risk! It'll only take one of them to try and attack and our whole pack will be in more danger than if we had a normal rogue raid!"

"Not entirely," he smiled and pointed at the map of their territory. It was always hanging up on the wall just behind Max and him. "You see, the outer safe houses are close enough to the border for the regular guards to watch as well. That way, we don't have to use extra men to watch over the rogues. If we just let them stay around the outer rim of our borders, then they'll be far enough for the pack to have time to move and attack. Then, all we lose is some supplies if they do decide to attack us."

"I don't think they would attack us," Ed said. "Not with a pregnant she-wolf in tow. It seems to be that they are just a group of wolves down on their luck."

"We shouldn't take our chances," Liam argued. "Not with one of them being a beta."

"He was the one who howled and made the formal request," Max said. "I understand your concern, though. For some reason, it was difficult to really read that wolf."

"Really?" Mr. Locke leaned in. "What was he like?"

"I think he's albino, by the looks of it," Max said. "But I don't know for sure. I know he never lied to me when he made the request, but there was something different about him that I can't put my finger on."

"Did he seem dangerous?"

"He tried to make himself as small as possible when I first saw him. He wasn't afraid, I could tell that. It seemed like he was trying to hide his strength almost."

"Interesting," Mr. Locke looked down as he thought. "If he's albino, then I'm sure Dr. Button would be interested in seeing him. His wife most likely has some history on the condition with werewolves in her library."

"Isabelle knows a little about it," Tyler said. "She had an issue with that in her old pack."

"It doesn't matter that he's an albino," Liam said. The old man looked tired, even when he was angry. It was long past all of their bedtimes, since Max waited until after the party to do this meeting. "He's still a beta, one that you can't read well. That's dangerous all in its own."

"I like Charlie's idea," Ed said. "It seems like a win-win situation: they're in a place where we can watch them and learn about them, without it being much of a risk to the pack. Besides," he winked at Charlie. "If they want to be in a pack bad enough, I think they'll take our test."

"That's never been done before," Liam argued. "It could wound our defense if they decide to attack."

"Or it could strengthen our defense," Charlie said. "I mean, the saying always goes: The Enemy of My Enemy is My Friend."

He could see that more people were starting to like this plan of his. The one thing that he enjoyed was finding a middle ground to things. That way there weren't as many disgruntled pack members. If they just accepted them, for example, much of the pack wouldn't trust them. If they turned them down and let them go their separate ways, then they risk getting attacked by them later. He had a good feeling about this.

"The reason I called this meeting wasn't just to get advice and opinions," Max said, trying to wrap things up. They were all exhausted and in need of rest. "I'm not going to make this decision. It affects the whole pack. I called this meeting to leave the decision up to you," he gestured towards the rest of the table. "Should we follow out this plan, or turn them down?"

Charlie loved meetings like these. It truly showed how much Max was willing to let the pack decide on matters like this. If it wasn't too dire, and affected the whole pack, Max would let the council vote on what they wanted to do. It kept the peace more times than not during Max's father's reign.

"I vote the plan," Tyler said. "But I think it would be best if we had our strongest guards around whichever cabin they go to. We don't know the strength of that beta yet."

"I'll make sure of it," Max smiled at his friend.

"I vote plan," Sam said. "We can't forget about that delta too though. They can be just as dangerous."

"The strongest guards could go with them on their running routes too," Charlie recommended. He squeezed Max's hand as his way of trying to support him.

"Great idea," Ed leaned back in his chair. "I vote the plan."

"We do too," Mr. Locke said, looking at his wife as he spoke. "I think there's been enough bloodshed. If they were kind enough to treat us with respect, we should do the same."

"I guess you don't need my vote, then," Liam stood. "I'm going to get some sleep."

The meeting was dismissed with that, and the people slowly walked out, dying to get some rest.

"Hey, Charlie," Ed elbowed him before he walked out. "Don't worry about Nick tonight. I'll make sure he's okay. You just get some rest."

"Nick?" Max looked over to them. "Where is he? Is he okay?"

"He isn't taking Katy's leaving too well," Charlie said. "He was crying when he saw the car pull away."

"I completely forgot about Nick throughout this," Max groaned and rested his head on his hands. "I was going to have a movie marathon with him to try and get his mind off of it all when the party was over."

"Well, you can't exactly ignore rogues," Ed said. "Don't worry about it, I got it this time."

They both thanked him and watched him leave. As soon as everyone was out of the room, Max rested his head on the table.

"Come on Max," he started rubbing his back. "Let's get some sleep."

Max grunted his reply and stayed there, making Charlie laugh a little. He kissed his shoulder and pulled on him a little bit. The coaxing worked and the bulky man slowly stood up.

"We have another long day tomorrow."

"It'll be fine," Charlie gave him a small kiss. "We were able to get through those meetings, we can get through this."

"Did I ever tell you just how much I love you?" he hugged him. Charlie could feel all the tension that the man had just melt away.

"As much as possible," Charlie started to guide his tired lover to their suite. "I love you too."

CHAPTER 7:

A Different Kind of Welcome

"How do we know he's going to come back?" Jackie asked. She was sitting on Herbs lap, enjoying breakfast. Herb was rubbing her stomach lovingly. It was nice to watch a couple being so loving to each other. He could tell that the ground was much too hard on the poor woman's back. There was already enough pressure on her spine with her bump growing so quickly.

She told Alistair that they were thinking it was twins. They had done the best they could to make sure that she was eating healthy.

"He will," Madeline replied. "He'll either want us out of here, or he'll bring us inside. Either way, he's not going to want some rogues to just sit here outside of his territory."

"That Alpha was the biggest I've ever seen," Herb said, wide-eyed. "I didn't even know werewolves got that big!"

"Alistair," Jackie looked to him. "Have you seen a wolf that big before?"

"I saw one close to it," he answered. "The Moon Goddess has truly blessed this one, though. She must be proud of this pack."

"I hope that means they aren't brutal," Jackie shivered. "They said that our pack was blessed by the Moon Goddess too."

"A true blessing isn't given to you," he looked over at the creek. Madeline had been able to catch some fish with some extra string she had. It made for a great breakfast. "It's earned through listening to the Moon and staying faithful to her."

"And you think our pack wasn't truly blessed?" Her brown eyes looked so curious at him. They always ate up every word that he said.

"I don't believe the Moon Goddess would take kindly to an Alpha allowing someone to steal someone's mate," he shook his head. "Mates are the people that she pairs together herself. I can only imagine your old pack going through hard times because of that."

"I hope so," Herb said. He was holding onto her tightly as he spoke. "I hope they're cursed for what they were trying to do."

"I don't want to wish ill on anyone," Jackie shook her head. Her long hair traveled with her as she moved. "I just hope they change their ways."

"I'm just glad we didn't stick around to find out," Herb said.

The morning birds were chirping up a storm as they talked. Alistair knew that they were still being watched. He could feel the eyes of the guards on him all night. It was another reason why he wouldn't sleep. He had gone plenty of days without it. It wasn't the best of ideas, as sleep always replenished his strength and the sharpness of his thoughts, but when it was necessary, he was able to do it.

"So, why did you say you wanted to be in the pack too?" Madeline asked. "I thought you were just going to try and pass."

"I wasn't sure yet," he told her. "But the pull got stronger when I met that Alpha."

"Really?" she cocked her head. "I've never heard of this pull of yours, Alistair, but I hope that it's leading you to good things."

"It must," he looked to the creek again. "I don't think I would be this excited for it if it was something bad."

"Sometimes feelings are hard to figure out," Herb said. "Sometimes you can think that they're good, and they're actually warnings."

"My instincts have never been wrong before," he shook his head. "That's why I only follow them."

"That's a good trait to have," Madeline said. "Being a tracker, you have to listen to your instincts a lot as well."

"When do you think he's going to come back then?" Jackie looked a little anxious. "Should we go back into our wolf forms until he comes?"

Before he could tell her his thoughts on the matter, he smelt something. He looked to the border to find that the guard had made himself seen. It was easier to look at him in the sun rather than the moon. He had dark brown fur that blended into the forest grounds. His eyes were dark blue, much like the night sky. There was another one with him this time that looked almost exactly the same.

They must be twins.

"He's coming now," Alistair said. "I believe it would be best to be our wolf forms before he comes, just so he can recognize us easier."

Jackie got up as quickly as she could and started to walk to a bush to change. Herb was right with her the entire time. The guards watched Jackie with gazes of inquiry. Their gazes seemed softer on her rather than Madeline and him. Alistair had gotten the heat of most of their glares. He knew that they still didn't trust him. Most beings didn't.

He threw off his shorts again and changed into his wolf. The guards looked shocked as they watched him transform. He didn't know why, but he made sure to lay down as soon as he could so they didn't think he was trying to attack them.

The last thing he needed was a whole pack trying to go after him. That was another reason he was so submissive to them. Alistair was strong, and his legs moved fast, but he was no match for this pack.

His smell was enhanced when he was in this form. He could smell the Alpha coming their way. He stayed in his place, the others soon following his laying position. Herbs wolf was holding the bag that had their things in it.

He gave a silent prayer to the Moon Goddess that this pack would accept his request. There was something in this pack that pulled him towards them. Even when they looked at him with laser eyes, he could not shake the feeling off.

The Alpha looked more magnificent than before. His fur glittered with red as the sun's rays bounced off from him. His deep purple eyes showed nobility. The stance that he took was a defensive one, as he walked up to them, past the border line.

"*Stand,*" he told him. He stood, and then the wolf looked at the ones behind him. He assumed that he had told them to do the same, because he did not growl at them when they stood as well.

"*Follow me,*" he ordered. The authority in his voice was enough for even the most defiant to obey. "*If you stray at all, you will be killed. Do I make myself clear?*"

"*I understand,*" he told the red wolf. "*I will do as you say.*"

"*Good.*"

He turned around and walked back to the border of the territory. They walked in a single file line as they followed him. The guards were all around him. Even with his skills that he had used all his years of being a traveler, he could not tell how many there were. This pack didn't seem very stranger friendly. He knew that when he first smelt their border line, but he had no clue that it was to such an extreme.

The pull was stronger as he crossed the border. There was something there that he so desperately wanted to find. But this was not the time to follow his feelings. He had to do as the Alpha said for now if he wanted to keep his life.

They didn't take them that far into the territory. He wasn't complaining, though. They had respected their small group enough to give them refuge in their territory. Just by that alone, he could tell that there was good in their hearts.

He stopped at a small cabin, just a little ways from the border lines. He smelt more people there, along with something freshly baked. It looked homely enough, even with its small size. When they were there, bones cracked as the Alpha changed his form. The human of the wolf they followed was a man of bright red hair that went every which way. He was well trained and strong, based off from the muscle that Alistair saw.

He told them to stay where they were, and went inside. Alistair did not move a muscle, for he knew that anything could be taken as an excuse to attack from the guards. Especially with their Alpha in his weaker form.

He came back out, changed into some light pants and a shirt. His purple eyes still held the same serious look that his wolf did.

"You," he pointed to Herb, who was holding the bag. "Drop it. It needs to be inspected before anything else."

Herbs wolf let out a small whine, but he dropped the bag. The Alpha picked it up and rummaged through it. All they had in it, from what Alistair knew, was clothing and supplies for surviving. There was a pan for cooking, and a hunting knife. Those were the two things that he pulled out of the bag and threw across the forest floor.

"There won't be any weapons while you are here," he told them. When he was finished rummaging through the bag, he put it on the porch of the cabin. "Inside will be clothes for you to change into. They're cleaner than the ones that you have. Change into them and come out."

They all let Jackie go first, as she was the one who needed her privacy the most. She looked a little scared to be the first to go, but Herb was right behind her. Madeline and Alistair waited for them to come out before going in themselves.

"Are you her mate?" The Alpha asked as Herb walked out with her.

"Yes, sir," he answered.

Alistair tried to listen to the questions that the Alpha was asking, but he got distracted. The cabin was the most beautiful thing he had ever seen. It was made out of polished wood, with racks of clothing all around. There were beds on the left side and closed off stalls that he supposed held bathrooms in them on the right.

"Well," Madeline said as she changed into her human form. "They're definitely well off."

Alistair said nothing. He found some clothes that fit and put them on. It felt strange to wear that many clothes on his body. He wasn't used to wearing clothing at all. But he could get used to them. They would protect his skin from the sun in the very least. He always healed easily from his skin condition, but that didn't mean that it was comfortable.

When he went back out there, he found that the smells he had noticed at first were stronger than before. He turned and noticed three people other than the Alpha that was standing out front. Two were older. One had fully white hair with light blue eyes. He didn't seem that strong physically, but his face showed that he had many years of experience in his profession. The other one had black hair that was just starting to grey. He had the same purple eyes as the Alpha. They looked like they were related from the way their faces were shaped and the stances both men had right then.

The third one was where the strangest smell came from. He was a petite man with blond curls and bright green eyes. The more he looked at the man, the curiouser he became. From his scent, he could tell that he was human. But there was a uniqueness to it that he hadn't experienced before. It was sweet, like fresh apples coming from a tree. He had a feeling that the man was at least a little bit wolf.

Then he realized something else about his scent that made him snap his head down immediately. He was mated.

And his scent was mixed with the Alpha's.

Alphas didn't like it when people stared at their mates. That's what he had learned. Even though the Luna seemed friendly, he wasn't going to take his chance on it. He was lucky that he didn't get attacked just for the eye contact that he shared with the Alpha's mate. They had stared at each other silently for a solid minute. Those emerald eyes looked full of wonder at him.

Of course, he wasn't one to judge the Alpha's mate. It was traditional for an Alpha and Luna to be male and female respectively, but not unheard of to be both male. He had seen that many times when he was in the North. Human Lunas were more common than male ones. It seemed as if this one was truly unique to this pack.

He wondered why the Moon Goddess wanted this for this pack? Lunas always had something that is their strength, no matter what gender or magical species they be. He wondered what this man's strength was for this pack.

"Look up," He heard the Alpha command. When he obeyed, he saw those purple orbs boring into his. His aura radiated dominance. "Why did you look down?"

"I did not want to disrespect you," he answered.

"How would you disrespect me?" he asked. His face had changed from domineering to confusion. He knew it would not last long.

"I was unaware that your Luna was here," he told the Alpha.

"Luna?" Madeline asked. "But there's only-!"

The Alpha growled, making her stop immediately.

"I suppose introductions are in order," he said, changing the subject. "I am Max, the Alpha of the Crescent Moon Pack. Tell me your name and the pack that you came from."

"I'm Jackie," the brunette spoke first. It seemed like she was trying to get the attention off Madeline for a little. "Jackie Green. The three of us came from the Citrus Valley Pack." She motioned towards Herb and Madeline.

"Why did you leave?"

"The Beta of the pack," she looked a bit shy as she spoke. "He had taken a liking to me, even after I had found my mate. When we talked to the Alpha about it, he gave the Beta permission to take me as his mate instead," she tried to hide a sniffle. "We ran before anything worse could happen."

"How far are you along, dear?" the older gentleman along the side asked.

"Just a few months, I think," she told him. "It's hard to tell time when you're on the run."

"Would you mind if I examined you?" he asked, taking a step closer. Herb took ahold of her hand, trying to be defensive of her as best he could in their situation.

"This is Dr. Button, our lead pack doctor," Alpha Max responded to Herb's reaction swiftly. "None of you will be hurt in this territory. Not unless you try and hurt anyone else."

Jackie put a hand on Herbs shoulder to comfort him. They looked at each other a moment before he reluctantly let her go. The doctor lead her to a seat in front of the cabin and started his examination. He had his tools in a portable case.

"What's your name?" he continued down the line.

"Herb Wiatt, sir," he stood up straight. His focus was slightly wavering as he glanced over to his mate a few times. "I was a builder in my pack before."

"What did you build?"

"Mainly houses," he answered. "Every once in a while, I would make a new bench or help re-shingle a roof. I also have some skills as an electrician."

"Interesting skill set," the Alpha smiled at him. "We'll have to put that to use some time."

"I always love to work, sir," he smiled back at him.

"You came here to find a better place to start your family then?"

"Yes," he glanced at his mate again. "We didn't know that she was pregnant until after we ran. Unfortunately, she hasn't had any medical attention for the entire time."

"She's still very much healthy," Dr. Button set his tools down and looked at him. "You did a great job tending to her."

"Thank you," his dark eyes showed relief as he heard the doctor speak.

"And you?" he asked the next in line. Alpha Max looked a little tense around her. It was probably due to what she was about to say about his mate. Dominant wolves are always possessive of their mates. "What's your name?"

"Madeline Tithe," she answered. Her head bowed ever so slightly out of respect for the man. "I was a tracker for my old pack."

"Why did you leave?"

"Besides the fact that I wanted to make sure these guys made it through the forests alive," she motioned towards Herb and Jackie who were now standing side by side. The doctor was checking him next. "I was going to get replaced from my career by someone younger than me. They thought that I had gotten too old to still be able to track as well as another delta."

"How old are you?"

"32" she told him. When she saw the Alpha's eyebrows furrow, she chuckled a bit. "It was confusing me too," she told him. "I had spent fifteen years tracking for that pack, and they wanted to replace me with a much younger delta, who they were trying to make me train beforehand."

"Your tracking skills might be useful for the task I need of you," he told her. "I'll be the judge of your tracking skills. That being said, we don't replace anyone until absolutely necessary. If you do get into a high tracking position, then you won't be replaced until you retire."

"Good to know," she smiled at him. Madeline seemed to have a knack for getting people to like her. The Alpha had already calmed down about her questioning of their Luna. He respected her for that ability alone. She had even calmed Alistair down about them when they had first met. It was a great trait to have.

It was a trait that he wished he had. But he never had many people to socialize with. The trees always talked and he would listen, or the wind would sing him a beautiful tune as he ran. There was hardly a need for him to be in his human form and talk. And he didn't need to most of the time.

Now the Alpha was looking at him. His domineering stare was intense. He wanted to look away, but he knew that it would make the Alpha angry. And that was the last thing he wanted to do. So, he looked into those purple eyes, hoping that they would show mercy on him, just like they had done before.

"And you?" he asked, his stance unwavering. "What's your name and what pack are you from?"

"Alistair Miles," he answered him without hesitation.

"What pack were you from?"

"I was once in a pack called the Borealis Pack," he told him. Bringing up that name always brought back horrible memories. He didn't have time to deal with that. Not right now. He needed to keep his mind sharp and clear. Something always happened when you were least expecting it.

"The Borealis Pack?" the Alpha asked. "Where is that from?"

"Far north from here," he replied.

"Where?" he asked again, this time he had more aggression in his tone.

"I don't know."

CHAPTER 8:

Newcomers

He didn't know?

This man was about to make Max's head spin. He was already a strange sight to see. It wasn't often that there were albino werewolves. They were always seen as weak. But this one wasn't. And that put him on guard even more.

"How do you not know?" he asked him. He knew that those bright red eyes weren't lying. That only made this more confusing. The man hadn't lied to him at all. He had complied easily to every order that he gave.

It wasn't like a rogue to do. They hated their freedom being taken in any way. But this one gave his so freely. It put him on edge just how willing he was to comply to him.

As much as he wanted to trust these rogues, he wasn't sure about this beta. The way he held himself showed hints that he was trained at some point. And a trained rogue was much more dangerous than untrained.

"I wasn't told," he stated everything so easily to him.

"Dad, are you reading anything off him?" he mind linked with his father. Since it was difficult to read the mysterious man, he had wanted to

bring him for a second opinion. Of course, he needed to bring Button, as he needed to get them all checked up on.

Charlie had just begged him to come over and over. Max had tried to argue that it was dangerous, but he failed to realize just how powerful his mate's skills were when it came to arguing.

He now understood how Liam felt.

"Honestly, I'm just as confused as you," His father replied through their thoughts. *"All he says is honest, but it's difficult to get any kind of reading off him. All I know is that he must have been traveling for a long time."*

"That's what I was thinking," he kept his eyes on Alistair's the entire time he mind linked. The man had pure white skin and muscles that were made for both fighting and running. His face was another thing that stuck out about him. His chin and cheek bones were a defined, though not sharp. He had straight white hair that reached to the middle of his neck. Even his eyelashes and eyebrows were pure white.

Max had met white wolves before. But he had never met one that was an albino. He knew that there was a difference, he just had no idea how great of a difference until now.

"Why did you leave your pack?" he asked. For a beta, Alistair was extremely passive. He even put his head down when he realized that Charlie was his mate. It wasn't like Max was expecting him to. It actually threw him off rather than anything else.

How could a rogue show respect like this? Respect was always earned with werewolves, especially rogues, yet he gave it freely to everyone. Even Desmond and Ray were surprised that he didn't once try and show dominance over them when they had seen him first.

"I was left for dead after an attack," he said. There it was. The little flicker of hurt that Max had been waiting for. The albino had been so calm throughout the morning that he wasn't sure if he had any other emotion.

The hurt in his eyes showed for a little while. He blinked vigorously a few times before it went away.

Control.

That's what he had. He had control over his emotions.

"Why?" he kept the brutal eye contact going. He wanted to see him show his human side more. He wanted to solve this mystery as soon as he could. This man was an enigma that was driving him insane.

"They thought I was going to die," Alistair told him, the hurt returning in his eyes. "When I tried going back to them when I was healed, they had already moved on without me."

"They're a traveling pack?"

"We had to be," he told him. "It was the best way to stay safe and find food in all the snow."

"Why didn't you try to find them?"

"I did," his red eyes were having a difficult time looking at him. It looked like he was reliving a memory. "By the time I had found their tracks, they had gone too far. They broke the bond with me."

"*Can that happen?*" Tyler asked. He was with the guards that were surrounding the area. Max wanted to be as safe as possible, especially with Charlie there.

"*You'd be surprised at what some packs do to misfits,*" Dr. Button answered. He was still checking up on the delta rogue. She seemed friendly, but he wasn't going to let down his guard around any of them.

"*Some packs that are traveling do so for survival,*" Max's father explained. "*Which means that anyone who cannot do their part in obtaining things to survive are useless to keep. There are exceptions of course. But most of the time they try to get rid of the weakest link.*"

"*I wouldn't exactly call him the weakest,*" Sam said. He stood on the opposite side of Tyler, listening in on Max's interrogation.

"Albino's have a history of being weak," Dr. Button said. He obviously seemed fascinated with the man. *"Their main flaw is their eyes. It could also be that this Borealis Pack didn't quite favor him. It seems as though he has some buried memories about them."*

"A yes," Sam sounded annoyed. *"Dr. Button: doctor, scientist, and psychologist extraordinaire."*

He could hear the guards laugh a bit at that through the link. Most of them stayed silent. Max decided to stop his questioning, as the doctor was just finishing up Madeline's check-up. The first three had stayed rather healthy during their journey. Madeline had gotten a wound that had just healed by the look of it. She told them that it was from an attack of some of the other rogues in the area.

Of course, it was. Those animals were wicked, and had always been.

"You've seen them?" he asked her.

"We were trying to pass through the area," Madeline explained. "Jackie just needed somewhere to rest and they didn't like that we were there."

"Where were you then," he asked Alistair.

"This was before we met him." She answered for him. "We met him after we had gotten away from them."

This was strange. These three are from the same pack, and stayed together in their adventures. And then they decide to have Alistair come with them? That wasn't like rogues. It wasn't like werewolves in general. They didn't like strangers.

"Are you saying that you just met him?"

"Not entirely," the woman's golden eyes went defensive as they talked. She must care for him in some way. "He helped us get to your borders and talk to you. We consider him a close friend."

"Why would they trust a stranger that they just met?" Sam asked. He seemed just as confused as Max.

"Why are we trusting strangers that we just met?" Tyler shot back at him.

"We aren't trusting them," Max answered. *"We're just giving them enough space to prove themselves."*

"He has a strange aura about him," Desmond answered. Max had asked him to watch them throughout the night. *"It's oddly comforting. Even the way he talks. It reminds me of the wind."*

"Should I tell your wife that she has competition now?" Ed spoke up for the first time. Max was waiting for him to find somewhere to tell a joke.

"I don't go that way."

"Sure, you don't." There was a mischievous glint to those golden eyes that Max hadn't seen in a while. He missed being around his friends when they didn't have to work all the time.

"What's your age, son?" Dr. Button asked Alistair. It was his turn to get looked over by him. The first thing that Button always does is paperwork, unless it's something dire.

"I...." Those red eyes looked to the ground for a second. When they looked up, he looked confused. Another emotion that Max hadn't seen on him. He wasn't even confused when he realized that Charlie was the Luna. He just accepted it.

"You what?" Dr. Button showed his concern for the stranger. He put a hand on his shoulder to keep him grounded.

"I don't know," he looked towards the doctor. "I lost track of the years long ago."

How...?

What *did* this man know?! Max was going to rip his hair out at this point. How could someone know so little about basic information that involved themselves?

He should have just chased them far away from the territory when he had the chance. But there was some part of him that was happy in the fact that they treated him with respect. They had done what no other rogue had, and asked.

And now he was left dealing with the consequences of allowing them to make his head big.

"What age were you when you were abandoned?" Max's father stepped up to him.

"I was 16, sir," he replied.

"Do you know what year you were born?" Button asked this time.

"I was never told the years," he said.

"*I think I understand him a little better now,*" his father mind linked with him.

"*Mind explaining?*"

"He's lost," he explained. "*It seems like his pack neglected him, used him, and threw him away. They only told him the information they thought was necessary for him to know.*"

"*What pack would do that?*"

"*Some brutal ones,*" he answered. "*There aren't many of them around anymore, but they still exist. If they thought of him as weak, I don't think they cared if he lived or died.*"

"Alistair," Max called him by name this time. The man looked a little surprised to hear it. "What was your profession in the Borealis Pack?"

"I was a warrior," his low voice vibrated through the forest grounds. Everyone's guard was immediately brought back up. A warrior was always trained to be the best in the pack. They were the fighters; the defenders. Max could tell that he had been trained. But hearing him say that he was a warrior was different than coming up with his own hunches.

"*So, they used him to fight and then threw him away?*" Ed asked.

Max stayed silent, even in his mind. He looked hard at the man. He could easily try to attack any pack members and hurt them. He could pick up on details faster than the average wolf and he knew how to fight. He was lucky that he didn't know the land that well. He knew there was a reason why he didn't trust him.

But, if he did prove himself worthy, Max would have another warrior. He would still need some training, but it wouldn't be as difficult as training someone who was completely inexperienced.

All of these rogues had some qualities that could be useful to their pack. Even Jackie. She had told Max before Alistair had come out that she was a nanny at a young age. It would be perfect for the children to have someone else to watch over them.

Those red eyes were mysterious. They held no answers to his questions, for they seem to be looking for those answers themselves. Yet they also seemed to have some knowledge that he wished he could ask him about. He was a clean slate and a wise man at the same time.

"Do you trust me?" Max asked him.

"Yes," his answer was quick, without any uncertainty to it.

"Why?"

"Because the Moon Goddess shines her blessing on you," he smiled at him.

"What do you mean?" This man was getting more confusing the longer he talked to him.

"I can't explain it," he shook his head. "But I trust you."

This level of blind faith was insane. But it made him a little less worried about him. He was still wary of any of these rogues going near the rest of the pack, but he would allow them to stay in their territory for now.

"How did you learn to shift silently?" he went straight onto the next question he had. He needed to get as much information from him as possible. His pack needed to know about these rogues before they could still feel safe. And that was something that even the warriors were dying to know.

Not even the sneakiest wolf could shift silently. The fact that he could was shocking to say the least.

Dr. Button examined him during the last bit of their conversation. He was taking blood samples at that time. Alistair just sat there, completely still as the doctor performed his tasks. He was as trained as a service dog, and twice as calm as one.

"I wasn't taught," he told him. "I had learned simply through my travels. There were many places I had to sneak past."

"Alistair," Dr. Button cut in on the conversation before Max could ask another question. He gave him a rather annoyed look as he did it. "Before you get pelted with more questions, do you remember who your last doctor was?"

"I believe it was Dr. Hyatt," he told him. "I saw him before I was able to transform."

"Alright," he jotted it down in his notebook. "I can try and pull up your medical records to see if we can find any information for you. You have some vision issues, and you're eventually going to need glasses. But, other than that, you seem quite healthy."

"Thank you," he said. The pricks from the needle looked ten times worse on his snowy skin. It bruised badly around the small puncture. But, just as quickly as it had come, it went. They all witnessed the wound heal quickly, looking as if nothing had ever happened to the smooth skin.

"*You trust him, Desmond?*" he asked one of his warriors.

"*I mean, as much as you can trust a complete stranger,*" he answered him. "*He never spoke badly of anyone the whole night. He stayed awake to guard the other three while they slept.*"

"*He may smell like a beta,*" Ed commented. "*But he doesn't act like one. If anything, he acts like a gamma.*"

"He's definitely a beta," Max answered. "I know it. His scent is too strong to be any lower rank. And he's definitely not an alpha because his scent doesn't match most alpha scents."

"Either way, it's good that he doesn't have an ego on him," Ed said. "Even beta's get them. I mean, just look at what Jackie's Beta tried to do to her. But this guy acts as if he's an omega almost. He's just a little more serious. I think they might do our pack some good."

"I just hope Liam wasn't right," Max told him. As much as he had wanted the council to decide on what to do with this group, he hated the idea of letting rogues in. He had grown up his whole life with them coming into his territory and causing havoc and destruction.

And then these four come out of the blue, requesting to join their pack.

He was already given another challenge from the Moon Goddess. As if he needed any more. Max found peace believing that once he dealt with the rogues that were attacking them, things would get better. He planned on getting rid of them by the end of the year, and failure wasn't an option for him.

"You are onto our territory," Max told them. "But not in the Crescent Moon Pack. If you truly want to be, you're going to have to prove you do."

"What do you want us to do?" Madeline, the delta, asked. Her eyes were golden, like Ed's. They were smaller than his, though. She put her shoulders back and stood straight at hearing him say that. He liked that she seemed up to the challenge.

"You will patrol with the rest of my warriors," he told them. "Jackie will be an exception to this. I can't have someone who's pregnant on patrol. You will stay here in this cabin during this time. While you are not on patrol, you are not permitted to go further than a mile perimeter of the cabin."

"What about hunting?" Herb asked.

"All your food will be provided," he told him. "Don't hunt on my territory at all. You won't need to."

"When will we start?" Madeline asked.

"Tomorrow," he said. "Today, you can get accustom to your living spaces. I will give you orders tomorrow morning about your tasks."

He looked at the four of them. They all nodded their head in understanding. Madeline stood straight to show her confidence in her new challenge, but Alistair just made himself look small. His red eyes would still meet his, but there was something about him that Max couldn't pinpoint. It wasn't anything threatening. It just reminded him of Charlie in a way.

He dismissed them into their new cabin. Once they were all inside, he slowly let all the warriors disperse and get back to their normal duties. Some were ordered to make sure to check the cabin every time they passed by it on their rounds. Other than that, he wanted them to be left alone.

The first thing he did when he turned around was grab Charlie. The blond was shocked, but hugged him back happily.

"I have a good feeling about this," he said.

"I hope your feeling is right," Max smiled at him.

He did hope that his feeling was right. Because all he could feel was worry.

This was going to be a difficult year.

CHAPTER 9:

A Challenge for the Luna

"Hey Charlie!" Ian made him jump.

Charlie smiled at his old friend. It was their last day at their house, as the territory meetings were finally over. He was glad that he had been able to talk to him about what had happened just a few months before. He talked to Ben, Ian's mate, to try and clear some things up. Thankfully, there was no hard feelings about how Ian and him acted when they first saw each other at Charlie's old job. It was all just a big misunderstanding.

"Hey Ian," he said. "You got any plans for your last day here?"

"Well, I was going to ask if you wanted to hang out for a bit, but," the man looked at the papers that Charlie was holding in his arms. "It looks like you still have a lot of work ahead of you."

"How about tonight?" he suggested. Unfortunately, this paperwork really couldn't wait. "We could all go out to eat." He had learned quickly that it was best not to plan things for just the two of them. Both Ben and Max get extremely jealous and possessive of the both of them if they even tried.

It wasn't like Charlie was the one who had openly ignored his boy-friend as soon as he saw him. Thankfully Max didn't see it that way. Charlie heard sometime after the incident that the two of them had gotten into a fight. Ian had told Max that he was just using Charlie, which hurt him to hear.

The two of them had gotten over it for the most part, but there were still some problems between them. Thankfully, neither of them let it get in the way of work.

"Yeah!" Ian agreed. "That sounds like a great idea. I'll invite Ben and Lenny."

"I'll see if Max wants to come," he knew that his love was going to say yes, no matter what. "And I'll ask Nick too. He's been super busy with work himself lately."

"Alright," he looked as happy as a child on Christmas morning. "I'll leave you to all the paperwork. I know how annoying that can get."

"It's not annoying," he shook his head. "Just tedious. I can do it easily."

Ian had been the Harvest Moon Pack's step-in Luna while Lenny's mate was sick. She's doing better now, though Charlie hadn't been able to meet her yet. Ian still helped her from time to time.

"It seems like you're made for it," Ian said. "It took me forever to get used to all the paperwork."

"You were never good at paperwork."

"I'm so glad I don't have to do it anymore."

"Don't you still help Wynona? Isn't she still taking care of her newborn?"

"Yeah," he gave a sheepish smile. "But I don't have to do as much. Even if she only takes a little of the workload off, it helps tremendously."

Charlie knew how that felt. It was easy to do, but there was a lot of it when you had to care for and document a whole pack. They were roughly at the three hundred mark as far as the population of the pack went. He had tried his best to learn all of their names at least. It was difficult when there were that many people.

That's why he was glad that Isabelle, Tyler's wife, had offered to help. Unlike the Harvest Moon Pack, their pack had someone who worked as an assistant to the Luna. Isabelle loved paperwork and was desperately trying to get a job that was closer to her children, so Charlie gladly gave her the title. She had helped him tremendously, even when it came to answering questions or giving her own perspective on things.

And she was one of the people who actually liked him.

It wasn't like the pack hated him. Actually, they were all ecstatic when Max and him first took their positions. All of them talked about the great things that they were bound to do. But tensions rose when time started moving along. Since they had to wait to do anything about the rogues, people were getting frustrated. And Charlie's position in those meetings posed a threat to them even getting accomplished.

He should have just stayed quiet through them. If he just tried to mind link with Max what his ideas were, then they could have made more progress much faster. It would have been better if he weren't in those meetings at all, with how the Alpha of the Blood Moon Pack looked at him. He still treated him with respect verbally at least. But there was some tension.

And now with the new rogues that came in, there were going to be more issues. He knew that Max didn't exactly like that they were there. He didn't blame him. The whole pack was not going to like this at all considering their history with rogues. But Charlie couldn't see why they wouldn't give them a chance. They were the only ones who actually asked, after all.

What Liam said had gone through his head over and over again that whole day. It was easier for them to attack the pack, even with the extra guarding. All that did was stretch their warriors out more.

As soon as the pack learned about this they were going to be shocked beyond belief. They were all going to know that it was his idea, of course. And this was all going to be on him if it messed up in any way.

"What are you thinking about this time?" Max's voice came into his thoughts. He still wasn't used to mind linking with people, especially Max. At first it would give him headaches. After a month of it, though, he got the hang of it.

What he didn't like was the randomness of it. Someone popping into your head sporadically throughout the day was a headache all on its own. It didn't help that Max liked to pop into his head whenever he started worrying about something.

"Nothing," he said. *"Just dealing with work."*

"You're a bad liar."

Charlie walked into his office and put his paperwork down on his desk. He had said goodbye to Ian long before reaching the third floor. The Luna's office was across the hall from the Alpha's. It was smaller, but it connected to another large room that held filing cabinets for anyone in the pack that ever lived. Mrs. Locke was insane when it came to organizing. She had turned it into the giant glory that it was.

"Can we talk about it when we're both not up to our elbows in paperwork?"

"As long as you stop overthinking it," Max agreed. *"Maybe we could have a nice hot bath tonight and just relax."*

He liked the idea, but he couldn't forget about the plans that he had just made.

"Ian invited us to go somewhere to eat tonight," he explained. *"I figured, since it was their last night, it would be rude to say no."*

"Is that what you're worried about?"

"No," he frowned. He sat down and tried to focus on his paperwork. But trying to do that while mind linking with someone was impossible. *"I thought we should invite Nick too. I'm sure he would love to get out."*

"That sounds like a great idea," Max said. *"I've been wanting to do something with Nick today anyway."*

"I hope he's okay."

"He'll be fine. I think he just doesn't want to be alone right now."

He really did feel bad for Nick. Out of all of this stress that the pack was under, Nick and Katy were the two people that he could always go to if he wanted to brighten his mood. They were always together; completely inseparable.

And now it was just Nick.

"Well, this dinner should be perfect for him then," Charlie said. The mind link didn't last long as they both had a lot of work to do. But the promise of something fun for once kept him going.

He was glad that he didn't have to tell Ian and Lenny about the rogues that had come. Max had decided to keep them a secret from the pack until they left. It would only bring about more questions from both the pack as well as Lenny. They wanted to wait and see how well these strange rogues would do before telling any of their ally packs anyway.

He couldn't put a finger on why, but he liked those rogues. They all seemed like they fit in with their pack. Jackie reminded him of a lot of the mothers here. Herb talked like he worked all the time and loved what he did. And Madeline had a dedication to her job too. If there was one trait that this pack seemed to all share, it was their dedication to their work. Whether it be something as small as washing dishes, or as grand as guarding the territory, everyone worked tirelessly for their family.

Alistair was the one that he could tell everyone was worried about. He had never met someone who was albino. It was shocking to see at first. But everything about him was calm and controlled. He looked like he had a lot more strength than he put off, but there was something in his eyes that reached to his heart. He wished he could have gotten a better look, but as soon as his eyes reached him, he put his head down. He saw fear for a split second in the man. It shocked him that he would be afraid of him. Although, it could have been more of a fear of Max.

He also was the only one that didn't question Charlie was the Luna. He was used to people asking questions about that or giving him strange glances. But Alistair just accepted it. Max told him that he was confused as to why he was so accepting himself, but they would have to ask about it later. It was mid-morning when they left that little cabin. And Max probably wouldn't let him go to see them again tomorrow.

A knock on the door snapped him out of his work. Looking at the clock, he had been doing his paperwork for about two hours now. His stack had depleted quite a lot though. Isabelle was off to deal with some issues with her baby sitter, but she would be back soon.

"Come in," he said. He was hoping that it was someone who was going to be able to get him out of his thoughts. It would be nice if it was one of the members asking to talk to him about something pack related. He seemed to handle that well, and it got his mind out of the crazy spiral that it always seemed to go in when he was stressed.

Instead, it was the last person he would expect to see. Liam walked into his office and took a seat in front of his desk. There were no words between them as the old man got comfortable and leaned back in his seat.

"You know there was a reason as to why I said what I said at the meeting last night, right?" He got straight to the point. As much as they talked in the meetings, Charlie rarely talked to the man outside of them. It didn't quite seem like there was a difference between the way he talked in different settings, though, so Charlie couldn't say much about it.

"I wasn't trying to make you feel like your opinion didn't matter," he told him. "I honestly love when you bring up issues with plans. It allows room for us to make a better one."

"I know, Charlie, I know," Liam sighed. For once, he didn't seem so menacing. Instead, he seemed like an old man. "Do you realize all the issues that could arise from something like this?"

"I understand," he told him. "That's why I suggested the outer cabins. We won't even need to stretch out our warriors that way." He hoped that was the case at least. It was still difficult trying to bury his doubts about his own plan.

"I don't mean issues for the pack," Liam sat straight at that. "I mean issues for you."

"How would they be an issue for me?" Charlie asked. He was curious as to why the man was even concerned about him. As much as he was great to debate with at their meetings, he didn't think they had gotten close enough for Liam to be worried for his sake.

"Charlie," he started. "As much as I've been hard on you throughout the months, I don't hate you."

"You don't?" he couldn't help but ask. Liam and him had always had issues, ever since he had first met him. Why was he acting like this now?

"Well, you actually do take everyone's opinion into account," he grumbled. It was too obvious that he wasn't used to giving compliments. "As much as I hate that my ideas get shot down all the time, you've done well to find a middle ground for everyone."

"Thanks," he said. That was the first compliment that he had gotten from him. He'd have to write down the date and time. Charlie almost laughed at the thought. "Your ideas are just a little too brutal sometimes, though. The pack doesn't seem to want that anymore."

"I know," he waved it off. "That's not the point of this. The point I was trying to make is that you just put your reputation at risk by doing this thing with these rogues."

Now it was Charlie's time to sigh. He really hoped he could just take a compliment from this conversation and have that carry him throughout the rest of the day. It would make everything so much easier.

That relaxing bath that Max was talking about didn't seem like a bad idea.

"We couldn't just kill them, though," he rubbed his eyes. They were getting tired from all the papers. "That would destroy the morale of the warriors."

"The Crescent Moon Pack hasn't accepted a rogue since my father's time," he explained. "And it was *that* very rogue that caused our first fall in the pack."

"They aren't violent," Charlie argued. He knew that they weren't.

"Not even that beta?"

"He had complied to every one of Max's demands, and answered every one of his questions honestly," he looked at those purple eyes seriously. Max's family had a history of those eyes. "Only two questions did he hesitate on, and that's because he didn't know the answer."

"He didn't hesitate at all?" Liam furrowed his eyebrows.

"He answered them with such surety," Charlie answered. "Look, I know my reputations on the line, but I don't believe these four are going to cause us any harm. They're different from the rogues that come to attack us."

He had personal experience from those wolves, even if it was just a couple of instances. Charlie could tell the difference between the skinny rogues that looked ready to kill anything and the sad ones that had followed in a single file line just to try and find a better life for themselves.

He still couldn't get those red eyes out of his head whenever he thought about all of this.

"It could be a trick from them."

"Then Max would be able to tell that they were lying somewhere along the road," Charlie told the old man. "And Alpha Leo was there as well, to try and get a good reading on all of them."

"Hmph," he slouched into his chair again. "This is the strangest thing. It's just not something that rogues do. If they seek sanctuary, it's usually either a trap or they don't like staying tied down and run again."

"I don't think any of them wanted to keep running," Charlie told him. "Maybe if you meet them you might get a better idea of what I'm talking about."

"When are you allowing the pack to meet them?"

"When they have proven themselves trustworthy," he answered. "We aren't taking the risk of them being too close right now. Max wants to see how well they do on patrol."

"At least you're playing it safe," he stood up from his chair. "Just remember that you can't keep it a secret from the pack for too long. That'll start more distrust. I know that Max will take the blame if this plan messes up, but everyone will know that it was your idea. Be careful."

"I will," he told the old man. Liam sighed and said his farewell. It wasn't until the door closed that Charlie let those words truly sink in.

He wasn't sure if he was meant for this leadership position. He shouldn't have said anything at the meeting. But his instinct had told him to find a medium in the extremes that they were shouting. And his heart wanted to give them a try.

Not even Max wanted this. He could tell just by how he was acting towards Alistair. He didn't like them. He was scared of them hurting the pack. And Charlie didn't blame him, knowing the history of rogues with their pack. That was another reason why he didn't want to talk to him about it. He felt like he was all alone in thinking that this plan could actually work.

"You look like somethings bothering you," Isabelle came in. Charlie was glad to see her. As Tyler's mate, they balanced their responsibilities so that each would be able to work and be able to care for their children. They had wanted to try for another child, but thought it best to wait. There was a lot of things going on with the pack. They thought it best if they waited until all of it blew over. Maybe Charlie wouldn't need as much help then.

"You could say that," he told her, rubbing his eyes again.

"Do you want to talk about it?" she asked. She always looked so professional with everything she wore. Her black hair was always done up in a bun with some strings coming out of it. It made her look so elegant.

"You'd have to be able to keep a secret," Charlie ran his hand through his hair. He needed to tell someone, and he was curious as to what Isabelle's opinion was going to be.

She just nodded and closed the door all the way. The offices around there were almost sound proof. The meeting room was the true place to tell secrets, but he didn't have time to sneak over there. He still had so much paperwork to do before he even thought about going out to eat with Ian.

He told her what happened with the rogues that requested membership and the council's decision. She seemed shocked at the whole story once he was done with it.

"We never have rogues request to join our pack," She shook her head. "That is very strange."

"That's what we all thought," he told her. "To make things more interesting, one of them is a beta, and an albino."

Isabelle froze for a moment, mouth closing before she even started to talk. At just the mention of the description he gave, her dark eyes seemed to be lost in a memory that was off limits to him. He was immediately curious as to what was going on in that head of hers.

"Albino?" she asked.

"Yeah," he told her. "He's the real reason why everyone's so worried about this."

"What's he like?"

"Honestly, we don't know much about him," he shrugged. "He doesn't even know how old he is."

"He doesn't?" she scrunched up her face in pain. "How does he not know his age?"

"He said that he lost track of time during his travels," he explained to her. "And he doesn't know how long he's been travelling either."

"That's probably why they don't trust him," Isabelle said. "It's hard to trust someone you don't know."

"Dr. Button's already working on it a little," he said. He was more concerned with his assistant than the rouges at the moment, though. "Are you okay?"

"Yeah, why?" she answered all too quickly. Her whole body was tense, and her face was emotionless.

"You just don't look like you're okay," he grabbed her hand and started rubbing it. "Did I say something?"

"No," she shook her head. Her hand was pulled away as she grabbed some paperwork that needed to be filed. "I just got lost in thought."

He knew that she was lying. But he wasn't going to push it. Maybe she would tell him eventually, maybe she wouldn't. As curious as she was about Alistair, he was hoping that she would tell him her views on the issue. But it didn't seem like she was going to talk about it now.

Instead of dwelling on it, Charlie went back to doing his paperwork. He still had a long way to go before he was finished with them all. There was a lot to catch up on.

While he worked, his mind continued to think about the rogues. He remembered hearing everyone say that the Moon Goddess always challenged the leaders of the packs during the beginning of their reign, so as to prepare them for any rough times ahead. Was this his challenge? To get this pack to see the good in something that they thought was bad?

If so, he hoped he could do it.

CHAPTER 10:

The Patrol

"That was easier than I thought it was going to be," Madeline sat down on one of the beds inside the cabin. "I think that request was the best thing we could have done."

"For us maybe," Herb told her. "The Alpha practically tore Alistair a new one."

"He's a protective leader," Alistair told him.

"I know that," Herb said. "But why would he be so hostile towards you? He wasn't nearly as bad around the rest of us."

"That's how they always react," he shrugged. "I come off as intimidating to most."

"But you're the kindest person we've met so far," Jackie said. She was resting her hand on her stomach as she sat down. "How can you be intimidating?"

"I can see it," Madeline nodded. "He's strong, and his wolf is pretty big considering most werewolf sizes. Not to mention he stands out a little bit."

"I suppose that answers it then," Alistair smiled. "I never knew the true reason, other than perhaps my strength. I simply knew that it happened."

"Well, you never told us you were a warrior in your old pack." She looked at him with curious eyes.

"I don't like thinking about those things." He looked out the window of their new home. At least he now had shelter from the sun. It gave him discomfort being away from the cool breeze that always helped to guide him, but he was used to discomfort. He had dealt with that his whole life.

"Were they bad times?" Herb asked. It shocked him just how intrigued everyone was about him. No one had ever asked him so many questions, other than those that regarded his appearance.

"Yes," he answered simply. Memories threatened to invade his thoughts, dampening his accomplishments with their black spindles of poison. Yes, this Alpha seemed to be guarded around him. But that did not mean that the world was ending. He could take another test from the Moon Goddess. He had gone through plenty of her tests as he journeyed.

It worried him that all of his tests wound up being more difficult than the last, but he had high hopes for this one. After this, he should be able to be at peace at last.

The pull was still there too. It was much stronger now that he was settled into the territory. He wished he could run towards it, like he was doing before. He wanted to find out what had pulled him so far, for so long. It had just started a season ago. The mystery of it was what kept him going. He needed to figure out what it was that pulled him so.

But it would have to wait. He didn't want to find the source of this pull right before getting slaughtered by this pack for breaking the rules that the Alpha set in place.

The next few days were simple enough. They each had a set time in which they would run around a part of the territory, making sure that no one passed through. Jackie was the only exception, and the doctor had been keen on visiting her every day to make sure that her child was healthy.

He met the other leaders of the pack through his patrols. Ed, the Gamma, would always be the one bringing them their meals. They had excellent food. He had forgotten how great human food was. One day, he was accompanied by the Delta, a man named Sam. He took a liking to Jackie and Herb. It was easy to see that he was a family man.

Tyler, the Beta, was the one who he patrolled with. He reminded him much of the Alpha. His face was always serious around him. And he only talked when he needed to. Alistair enjoyed that more than they probably thought. He liked the silence, for through it, he was able to hear the wind speak.

They patrolled at night. The darkness never frightened him. His mother had always told him that the Moon Goddess was watching over them at night. She would tell him that on the nights he would wake up from a nightmare.

The doctor was right about his eyes. They were never the best. Alistair had always depended on his ears and his nose to help him in dangerous situations. But he was grateful that he wasn't blind. Then he would never be able to see the colors of the world. He loved colors. They helped bring everything to life. Even the night time had a color to it.

This forest had to be one of his favorites, and it wasn't just because of the pull that kept tempting him. The water was clean and light blue, with plenty of fish in them. And the trees were thick and reached out to the sky. The ground was soft when they weren't by the rocky areas. He would love to explore the area more.

The air was nice here, too. Even with all the cities around, the forest wasn't overwhelmed with the sounds or the smells of it. Although the smell of city food was always a good one for Alistair.

He really loved human food. They all had different tastes that made them unique. Even if it was the same dish. If someone else was cooking it, there would be something different about it every time. He remembered when he first set out on his adventure and he would try to eat all the different kinds of leaves in the first forest he went into. He was lucky enough that he threw up most of them. He learned the lesson to watch what he ate quickly.

That seemed like such a long time ago. Instead of the snowy terrain that he was born in, he had travelled somewhere that was completely different. Instead of there being only one color to look at, there were countless. Instead of their just being snow and some trees, there were trees everywhere, and dirt.

He wondered what the winter would be like here.

For now, he would be happy with only being allowed along the edges of the territory. He wasn't picky. It felt nice to be running with a cause too.

Another thing that he enjoyed about this forest was all the different colors that these wolves were. Tyler's wolf, for instance, was a bluish grey. It fit his human half well. Even his wolf looked calculated. He traveled through each area gracefully, knowing all of the cracks and crevices of the forest.

That was one thing that Alistair was never able to do. He never stayed in a forest long enough to really know it. He prayed that it wouldn't be the case with this forest. It truly fascinated him.

A slight change of wind made Alistair halt. It was the third day of his patrol. The other two had gone well, but he sensed something wrong today. With the wind change, there was a new scent that he didn't recognize as anyone familiar. It was just a small hint of one, that disappeared as fast as he had caught onto it, but Alistair had learned to take those smells with heed.

How would he tell this to the Beta? He couldn't mind link with him. And shifting to his human form would make him vulnerable to them. Thankfully, Tyler noticed that he had stopped and turned around to see what the issue was.

He sneezed, wrinkling his nose and shaking his head. Tyler cocked his head. Obviously, he wasn't used to trying to communicate like this. But it didn't take long before some other warriors were over there, trying to see what the problem was. Alistair was hoping that they would take his stance as a hint. He wasn't sure if the Beta was going to attack him as punishment for not following orders, so he put his head low to the ground.

He recognized most of the warriors by now, although he did not know their names. The twin wolves were there, looking just as confused as the Beta.

Then he heard something. A twig snap nearby. They were right by the border to the territory. His ears perked up and he lifted his head towards the sound. The rest of the warriors followed his actions.

It was coming from the other side.

It was dark out that night, as clouds from summer rain had covered the dim sky. But he didn't need his sight to hear the faint breathing of a wolf on the other side of the border. He could tell it was a wolf from the sound that it made when breathing out of its nose. It was faint, almost like the wind itself.

Then he heard another.

And another.

Alistair sneezed again and growled lowly. He hoped that the pack didn't take it personally. He faced the invisible wall, but his growl was quiet; a subtle warning to see how far these strangers would go. The other warriors were still confused. With all the wind changes, he knew that it was difficult to pick up on scents. But he could hear breathing. And that he was sure of.

There was a calm, where everything was silent except for his low growling and the wind. The forest was frozen in time as they all waited for something to happen. Someone had to make the first move.

He couldn't see anything but a blur, but he knew who they were going to go for. As soon as he heard them move in for their attack, Alistair jumped in front of the Beta. Just as he thought, the rogue bit into his back with a ferocious growl. He yelped out in pain, but he wouldn't let the beast do any more damage. He thrashed back and bit into its leg.

There were only three of them this time, but their fighting skills were good. The other two had gone for the rest of the warriors. But the first rogue had already failed in his surprise attack. Alistair had gotten a few more wounds before being able to get him on the ground. Tyler went straight for the neck. The rogue yelped and struggled as the Beta snapped the thick bone. Alistair had been pressing down on the wolf the whole time so that it wouldn't be able to escape.

That wolf must have been the strongest of the three. For the other two were already dead by the time that they were done. Their dead bodies the cold reminder of why this pack had such an issue with rogues. Alistair understood them more now.

None of them had bad wounds. Most were shallow. They were all healing already. Alistair knew that his would take a while to heal, but he could still stand and move around. The warriors watched him curiously. He tried to show them that he was fine, but he wasn't sure if they understood.

He shook his coat, fur flying off him. His winter coat was shedding. Which could make the healing of his wound longer if it got in it. The heat of his coat was the most discomforting out of everything else.

The warriors looked to the Beta. It was obvious that they were talking amongst themselves. The twin wolves went up to him and looked at his wounds. He let them. He trusted them, as they had never done anything to show harm towards him.

They licked the wound, trying their best to clean it. After a few minutes, however, they moved away. Tyler looked at him and motioned him forward. They set a steady pace, walking more than running. It didn't take long for him to realize that they were taking him back to his cabin. He was sure that the moon had traveled far across the sky, but he had no longing to stop his work. He wanted to keep patrolling with them.

But a wounded warrior is never a good warrior. He remembered being told that a long time ago. He didn't like that memory. But he would take the message from it.

The cabin came into view. It was a nice home to call his. He realized quickly just how more comfortable beds were than the forest floors. He slept in the afternoon, as it was the best way to be sure that he could do his job to the best of his abilities. However, with the rest of his friends doing different shifts, and Jackie needing special attention, it was difficult to rest without getting woken up at least once. He mainly napped throughout the day.

The last couple days he had come home to calm doors, with the promise of breakfast soon. He would be lying if he said that he didn't enjoy his living conditions. Even if he wasn't fully trusted, he could live like this comfortably.

They treated him better than most.

When the cabin came into view this time, however, it wasn't calm like it had been. In front of the cabin stood a sleepy Madeline, looking worriedly at him. The Alpha was there too, with the doctor next to him.

"Change," he ordered.

He didn't like changing into his human form when wounded. It took him longer to heal that way. But maybe this would keep the fur from getting in his wound. That was the one thing that Alistair was worried about.

He obeyed. His human form looked worse than his wolf. He could feel the blood trickle down his side. Transforming must have opened it back up. He could also feel the wound that was on his thigh more in this form, as he was only on two legs now.

The Alpha then did something that he wasn't expecting. He walked up to him and wrapped a piece of cloth around him. His eyes were softer, if by just a little, than when he had seen him last. He looked worried.

"Can you walk?"

"Yes," he nodded. He had never had an Alpha be worried for him. It surprised him.

"Good," the man put an arm around his shoulders. "Then come inside. You need to get treated."

He nodded and walked into the cabin. The wound on his thigh made him limp a little, but it was tolerable. He had felt much worse pain.

The warriors that had come with him had shifted as well. Alpha Max threw them some shorts. It was just three of them. The rest had gone back to their duties. It was interesting to see the twin wolves as humans. But Alistair couldn't focus on them right then. They followed him into the cabin.

Herb and Jackie were inside, looking concerned as well. As soon as Jackie saw him, tears started forming in her eyes.

"Alistair!" She would have jumped up if it weren't for Herb holding her down. "Are you okay?"

"I'll be fine," he smiled. He wasn't used to people of his own kind being concerned for him. Especially not people that he had just met. "I've been through worse."

"You have to tell me how you did that!" He looked to see one of the twins looking at him in wonder. His dark blue eyes sparkled in a way that made him look like a child.

"Did what?"

"He's not explaining anything until I treat him." The doctor put a hand on his shoulder and put pressure on it. He sat down on the bed and allowed the doctor to work. He learned to appreciate doctors. They had always taken care of him.

"I would have healed faster if I was in my wolf form," he said. He knew he shouldn't have said anything that sounded rude, but he hated how much blood his human form always lost. It left him feeling dizzy and fatigued.

"If you were in your wolf form, your wounds would have gotten infected by your own fur," the doctor said. He stayed silent as his wounds got cleaned up. The dirt from the fight had also caked onto his human body. He wished he could clean himself.

Once the wounds were cleaned and inspected, they were wrapped. It didn't take too long. He only had two deep wounds. The rest had already healed. The one on his back was going to take the longest. He had let the wolf sink his teeth deep into him in order to protect the Beta. He should still be able to do his next patrol, though.

"Well, it seems as though your immune system is working well," Dr. Button said. The cloth that the Alpha had wrapped around him now simply covered his private parts. "Your wounds should heal quickly. Though I still suggest you take a day to rest."

"Can we ask him questions now?" The warrior perked up again. Him and his twin were rather short, for men. But their muscles showed that they were a worthy foe if threatened.

"So, he's going to be okay?" Madeline asked the doctor. She completely ignored the twin.

"He's going to be fine, dear," Dr. Button assured her.

"These two warriors are Ray and Desmond," Alpha Max introduced the two of them. "I know that Alistair has met Tyler, but I know that some of you haven't. He's my Beta." He introduced Tyler and the twins to their group as well.

"Nice to finally meet you as a human," Desmond said. There was a small part in their hair that helped him tell the difference between the two. "Now, can I ask you a question?"

"Besides the one you already have?" Alistair couldn't help but smile. The man had been practically bouncing ever since he got inside.

He was surprised to hear a snicker come from Tyler. It was a small one, but he could hear it.

"How were you able to tell that those rogues were coming?" Alpha Max asked. He sat on the other bed, right next to him. His purple eyes looked curious.

"I heard them," he told him.

"How?" Ray asked this time, he seemed calmer than his brother, but still just as curious. "Desmond and I have the best hearing and we couldn't pick up anything."

"I heard them breathe," he explained. "Every creature has a different way they breathe, especially if it's through their nose."

"You heard them breathe?" Madeline looked just as shocked as the rest of them. "How the hell do you hear a rogue that's sneaking breathe?"

"That's what I want to know," Max said.

"I listen to the wind all the time," he told them. "I believe that's how I started noticing the difference in how they breathe. I've had to run away from enemy wolves in the past as well."

"That takes a lot of discipline," Dr. Button said. "It's not often that a wolf can train their ears to hear something like that. Usually, we go by sense of smell."

"The wind can keep the scents away if they are sneaking," he said. "That's what was working against us in that fight."

"How did you see them attack me?" Tyler asked this time. He had been silent most of the night until now.

"I didn't," he told the Beta. "I just knew they were going to attack you first."

"How?" Tyler asked.

"You were the strongest one in the group," he told him. "If they had the advantage of surprise on their side, the strongest one should be attacked first."

"And you went in front of him and took the bite?" Max looked for affirmation. Even Jackie and Herb looked shocked at the information that he was giving them.

"Yes."

"Why?"

"Because it was my duty," he told him.

"Duty?" He raised an eyebrow. "Is that what your last pack taught you?"

"Yes," he lowered his head. He didn't like it when the Alpha brought up his past so much. He understood why he did, but he didn't wish to relive it.

There was some silence in the cabin. He was sure that the Alpha was talking to his pack through their mind link. He kept his head low throughout this. He did not wish to see the anger that might be in the Alpha's eyes.

"You did a good job," Alpha Max finally said. He looked up to see that he wasn't angry. "Get some rest for now. You have the next day off."

They all left in silence. Dr. Button made sure to tell him to stay off his feet until he had healed completely. He could see that Jackie would try and make sure of that. She still seemed quite worried for him.

He was more in shock at what he just heard. Alphas never complimented him, or told him he did a great job. No one did.

No one ever treated him like anything other than a beast.

CHAPTER 11:

Mint and Fresh Snow

The hustle and bustle of the kitchen was always a welcome sound. The chaos that came from making a bunch of different food at once was what made the place feel like home for him. Aldi had told him that the kitchen, even if it seemed crazy, always had an order to it. It only took him a few months to understand what he meant.

When Nick was first starting out as a chef there, he had no idea what to start with. It was overwhelming when you looked at all the orders that came in from all the people in the mansion. They all wanted something different. Parties were a completely different story, but the everyday life could easily overwhelm anyone who was working in the kitchen.

It was like its own little dance. And it didn't take too long for him to get into the groove. His father always told him that the world was a song, just waiting to be danced to. He really did love the stage.

"Don't you think it's something to worry about though?" Alan said. He was another chef on the morning shift. "I mean, we've never welcomed rogues onto our territory."

"And we've never had a male Luna," Nick argued with him. "And we've never had a delta as a chef. There's always firsts for everything, Alan."

The kitchen was also the main gossip hub. All the workers went there to hear the latest news on everything and everyone. Even with all the sounds and clashing of pans that came from the kitchen, you could always hear at least one person talking about something that happened.

"But they're rogues!" The man grabbed a pan and slammed it on the stove. He was on egg duties. And there were a lot of people asking for omelets today. "Why should we trust them?"

"I don't know," Nick shrugged. "Max said that it was agreed upon by the council. They hadn't even gotten on our territory until they were let in."

Max had made the announcement about the rogues being allowed a chance to prove themselves about a week ago. It was the day after the Harvest Moon Pack left. He told everyone that they had asked to join the pack, and the council agreed to try and test them. It seemed a little risky to him, but he trusted Max and the council.

"Did the council really agree on it?" the blue-eyed man muttered. "Or was it just Charlie convincing them?"

"You really think it was all just Charlie's idea?" Nick cocked an eyebrow. "Man, you must think that pigs can fly, huh?"

"He's the only one who would come up with an idea like that!"

"I hear that the rogues are actually pretty good people," one of the dishwashers said. She was a blonde named Daphne. "The warriors talk well about them."

"I heard that one of them saved Tyler," another dishwasher said.

Remember how he said that this was the main gossip hub?

"How did he save Tyler?" Alan shook his head in disbelief.

"He went in front of him and saved him from an attack," they told him.

"Desmond was telling me that he could hear the rogues breathing from the other side of the boundary lines," Nick added. He liked hanging out with Desmond and Ray. They had been really interested in the rogues lately, though. There was something about one of them that they couldn't figure out apparently.

"I just don't like this," Alan shook his head. "It's right when we're trying to push them out of here, too."

"Max wouldn't let them come in if he thought they were going to harm us," Nick assured him. "You know how he is about that."

"I know, but what if he's just blinded by the Luna?"

"Alan, I don't get you," he shook his head. "Just a few months ago, you were talking about how he was going to be the best Luna for our pack. Now you're saying that he's blinding Max? You need to make up your mind, man."

"Nothing's been happening!" he argued. "We've been talking about dealing with these rogues, and instead of doing anything about them, we're inviting them in?"

"These aren't the same ones that were attacking us though," Daphne said. "One of them is a winter wolf. And another one's pregnant."

"And look what's happening with the other rogues that have been attacking us?" Alan sneered at her. "Nothing."

"No one's hurt right now," Nick told him. "That's what you should really be thinking about."

"No," Aldi's voice carried over to their side of the kitchen. "What you two should really be worried about is finishing those orders."

"What do you think about this all, Aldi?" Alan asked.

"I think that your eggs are burning," he grumbled. It was Aldi's last day until his vacation with his wife. Nick was sure that he was grateful for the time off. The workers were slowly getting their vacations in, little by little. Nick didn't want one, though. He'd much rather keep working through it all.

He still had that car to save up for, after all.

The morning went by with more talk about the rogues. There were rumors galore about them, but Nick knew which ones to filter out. There were always crazy ones that people liked to say. Whether it be the way they talk about the rumors, or just who the one saying it is, he could tell for the most part which was true and which wasn't.

He tuned most of it out, though. He wasn't worried about it. They all grew up with Max. They knew how protective he was of the pack. It didn't matter that he found his mate and was the Alpha now. He hadn't changed a bit.

They still talked a lot actually. He'd eat his lunches with him and Charlie. Max said that it got them both out of their offices for a little. And Charlie still had an issue with forgetting to eat when he was diving into work. It was a good thing that Isabelle was there to help keep track of that.

He was glad that their workload had lifted some. The couple had been so stressed out with all of the meetings that had taken place. After a few days of catching up on paperwork, they were finally back on their normal routine. Which meant that Charlie could finally start making pies with him again.

He was sure that Ryan had missed him the past month. That human chef was enjoying the little business that he had finally gotten. If it weren't for Max's father helping him buy it, he would have been trying to find a crappy job elsewhere. The restaurant he used to work at, the one that Charlie was at too, closed down quickly after all the workers quit. It was good to see some karma taking place.

"Hey, Nick," Daphne grabbed some of the dirty dishes next to him. "Have you heard anything from Katy?"

The pancake he was flipping almost fell onto the stove. He had been so lost in work and his daydreams that he almost forgot about her. It wasn't like he was trying to forget his best friend. He was just...

Sad.

And he was really trying to not be sad.

"No," he answered. He tried to force a smile. "She's probably just getting used to that other pack."

She had told him that she was going to call him every day. She told him that the night she left. But she didn't. And not having her voice in his mind was making him spiral in a greater depression than he already was in.

"You should have gotten her when you had the chance man," Alan shook his head.

"How many times do I have to tell you people," he shook his head. "We're just friends! Does that compute in that hollowed out head of yours?"

Alan rolled his eyes. "Men and women that aren't related can't be friends," was his answer.

"I think that's just you, bud," he said. "And just because you're upset that you haven't found your mate yet, doesn't mean that I should have tried to take someone else's."

Alan was 35 years old and mateless. There weren't any others in the pack that were at that age, and he had tried dating others to no avail. Everyone tried to be there for him, but he was more of a loner than anything else. Nick thought it just made him grumpy.

Oh jeez.

He was going to be mateless the rest of his life.

Did that mean he was going to be grumpy like Alan?

Goddess, he didn't want that to ever happen.

"At least then she wouldn't be with some asshole."

"No, she would," Nick answered. He was just cleaning up his station now. "I would just be used as a chew toy for him."

Before they could say anything else, the door opened and in popped Ed. It seemed like his pack duties had lessened quite a lot after the meetings were over. Ed usually came around both breakfast and lunch time to get food for the rogues. He was just the person Nick was looking for to change the subject.

"Hey Ed!" he grabbed a container. He had kept it in the fridge that whole morning. "I have something for you."

"Great!" Ed smiled. "I actually don't have that much time today. I'm running a bit late."

"Hey, I get it," he shrugged. His heart sank at the fact that he was going to be alone the rest of the day. "Just bring this to the pregnant lady. It's what my mom always drank when she was pregnant with me. She told me it worked wonders."

"Oh, thanks," Ed grabbed the container. He was putting the rest of the food in a large lunch pail. Nick usually got the pail all set up for him beforehand, but it had gotten a little busy that morning. And he had gotten lost in thought.

He had been lost in thought a lot lately. It didn't help that it was getting more difficult to sleep. He didn't want to sleep at night. The moon was oddly comforting. It made him happy, even if only a little. So, he stayed up late, and got up early. It usually resulted in him taking a nap in the afternoon. But he always tried to see if anyone wanted to hang out first.

"No problem," he smiled at him. "Here, I'll help you load it into the Jeep."

"Sounds good to me," They walked out of the kitchen together. It was the end of his shift and he had already cleaned up his station, so there was no need to stay there any longer than needed. When they got far enough away, Ed put an arm around his shoulders. "Is Alan being an ass again?"

"When is Alan not an ass?" Nick joked. "He's a great chef at least."

"Yeah," Ed sighed. "There's always those people in every pack, I suppose."

"Oh, it's every family, really," he said. "There's always the ones that won't agree with others. Just like there are always drunk uncles and grandpas that tell old war stories."

Having a big family helped him understand how the pack worked. He had plenty of family members. Some of them didn't like him, and some did. The point was that they all got together when shit really hit the fan.

"So," Nick broke the silence once more. "What's the rush this time?"

"Max wants me to try and warm these guys up a little," Ed said. "You know, get them more comfortable so they'll talk a little more about themselves. That was kind of the whole purpose to me bringing them food every day."

"And they still haven't talked to you?" It was surprising to hear that. Everyone warmed up to Ed easily. He was as easy to talk to as Charlie was.

"They've said bits and pieces," Ed explained. "It's a little complicated."

"You could always start it off with stories about us, you know," he pondered out loud. "Maybe if you answered some of their questions, they'd be more open to answering some of yours."

"I could try that," Ed frowned. "But they see me as one of the leaders of the pack, so they don't act as normally as you and I would around each other. They just see me as someone trying to pry into their lives."

"Ah," he said. "That's a tricky one. If they saw how you acted around everyone else, it might help. But I doubt Max would want anyone else going to see them."

"Hmm," Ed paused in his actions. They had just finished loading the food and securing it in place. It needed to be nice and snug for all the off-roading that was required for getting to those cabins.

Before Nick could ask him what he was thinking, he saw those golden eyes sparkle and that old mischievous grin spread across his face for the first time in a long while.

Oh no.

"Why are you giving me that look?" Nick asked. When Ed pointed that look at someone, it usually meant that he had a plan, and wasn't going to back down from it.

"You're coming with me," Ed's smile got wider.

"I'm going with you?" Nick asked incredulously. "To talk to the rogues?"

"Yup!"

"Isn't Max going to get mad?" He stood by the passenger door. It seemed better than going back to his room and trying to take a nap, but he really didn't want to go against an order.

"Not as long as you're with me," Ed got in the driver's side. The passenger door had already been open as some of the food had been put at the foot of it. "I'll just tell him that it was a strategy to get them to talk. He'll be fine with it."

"I don't know," he warily looked at the man. He wasn't sure about these rogues. It was in a werewolf's nature to hate rogues, especially when they had been threatening their pack for ages. He remembered almost being attacked by one once. Max had to save him that time, too.

"Come on, Nick," Ed begged. "I know you're just going to be bored in your room anyway, why not go on an adventure?"

"Because I'm just a tiny omega?" he felt tiny at that moment. He was tall and lanky. But he wasn't strong, and he wasn't good at fighting. It wasn't in him.

"I got you, Nick," Ed stretched his hand out to him from the driver's side. "If anything happens, which it won't, you'll have me, plus a couple other warriors to protect you. They patrol that place too, you know."

He couldn't help but let his friend convince him. There was a part of him that was so curious as to who the people were that made Max want to take a chance on them. He always did love meeting new people anyway.

And it wasn't like he had any other plans. Max and Charlie were going to be busy the whole day.

They didn't talk much as Ed drove them to the cabin. It was one of the few at the far end of their territory. The Jeep that Ed was using didn't have AC, so they opened the windows. It made everything ten times louder, but the wind felt nice going through his hair.

He felt nervous the closer they got. But there was another feeling that was foreign to him. There was something about where they were going that made him wish that Ed could go faster.

The smells were so strange when they got near. There were four main scents to the cabin, but the one that he focused on the most was a minty scent. It smelt like fresh snow and pine. He had known the smell of snow in this forest his whole life, but, for some reason, this scent was different from those winters here. It made him feel cold, and warmed his heart at the same time.

He wished he could have a candle of that.

"Alright," Ed parked the car. "We're here."

They opened the doors and started getting out the food. As soon as they did, one of the strangers were already coming outside to greet them.

"Perfect timing," she said. It was a woman with gold eyes just like Ed! "I'm starving!"

It seemed like she hadn't noticed him yet, as her main focus was on the food that Ed was holding. Ed had a protective tension to him. It helped Nick understand why they might be so difficult to get comfortable around them.

Sometimes, you just had to leave stuff like this to an omega.

"Good," Nick answered with a smile. "Cus it's nice and hot."

"Oh, I'm sorry," the woman put a hand to her heart. "I didn't see you there."

"Hey, it's always hard to focus on an empty stomach," he shrugged. Omega's scents were so small usually that it was easily masked with other smells. Especially if you were hungry. "I'm Nick, one of the chefs of the pack."

"Madeline," she smiled at him. "I would shake your hand, but it seems like it's full."

"Don't worry about it," he shrugged as he carried the food inside. Ed was right behind him. "I'm not the formal type. A simple 'hi' is fine with me."

The inside of the cabin had all kinds of smells to it. It felt homely in a way. Usually, these cabins didn't. It was neat that they had made due with what they were given.

"You must be the lucky lady expecting," he smiled at a young woman who was sitting on one of the beds. She was a pretty little omega, with soft eyes and a kind smile.

"I'm glad you can tell," she joked. Her voice sounded like honey. He could see why her mate was holding her so protectively. "It's nice to meet you, I'm Jackie."

"And I'm Herb," her mate said. He looked like he was trying to be respectful at least. His wilder look made him seem more scarier than he came off as, though.

"I'm Nick, one of the chefs of the pack," he nodded at them. "Actually, I wanted to give you guys something." He rummaged through the containers of food until he had found the one that was his.

"What is this?"

"It's something my mom made," he told her. "She drank it when she was still pregnant with me. She said that it helped her through her pregnancy. I hope it does the same for you."

"Thank you," she smiled. "I hope I can meet your mom eventually so I can thank her as well."

"Oh, I'm sure she'd love you," he said. "She comes off as a bit frank though, just as a fair warning."

The sound of one of the doors of the cabin opening snapped him out of his conversation. He stood there transfixed on what he saw before him. A beefy man with pure white skin stood in the doorway to the bathroom that the cabin had. His bright red eyes stared at him, but it wasn't with any hatred in it. His gaze was soft, curious, and had a pull to it that Nick couldn't explain.

And he smelt of mint and fresh snow.

CHAPTER 12:

The Answer to His Mystery

He was in the bathroom cleaning up when he felt it. The pull. It had gotten stronger when he had gotten into the territory, and even more so when he met the Alpha. But it was getting stronger. He wasn't sure how much longer he could control his urge to follow it. He knew it would likely be met with his demise, but there was something so tempting about solving his mystery finally.

He closed his eyes and took a deep breath. This was going to be a test of his control. He wouldn't be able to find out why the Moon Goddess brought him there if he acted on impulse.

He wished he knew what it meant, though.

He washed himself quickly and got out of the shower. It was nice that they gave them the luxury of something like this. He could even change the temperature if he wanted. Although the rest of them seemed to like hot showers, he preferred cold. It was hot enough outside already, and these showers were the best way to cool off.

He dried himself off quickly, and got into some clothes that were given to him. As much as he hated wearing shirts, he felt like he needed to when the pack Gamma, Ed, came over to bring them their meals. He felt it was disrespectful not to. As it may show that he had gotten a little too comfortable in this lovely cabin.

He loved wearing colors. That added to some fun of wearing these clothes. This time, he wore jean shorts with a light pink shirt. The color of the shirt reminded him of fish. He loved fish. They were as much fun to watch as they were to catch and eat. He had spent many hours watching fish before he would head off to the next area.

The one thing he had still not gotten used to was shoes. He had always hated wearing them as a child, even when his toes would feel like they were going to fall off from the chill. They crunched his feet and wrapped around them so tight. And now that it was so hot, he didn't want to wear any more clothing than he had to. Shoes made him warmer, not cooler.

His stomach growled for food. It seemed to already be getting used to the three meals that they were given. What he would do many times in his travels was eat once a day, so he could have more time to run. Sometimes it would be bad, and he would have to go without eating for a couple days. He was grateful that this pack had given him so much, even if they didn't know him that well.

He walked out of the bathroom door and was hit with another wave of the strong pull. He thought that the smell that had come across his nose had been the food that Ed had brought. Instead, it was a lean man that was looking at him in awe.

He couldn't stop looking at those hazel eyes. He was frozen in place by the scent that the man was giving off. It was a sharp smell, like a foreign spice that he had not heard of. He longed to go to this man and feel his long dark hair. It was pulled back into a ponytail. He wanted to see what the man looked like with it resting on his shoulders. He wanted to know how it felt.

He wanted to know how those lips felt. They were parted slightly. It made him want to touch them. Everything about this man made him want to touch him.

He averted his gaze only after hearing the Gamma clear his throat. He looked protective of the other man. It made him more curious, but he would not try and pry. That wasn't a good idea. Instead, he dropped his gaze and put his head down.

"Nick, this is Alistair," he heard Ed say. He didn't want to look back up at the man, for fear he would get lost in those hazel eyes again. "Alistair, this is Nick, one of the chefs of the pack."

"It's nice to meet you," Nick said.

"You as well," he nodded. He should go to another room. If Ed was protective of this man, then he must be wary. Protective werewolves are not ones to mess with.

The pull got stronger, as well as the scent that danced along his nose. He should have backed up, but he stayed frozen in place. This pull was enough torture for a whole lifetime. He struggled against it.

"Hey," Nick's voice came to him like leaves to grass. It was as if color had a sound to it. "You can look at me, you know. I don't bite."

"He's worried about your Gamma," Madeline replied for him.

"Me?" Ed said. "I didn't do anything."

"You were when he was looking at him," Herb muttered.

Alistair stayed quiet. He had to find a place to escape. His instincts were telling him to find the source of this pull immediately, but he feared that it would only do bad. He didn't wish to create conflict. It seemed to follow him everywhere he went, but he still tried to avoid it when he could. He had just gotten on good terms with the Gamma, as well as some of the other warriors. He couldn't tarnish that now.

"Come on," he felt a hand on his arm. "Food solves everything."

His touch made his gaze snap back up to the chef. It sent waves of electricity through him with every second it stayed there. There was a warmth that he longed for in those mesmerizing eyes. He wished he could have stayed in that position.

He was the pull.

This man was the source of the pull that had been pushing him along for all this time. The Moon Goddess had brought him to this pack, this cabin, to meet this chef.

He couldn't help but smile when he came to this realization. Nick seemed just as mesmerized by him. He liked when he looked like that. His gaze seemed lost in a sea of thoughts. But he smiled after seeing Alistair do so.

Alistair nodded his answer to what Nick had said before and sat down at the small table. It had been placed in a small corner of the room, but it worked for them.

"So, you're the one that can hear wolves breathe, huh?" Nick asked. He put down Alistair's food in front of him, looking as if he had done it so many other times.

"You heard about that?" he asked. Even Ed seemed a little shocked himself at hearing the chef ask that. Nick just casually shrugged at the man and went to sit in his chair.

"If there's one thing you should know about the kitchen," he replied. "It's that it's the biggest gossip place in the entire state, I swear."

"Reminds me of the kitchen in Citrus Valley," Herb said, rolling his eyes. "I would be fixing one of their ovens and I would hear the craziest of stories."

"You used to fix stoves?" Nick looked at Herb. Alistair's mood seemed to fall when he did. He liked when the chef was looking at him.

"Oh yeah," Herb answered. He wiped away some of the food that had fallen onto his beard. "I fixed just about everything that place had. They didn't want to hire anyone to do it. That was how I convinced them to let me go to school for it in the first place."

"Sounds harsh," Nick's face got softer at hearing that. "Did you guys really get out of there because of that Beta?"

Jackie and Herb nodded. Herb then put an arm around Jackie to try and comfort her. She didn't like thinking about those bad memories, much like Alistair didn't like to think of his own.

"They were all a bunch of assholes," Madeline said in between bites. They were all starving. "Even the ones who were in charge before them."

"I can't believe they really wanted to replace you," Ed said this time. His tension seemed to go away as they talked. Nick seemed like a good person to help people calm down. He looked so relaxed around them that it helped Alistair calm down as well.

"Oh, they hated that I was their head tracker just about the whole time I had that position," Madeline started. "I was appointed it by the last one who retired. He taught me everything. But they had this whole notion that I should be inside caring for children or something like that. Ever since that, they were trying to find ways to get me out of that position."

"You aren't mated?" the chef asked.

"Nope," the woman shook her head. "Never found the right man, I suppose. I just turned any frustration I had towards it into my profession. I was damn proud of that job too."

"Reminds me of Alan," Nick laughed. "Only he's ten times grumpier than you."

"He's mateless I take it?"

"Yeah," Nick shrugged. "He even tried dating for a little bit. Nothing really worked out for him. So, he's mainly been focusing on his career in the kitchen."

"It's actually pretty amazing when you can turn it into a love for your passion," Madeline lit up. "It really helps you see life in a different light."

"You'll have to teach him how to do that," he laughed. "I'm afraid there isn't much left in the man other than a love for gossip and cooking."

"Do you have a mate?" Jackie asked him. Alistair was curious about this as well. He didn't know why it intrigued him as much as it did, but he found himself focusing hard on the man for his answer.

He seemed like he should have a mate. He was talkative, but also calm. It seemed like he would have gotten a mate easily. He was handsome enough as well.

He still wanted to feel his hair.

"Not yet," he said. "Hopefully they'll be out there somewhere," he glanced at Alistair for a split second. It was during that second that he started to wonder if Nick could feel it too.

Could he feel this pull? Was that why he was with Ed today?

"Can I ask you a question?" Jackie said. Ed had gone to the bathroom, so it was just them and Nick for a few minutes.

"You know you could ask around Ed too, right?" Nick chuckled a bit. He seemed amused at their wariness of the man. "He's not as scary as you think."

"I'm sorry," Jackie looked down. "I just didn't want to offend any of you."

"What's the question?"

"Do you really have a male Luna?" Jackie asked shyly. "We saw him for a little bit when we first came here, but I've never heard of a male Luna before."

"Yeah," Nick chuckled a bit. "It's a first for us as well. But he's done a pretty good job so far. Trust me, you'll love him when you finally get to talk to him. He's great at baking too."

"Is that why he smells like apple pie?" Madeline asked.

"No," Nick laughed again. "But that is why we nicknamed him Apple."

"I've never heard of a male Luna either," Herb said. His eyebrows were all scrunched up. They were so bushy, it made his whole face look fuzzy.

"They're pretty common up north," Alistair said. It was the first time he had spoken for most of the lunch.

"What did I miss?" Ed sat back down with them.

"Wait," Madeline completely ignored Ed and looked at Alistair. "You've seen other male Lunas?"

"I've seen quite a few in my travels," he answered. Now even Ed and Nick were looking at him. "Most of the time the Luna males were small, and their Alphas extremely protective." That was why he had put his head down immediately when he noticed the Alpha's scent on the man.

"Well, it's good to know that we aren't the first pack like that," Ed said. "I didn't know there were that many."

"What else did you find on your travels?" Nick asked. He liked that the chef was giving him his attention again. He had already grown fond of the man.

"Many things," he shrugged. "It's difficult trying to remember them all when on the spot, though."

"Did you fight a lot?" the chef asked.

"Only when I had to," he shook his head. "I wouldn't have survived this long if I had tried to fight everything I could. There were some dangerous creatures in some of those forests as well."

"What was the craziest fight you got into?" Nick's eyes were wide with wonder. It felt nice to have someone look at him in such a way. Instead of being on guard around him, or being afraid of him, Nick simply treated him as a normal being.

"The craziest?" he racked his brain for one of the many things that he had done on his travels. "I'd say that would have to be the werebear."

Everyone looked at him in horror. Nick just about dropped his fork as he heard it.

"Those things actually exist?!?!" Herb asked. "I thought they were just stories that parents tell their children so they don't try to get away from pack territory!"

"They usually keep to themselves," he answered. "That's why it's not often you get to see them."

"So, you fought one?" Ed said.

"Yes," he answered. He was going to leave it at that, but then he saw Nick's hazel eyes looking at him again. "It had gotten mad with a sickness that I hadn't known that much about. It was a sickness that made them try to attack everything they saw."

"So, it attacked you then?" Madeline asked. They were all listening intently to him.

"Actually, it was attacking some human hikers," he answered. "I jumped on its back before it could hurt them too bad."

"What happened after that?" Nick persisted.

"I didn't win that fight, if that's what you meant," he gave a sad smile. "I had barely gotten a good bite into its back before it threw me off. It eventually ran off, but I was pretty hurt in the process."

"Why did you save the humans, then?" Herb asked. "Why didn't you just keep on running? You would have gotten away without any harm done to you."

"That seems like the logical thing to do," he smiled. "But I like humans. They always helped me when I needed it."

"Really?" Jackie asked. "That's sweet."

"That's how I survived that attack," he told her. "After the werebear ran off, those hikers came back to find me."

"What did they do?" Nick was asking so many questions, it reminded him of an excited child when their parents were telling them a story.

"They brought me to a wildlife doctor," he told him. "After that, I lived in a zoo for about a year."

Laughter escaped him when he saw the look on all of his friends faces. He didn't expect that telling these stories would be as fun as it was. He had so many, but never had anyone to share it with.

Talking wasn't so bad when he had people like them.

"You were in a zoo for a whole year?!" Madeline looked astonished. "How the hell did you manage that?"

"I would have thought someone like you would have gotten out after a week at most," Herb said.

"At first I was there because it took a while to heal from the attack," he explained. "Then I became curious about the place and wanted to learn more about it. Once I had learned all that I had wanted to, though, there was the issue that I didn't want to get seen changing form and bursting out of there. There were cameras everywhere."

"How did you get out then?" Nick asked. He loved when Nick asked him questions. It made him happy just hearing that voice of his.

"The electricity had gone out throughout the whole zoo," he answered. "I used it to change forms and break through the cage. Then I went to the locker rooms for the workers and changed into some extra clothes that they had."

"Then you just walked out of there?" Nick asked. When he nodded his answer, the man laughed. "That's the most James Bond method of escaping I've heard!"

"James Bond?" he tilted his head. He was too used to doing that to show confusion when he was a wolf. He forgot that humans don't normally do that. They use their faces and their words.

It still made Nick smile though. He was happy to make the chef smile so much. It seemed like he had even gotten on good terms with Ed again, as he was finally comfortable around them.

This short time in his life had given him the happiest moments he had. He hoped that he could gain the packs trust soon.

He hoped he could gain Nick's trust too.

They talked for a while after that. Everyone had finished their food, but they still sat in their seats at the table, talking about so many things. There were many stories that Nick had as well. Many of them were kitchen stories. But they all made everyone laugh.

They talked about this pack as well. Both Nick and Ed told stories they had from growing up. It was nice to hear good stories of packs rather than horrible ones. Jackie and Herb looked happy hearing that as well.

"Well, we should probably get going," Ed said. His heart sank at hearing that. He looked at Nick, and found that he had been looking at Alistair first. They had both been glancing at each other from time to time. He looked a little sad to leave as well. But he still picked up the dishes that were left on the table.

"Well, it was nice meeting you Nick," Jackie smiled at him. She was so nice with everyone. "I hope we can all talk like this again."

"We should be able to," Nick smiled at her. "I'll bring more of my mom's food over for you. It really does help with women who are expecting."

"Thank you," she said. "I'd enjoy that."

They all said their goodbyes. By the time that Nick had gotten to him, he stuck out his hand to shake. He had seen humans do it plenty of times. He grabbed his hand softly, and the sparks flew through his veins. He enjoyed the sparks.

"Welcome to the Crescent Moon Pack," Nick smiled at him. His tanned face looked heated as he said it. Alistair wished he could touch his face to see if it really was warm.

"Thank you," he smiled back at him. It made him so happy just to have someone who treated him so kindly. Kindness always warmed his soul.

It hurt to watch them leave. He could feel the pull stretching as they drove off. It was still there, ever constant in his being. But it didn't feel as amazing as when Nick was there.

"I take it you have a liking for him?" Madeline asked. They were standing just outside the doorway, watching the vehicle go through the trees. The sun was slowly descending in the sky.

"He's the pull," he answered. It was as simple as that. Nick was the pull. The whole reason why he was there.

Nick was his gift from the Moon Goddess.

CHAPTER 13:

A Talk in the Moonlight

He needed someone to talk to. So badly. Nick needed someone to talk to about that man. They had only been talking to him for an hour, but it seemed like mere seconds. He wanted to talk to him more. Alistair seemed to have countless stories.

And there was that strange feeling he got when he was with him. Nick hadn't felt anything like that before. There was something about those red eyes that always had him wanting to look at him. He did a good job playing it cool after he first saw him. But he couldn't deny the feeling that he got when they touched.

He had felt so bad when Alistair put his head down. He had a lot of muscle, it was easy to feel intimidated by the albino. But he looked so scared when Ed growled a bit at him. That was how Nick knew he was harmless. He seemed much more like a gentle giant than anything else. Ed was happy that Nick had gotten him to talk. Apparently, he had only answered the bare minimum when they asked him questions.

When he touched his arm to try and get him to not fear them, he felt something he wasn't expecting. Sure, Alistair seemed to have a unique scent that Nick couldn't seem to get over, but he couldn't just leave it at that after he felt those sparks.

There was only one reason that a werewolf felt sparks when making any contact. And it shouldn't be possible. Not for him.

Which is why he desperately needed someone to talk to.

Nick pulled out his phone. It was charging by his nightstand. He had been busy with Ed for the rest of the afternoon. There was no way he could talk to him about it. They still didn't trust Alistair. If he said that Alistair might be his....

Well, he just didn't know how Ed might react to that.

It wasn't too late. She might be a little busy with her mate. But she never ignored her phone. And she was the only person that he could talk to about this. She was the only person that Nick could talk to in general. Charlie was a good person to talk to, but he wasn't Katy.

"Please answer." It was night now, and he had been tossing and turning trying to get some kind of sleep for work tomorrow. He just couldn't, though. He kept on thinking about how warm that pure white skin felt.

Every ring was torture. He needed to talk to her. At least once. It had been a week since he had seen her, or heard from her.

"Hello,"

"Katy! I'm so glad that you answered. There's something I need to-!"

"This is Katy! If you got to this, it means I'm not at my phone right now! Leave a message after the beep!"

His whole being shrank. Of course, he would get tricked on the voice-mail. He had never had to hear it before. She always answered her phone. When the beep came, he didn't know what to say. His throat got thick.

"I miss you," he choked out. That was all he said before he hung up. He put the phone back on his nightstand and curled up in his covers. He felt so lonely without her. The only thing that comforted him, at least a little was the moon that shined through his window.

He couldn't keep crying about this. This happened all the time. It was only natural that people move on with their life. He just had to get over it, and move on with life.

Whatever life he had.

He looked out his window at the moon. It had been bright the whole week. He liked to think that it was to comfort him. But it was probably just the fact that it was summer, and the moon always shined brightly in the summer.

Nick wondered if Alistair liked looking at the moon. He had been to so many different places. He wondered if the night sky looked any different up north.

He wanted to see him; to ask him more questions. He wanted to talk to someone, just to hear another voice. He liked Alistair's voice. It was low and calming. He could probably fall asleep to it if he ever got the chance.

Screw it. Nick got out of bed and grabbed a pair of shorts. Max was going to kill him if he found out he was doing this, but he was going to go insane in this little room. He had to talk to Alistair.

It was quiet in the manor. His section didn't have much footwork, as it was mainly for the workers who didn't have families of their own yet. Alan lived just down the hall from him. But there was a whole chunk of them that were off on their vacations. So, that night, it was dead.

He stopped by the kitchen really quick and grabbed a bag from the pantry. The kitchen had closed a while ago, so no one was there. After that, the door out of the house was just a couple steps away.

Nick actually loved the heat of the summer. He loved napping in the sun, especially in his wolf form. It relaxed him. And the fresh air of the night seemed to have a similar effect.

He walked into the trees and took off his shorts. It wasn't often that he went into his wolf form. He mainly did it when he wanted to have fun or was trapped in the house a lot. With the rogues around, the members of the pack like him had to stay as close to the packhouse as possible when in their wolf forms. Max didn't want them getting hurt, and he understood. He didn't exactly want to get killed by a rogue.

It felt freeing with the breeze going through his fur. He took from his mother's side a lot, even in wolf form. Many people didn't know that India had different looking wolves. He had gotten bullied for it a few times. There was a whole point where he didn't want to ever shift just because of all the bullying. It took Katy and a few others to convince him that his wolf wasn't something to be ashamed of.

He sniffed around at all the familiar smells of home. He enjoyed his heightened senses for a bit before he grabbed the shorts and bag that he had and started his personal journey. He hoped that the warriors wouldn't notice him running around. But he figured he'd just tell them that he was going to enjoy a midnight snack to get his mind off things. He'd get yelled at, but it wouldn't be near as bad as the punishment for what he was actually doing would be.

It wasn't long before he got to where the cabin was. He decided to shift behind some trees just in case someone saw him.

Normally, he wouldn't care, as they had all seen each other naked before. But there was something about Alistair that made him suddenly insecure about himself.

He started walking up to the cabin, trying to think about what he was going to say, when something stopped him. Alistair's mint scent wasn't as strong over here. He caught a whiff of it coming from another direction.

He turned around to see a pure white wolf staring at him from afar. He looked magnificent in the moonlight. Nick felt ten times better just seeing him there. He didn't know that he had been holding his breath until then.

"Thought I'd bring a snack," he held up the bag that he got. The wolf cocked his head, reminding him of when Alistair did that earlier that day. It made the man look adorable.

His shift shocked Nick. It was completely silent. Werewolves never shift silently. There's always at least the sound of bones breaking. How had he learned to do that?

"What is it?" Alistair asked. His head cocked to the side again.

"Snickerdoodles," Nick tried to suppress a laugh. He wished he could make him cock his head like that more. It made him seem like a puppy. "I have a feeling you've never tried them before."

"I don't think I have," he smiled at him. He was gorgeous when he smiled. Nick was slowly losing control over his own thoughts. He wasn't supposed to be thinking about how gorgeous this man was. He couldn't be. He wasn't supposed to have someone like him. He was supposed to simply be the cool uncle to his family.

He wasn't supposed to have a Happily Ever After.

But, the more he looked at Alistair, the more those thoughts seemed to fly away. This man was supposed to be this scary rogue that everyone was watching carefully. No one knew much about him. But he looked so nice when he talked. His whole demeanor was calm; watchful.

"Let me get something to wear," Alistair broke him out of his thoughts.

Oh no. How long had he just stood there like an idiot staring at the man?

Wait.

How had Nick not realized that the man was naked?!

It was supposed to be common sense. But that had all gone down the drain that night. He nodded at the man and let him past him into the cabin. His eyes were trained to his feet. He knew that if they looked anywhere else, they would be traveling to areas that Nick did not want them to.

It only took a few minutes for the man to get changed. Nick used that time to try and get rid of the heat that had risen to his cheeks. Men weren't supposed to blush. He wasn't supposed to, at least. When Charlie did, it was cute. The Luna was an adorable plush that everyone seemed to love. Nick was just a cook.

He wondered how Alistair would look when he blushed.

Nick really needed to stop thinking about this. He needed sleep. He hadn't been able to sleep well for the past two weeks. Ever since Katy got mated, he wasn't sure what to do with himself.

He found himself staring at the moon when Alistair sat next to him. They were just on the porch of the cabin. Nick smiled at the man and handed him the bag of snickerdoodles.

"So, you've never had them before?"

"No," Alistair opened the bag and pulled one out. "Are they sweet?"

"Yeah," he told him. "They're loaded with sugar."

"I love sweets," Alistair smiled again. The look he gave Nick seemed like a nostalgic one. "I never got that many when I was a kid. But I remember my mother would give me some on my birthdays."

"You didn't get any on your adventures?"

"I was a wolf most of my travels," he shook his head. "I didn't get much of a chance to try a lot of food in general."

"Really?" This only made him more curious about the man. "So, you only ate what you killed in the wilderness?"

"For the most part," he said. "I've grown to enjoy the meals that were given here." Those ruby eyes looked at him again. "I forgot to thank you for those meals."

"Oh, don't worry about it," Nick brushed off. "It wasn't just me who made it. We have a ton of people in that kitchen."

"Do you like cooking?"

"It's a passion of mine," he grinned just thinking about it. "It's fun making all kinds of foods. I'm usually on the morning shift, though. But!" he put a finger in the air. "I've perfected pancake flipping!"

"I hope there's one day when you can show me," Alistair said. He ate the cookie that he was holding and Nick had to hold make a laugh as he saw the face that he made. It was like a child finding out what chocolate was for the first time.

"Do you like it?" he snickered.

"It's amazing!" he told him. "Did you make this yourself?"

"Yeah. It's super easy to make," Nick said. "I used to make them all the time when Katy and I were…" he paused and looked up at the moon. He had almost forgotten about her. "When we were working together."

"Is Katy another cook?" Alistair asked. He could tell that the man was looking at him, but he didn't want to meet his eyes. He didn't want to start crying in front of a stranger, even if that stranger was nice to him.

"She was my best friend," Nick explained, keeping his eyes on the moon for comfort. "She left about a week ago to her mate's pack."

"Oh." His low voice paused a moment, letting the silence consume them for a second or two. "Is it far away?"

"Not really," Nick rested his head on his hands. "It just seems that way."

"You two were really close, then?"

"You could say that," he smiled a little. "Many people thought we were joined at the hip. We did just about everything together."

There was another pause as he stared at the moon. He shouldn't have come here. He thought, for some reason, that it would help him feel better. That coming here to see this strangely fascinating man, would somehow distract him from the pain of losing his best friend.

"I'm sorry," Alistair finally said.

"Sorry?" Nick looked at him finally. His face had fallen into a worried one. "What are you sorry for?"

"I'm sorry that you feel sad," he answered. "I've never had someone that I was that close with. I can only imagine losing them."

"I haven't lost her," he shook his head. "She'll talk to me again, eventually. And we'll be able to hang out again. I'm just whining."

"I don't think it's whining," Alistair's feathery hair moved in the breeze. It looked so light and thin. "Good friends are hard to come by, no matter where you are."

"I guess you could say that."

"We all had a fun time with you today," he said. "If you would like, I'm sure we would all like to be friends with you."

"I have plenty of friends," Nick told him. "They just all have their own things to do. Whether it be work, or family. Everyone's just moving on without me."

"I won't be." The way that Alistair said it made it feel like a promise. Nick's heart wanted to believe him. But he wasn't sure about the stranger.

"How do I know you're going to actually stay here?" He asked the albino. It was well known that rogues didn't like to settle into packs. Even if they did, it was likely that they would try running off again at some point.

"Because the loneliest way to live is through never having a home," Alistair said. Nick looked at him, but the man was staring at the moon now. "I've been running for a long time. Some friends were made throughout my journeys, but none ever lasted. The only friend I ever truly had was the wind and the moon."

"Really?" he asked. "But you've gotten to see so many things! Don't you enjoy the adventure?"

"Not when there isn't anyone to talk to about it," Alistair answered.

Nick's heart broke for the man. He understood where he was coming from. He was feeling the same thing that Nick was: loneliness. As much as he remembered all the things that he had heard about rogues, Alistair didn't seem to fit into that category.

"Alright," he agreed. "I'll be your friend." He felt like he was in elementary school saying it like that.

"I'm glad," Alistair smiled again. "I'd love to try some more of your cooking."

"Can I ask you a question?"

"Sure."

"Why are you so nice?" he looked into those ruby red eyes again. It wasn't common for any rogue to be this kind. Especially not one who's as strong as Alistair seemed to be. Rogues were always brutal and vicious. Alistair seemed more like a pet who had lost his home.

"Do you see the moon shining down tonight?" The albino asked. They both looked at it at the same time. "The Moon Goddess shines down on us. Sometimes it is to bless us, and sometimes it is to teach the ones who have strayed from her guidance. My mother always told me that it is through her that you live your life through. She told me that love and kindness go a long way. And, if you follow the path of the moon, you will be forever blessed with her gifts."

"Wow," Nick said. "I've never heard something like that before." They always talked about the Moon Goddess, and the blessings and curses that she had put on their pack throughout the years. But they never talked about her in such a tangible way. And he had never heard someone say that about the Goddess.

"I'd like to believe that's why I was brought here," Alistair told him. "So that I could finally find the thing I was looking for the most."

"And what was that?"

"A family."

"You didn't have a family with your other pack?"

"No," Alistair frowned. "They never treated me like the families that I've seen through my travels. They treated me like I was just a tool to be used."

"But your kind of being used here," Nick said. He didn't exactly want to speak poorly of his pack, but he couldn't make the man disillusioned with the position he was in.

"Not entirely," he told him. "I'm still allowed days to rest, for instance. It surprised me to hear that tonight was the one that I had off."

"They didn't let you have a day off in your old pack?"

"No," Alistair shook his head. "That's why I'm grateful for all that I am given here," He smiled at him. "You and your pack have truly been a gift for me."

Nick wasn't sure what to say to that. He had never met someone who was so happy just over little things like getting a day off. His heart went out to him. He wanted to give him a hug or something, but he wasn't sure how the man would react to that.

Instead, they just talked about random things. Alistair talked about the most annoying thing in his travels. Nick laughed when he said that it was a bird that had been following him all throughout one of the forests that he had went through. He was a funny man, once you got him talking.

He didn't think he would actually feel better by end of the night. But, the more he talked to this mysterious man, the happier he seemed to be. He was so happy about it, he promised to talk to him again the next night, as the man had that night off as well.

For once in two weeks, Nick actually felt excited for something.

CHAPTER 14:

Some Rest and Relaxation

"Are you sure you're okay with it?" Max asked Nick. His childhood friend had been one of the reasons for his worry for a while now.

"Yeah, I'm fine, Max," the chef said. "I was planning on going to lunch with Ed anyway. He's been getting lonely with Emily still gone on her internships."

"Alright," he frowned. He had planned on having lunch with him that day, but him and Charlie had finally gotten a day off together and he had missed having a whole day with his mate. "As long as you're okay with it."

"I'm doing fine, Max," Nick smiled at him. He had been unusually happy the past week. Everyone that knew him was relieved to see the old Nick back, rather than the hollowed-out man that he was when Katy left.

Max still felt bad about that. He worried about one of them finding their mate before the other. Both of them would be devastated. He had hoped that they would both find their mate around the same time. But it seemed like that wasn't going to be the case.

He knew that Nick was destined to find a mate though. Whether or not the man thought he did. If anyone heard the story of how he was born, they would think the same way too. There was a reason why the chef's mother told him that he was a blessing from the Moon Goddess. And Max believed that the goddess wouldn't ever want him to go without someone.

For now, he was glad that Nick found something to make himself happy. Maybe his brothers brought up his spirits or something. Max had been so worried, he contemplated calling Nick's oldest brother to come and visit him. Nick was always so happy to see him.

Max left the kitchen with a weight being lifted from his shoulders. Now that he didn't have to worry about Nick, he could actually enjoy the day with Charlie. Hopefully the man would still be asleep, but he doubted it. Charlie never stayed asleep long after Max got up. They had gotten so used to sleeping next to each other, it was impossible for them to not.

He was going to just talk to Nick through mind link, but that would take out the personal feeling to it. And he wanted to make sure that Nick was going to be alright before canceling their plans. Now, it seemed like the man was happier that he did. Whatever him and Ed were doing was making him happy. And Max was just happy that his friends were happy.

Ed seemed to find more information on the rogues than he thought he was going to be able to. Sometime last week, they had started to open up to him more. It was fascinating hearing all the stories that these strangers told.

A part of him wished he could go and talk to them all himself, but he had already tarnished all possibilities of him being able to talk to them normally. He made himself appear as the serious leader so that they wouldn't see him as weak in any way.

Getting them to talk more about themselves was more Ed's expertise anyway.

Max walked into his room and, low and behold, Charlie was nowhere to be found.

"You better be in here somewhere, Apple," he mind linked with him. It was nice to be able to do that with him now. Especially if he missed him when they were both stuck in their offices.

"I'm in the bathroom!" Charlie yelled. He didn't like using the mind link unless he absolutely needed to. Max had learned just how taxing it was for his mate from the first month of him being a member of the pack. He would get horrible headaches from it. When they went to Dr. Button about it, he told them that it was something that would pass. Max was grateful when it did.

Breakfast was already out on their dining table. Most times, the pack didn't all eat together unless it was a holiday. It would be too difficult trying to get everyone together for that three times a day anyway. And it allowed the pack to pick out what they wanted to eat rather than have to eat whatever the Alpha wanted.

"Dealing with some more work?" Charlie asked. He came out of the bathroom with nothing but a robe on. Since it was so hot, they rarely wore too much clothing in their room.

Of course, there was another reason they didn't wear much clothes, but that was a thought that he'd rather entertain when he was done eating.

"I just had to talk to someone really quick," he pecked him on the cheek and pulled out a chair for him. "I don't have any other plans today."

"Are you sure?" The blond looked a little guilty from the other side of the table. "I don't want you canceling plans because of me. I know how busy we both can be."

"I'm all yours," Max winked at him and took a bite out of his food. He knew how much days like this meant to Charlie. It meant the world to him too. Just being able to relax with him for a whole day was enough to get him through a whole month.

"Well," A smile spread across his love's face, reaching those emerald eyes. "Since we finally have a day off together, I was thinking of something."

"What is it?" He tried to hide his disappointment. He wanted to just have a day with Charlie, in the room that they only seemed to sleep in. He wanted to enjoy some peace and quiet with him.

"Hmm," The hum to his voice was like music to his ears. He couldn't be mad at him. He was probably dying to get out of the house after so much paperwork. "Maybe I'll keep it as a surprise for you."

"A surprise?" Now Max was more than curious. "I'm guessing you already planned it then?" He learned quickly just how well Charlie was at planning the perfect thing for them. Ian was a big example of that. Since Charlie knew that Max didn't want him to be alone with the man (he wasn't sure if Charlie really did either) he always planned their get-togethers as a group date. That way, they had Max, Ben, and Leonard to keep Ian in check.

The man wasn't bad. He was really loving to Ben, and exceptionally nice to Max after their disagreement all those months ago. But neither Max, nor Ben, liked the certain look that the man got when he started talking to Charlie. It was as if he never got over his crush on the man at all. And it made Max all the more possessive of his mate.

"It's not something that big," Charlie shook his head. "Just something small that I had been thinking about for a while now."

"Where is it?" he asked.

"I don't know," the blond teased. "You'll have to find out after breakfast."

Max rolled his tired shoulders and sighed. "As long as I can get a nap in at least, I'll go anywhere with you."

"You'll get your nap in," Charlie giggled. "I promise you that."

They talked a little as they ate. They tried to stay off from the topic of work whenever they could. It was stressful if you talked about work all the time. They had already dealt with that enough during the week of hell that was those meetings. As much as they were still working quite a lot now, it wasn't nearly as bad as dealing with those meetings.

Sam's new twin boys were the main thing they loved talking about. Charlie lit up when he talked about children. Max hadn't gotten a chance to see them too much, but he wanted to. They were adorable babies that looked so much like their dad. The man's parents had pulled out baby pictures of him just to compare them with the twins when Charlie was there. Max knew just how embarrassed his friend was without even being there.

Sam got embarrassed easily. It was something that Leah had quite enjoyed finding out about when they were first mated. She loved embarrassing him like his parents did: with compliments and cute pictures of him.

It didn't help that Ed would egg her on a bit with them. Ed was always the jokester. Max could tell that the man was desperate to have children of his own soon, though. Emily only had one more year left before she would graduate from college. Then it was a lot of work after that. But she said that she'd want to take a little break before doing more schooling to be with Ed and relax a bit.

And Ed just couldn't wait.

Of course, Tyler and his wife, Isabelle, were a power couple. Both of them did their jobs and managed their children perfectly. Isabelle had been working a little more to try and help Charlie out with the backload of paperwork (another consequence from the weak of hell) but it wasn't difficult for Tyler to take some extra time off. Now that it was calmer in the pack house, Max was letting anyone who needed it go on vacation. They needed rewarded for their hard work.

"Alright," Max leaned across his empty plate and looked into his mate's playful eyes. "Are you going to tell me my surprise yet?" He was already too awake for the day, there was no chance of him being able to go back to sleep. And he was too curious as to what this grand secret that his lover was keeping from him was.

"I have to get it ready," Charlie said. He then got up and walked to the bathroom, confusing Max.

What did he have to get ready? Why did it involve the bathroom?

Was he going to get a striptease?

Max laughed at himself at that. There was no way he would ever get Charlie to do that. At least, not of his own planning. They've had some fun times with clothing, but Max liked it better when he was the one taking Charlie's off. It allowed him to touch him more.

So, if this wasn't a striptease, what was it? This was too early in the day to be anything too grand. Max made sure to lock the door to their suite though, just in case.

It seemed to take forever until Charlie came out of the bathroom again. When he did, the door let out a cloud of steam.

"Okay," the blond gently took his arm. "It's ready."

"You planned a bath?" he smirked at him. He let the small man lead him to their bathroom.

"Something like that," he smiled. When they got in the bathroom, a cloud of warmth washed over him.

Their bathroom had been changed into some kind of luxury spa. Candles were laid out everywhere, and the bath was a beautiful turquoise color with red petals floating on top.

"I thought you deserved a spa day," Charlie finally told him. He looked so happy when he said it. Max couldn't help but smile at him.

"Me?" He pulled Charlie closer to him. "Who's to say this shouldn't be about you?"

"Because I'm not the one who has knots all over my back," Charlie's hands went up to his shoulders. "And you work so much. You need a day to relax for once."

"Don't you?"

"Not as much as you," Charlie kissed him lightly. His robe was clinging so delicately over his skin, it made it easy for him to slip his hand under it. Just as soon as Max was going to deepen the kiss it, though, he pulled back. "Don't distract me," the blond giggled. He was so cute when he giggled. "This is supposed to be about you."

"And what if all I want is you?" He pulled him in closer to him. The closer he was, the more Max wished he could never let go of him.

"Then I promise you this'll be worth it," Charlie batted at the hand that was going lower down his back. "Now get out of these clothes."

"Yes, sir," he smirked. Charlie laughed when he said that. But he wouldn't let Max hold him until he was finished taking his layers of clothing off. Then he was ordered in the tub. Max thought it was fun being ordered around in such a caring way.

He was expecting Charlie to get in with him. He loved having baths with him in his arms. It was the most relaxing thing to him. Instead of stepping into the warm water, though, Charlie started washing his hair.

He remembered the first time Charlie had done his hair. It felt like complete bliss to him. He never thought it would feel any better until he felt those beautiful hands massaging his scalp. His head fell back and he let out a moan of relief as all the tension in his head and neck melted away.

Then he felt lips on his, ever so gently. He smiled as he tried to kiss them. As fast as they were there, they had left. And he heard more giggles coming from above him. He tried to open his eyes, when a rag was put on them.

"Don't," Charlie hummed. "I don't want any soap getting in your eyes."

"You're such a tease," he smiled and shook his head a bit. "You know that?"

"This is supposed to relax you," Charlie argued, clear amusement in his voice, "Not excite you."

"Why can't it do both?"

"It can't do both right now," Those hands cradled his head and went down to massage his neck. "After all of these knots are out, and you're not all wound up, then maybe I'll work on exciting you."

Just him saying that was enough to do the trick. Max had no idea how nice it was to get pampered like this. The smells were calming too. He didn't smell too much. Spa items always threw him off with all the strong scents that came from them. Right then, all he could smell was lavender and vanilla. They weren't that strong, so he wasn't complaining.

Once his hair was thoroughly washed and rinsed, he was gently nudged forward and those hands traveled to his shoulders and back.

"I don't know where you learned that," he moaned as the man worked out all of his knots. "But don't stop."

"You'd be surprised what you learn as a baker," Charlie explained. "Massaging is a lot like trying to make bread."

"So, you're a cat then," Max smiled thinking about how cats liked to knead on pillows or people.

"I guess you could say that," Charlie chuckled. "I had no idea that you had gotten so many knots."

"Me either," he sighed. "I'm glad this job isn't like when my ancestors were alive, or I'd never get a break."

"Was it really that bad?"

"Kind of," he answered, thinking back to when his father would tell him the stories of the pack's history. "This used to be a much larger pack than it is now."

"Really?"

"Mmmhmm," he felt his body relax as more and more knots were worked out. "I believe the largest population we had was two thousand."

"Two thousand?" Charlie sounded surprised. "When was that?"

"During my great, great grandfather's reign," Max said. "After he died, the pack started to go through a lot of dark patches."

"How did it go from two thousand all the way down to two hundred?"

"My dad told me that it was due to the Moon Goddess being angry with us," he sighed as he remembered the story. "This pack wasn't the best one. It had its goods and bad. It still does. That's why now there's a history of the Alpha's going through extreme trials during the beginning of their leadership."

"But what happened to all of those people?"

"Some ran from the pack," he explained. "As it had gotten that bad. Plenty died at the hands of my great grandfather. He was a tyrant to say the least. Then there were the rogue wars of his reign which caused many deaths. And, of course, the civil war that happened here during Liam's reign. During that time, there weren't a lot of people starting families either, and more pack members were having difficulties finding their mates."

"That sounds horrible," Charlie said. Max had been so caught up in the story he was telling that he hadn't notice the blond had gotten in the tub with him finally. His robe was laying on the floor next to it.

"It's a lot to take in," Max said. He remembered when his father first started to tell him those stories. He hadn't wanted to believe them. It sounded straight out of a story book. All of the things that he had learned about horrible leaders, bloodthirsty tyrants with no thoughts for anything but themselves. He didn't want to believe that he was related to someone like that. Or that such horrible things had happened to the people that had helped raise him.

"Is that why you're so worried about keeping everyone safe?"

"Yes," he grabbed the leg that had been lying next to his and pulled Charlie around to the front of him. The blond didn't expect it and gasped a little. But he calmed down when Max put his arms around him finally. "Including you."

"I'll be fine," Charlie shook his head. "You've done enough taking care of me. It's time for me to take care of you today."

"Apple," he held him tighter in his arms. "I've never done enough when it comes to keeping you safe." He cupped his face with his hands and made him look up at him. "You're the love of my life."

"And you're mine," Charlie smiled. "But that doesn't mean that I can't pamper you today."

"You should do more than just pamper me," His hands started to wander down his lover's body. He never got used to the feeling of his soft skin, or how he reacted to even the smallest of touches.

"Well," The blond smirked a little. "You do seem more relaxed now."

Max stopped whatever conversation that was going to happen. He just kissed him. As much as he enjoyed the flirting that Charlie was finally comfortable with doing, he couldn't hold back anymore.

"Let's enjoy the rest of the day," he smiled. Then he quickly picked him up and carried him out of the tub. Once they were dried, he would bring him to bed and they'd hopefully stay there the rest of the day.

CHAPTER 15:

Answers and Questions

It was a normal day in of paperwork for Charlie. He was close to finally finishing off the extra work that had accumulated from all the meetings that had taken place the month before. That was another reason why he was glad that Max and him had finally gotten a day off together. Recently it had been so busy dealing with the aftermath of everything, that they hadn't had much time with each other. They always came back to their suite though.

The suite was something that he hadn't expected when he had become Luna. The Luna and Alpha always get the best room in the mansion. So, they had a lot of moving around to do. At first, he thought that they were taking Max's parents room, but it was actually a spare room on the second floor that had been renovated into a beautiful suite.

And it had a balcony.

He rarely got to use it, much like the one that he had at his old apartment, but it was nice to wake up to the sunlight that shined through it. Max had thought of him when he picked the room. It was yet another birthday present, one that Max didn't give him until a week after his birthday.

He remembered those days fondly. They weren't that long ago, but it seemed that way when he thought about all of what had happened the past few months. He had spent a lot of time with Max that whole month of his birthday. Then there was the rigorous Luna training that he went through. It was two weeks of constant paperwork and werewolf history. Even then, he still didn't know as much as he would like to.

Like he didn't know that this pack used to be so large. He had thought that having a pack of almost three hundred was bad, Charlie couldn't imagine the work that went into dealing with thousands of them. Then again, Max's mom had made a system that worked well, even with a possibility of a quick population increase. That had been the past Alpha's mission during his reign: to grow the pack.

If they had these rogues out of their hair, they would be able to grow faster, with more land to grow on and no dangers lurking in the trees.

"Charlie," Max popped up in his head. *"I need you in my office, please."*

"I'll be right there," he answered. Isabelle had long gone to take care of her kids, so it was just him again in the office. He didn't like the fact that Max called him to his office, though. There was a tone, even in his thoughts, that worried him. It sounded stressed and frustrated.

He had just helped him deal with that.

He walked across the hall after making sure that his paperwork was all nice and neat. It would throw him off if he went back in there and tried to get right back to what he was doing. It made it easier when it was organized no matter what.

What was going on this time? It seemed like the problems would never stop. They still had rogues to deal with, and he was enjoying the peace that the other packs leaving their territory gave them. Everyone was slowly coming back from there holidays and everything was slowly getting back to their normal pace.

Charlie really hoped that there wasn't another issue with the neighboring packs. The Harvest Moon Pack was easy. They were logical and had a modern way of thinking. The Blood Moon Pack was the one that liked to butt heads with everyone. They always wanted the most of everything because they thought it was what they deserved.

What they really deserved was a swift kick in the-

Charlie knocked on the Alpha's door before entering. He always did it just in case there was someone else that Max was talking to in there. He didn't want to just barge in right when they were in the middle of a conversation.

"Come in," he heard Max say. He opened the door to see Dr. Button and his wife, Adelle, in the office. He closed the door before anything was said. It was something that he had grown a habit of since he heard that people liked to eavesdrop on this floor. It was mainly guests, such as the other packs visiting, but it was always better to be safe than sorry.

"What's going on?" he asked. There was a look to Max's face that worried him. It looked just as his tone sounded through the mind link.

"We found some information on the rogues that are staying with us," Button said.

"What did you find?" he sat down at one of the chairs that the office had. It was designed for many people to be in if need be.

"First off," he pulled out three folders, "The three from the Citrus Valley Pack were telling the truth. Their stories match up with the records I found in the database. Herb was a builder, Madeline was a tracker who was about to be replaced, and Jackie was only just eighteen when the Beta started taking interest in her."

"That's horrible," he said, he flipped through the folders to see the information that was held within them. It showed basically everything that the doctor had said.

"Her family was devastated when she ran, apparently." The doctors face softened a bit. "I doubt they would have wanted her to live like that."

"The Citrus Valley Pack has a habit of doing things like that," Adelle said. "They like going against the mating rules if it's for the sake of their leading lines getting stronger. It's probably the reason they haven't grown that well over the years."

"What about the fourth one: Alistair?" he looked at Button questionably.

Ah, there it was. That's where the tension lied. The whole room seemed to freeze as Button and his wife looked at each other.

"Well," Dr. Button adjusted himself in his seat. "I found a few documents on him, one including his age."

"What is it?"

"He's 26, born in Alaska," he put down another folder. "There are many medical documents of him from a human doctor, but not any past the age thirteen."

"I wonder why..." His eyebrows furrowed as he looked through the new folder. There weren't that many papers in there, and most were medical. He was a very sickly child it seemed. The pictures they had of him as a child were adorable, though. His smile made him look like he didn't have a care in the world.

"Because when you turn thirteen, you're able to shift for the first time," Max answered. Charlie wished he knew why the man looked so frustrated. "And since he was a warrior for his pack, they probably took him away to fight for them."

"Did he get any schooling?" He couldn't find any school paperwork. The other three rogues had them, but Alistair didn't.

"It seems as if he was homeschooled for most of his childhood," The doctor answered. "In a pack, that could mean that he wasn't taught anything."

That was sad. He hoped the man at least knew how to read or write. And how was he supposed to use things like money if he didn't know any math?

"We're missing the point," Max said. His tone was as cold as ice.

"What's the point, then?" Charlie asked. He was a little annoyed by his lover's tone, but decided to ignore it. It wasn't worth getting mad over.

"The point is," Max explained. "That he's been a rogue for ten years, and has somehow survived traveling through a whole country until getting to us."

"It's not likely that rogues can last that long," Adelle answered. Her silver hair was tied up neatly in a bun, as usual. "Especially if they're traveling as much as he seemed to have. I've looked at the Borealis Pack as well. They're a traveling pack, and a powerful one at that. They pride themselves on their survival tactics that they've learned through their ancestors."

"He's dangerous," Max told him. "That's what this all means."

"But he hasn't done anything to our pack," Charlie said. "I understand that this means he's strong, but how do we know he's going to use any of that strength against us?"

"How do we know that he won't?"

"We need to find out more about him," Adelle continued. "The more we can learn about his adventures, the more we can understand his character."

"I don't understand," he furrowed his eyebrows. "Are we putting more restrictions on them? Or leaving them to the same plan?"

"We're putting more restrictions on them," Max ordered. "I don't want to risk him attacking anyone."

"He's been running with our warriors for two weeks now," Charlie said. "And he hasn't done anything to even indicate that he was going to hurt us. He even saved Tyler from getting attacked."

"That's true," Button agreed. "None of the warriors were wounded due to him taking the first blow."

"He was able to hear those rogues breathing from the other side of our lines," Max's eyes flashed with anger. "I don't trust someone who is that connected to nature. It means that he's that much closer to his wilder side, and your wild side is much more dangerous than your human side."

"You're treating him as guilty until proven innocent," Charlie looked at his lover. "Instead of the other way around. I understand the restrictions that we already have on him, but I don't think it's necessary to tighten his leash."

"We have to because we don't know just how dangerous he is," Max argued back.

"I wasn't seen as dangerous after I saved Sam."

"That's because you were a human."

"But I could have easily been a hunter." He didn't know why he was doing this in front of Dr. Button and Adelle, but there was something that just felt wrong about this. He didn't like the idea of punishing him for following the rules that he set in place. "You didn't know."

"That's not the point."

"Isn't it?" He was trying to still sound calm, but the man had lit a fire in him. After years of schooling in a place that taught justice for innocent, he hated this idea. "He hasn't acted hostile in any way, shape or form."

He remembered the look of fear in those bright red eyes when he saw him that day. If there was anyone who was scared, it was Alistair to them.

"That calling, actually," Adelle butted into the conversation. "The howl that he made to get your attention, it's called 'The Traveler's Request'. It used to be used when there were many other traveling packs. But it was thought to have been extinct in its use as the traveling packs decreased. Rogues don't like to follow any rules but their own. This request was usually done through Alphas of the travelling packs, to request permission to pass through the pack's territory."

"So, it was something else that he had learned from his pack."

"Not entirely," Adelle answered Max. "The only traveling packs in existence are ones that live in environments that are difficult to live in, such as the icy tundra that is Alaska, or rogue packs. Neither of them would have a need to learn such a request."

"Then how did he learn it?!" Max almost slammed his fist on his desk. He looked at Charlie with fire in his eyes. "This is what I mean! The more we try and learn about the man, the more questions we have than answers."

"Have you thought to ask him?" he suggested. "He seems open to answering any questions as truthfully as he can."

"I would, if I was sure that he knew the answers himself," Max frowned. "We've tried asking him questions. He's just been traveling for so long that he doesn't know much about location names and doesn't know anything about how long he spent there."

"Okay." Now he understood where the frustration was with his lover. This rogue just came into their lives, asking to be a part of it when they were in the middle of trying to rid themselves of other rogues. Then, he comes in with no answers to their questions, and more mystery that they were comfortable with. "I still don't think that's a justifiable reason to put more restrictions on him."

"Dr. Button, Dr. Adelle," Max looked at the two that sat in front of his desk. "Thank you for the information that you've found. You're dismissed."

He didn't like how he said that. He should be scared at how mad the man looked when he let the doctors go, but he was dead set on trying to figure out some way of convincing him out of this.

"We'll keep looking for more information," Adelle said. They both said their farewells and left the office.

And then it was just him and Max.

"You don't understand the seriousness of this, do you?" Those purple eyes burned into his. "Do you know how many stories there are of rogues tricking packs into letting them in just to destroy them?"

"I'm not saying we should let him in the pack," he said. "At least, not yet. I'm just saying that the patrol is the only way that he could possibly prove himself to us. Without that, how are we ever going to trust him?"

"If we keep him on patrol, how do we know that he wouldn't just attack our warriors with the rogues that are coming over the territory lines?" He grabbed his red hair in frustration. "We don't know for a fact that he could truly hear those rogues. For all we know, it was just a plan to get us to trust him more."

"That's why I'm not telling you to lessen the restrictions that we already have on him." How many different ways did he have to say this for it to actually make sense to this bull-headed man? "But how is he going to prove himself if not through that? Shouldn't we consider him innocent until proven guilty?"

"No!" Max yelled at him. It almost made him jump with how loud it was. "I don't want to give him any leeway until I know everything about him and his travels."

It hurt to have Max yell at him like that. Max had never yelled at him like that. He wanted to just run out of the office and hide somewhere. But he couldn't. As much as Max was stubborn about this stranger, so was he.

Charlie remembered what Max had said about wanting to protect this pack. It seemed like he was being overprotective at this point, but he could at least try to understand where he was coming from. This pack had just gotten back on its feet after nothing but war after war that had plagued it. About a tenth of its original population still remained after those wars.

He wanted to protect them. Charlie could see it in his eyes. As much as he wanted the man to see the logic that he was presenting to him, those eyes showed that he wasn't going to take it at all.

"Okay." He nodded his head, shocking the man. They had been staring at each other in silence for a bit before he had finally spoken. "Give me three days."

"Three days?" The anger in his eyes almost went away.

"I'll find everything about the man in three day's time," he told him. He was determined to help figure this out. "Then I'll report it back to you."

"Charlie," Max sighed and rubbed his face. "We could barely find out this little bit of information in two weeks. How do you expect to find out everything within three days?"

"I'll leave that as a surprise," he answered. He wanted to smile at him and show that he wasn't angry with him. He understood where the man was coming from. He just didn't agree with it.

Plus, this plan with these rogues were his idea in the first place. It was just like what Liam said: if it failed, then it was Charlie's reputation at stake. He couldn't have that. It took him a lot to gain the reputation that he had right now, even in such a short time. He needed this to work, and he knew it would.

"Why are you so adamant about him?" Max asked. "Why is this the one thing that you're being stubborn about?"

"Why is this the one thing that you are being stubborn about?" Charlie asked him right back. "It was my idea to let them into our territory. I'll take full responsibility if it fails. But I will try to see this plan through to the best of my capabilities."

There was another silence as they stared. Both of them seemed to be fighting with each other through their gazes. And neither of them wanted to back down.

"Alright," Max finally said. "Three days. I expect a full report."

"And you'll have it," he said. There were so many things that he was already thinking about to start this mission of his. He dismissed himself from the Alpha's office and started walking back to his.

The first thing he did, though, was put a mental block on the mind link. He knew that Max wasn't going to like it, but he knew that the man had done it to him. And he was going to need as much focus as he could get.

It was time to get to work.

CHAPTER 16:

Brushing

He didn't quite know why he was forced to stay to the cabin now. He must have messed up in some way. Alistair thought that he had done everything that they had wanted. But he also knew that this pack was very cautious. Even the twin warriors, Ray and Desmond, were still slightly warry of him.

They talked to him at least, those warriors. They seemed to enjoy the stories that he had told Nick and Ed. It was interesting to find out just how fast his stories traveled throughout the pack. He didn't mind everyone knowing. It brought him joy being able to tell them the stories of his travels. He just hadn't known that it would.

He told the twins more about his stay at the zoo. Even though it was just for a year, he had gotten plenty of stories. It was nice seeing all the children staring at him in wonder. He had also told them about when a child had fallen into the place where he was held.

Of course, his conversation with Nick the first day that he came had also made Madeline, Herb, and Jackie curious about him. It wasn't that he hadn't wanted to tell people his stories, he just wasn't used to talking. He had spent most of his life living as a wolf. And hardly any of that time was spent talking with anyone.

It was extremely lonely.

He talked to Madeline and Herb about Nick. When he told them that he was the source of his pull, they seemed a little confused at first. Herb was the first one who seemed to understand what it meant.

"It's a mate bond!" he told him. "You've been following a mate bond this whole time!"

"A mate bond?" He hadn't known that he was going to be blessed with a mate. His old pack had always told him that he wasn't worthy of one. That his only use was his skills in battle. He thought that this pull was leading him towards a good future for himself; a place where he could finally be at rest.

"You know what a mate bond is, right?" Herb asked. None of them were sure what Alistair knew at this time.

"Yes," he answered. "I just didn't think that this pull was it."

"You two are obviously made for each other, then," Madeline laughed. "Because you both acted like you didn't feel a thing for each other."

"They were staring at each other quite a lot," Jackie pointed out. "I think Nick feels something."

"If that's the case," Herb shook his head. "Then you two are the strangest couple I've met. Usually when you first find your mate you can't keep your hands off each other."

"He doesn't seem like that type of person," Jackie argued with her mate.

"It doesn't matter what type of person they are," Herb said. "That's how mates always react to each other. It takes a lot of control not to."

It did take him a lot of control. He remembered when he first saw him, and how many times he had wanted to close the distance between them. He remembered the feeling that he had gotten when the man first touched his arm. It was a sensation that he had never felt before. It was something that he had never thought he'd be able to experience.

"Well, since we know it's a mate bond now," Madeline stopped the bickering couple. "I can't believe it was so strong that you could feel it from as far away as you did."

"How far were you when you felt it?" Herb asked him.

"I don't know the exact location that I started feeling it," he answered. "At first, I had just ran in that direction, without knowing why. After a while, I felt it and realized that it was the reason why. I have been following it for a whole season."

"A whole season is roughly three months," Madeline said. "And, judging by how quickly you seem to travel, I'd say you were pretty far to have felt it."

He didn't know why it was shocking for them to hear that he had been following it for so long. All he knew was that he had finally found the source of it. He had finally solved his mystery.

And that had only made his need to have the man near grow.

Nick had started to come by every day after that. They'd all share their lunch together. Of course, Ed was there each time as well. He supposed that it was to keep the omega protected, in case they became hostile. Alistair never knew how difficult it would be to gain a pack's trust. He didn't know just how far their hatred towards rogues had gone.

When Nick would visit him at night, those were the best times. He loved talking to the man. It was obvious that he was lonely when he talked about his friend leaving the pack to go to her mate's. He could see the hurt in those hazel eyes. He wanted to be there for him, even if it was just as a friend. He wanted to be able to make him happy.

"How do I know you're going to stay here?" Nick had asked him that night. He was surprised that he would ask him something like that. Why would he be going through all of these trials of this packs if he didn't want to stay here for the rest of his life? Where would he go if he left here?

His answer seemed to surprise the chef. He looked at him as if something had clicked in his brain.

They talked a lot since then. Nick usually came at night on Alistair's days off, or in the morning, right before Nick's shift in the kitchen. He loved the conversations that they had. They could talk about anything and it would be complete bliss. Usually, it was stories that they would tell each other. He loved making the man laugh. He came to life when he really got into a discussion.

Sometimes he would have a desire to touch him during their talks under the moon. He refrained, though. As much as the man pulled him to want to be as close as possible, he didn't want to jeopardize what they already had. They had just met.

Maybe Nick would come tonight. He could use the company. Everyone was asleep for their patrols the next day. The Beta, Tyler, had told him that he was off from that duty for at least three days. He didn't know why, but he wouldn't ask. Asking a superior why they gave out an order was grounds for death.

But maybe Nick would have heard something during work. He didn't want to just lay around in the cabin. He had plenty of energy. So, he would guard the cabin at night. They were still close to the territory lines. It would be easy to see if any rogues were breaking through on their side. He was used to sleeping as a wolf on the forest ground, as he had done it many times. He was a light sleeper. He needed to be. If the wind changed, even a tiny bit, it might be time for him to leave.

It had only been one day that he had been stuck to the area around the cabin. He wouldn't complain, as he was still given his meals, and still allowed his friends to talk to. He just wished he knew what he had done to cause this. If it was something that he had done, what if he did it again?

He didn't know the culture of this pack enough to know if he had done anything wrong.

The pull grew strong again, distracting him from his contemplations. The moon shined brightly, even though it was slowly turning into a new moon. He hated the nights of the new moon. Those had always seemed to bring bad things to him. The Moon Goddess turned her head to rest on that day, and it was up to Alistair to fend for himself, without her guidance.

Those were the darkest nights as well. And his eyes were never the best.

He was going to change into his human form, as he could feel Nick come closer to the cabin, but then he heard an engine. Too curious to turn away, he followed the sound to see Nick alone in one of the vehicles that Ed used to bring them their food.

"Hey Alistair!" Nick smiled as he parked. "Do me a favor: don't change out of your wolf form."

Don't shift? But then he wouldn't get to talk to him. It wasn't like he had a mind link to share with him. He was sure that once they were officially mated they would. But for now, talking in their human forms were the only thing he could do.

Nick laughed a bit when he cocked his head. Alistair liked making him laugh, so he did it a lot.

"No offense, Mr. Snow Wolf," Nick told him. "But you look adorable when you do that."

His heart skipped a beat when he heard that. He didn't get compliments like that very often. He barely got compliments as it was. It was nice to hear Nick give him one.

"Alright," Nick had already gotten out of the car and was rummaging through one of the back seats. "I figured, since you were talking about how you were shedding so much, I could help you with that a bit."

Help him? Alistair watched curiously as Nick brought out a trash bin and a large grooming brush. They smelt interesting. He wanted to get closer and sniff them. Nick saw his nose twitching over to the new items and laughed.

"You act like a dog sometimes," His smile could light up the whole forest. "You know that?"

Nick went to pet his head. His hand had traveled slowly, cautiously. There was still a bit of uneasiness in him. It upset Alistair when he saw it. He didn't want the man to think that he would hurt him in any way.

He closed the gap with his nose and nudged his hand over his head. Nick smiled at that, shaking his own. He pet him a little. When he ran his hands through his thick fur, he could feel the sparks flying through him. It excited him and soothed him at the same time.

"Man," Nick broke the silence. "You really aren't doing well in this heat."

It was true. He hadn't been comfortable in his wolf form due to the intense shedding that his coat was undergoing. He wasn't used to such hot temperatures and it showed. Not only was he having to stop to drink water more, but his fur was so bad that Nick could pick gobs of it out.

He went to work on his coat, picking out the really bad patches, and brushing out the other ones. It was relaxing to have someone brush him. The brush felt good as it got all the extra fur off his body. Nick would take the fur and dispose of it in the trash bin that he brought.

There wasn't much talking in between them. Nick quietly hummed as he worked. It was almost enough to make him fall asleep. He would have if he didn't feel like he needed to keep watch of the cabin. Having Nick here alone made him more alert. He wanted to protect him. He was sure that this pack would never forgive him if he let something happen to the chef. He could tell that he was well known. Ray and Desmond seemed to know him well. They would all be devastated if rogues came and hurt him.

Of course, there was also the fact that he would be upset with himself if anything had happened to the man. There was still so much he wanted to know about him. A part of him was happy that Ed always came with him during the day. It was nice knowing that he was being protected, even if Ed was mainly trying to protect Nick from him rather than rogues.

Whether or not he seemed like he was weak, Nick was still an omega. It was obvious. He so perfectly calmed people down, and got them comfortable enough to open up. Yet, as much as he shared the similar traits of omegas, there was something unique about him. He didn't get scared easily, for instance. Or he didn't show it. He talked through sharing stories, rather than trying to be comforting in other ways.

He came off to people as a friend that you could tell anything to.

Which is why it hurt Alistair to see just how lonely the man was. He always brightened up when he was talking to someone, though. And he seemed happy around him. Alistair liked that he was happy around him.

"Jeez," Nick stopped humming for a minute. "I could make at least three of you with all this extra fur."

Alistair shook his head, making more fur fly off his neck.

"Hey!" Nick laughed as he tried to cover his face. "You're going to make me sneeze!"

He turned his head to look at the man. He had been working on the area near his tail. That was the part that he couldn't shed the easiest. The rest he seemed to be able to scratch off or rub off on some brush. He hated doing it, as it made it easier for people to track him, but sometimes it was necessary.

"I can see why this made you so uncomfortable," Nick said. "I can't imagine carrying all this heavy fur on my wolf. I'd probably wind up grumpy."

He perked his ears up. He hadn't had the chance to see Nick's wolf. He wondered what it looked like. Most people have wolves that match their hair and eyes, but that wasn't always the case. If you were born into a family of grey wolves, for example, your human hair wouldn't be grey, even if your wolf was.

Other than that instance, though, he had noticed that many of the members of this pack had different colored wolves. It made him curious as to why that was. Packs were typically all one or two colors, but this pack was every color imaginable. They must have been from many different families in their past.

His curiosity of what Nick's wolf looked like only grew at those thoughts. It would be fun to play as a wolf again. He hadn't gotten the chance to play since he was thirteen. And that was only for a short time before the Alpha of his old pack wanted him to be trained as a warrior.

He had a feeling that Nick's wolf would be playful. He would love to play with him, or run around a bit with his wolf. Maybe he could ask him sometime. It could be a good distraction from the boredom that he was trying to fight off.

"You know, I've never seen a white wolf until you," Nick told him. "I remember hearing stories about white wolves. Most of them were just tall tales that you hear as a kid though. It would be fun to see where you grew up. Just to see how much snow is there."

There was a lot of snow. He could remember that easily. If there was one thing he missed about that place, it was the beautiful snow that lay untouched by any being.

"I'd probably freeze to death there, though," Nick continued his rambling. "I don't exactly have the thickest of skin, or coats in my wolf form. That, and, growing up here, I got too used to the weather in this forest. It's still fun to play in the snow. I know that sounds childish, but I kind of like doing things like that from time to time."

Alistair didn't know why the man was trying to defend himself. He loved the idea of playing in the snow. Just because you aren't a child anymore doesn't mean that you have to stop doing what you find fun.

"But it's too much fun to lay in the sun too. I don't know how that works with you having a condition like that, but I love it. It's like a warm blanket, especially on the really sunny days in the winter."

There were so many things he wished he could say. He wanted to talk to him, instead of just hearing him go on and on about different things. He loved the sound of Nick's voice. His was higher than Alistair's, as everyone else's was, but it wasn't feminine in any way. His voice had a casual sound to it that made Alistair feel like he was on vacation from all the trials of his life whenever he talked to him. He just wished he could say something to the man so that he knew that he agreed with what he was saying.

Nick always seemed to only wear shorts when he went to see him at night. His tanned skin glimmered in the moonlight. Alistair liked seeing him without so many clothes. He had a little bit of black hair on his chest. It was thick, like the long hair that was always put up in a ponytail.

He didn't look like he had much muscle, but that was common for omegas. And he was only a cook. Alistair noticed that he had some muscle on his arm and legs, though. Other than that, he had such a slender frame.

He didn't look delicate, but he did look easy for Alistair to hold and lay with.

"At least you never have to worry about feeling the cold breeze," Nick took him away from his thoughts. "I should have brought a shirt or something."

His instincts kicked in before he could stop them. Alistair gently curled around the man, making sure that he nuzzled him to tell him that he meant no harm. Nick didn't say anything to his action. He just laid down with him. He had brushed enough fur off from him to where he could finally be comfortable again.

"I guess this works," Nick chuckled. "I was just going to say that I could use all the extra fur from you as a coat."

Wouldn't that be itchy? He cocked his head at the man again.

"It was supposed to be a joke," Nick patted his head, his smile reached up to his eyes. It was nice to see. At first, they just laid there, looking at all the stars in the sky. Nick would lazily pet his neck as he was closest to that.

Eventually, Nick had put his hands around his neck. He buried his face in his fur and sighed. Alistair never thought he'd ever feel something so amazing in his life. The sensation had his heart pounding loudly in his chest. He didn't want this to end.

He kept an ear out for the wind, just to make sure that no one would sneak up on them. He felt the need to protect this man the most out of all of the people he had met. Originally it had been Jackie, as she was carrying another life in her. He would still protect his friends with his life.

But he felt strongly about the one that was curled into him. He needed to protect the one that had pulled him all the way here. If it weren't for him, Alistair would have been much further south, most likely regretting the decision due to the heat. He would have never found this pack that was so generous to let him be in their territory.

He would have never been this happy.

After a while, the petting stopped. He heard light snoring coming from Nick. He looked at him. He looked so peaceful when he slept. It made him happy to see the man peacefully sleeping with him. He wished they could do it regularly.

The light snoring had a lulling effect on him. Soon, his eyelids were heavy, and he couldn't keep them open anymore.

With his ears towards the wind, Alistair fell into a deep sleep.

CHAPTER 17:

Unwanted Advice

Great. This was absolutely fantastic.

Now Max had fucked up beyond belief. He didn't think he could make such a grand mistake. He had tried so hard to be as careful as possible when it came to decisions so that there wouldn't be any. But there was something that he hadn't thought of when it came to his work.

And that was Charlie.

If he didn't know that Charlie was Luna material then, he sure did now. He was perfect at figuring out the best way to push his buttons too.

No, not all the time. He couldn't say that. It was only this once, actually. And it was about, out of everything else that they were dealing with, a rogue.

Didn't he understand anything? They had a pack to protect. Almost three hundred people were under their protection. And Charlie was going to be head strong about a rogue that they didn't know enough about? He knew that the blond understood how dangerous rogues were. Yet, for some reason, he felt compelled to fight with him over this one.

Werewolves are dangerous, and rogues are more so. With the average werewolf, they have a code to follow: a set of rules designated by their pack. If the pack was a good one, then so was the werewolf. But rogues were on their own. They had no laws to abide by and no rules to follow. They were the main ones that terrorized humans as well as any packs they could get ahold of.

If a pack were to take in a rogue, as many have and do regularly, it's best to know everything there is about that rogue beforehand. Secrets are a clear indication that they are trying to hide something from you. And that could be dangerous.

But Alistair didn't have secrets. He just had a clean slate for a memory when it came to the basic information that they needed. It amazed Max that he could even remember the name of his former pack.

It took them two weeks to find just the basic information on him, and Charlie expected to find everything else within three days?

Technically one now. Max had been losing his mind over just how much his mate seemed to dive into this project. He also hadn't been coming to bed and had shut him out of his mind. It hurt him to no end that he couldn't sense what his mate was feeling right at that moment. He wished he never taught him how to do something like that.

Which brought him back to how much he had fucked up.

Charlie had asked him why he was treating the man as if he was guilty until innocent. But he doesn't understand how dangerous a rogue like him is. The stronger the rogue, the more likely they were power hungry, or worked for an even stronger one. He could be a second in a rogue pack for all they knew.

And he had been traveling for ten years! That fact alone was enough to set off an alarm in his head. A rogue that can survive ten years by themselves is strong. The average rogue lasts about five at most. Usually during this time, they either join a pack or go into a rogue pack. That's the way that they survive as rogues.

But Alistair hadn't seemed to do that at all. He had simply traveled. He had traveled all the way from Alaska, through an entire country, to come here. It raised too many questions. Why did he decide this pack, out of all the other ones? Surely there were plenty of packs up north that would have accepted him. Why did he not settle down somewhere? How strong was he?

Max knew that the man's survival instincts were strong. The rogue seemed to be well aware of his surroundings, and easily remembered any new land that he entered. Tyler had told him just how quickly he had learnt the patrol path that he had been on.

Yes. He had saved Tyler from a vicious bite wound. But that could have easily been a plan to gain their trust. Max didn't trust it one bit. The rest of his warriors were left unharmed as well. He wasn't sure how to feel about that.

He was good at what he did, Max would give him that. But he wasn't sure that he could trust the man yet. And, with the little information that he was given about him, Max wasn't willing to let him stay on patrol until he trusted the man.

But, for some reason, Charlie was really adamant on it.

"It was my idea," he had told him. "I'll take full responsibility if it fails."

Charlie had looked so serious when he said that. As much as he was angry with him, he couldn't get over the fire in his eyes when he told him that. He just hated that it was being pointed at him. The man had truly grown over the few months of leadership, as did Max. They were the power couple of the century. They were able to get anything done, even when it came to convincing the Blood Moon Pack to get their heads out of their asses.

And it was all ruined over one rogue. That was what they disagreed on.

He must have really pissed Charlie off, because he hadn't let up on the barrier he had put in his mind at all. Max was completely cut off from his mate and he hated it. From what Max had found, the man had been keeping himself in his office for the past two days.

Meanwhile, Max couldn't even get any sleep without him around. He wanted to burst into that office and apologize, but something got the better of him. He worried too much for the safety of his pack to just give into him. Even if Charlie was able to find out everything about this man, he wasn't going to apologize. This was something that he had felt passionately about. And he wouldn't risk his pack's lives just because of a quarrel that he was having with Charlie.

Their first quarrel, he might add.

Max had been pacing in his office for some time now. He had gotten all that he needed done, and then some. Since he couldn't seem to sleep, he had spent his nights working himself to the bone. But now, there was nothing to do other than overthink what had happened between him and Charlie just a couple days ago.

When would this torture end?

A knock on the door almost made him jump. He had been so busy drowning in his thoughts that he was making himself jumpy. He was sure that the insane amount of caffeine that he had been drinking didn't help either.

"Come in," he said. He really hadn't wanted to talk to anyone. Ever since what happened between him and his mate, he was worried that he would snap at someone.

Dr. Button came in, followed by Max's dad. A feeling of dread filled him as he realized what this might be. It made him feel like a child again.

He wished he were a child again at this point. At least he wouldn't have to deal with a lover that hated him at the moment and a rogue problem that was threatening his relationship.

"I had a feeling you would be in here still," his father said. He took a seat in one of the chairs that were against the wall.

"Is it an emergency?" he asked. He didn't want to deal with any beating around the bush. He was already close to losing his mind as it was.

"A health one," Dr. Button said. "Sit down Max, let me check up on you."

"Me?" he looked at the doctor, dumbfounded. "I'm perfectly healthy."

"You look more like you've gotten lack of sleep and too much coffee." Those cold eyes wouldn't give into him. "It's in the pack's best interest if I give you a check-up. It's either that, or I speak with the council about it and make it a forced visit to my office."

Button always had a way with words.

For the record, that truly was something that the pack doctor could do if he felt that the Alpha needed medical attention but was refusing it. As much as it was his right to refuse the check-up, his health was absolutely crucial in the success of the pack. Therefore, he had no say in the matter.

Max reluctantly sat down in one of the chairs that Button had pulled forward. He didn't want to sit down. He needed to go for a run or do some training. He needed to do something to clear his mind.

But he couldn't stand being any farther away from Charlie.

The only thing that had been keeping him sane at the moment was that he could still feel his mate bond. His emotions were cut off from him, and he wasn't able to mind link with him, but he could still feel that he was near. Their offices weren't that far apart.

"So," His dad put his hands together and rested his chin on them. "Do you mind telling me what's going on between you and Charlie?"

"Yes, I do mind," he said. He'd rather not tell his father about this. All the man was going to do was tell him that he was an idiot and to go apologize.

As if he could go apologize right now.

Much to his surprise, his father chuckled at his response and shook his head.

"You know," he started. "Your mother and I had quarrels over work before. It was absolute hell having to deal with her when she was mad at me."

"I can only imagine," Max said. He was itching to get out of the chair that Button was forcing him in. The doctor was ignoring his antsy behavior while jotting some things onto his paper.

"We learned our first year that it's best not to take our disagreements to heart," his dad went on. "It only leads to hardships and difficulties."

Oh, his father had no idea what was going on. Max didn't even know where to start with all of this.

"It's a little different than you and mom," he told him. He knew that he would cave to his father eventually. "And it should only be one more day."

"What is it?" Those purple eyes pushed him to go on.

"This has something to do with Alistair," Dr. Button said. "Doesn't it?"

"Yes," Max buried his face in his hands. This was all so frustrating.

"Ah, yes," his father said. "The mystery rogue."

"Is it really wrong for me to restrict him more if he's been able to survive for so long as a rogue?" he asked him. He didn't want to get into this with anyone, but he didn't have a choice with his father. It wasn't like he didn't try to keep his love troubles away from everyone else.

"It's one method to deal with an issue," his father answered. "I'm assuming that Charlie had a different idea?"

"He thinks that I should keep him on patrol." He looked at his father incredulously. "How can I do that when it could easily be giving him the information he needs to give to the rogue pack that keeps attacking us?"

"How do you know he's working for the rogue pack?"

"How do I know that he isn't?" he fired right back at him. "The point is that there are too many unknown factors about this werewolf."

"I doubt he's in any rogue pack," Dr. Button said. "Not only are Albino werewolves seen as weak in comparison to any other wolf, they are usually killed by both pack and rogue alike for their white fur."

"He's stronger than the rogue's we've fought," he answered. "If there's one thing he's not, it's weak. His healing abilities are better than most of the pack members and his awareness of his surroundings is more enhanced than any of our trackers."

"And I'm sure Charlie brought up the fact that he hasn't done anything harmful to the pack?" His father had leaned back in the chair he was in, taking in all that he had said. "And has been respectful towards us?"

"Yes," he frowned. Great. Was his father on Charlie's side too? Would no one see his view on this? "I don't trust him. There have been countless stories about rogues gaining pack's trust and attacking the pack from the inside."

"He does have a point," Dr. Button said, looking at his father. "Liam would probably agree that it would be best to restrain him more until further information was acquired."

"Very true," his father said. "But there was no scent of the other rogues on the man."

"There are plenty of ways to get scents off," he said. "Creeks, trees, dirt, mud. Any of those things could be used to take away any smells that linger on you."

"Another good point." His father smiled at him. He always seemed to look proud whenever he was talking to him about the pack.

"Glad someone agrees," he sighed. Dr. Button finished his check-up with him, allowing him to stand. He went over to the chair on the other side of his desk and sat down. It was interesting how just a few short months ago his father would be the one sitting there. It was strange realizing just how much could change in a short amount of time.

"So, that leads us to the final question." His father moved his chair to face him.

"What?"

"What is it that you want for this rogue?" he asked. "What did you feel the first time you met him?"

"Confused," Max answered.

"Why?"

"Because he didn't act like a rogue usually did," he told him. "He was powerful, but never once tried to show it to me. I was confused because I had never thought that I would see the day where a rogue would actually ask to come onto our territory, and become a member of our pack."

"When you were questioning him," his father started. "The first day that he was brought into our territory, what were your instincts telling you?"

"That he was telling the truth." He rubbed his temples. "That he was willing to listen to me through any order I gave him. But that doesn't mean that I should just follow my gut and let him right into the pack." He looked at his father again as he spoke. "If I just follow my gut, then I run the risk of being too impulsive. And an impulsive leader is a foolish one."

"You've been trained well for your title," his father smiled at him. "Just remember that it usually takes both your instincts, as well as your knowledge to make a decision on something. And that's where your Luna comes in."

"What do you mean?"

"The Alpha and Luna are opposites, yet the same," his father explained. "If one is impulsive, the other is grounded and thoughtful. If one is keen to listen to their gut, the other usually listens to their logic.

They are the yin and yang of each other. But, without being able to work together to find a balance, you wind up with disarray."

"Can you just tell me what you're talking about already?" Max rubbed his head again. This was all giving him the biggest headache. "I haven't had enough sleep for this."

"What I'm trying to say is that you two need to work together in issues like this," his father told him. "If you both have a disagreement on something, then it needs to be worked out, before it turns into a greater issue."

"Look." He put a hand up to stop him. "I've already messed up on this. There's no going back. Charlie will tell me tomorrow if he's actually found all the information he could on Alistair, and then, hopefully, this can all be resolved then."

"And do you plan on living off from coffee until then?" Dr. Button lifted an eyebrow at him. "Because you would have had at least five heart attacks with how much caffeine is pumping through your system right now."

"I'll take it easy on the caffeine." He told the doctor. "I promise."

"I'll tell Aldi to get someone up here to bring you breakfast," Button said. He couldn't believe that it was already morning. It felt like just a minute ago it was mid-afternoon and he was up to his elbows in paperwork.

"Just think about what I said." His father patted him on the back. He nodded his response and watched them leave his office.

Hopefully Button would check up on Charlie next. As much as Max could handle not eating much for a couple of days, he didn't want his love to try that.

Should he have listened to him more? He didn't know anymore. All he knew was that he wished that it was tomorrow already. This was enough to drive him crazy. He already felt like he was going insane.

Okay. He would let Charlie complete his assignment. Then he would talk to him about this. They needed to have a nice long talk, and it wasn't just because Max missed him. They needed to figure out how they could resolve a conflict like this without it resulting in the silent treatment. His father was right, this wasn't healthy.

And he never wanted to fight with Charlie. He had worked hard so that he wouldn't fight with the man. After he had opened up to him, Max had always wanted to be there for him. He wanted to be the one that Charlie could always turn to when he needed someone. And he still did.

But work got in the way of those thoughts.

They had both been so caught up in it that neither of them were able to be there for each other, or talk to each other much. They worked great together when they agreed on something. But they needed to be able to work out a problem rather than doing whatever this was.

Charlie was right. They needed a vacation.

"Hey Max," Aldi's voice invaded his thoughts.

"Yes?" He really hoped that this was just about what food he wanted, or something silly like that.

"Do you know where Nick is?" the chef asked. *"I can't seem to find him anywhere."*

"Isn't he on the morning shift?"

"Yeah, but he hasn't shown up," Aldi answered. *"He's never been this late."*

Now a whole new kind of panic surged through him. One that he was hoping he would never have to feel. As quickly as he could, Max ran out of his office and off of the third floor.

Where the hell was Nick?!

CHAPTER 18:

Heat

It was bright in his room. He usually pulled the curtains over the windows before he went to bed, but he guessed he must have forgotten. It threatened to force his eyes open, but Nick just liked the feeling of the warmth that it gave.

The summers were the best for him. The sun always felt so good on his skin. It warmed him to the bone. Usually, the pack house had the AC on so that he couldn't feel the heat when he woke up.

He should be getting up. The kitchen probably needed him right now. But everything was so nice where he lay. He actually felt like he had gotten some decent sleep. He hadn't slept well for a while now. He had a dreamless sleep as well, which was another thing that hadn't happened in a while. His dreams had left him tossing and turning all night. But now they were quiet.

He wanted to stay asleep all day. He would tell Aldi that he wasn't feeling well or something. And just enjoy the peace and warmth that he had now. He could forget everything that he was worried about; every troubling thought was tied up and thrown out. He could finally just enjoy life.

Then he felt something nuzzle against his neck.

Nick opened his eyes to find that he wasn't in his room. He was in the forest, far into the forest. Although his body seemed unwilling to start functioning, his brain was forced to try and recall what had happened the night before. Slowly, but surely, he remembered what he had done.

Oh no. He had fallen asleep when he was hanging out with Alistair.

What time was it? Aldi was going to be pissed and start looking for him if he wasn't in the kitchen at a certain time. Looking at the sunrise, he was already late for his shift. The morning shift started as soon as the sun started to rise in the summer. In the winter it was before sunrise, as it took its sweet time shining in the sky then.

He tried to move, his eyes still adjusting to the bright sunlight that was around them. That's when he noticed arms around him. They tightened and pulled him closer. He looked to see who the arms belonged to, and saw Alistair snuggled up against him.

He couldn't say that it didn't feel nice. His touch calmed him. Alistair was beautiful even when he was asleep. His pale skin stuck out in comparison to the forest floor, or Nick, for that matter. And his white hair went every which way as he slept. Even his scent was calming. And his hold on Nick felt more like pillows than anything else. Nick must have curled into him in his sleep, because he didn't remember being this entangled in the man.

Wait a second.

Wasn't he a wolf when Nick had fallen asleep?!

Nick shook his head a little. He didn't have time to think about all of this. He was about to get yelled at so badly that his ears were going to fall off if he didn't get home soon. He forced his body to move again, grabbing onto Alistair's arms to lift them. Hopefully the man was a heavy sleeper and he could just explain all of this the next time he saw him.

Nope.

Those muscular arms moved, but not off from him. Instead, they started rubbing his sides. He gasped at the foreign feeling it gave. Nick tried to force himself to fight against the feeling, but was quickly met with the man shifting to be on top of him. Those red eyes were hazy, yet intense. Nick couldn't say that he didn't like the way the man looked at him.

"Don't leave." Alistair moved his hand up to his face. He rubbed his thumb across his cheek, sending electricity all through him. "Please."

He should have told him that he needed to go; that if he didn't, they might both be in trouble. But there was something about that low baritone voice, and those hypnotizing eyes that stopped him. Instead, he nodded. He had a feeling that his body wouldn't let him leave even if he tried. The sensations he was getting from Alistair's touches were enough to keep him in his arms for an eternity.

Alistair leaned in closer to him. His hands were starting to gently travel all over his body. It felt good to be touched like this, or held for that matter. He had never been touched like this. As much as it was gentle, he could feel the desire that came from them.

He was frozen, unsure of what to do or say. He didn't really have any experience with this kind of stuff. He didn't even know just where this was going to go. All he knew was that Alistair's touch felt good. And his minty scent was something that he would love to have as a cologne.

The man's breathing was light as his face dipped down closer to him. Their faces were so close now, their noses could almost touch. He could see the careful look that Alistair had in his darkening eyes. He was trying to be cautious. But Nick had no idea what he planned on doing with him.

Then their lips met.

Did he say that he was new to this stuff? Because, he was. Even when it came to kissing. He wasn't one of those kids who experimented or anything when he was younger, which made this more embarrassing. But he didn't have time to feel insecure about any of it. He kissed him back, of course. The man had already worked his way into his mouth, and was easily taking charge of it. His hands continued their exploring of every bit of exposed skin that Nick had. It was summer, so he had only decided to wear shorts. Now, he wasn't sure whether the idea was a horrible one, or a brilliant one.

His mind was hazy at the moment. He was focusing solely on the sensations that this man was giving him. Alistair was in complete control of his body and he didn't know how to feel about it. All he could do was enjoy the amazing feeling that came from their bodies touching.

He felt his hair come loose from its ponytail. Alistair's hand threaded into it, pushing his head closer to him. The kiss only deepened as he did this. Nick couldn't help but put his arms around the man. He felt completely helpless to his touch. It felt so good. It was warm, but it left his skin with goosebumps. And the kiss was enough to keep him in that spot forever. He didn't care if anyone would find them at that moment. He didn't care about the fact that he had barely met the man. All he cared about was this feeling right now.

Nick gasped for breath as the man broke the kiss. But Alistair just used the break to scatter kisses over his neck. He leaned into each one. It felt like he was drowning in a feeling that he wasn't used to. His whole body was lit up, and he was squirming under the man's caressing.

Alistair's hand had moved from his hair back to his bare torso. Everywhere the man touched, he leaned into him. He wished he could say something to him. But everything the man was doing was overloading his senses. All he could do was weave his fingers into the man's soft white hair, as his mouth continued its assault on his neck.

He was heavy and light at the same time as he put more pressure on him. His leg had wound up in between Nick's, slowly putting pressure on an area that hadn't had attention in a while. Nick gasped. A part of him desperately wanted this. He wanted to submit to this man that he had just met.

Was this how mates normally felt? He barely knew Alistair, and had only met him a short while ago, but his whole being felt like it belonged to him. He wanted the man to keep doing exactly what he was doing and to never stop.

But there was also that problem of his. The problem that was the whole reason why he didn't think he was ever destined to have a mate. The problem that had left him fighting off depression as a teenager and left him pulling himself together time and time again.

Although the sparks were doing a damn good job at lighting up most of his body, it wasn't doing much for his lower half.

That was, until he felt something else rub against him.

It twitched.

He wasn't sure what to think. But his brain decided to finally function at that point. And, through the art of surprise alone, he got out of Alistair's hold. His heart was pumping with fear. He stood a good distance away, wide-eyed and catching his breath.

He couldn't believe he had almost done that. He couldn't believe that he had almost let that happen.

He looked into those red eyes one last time. They were darker than usual and filled with lust, yet shocked at the same time. Nick was grateful that he didn't try to move closer to him. It gave him a second to truly see the situation that he had put himself it.

Alistair was naked, probably from shifting into his human form. His labored breath was the only thing that he could hear through the quiet forest. And he had been on top of him, holding him down.

It wouldn't take an expert to figure out what was going to happen if he didn't pull away when he did.

"Nick," he finally said, those red eyes had lost their lustful gaze and was changing into guilt. "I'm so-!"

He didn't give him time to speak. He just ran. He shifted into his wolf form and ran. His shorts were now shredded, but he didn't care. He had to calm that beating heart of his. His brain was a scattered mess of feelings and memories as it tried to piece together what had just happened.

He had almost…

With…

Maybe it wasn't a good idea that he went out to visit Alistair alone. He knew that it wasn't a good idea in the first place, but there was something about the feeling that Alistair gave him when he talked to him that he loved. He wanted to hold onto that feeling. It was the only good thing that he had right now.

Sure, he had his work. And he loved his work, but he could only do so much in that kitchen before he was done with his shift. Ever since Aldi had come back from his vacation, he had been making sure that Nick didn't stay too late. He told Nick that he was working himself too much.

Alistair kept away the feeling of loneliness that threatened to drown him. He knew that the man was his mate, even though he still wouldn't say it out loud. There was only one person he would ever say it to, and she still wasn't picking up her phone.

And what just happened between them left a whole bunch of mixed feelings surging through him. When you first find your mate, the first thing that you want to do is mark them, and make the bond stronger. He could tell that Alistair was planning on marking him right there and then. It was plain to see in those lustful eyes of his. He wanted to claim him. It was something that the dominant one always wanted to do.

But Nick wasn't ready for that. There were so many things that they didn't know about each other. That and he had no idea how the pack was going to react to it. He knew that they wouldn't do anything to him, but they could easily do something to Alistair.

Then there was also the fact that he couldn't get it up.

After all of those sparks and all of those good feelings that were surging through him just those few short moments ago, all it did was make it twitch.

Of course, that was way more than even he had been able to do with it, but it wasn't going to be enough to appease a lustful beta. He was hoping that he wouldn't have to tell him for at least a while. It was embarrassing to talk about, and usually only resulted in him having to tell his whole life story.

Why did everything have to be so complicated now? He already missed the days when he was just hearing about all the gossip of newly mated couples. Back then he could just laugh and shake his head, maybe make a few jokes. Now he supposed it was his turn to deal with the drama.

"Nick!" He almost jumped when he heard Max's voice in his head. *"Where are you?"*

"Just headed home now," he answered. *"I accidentally fell asleep in the forest."*

"Get to the kitchen," Max ordered. He held a seriousness to his voice. *"Now."*

A new kind of worry filled him as he ran home. He wasn't as fast as the warriors, so it took a bit longer to travel through the forest for him. Usually, he wouldn't mind. But now he was sure he was going to be slaughtered for his tardiness.

He wasn't even going to have time to shower.

Oh, he was in more trouble than he thought! Now he simply wished that he was back to dealing with his problems with Alistair. At least then he wouldn't have the Alpha's rage to deal with.

He wouldn't be worried if it were a week ago. He knew that Max was pretty lenient when it came to certain rules. But right now, he was dealing with a quarrel with Charlie.

And when the Alpha and Luna are fighting, it only means the worst of the worst for the rest of the pack.

He quickly ran through a pond to try and rid himself a little of Alistair's scent. The rest of the run quickly dried him off. When he got back to the house, he changed forms and threw on his uniform before bolting to the kitchen.

"Nick!" Aldi stood right by the entrance to the kitchen. "Where have you been? We've been worried sick about you!"

"Sorry about that," he said. "I couldn't sleep last night so I went into the forest to clear my head. I guess I must have fallen asleep out there."

There was no way in hell he was going to look at Max right now. His childhood friend was standing right next to Aldi, looking like a steamed vegetable.

He hadn't really seen him for the past few days. Everyone was saying that he had thrown himself into his work now that him and Charlie were fighting. He couldn't believe that the two of them were arguing. They were such a power couple before all of this. No one seemed to be able to figure out what they were fighting about either, as neither of them were coming out of their offices.

"And you didn't hear any of our calls?" Max asked him. His tone was dark and demanding. Nick had never heard him talk like that before.

"I haven't really been getting that great of sleep," he told him, keeping his head down. "It won't happen again."

Aldi seemed okay with his answers. They weren't lies, so he knew that Max wouldn't yell at him for that. But he was an idiot to think that he was out of the deep end just yet.

One thing that not many people knew about Max: when he was pissed, he had an aura about him that could absolutely paralyze whoever it was aimed at. Nick knew because there were plenty of time when he had seen Max mad at other people. This was the first time it was actually getting directed towards him.

He could feel him getting closer to him, and hear his footsteps.

"Nick," Max said. "Look at me."

He did as he was told. Max looked like he hadn't slept in days. His hair was still combed, but it was disheveled in a way that made it seem like he had run his hands through it way too much. His purple eyes were darker than usual.

Nick was so fucked.

"Why do you smell like him?" Max asked.

Of course, he wouldn't have been able to get Alistair's scent off just by running through a pond really quick. The man had only kissed the entirety of his neck. He should have taken a shower before he tried to go in the kitchen, but he knew that doing that would raise suspicion as well. And that would be going against an order.

When an Alpha tells you to do something now, you do it now.

"I was helping him with something last night," he answered. There was no beating around the bush with Max. That only pissed him off more. And, needless to say, Nick was already terrified of the man right now.

He was good at staying calm around people who were stronger than him, but that didn't count when it was this bad of a mistake.

"How do you even know him?" Max asked. "How long has this gone on?"

"Since Ed brought me there to try and loosen them up," he said.

"Ed brought you there?!"

Oh boy! Looks like Nick wasn't the only one that Max was going to kill today.

"Sorry in advance, Ed," he said through the mind link.

"He said that I was the perfect one to help get some more information out of them," he told him. Max's eyes were only getting darker the more he said, but if he tried to hide anything from him, he would only be getting himself in more trouble. "We both got some good information out of them."

Why didn't Ed tell Max that he was bringing Nick over there? That was something that left him a bit confused. With these rogues being such a serious issue for the pack, he was sure that Max had wanted to know every detail regarding them.

"No one is allowed to go there without my permission," Max told him. Nick cowered under his intense gaze. "No matter who you went with."

"S-sorry," he couldn't help but fear the man right then. He didn't look like he was in the best of minds either.

"What did you go to help him with?" Max asked.

"He was talking about how uncomfortable it was in his wolf form because of his shedding," he answered. "I kinda went out there to brush him."

That reminded him. The jeep and trash can were still out there.

"You went all the way to the edge of our borders," he started. "Just to brush him?!"

"Yes," his voice was small. Max really looked like he was going to hit him. Max. The man who had always stood up for him when they were kids. Nick never thought he'd see the day when he'd fear his childhood friend so much.

"Max," Aldi stepped closer to them. "Please, let's just be happy that he's okay."

He never took his eyes off from Max. He watched as those purple eyes closed. Max took a deep breath for a second, pinching the bridge of his nose while he did it. It was a calming method that Nick had seen him do a lot when they were kids. Thankfully, the next time he opened them, his eyes had almost gotten back to their normal color.

"Never do that again," he ordered.

"I promise," Nick said. He really just wanted this to be over with.

"Good," Max said, his voice was still low, but it had lost its intensity. "You're under house arrest until further notice. I don't want to see you outside of the pack house grounds."

"But-!"

"I will not change my mind!" Max hollered. Nick almost fell with how powerful his voice was. "If you go anywhere near that forest, or anywhere outside of our property, you will be punished! Do you understand?!"

"Y-yes," he answered.

Max left at that. Aldi tried to comfort him, as his nerves were more than frayed at that point, but there wasn't much the cook could do.

He wasn't going to be able to see Alistair at all now.

Now he truly was alone.

CHAPTER 19:

The Albino

Papers were scattered on the desk, none of them as organized as they were when he had first tidied up his office. He tried to keep them in their separate piles, but there was only so much he could do when he was trying to focus on something.

Charlie had been making phone calls and looking through news websites for the past two and a half days. He told Max to give him three. And he was going to be damned if he wasn't going to find every bit of information he could about this man that he was so worried about.

When he was in the charter school for law, he had to do study sessions like this. Of course, it was never for this long. But he had remembered staying up all night plenty of times just to get his work done. He was a perfectionist in school. You had to be if you wanted to keep your grades up. And he had still graduated with honors.

Of course, it didn't do too much for him. But it helped prepare him for this kind of situation at least.

He hadn't slept much other than the times he would pass out on his desk. Heather, one of the maids, would come in every now and then to give him his meals. She was a nice woman. Isabelle was the main one who had helped to make sure he ate. Although no one could convince him to get some sleep. Not even Dr. Button could. He had come in with Mr. Locke to check up on him a short while ago.

Thinking about that reminded him of Max. He really wished he hadn't put up that mental block on him. He had acted out of anger when he did it. Well, he had said to himself that he wanted to concentrate. It wasn't entirely a lie. He was sure that Max would try and distract him in one way or another if he hadn't done it. But he missed him now, and he knew that he was going to be hurt when he finally decided to talk to him.

He also didn't know how to take down the mental block.

He had learned about it before. But his brain was so full with information on his own project that he couldn't remember how it was done. He was sure that he didn't have the strength to do something like that right now anyway. He was absolutely exhausted, working off from maybe two or three hours of sleep in the couple days since he started this assignment.

But Charlie had been in worse situations. He had been doing twelve hour shifts in a crummy restaurant with no food before. It wasn't the healthiest way to live, but he lasted a week doing that. He could last a few days with little to no sleep.

He also had to stay in his office in case anyone called him back. There were quite a few time differences in the places he was trying to get ahold of. They could call him at any time of the day or night. Charlie couldn't miss a call, not even if it meant staying up crazy hours.

He had noticed something when he started digging into Alistair's past: he had more run ins with humans than he had beasts. There were countless stories about a huge albino wolf in local papers all across Canada.

He made sure to talk to Ed to see what Alistair had told him about his past. So far, he had been able to prove almost every one of his tales as true. In the news articles that he found it always wrote him in as helping others. If he was seen, it was to help people rather than hurt them.

The fight with the werebear for instance. Charlie couldn't confirm that it was a werebear, but there was a newspaper in the local town about an albino wolf risking its life to save two hikers from one. The article confirmed that a wildlife veterinarian had taken him under their care to make sure that he would heal properly. He was brought to the local zoo afterwards. There was even a news article in that same town about the wolf escaping almost exactly a year after the first article on him. Just as he had told Ed.

Other than that, he had Isabelle find some numbers to some of the packs in Canada. There weren't any in Alaska that could confirm that they saw him, and he was wary of calling the man's old pack, if they had a number to call them at all. But there were plenty of packs that had seen him during his travels. Most were wary of him, but they said that he hadn't harmed them in any way.

There was a few that didn't favor him. They seemed like they had biased opinions, though. They had told him that he had threatened them or tried to hurt their women and children. It would be an alarming thing to hear, if Charlie didn't research into the packs that he was calling. The packs that were saying those horrible things about Alistair were well known for their bad reputations and brutal ways.

There was also one that had told him of the werewolf doing the exact same thing that he had done with them, only it was just to pass through their territory. They told Charlie that he had howled to get the Alpha's attention, and then requested permission to pass through their territory. It was, by far, the strangest thing they had dealt with from a rogue. But they also told him that he looked dehydrated and desperate for food and water. And yet, he did not stop while in their territory to drink or hunt.

He followed the Alpha's advice to the letter. Just like he had done with Max's instructions.

He had gotten a map of the entirety of Canada, and had started to tack down every place that he had evidence of Alistair being in. The only thing that he hadn't been able to track down was exactly where he had been abandoned by his pack. He had tried calling some wildlife vets in Alaska to see if they had anything in their records of him, but they hadn't answered, and he was still waiting on them to call back.

In the meantime, he had called Alistair's old doctor, the one that he had when he was a child. The doctor was quick to tell him everything other than his medical history, as that was illegal unless Charlie had his consent for him to disclose.

The doctor had told him that Alistair had shown signs of child abuse. He had tried to get CPS involved with the boy, but they had done nothing on the matter. His mother, Iliana, had passed away due to a horrible sickness that was plaguing Alaska and a part of Canada during the time.

He was only fifteen when she had passed.

As far as a father, a name wasn't written down on his birth certificate. Charlie had read about disabilities with werewolves in a book that Dr. Adelle had brought him. He could easily make the assumption that the father was too ashamed of Alistair being albino to admit that he was his son. But Charlie had no evidence of that, so he wouldn't be telling Max that.

He had found out almost everything about the man within two and a half days. And he was proud of his ability to do so. It wasn't just him, though. Isabelle had actually helped him quite a lot. She had even stayed up with him all night while making calls. Charlie was grateful for her help, but he also wondered why she seemed so dead set to help him on this topic.

Charlie was doing this to prove himself as a good Luna, and because he didn't believe that the man should be punished for doing nothing wrong. But Isabelle had no reason to stay any longer than what she was scheduled for. And he hadn't pushed her to stay at all. In fact, he had told her to go and check up on her kids many times, but she always came back after an hour or so.

She seemed just as headstrong about this man as Charlie was. And he sensed that there was a different reason behind her motivation.

"You know you don't have to stay to help me," he told her. She looked almost as exhausted as he felt. "I'm already done with all the extra paperwork for the pack, and we're just waiting on one last call until we're done." He was excited to show Max his findings. He was sure that he was going to be amazed.

Maybe he'd take a few days off after this. He had done all his Luna paperwork for the next week while waiting on phone calls. It really passed time. But now he was all done, other than tidying up his office a little more.

He was excited to have those few days off after this. Maybe he'd be able to apologize to Max for putting up the block and they could just spend a day or two together. If the man didn't have his own duties to do still. Charlie wasn't exactly sure. Other than going to the bathroom, he hadn't really left his office.

"I can wait for one more phone call," Isabelle answered. She was carefully putting papers away. "They should be calling any minute now, anyway."

"That's why you should be with your kids and Tyler," Charlie gave her a gentle smile. "I can handle the last phone call." He had actually gotten used to talking over the phone by doing this project of his. He still didn't quite like it, but if it was for work, then it was much easier.

"Tyler can handle the kids for an hour more," Isabelle argued. She grabbed more papers off from Charlie's desk. Her bun was slowly starting to come undone, and strands were starting to come out of it. "And I could say the same about you and Max."

"This is the last thing I need before I can talk to him again." He really did want to prove himself. It wasn't just to this pack, but to Max as well. If there was one thing he had noticed in the argument that they had last, it was that Max didn't seem to trust Charlie as the Luna. Of course, him being human, there were some things he didn't quite understand, but Max had treated him as if he had no idea what he was talking about when they were arguing. He was looking at Charlie as if he was just that waiter that he had met last year, the one that didn't know a thing about werewolves, or that they existed.

He had poured his heart and soul into learning about this pack. He was going to prove his dedication. And he knew in his heart that Alistair was a good man. Everything about him showed kindness.

He looked like how Charlie looked when he was younger: lost.

Maybe that was another reason why he had wanted to fight for the man.

"He's probably really worried about you right now," Isabelle told him. "I heard from Tyler that he hasn't left his office other than one time the past three days"

"I didn't want him to worry," Charlie told her. "I just wanted to be able to focus on this."

"I understand," she said. "The mind link can be too much if you're really trying to get to work. Many warriors put up mental barriers when they're out on patrol so that they can focus on the task at hand."

"I'm glad I'm not the only one then." He smiled and shook his head. He couldn't wait to curl up in his bed after this. He swore he could sleep a whole day away.

They worked in silence, just cleaning up the office one last time. Charlie was sure that there was going to be more paperwork coming his way soon. But, for now, he could be proud that it was all done and he finally didn't have any work left on his plate.

"Isabelle," he broke the silence. "Can I ask you something?"

"Ask me anything," she said. She usually hummed while she worked. But the past couple days she was just as quiet and focused as Charlie with this project, which left him curious.

"Why are you so interested in finding out more about Alistair?" he asked her. "I know that he saved Tyler, but it seems like there's another reason underneath the surface."

Isabelle stopped what she was doing, standing in place as if she were frozen. He looked over to see that her dark eyes were lost in a sea of memories.

Maybe he shouldn't have asked. But he was too curious why the woman seemed so passionate about a man that she hadn't even met yet. Only a handful of people had met Alistair, as Max had ordered that no one try to meet him unless they had his permission. Although Tyler had met him, as he had been going with him on patrol most of the time, Isabelle hadn't.

What was making her so lost in thought?

"Before I met Tyler," she started. Her head was tilted downward, as if she could find her memories there. "I was in the Bloodtooth pack. We were a smaller pack, but we were strong. The Alpha had it in his head that we would all have strong offspring so that the pack would grow stronger." She paused in what she was saying. Charlie wasn't sure if she was going to continue or if she was going to drown in the sea of her own memories.

"And then?" He pushed her a little.

"Then my mother gave birth to my younger sister," Isabelle answered. Her voice was quieter than before. The hurt was clear to hear. "She was a beautiful baby of pure white skin and red eyes."

"Your sister was albino?"

"She was," Isabelle nodded, sniffling a bit. "My parents fought the Alpha tooth and nail to keep her alive. You see, Charlie, many packs aren't accepting of different kinds of beings like this pack. A lot of them will kill an albino werewolf right as a baby. They're seen as the weakest link of the pack, because they have so many health issues."

"Did the Alpha kill her?" He felt afraid to ask. He didn't like the idea of anyone killing off something that was innocent just because they think they are weak.

"No," she shook her head, sniffling a bit. "She passed away when she was ten. She had gotten too sick for the doctors to be able to help her. She," The sniffles became louder and Isabelle covered her face a bit. "She wasn't even able to meet her wolf. She was my best friend growing up."

Charlie didn't know what else to do, so he pulled her into a tight hug. He had no idea that this was such a serious topic for her.

"Albino werewolves are rare," Isabelle pulled away from his hug. "There isn't many that live as long as Alistair has. If they can survive long enough to meet their wolves, then most of their health problems can be managed easier. I've noticed that from the information that we got about Alistair."

"So, albino werewolves get sick a lot?"

"Yes." She nodded her head. She was carefully dabbing her tears away with a tissue to try and keep her makeup intact. "But my sister was just the unlucky one. Most albino werewolves won't die from their sicknesses if they are given the proper treatment as children. Most of them die from their packs."

That was enough to make Charlie shiver. He couldn't believe that anyone would just kill something that was innocent. It reminded him of culling, something that they had done with Labrador dogs in the past, when they thought that the yellow ones weren't as great of hunting dogs as the black ones.

Only this was with human beings. Charlie didn't care whether they could turn into wolves or not, they still had a human side to them. And killing them off just because they were albino is horrible in both the animal kingdom, as well as for humans.

"Well," He put a hand on her shoulder. "Alistair isn't your sister. But we'll still treat him as best as we can. He still has to gain Max's trust, though."

"Max doesn't trust him because he's travelled so far and for so long," she told him.

"I know," he answered. "Hopefully, this will help him trust him a little bit more."

He could only hope. This was just about the extent of Charlie's capabilities. He just hoped that it was good enough to meet Max's standards for him.

He really missed the Max that would look at him with soft, loving eyes, rather than the hard, cold ones that he had last seen. He missed the softer side of his mate.

He guessed that being the Alpha, and dealing with the stress of that can make you forget about the other parts of yourself. Maybe Charlie was the one being too hard on him. After all, he was just trying to keep his pack safe.

The phone ringing snapped both him and Isabelle out of their daydreaming. Charlie was the first one to reach it.

The phone call only lasted ten minutes, but it was enough to give Charlie the last thing he needed to finish his project. He hung up the phone and looked at Isabelle with tired but excited eyes.

"We got it!" He told her. He put the last tack in place on the map and headed out of his office. He had to find Max. He had to finally end this mess that they had both put themselves in. Charlie was so happy that he could kiss him right then.

He told Isabelle to head to her room. She needed to check on her kids before Tyler went on patrol. It was close to night time now, as the sun was slowly setting on the horizon. Charlie had been worried that he wouldn't be able to finish his mission on time. He was absolutely ecstatic that he had completed it.

He was a little nervous when he got to the Alpha's office. He hesitated before knocking on the door. He hadn't seen Max in almost three whole days. He wondered how he was going to react to seeing him there.

Did he look okay?

Should he shower before he did this?

Oh, there was no time for all of that! He needed to show him what he had found, and he needed to show him now! Charlie knocked on the door quietly at first. After a second of no answer, he tried a little louder.

After not getting an answer the second time, he grew impatient. He opened the office doors, praying that he wouldn't walk into some sort of meeting. Surprisingly enough, the office was empty.

But he had heard that Max had been in the office the entire time. Where was he when Charlie needed to talk to him?

The next thing he tried to do was call him. Max always picked up the phone unless he was patrolling with the warriors.

No answer.

Okay, now it was Charlie's turn to get worried. He supposed that this was karma for not talking to him for three days and blocking him out of his head. That's okay. He could deal with that as long as he figured out where the man was.

"Hey, Sam!" He noticed the Delta as soon as he got off the third floor. "Do you know where Max is?"

"He's not in his office?" Sam asked. He was holding one of his twin babies in his arms. But Charlie didn't have time to coo over the adorable thing now.

"No," he told him. "Did he tell you where he was going?"

"Well, he might be out patrolling," Sam answered. "I saw him head outside mid-afternoon. If he did go on patrol though, he should be on his way back now."

"Thanks!" he said before running off. He didn't want to deal with Sam asking why he couldn't just mind link with him. He was too exhausted to try and take down that mental barrier. So, he was going to do things the old-fashioned way.

It was a good thing that Max had taught him how to drive for the most part. He hadn't been able to find time to try and get his license, but he could drive one of the small jeeps around. He was shocked that this family had so many jeeps that they owned, but they were perfect for off-roading, so he guessed that was why.

He knew where Max usually patrolled. Of course, he wasn't going to go all the way to the edge of the territory, but he could meet Max half way.

He had a lot of things to be excited for.

CHAPTER 20:

Snowstorm

"There you are," Madeline sat next to him. He was outside of the cabin, looking at the sun as it left the sky. "We were wondering where you disappeared to."

"I'm sorry," he told her. "I didn't want to worry anyone."

"Alistair, you say sorry too much," Madeline chuckled a bit. "Mind telling me why you've been so distant lately?"

"Distant?"

"You've been quiet the whole day." She put a hand on his back. "All you've been doing is staring off into space."

"I've been thinking," he told her. He had been praying for forgiveness, and hoping that the Moon Goddess would grant him one more chance.

He knew he didn't deserve it, but he knew that the goddess was a merciful one. If not, he wouldn't have lived this long.

"Is it about Nick?"

"Yes," he answered. He had a feeling that the woman was able to read people well. Maybe that was why she trusted him so easily. He hadn't had anyone trust him as quickly as Madeline had. Although Jackie was close behind her on that list.

"I had a feeling," she answered. He looked at her to see that her golden eyes were watching him like a mother to a child. "Mates are never easy. Especially in situations like this one."

"You have experience in this?"

"No," she chuckled. "I haven't been lucky enough to find my mate. But I've heard enough stories, that I'd like to think I'm good at giving advice."

"I'm not sure if there's any advice you could give me," he said. It pained him that he could feel that pull so far away again. He wished that he could be as close to him as he was that night. But he had made the mistake of going too far.

"What did you do?"

"I let myself lose control," he explained, shaking his head. "I think I pushed him too far."

"By doing…?" she insisted.

"It would be embarrassing to say," he turned away from her. She just laughed at his words.

"Alistair, we're all werewolves here. And, trust me, I've probably heard worse."

He didn't feel like he had a choice. He had found that Madeline was stubborn in her ways, and she wasn't going to give up if it was something she really wanted to know. She had done the same with Ed before, shocking the Gamma.

He slowly told her what had happened that night. He told her that Nick had come late into the evening to brush his coat. That he had fallen asleep. Alistair had turned into his human form while sleeping with him, something that he hadn't done before.

Then he told her what had happened when they had both woken up. The feeling that he had felt when he was touching the man was foreign to him. The man was addicting to touch, so much so that he had started to let himself enjoy the moment.

"So, you tried to mate with him," Madeline said. "That's not that bad of a mistake. It's actually pretty common for mates to want to do, hence the word 'mate.'"

"He wasn't ready for that," Alistair sighed. "He ran from me."

"Is that why he hasn't come over at all the past couple days?" she asked.

He just nodded. It hurt him more that he couldn't even see him for lunch like he usually did. Not even Ed showed up to deliver their food. Ray and Desmond were the ones who had come the past couple days to bring them their meals. He wasn't sure why there was a change in the people who came over, but he was sure that it was his fault.

He could still feel Nick's soft skin glide across his palms. And the feeling of his lips on Alistair's was one that he would never forget.

"He'll come back," Madeline patted him on the shoulder. "That happens way more times than you think. If they're not well taught in stuff like that, then they're first time is usually scary for them. If they run, though, they'll always come back. I think Nick probably needs some time to think."

"How do you know this?"

"Mates were really important in the Citrus Valley Pack," she told him. "The males were always taught that they needed to be gentle with their mates the first time. It was interesting to overhear when I was a girl."

"Interesting indeed," he said. He hoped that it was the case for him. He hoped that he could at least apologize to the man. That wasn't how he had wanted to do it. His instincts just got the best of him. The need to keep him there and get as close to him as possible was strong.

But the hurt that Alistair saw in those hazel eyes weren't worth the physical desire that he had for him. They looked scared of him. Nick had never been scared of him, even when he first met him. That's what hurt him the most. He had never done something to scare someone off like that.

And, even though he didn't know him that much, he really did love Nick. His world looked brighter when he was around him. Now it was dark and grey.

Much like the sky when the sun went down. It had gone down quickly that night, leaving the stars twinkling. It was a new moon as well, which only made him feel more uneasy. He didn't like the new moon. It made him feel as if he couldn't see at all.

But he could hear well.

"Madeline." He stood up from where he was sitting. "Go inside."

"Why?" she asked. She became alert just through his tone of voice. She was tough for a delta, but Alistair didn't want any harm to come of her.

"Please," he said. He would push her in the cabin if he had to. "Go inside and block the windows and door. Protect Jackie."

She must have sensed the seriousness in his tone, because she listened to him without any questions the second time. As soon as the door shut, Alistair transformed into his wolf form, shredding the clothes that he had once worn.

They were here. He could hear their raged breath and smell the foul scents that they gave off. He didn't have any way of communicating with the warriors on patrol other than howling, and that would lead them right to the cabin.

He couldn't have that. He didn't know how many there were.

He couldn't risk his friend's lives.

Alistair ran towards the sound that he was hearing. It was right by the territory line, just a little bit further than the cabin. The Alpha had told him that he couldn't go further than a mile away from the cabin when he wasn't on patrol. He hoped that this instance would be an exception to that rule. If not, he would gladly sacrifice himself for his friend's safety.

He decided to be the first to attack, not wanting them to get any further into the territory. It wasn't a great idea, as it was just him going against them, but he didn't have a choice at the moment. He went for the one who was in the leader of the party, still unsure about how many there were. He had gotten a good bite on the leader's neck when he felt a sharp pain on his back.

A yelp escaped him, but he kept his hold, locking his jaw in place. It only took a couple thrashes for Alistair to rip the piece of meat off from the wolf. After that, he tried to find a new target. They had all set their eyes on him now. He quickly became their target.

He sensed about ten of them, including the one that he had just killed. The leader of the group lay bleeding out on the ground before him. He was outnumbered largely. But he knew better than to back down.

"Never back down from a fight!" He could still hear his old Alpha scream in his face. *"I don't care if you're soaked in your own blood! You will fight until the bitter end!"*

They all jumped on him at the same time. Every time he got a good attack on them, they'd hurt him tenfold. He got many of them in the hind, and ripped one of their ears off, but it wasn't enough. His skin was easy to tear, even in his wolf form. He was covered in the blood of his enemies as well as his own.

He couldn't last much longer. And he knew that it might take the warriors a while to catch onto the rogue's scents, as they very well could be far from this area.

He collapsed onto the ground, his legs unwilling to work for him anymore. He could do nothing but let the group tear him up. Alistair prayed to the moon for help, but she would not listen. It was a new moon, and bad things always happened to Alistair on new moons.

It was a new moon when he was first abandoned.

His eyes were blurry now, but he forced them to focus. The rogues must have thought that he was dead with how much blood he had lost. They had run off into the territory more.

But Alistair wasn't dead. He hadn't died when his old pack had left him either. He could see them running away from him. The forest transformed into a snowy tundra for that moment. The wind was whistling in anger and the snow was hitting everyone with more force than he could remember.

They had fought a monster of the waters while trying to fish. Alistair always stood in front of the rest of the warriors. He had to protect them. He had to take the blows so that they could focus on their attack. That was his duty.

It had strong teeth when it dug into him. He took most of the pain. Pain was nothing but a state of mind. That was what his Alpha had told him. He could last through pain.

But it was worse this time than the others. He couldn't move. He had tried to get up multiple times, but his body had simply lied there, limp. He looked to the warriors that were with them. He whined to tell them that he was still alive; that he needed help. He knew that they had heard him. He could tell by the way that their ears had twitched every time he made a sound.

Yet they left him.

Rage filled his being. A rage that he had not felt in a long time. Alistair stood from his bloody puddle. He would not back down this time. He would not go without a fight.

There were still people he needed to protect. His old pack was not nice to him. No one other than his mother treated him like anything other than an animal. But there were so many people here, where he was now, that had treated him like a man. Even the Alpha here had treated him with respect. He could have declined his offer when he first asked to be a part of his pack. But he decided to give Alistair a chance.

It hurt to stand. Every part of him was in pain. But he could get over it. He could forget about the pain. He stood anyway. And, when he did, he made sure to take in a deep breath.

He howled as loud as possible. He needed them to know that there was danger around. His howl echoed through the land, and, even though it was a low howl, he was sure that it could get picked up by the pack.

Then he started running. His vision was red, as his old rage resurfaced. He would not let these wolves hurt the ones who had been nice to him. Their kindness meant everything to him. It was through people's kindness that he had lived as long as he had.

His vision had changed. He saw through it both the snowy tundra and the wolves that had left him behind, as well as the forest around him now. The rogue's scents weren't difficult to find, but they were fast. Alistair used his emotions to pump his legs to go faster. He had their scent in his nose. They were headed closer to where his pull was.

Nick.

He wouldn't let them touch him.

Then he caught onto another scent. One that he had only smelt once. It was sweet and calming. He recognized it the second that it hit his nose. It had made his legs move faster as well.

That was the Luna's scent.

And the rogues were heading right to it.

The pain had all but slipped away as he dodged every tree and jumped over every bit of brush he could. His life didn't matter anymore. All that mattered was that these people weren't harmed.

He caught up to them right before he heard it.

"Max! Help!" He heard in his mind. He had no idea who it was that was asking, but he knew that he wouldn't let those wolves get as far as the pack house.

There was a wolf lunging for a car. He could smell the Luna's scent nearby. His own instincts came over him and he jumped to collide with the attacking wolf. They both hit the ground at the same time. But the wolf that he had stopped from lunging had pushed him off before he could sink his teeth into him.

They were in a clearing in the woods. Alistair could smell the scent of the Luna from the car. The wolf stood and tried to circle around the clearing with him, but Alistair would not budge. He stayed by the car, guarding it with his life. It had been difficult for him to stand up again, but he still managed to do it. One of his back legs had been hurt badly. He limped a bit on that one.

He howled again, to try and get someone's attention. This wasn't about him anymore, this was about the Luna. He was a human. There was no way he would be able to defend himself against all these wolves.

He knew that they were waiting for some sort of distraction. They attacked him right in the middle of his howl. This time, they showed Alistair no mercy. They all piled onto him at once, sinking their teeth into whatever part of him they could.

He thrashed around all he could, but he knew that not even his rage could keep him alive for very much longer. Alistair didn't care if his life ended at that moment. He just wanted to save the life of an innocent.

Weight got lifted off his shoulders as a wolf got knocked off him. He was surprised to see the Alpha growling and fighting viciously. The red wolf showed no mercy over the wolves that had started the attack. His other warriors weren't far behind. But Alistair stayed near the car no matter what.

He looked inside to see those green eyes staring back at him. They were absolutely terrified. It wasn't every day that even werewolves saw something as horrible as this. He wanted to try and comfort him, but there were too many enemies nearby that he couldn't risk it. He was afraid that he didn't have much fight left in him either. The rogues had taken most of his strength from him.

That was when the rest of the warrior's must have caught up. He laid down near the car, unable to stand any longer, as they tore up the trespassers. Relief flooded through him when he realized that no one had gotten hurt.

The Alpha immediately looked at him when the battle was finished. He didn't have any energy to move from the car that he was leaning on. He barely had enough energy at all.

"Alistair!" He heard a sweet voice come from the car. The door opened and closed, and those green eyes were soon right next to him.

"*Stay still*," The Alpha ordered. His labored breathing was now the only thing to be heard throughout the dark forest. Some of the warriors had left. He was assuming it was to check to see if there were more. He was surprised to see that most of them stayed, watching him.

Then he felt something wet on his side. He tried to jerk his head, but the Luna had moved it to lay on his lap. He didn't remember him doing that. But it was nice to hear the quiet shushing and the small pets on the head from the sweetly scented man. It reminded him of his mother in a way.

Maybe tonight was the night he would finally be able to see her again.

He had forgotten that werewolves could help heal another through licking. He remembered doing it a couple times in his old pack, but it wasn't much. Alistair was always told to fend for himself when he got hurt. He wasn't expecting this pack to show him any kindness.

It wouldn't help with the extremely deep wounds that he had gotten, but it gave him enough energy to stand. His legs were weak still, as that gash on it wasn't able to be healed. But he was sure that he could survive through it.

"*Shift*," the Alpha told him. He whined at him. If he shifted, he wasn't sure if he was going to stay awake. At least in this form, he could push himself further, if only by a little. His human form would be too hurt to even stay conscious.

He wanted to tell the Alpha this, but he couldn't. His mind was too focused on trying to stay awake and standing. He just looked at the Alpha with fearful eyes. He didn't want to die. He wanted to live. He wanted to finally have all the blessings that the Moon Goddess was promising him. He had worked so hard to get to this point.

Those purple eyes understood him, even without any words. They grew softer than he had seen them before, looking over his bloody and battered body.

"Trust me," he told him. *"I'll make sure you're taken care of."*

Trust him. That was what he had done from the moment he stepped foot into this territory. He remembered when he first fought these rogues. He had blocked one of them from attacking the Beta of the pack. He remembered how the Alpha had been waiting for him at the cabin. He had made sure that he was taken care of then.

He didn't have time to think about all the things that could happen. His strength was slowly depleting. The bad wounds were still open and bleeding. He had to come to a decision quickly.

He changed forms, feeling the pain soar through him as he became a human. His instincts were the only thing he had left in a situation like this. And it had told him to trust the Alpha.

He remembered being wrapped up in something warm and being put on something with cushions. It was comfortable right then. He also remembered that there was some yelling and demands that were being made. He couldn't figure out what most of it meant. He wanted to try to listen to what was going on around him.

But his body was too weak, and his senses were too tired.

He fell into the black void that was sleep.

CHAPTER 21:

Blood

"Max! I need to talk to you!"

"I don't have time for this, Nick," he said. He knew that the omega was still following him. He had just finished going on patrol with some of the warriors and there was already so much to deal with.

He needed to get to the Luna office. The three days were officially up and, knowing Charlie, he'd be ready for him right on time.

And he desperately needed to talk to him. He needed this Hell to be over with.

Of course, he felt bad for going off on Nick that day. He had used his authority to threaten him. He had never done that to him before. Thinking back to that memory, he had never seen Nick so scared of him before. And he hadn't heard him stutter like that since they were in elementary school.

But Nick took it too far. He had gone against his orders. And, while Max knew that the man had a habit of doing so, he never thought it would be an order that concerned his safety, as well as the packs.

"I just need one minute," Nick said from behind him. "Please." He sounded like he was desperate. Max didn't know why he seemed to be so interested in seeing the rogue. He knew that Nick liked to find someone and hang onto them as much as he could, but he never expected him to do it to the most dangerous rogue that they had let in their territory.

Why him?

"Why did you do that Nick?" He turned around to face the cook. "I know that Ed said that it was okay to go with him. But, what on earth made you think it was alright to go and see this complete stranger? What if you got hurt?"

"He wouldn't hurt me."

"How do you know?" he asked him. The man's eyes darted all around before landing on the ground.

He couldn't do this. He needed to figure out his own problems, before he lashed out on his friend more. He had already tore Ed a new one. The man didn't even think of asking him permission to bring an omega to the rogue's cabin. He knew that he hurt Ed with what he said as well, but he couldn't say the man didn't deserve that. He had jeopardized the safety and health of a pack member.

He knew that Ed would get over what he had said within a day or two. But Nick he wasn't sure about. It might take some apologizing to repair the friendship that they had.

"Look, Nick," he cut through the awkward silence that had come between them. "I'm not in the right mind to deal with this right now. I have about a thousand things to do and not enough time to do it. Let's talk about this tomorrow." Hopefully he'd get some sleep by then. Or, at least, all of this mess with him and Charlie would be over with.

Nick didn't respond at first. So, Max decided to walk away from the situation. He would talk to him when all of this was done. All Nick had to do was last one more day on house arrest and they could talk this all out.

"He's my mate," Nick said.

Max stopped in his tracks.

"He's your…" His eyebrows knitted together. He turned around again to see that Nick had his head up, looking at him.

"That's why I went to see him," Nick told him. He looked a little guilty while he talked. "That's why I've been going to see him for a while now."

There were so many things for Max's tired brain to process.

"I thought you were…"

"Yeah," Nick chuckled a bit. "I thought so too. I guess I won't be sweeping anyone off their feet."

"Is that why his scent was all over your neck?"

"Yeah." The cook started rubbing his neck as soon as he mentioned it. "He's not really that bad of a guy, you know."

"Nick," he sighed. This was a whole new level of complicated. "Why didn't you tell me this before?"

"Because he's a big scary rogue that the whole pack has been freaking out about and you haven't exactly been happy about it."

"True," Max frowned. "But telling me that would have made things easier to understand."

"I just didn't know whether you were going to get pissed off at me or not," Nick said. "I was hoping to tell you after he got ac-!"

They both turned their heads to the forest. A howl in the distance had put Max on immediate alert. He knew that the low howl could come from one person and one person only.

"Alistair!" Nick said. Max instinctively put a hand out to stop whatever movement he was trying to make.

"Stay here, Nick," he told him.

"But Alistair!" His friend's face had never looked so worried before.

"I'll take care of him," Max said. "I promise."

He didn't have much time to see if the man would follow him, he just prayed to the goddess that he wouldn't. It only took a second to change into his wolf form that he had been in only a few short minutes ago.

The howl came from the cabin that the rogues were all in. Even if that small group weren't in the pack officially, he wasn't going to just let his enemies hurt them all.

Martha, an elder warrior with many years of experience in battle, was the one on patrol of that section. She wasn't that fast, but she was powerful, and she could take quite a lot of damage without needing much medical attention.

But he knew that she wouldn't be able to get there in time.

It was a good thing that Max had practiced running through his territory so much before becoming the Alpha. He knew how to dodge every tree and still went as fast as possible. The other warriors were closing the distance between them and the cabin as well. He made sure to mind link with Tyler, Sam, and Ed to get them to help with the fight.

He was the first one that got to the cabin that the four were staying at. The cabins that they had made were sturdy. They were built out of the trees that grew in the forest, and made to handle a fully sized wolf ramming into it. Another reason why they were first built was to be a safe house for those that might need it.

He could smell them before he could see them. Three enemy rogues were attacking the cabin. And only two of the group were trying to fight them off. From the scents they gave, he could tell it was Herb and Madeline. He could hear Jackie inside, screaming in fear.

Max tackled one before it could lunge at Madeline. With one quick bite, the wolf's neck snapped. Then he went to the next one, which Herb was fighting off. He bit its tail to get its attention. After it yelped, Herb went for its throat. Max helped him take down the enemy before going to the last one that was there. By then, the warriors had finally arrived, breathing heavily. They took down the last one that had been attacking Madeline while he was finishing off the other one.

"*Where's Alistair?*" he asked Madeline. She seemed to have some deep wounds, but it wasn't anything that wouldn't heal with the help of Dr. Button.

"*We don't know,*" she told him. Even as a wolf, she looked concerned. A whine escaped her snout. "*He told us to barricade the door and windows one moment, and the next thing I know, he howled and there's three of them coming at us.*"

"*Alpha,*" Martha got his attention. She wasn't there, but it seemed like she was on her way. She should have been the first to get to the scene other than Max, though. She wasn't that slow of a warrior, and she wasn't one to mess around.

"*What?*"

"*I found something,*" She told him. "*Right by the border, there's one of the rogue's bodies, dead. The albino's blood is everywhere.*"

"*Is he there?!*"

"*No,*" she said, making his heart race. "*There's more to it than that. There are ten new scents that I'm picking up that are foreign.*"

Ten?

There hasn't been a group of ten of them in a long time. Max sent out most of the warrior's that were around them to scan the area. If there was one dead that Martha found, and three that he had helped kill. That meant that there were six left.

"*Come over to the cabin,*" he ordered. "*I need you to escort the three here to the packhouse. They may need medical attention.*"

"*On my way,*" Martha said.

As much as Max didn't get too much sleep, he felt wide awake now. Adrenaline was pumping through him as he waited for news on where these rogues were in his territory. He had a feeling that he was going to have to follow Alistair's scent. If the man had lost a lot of blood, it was likely that he was injured badly.

"*This is Martha,*" he told the three of them when the elder warrior had come. Jackie had poked her head out to see if everyone was okay. Her husband nudged her hand to comfort her. "*She's going to escort you three to the packhouse. There, you will get the medical attention you need.*"

It was too risky to keep them this close to the territory lines now. Their lives would be in danger if they were to stay in the cabin any more. He could figure out where to keep them all at another time. Right now, he needed to keep them safe.

"*What about Alistair?*" Herb asked him.

"*Leave that to me,*" he promised. "*I'll find him.*"

As much as the man made him wary, he wasn't going to let him die. He hadn't done anything to deserve death. At least, not to their pack. And he had been the first line of defense that they had that night.

The idea of him going up against ten wolves at once seemed absolutely insane. He hoped the man wasn't dead already.

"*Max!*" He heard a familiar voice in his head. "*Help!*"

A new surge of adrenaline pumped through Max as he finally was able to feel his mate's emotions again. Charlie had finally taken down the mental barrier that he had put up for three days. Fear was the one thing that Max could feel in his mate.

He ran as fast as he could, following the scent to Charlie. Even this far into the forest, the man's scent was strong. That was why the rogues always seemed to go towards his scent. That was why Max almost always kept him in the pack house.

Where was he now?

He noticed the rogue's scents as he ran, but there was also another strong smell. There was a blood trail as he went deeper. It only took him a few seconds to remember the smell from when Alistair was wounded the night that he saved Tyler.

Alistair was chasing after them.

This would have been the perfect time for him to be able to mind link with the albino. But he didn't have time to think about that now. Now he had to find both Charlie and Alistair. And hope that he could do so before it was too late.

There was so much of the albino's blood on the forest floor that he very well could be dead. Max didn't want that. He needed some kind of sign that he was still alive. There was no way he could let Nick's mate die by the hands of these wolves. There was no way he could have him die at all.

Another low howl could be heard. This time, it was close to the packhouse. The warriors wasted no time changing courses for the sound of the howl. Max was already on his way. And Tyler, Sam, and Ed were right behind him.

He growled and jumped as he reached the clearing. The rest of the rogues that Martha had smelt were there. And all of them seemed to be attacking one thing. Max killed off one in an instant, immediately going after another. There was no time to look around or figure out the situation that was going on there.

Tyler took care of another, and Ed and Sam were attacking some of the ones who were trying to run from them. Ray and Desmond were there next. They all gave no mercy to their enemies. That was the mistake that Max's father had done with them.

When they were all dead, he finally looked at the thing that they had been attacking. It was a mess of white fur and blood. It was slouched over a jeep.

"Alistair!" Max heard Charlie before he saw him get out of the car. Those green eyes had never looked so terrified before. He went into action and knelt down by the ball of white fur.

Alistair. He had been protecting Charlie.

"He looks hurt badly," Tyler said. *"I don't know if he's going to make it."*

"He took all of those rogues on at once!" Sam said. *"I'm surprised he's even alive right now!"*

"We have to help him," Max told them. He may not have liked the albino at first, but he had a heart. He wasn't just going to let the man who protected his mate bleed out and die.

Max looked at Alistair. His red eyes had a helpless look to them. A whine of pain came from his mess of white fur. Charlie had been watching Max the entire time. He had grabbed Alistair's head and put it on his lap, petting it gently.

"Stay still," he ordered. He told the ones who were there to lick the wounds. It was something that warriors did a lot to help the wounded to heal faster. There was a certain magic to it that no one could seem to explain.

They were able to close some wounds, but not the deep ones. They still bled profusely.

"We need to get him to Button," Tyler said. *"These wounds need to be stitched up."*

He agreed with his beta. But he wasn't sure if the wolf was willing to transform into his human form so that they could get him there faster.

They all backed away from the albino as he tried to stand. He was limping really bad on one of his hind legs, and his panting was getting worse.

"Shift," he ordered him. Those red eyes grew fearful with hearing his words. A whine escaped his snout again. Max knew then that the man was too weak to mind link with him, but he had to save him.

The large white wolf suddenly shrank ten times smaller when he looked in his eyes. They were brought back to a younger time, one of fear. Max remembered that he had gotten abandoned by his pack. He told him it was after an attack. They left him for dead. By the looks of how Alistair was now, he had a feeling that the wolf thought that he was going to be left behind by them as well.

No. Max wasn't going to leave him to die.

"Trust me," He went up to him and nudged him a bit. *"I'll make sure you're taken care of."*

Alistair had said that he trusted him before. This was a true test of that, he supposed. One that was answered immediately. Alistair transformed silently into his human form. As soon as Max noticed him start to change, he did as well.

"Charlie," he told his mate. "Get the-!"

"Already on it," The blond had a blanket from the Jeep that he wrapped around Alistair's body. Max and Tyler helped put him in the back seat.

"Tyler," he looked at the Beta. "You guys guard us."

He got into the driver's side, letting Charlie get into the passenger's seat. He had already told Button the situation through the mind link so that he could prepare.

"Why are you outside of the pack house?!" Max asked. He was speeding as fast as he could to the house.

"I was trying to find you."

"And you couldn't just mind link?!"

"I was too tired to figure out how to take down the mental barrier," he answered, looking back at Alistair. "I didn't know there were going to be rogues this close to the house!"

They had gotten close to the house. Charlie didn't seem like he had even gotten that far. It only took a minute before he could see the manor. He parked as close to the entrance as possible. Tyler and Ed changed forms and opened the doors as soon as Max had stopped.

"Clear the way!" Max told Sam. They all bolted for the infirmary. When they got there, Dr. Button had already had an operating table set up, along with an I.V. bag of blood.

They were rushed out of the infirmary as quickly as they had gone in.

"Max!" Nick raced up to him. "Is he okay?!"

"He's in surgery right now." He wasn't going to tell him that he might not make it. He had seen the amount of blood that he had lost. The fact that the man was conscious for so long was enough to tell Max that he was strong. He just wasn't sure if he was strong enough to last through this.

"I couldn't believe it," Charlie shook his head in disbelief. "He took on six of them! By himself!"

"He did?" Nick looked so worried, it hurt Max.

He should have never been so harsh on the man. He should have never been so harsh on Nick, or Charlie.

"Nick," He looked at his childhood friend. "I need you to go in there."

"What?!" Everyone looked at Max as if he were insane. But, if there was one thing he knew, it was that mates helped each other, even with drastic health problems like this. He had heard many stories of werewolves surviving near death experiences because of their mates.

"It's going to be bad in there," he continued, ignoring everyone else. "But he's going to need you."

Nick just nodded and slowly turned the nob.

"What did you mean by that?" Sam asked. "How is Alistair going to need Nick?"

"They're mates."

And he was going to have to do a lot of praying tonight.

CHAPTER 22:

The Pull

It was cold. He wasn't used to being cold. Even in the icy tundra, it would take a lot to chill him. But this was a different kind of cold. This was the kind that went to his bones. The kind that left you unable to move, no matter how desperate you were to search for warmth.

He didn't want to accept this immobilizing cold. He wanted to be warm. He didn't want to live like this.

Was this what the Moon Goddess wanted? When she had brought him all the way to this forest? A flash of purple eyes came into his mind. They were calm, assertive, yet gentle at the same time. They actually looked concerned for him. Out of all the faces that he had seen in his life, he had never met so many kind ones as he had when he was here.

His adventures to new places were finally over. He was happy with the friends he had made. They had made him laugh and smile. He hadn't felt so good in a long time. He could be happy that he had lived through even the shortest of moments in his life such as that.

He could die happy knowing that his friends were safe. That had always been his destiny: to sacrifice himself for others. At one point, he thought of living for himself. But his life wouldn't have purpose if he did that.

He was slowly falling deeper into the arctic water. His bones getting colder. But then he felt something pulling him up. It enticed him; sparked a feeling in him to keep trying to stay afloat. He didn't know what that feeling was, but he couldn't stop himself from listening to it.

Soon the heat returned to his body. He heard distant voices, but he would not try to focus on them. He had grown tired of all the swimming that he had done. But he was closer to the pull than he had been before. He wanted to push himself closer to it, but he couldn't. His body was too weak, and his eyelids heavy.

He could feel a hand intertwined with his, and another caressing his head. They felt so nice, he hoped they never left. They were the ones that had pulled him up from the freezing water that he had been submerged in.

He didn't know that he had fallen asleep during that time. He just remembered those soft hands holding him in loving ways. When he opened his eyes finally, he was shocked to find himself in what looked like a doctor's office.

He hadn't been in a doctor's office since he was a mere child. It was a little different from a veterinarian's office. He had been to those plenty of times. Here, though, they had more tools scattered around the counters.

The one thing he was used to seeing was the I.V. of blood. Usually, he was laying on his side when he woke up to things like this. That was the easiest way for the wildlife vets to treat his wounds. They were always really nice to him, making sure to talk to him, even though he couldn't talk back.

The first time he had gone to one, he had been confused. He was too weak to try and stand up, but the foreign place was much different from the icy home that he was used to.

Now, he was used to waking up in places like this. It always took a while for his memory to come back to him, but he knew that it would. He relaxed into the mattress he was in, trying to stay as quiet as possible.

The sun was up, shining brightly in the room. He liked that the sun-rays had a color to them. Yellow was a nice color. He remembered seeing many yellow flowers during his travels. And the trees would sometimes have yellow leaves. He was happy that the room had color to it. The light blue on the walls were calming, as were the pictures and paintings that adorned them.

Then his eyes traveled to a man: one with long black hair and a slender face. His skin was caramel. He liked the look of this man. He was asleep, curled up on the chair right next to his bed. His eyelashes were long. He had realized that a lot of men have long eyelashes rather than women. It always fascinated him.

His body started to wake up, and he was able to feel more around him. The pain was the first thing that he felt. He had to close his eyes and curl his hands to make sure he didn't make a sound. Sounds were danger-ous, no matter where you were. And the pain would pass. He was always able to overcome pain. He just had to wait until the initial period was over.

Then he realized that there was something in one of his hands. He wanted to look, but he feared he would lose concentration. It felt nice, though. It intertwined with his fingers, soft and gentle. He hadn't felt some-thing that gentle in a while.

"Is he awake?" He heard someone whisper. A door quietly shut behind him. He heard a lot of bustling going on as it had opened. It was a good sign that his senses were waking up.

"I don't know." Another voice said. He liked that voice. It made him want to smile through his pain. "He just started to clench his hands."

There wasn't any more talk after that. It made him sad. He wanted to hear the beautiful voice again. Instead, there was just some shuffling around. Papers moved. He liked the sound of paper. It was such a small sound, yet it was one that he could hear just through picturing it.

He took deep breaths to try and calm his body down. The pain was slowly going away. He hoped it would soon. He wanted to see that man again.

Cold hands held onto his arm. He was used to cold hands, but they still surprised him. His eyes snapped open once again. An older man was the one who had the cold hands. It was easy to see that he was a doctor.

Then his sense of smell woke up, and he started to realize exactly what was caring for him.

His hands moved to his head as his memories all decided to flood his mind at once. He couldn't see anything other than the vivid pictures of everything that had happened in his life. It had never been like this. He hadn't had it this bad in a long time. Usually, if he remained calm throughout it all, his memories would slowly settle into his mind and he could figure out his next move.

But the pain hadn't gone away. He wasn't strong enough to overcome it. There was only one other time that he wasn't able to overcome the pain. And it was that memory that he feared the most.

"Alistair!" He heard someone yell. It was that melodic voice again. It brought him back from that memory that he was drowning in. "Dr. Button, what's going on?"

"He's just coming to his senses, Nick." The other voice said. He couldn't open his eyes again. The pain was too intense.

"Something's wrong," Nick said.

"Pain," he spoke through his teeth. It was the only thing he could say. Everything hurt: his stomach; his legs; his head. He wasn't strong enough to block it out. He always blocked out his pain. That's what had helped him survive. But this was too much. It was overloading his senses.

He didn't hear much. But he did feel a prick on one of his arms. There was a strange warm feeling that he had remembered all too fondly. It traveled from his arm to the rest of his body, and he could feel his heart calm. The pain slowly went away.

He took some deep breaths as his body finally relaxed. His eyes grew heavy again, and he couldn't keep them open. The cold hands that he assumed were the doctors were still on his arm, putting some pressure where the prick had been. Warm hands were holding onto his other arm. They had gently brought his arm away from his face. It kept him in the present, fighting off the shadows that were trying to pull him under.

"Give him some time, Nick," the doctor said. "He's not going to be able to jump out of bed right after an attack like that."

"Nick?" The sound of his own voice was strange to him. But his memory of Nick finally came to the center of his mind. He forced his eyes to open and see those hazel eyes again. They were the most beautiful eyes he had ever seen.

"Take it easy," Dr. Button caught his attention. "You have quite a lot of stitches right now."

He tore his gaze from Nick to look at himself. He was wrapped in bandages everywhere. And one of his legs were in a cast, lifted up on a sling. He had two I.V.'s in either arm: one had blood, the other had a clear liquid. He couldn't quite tell if it was water or something else.

"Is everyone okay?" he asked. He remembered just how many of those rogues there were. He couldn't imagine all the people that could have gotten hurt.

Was Madeline and the others okay?

"Everyone's doing just fine," Dr. Button answered, sending a wave of relief through him. "You took most of the damage."

"The Luna." It was still difficult for him to talk right then. The medicine that had helped the pain go away was making him drowsy all over again. "They were going after the Luna."

"He's just fine," the doctor reassured. "The only people that were hurt, besides you, were Madeline and Herb, and they just had some minor injuries."

"Are they-?"

"They're fine," he stopped him. "They healed from them overnight."

He slowly nodded and let the doctor do his job on checking up on him. During that time, his eyes wandered back to Nick. The man looked so worried about him. He didn't want to see him worried. He wanted to see him happy, like the first time he saw him. He wanted to hear that laugh of his again.

He still needed to apologize to him. But he wasn't going to do that with the doctor there. He had a feeling that the doctor had already been told that they were mates, but he still wanted to apologize when they were alone. He wanted to talk to him again. They had talked merely days ago, but it felt like eons.

"Well, I'd say you're on your way to recovery," Dr. Button told him. "You have several severe injuries, including some deep bites that had to be cleaned and stitched. Your leg is broken, with the other one being fractured," he was looking at his medical paperwork as he said all of this. "I'd say, with how fast your metabolism is, you'll recover within one to two weeks."

He wondered what the Alpha was going to say to that. Was he going to let him stay there? He was sure he could think of something. But right now, he could barely move.

"Thank you, doctor," he said.

"There's no need, son," his soft smile reached his bright blue eyes. "You put up one hell of a fight, both in battle and in the surgery room. Get some rest now."

He nodded his farewell to Nick before leaving the room. Alistair stared at the door for a second. He wasn't used to being treated this well by his own kind, even if it was a doctor. It gave him a strange feeling, but a good one, nonetheless.

"Alistair," Nick got his attention. "Are you okay?"

"I feel better." He smiled at him. He didn't realize just how much he missed the man until that moment. "The pain is gone for the most part."

"That's good." He smiled back. He linked his hand with Alistair's again. "I'm glad you're feeling better."

"I haven't been in that kind of pain for a long time," he told him.

"Well, you did get really beaten up," Nick said. "I wasn't sure if you were going to survive or not."

"Something kept pulling me back," he said. He squeezed Nick's hand a bit, enjoying the calm feeling that it gave him.

Nick didn't say anything after that. They both enjoyed the silence together for a minute or two. Alistair had no idea just how nice it was to have a mate. It made everything better, even when he was in pain like before. He'd hate to think that he would ever lose him.

"Nick." He caught the man's attention. "I wanted to apologize to you for what happened the last time we were together."

"What?" He looked a bit confused. His brows knitted in a way that looked cute on him. Alistair wished he could reach out to touch that face. To have him in his arms again.

"I lost control that morning," he said. "I know it's too early to push you to do that. I just got caught in the moment." He slowly and carefully pulled the warm hand close to his mouth. "I promise it won't happen again."

"Alistair," Nick shook his head. He couldn't tell if the man was laughing or crying. "I can't believe it. You just risked your life, almost died, to protect my whole pack. And, when you finally come to, after a whole night of us fighting to keep you alive, you apologize?!"

"I don't want to lose you," he answered. He didn't know what he would do without him. He had spent so long trying to find his purpose in the world. Now that he had finally found the one who gave him purpose, he would rather die than lose it.

Lips met his faster than he had time to react. They were soft, just like before. Those warm hands came up to his face, as if to hold him there forever. His arms instinctively wrapped around the man's waist as best as they could. The feeling of Nick all around him was addicting, as was the scent that lingered around him. He wanted to deepen the kiss; to make this feeling last a little bit longer. But Nick broke it off before he could.

"You're not going to lose me," he told him. His eyes were wide, and his breath heavy as it hit Alistair's face. "I almost lost *you*."

He had never seen someone look at him in this way. There was so much fear in Nick's eyes, but it wasn't of Alistair's strength. It was a fear *for* him. All of the emotions that the man had the night before came to the surface for a second; all of them showing Alistair what he had gone through. The fear that he might not make it was the one that was strongest flashing in his eyes. Along with the relief of talking to him and seeing that he was okay. He saw it all in the mixes of brown and green that colored it, painting his very soul.

"I'll be okay." He slowly moved his hand to hold Nick's face. The I.V.'s in his arms made it difficult to move them. "I promise."

A tear escaped Nick as he leaned into his hand. He wiped it away with his thumb, giving him as much comfort as he could. The man was hovering over him, so as to not put any pressure on his wounds. Alistair wished he could pull him towards him. He wanted to hold him as close as possible.

A small knock on the door snapped them both out of their daze. Alistair had gotten lost in those eyes so easily. Now they were taken away from him as Nick moved. He wanted to tighten his hold on him, but he didn't have the strength, so he let him go. He got back in the seat next to his bed just as the door opened up.

Alistair tensed. The Alpha and Luna walked into the room. He wanted to see if the Luna was alright, but he didn't want to anger the Alpha. So, he kept his gaze towards the Alpha instead.

"How are you feeling?" the red head asked. His face looked different than the other times he had spoken with him. They looked softer, with a sense of worry rather than the anger that he had seen in them before.

"I'm feeling alright." He tried to shift in his bed, to sit up a little more. But he couldn't seem to get his arms to lift himself up. "I should be healed in a week."

"Dr. Button said one to two weeks," Nick told the Alpha. Alistair was surprised that an omega could talk to someone like an Alpha with such confidence.

"That's funny," the Luna said, a smile on his face. "He told us that it would be two."

It was hard to keep his eyes off the Luna. He had a gift for making people comfortable through his scent alone.

"Knowing Button, it was because he didn't want you to try and get out of the infirmary before you were ready," Alpha Max smiled at him. He hadn't had the Alpha smile at him before. "It would be best to listen to Dr. Button and stay down until he says. He gets rather annoying if you do otherwise."

"I'll listen to his orders," he told him. He already missed the feeling of Nick's hand in his. He wanted to hold him in some way.

"Good," Alpha Max sat down on one of the seats.

He got distracted by a hand on his. It wasn't Nick's, he could tell because it didn't give him the same amazing feeling that Nick's touch gave. He looked up to see emerald eyes, blond curls and a smiling face.

"Thank you for saving me," he said. It was difficult to keep his eyes off from him.

"It was my duty." He avoided his gaze by looking at the ceiling.

"You can look at him, you know," the Alpha said. He looked to see that he was watching him with a strange expression. "I'm guessing in your old pack you weren't allowed to make eye contact with the Luna?"

"No, sir," he answered. "We weren't allowed to look at any of the superior's mates."

"We don't work that way," he told him. "You won't get in trouble for looking or talking to them."

"I think we have a lot to learn about this old pack of yours, Alistair," the Luna said. He looked at him for the first time since he had been brought into the territory. "I'm really glad you're feeling better now, though."

"Thank you, Luna." He smiled at him. He really liked humans. They had been nothing but kind to him. This one seemed to be a little special. It was easy to see that he was fit for his position.

"You can just call me Charlie," The Luna smiled. "I forgot that we weren't officially introduced when we first met."

"It's not common to call a Luna by such a civil name," Alistair said.

"We aren't really a common pack," Nick butted into the conversation. "It's a little strange around here. But in a good way."

Every time he looked at Nick, he couldn't help but smile.

"Now," Alpha Max leaned in from his chair. "Do you remember what happened?"

"Yes," he nodded. He proceeded to tell the Alpha what he had done. When he had heard the strange sounds and the fact that he hadn't wanted to howl near the cabin, as it would bring the enemies to Jackie. He told them about when he first spotted them at the border, and his attack on the leader. They didn't do as much damage to him then, but now he knew that it was because they had a mission.

"So, you ran after them?"

"Yes," he told him. "That was when I also caught onto the Lun-I mean – Charlie's scent."

It didn't take long before he was finished. Charlie was now sitting next to the Alpha, both of them transfixed with the story he was giving. He looked at Nick to see that he was just as interested. He liked telling his stories to Nick. The man loved his tales.

"Well," the Alpha said once he had finished. "That matches everything that we found. I tracked your blood all the way to where Charlie was."

He remembered when he had finally come. He was the one who got one of them off from him. He had a feeling that an Alpha wolf as large as his would be fast as well.

"You showed your loyalty to us through your willingness to sacrifice yourself for others," Alpha Max stood up. He looked like a king when he spoke now. But there was a sparkle to his eyes, showing a happiness that confused Alistair. "Because of your bravery in battle, as well as your friends that were with you, I welcome you to the Crescent Moon Pack."

He looked at him in disbelief. He hadn't done any of that because it was what was needed to be a part of the pack. He just did it because it was the right thing to do.

"Welcome to our family," Charlie said.

"I don't know what to say," he told them. After all his days of traveling and suffering, he never thought he would see the day where he would finally have a home to call his again.

Now he had that, and more.

CHAPTER 23:

Charlie's Office

It was early afternoon when they woke up. They both awaited the doctor's news about Alistair in the waiting room. It was already late in the night when he had finally told them that the man was stable. That, along with the fact that neither of them had gotten any sleep the past three days, made it difficult for them to even reach their suite.

They were barely able to get a shower and wash themselves before collapsing into bed. Max didn't let Charlie go the entire time. He knew that there was going to be a lot of explaining that he was going to need to do, but not now.

The first thing that Charlie did when they woke up is tell him that he was sorry. He somehow convinced him to get dressed and follow him into his office. He had to show him the reason why he had been locked in there for so long.

"How…?" Max couldn't even finish his question. He just looked around the office in awe. Charlie hadn't just put a map up on one of his walls. He had made his walls the main presentation of his project.

"The Buttons were looking at the werewolf databases for more information," Charlie said. "But, from what Ed said, it seemed like he had been more involved with humans rather than his own kind."

"And you got all of this information," He looked at him in absolute shock. "In three days?"

"I told you I could do it," he said, looking shyly at the man. "I wasn't doing this out of anger. It was just my way of trying to help you so that we wouldn't be arguing over gut feelings anymore."

"What's this?" Max pointed at the map of Canada that he had gotten.

"It's all the places he's traveled that I could find," he answered. "There are still some missing gaps, of course, but I was able to find all the important landmarks that he had been to."

The only one he was waiting on, before all of this happened, was to find out where the albino was brought when he was first abandoned by his pack. He had a track history of vets in the past. Charlie had forwarded all the medical information that he found from them to Button.

Even the doctor seemed impressed with him.

"You know, Charlie," Max looked at him. "It wasn't just your responsibility to make sure that this plan works out. It was all of us who agreed on it."

"I know," he said. "But I was the one who gave the idea out. And I wanted to show you I could do it."

Max pulled him closer and buried his face in his shoulder. He couldn't help but hug him back. He missed Max's hugs, even though it hadn't been that long. He liked the feeling of him sighing into him, and feeling all of his tension leaving him.

"We can't do this every time we have a disagreement on something," he told him. His voice was a little muffled in his shirt. "It'll only get worse for the both of us."

"I know," Charlie sighed. "I'm sorry, I shouldn't have put up that mental block. I just wanted to concentrate and it just made things worse."

"It's not just that, Charlie," he said. "If we don't agree on something, we need to work it out then and there, or we risk our emotions clouding our judgement and being distracted if something else happens."

"Okay." He pet his head. It was nice seeing this part of Max again. "Then when it happens again, we'll both handle it better."

They were both still new to their leadership roles. Max's parents had told them that they were going to make mistakes no matter how well prepared they were. Charlie knew that Max used their statement as a means to be as careful and cautious as possible. But he believed that mistakes were going to be made no matter what. The best thing they could do was learn from them.

"Apple," Max's voice got lower as he moved his face closer to his neck. "You need to promise me something."

"What do I need to promise you?" A smile reached his face as he felt his lover's hands travel under his shirt. They were rubbing his sides.

"Two things," he started nibbling his neck, quickly traveling to his ear. "The first one is that you'll never block me out again."

"I can do that," Charlie said. He didn't think that he would ever want to do it again after how difficult it was to take down. And Max hadn't seemed to want to stop holding him once he did. He felt bad that he made him so worried about him.

It always made him a little jealous that Max had such a hold on him though. As much as he told Charlie that he was his, Charlie didn't have the ability to feel what Max was feeling. He was marked by the werewolf, showing everyone that he belonged to him. But there was nothing showing people that Max was his.

"The other one," He got to his ear, distracting him from any thoughts going through his head. His breath was hot and his hands had traveled lower than they were before. "That you need to promise me," He nibbled at his ear. "Is that you'll be mine forever."

"You already have a mark to prove it," Charlie chuckled. The Alpha's possessiveness was in control at the moment, and he held onto Charlie as if his life depended on it. He couldn't say that he didn't like the feeling of all the attention he was giving his body.

"I need more than a mark, Charlie Fairchild." There was a low rumble coming from his chest. He wished he could feel it in his hands. He loved running his hands over Max's chest.

"I promise you." He leaned into the man. It was too easy to get him to fall for him all over again. "That I will be yours forever."

Max kissed him hard. He didn't know what was going on at that exact moment, in the flurry of it all, but he wasn't going to complain. He kissed back, making that rumble in his lover's chest get just a bit louder. His hands lifted him off the ground, sitting him on the desk that was there.

Oh yeah. He almost forgot that he was in his office. He wanted to ask if they should really be doing something like this here, but there was no fighting with that domineering mouth.

He heard a drawer open, but couldn't look. While one of those hands were away from his body, the other one was in his hair, keeping his head in place. He couldn't help but wrap his legs around him. He missed his touch so much. He missed being in his hold.

Wet fingers slipping into his pants were what made him break the kiss.

"How did you-?" He couldn't finish his question as those fingers slid inside him.

"Did you really think I wouldn't have planned for something like this?" Max nibbled his ear.

How did Charlie not see something like that in his own office? He had questions for this sinful man. But there was no way he was going to be able to get any answers when he was touching him like this.

Whatever little things that were on his desk were knocked off as Max laid him down on it. Charlie grabbed the man's shirt. He couldn't help but want the man just as much as he wanted him. His clothes were almost all the way off. But he wanted Max's off as well. At least his shirt. He wanted to feel his hot skin on him.

Max complied, throwing the thing off as fast as he could before getting his hands back on Charlie.

He slowly entered him, torturing him with every second longer that he took. Charlie was a mewling mess underneath him. It had been months since they had gone even a day without touching or holding each other. It made this all the more enticing.

"Max," he mumbled. His arms were wrapped around his neck, holding on for dear life. "Please," he begged.

"Please what, baby?" Max asked. He could feel him smirk on his neck.

He hated when he teased him like this. It was sweet torture that had him turning into a hot mess every time he did it.

"Faster," he begged. He needed release now more than ever. He needed Max.

"I don't know," Max's voice was husky as he kissed his neck lightly. "You haven't exactly been the nicest to me."

He wanted to say something, but Max pushed into him quick, making him forget how to make words.

"But," he whispered into his ear again. Charlie couldn't really seem to do anything but cling to the man. "You did make those promises to me."

"You," He lightly hit Max's back. "Are a tease."

"Hmm," Max smiled against him again. "That's funny, I remember saying the same thing to you earlier this week."

He let out another quiet moan as he pushed into him. He needed him so badly. It had been too long since they had done this. It didn't take long for Max to cave into him. They both held each other tightly as he moved quickly in and out of him. He could feel the muscle on his arms as he tightened his grip on him. He never wanted him to let him go at that moment.

He finished deep inside him, making him climax right along with him. Max always knew how to make him feel the greatest when he was in his arms. Whether it be sexual or not, it made Charlie love him more than ever.

"I missed you," Charlie buried his face into the man's shoulder. It wasn't exactly comfortable on that desk, but neither made any motion to move from each other's hold.

"I missed you too," Max said. "You had me losing my mind for those three days."

"I'm sorry." He shook his head. He really did feel guilty. "I messed up."

"Charlie," Max shifted to where his face was in the man's hand. He lifted his head up to face him. Those purple eyes had never looked so loving towards him. "No matter what happens with anything, I will always love you."

"I know." He smiled at him. "You know I'm always going to love you too, right?"

Max practically purred at his words, nuzzling the part of his neck where he marked him. Charlie loved when he did this. As much as there were plenty of heated moments, his favorite ones were always when they could cuddle and hold each other. Of course, when it was both, that was the best.

"We should get out of here," Max said after a moment or two. "Now both of us need to shower again."

"You aren't throwing that condom away in here." He chuckled as the man went to look for his shirt. "I don't want anyone knowing that we did something like this here."

"Of course," Max winked at him, pulling on his shirt. "This is our little secret."

Why did he have a feeling that Max was going to try and do this more often?

Thankfully they were able to get to their suite without anyone seeing them. Charlie knew that they would be able to smell them, and he'd rather not go through the embarrassment of that getting spread around the pack.

Max held him the entire time. The clinginess of their bond was stronger than ever now that they had been away for a while. He didn't know how he lived without him before.

After their shower they were told that Alistair was awake. The doctor told them that he was going to recover in two weeks. He had the same look in his eyes that he did when he had Charlie under his care. He was happy to see that Alistair had gotten into one of the pack member's hearts.

Besides Nick's that was. He wished he would have known that Alistair was Nick's mate before. He was so happy to hear that the chef had found someone. Now he just hoped that the albino would be understanding and patient with his friend.

Maybe that prayer had worked after all.

It was strange to see Alistair avoid his gaze again. The man had saved his life, yet he was still so fearful. When they found out that he wasn't allowed to look at the superior's mates before, it made a little more sense. He just hoped that the man would get out of that habit. He wanted him to be comfortable here now that he was finally going to be a member.

He looked so bad, wrapped up in all of that gauze. He looked like he was in a lot of pain, but he told them that the doctor had given him medicine for it. That was all the doctor could seem to do, other than to continue to give him more blood through an I.V.

He was so happy when Max made the announcement that he was joining the pack. Even Nick looked happy. Max had brought the man out to apologize to him for being so harsh on him. He told Charlie that he yelled at the man after finding out he was sneaking over to the cabin to be with the albino. Thankfully, Nick understood. He seemed a little wary of Max, but he told him that there were no hard feelings. He was just happy that he was alive.

He did tell them that he wanted the fact that they were mates to be a secret for now. Charlie already had a feeling he would. He had told Max ahead of time to tell Ed to keep it quiet for now. He knew the rest wouldn't be talking about it. They were all busy with other things. Ed was the one who was the gossip.

The next people they had to talk to were the other three that were with Alistair. Charlie hadn't gotten much time to talk to them before, or any time for that matter. Dr. Button said that they didn't suffer from any major wounds, and Jackie's babies were still okay in her womb. He found out that they were triplets when he did his check up on her last night.

"Is Alistair okay?" Madeline asked. Right when they walked into the room that the three of them were in, all of them jumped up. They looked so worried for their friend.

"He's recovering well," Max answered her. "He can't have many visitors now, but he's said to be healed up in two weeks."

They all gave a sigh of relief at that. Charlie thought it was sweet how easily they befriended him. From what he had found, they really hadn't known him for that long.

"So, you're the Luna?" Jackie asked. He remembered her by how long her hair was. She looked so sweet and kind.

"Yeah." He put out his hand for her to shake. "You can just call me Charlie, though."

"It's nice to meet you, Charlie." She smiled. "Nick told us a lot about you."

"I'm glad to officially meet you," he told her. "I'm glad to meet all of you, officially."

He could tell that they weren't used to a male Luna. But they were still kind to him. It was mainly Max that did all the talking, just like with Alistair. He just tried to make them feel a little comfortable.

When Max told them that they were granted membership into their pack, they were ecstatic. He could see Herb and Jackie give a relieved sigh. Madeline seemed a little on edge about it, though.

"Is Alistair allowed membership too?" Her golden eyes were defensive.

"Yes," Max told her. "He's in your group. All of you will have a ceremony to join our pack. We'll set it for when Alistair has regained his health."

It would have been ridiculous not to allow them into the pack after what just happened. Alistair risking his life like that, to the point of almost death, to save him was enough to show where his loyalties lied. As far as the others, they had done well in taking care of the three that had come their way. It was easy to see that they were good people.

Madeline nodded at his answer, her face softened and she smiled. Charlie could already tell that she had a certain spunk to her. She was protective over the people she got close to. He could tell that by her reaction about Alistair. There was a mothering air about her that Charlie liked to see though.

"Your rooms will be on the first floor," Charlie said. "I'll have Heather give you guys a tour when you're ready."

"Heather?" Herb asked.

"She's one of the maids here," he told him. "Don't worry, she's a quick call away if you need her."

They nodded and Charlie and Max said their farewell's. As soon as they walked out of the door, Max was practically pulling him in the direction of their suite.

"I'm assuming you got all of your paperwork done?" Charlie chuckled at the man's excitement.

"When you have nothing to do but work for three days straight," Max opened the door for him. "You tend to get a lot done."

"I was actually really looking forward to having some time off after that project," he told him. He was immediately wrapped in Max's warm embrace. "Maybe we can have a break for a day or two."

"Maybe?" the man mumbled into his ear. "I'm counting on it."

He could already tell where this was going to go. Neither of them had completely satisfied the lust and need that piled up when they were apart. Even though Charlie had finally gotten to a healthy weight, Max still picked him up like it was nothing.

But, instead of doing their usual routine of throwing off their clothes and colliding into bed, Max sat him in a chair and knelt by him. He held his face in the palm of his hands and looked at him with those beautiful amethyst eyes.

"Charlie, there's one thing that I've been neglecting to ask you for a while now," he told him. "One that I've been wanting to ask from the moment I saw you."

"Max, what's this about?" A bit of worry made his heart beat faster. He didn't know whether this was going to be a good question or a bad question.

"If there's one thing that I realized from just these three long days," Max said. "It's that I really can't live without you, not even for one day. I need you to be mine forever." His hand moved to the mark that he made on Charlie's neck. "And that takes more than just a mark. I want to prove to you that I love you and will love you for the rest of my life."

Then he pulled something out of his pocket. It was a small jewelry box.

Wait.

This couldn't be happening.

"Charlie," He opened the box to show a gold ring with garnets and diamonds in it. "Will you marry me?"

He didn't know what to say. He knew that it was going to come sometime, but he didn't expect it to come now. He truly wanted to stay in that moment forever, just to always be able to remember the look in Max's eyes that were filled with love, and the amazing ring that he was holding. He never really had much jewelry before Max.

Now he was going to get the best one.

"Yes!" He collided into him, wrapping his arms around his neck. "Of course, I will!"

His true dreams had always been to find love and have a big family. Both of them seemed to happen in less than a year.

He couldn't be happier.

CHAPTER 24:

The Moore Family

"Okay," Nick opened the doors to the infirmary. "It's time for one of my all-time favorites: Curry."

"What's that?" Alistair asked. It had been a week since he had almost gotten killed from the rogue attacks. He seemed to be healing quickly, just like Dr. Button had said, but he was ordered by the doctor to stay bed-ridden for one more week. He still had more stitches waiting to get out.

"Oh, I've heard of curry," Madeline said. Her, Herb and Jackie had been visiting Alistair every day, along with Nick, of course. "Isn't that an Indian dish?"

"Yup!" He set a bowl down in front of everyone. The one thing that he enjoyed doing was having lunch with the people who were stuck under Dr. Buttons care. He did it all the time with Charlie when he was first brought to the pack house. "I learned how to make it the traditional way from my mom."

"Finally." Herb rubbed his stomach. "Something spicy!" He had finally been able to trim the crazy beard that he had going on when he first met him. Now it was much shorter. It made him look much younger and less crazy than before.

"Sorry, Herb." He smiled as he put down a bowl for him. "This isn't the spicy kind."

"What?!" He looked at him with the most surprised eyes. "How in the world do you make curry that isn't spicy?"

"That's easy." He laughed. "You become a chef. Besides," He put Alistair's bowl down last. "I don't know if you guys can handle the true spices of India."

"Are you challenging me?" Herb asked. His shoulders straightened and he gave him a playful look.

"It's probably not best for Jackie, anyway," Madeline said.

"Spicy food is good for babies," Nick told her. "At least, that's what my mother always said. She ate spicy food all while she was pregnant with my brothers and sisters."

"I'd take that challenge," Alistair said. His smile reached his eyes when he looked at him. "I could handle it."

"Have you had spicy food before?"

"Skunks don't count," Herb said before Alistair could answer. The room erupted in laughter.

Nick missed times like these. It felt like he was with his family when they all decided to come down. They were the one omega family that had reunions where they would all visit each other. But they only happened every three or four years.

It had been absolutely terrifying watching Alistair fight for his life on the operating table. Dr. Button had put a curtain over his body so he could only see his head. Of course, he had to tell the doctor that they were mates. The doctor didn't really have time to react when he was working on him. Afterwards, though, he congratulated him.

"Finding your mate could very well help with your health problem," he told him. "It's happened before."

He really didn't want to talk about that right then. He didn't want to talk about that at all, but especially not when he just witnessed the man almost die right in front of his eyes.

That was why he couldn't really be mad at Max, though. He at least said that he could go in there and be with him while the doctor was operating on him. He did apologize for snapping at him, and Nick understood why he did. He just hoped that he never got yelled at by the man again.

"One of the children at the zoo gave me a chip that was spicy," Alistair answered the question. "It didn't taste too bad."

"Man," Herb laughed. "It sounds like you got pampered when you were there."

"There were a lot of really nice humans there." He smiled at the memory. Nick loved watching him like this. He was so comfortable around them all. He loved hearing his stories as well. He always seemed to have a bunch of them.

And he loved just about everything that Nick gave him to eat. He was having a blast making all these different foods for him to try. Surprisingly, he hadn't found a single thing that he didn't absolutely love.

"So, what do you guys think?" Nick asked, motioning to the food.

"It's not spicy enough," Herb complained.

"Herb!" Jackie smacked his arm. "Where are your manners?"

"I'll give you the spiciest curry of your life next time," he told him.

"You better," Herb grinned.

"I think it's amazing," Jackie said. She had gotten a big appetite now that she had to eat for more than just herself. It was crazy to hear that she was going to have triplets.

"It really is," Madeline wiped her mouth. "You're a good cook, Nick."

"Thanks." He smiled at them. "I love cooking."

"You have a talent for it," Alistair said. Every time Nick looked at him it was hard to move his eyes off from him. He was wrapped up in bandages still, but he was still as handsome as ever.

He was pretty sure that Madeline and the others knew that they were mates. As much as Nick was pretty good at hiding things like this from others, there was always a certain look in all of their eyes that hinted at it. Whether it be a playful look, or merely a happy one, there was just something about it.

He was going to say thanks and pick up the dishes when there was another knock at the door. Nick noticed some familiar scents from behind it.

Oh boy.

"This rooms going to get pretty crowded," Nick told the others. They all looked at him curiously. He should just turn them away, due to Alistair's condition, but he knew that they weren't going to take no for an answer. So, instead of fighting it, Nick went up to the door and twisted the doorknob.

"Guys," he smiled. "Meet the Moore family."

He opened it wide and four people walked in at once. They all talked almost at once as well.

"Bakshi!" His mom came over to hug him. She was a smaller woman, and was shrinking the older she got. Since the rest of them were so tall, they always had to bend over to hug her. "I haven't seen you in so long! Why don't you visit us more?"

"I haven't talked to you for a week, mom." He shook his head. Her thick accent had stayed with her, even with the many years that she had spent in this pack.

"That's too long." She waved a finger at him. Her jet-black hair was just starting to grey. It was put up in a tight bun. His father had tried to convince her to keep it down plenty of times, but it wasn't in her culture to keep her hair down unless she wasn't mated.

"We were starting to worry that you went mute or something." Barry winked at him. He looked around the room. "But we also wanted to greet the newcomers to the pack."

"Guys." He looked at the friends that he had just ate lunch with. "This is my family: my brothers, Barry and George. And these are my parents, Myra, and Alex." He went down the line of the people that had just entered the room. Then he proceeded to introduce all of his family to them.

"Nice to meet you all." His dad smiled at all of them. He had the best smiles. Being a dancer for Broadway himself when he was a kid, he maintained his shape well, even in old age. His light brown hair and light skin was what was passed down to most of his sons. Nick was the only one that looked like a carbon copy of his mom.

Only taller.

And, not a woman.

"It's nice to meet you too!" Jackie said. She tried standing up, but was gently pushed back down by Nick's mom.

"No, honey," she told her. "You don't need to get up. Here." She handed her a bowl of her special drink. "Drink this."

"Oh, thanks!" Jackie smiled. Herb seemed to like that his mate was being pampered a bit. "Nick gave me this a while back actually. He told me you were the one who made it."

"No woman should have to go through what you did." She shook her head, giving her a look of sympathy. "This is what I drank when I was pregnant with Bakshi, it will help your babies grow big and strong like him."

"Bakshi?" Alistair asked. He was always shy to talk to new people, but Nick had found that he was getting more comfortable with it. "Who is that?"

"It's my middle name," Nick said. "Nick Bakshi Moore."

"It's a Moore thing," George explained. He was handing out these bags that Nick could only assume were clothes. "Mom likes to call us by them."

"They're from my old home," she told them.

"So, it's an Indian name?" Madelyn asked.

"Yes." She nodded her head. "It means Gift."

"Aww!" Jackie said. "That's so cute! Herb, we need to think of baby names and make them as cute as that."

Nick couldn't help but laugh at the look on Herb's face when she said that. He looked like he had forgotten that the babies needed names. Madelyn laughed with him.

"Don't worry." His dad patted him on the shoulder. "If you look in the bag, you should find a baby book. We have tons of them."

Nick watched as they all opened up the bags that had been put on their laps. There were some clothes, blankets, and personal hygiene items that they probably desperately needed. For Jackie and Herb, though, it seemed as though his mother had gone all out. She had given them about a dozen baby clothes as well as some books for new parents. There were diapers and some dried baby formula too.

"You really didn't have to do this," Herb said. "Jackie is only two months pregnant."

"Trust me," his father told him. "You're going to have to stock up as fast as you can. We have more in our suite, actually. You can have the rest if you'd like. We won't be needing it anymore."

"Yeah." Barry elbowed Herb. "Once you have, like, twelve of us, you tend to want to stop."

"Twelve?!" Madelyn almost choked on her water. "There's more of you?"

"There's always more of the Moore's," George said. "We're the biggest family in the Crescent Moon Pack, possibly the country – don't hold me to that – and we're the richest omega family as well."

"Oh boy," Nick sat down next to Alistair's bed. "Here comes the story again."

"What story?" Alistair asked. His wore a confused smile. Nick was happy that he wasn't feeling overwhelmed by all the people that were in the room. It wasn't like it was a small one, it just felt that way when you had this many people in it.

"The Moore family story," Nick said.

"Well, since you're being so fussy about it," Barry folded his arms dramatically, "Why don't you tell it this time?"

Nick smiled as his friends and new pack members leaned in, as curious as can be.

"Long, long ago," he started, "In the ancient times, the young Alex Moore set out to New York. He somehow convinced the Alpha of said ancient time to let him travel, becoming the first in the Crescent Moon Pack to do so. He learned how to dance, and sing, and swing. And quickly climbed the ladder to being a Broadway star."

"He traveled the world, performing for both large and small crowds. Until one day, he met a woman who was – is! – the most beautiful woman in the world." He looked at his mom and smirked. "He told his Alpha that he had met the love of his life, in a small pack in India. He had acquired much wealth during his travels. So much so, that the Alpha of his mate's pack was in awe. He couldn't believe that a little omega could gain such wealth."

"He vowed to love this woman for the rest of his life. He taught himself her language and told her that he wanted to grow a family with her. Needless to say, she fell for the handsome devil. The Alpha's of each pack talked and allowed the gorgeous woman to be brought to his pack in exchange for some money that her pack desperately needed."

"They wed immediately, under the full moon. Some say that the Moon Goddess blessed them on that day. For she blessed the woman with fertility. A blessing that the Crescent Moon Pack had not gotten for a long, long time."

"They had twelve children, all of them talented in their own way. Their father forced them to learn how to dance, and their mother taught them the ways of her old culture, so that they might never forget where they came from."

"And you said that I told it dramatically," George rolled his eyes.

"You can travel in this pack?" Madelyn asked.

"We used to," his dad answered this time. "Once the rogues started causing issues with our pack, it became dangerous and was banned."

"How long have these rogues been attacking you guys?"

"A long, long time." His father sighed. "Our pack has gone through a lot of troubling times. We're just glad to be blessed enough that none of our children have died."

"Max isn't going to let anyone die." Nick shook his head. "That's one thing he's always promised."

"I'm glad," Jackie said. "He seems like a good leader."

"He may have not been the kindest to you all at first," Nick said. "But he does care about everyone in the pack. He's a bit overprotective in that sense."

"I had a feeling," Madelyn said. "He was giving Alistair the hardest time."

"We truly do have to thank you." His mom looked at the albino. His ruby eyes were soft when he looked to her. "You protected this pack that has been hard on you the whole time you've been here. You protected it with your life, and saved us all from the harm that they could have done."

"The Alpha hasn't been as harsh as you all think," Alistair said. "When I was traveling, I would be lucky to have even one meal a day, and shelter from storms were rare. The Alpha provided all of us with shelter and three meals a day. He helped me when I needed it the most. And, for that, I am eternally grateful of him."

Nick didn't think about it like that. He couldn't imagine only having one meal a day or not having shelter from all the storms that this forest had. It explained why Alistair never looked disgruntled when Max put those restrictions on him.

The small woman smiled and went over to him. She kissed the top of the albino's forehead and gently patted his shoulder.

"You are just like Bakshir, then," she told him. "You are a gift to our pack."

They talked a little more. A little to Nick's family usually was another hour at least. They all loved to talk. That was a family trait that had passed down to everyone. His family had a habit of befriending people easily as well. They were the storytellers; the dancers; the jokers.

Nick wished that he could freeze time and be in this moment for just a while longer. Nowadays it was rare for much of his family to spend time together. George and Barry had wives and children of their own to take care of. His parents were always doing something to help the pack, even in their old age. They were all so busy working and having their own lives that it was difficult to even get these four together at the same time.

It didn't last, though, much like the many good things in his life that had been slipping out of his grasp. Jackie was getting tired and his brothers had to go check on their kids. Alistair needed to rest a bit anyway. Soon the busy room was empty, and it was just Nick and Alistair again.

"You miss your family." Alistair broke the silence. "Don't you?"

"I never used to," he answered honestly. As soon as they were gone, he wove his hands into Alistair's. "I think I'm still just sad cause of Katy."

"Your mother's a wonderful woman," he told him. "She reminds me a lot of mine."

"Is your mom still with that old pack of yours?"

"No." He shook his head. Nick could see pain in those eyes of his. "She passed away when I was fifteen. My Alpha wouldn't even let me bury her."

Just the thought of that alone was enough to make Nick cry. He couldn't imagine if that had happened to his mother. She was stubborn and bossy, but she had cared for him and loved him from the moment he was born.

"What did she look like?" he asked.

"She had blonde hair," Alistair started. "The kind that any light would catch onto. She wasn't that tall, if I remember correctly. But her eyes..." He stared off into the distance, reliving a memory. "Her eyes are what I remember the most. They were light blue. But, under the moonlight, they looked just like the full moon. I will never forget her, or the lessons that she taught me."

There was a tear that escaped the man. Nick saw it before he could try and wipe it away. He put his hand on the man's soft white cheek and brushed the tear away with his thumb.

"I think my mom was right." He smiled at him. "I think you really are a gift to this pack." He leaned into him and hugged him as best as he could. Alistair's arms quickly wrapped around him. It felt good to be in his hold again. He never thought it would feel this nice just to have someone hold him like this.

"I think you are a gift to me," Alistair said. Nick looked up to see a twinkle in his eyes. "Bakshir."

CHAPTER 25:

A Kitchen Throwback

There weren't that many cooks working that morning. Most of them were planned to do the afternoon shift that day. That way there would be enough workers to help cook for the party as well as the regular meals. For anyone else, it would mean that the morning crew had to work extra hard on making meals. But when it was Nick and Aldi working on the same shift, they could get anything done.

Including some talking.

"So, there I was." He flipped another pancake. "Soaked head to toe and laughing my ass off."

"I can't believe they actually sprayed you with a firehose!" Jackie looked absolutely mortified by his tale. Herb, however, was getting a good laugh out of it, which was nice to see. He had a lumberjack's laugh. It was loud enough to fill the entire forest with sound.

He knew it was going to be dead in the kitchen. Not that many people were scheduled to work and there weren't that many orders with everyone sleeping in. So, he asked Aldi if he could bring the newcomers to the kitchen to meet some more of the pack. Aldi usually didn't like anything that distracted the workers, but he seemed pretty curious to meet these newcomers himself.

"It'd be nice to meet the one who made you smell like that when you came back that morning," he told him. That had to be the most embarrassing thing the chef had said to him. And Nick didn't appreciate the smile on the old man's face when he said it.

But he got to bring all his new friends to the kitchen. It didn't take long for all of them to fall in love with Jackie. She was adorable, and easy for anyone to befriend. Herb and Madeline were easy as well. But there was always Alistair that made everyone tense.

The kitchen was silent for a second when the albino walked in. Everyone was trying to get a good look at him, and Nick could feel the stress build up on the man's shoulders because of it. When Alistair had gotten out of Dr. Button's care, they had given him a room to live in on the first floor. It was obvious then that he wasn't used to being around so many people.

The fun thing was that Nick was able to get him out to talk to everyone easily. As soon as he started the conversation, Alistair would find an easy way to add himself to it, and then he would relax. It was nice seeing him relax after talking to someone. Everyone was shocked at his appearance, but it didn't take long before they started to warm up to him.

Surprisingly, Aldi warmed up to him immediately. When the whole kitchen was quiet, he stopped what he was doing and went to shake his hand.

"Welcome to the pack, son," he told him. Nick didn't exactly know what the head chef thought of the newcomers, so he was happy to see him take Alistair in so easily. A part of him wanted to ask him why, as Aldi wasn't too keen on strangers. But there was something about that all-knowing smile that he had on his face before that held Nick back from satisfying his curiosity.

Him and Dr. Button were the only ones that could make that look, he swore. It was the one that made you really start to ponder just how much they knew.

It eased the tension of the kitchen quickly at least. Of course, Aldi was also barking at all of them to get back to work, so that helped a lot too.

"It was my idea," Nick told the group of friends. He could see Aldi shaking his head from the corner of his eye. The old cook had heard Nick tell this tale many times before. "Max and Tyler just wanted to see their parents faces when they got an 'A' on the project."

"I can't believe Max would do that to you," Charlie popped over to him to grab some things from his work station. He was baking pies for the party. It was something that Nick knew he missed a lot. The blond absolutely shined in the kitchen.

"You should be glad you didn't meet him in high school," Nick just laughed. "He was the most defiant 'good boy' you'd ever meet."

It took Madeline, Herb and Jackie some time to get used to Charlie being in the kitchen. Alistair still wanted to keep his head down around the man. Nick challenged this by finding ways to get him to look up again. Him and Charlie had a secret mission to get the albino to be comfortable in the pack.

Even though he wasn't officially in the pack until tonight.

Charlie's scent alone made it easy for people to like him. Jackie warmed up to everyone. But, surprisingly, it was Madeline that started to like him first. Nick found out that she was just a bit protective of Alistair, which threw him off.

"I just don't like the way that everyone looks at him and treats him when they first see him," she told him a few days ago.

"They just aren't used to seeing something like that," he told her. "And Max wanted to make sure that the pack stayed safe."

"If he saw how that man acted when we first saw him." She shook her head. "He would have a completely new perspective on the man."

"What do you mean?"

"There was just something to him," she told him. "As much as he seemed like he didn't know much when the Alpha was questioning him, he knows a lot. He's keen on his instincts and follows it religiously. He's wiser than his age. And I honestly don't think he would ever cause harm to anyone who was kind to him."

He liked that thought. Alistair really did seem like the wise gentle giant. Even compared to Nick, who was 6'3", the man towered over him. But he always made himself shrink whenever he noticed that anyone was afraid of him. He made himself look as small as his large body could be. Nick hated when he did that.

At least in the kitchen, he could always give him some food to try. The man absolutely loved trying everything. Aldi already loved him because of it. As soon as Alistair said that he loved fish, the cook looked as happy as a clam. Aldi's signature dinner dish was salmon. And, sadly, not a lot of people requested it from the old man anymore.

Of course, Charlie all let them try his pie fillings. The man made the best pies in the world. He was baking other things for the party, of course, but the main thing that everyone wanted from him were his pies.

"So, did it actually work?" Herb asked him, bringing him right back to the story he was telling.

"Nope." He shook his head, "The conditioner was still in it a bit."

"How the hell does a firehose not get conditioner out?!" Madeline laughed. "This can't be real!"

"I still have the graded report from it." He stood proudly. "We almost got in 1st place at the science fair, too."

"You mean to tell me." Madeline pointed the fork she was using at him playfully. "That a project about using hair product on different types of hair, almost won in a science fair?"

"Yup!" He laughed at her reaction. Even Charlie seemed shocked at that. "Our opening pitch was: Three men; Three hairstyles; One Firehose."

"It was the talk of the pack for at least a month," Aldi shook his head. "None of us could believe that those three could do something so ridiculous and still manage to get a good grade on it."

"You should have done it on beards," Herb said. "I can only imagine trying to use a firehose for that."

"Then we would have needed to convince others to help us," Nick said. "This was before Tyler could even start to grow a beard."

"Your hair's really that thick?" Alistair asked. His low voice always made him feel a warm pull towards him.

"It may not look it when it's up in a ponytail, or braided," he answered. "But I got a lot of my mom's genes. And her hair used to break rubber bands with how thick it was."

"That sounds beautiful," Jackie said. "I wish I had thick hair."

"Trust me when I say you don't." He shook his head. "It really is a pain and a half trying to wash it and get all the conditioner out."

He wished he could mind link with Alistair already. Those red eyes were giving him an intense stare that had him wondering exactly what he was thinking. He remembered when they first kissed and how the man had taken his hair down just to run his fingers through it.

Just the thought of that alone made him shiver.

They were still close in their relationship. Alistair was taking it slow, and Nick was enjoying that he was. He still had to find the perfect time to tell him about his own problem. He wished that he was like every other person and he didn't have to worry about something like this. But he wasn't that lucky.

Alistair was a cuddler, surprisingly. Someone who was as toned as him, Nick would have never thought that he would be as cuddly as a teddy bear. He almost wanted to start calling him that when they were alone. The way he held him when they were just lying in bed made him so relaxed. It was like he was floating on clouds.

"Alright," Madeline got up from her seat. They were all sitting down at a counter that no one was using at the moment. "I'm going to head to the bathroom, before it's too late."

"I'll make sure to tell all my stories while you're away!" he yelled as she walked out. He could see her shaking her curly head as the door closed behind her.

"I really hope you don't tell us any stories while she's gone," Herb sighed. "Knowing her, she'll have me retell them to her later. And I suck at telling stories."

"You could easily just ask Nick for it again," Charlie said. "He tells these stories all the time."

"Hey!" He faked an appalled look. "You never heard the last one I told."

"I love all of your stories," Charlie smiled at him. "No matter how many times you tell them."

"Thanks, Apple."

"What's the story behind your nickname?" Jackie asked Charlie. Nick couldn't help but laugh at how interested Alistair seemed to be with it too. He looked like a puppy when he was curious.

Did he mention that he was adorable?

"Aldi nicknamed him that when he first met him," Nick told them. "After that, it's been a nickname that kind of stuck."

"Was it because of his scent?"

"That was a part of it," Aldi answered the question this time. "The other reason was the boy loved talking about how he made apple pies better than the rest."

"I still think Ryan makes them the best," Charlie argued.

Nick loved whenever Charlie was in the kitchen. Today reminded him of when he first met him. They were all so curious as to why there was a human in the pack house. Then there was his scent that threw all the workers off. It was the only smell that could stand out in a kitchen of food, scents, and steam.

"You were so thin back then," he told him. The memories of those days made him smile. They were when he was much more carefree. Charlie was easy to make friends of too. Even though they were told to be cautious with him, he always talked so easily to them.

He missed those days. Even though it wasn't that long ago. It felt like forever. A part of him wondered how Alistair would have reacted to Charlie back then. He really did like the human, whenever he finally did allow himself to look at the man. They were on their way to being good friends, which made Nick happy.

"Nick!" Alan came in before any of the newcomers could ask more questions. "What are you cooking? It smells amazing in here!"

"Uh." He paused to look at the chef. He had just come in, and, surprisingly, he had a smile on his face. "I'm just making my usual Alan. It might be the fact that Charlie's here, though."

"No, that's not what I mean," Alan furrowed his eyebrows. "It smells different in here."

Nick had no idea what he was talking about. Other than the scents of the new wolves that were going to join the pack that night, there were no new smells. He was flipping pancakes like he always did. And Aldi was preparing the dinner for the party. It was all things that they had done before, if not regularly when you worked in the kitchen long enough.

"I have no clue what you mean." He shrugged his shoulders. "You want to say hi to the newbie's though?"

Alan's face fell when he said that. It went from a slight excitement to his dull working face again. Nick almost felt bad that he had said that, but he had no clue what the man could have smelt.

He introduced them just like he had done everyone else. It was fun having people meet others. Nick was the best at getting them to actually talk. Of course, it helped that Jackie was as sweet as honey with everyone, and Herb calmed down as soon as Jackie had warmed up to them. She was so young, being that she was only eighteen. It seemed to make all of them want to protect her.

"Oh, you're the other mateless one," Herb said. He seemed to be getting more comfortable in the pack house the longer he stayed.

"Yeah, yeah." He waved them off. He had started on working at his station as they were trying to talk to him. "Laugh all you want, I'm sure that beta of yours is having a laugh that I'm this old and mateless too."

"Why would I be?" Alistair asked him. Nick tensed when Alan mentioned him. He didn't want the man to pick on him. Alan wasn't too much of a bully. But he did get hurt easily. And, when he was hurt, he liked to say hurtful things back.

"I'm sure you already found your mate," Alan told him. "Alphas, betas, and omegas always find their mate fast. It's always the deltas and gammas that have the hardest time."

"I don't think that's true," Alistair said. "I never thought I'd ever find my mate, no matter how much adventuring I'd do."

"You're mateless too?" Alan looked at him dumbfounded. "Oh, great, join the club, buddy. We got jackets."

"There's a club?" Alistair cocked his head to the side, as he did whenever he got confused. Nick had to hold back a snicker.

"Madeline would be the boss of that club." Herb chuckled. "She hasn't found her mate either and she's proud of it."

"Why would anyone be proud of it?" Alan looked disgusted that he even said that.

"She just turned it into her devotion to her career," Herb said. "You should hear her talk about it. She can go on and on about something as small as a bird feather."

"That's not natural," the cook huffed. He seemed extra emotional today and Nick didn't quite know why.

"Try telling her that." Herb shrugged. "Although, I'll warn you, she may tear you a new one if you say it like that."

"It's not about the whole 'women should be making babies' speech." Alan rolled his eyes. "It's in our nature, even as humans, to want to grow our families. It gives you something to live for in the long run, when you can no longer work. It's so that you can have someone who will be there for you when you are at your lowest, and celebrate with you at your highest. That's what mates are truly for."

Nick looked to the chef to find that his expression had gotten much softer. He knew that Alan hadn't always been a grump, but it was different when he saw the man almost go back in time right in front of him. Even though he dated, Alan never seemed to find the right one. Now Nick understood him a little better. He was just like him.

He was lonely.

"I understand where you're coming from." Alistair smiled at him. "It's easy for some people to find their mates. But others the Moon Goddess likes to challenge. I'd like to think that when they pass those challenges, though, she will reward them."

Nick was having a hard time focusing on the food he was cooking. He could feel those ruby eyes on his back the whole time he was talking. Alistair had such a weird effect on him. Every time Nick's senses picked up on anything that related to the man, they heightened. They tried to pull him towards him even when there were people around.

He had told Alistair that he wanted to keep their relationship a secret for a while. The important people knew already, so it wasn't like they were going to get in trouble for it. Truth be told, he feared his mother's reaction to his mate. She hadn't exactly been happy when his oldest brother was found to be gay.

"How old are you?" Alan asked Alistair.

"Twenty-six," he told him. Nick didn't know that Alistair didn't even know his age until Button came into the infirmary and said it. He had a feeling that it would be easy to lose track of time when you were traveling to be a wolf, but he had no idea it would be that bad.

"Wait until you hit thirty," he told him. "You'll start believing that mates don't even exist."

"I would never lose faith in something like that." Alistair shook his head. "Mates are one of the many reasons why the Moon tests us so much. For each individual, she designates a specific trial that they must overcome in their life before they are to achieve happiness."

"Then what would mine be?" Alan looked at him. His light brown eyes bored into the albino's with nothing but frustration and annoyance shining through them.

"Perhaps it would be the trial that she's given me," Alistair pondered out loud.

"And what's that?"

"A trial of patience and waiting." He smiled at him. Nick had never thought that Alistair would talk to Alan that much, let alone start talking to him about this stuff. His stories about the Moon Goddess were so much different from the one's that Nick was taught. It was fun to listen to though. The man was truly devoted to her.

"For seventeen years?" Alan looked at him dumbfounded. "That's the most ridiculous thing you could ever say."

"It seems like a long time," he told him. "Until you start to realize just how long of a life we truly have."

Wow.

Madeline was right, Alistair really was a man wiser than his age.

"Alright!" Madeline's voice boomed as she walked back into the kitchen. "What are we trying now? It smells amazing in…"

Nick looked over his shoulder to see why the woman had stopped in the middle of her sentence. It turned out that he wasn't the only one looking at her. Alan had completely stopped what he was doing and stood frozen while facing the woman that had just walked in.

No, they were looking at each other.

Wait a second…

"Mine!"

CHAPTER 26:

Suit and Tie

"Mine!"

That was the last thing Alistair heard before Madeline and Alan grabbed each other. He was pleasantly surprised to see that his point was proven almost immediately. He'd have to thank the Moon Goddess for that favor.

He had simply wanted Alan to realize the bigger picture. Many people look at the smaller picture and think that the tiny portrait is the whole story of their life. But there's a canvas when it comes to life, full of ups and downs that forever happen, whether you find what you want in life or not.

He really wasn't expecting Madeline and Alan to be paired with each other. Looking around, though, it didn't seem like anyone else did either.

"See?" Herb broke the silence. He gestured to the new couple while looking at her. "No matter how their personality is, they always do this."

Alistair couldn't help but laugh a little. It seemed just like Herb to bring up an old conversation at a serious time like this one.

"Just because they're doing this, doesn't mean that everyone does," Jackie argued back, her arms folded. She didn't look like she was truly angry with her mate. It was fun seeing her tease Herb for once.

"What are you two talking about?" Nick asked them. Those hazel eyes glanced at his again. He loved just how much the man looked at him. It looked like there was a tiny battle going on in his eyes to not glance his way. He knew that it was due to him not wanting everyone to know. Alistair understood. Nick seemed completely innocent to all of this, which made him feel more guilty for what he had done before.

"Don't worry about it," Herb told the chef. "It's just something we've been talking about for a while now."

"Alright you two." Chef Aldi stopped what he was doing to go over there. "Out of the kitchen." He shooed them away. "We can't celebrate for the welcoming of new pack members, and new mates, without food."

They stopped for a second and looked to the chef. Madeline was red in the face, still trying to catch her breath. Alistair was sure that not even Herb had seen her like that. And the man seemed to have known her for quite some time. Alan seemed embarrassed as he looked at the head chef.

"Aldi, I'm sorry, I-!"

"Don't be sorry." The chef smiled at him. "Just go and enjoy your week off. I'll tell Max about it."

They watched as the two ran out of the kitchen. Alan looked young. It was as if he had shed off all those years of waiting for his mate. Alistair was happy for him.

"Well, I'm glad he's got a week off." Herb shook his head. "He looked like he needed a vacation."

"Everyone gets a week off from their duties when they're first mated," Nick said. He had hopped over to Alan's work station and was taking care of the food that the man was making. Alistair loved watching him cook. He looked as though he was dancing with all the multitasking he did.

"Really?" Herb looked surprised. Alistair couldn't say he wasn't as well. "That's the first that I've heard of a pack doing that."

"All the packs around here do it," Nick explained. "It's to keep the mates from obsessing over each other and getting distracted from their duties."

"Makes sense." Herb nodded his head. "When I first met Jackie, it was when I was re-shingling a roof. I was lucky that my friend at the time was there to stop me from nailing myself in the hand."

"I've heard worse horror stories," Chef Aldi said. "Nick, can you handle both orders today?"

"Yup!" The man flipped a pancake as he answered him. The way he did everything so gracefully left him awe-struck. "Easy as pie."

Alistair wished he could talk to him privately more. They only are able to at night when they both need to get some sleep. Nick had been so concerned with having him meet everyone that he walked him around the pack house at least ten times over. Alistair didn't mind though. He just wished he could ask him some things.

He wondered if the reason why he wanted them to be a secret was because of his career. The chef really looked like he loved what he was doing. He wondered if he was worried because he didn't want to go on this week break that the pack did for mated couples.

He wished that Nick would open up to him a little more. He loved telling stories about himself, but there was something that was keeping them from being closer.

"I'm so glad he finally found someone," Charlie said. He had been multitasking as well as Nick. He worked well when he was in the kitchen, and Alistair truly loved the pie filling that the Luna had made.

"I wonder how he's going to act now that he found her." Nick looked at him really quick. It was interesting seeing an omega talk so freely to a

Luna. But it was more common than one talking comfortably to an Alpha. It was surprising for him to hear that they were friends.

It also explained why everyone was so protective of the omega. This pack was a strange one, but it was a good one. Alistair was proud that his instincts had brought him here. He hadn't been this happy in his entire life.

"How who's going to act?"

He stiffened a bit as he heard the Alpha walk in. Charlie looked over to the entrance and immediately smiled. Their love was nice to see, but Alistair still didn't dare to keep his eyes on the Luna for too long. If the Alpha was protective over his pack, then he could only imagine the possessiveness he had with his mate.

"You aren't taking Charlie away from us this time," Nick said over his shoulder. "We're already short staffed as is."

"What's going on?" The Alpha furrowed his eyebrows. He had gone over to Charlie and held him anyway. The Luna chuckled and hugged him back.

"Alan found his mate," Aldi said.

"Really?!" Alpha Max looked excited for the member of his pack. He still kept ahold of his mate the entire time he talked. "Who?!"

"Madeline," Aldi answered. He seemed like he was having to focus more on his work. "Nick! Did you get those eggs done?"

"Right here," Nick placed a plate down with two eggs, sunny side up. It looked perfect. "The next three should be ready in a minute."

Nick was fully focused on work now. Those beautiful hazel eyes were concentrated on the many different things that he was doing. And the way he went from stove to stove made him look like he was dancing with the food he was making.

"Well, I guess this is the best time for you guys to get ready." Max walked away from his mate and towards Alistair and his friends. "It's going to be too busy for Nick to even try talking. Come on, Leah and Sam are ready for you guys."

"Is Leah Sam's wife?" Jackie asked. Sam had already befriended the couple quickly with his stories about his children. They had all stood up and started to follow him.

"Yeah," Max told her. "She's still a little tired from all the kids at the moment, but she's been dying to meet you."

They all started walking out of the kitchen, including Alistair. He knew it would probably be best to leave since they were so busy. Nick needed to focus on his job right now.

"Later guys!" He heard Nick say from his stoves. When he looked back over, he saw Nick's eyes meet his. "I'll see you all at the party!"

They said their farewells and left. Alistair was surprised when the Alpha wanted him to follow them. He was just leaving so as to not seem rude. But Max insisted and lead him to the second floor. They stopped at one of the doors.

"I'll let you guys go in first," Max told Jackie and Herb.

Herb looked at Alistair with a cautious glance before complying to the man's wishes. Alistair wasn't scared to be alone with the Alpha. He knew the man wouldn't hurt him. Not after he had gone through so much effort to save him.

"Madeline might be a little distracted to get ready," Alistair told him. He didn't want his friend to get in trouble.

"Yeah, that was a little unexpected." The Alpha ran his hand through his hair. He looked a bit stressed. Alistair wasn't sure if it was because of Madeline or just the fact that he was away from his mate. After the rogue incident, the Alpha hadn't wanted to let his Luna leave his side. "I'll have to tell Leah to go to her room. Alan and her picked a bad day for this."

"I don't believe it was planned," he told him. He liked that he could talk to him a little more. He wasn't staring at him like he had when they first met. Now, he seemed calmer. It was nice to see in a leader.

"If Alan was planning it, he would have had his mate when he was sixteen." Max laughed. "He used to be a hopeless romantic when he was younger."

"I'm happy for him." Alistair couldn't help but smile. It warmed his heart that his friend, Madeline, was also finding her mate. It meant that they were all fated to be there. The Moon Goddess was happy that they had listened to her.

"Alistair," Max looked serious for a second. "Can I ask you for a favor?"

"Anything." He bowed his head towards the man.

"Be patient with Nick," the Alpha said. "He's not used to anything regarding mates. I'm not at liberty to say, but I'm sure he'll tell you soon."

"I will," he told him. He had waited this long to find him. He could wait a little bit longer. "He told you about us, then?"

"Right before the rogue attack," Max said. "He was so worried about you."

He remembered all the nights that they spent talking in that infirmary. It didn't take long for Nick to start spending the night in that chair by his bed. As soon as Alistair was healed enough, he would convince him to sleep on the bed with him. The most peaceful sleep was always when he was in his arms. Nick would relax into him. Then they would talk a little, until Alistair had lulled him to sleep.

"Can I ask for your opinion?" Alistair asked.

"About Nick?"

"Yes."

"Well, I'm not as close to him as Katy was." He sighed. "But I'd say the best thing you could do is keep talking with him. And be as honest as you can be with him. The more honest you are with him, the more likely he'll open up to you as well."

"Thank you." He smiled. "I'll try that."

"You really are different, Alistair," Max told him. His purple eyes held a curiosity in them that he hadn't seen in many. "I'm glad to have you in this pack."

"Thank you," he said again. "I'm glad to be here."

It took a while before Jackie and Herb came out. Both of them looked amazing. Jackie was in a long green dress that flowed with the breeze. It hid her stomach in the few layers that it had. Herb was wearing black pants with a matching green dress shirt. There was a vest over it that had some flowers in the front pocket.

When he went in there, he was surprised to see that Leah was excited to see him as well. She talked most of the time. Sam had seemed a little unsure about him still, but he warmed up as soon as his wife started talking.

He was told that he could pick whatever color he wanted and they would find something. He didn't want to wear something that would make him more noticeable than he already was, so he decided on light brown. It reminded him of the forest floor that surrounded him. He felt like it was the best color for this occasion. He hated wearing black, as it always made the sun burn into him more. That and he thought it looked horrible on him with how white his skin was.

They picked out a light brown and off-white suit for him to wear. It fit him well. He liked it. It reminded him of the little television that he got to watch as a kid. He mainly saw it when he went to the doctors. But there were many gentlemen that wore outfits like this one, and they were always seen as respectful.

He wasn't entirely happy about having to wear shoes, but he wasn't going to complain about it. This was a gift. And it would be rude if he complained about a gift.

The party started at sunset. It was still hot, and he didn't quite like all the layers of clothing that he had to put on for this. But it was much cooler than earlier that day. Alistair didn't have anything else to do, so he went to the party early. He sat at one of the back tables, so as to not bother any of the workers who were still setting up.

"Alistair?!" He heard Nick before he saw him. He turned to see the man had changed from his work attire. He had on black pants with a black vest, much like Herb's outfit. Only Nick's dress shirt underneath was pure white instead of green, and he had a red rose on it.

He looked amazing. Alistair couldn't help but smile at the chef. He wanted to hold him, but he knew that it would be stepping out of line if he did. If there was any time that he needed to practice his control, it was now. He would rather die than lose Nick.

"You look great!" Nick told him. "I didn't think you were going to pick brown, though. Did Leah not have a more colorful suit for you?"

"Brown is a color," he said. "I thought it would be the best fit for this."

"I guess you're right." Nick smiled. "You do look really good in that."

"I could say the same for you."

"What, this?" The man looked down at his suit. "This has been tucked away in my closet for way too long. I figured it would be the best suit to dance in too!"

"I remember you saying that you liked to dance," he said. That was one of the nights he would talk about Katy. They were a dancing duo and would dance at all the parties that the pack would have.

"Yeah!" Those hazel eyes got brighter the more he talked about it. "My whole family dances. It's something my dad forced us to learn as kids."

"I'm glad you enjoy it, then." He chuckled. He loved the excitement that Nick had when he talked about the things he loved. "Is your family going to be dancing with you?"

"Probably not." Nick looked away. Alistair could feel the excitement leave the man's body as he said it. As much as he had tried to hide it, he looked disappointed. "They have their mates and their children to take care of. And at parties? The kids always go wild."

"I'll dance with you," he said. It was one way that he could be there for him without pushing things too far. At least, that's what he thought. "If you want, that is."

"You know how to dance?"

"No." He shook his head. "But I like trying new things."

"I thought that only was for food with you." Nick's face had brightened at what he had said. He was happy that he had decided to come to the party so early.

"Well, this was my first time asking to be in a pack," he said. "You can't truly enjoy life if you don't keep trying different things."

"I guess that's true." Those hazel eyes had gotten a sparkle to them. "Alright, I can teach you some of the basic dances before the party starts at least."

He ran over to where the music was going to be controlled and started talking to one of the workers there. They nodded at him, and started pressing some dials. The next thing Alistair knew, some slow music was playing.

"Okay." Nick walked up to him. "The first thing you always have to learn is the slow songs. Because there's so many of them, especially at weddings, and you're probably going to wind up dancing at weddings."

"Are you going to be at the weddings?" He smirked. Nick had put his arms up in a position and gestured for him to hold his hands.

"Probably," he answered, rolling his eyes dramatically. "There are so many weddings that happen here, you wouldn't believe."

"I've never been to one before." He watched as Nick moved his hands into the right position. "I've seen some, though. They're very beautiful."

"Any weddings in the woods?" He slowly started moving in a pattern, matching the music perfectly. Alistair was surprised that he could match the pattern as well as he did.

"Some," he replied. How did people talk and dance at the same time? This was one of the most difficult skills for him to learn. He liked how nice it felt to be this close to Nick again, though. They had only been apart for a little while, but it felt like forever.

"You catch on pretty quickly." Nick looked shocked as the song slowly came to an end. "Are you sure you've never done this before?"

"I'm not lying to you." He shook his head. He liked seeing the chef looking pleasantly surprised. It made him want to learn more things to impress him. "It's not that difficult when you use the rhythm to guide you."

"You must be a natural, then." Nick smiled. "My dad was surprised when he first started teaching me to dance too. He said that I was going to be the next Broadway dancer."

He was able to learn a few more dances before the party started. It didn't take long before more people started trickling into the area. They stopped dancing as the music was starting to change to lighter songs, setting the mood for the celebration.

Alistair took a deep breath as he saw the Alpha and Luna come into the area, indicating that the celebration had really begun.

CHAPTER 27:

A Moonlit Celebration

"I told you he was going to dress up," Charlie smiled as they walked into the party. This wasn't their first big party that the pack had with them in charge, but it was still nerve-wracking at the same time. As much as he had found out that he was a great host, it took quite a lot of work to host for a party with almost three hundred people in it.

"If he keeps this up, then the whole pack's going to find out without anyone saying anything," Max shook his head a bit. Not everyone was there yet, so they were walking around greeting the ones who had come early.

"I don't know," Charlie said. *"I don't think people see Nick as anything other than a goofball at parties."*

Nick and Alistair were the first ones they saw. They were standing around talking on the dancing area. Seeing Nick actually dressed in something that wasn't pleather or shiny at a party for once was shocking to say the least. He didn't even know the man had any other party attire. He wore that suit at Katy's farewell party, but this outfit was much more fit for parties.

"He's got tap shoes on," Max told him. Of course, they were talking about this in their mind link. It would be bad if someone overheard them. Especially since they promised Nick they wouldn't tell anyone.

"Tap shoes?"

"For tap dancing." The man explained. Charlie looked over to his friend once more to see him wearing all black dress shoes. *"This parties going to be a blast."*

"How do you know they're tap-dancing shoes?"

"His family has done too many surprise group dances," Max told him. They were still greeting people in between. Max was moving around the room in a way that they would get to the center last. Charlie guessed it was to get a good look at Nick subtly and without actually going up to him and asking. *"That's probably what everyone is thinking they're going to do with how Nick's looking. But he usually wears something over his dance outfits to throw people off."*

"So, there's not going to be a group dance?"

"Probably not. But Nick is definitely going to put on a show for Alistair."

They cut off the mind link at that. There were too many people trying to talk to them now. It was fun to see Nick looking so excited for once, though. The last party they had he was so sad and just wandered around the edge of the rooms, watching Katy. Charlie wished that her mate would have let her have some more time with him. But he already looked so possessive of her. It didn't sit right with him. Max had always been clingy to Charlie, even when they first met, but he never stopped him from going to see his friends or doing the things he wanted to do.

Even when those things didn't help him in the long run.

Now Nick was back to being the center of the stage. He was always so theatrical at parties. Katy played a good part in that, he guessed. The only difference was that this time he had Alistair with him. The two complimented each other well. They both looked completely different from each other, yet had a similar calm aura about them.

What surprised all of them was how easily Nick opened Alistair up. The man used to only answer with as little words as possible. Now he was another story teller, just like Nick. It was fun to see the two bounce off each other's stories.

Charlie didn't think the man would go with a brown suit. It reminded him of a business man kind of. He was surprised at how good it looked against his pale skin.

"Well, Nick seems to be all dressed up." Sam met up with them. Him and Ed were glancing over to the chef too, smirking.

"I should have known." Ed shook his head. "The way those two looked at each other when they first met should have been the first indication."

"I'm still pissed that you did that without asking." Max glared at his friend. Charlie could tell that he wasn't too serious with his statement. There was a hint of happiness in his eyes.

"Hey." Ed put his hands up dramatically. "I was in the wrong there, I'll admit it. But!" The mischief was back in those golden eyes and they were shining in the party lights. "You can't say that it didn't work. Without Nick, I would have never been able to figure out a thing about him."

"It actually wound up helping my little project too," Charlie shrugged. "I started at that zoo when I was first making calls."

"Oh yeah?" Ed asked. "Do they still remember him?"

"They said he was the most well-behaved wolf they had ever seen," Charlie laughed. "They almost thought that he belonged to some kind of circus with how well he acted."

"He may have." Ed laughed. "Knowing all the things he's said that he's done, I wouldn't be surprised."

They were slowly walking over there. It seemed that there was a bit of a crowd forming over where Nick and Alistair were. Nick was the best at bringing crowds together. Charlie noticed that Alistair usually didn't do well in crowds. It took a while for him to relax in one, and he was never fully calmed until the crowd had dispersed a bit. But this time, he seemed happy.

Herb and Jackie were in that crowd. They talked a bit, but Jackie could only take so much standing around. Since she was having triplets, it made her look as if she were much far off in her pregnancy than she really was. Of course, that made all the mothers and expecting flock to her. Thankfully, Herb wasn't as protective of her now that he knew that it was a safe place.

He remembered seeing how he always tried to protect her. It reminded him of Max. He knew they were a good couple from the moment he saw them.

Madeline had made it last to the party. She looked a little embarrassed when she went to greet her friends, but happy nonetheless. Her golden eyes shimmered in the lights, along with her dark blue dress that was made to look like the night sky. It fit her complexion perfectly.

"Aren't you proud of me?" Leah asked Max. "They all look so amazing!"

"You can make a donkey look amazing, Leah." Max chuckled.

"Yeah," Ed smirked. "I'm sure you've made Sam look great so many times."

"Hey!" Sam looked a bit hurt, but they were all laughing too hard to really feel bad for him. Charlie felt worse for him when he went to try and wrangle all of the kids back to one spot.

Leah's sister, Heather, was only a couple years older than her. They loved to joke around about their little competition of who can have the most kids. Charlie had no idea why they did that, but they did.

Now that Leah had given birth to her twins, she had four in total: one girl and three boys. When they found out it was going to be twins, Heather seemed to be upset, but it was more in a playful way. She only had three at the moment, but she found out that she was pregnant just before Leah gave birth. And she was hoping for twins to beat her sister.

Needless to say, their respective husbands did not like this friendly competition.

When Charlie tried to meet all the children of the pack, it was insane. He had no idea that there were so many children that he had to try and remember the best he could. It didn't help that almost every month they would multiply. Max said that it had been a long time since the pack had been this fertile.

According to Dr. Adelle, when he talked to her about it, it started with the Moore family. As they had the most children than anyone in their pack. Mrs. Moore hadn't miscarried once in all her years. Their children also helped the Crescent Moon Pack strengthen their relations with many others. A lot of them were mated to members of other packs and left to join them.

Nick was actually the last one in his family to be mated. Then again, he was the youngest. Charlie wasn't sure how Nick's family was going to take Alistair, but he hoped for the best. Maybe if he sent out another prayer it would work again.

"So, you ate leaves?" Isabelle asked Alistair. They had finally gotten to the center of the room after greeting everyone. Isabelle had been interested in meeting Alistair since she found out about him. Her dark eyes looked curious, but also motherly. Charlie wasn't sure how many people knew about her sister's story. He wasn't even sure if Tyler knew.

"Yes," Alistair laughed. He had such a low voice that his laughter sounded like a vibration. "I was young and it was the first time I had seen so many leaves of different colors and shapes. I learned my lesson on what to eat after I threw them all up."

"That reminds me of Clara," George laughed. Nick's two closest brothers surrounded him in the crowd. "When she first transformed, she acted like a puppy. She bounced and yapped. We made fun of her for years about that."

"Is Clara one of your sisters?" Alistair looked at Nick.

"Yup!" Nick answered. "She's here somewhere."

"Knowing her," Barry laughed. "She's probably sneaking into the kitchen to eat all of the pies and sweets that Charlie baked."

"I am not!" They all heard a woman's voice squeak over the crowd. It only seemed to make the three brothers laugh harder when she spoke.

The crowd slowly cleared out when more people started dancing. Charlie and Max were both surprised to see that Alistair could dance. He wasn't the best at it, but he seemed to pick up on it quickly enough. Even when he missed a step, he never stepped on Nick's feet at all throughout the short time they danced.

"Observant and controlled," Mr. Locke said when he came up to them. He had been watching them dance as well. "An interesting werewolf, to say the least."

"He's definitely a mystery," Max told his father. Charlie loved how the two were still close, even with their duties to the pack changing. Mr. Locke would still occasionally run with the warriors. He didn't want to get out of shape in his retirement, so him and Max would still train together.

"*Liam headed Alistair's way,*" Tyler's voice popped up in their heads. Charlie looked to see the beta was tense as his mate talked to Alistair more.

"Not again," Max muttered. He pulled Charlie with him as they went into the crowds to where Liam was.

Charlie was a bit worried about this himself. He knew from first-hand experience that the man didn't like new people coming into the pack. It took Charlie about six months to officially get on his good side.

They had just gotten Alistair to open up too. They still had so much to figure out about him. What if Liam tore him down just like he tore Charlie down when he first met him?

"So, you're the beta?" he heard Liam say. It was still tough to look for him through all the people they were shimmying past.

"I am a beta, yes," Alistair told him.

"Why did you come here?" His voice was tense and cold. It almost sent shivers down Charlie's spine.

"Because I wished to end my travels," Alistair answered simply. They finally made it to the clearing where everyone had been giving the two space.

It seemed as though Liam had that effect on the pack. When he started questioning, everyone moved out of his way.

"Why?" Liam's face looked just as he sounded.

"Liam!" Max barked. He looked enraged that the man would try something here when they were accepting Alistair into the pack.

"I'm allowed to ask a question!" The old man boomed before Max could get another word in. Max's family seemed to have stubborn as their dominant trait.

"I'll answer your questions," Alistair said. He had shrunk again. Charlie noticed that he shrank whenever he was worried that someone was intimidated by him. "I wished to end my traveling because I was tired of running without a purpose."

"Without a purpose?"

"Yes." The albino nodded. "The Moon Goddess brought me through many trials. I have grown much from the time I was left by my old pack. I no longer want to be alone, to face the unknown by myself. I wish to belong."

The way he talked was moving. There was always something about him that made people want to know more. Even his low voice brought people closer to hear it. It was soothing, like calm waves of the ocean.

"Good answer." Liam smiled at him. Charlie was shocked at the old man's reaction. "Are you spiritual?"

"Yes." He nodded again.

"There are three beings that you must notice when you step into unknown territory." Liam started. "One is wise; one is a guide; and the third is a gossip. What are they, and which one do you listen to first?"

He could tell that Max was going to say something, but he squeezed his arm to hold him back. There was something about this that made him want to hear what Alistair's answer would be. He had read of this riddle in one of the books that Liam had written. He loved riddles, even though he never had been great at solving them.

There were a few seconds of silence, but it didn't last long. Alistair had met Liam's eyes with a kind smile.

"The wise are the trees," he answered. "For they have been there the longest. The guide is the moon, for she is who we all seek advice from. The gossip is the wind, for it speaks what everyone says."

"Correct," Liam looked impressed at the albino. "Which one do you listen to when you first get to the unknown land then?"

"The wind," Alistair answered.

"Why?"

"The trees only speak through it their toils and victories that their land has gone through," he told him. "And the moon can only guide you through clear night skies. The wind is the one that you should listen to first."

Everyone was silent at his answer. Charlie didn't know whether it was because of what Alistair said, or because of them waiting for Liam's response. He was surprised that Alistair could answer that riddle. It was one that Liam had made himself.

Was there a book about this religion of theirs? Charlie really wished he could read it if it existed.

"Correct," Liam said again. "How did you learn that, Alistair?"

"My mother, sir." Those red eyes grew sad. "I have her to thank for my knowledge of the Moon Goddess."

"Don't ask where his mother is," Charlie mind linked with the old man. His purple eyes glanced at him for a split second before going back to the albino's.

"Why? Do you know what happened to her?"

"She died before he was left for dead in his pack," he told him. He knew that it was personal information that he was sharing. But there was no other way to keep the man from asking him. He knew that he wouldn't tell anyone either. Liam wasn't much of a gossip.

Those purple eyes glanced at him again, looking a bit softer. His demeanor changed slightly. It was barely noticeable to anyone who wasn't watching him intently like Charlie. But he looked a little softer than before.

"You make for a good warrior, boy," Liam interrupted the silence. He stuck his hand out for the man to shake. Once he did, he smiled again. "I'm Liam Locke. Welcome to the Crescent Moon Pack."

"Thank you." He smiled, shaking his hand.

"*What did you tell him?*" Max's voice popped up in his head.

"*Just to not ask about his mother,*" Charlie answered. "*The rest of that was his own reaction.*"

"*I think you softened him up quite a lot Charlie,*" Mr. Locke said through the mind link. When he looked over to him, he noticed that his eyes had a sparkle to them. "*I don't know what you may have done to make him this way, but it's something that not even I could do. And I'm his son.*"

"*I really didn't do anything,*" He chuckled to himself. He was happy that Liam was starting to understand people a little more. Although Charlie was sure that the answers that Alistair gave helped him in his understanding.

The party went in full swing after that. Many of the elders were talking to Liam in the corner, shocked at his reaction as well. Nick did wind up tap dancing, much to Charlie's surprise. He didn't know that tap-dancing shoes had covers on the bottoms so that they wouldn't click every time you walked in them. When he didn't hear the clicking when Nick was just simply walking, he thought that Max hadn't seen right and it wasn't the right kind of shoes. But, when he saw the man kick the covers off and start tap dancing in the middle of one of the songs, he was happily surprised.

It was funny seeing Alistair's reaction to it. He looked at the man in complete awe.

"I guess he is going to sweep someone off their feet and win them over with dance," Charlie whispered into Max's ear. They both laughed as now Max was seeing exactly what he was talking about.

Since they knew that Jackie wouldn't be able to stay for the whole party, they changed up the schedule so that the uniting of the rogues into the pack would be in the middle of the party rather than at the end which was more traditional.

All four of them went up one by one to the middle of the backyard. It wasn't that hot of a night out thankfully. It had rained earlier that day and the wind was cooling them off quite a lot. Max and Charlie stood in the middle, each of them wearing their necklaces that showed their titles. The lights had dimmed down to have the moonlight shine down on them.

The moon was full and bright, just like the last party. For the pack, it was a good sign that this is what the Moon Goddess wanted. Charlie just couldn't believe that it had been a full month that they had met these strangers. It seemed like eons ago they were discussing what to do with them.

If there was one thing that Charlie realized throughout his time in his role, it was that time could either fly by, or seem like an eternity. He loved his job, though. He truly couldn't be happier, even with all the challenges that they've already gone through.

"As Luna of the Crescent Moon Pack." Charlie looked at the four of them, holding the symbol that the past Luna had given him. "I, Charlie Fairchild, welcome you to our family."

"As Alpha of the Crescent Moon Pack," Max spoke right after him, doing the same with his symbol that his father had given him. "I, Max Locke, welcome you to our family. May the Moon Goddess bless us with prosperity and strength."

CHAPTER 28:

Training

The training grounds was a big part of the yard. There was a room of course that people could train in, but it was mainly outside that werewolves did most of their training. Their pack usually started training its warriors at a young age, but there was always that one member that decided to be a warrior later in life. No one judged. They were all a family there.

Most are born to be a warrior. They have that innate desire to protect the pack that was imbedded deep in their bones. They will do it at whatever the cost. In the past, many died because of their obedience to their Alpha. In order to have the best army for the pack, you need a leader that knows each and every one of his warrior's strengths and weaknesses. That way, he can best place everyone in their right position in battle.

That's why the training grounds had a balcony above it. It was the best way he could watch the warriors train and figure out what they needed to strengthen. Of course, Max had trained with all of his warriors since he was a boy. They all knew how well he could fight, and he knew how well they could fight.

It was why he had been wanting to attack the rogues for so long. He knew that his warriors could do it. They trained hard to ready themselves for the day they would finally get to sink their teeth into their enemy's fur. They all hated waiting for so long. Max knew that they were getting antsy about it. They had been ordered not to go off the territory for the entirety of his father's reign. His father was so focused on making the pack safe and letting it grow that he didn't allow the warriors to use their true strength.

Max knew that they were still antsy, if not even more so. Now that they finally had an Alpha that wanted to fix this problem that plagued them, they had to wait for the political side of things to clear out. And the fact that they accepted some rogues into the pack didn't exactly help.

He knew that Alistair could change their minds about this whole ordeal. He had already impressed Tyler, who was extremely warry of the rogue, as well as Ray and Desmond. He was sure that the more who patrolled with him, the more of the warriors would like him. And training together was what bonded warriors. It connected them in a way that simply being a part of the same pack couldn't.

Max wasn't having anyone train with Alistair today, though. He needed to see how the albino matched up to everyone else. He knew from the incident with Charlie that the werewolf was strong. He could withstand a lot of pain, and trusted Max when he gave him an order. He'd like to say that they both gained each other's trust that night.

Max was putting Alistair through it all: the Stamina Check; the Awareness to Surroundings Test; Intelligence in Battle, the list was endless. He had warned him ahead of time that the day was going to be long and hard, but the man took it with confidence. Max assumed it was because of all the traveling that he had done that he was able to get through the morning tests without being too tired. His only downfall was the water that he had to drink in order to keep going. His thick coat was meant for the heavy snow in Alaska. He could only assume that the summers here were going to be bad for him.

They actually brushed his coat out. By them, he meant he had Nick do it. It was kind of funny that Nick had literally been doing that and fallen asleep that one morning that he was trying to find him. And he needed to test the skills of the man without any obstacles in the way.

Nick had actually gotten some of the kids to help him. It was fun to watch all the kids go up to the calm snow wolf and help brush him out. The parents seemed rather amused by it too, but they were mainly grateful that they didn't have to deal with their kids going on another burst of energy.

He looked much less ragged than before, that was for sure. His white coat shined after they got the winter coat of his off. Charlie had told him that it took at least five trash bags full of fur until they were all done. He got there at the tail end to try and help. Max was still busy with his duties.

It was mid-afternoon when the tests were all finished. Alistair had gone through them without much need for a break. He did well. Max could tell that he had amazing stamina, and his speed was in between Tyler and his. Tyler was on the slower side of the betas. He made up for it with his skills in battle, though. That's what made him the true Beta of the pack.

There was an issue with his appearance that would be a problem in battle. Alistair showed his skill at hiding through bushes, and his paws were made for being quiet, as he had snow paws. But when he ran, he was as easy to see as a neon sign.

He was good at attacking, and quick to pick up on even the smallest sounds that could potentially be threatening.

How the Borealis Pack didn't want to keep him was absolutely baffling. Max felt like he had just struck gold. Alistair could easily be the extra warrior he needed for taking out these enemies for good. The rest of the warriors were starting to see it as well. They watched from the balcony too. They needed to know how their new member was going to fight.

As much as they were all a family in the pack, the warriors held something even closer. It was like soldiers sent in the same battalion for a war and surviving through it together. There was a connection: a bond that they all shared. When they mind linked in battle, for instance, there wasn't much time to think a word. They spoke through feelings and memories of what they saw. And they were all connected so much in battle that they understood immediately.

Max had used it plenty of times in battle before he was the Alpha. If he got enraged in a fight, the others that were fighting with him would feel it too, and they would use that as their own fuel to do more damage.

"*Stop.*" He commanded. The albino listened immediately. His halt was quick and silent.

Martha was the one that was giving him most of the orders through his training that day. She had a long history with the pack that dated back to Liam's father's reign. She was one of the warriors that had lived through it all, and somehow survived. The burly woman had plenty of scars, but she considered them accomplishments as wounds she was able to overcome.

"*Change and put some clothes on,*" he told Alistair. Martha wasn't too far behind him. "*Meet me under this balcony.*"

The wolf nodded and followed orders. He could see that he had worn himself out, but Max had a feeling that he could continue for much longer. One of these days of training, he was going to have to see just how far he could be pushed. That was one thing that he needed to know now that he was his warrior.

Martha did the same thing. Her clothes were always plain, but she mostly had to wear men's shirts as her shoulders were too broad for most dainty shirts that are made for women. She was short too, which made finding clothes difficult for her. He remembered just how happy the old lady was when Leah and Sam opened up their clothing business. They had gotten her clothes down perfectly.

"Martha." He looked to her when Alistair had come out. "What's his stats?"

"Pros are: Stamina, Strength, Agility, Speed. He has strong teeth, but I'm unaware of his attack power on them just yet," she told him. She was the first warrior to train Max when he started as a child. She was known as a tank in battle, as she wasn't fast at all. But, when she got a bite into a werewolf, she clamped down and would tear a chunk out. She was also one of the best when it came to finding a warrior's strengths and weaknesses. Max trusted her with all of the warriors that he had right now, as well as the ones that he would get in the future.

"Why don't you know his attack power?" Max looked at her confused. Usually, she would know everything after the initial trials. This was different for her.

"The other pack that trained him didn't train him for the right position in battle," she told him. Alistair was looking at her confused as well. There was sweat pouring off from him in the summer heat. He was glad that there was shade under the balcony so that the man wasn't too uncomfortable.

"I was noticing that too," Liam came out. He was still considered a warrior since he was a former Alpha. Martha was the oldest compared to all of them, but he was next to take that position.

"Before we get into this," Max stopped Liam. When it came to training warriors, Liam loved to get ahead of himself. "What are his weaknesses?"

"His cons are: Soft Skin, as we witnessed when he was trying to save Charlie; bad vision, which gets balanced out through his other senses; and a misplacement in his training before, which could lead to an issue in attempting to retrain him for the right position. And," she took a deep breath. "It doesn't seem like he was trained to link with other warriors."

"What do you mean?" Alistair asked this time.

"When you fought with your old pack," She turned to face him. "How did they give you orders? Would they tell you them, or would they show you?"

"They would tell me," Alistair told her.

"What was the first thing they taught you when you were in battle?" She asked.

"To protect my pack."

"They didn't seem to do a good job at protecting you," Martha frowned. Max knew it was the best thing to have her do the initial training. She could read a warrior like a book.

"What are you trying to say. Martha?" Max asked. She normally never had answers like these whenever she talked about a warrior. Her answers were always frank and precise. She never was one to beat around the bush.

"He was trained for the wrong placement," she told him. "The way he fights is like a Tank: someone who can defend while taking a couple wounds and still keep going. However, his skin is too soft for the Tank position, even with his fast healing."

"What should his position be then?"

"In my opinion," she started. "It should be Frontline Attack. He's got the speed for it. And, I believe he's got the bite for it, but I won't know for sure unless he's trained more to attack rather than defense."

"What was a typical battle like for you, Alistair?" he asked. The man looked like he was trying his hardest to take all this information in.

"I would go out in front of the warriors," he told him. "I don't believe I was a Tank, though. I was taught to protect the pack with my life if I had to."

"Wait," Liam stopped them all. "By protect the pack, did you also try to protect the warriors as well?"

"Yes." He furrowed his eyebrows. "Why?"

They were quiet for a second or two. That description only fit one position, and it was one that had been banned throughout all the packs for centuries.

"Alistair," Liam told him. "You weren't used as a Tank. You were used as a Sacrifice."

"What do you mean?"

It all made sense now. Every time the man fought, every time he was in any bad position, he took it and kept going as if his own well-being didn't matter. That was what he had seen in those red eyes every time he fought and trained.

"A Sacrifice position," Max explained to him. "Is almost self-explanatory. They are the ones that the warriors send out first in battle to distract their enemies with. It's so that their enemies will focus on tearing up the Sacrifice and they can, in turn, size their enemy up and attack with the best strategy."

"I..." A wave of understanding hit those ruby eyes. Max could see the hurt and the pain that were in them. As much as they had been closed off to everyone when he first met him, they had opened up a bit more. "I don't know what to say."

"You said you fought as a warrior for them for three years?" Desmond hopped down from the balcony. He had the lightest feet. His dark eyes looked concerned for Alistair to say the least.

"Yes," Alistair nodded.

"It's a miracle you survived in that position for so long," Liam told him. His eyes had gotten softer as well. "Normally, anyone in the Sacrifice position wouldn't last longer than a year."

The Sacrifice in packs were the weakest members. They would use this as a way to make them more 'useful' to the pack. That was how omegas had almost gone extinct. The closest thing to the position that their pack had in the past was Martha's first position when she was allowed to be a warrior. They had put her as Frontline Tracker, misplacing her so much that she got many wounds due to it. Thankfully, she outshined her other warriors in battle by overcoming the obstacle and surviving every battle that the pack had gone through, until Liam put her in the place that she had belonged.

This pack had gone through some bloody times, but they never did something as brutal as what Alistair had gone through in his pack.

A werewolf that could survive being a Sacrifice in battle was a strong one, and needed to be respected. Max would make sure that Alistair got all the respect he needed. Right now, though, he just looked lost again. As if he wasn't sure what to do at that moment.

"The first thing I want to train you on is for Frontline Attack," Max told him. He looked into his eyes to ground him. The man already seemed calmer with some sense of direction. "The patrol and training should give you a good idea of the Warrior Link that all of us share in battle. But there's one thing I want you to do along with your training."

"What is it?"

"This pack fights alongside each other," he told him. "We help each other in battle, but we do it through attacking the enemies, not through taking the bite for someone. I want you to think of this as you are training each time."

He needed him out of the mindset that his old pack had put him in. It was obvious that he had been abused by that pack. And, with how little packs lived around areas like that, it was easy to do things like what they did to Alistair without getting known for their illegal deeds. They probably hadn't gotten checked up on in a long while.

"I'll do my best," he said.

"You know," Martha looked at him. "You said that you fought a Werebear before?"

"I have," Alistair answered. "But I didn't win that fight."

"You could have," Martha told him. "Werebear's are well known for reacting slower than most supernatural beings. If you had tried a different fighting tactic, the one that you should have been trained for, it would have been easy for you to take down."

"You know how to take down a Werebear?" Alistair looked at her with a shocked expression. The one thing that Max liked about the man was just how much respect he gave everyone he met. It already had given the warriors a better perspective on him.

"I've been trained to fight off many things," she nodded. "Just in case the pack might come across the problem. If you used your agility rather than just trying to sink your teeth into it, you could have worn him down through multiple gashes."

"I…I hadn't thought of that before," he smiled at her. "Thank you."

"It's always better to face things as a pack," Martha smiled at him. "You're more powerful than you think. It's going to be tough to train you for your position. However, if you are willing to go through the rigorous training, I guarantee you won't regret it."

"I will take on your challenge, then," he told her.

Max smiled at them. It wasn't very often that someone warms up to Martha that quickly. He would have thought that Alistair would be intimidated by the old battle axe of a woman. Today proved to be good for helping the pack grow.

"Tomorrow take the day to rest," Max told him. "The day after is when the training starts. Since it's rigorous, you will be excused from the patrol duties until you are deemed ready by Martha."

"I understand," he nodded. He looked like he had a lot to process, but he seemed ready for the challenge. Max was happy to see him so willing to learn something new.

"Good," Max gave him a smile before dismissing him. The training room in the house had its own showers for warriors that needed to cool off or wanted to clean before heading to their rooms.

"I didn't think I'd see the day," Liam shook his head. "When I would meet a Sacrifice."

"I can't believe they would use him like that," Desmond said. He almost forgot that the brunette was even there. "No wonder he enjoyed that little shed on the outskirts! We treated him better as a rogue than his old pack did as an actual member!"

"He's going to need more than Martha to help him train into that new position," Max said. By that time, all of the warriors had come down from the balcony. Out of almost three hundred members of his pack, there were 83 that were warriors. It didn't seem like much, but they had trained hard enough to each have the same power as five normal werewolves. Max looked to them. "Are you ready for it?"

They all nodded. It would have caused a scene if they answered all together. And they had all been trained to keep as quiet as possible.

The warrior link was buzzing with information about Sacrifices and the things that they had heard about it. Martha was the only one who experienced the closest thing to it. And her memories were nothing to laugh at. She had gone through some bloody battles and barely made it out alive.

This was going to take all of them. Because warriors are one. They aren't many, not when it came to battle at least.

"Help him reach his greatest potential," Max told them. "And we reach our greatest potential."

He dismissed them with that and let them go and do what they wanted. It had been a long day for all of them as they sized up the new recruit. They would have to one more time for Madeline, since she was a tracker. She was still on her vacation. And, knowing how that usually goes with new mates, she could easily wind up pregnant after that week was up.

Max was proud to have two new warriors added to his pack nonetheless. He just hoped they would be ready in time.

Because he wasn't sure just how much time they had.

CHAPTER 29:

Opening Up

He really shouldn't be worried. There was nothing bad that could happen. The territory was safe and the pack house was even safer. The warriors were always around if a rogue came or something of the sort.

Yet, here Nick was, pacing around his room like an idiot.

Was it normal to act like this? He wished he knew. There were so many questions that he had about mates. He remembered Katy talked about it a lot, but he zoned most of that stuff out. He never thought he'd need it.

Oh, if he only knew what troubles lied ahead for him.

It was mid-afternoon and he still hadn't heard anything from Alistair. He would mind link with him, now that he finally could, but it was strictly against the rules to mind link with a warrior who was in training unless it was an emergency.

But training usually took up half a day. Nick didn't know that much about all the things that warriors underwent, but he knew that their training usually didn't take that long. He hadn't seen or heard of any of the warriors either, for that matter. They had all gone to watch the initial trial.

It was something that Nick had known about, but was never able to witness himself. Only warriors saw the trials.

Was he being clingy at this point? It wasn't too late into the day. And if something was going on in the pack, Max would have told them all. He would have given them an order to stay inside or something. So, he knew nothing was wrong.

Why was he still worried?

Dammit. He still didn't have anyone to talk to about all of this. Having a mate was confusing. And he felt like a teenager all over again when it came to emotions. When he was around Alistair, he felt happy and calm, but when he wasn't and his mind was no longer focused on work, he was anxious. They had only started their relationship and Nick was obsessing over the man.

Was this because he didn't have anyone to talk to? Was it because Katy was gone? He was sure that it might be a part of it, but he doubted that it was the whole thing. He couldn't exactly ask Ed for advice because he was with the warriors right then. He wished they would allow him to sit and watch at least once. He just wanted to be able to see Alistair again. Just once.

Screw it. He knew one person who was available to talk to at least. As much as this was going to be embarrassing.

"Dr. Button?" He made his voice quiet in the mind link just in case the doctor was busy with something. Button had helped him a lot with his health problems. Hopefully he could help him understand his strange bond too.

"Yes?" Button asked. Nick released a breath from his lungs that he didn't know he was holding in.

"Are you busy at the moment?"

"Not really, why?"

"*I, uh, just wanted your advice on something.*" Jeez, he hadn't felt this embarrassed in an eternity. He truly did feel like he was a teenager all over again. And he was twenty-one.

"*Is it about your mate bond?*"

"*How'd you guess?*"

"*Let's just say I had a feeling you were going to be asking for advice for it eventually,*" the doctor answered. "*You haven't really had a lot of experience with it either.*"

"*You got me there,*" he joked. After a few seconds of silence, Nick sat down on his bed and started to focus on what his first question would be. "*Is it normal to be nervous when they aren't there?*"

"*Yes,*" Button sounded like he was getting a kick out of this. But his tone was gentle, so he wasn't going to complain. "*Especially in the early stages. Although Max and Charlie's bond has only made them clingier towards each other.*"

"*Do you think I'm going to be too clingy?*"

"*I doubt Alistair would be mad if you were, Nick. You forget that you're mated with that person for a reason.*"

"*What if...?*"

"*Are you talking about your health problem?*"

"*Yeah,*" He felt defeated every time he had to mention it. "*What if it doesn't work when he tries to...?*"

"*You'll have to talk to him about that,*" Dr. Button told him. "*The best way to keep a relationship working is through communication.*"

"*But what if he rejects me because of it?*" He had heard about mates when they got rejected. Most of them would commit suicide because of the pain that it caused. Others would just lose the will to live or be happy. If there was one thing that Nick had been trying his hardest to fight off, it was the sadness that was always trying to consume him. Sure, he had Alistair. But there were so many things that he still had to tell the man. Katy just knew him. There was no hiding anything from her. She simply knew him, just like he knew her. It still hurt that she was gone.

He could only imagine the pain of being rejected. He wasn't sure if he would be able to handle that.

"He doesn't seem like the type to reject his mate, Nick," the doctor comforted. *"If he rejected you, I'm sure that he would need quite a lot of stitches for what Max might do to him as well. I understand your fear, but I don't think that hiding information like that from him is going to help the situation either."*

Nick laid back on his bed and stared at the ceiling. He remembered how those ruby eyes looked at him with such want that morning that he first woke up in his arms. He remembered how the man touched him, how it sent shivers down his spine. He remembered how Alistair had told him after he had met his mother that Nick was his gift from the Moon Goddess.

Man, this guy was sappy.

Nick loved sappy.

He was just going to have to tell him. Maybe he'd do it right when he saw him after his training, just to get it out of the way. He had to tell him soon, before he lost the will for it. Before he wound up in those strong arms and all of his thoughts started melting away.

A knock on his door snapped him out of his thoughts. He cut his mind link with the doctor off and tried not to rush too much to open it. The scent of his was too easy for his nose to pick up on. He knew who it was as soon as they knocked.

"Hey!" He opened the door to let Alistair inside. "How was it?"

Alistair didn't say anything. He just held him. He wrapped those arms around him and pulled him close. Nick could tell that he had taken a shower before because his hair was wet. He made no move to get out of Alistair's hold. It was too nice and warm being this close to him.

They had gotten used to this at least. As much as they hadn't tried any sexual things, they still held each other and kissed.

You know, like a bunch of innocent teenagers.

It didn't take long before Alistair had brought the two of them to Nick's bed. He laid on top of him with his face buried into the crook of Nick's neck. He loved the feeling of the man's breath on his skin. He loved the way the man touched his sides. They always seemed to slip under his shirt, which only made him want his touch more.

"That bad, huh?" He broke the silence. He didn't really know what to say to comfort him. He was always bad at comforting people, even if Max told him otherwise. He usually told jokes or something to compensate for his lack of advice on the topic.

"I was a sacrifice," he told him. His mouth was still close to his neck. He almost shuddered at the feeling.

"A what?"

"A sacrifice," Alistair said again. He held Nick tighter after he said it that time. "In my old pack, that's what I was trained to do."

"You were trained as a sacrifice?" Nick hadn't been taught that much about the warrior stuff, but they all learned about what the basic laws were for every pack. "That's illegal, though."

He heard about sacrifices a little. Many of them were omegas because they seemed to always be the slowest and the smallest. It wasn't until the omegas almost became extinct that the Moon Goddess really started to punish the packs severely for the mistreatment towards them. She gifted omegas with fertility so that they could repopulate themselves. It was a horrible story that he hated hearing about. Omegas had an important role in each pack, much like the rest of the types did.

He didn't think that other packs still did something like that, though. And Alistair wasn't weak, either. The idea of sacrificing one of their own just to win one battle was horrible, and a dumb battle strategy.

"That's what Desmond had said," Alistair answered. "I was too young to realize what they were doing was wrong. I just listened to the orders that the Alpha gave me. That's what I was taught."

Nick tightened his hold on the man this time. It was a terrifying thought that he could have easily died before Nick would have even been of age to feel the mate bond. He never wanted to lose Alistair.

He was his teddy bear.

"I'm so glad you're here." He put his face into the thin white hair on the man's head. There was so much of it, yet it didn't look like it.

"Why would they want me dead so much?" He sounded like a scared child the way he asked that question. "My mother and I hadn't done anything to harm the pack in any way. They wanted me to be a warrior. Why would it just be to use me as a sacrifice?"

"I don't know." He shook his head. He felt the pain that Alistair was feeling. It hurt. They weren't even officially mated, but he could feel the man's pain. "But you're never going to have to deal with that again."

He knew the warriors. They were all dedicated to protecting the pack. He knew that they wouldn't let Alistair die in battle. All of them had trained so hard just so they wouldn't die in attacks. They might not seem all that powerful when you looked at their numbers and compared it to some of the other packs. But there was a reason why the rogues hadn't been able to kill anyone.

Alistair moved his head to hover above his and looked at him. Those ruby eyes looked glossy almost, and fearful.

"Do you really think so?"

"I know so," he told him. He couldn't help but rest a hand on Alistair's cheek. It was an instinct to comfort that Nick didn't know he had. "We protect each other here. There aren't going to be any sacrifices or anything of the sort."

There was some silence. Alistair held Nick's hand, his ruby eyes shimmering with hope. Nick never thought he would see the day that anyone would give him that look. Because if one did it meant that they really were hurt before. It pained him to think that anything bad happened to such a kind soul like him.

He didn't expect for that moment to end by Alistair kissing him, let alone with all the force that he used. There was a passion to it that Nick hadn't felt before. Those lips begged his to part, burning him with desire. He submitted to the beta and opened them for the first time. It was such a foreign sensation. Nick didn't quite know what to think about it. But it made the sparks fly all throughout his body.

It didn't help that those sinful hands were starting to explore his sides again. With every touch, he leaned in more to the man.

Then his heart started to race about a mile a minute as he started to spread his legs and put pressure there. Nick could smell that his mate was aroused. He desperately wanted to help him with his problem. But he wasn't sure if it was possible.

He wanted this. He wanted this so bad. Nick had heard that werewolves with this problem usually get them solved once they find their mates. It would make it so much easier if it would just magically work and he wouldn't have to go through the embarrassment that was telling the man what was wrong with him.

It's not like he didn't try. He leaned into the foreign pressure, creating some friction. The only thing it seemed to do was make it twitch again. He knew Alistair was enjoying it. Why couldn't he?

Why couldn't he just have one good thing?

"Nick," Alistair broke of the kiss and pressed his hips down to the bed. The man smelt so good when he was aroused. He wanted to enjoy it, but he was too focused on the beta that was now looking deeply into his eyes. He was panting heavily. So was Nick. He liked just how passionate the kiss had been. He liked that it was Alistair who was the one that kissed him like that. He liked the feeling of the man's hands running all over him.

He just wished that he could have something work out for him.

"Yeah?" Nick asked. He was so scared of Alistair's reaction, his voice almost came out as a squeak.

"What's wrong?" His eyes were still dark due to his arousal, but they looked more concerned that anything.

He really didn't want to have to say this. He didn't know whether he was going to reject him or not. There was so little that he did know about this all. But those red eyes only grew softer the longer he waited.

"I can't." He shook his head. Just before his emotions bubbled over the man grabbed him and held him in a tight hug again. Nick just buried his face in the man's chest and burst into tears.

This was why he never thought he would have a mate. A part of him never wanted one, just for the conversation that he knew he would have to have with them about this.

"Shh," Alistair moved them to have Nick in his lap. The man's back was leaning on Nick's head board. "I'm sorry. I pushed too far again."

"No." He shook his head. He could barely get the words out through the sobs that his body gave. "No, you didn't. I just can't."

"Can't what?" he asked. His low voice was soothing, just as his hands were that rubbed his back. "Nick, please tell me what's wrong."

"I'm afraid," he admitted.

"Afraid of what?"

"That you'd reject me." It almost tore his heart into pieces just from him saying it out loud.

"Nick," Alistair lifted his head up to look at him. His face was soft and concerned. "I'd never reject you."

"But I can't mate," Nick choked out. His body was desperate to cling onto his mate with all that he could. "I can't even get it up."

"Are you infertile?" He looked just about as confused as Nick did when he first heard the news. "Did someone hurt you?"

"I have Erectile Dysfunction," he finally said. His sobbing had calmed down just a little bit. He was still afraid of the man rejecting him. "I could take a whole bottle of Viagra and it wouldn't do shit other than make my heart race like a madman."

"I see," Alistair said. "Has it ever worked then?"

"Once in a blue moon," Nick shrugged. "I never know when."

He wanted to beg him to not leave him. He would do anything to stay with Alistair. He hadn't known him for all that long, but he felt like he belonged in those arms. He hated the idea of losing someone again.

"Once in a blue moon?" Alistair smiled at him.

"Why are you smiling?" He hadn't thought that telling him something like this was going to make the man smile. Was he going to laugh at him?

"I've seen plenty of blue moons," the man answered. "I think I can wait for one more."

"You know that was a figure of speech, right?"

"I don't think it was just a coincidence that we found each other when we did, Nick," Alistair held him close to him. Nick couldn't help but put his arms around the man again. "If I need to wait a little longer to mark you as mine, I will."

"You will?" He was so shocked by his answer. Usually, people freak out about stuff like this. From what he had learned, it lead to a lot of people just up and leaving. Nick hadn't wanted that. He wanted to stay with Alistair.

"Of course," Alistair kissed his cheek. "I love you."

"I love you too." It felt strangely relieving to say it. A part of him worried that he was moving too fast, and saying too many things that would hurt him in the long run. But, if Alistair was willing to wait, then he could still have time to get to know him even more.

"I'll never leave you, or reject you, Bakshir," he mumbled into his ear. It was oddly comforting hearing him call him by that name. "Why would I?"

"Because I'm broken." All of his insecurities about this were flying out of his mouth as Alistair quietly comforted him. He didn't know how the man was able to do it.

"You aren't broken," Alistair said. Every word the man spoke was like butter to him. "You're just different."

"I am?" His face was still buried in the man. He was too embarrassed to show him the tear-stricken face that he had now.

"Of course, you are," he soothed him. "The Moon Goddess doesn't make mistakes. And she definitely made you."

"You're adorable," Nick chuckled. "That had to be the cheesiest line I've heard."

"Cheese sounds good right now."

"Yeah," he agreed. "Let's go get something to eat, before the kitchen closes and it's too late."

They got up and started walking towards the kitchen. Nick didn't know why, but he felt lighter than he did before. Lighter than he had in a while now. It felt like a weight had been lifted off his shoulders, one that had been there ever since he was thirteen and found out about this little problem of his.

He really hoped this blue moon would hurry up.

CHAPTER 30:

A Visit to the Past

"Are you sure you want to do this, Apple?" Max asked him. They were just about to leave the pack house for the day.

It was going to be a long drive, but they had another meeting to see how the other packs were progressing with their warriors. This time they decided to have it in the middle so that it wouldn't be too much of a hassle for one pack.

"I was going to have to see them again sooner or later," Charlie told him. He had to get over this anxious feeling. He knew they would be glad to see him no matter what he had done with his life.

Max stopped loading the Jeep and pulled him in close. It was nice to melt into the man's arms again. He loved how much Max could calm him, even if he was really nervous.

"You don't have to go, you know," he whispered into his ear.

"Then they would really see me as weak," Charlie told him. A low growl rumbled in the man's chest at what he said. "No matter how angry that makes you, it won't change their minds. And, like I said before, I was going to have to see them again eventually."

"You're the strongest Luna that we've ever had." Max held him tighter. "Even if you can't do what other Luna's can do physically, you are strong in every other way."

"Are you going to say this stuff every time I talk about being weak?" He chuckled and started playing with his hair. There wasn't anyone out at the time. It was early in the morning, and the air was full of fog. It looked like it might rain, but Charlie never knew if it actually would. The clouds were tricky sometime.

"Yes," Max kissed his cheek. "I never want you to believe you're weak again, Charlie."

His past had come to haunt him that morning, which was another reason why they were up so early. The nightmare wasn't as terrifying as before thankfully, and Max was able to wake him up in the middle of it. But there was just something about this trip that was keeping his nerves from calming.

Max had been good at clinging onto him that morning. He would barely let him go when they needed to pack their things. It was only going to be a day trip, but it was going to be long.

And, knowing them, there was going to be a lot of talking. Which was why Charlie was wanting to head out early so that they didn't have to wind up staying the night.

As much as he loved them, he didn't want to stay in that house again.

"We should get going," Charlie gently pulled out of the hug. He could tell that Max wanted to pull him in tighter, but the man let go. "It's going to be a long drive to Sun City."

The place where Charlie had grown up in. That, of course, was where the meeting was taking place. The middle ground for all the packs was actually the Cooper's house, where Charlie had lived for almost a year while getting emancipated.

There were many memories in that city. Memories that he never wanted to ever think about again. He had told Max everything, of course, but he didn't ever want to go there and see all those buildings again.

But he had to. He had a job to do and a responsibility to the pack; his family. And he wasn't going to let any of them see his family as weak. They were all strong and dedicated. And the Blood Moon Pack, which was going to be traveling to the Cooper's as well, couldn't see that. So, he was going to do his best to get them to see just how strong their pack was.

Max opened the door for him. They had already said their farewells to the ones that were awake that early. Aldi had gotten a pail of food ready for them for the trip there and back. It was full of snacks to keep them from being too hungry when they got there. Of course, Charlie also decided to bring some of his pies. Ian and Lenny had been dying to try them ever since he talked to them about it.

Their journey there was mainly silent. They talked a little bit to kill some time. He mostly just looked at the scenery, though. He recognized so much of it when they passed Gila. He missed the manor already.

They didn't need anyone else going with them. Max wanted their territory to be as guarded as possible with them gone. His father was told to take charge of the Alpha duties in the meantime. He happily agreed to it. It was only going to be one day, after all.

"So, how's Alistair's training going?" he asked. He really needed to distract himself as they got closer to the nightmare that was his past.

"Pretty good," Max said. He grabbed his hand and squeezed it. Charlie loved that the man knew exactly what he was doing when it came to things like this. "He's struggling a bit when it comes to attacking, though. He goes for the legs instead of the neck when he has a chance to."

"That's such a strange thing to train him for." He shook his head. "The first thing I noticed about his wolf was how sharp his teeth looked."

"They were just trying to kill him," Max said, sighing. "I don't know whether it was because he was albino or something else, but they treated him like crap."

"How are the warriors with him?" Charlie had heard that they weren't too happy with rogues being brought into the pack. They were loyal to their Alpha until the end, but it still wasn't good when they were disgruntled.

"They warmed up to him pretty well actually," Max smiled. "He seems to have that effect on people. He learns from them quickly and always tries to take their advice. The only thing I can't seem to get him used to is the warrior link."

"Warrior link?" he asked. "Is that a private mind link for warriors or something?"

"Just about," Max answered. "It's something that kind of happens when we're in battle. Instead of using words to tell everyone what's going on, we can link our memories and, sometimes, our feelings."

"That's interesting." No matter how many books he read about werewolves, there was always so much more to learn about them. That was another reason he enjoyed being a part of this pack, though. He absolutely loved learning new things.

He let the conversation die out when he saw the sign welcoming them to Sun City. It was just like how he remembered it all those years ago. Nothing really changed. As much as there were beautiful buildings and houses, there were also some tattered ones. He wished he could just close his eyes and wait until they got to the Cooper's, but his body wouldn't let him. With every familiar place, an old memory would pop up.

Then he saw the old apartment that his parents had last. The one that he had to run out of; into the forest behind it.

"Charlie?" Max squeezed his hand tighter. "Are you okay?"

Charlie just shook his head. His hand slipped out of Max's and he covered his face. He wanted to stop the hot tears from coming, but he wasn't able to. He let them fall silently in his hands. His mind was recalling what had happened vividly. It was almost like he was there.

He didn't hear what Max was saying, or the car stop. All he could hear was that man's sickly voice.

"You could get all the money you wanted if you sold this precious one."

He couldn't be dealing with this. He had something important to do. He needed to be there for his pack; his family. He couldn't be selfish right now. He had to pull himself together.

"Do you know how many people would spend millions on a gorgeous face like this?"

"Charlie!" He flinched at the arms that grabbed him. He was so lost in that horrible memory that he hadn't known they were Max's at first. "It's okay baby." He rubbed on his back. "It's just me."

He slowly unraveled himself. He hadn't known that he had curled into a ball until then. That, along with the nightmare that he had woken up from, was tormenting his mind. But Max's soothing voice was gently bringing him out of it.

"It happened there," he mumbled, still in tears. "In those apartments."

"It's over now, Apple," Max told him. The sound of his nickname helped bring him back to the present. "I'm never going to let anyone hurt you again."

He didn't know how long it took for the sobs to stop. Max's shirt was probably soaked by then, but the memory finally faded away. And he was slowly brought back to the present.

"I'm okay now." He took a few deep breathes and pulled away from the man. They had pulled over to the side of the road, and Max was holding him tightly. "Sorry, I-!"

"Don't say sorry, baby," Max comforted. "We shouldn't have come here. I should bring you back home."

"No." He shook his head. "We both need to be there for the meeting. I'll be fine, I promise."

Those purple eyes bored into his, looking to see just how truthful he was being. As much as Charlie hadn't wanted to go back to Sun City, he did want to be at this meeting. He had to prove to all of them that he was a good Luna, and that the Crescent Moon Pack was strong.

"Are you sure?"

"Positive." He gave him a small smile. "Besides, this might be the only way I actually get over this."

"Do you want to talk about it?"

"No." He shook his head again, still smiling. "I don't need my Alpha to be angry when we finally get there."

Max smiled back at him. "You are going to tell me then?"

"I tell you everything," he said. "Just, not right now."

They started driving again. This time, Charlie mainly focused on the cargo that they had. Tidying it up, or pulling out the pies. Sun City was big, but it wouldn't take too long until they were finally there.

The house looked like a law firm with how it was designed. Dark bricks covered most of the outside, with some flowers hanging from the walls to decorate it. They had some beautiful gardens. Charlie noticed that they had changed the types up. He remembered that they were blue and yellow when he first lived with them. Now they were pink and purple.

Max opened the door for him, as it was now their normal routine. They both grabbed some of the things from the back seat and headed for the door. Max made sure to wrap and arm around him and pull him close. His touch always made Charlie feel better.

"Charlie!" He heard Ian before he saw him. The man looked excited to see him when he opened the door, but his expression changed slightly when he saw how tightly Max was holding him.

Oh, the drama between these two. Charlie wondered if it would ever end.

"I brought some pies over." He broke the short silence. He wasn't going to let it get awkward while they had so much stuff in their hands. "I figured it was the perfect time to have all of you try them!"

Ian was the worst at reading him, which was more of a good thing than a bad thing. He didn't notice the slight redness to his eyes or the hint of sadness in his voice. But Max noticed. The man held him tighter because of it.

Ben and Lenny were the next two to come out. Lenny seemed to see that something was wrong, but he simply helped by grabbing some of the things out of their arms and leading them inside.

"Charlie," Lenny said. "You haven't met my wife yet." He then took the hand of a beautifully tall woman with long black hair and blue eyes. "This is Wynona."

"It's a pleasure meeting you," Wynona said. Her voice sounded like the wind.

"The pleasures mine," Charlie smiled at her. "I'm glad to hear that you're doing well."

"Oh, Lenny told you I was sick, didn't he?" She shook her head. "That man can't ever seem to keep anything to himself."

"I guess he hasn't changed much then." Charlie laughed. It looked like he wasn't the only one who disliked just how much the man talked about them.

"I'm trying to get him out of that habit," she told him. "It's slow progress, but I think it's working."

"I'm sure he's talked a lot about me."

"A little." She told him. "The best way I found in teaching him not to do that is by not listening to him."

"I'll have to try that when I talk to him, then," Max laughed a bit.

"What are we talking about?" Lenny came back. He had gone to the kitchen to unload some of the food they brought over.

"Oh, just how excited I was about Charlie's pies!" The woman winked at the two of them again. Charlie liked her already.

"Well, I'll be damned." A familiar voice come from the one of the hallways. "If it isn't Charlie Fairchild."

He looked to see Mr. and Mrs. Cooper in one of the doorways. Each of them looked like their sons. They both had dark, curly hair with the same colored eyes. Lenny's eyes he had gotten from his mom. Ian's were inherited from his father.

A whole other wave of memories hit Charlie. This scene reminded him of when he left for Gila. They had all looked so sad then. He had really wanted to make them all proud, especially since they helped him so much. Right now, he wasn't entirely sure if he had or not.

Would they be happy that he was a Luna now?

"Mr. and Mrs. Cooper!" He gave them his customer service smile. He still seemed to have it when he was hiding his nerves from everyone. "It's good to see you again."

"I'm so glad to see you, Charlie," Mrs. Cooper ran up to hug him. Her hair was put up in a braided bun, just like it always was. Only this time there were a few gray strands in it. "Lenny told me all about you being Max's mate."

He looked at Lenny for a second. Apparently, the man was too busy getting the stink eye from Wynona. The woman might look a bit weaker than the average woman, but there was a certain strictness to her stare that could take down even the strongest willed man.

"I like her." He mind linked with Max.

"Me too, her and Leonard were always a fun couple to watch."

"Does she always do that to him?"

"Yup." He could tell that the man was smiling just through the tone of his voice in his head.

"Yeah." He finally answered the Cooper's. "I'm now the Luna of the Crescent Moon Pack."

His heart raced at saying it. He never thought he'd see the day when he would finally tell them what his chosen profession was. After his schooling didn't go too well, he was hoping that he would never see them again. Just so he wouldn't have to tell them that he had failed.

"That's a big change for your pack," Mr. Cooper looked at Max. "You were able to get them to accept it this quickly?"

"Come on," Ian butted into the conversation. "It's Charlie we're talking about! He can charm his way into the devil's heart if he needed to."

"Where's the Blood Moon Pack?" Max changed the subject. He could feel the man tense next to him. Max always got more possessive of him when Ian was around. Honestly, Charlie liked that he was. He really didn't want to deal with a fight if Ian accidentally took things too far, or if Ben got angry with him. It was better this way.

"Charlie! Max!" A shrill voice filled the front room as a familiar face ran up to them.

"Katy!" Charlie hugged her. He had missed her almost as much as Nick did. He knew that Max said he would be fine after a bit, and he looked happy with Alistair, but he knew the man was still sad that he didn't have his best friend anymore.

"I missed you guys so much!" She hugged Max next. A slightly peeved Owen watched them both behind her.

"We missed you too!" Charlie told her. "Nick had been trying to call you for ages now. He's been a mess since you left."

"Really?!" Her face fell. Charlie could tell that she had been stressed for a little while now. She looked like she hadn't gotten much sleep at all. "I'm so sorry! My phone doesn't have service over where I am now."

"No service?" Max gave Owen a curious look. "You guys didn't set up cable for that yet?"

"We never really needed to use something like that before," Owen shrugged. "We're setting it up now, though. Our place should have service in a couple of months."

"It's a good idea to have internet, no matter what," Max told him. "That way you can get into the databanks."

"I'll see about that," Owen frowned. "My father kept us in the stone ages for his whole reign."

When Charlie was looking into the packs around them, he found out that they each had their own levels of technology advancement and involvement in human lives. The Harvest Moon Pack had the most of both. They had technology everywhere and thrived off from it, and they actively helped the humans in their territory in every way that they could.

The Blood Moon Pack was the opposite of that. They didn't look after the humans in their territory and mainly kept to themselves. They also, apparently, didn't have any service wires for phones or internet. Charlie now understood why she hadn't been calling them at least.

The Crescent Moon Pack was somewhere in the middle of the two. Charlie liked it that way, as it seemed to keep the peace a little better.

"I feel so bad that I couldn't talk to Nick." Katy walked with Charlie. They were all headed to the meeting room that their manor had. "I wish I could see him again."

"Well, it's still early in the day," he told her. "If this meeting goes by smoothly, then maybe you and Owen could stop by our place for an hour or two."

"Charlie, you're a genius!" She hugged him again. He missed how theatrical she was about everything. "I'll ask Owen when this is all said and done."

They both walked into the meeting hall with smiles on their faces. This was another reason for Charlie to be excited to get home.

He couldn't wait for this meeting to be over.

CHAPTER 31:

Mud Fight

"That training was some of the most difficult I think I've ever done," Madeline said. Her and Alistair had been on the same training schedule for that day. She had to go through the same initial test that he did, but it seemed like she had a more difficult time with it.

"It doesn't surprise me that the warriors are all strong here," Alistair told her. "They train hard to protect their pack."

"I don't know how you can do your training so easily." She shook her head. "This stuff makes me feel like an old woman."

"It won't after a while," he assured her. "Right now, though, you can get a great night's sleep."

"Yeah," she said. They were inside now, but they were still soaked from head to toe. The summer rain had decided to pour down on them right in the middle of training. "If Alan will let me sleep."

"He doesn't let you sleep?"

"It's just a joke." She laughed. "We're both not used to this whole mating thing. It's hard to figure out a routine so that you don't wind up forgetting about your responsibilities."

"Ah." He understood that. Whenever he was holding Nick, he never wanted to let him go. The chef had to remind him that they were going to be late before he would finally get up. He didn't want to anger the Alpha by showing up late to his duties, no matter how nice it was to have his mate in his arms.

"How are you and Nick, by the way?" She grabbed a towel to dry her face off. "Still taking things slow?"

"Yes," he told her. "It's better this way."

"You two really are some strange mates," Madeline laughed. "But I can respect that. If anything, you have a lot more control than anyone else that I've met."

"It was how I was trained," he told her. The most difficult thing for him at the moment was trying to retrain his mind to meet the needs of this pack. Martha had told him that the progress was slow, but there was progress. He just wished he could make them proud. No one had ever believed in him as much as the warriors that were teaching him.

"Well, you learned that pretty good." She snapped him out of his thoughts. "So, what are you worried about?"

"What do you mean?"

"You always get distant when you're worried about something," she told him. Her wet hair was stuck to her face when she looked to him. "You know I'm still your friend, right? It doesn't matter whether I'm mated or not."

"Thank you." He smiled at her. Then he looked ahead of him and sighed. "I'm worried that I'm not training hard enough. There's much that they want me to learn, and I'm not sure if I can learn it as fast as they are hoping."

"You train harder than anyone I've seen, Alistair." She put a hand on his shoulder. "If I can give you some advice, I'd say that sometimes, the harder you try at something, the more difficult it's going to be for you."

"That…" He furrowed his eyebrows. "That doesn't make sense."

"It does when it comes to training the body," she pointed out. "And the mind for that matter. When you want to learn something and it's just not happening, the frustration of it holds you back from getting it. Sometimes, you just have to take a step back, and wait for nature to do it's magic."

"Frustration is holding me back?"

"That or anxiety from other's expectations." She wrapped the towel around her short hair. "Just something to think about. If you can stop thinking that you can't do it, or stop thinking about the fact that they might be pushing you to do it, then you might find out that you'll learn it naturally."

"But I want to impress them," he told her. "I want to prove to them that I can help fight."

"Alistair, what you did when you almost died proved that." Her gold eyes looked at his with such sincerity in them. "If those warriors don't like you after you saved the Luna of their pack, then they're idiots, and you shouldn't listen to what they have to say."

"It's not that," he told her. "This pack has done more for me than anyone else in my entire life. I just wish I could do more for them."

"You're doing the best you can." She hugged him. "And that's enough. Don't beat yourself up about the things you can't control. It's just like you said: The Moon Goddess will guide you in the direction you want to go and help you with what you need."

"Thank you." He hugged her back. "I never thought I would need to hear the words that I spoke to someone else."

"Sometimes it's hard to listen to your own advice." She shrugged. "We're all human after all, even if it's only partly."

She left after that, talking about needing to take a shower. She had been training with him for only a day, but Alistair was enjoying having her company again. She was a good tracker.

He took a quick shower to rinse off all the dirt that had caked onto his feet when he was running in the mud. It was nice to train in the rain rather than the normal summer heat. The water was warm, but it still cooled him off. He was grateful for that.

When he changed, he walked slowly to Nick's room. As much as he appreciated the room that the Alpha had gifted to him, he liked being with Nick in his room. It had a personal touch that Alistair hadn't been able to give to his room. Nick told him that he would have to take him shopping when they could, but Alistair simply enjoyed being around the man. He truly was nice to talk to.

Nick's scent wasn't strong by his room. It didn't seem like he was in his room at all.

"Nick?" He was still trying to get used to mind linking with someone. He hadn't done it in so long that it was now a foreign concept for him. It wasn't too difficult to get the hang of, though. He just hated the idea of bothering someone.

"Hey, Alistair," Nick replied. It felt amazing to hear his mates voice in his head. It felt as though he were right there next to him. *"Are you done with training already?"*

"I'm usually done around this time."

"Oh." The man paused a second. *"Wow. Sorry, I lost track of time."*

"That's okay," he told him. *"Would you like some time alone?"*

"Not really," Nick said. He could feel that the man was sad through their bond. They hadn't officially mated yet, but it had been getting easier to pick up on his emotions recently. *"I never like being alone."*

"Where are you?"

"On the back porch," he answered. Alistair started walking there immediately. He was worried that Nick was going to overthink something. If there was one thing that he wanted, it was to be there for his mate. He

had never had someone to care for in this way. Nor did he have anyone who cared for him like Nick did.

The back porch was big, but it didn't take too long to spot him. He was sitting in a chair right by the edge of the covering. His hazel eyes looked lost in the downpour. Alistair sat down next to him, watching him carefully.

"What's on your mind?" he asked him.

"Nothing really," Nick sighed. "I just really like the rain."

"You do?" That brought a smile to his face. He loved to run and play in the summer rain. It was always fun for him.

"Yeah. I used to go on walks in it all the time with Katy." His eyes got lost in the rain drops again.

Ah, this was about his friend again. Alistair really did hope that he got to meet her sometime. Nick spoke well of her, and she must be a good person if she was close to Nick. But he truly just wished that she would talk to him again. He could feel the pain that his mate had at the thought that he might not ever talk to her again.

"We should walk in it, then," Alistair stood from his chair.

"Do you actually want to?" His hazel eyes met with Alistair's finally. "Or are you just trying to comfort me?"

"I love running and playing in the rain," he answered, offering him his hand. "It's a lot of fun to do as wolves too."

"I used to love playing in the rain as a wolf," Nick smiled. He looked like he was going to laugh with all the memories that flooded his eyes. "My parents used to yell at me for tracking mud all the way through the house."

"Let's have some fun then," he said. He had just showered, but he wasn't worried about getting dirty again. The mud was fun.

"I don't know," Nick shied away from him a bit. "I'm not sure what you'd think of my wolf."

"Nick." He took the man's hand and held it gently. "I'm never going to think that you're ugly, or strange. It doesn't matter what you do or how you look, I will always love you."

Nick smiled at that. Instead of answering him, he simply ran out to the rain and started racing through mud piles. Alistair followed. He always enjoyed a game of chase. He really didn't get a chance to play much when he was young. So, he liked to take every opportunity that he could.

He caught up to Nick quickly. They hadn't changed into their wolf forms yet. Instead, Nick had started to throw mud at him. They laughed as mud was starting to cover them all over. As much as it was fun to throw mud at each other, they mainly chased each other through the rain.

Alistair was the first to shift. He took off his shirt and shorts and shifted right as Nick was trying to run away again. He raced up to block his path with his wolf form. He had been curious of his mate's wolf. The fact that he was so insecure about it only piqued his curiosity for it more.

"Hey!" Nick giggled at the fact that he had been caught. "No fair!"

"It might be a little more fair if you changed into your wolf," he coaxed. He enjoyed how happy Nick looked by all of this. His face showed a child-like happiness that made the world around him bright.

"I don't know," Nick smirked. He went to scratch his neck. "It might be fun seeing if I can outrun your wolf as a human."

He didn't know why the man was being this persistent about not showing him his wolf, but it worried him. Nick had finally opened up to him about his health problem. It didn't take long for Alistair to realize all of the man's insecurities that came with it. He needed to overcome this obstacle if he wanted to strengthen their bond.

He didn't care that they couldn't mate at that time. He was a patient man. He could wait until the time was right. If there was one thing that his trials on his journeys had taught him, it was that patience was the most important thing to have. It was the one thing that he had used all throughout his life. Without it, he probably wouldn't have survived as long as he had.

He could still hold Nick and kiss him. He could still fall asleep with him in his arms and talk to him as much as he wanted. He was happy with what he was given.

Now he just needed to get the man to show him his wolf.

Alistair whined and used his nose to nudge his shirt a bit. The man laughed at his actions, scratching his neck more than before.

"Alright, alright," he told him. "But you have to promise you won't laugh."

"I'd never laugh at you," he told him. The best way to communicate as a wolf was through the mind link. He was so happy that he could do that now.

Nick shook his head and started taking off his clothes. They were covered in mud. They were far enough from the manor at that point that no one would be wondering what they were doing. He quite liked watching him undress, but that was a thought that he would save for later.

His transformation took longer than Alistair's usually was. He guessed that it was because he didn't use his wolf form as much. Alistair still changed to his wolf whenever he was outside. It helped him enjoy the forest more. And he was more comfortable that way.

A light brown wolf showed itself in the spot where Nick once was. He looked different from the other wolves, but not as much as he always told Alistair. His fur was shorter than most, and his ears were larger. They stood straight up in the air. It was a slender wolf, with some darker designs along its back. The first thing that Alistair noticed was how small he was.

"And you call me adorable?" he joked. Those hazel eyes looked shy at first, but they brightened after Alistair said that.

"You don't think it's weird?"

"*Why would I?*" Alistair went closer to the small wolf and nudged his neck. "*You aren't that different.*"

"*My mom says that wolves in India look like this,*" he told him. "*I kind of got bullied for it when I was a kid.*"

"*You look graceful,*" Alistair told him. He was enjoying watching his mate's insecurities go away. It took Alistair a long while to come to terms with how he looked in both forms. If it wasn't for his mother, he probably would have still been insecure about himself. But Nick didn't have anything to be worried about. His wolf looked lean, even with his size. Slender muscles on his thin legs showed that he was built for running.

"*I wouldn't exactly say graceful,*" Nick said. He still seemed nervous about the whole thing.

He could have showered him with compliments the whole rest of the day, but then the sun would come up, and they would miss their fun in the rain. So, instead, he rubbed his body on Nicks as lovingly as he could. His wolf was much larger than his, so he tried his best to be as gentle as possible.

Then he nipped at the fluffy tail.

Nick's wolf yelped, snapping at him. After that, their fun had started. They chased each other through the woods, getting mud all over their paws and fur. Nick had rolled in the mud at some point, turning to be on his back to show surrender. Alistair wound up getting mud all over himself after Nick had jumped up and started running again.

Even though he was small, he was a pretty fast runner. Of course, Alistair could still keep up with him easily, but there were much slower werewolves that he had come across. Martha was a great example. Not every wolf was fast. Sometimes they had to use their strength or their smarts to balance out the lack of speed that they had. That's why he liked Martha. She was an elder warrior who had pride in her pack and her position.

"*Okay! Okay!*" Nick said. Alistair had pinned him in another mud puddle again and was nipping at him. "*You win!*"

"What's my prize?"

"Whatever you want!" If Nick were in his human form, Alistair wouldn't be surprised to see him giggling like a child underneath him. "Just stop it!"

"Come on." He got off from him and nudged him to get up. "We should get inside. The rain is slowing and it's going to get humid."

"Aww." His wolf looked up at the sky. The clouds were slowly clearing, showing the blue sky that they were covering. "I wish we could do this all day."

"There seems to be a lot of rain showers here," he told him. "We should try and do something like this more often. It was fun."

"I haven't done something like this in forever!" They slowly started walking back to the manor.

"I've always wanted to do something like this."

"You haven't before?"

"No." He looked over to see the wolf was already staring at him. Those hazel eyes looked sad at that moment. "That makes this all the more greater."

"Well, then we'll have to do this more often."

Nick lead them to a shed that was near the manor. It was a small cabin, much like the one that he had been brought to when he was first allowed into the pack territory. Then he changed into his human form and motioned for Alistair to do the same. They both went into the cabin to throw on some clothes.

"You really do look graceful," Alistair told him. He pulled him into his arms as soon as he was able to. They were both so muddy that the new clothes were just going to get dirty all over again. "In both of your forms."

"No one's ever said I was graceful before." Nick shook his head. Alistair liked how he leaned into his hold, though. "Is that just another way of saying that I'm skinny?"

"I could call you beautiful." He kissed his cheek. He could feel the warmth coming from them.

"That's for women."

"Beauty is for everyone and everything," Alistair argued. "It doesn't have a gender."

"Then why does everyone only call women beautiful?"

"I don't know." He nuzzled into his shoulder. "Why think about what others say?"

"You," Nick chuckled. "Are too good with words. I thought Ed was the best with wordplay."

"I don't want you to think you're ugly just because you're different," he told him honestly. "My mother always told me that different never meant ugly. Some people just get scared of different."

"Did you learn most of these things from your mom?"

"She was a wise woman." He smiled thinking about her. As much as it hurt him that she wasn't in this world anymore, he always remembered the good memories he had with her. Before Nick, she was his color.

"Okay Teddy Bear," Nick started squirming. "We need to take some showers and get some food."

"Teddy Bear?"

"You're cuddly like one," he explained. Alistair liked that. It was funny. "Now come on, before someone comes in and starts wondering why we have a bunch of mud all over us."

"Wait," Alistair stopped him one more time. "You said I get a prize, right?"

"Maybe," Nick smiled at him. "What would you want? Some more snickerdoodles?"

"How about a shower?" Alistair smiled back at his mate. "Together?"

CHAPTER 32

A Welcomed Surprise

No. Nothing weird happened in the shower.

At least, nothing that Nick thought was weird for two mates. He was worried that Alistair might try something. He didn't exactly want a repeat of the night he had to tell him that he couldn't get it up. He had been worried about a lot of things that day. Alistair seemed to take most of them away by simply having fun in the rain with him.

Graceful. No one ever said that he was graceful. He didn't know how, but the man always knew the right thing to say at the right time. And he was slowly falling for him more and more.

He didn't even have that much fun in the rain with Katy, and they had played in it quite a lot when they were younger. Alistair kept on trying to nip his tail, which was annoying and fun at the same time. He tried doing the same to him, but he just used it to topple him over.

The giant teddy bear seemed keen on showering Nick with compliments the whole time they were supposed to be showering themselves with water and soap. He had a feeling that Alistair was just using this as an excuse to hold him longer. And wash Nick's hair.

"Why are you obsessed with my hair?" He asked. It was soothing having someone wash it for him, he couldn't deny that. But the man always wanted to weave his fingers in it, or comb through it with his fingers.

"It's soft."

"That's your only reasoning?"

"I like soft things," He held him tighter. "Like you."

Jeez this man was corny. Nick couldn't help but laugh at it. He was just glad that his day didn't wind up turning out as sad as he thought it would be. Every one of the warriors were patrolling the territory that day since Max and Charlie were gone. With Alpha Leo in charge, he was told to keep everyone as well guarded as possible.

Of course, that meant that Ed, Sam, and Tyler were all gone. A lot of his friends were either with their families or on the patrol. He was lucky that Alistair was still in training. Or he would have truly been alone.

"What are you worried about?" Alistair asked him. They had gotten dressed after the man finally let him go, and were headed to the kitchen to get something to eat.

Nick didn't know why or how, but their bond had grown strong enough for both of them to catch onto faint emotions of each other. Usually, it was just the extreme ones. Alistair seemed to pick up on his easier than he was able to pick up on Alistair's, though. He wanted to ask Dr. Button about it, but he wasn't sure if he should bother the man too much about all of this stuff. He was always up to his elbows in work.

"I'm just worried a little about Charlie," he answered as they walked down the halls. "He hasn't been past Gila City in ages. And, knowing his scent, he could easily bring some rogues to him."

"I'm a little worried about that too," Alistair slowed his pace. "You should always protect ones that the stars bless as well as possible."

"What?" He stopped to look at him. What was he going on about now? Those ruby eyes seemed lost in a memory. It frustrated him that he had opened up to the man so much, yet he still didn't feel like he knew much about Alistair. The man was nothing but mysteries that unraveled into more mysteries.

Before he could even think about trying to press the man for answers, a familiar scent danced along his nose. One that he hadn't smelt in what had felt like an eternity. He didn't even have to hear the doors to the manor opening, or the sounds of Charlie and Max coming home. He just ran over to the entrance.

"Nick!" He heard her before he saw her. Like a flash, Katy was in his arms giving him the tightest hug he had ever received.

"Katy!" He hugged her back. He felt so relieved to see her again; to hear her voice again. He almost spun her around if not for the glare that he could feel bearing down on him.

"I missed you so much!" Katy said. Her voice was a little muffled in his shirt. He remembered when she had her first sleep over at a friend's house without him. They were only ten, but the parents said that there weren't any boys allowed. Katy had missed him so much that she had bawled to her parents to pick her up early, only to jump on him when she got home.

"I missed you too!" He told her. "Why didn't you call me? I thought you said that you were going to try and talk to me every day?"

"They don't have any service," Max answered. He looked happy at least. Him and Charlie must have planned this. Because there was no way that Owen had. He looked so pissed that she was still holding him.

Oh. He must have found out that they weren't blood related.

So, he was going to wind up as the man's chew toy.

"I'm so sorry, Nick!" Katy was crying at this point. She was always a big crier. "I wanted to go somewhere to call you, but I had to train to be Luna, and there was all this stuff I had to do."

"At this point we might as well be pen pals," Nick laughed. He was so happy to see her. Her hair was as untamed as ever. The humidity that came after the rain always made her hair impossible to calm down. He was sure that her parents still had pictures of her in a lion onesie that they had gotten her. With her hair the way it was, it was perfect for her costume.

"We have so much catching up to do!" She finally stepped away from him and jumped excitedly. "I have so much to tell you!"

"I was just about to get some dinner," he suggested, pointing behind him to the dining hall. "If you all want to join."

"I don't like how that Alpha's staring at you," Alistair popped into his head. He hadn't realized the man had followed him here. Nick looked behind him to see that he had stayed by the wall, watching quietly.

"He shouldn't do anything with Max around," he told him. *"He's just a bit possessive. He'll get over it when she goes off on him."*

"Who's this?" Katy asked.

"Oh, uh." He put his hand on the back of his head. He was always able to talk to Katy about everything, but he didn't exactly want to tell her it in front of everyone. He hadn't even told his parents yet.

"This is Alistair," Max answered for him. "He's our newest warrior."

"Oh!" Katy caught on quickly to the tone of Max's voice. She gave a look to Nick saying that he was going to have to fill her in later. After a split second, she turned to Alistair and stuck out her hand. "I'm Katy. It's nice to meet you!"

"The pleasure's mine," Alistair smiled kindly at her. He shook her hand. "Nick talks about you a lot."

"Really?" She looked back to him. Alistair seemed to be enjoying his discomfort in all of this. He gave him a small smile before anyone could notice. "Were they all embarrassing?"

"Just child hood memories," Alistair told her.

"Come on," Charlie held onto Max's arm and they started leading them all to the dining room. "Let's get some food."

Alistair stayed close to him as they walked. He had this protective stance about him. It only took one quick glance at Owen for him to understand why, though. The Alpha looked piping mad. And his anger was shooting out at him like daggers out of his dark maroon eyes.

It seemed like the pup still needed more training. He could tell that there was some tension between the couple already. As much as he said that he wanted to see her go off on the man, he didn't really want her to be miserable with her new mate. He was younger than her, and if he was bull-headed, then it was most likely that his youth wasn't helping either.

He really did want Katy to have her Happily Ever After. He wanted her to be happy. Her feisty nature was perfect for a Luna, and he was sure that she would make a great leader. He just wished that he didn't have to see so much stress on her right now. Because it didn't seem like her mate was helping her with it.

Come to think of it, Charlie didn't quite look right, either.

"Hey Max," He mind linked with the Alpha. *"Is Charlie okay?"*

"He should be fine," Max answered him. *"We might take a day off from our duties tomorrow, though."*

"What happened?"

"I'll tell you later," he promised him. *"Right now, let's just enjoy some dinner with Katy, now that we know she's alright."*

Aldi came out to bring them their food. Katy had always been a touchy person, so, of course, she hugged the chef. He told her how much he missed her in the kitchen and all the other things that came with seeing a person for the first time in a long while.

It had been a month and a half at that point. And Nick could still see the black car of the Blood Moon Pack driving off with her that night.

Owen only seemed to be calm and happy when she was next to him. It was easy to see that they were still in love. But Nick was worried that Katy was giving up a part of herself to be what he wanted her to be. Her light brown eyes didn't have the same sparkle that it did before.

"I'm going to go to the bathroom." He excused himself from the table. "I'll be right back."

It didn't take long before he found out that he had been followed. He thought that it was going to be Alistair. He was probably worried about him. He was surprised to feel slender hands grab his arm and drag him to one of the guest rooms that were right next to the restrooms.

"Nick!" Katy shut the door. "You are telling me everything."

"You first." He crossed his arms. "Mrs. Can't-Even-Write-a-Letter."

"I'm sorry!" Tears were starting to well up in her eyes again. "They really don't have service over there, and they were keeping me there so that I would be safe."

"What about the letter part?" He was mainly just giving her a hard time at this point. He was hurt that she hadn't tried to talk to him at all, but he wasn't going to let that ruin their friendship.

"There's been so much Luna training that they've been making me do." She plopped down on the small bed that was there. "I've barely been able to get a good night's sleep! I keep having nightmares about paperwork."

"Katy." He sat down next to her, "Are you okay?"

"I'm fine," she assured him. "Great actually. It's just that they've been trying to get me to learn all of these things as fast as I can so that Owen's mom can retire, and it's been so stressful."

"Reminds me of when Charlie was training," he said. "If it weren't for Max, I'm sure he wouldn't have gotten any sleep."

"Oh, that man is a genius." She shook her head. "He could do paperwork with his eyes closed. And he still doesn't give himself enough credit for it."

"Well, it is Charlie we're talking about." Nick smiled.

"That's true," she sighed. "I missed you guys so much."

"We all missed you too." He hugged her again. He really hoped that she hadn't heard any of the voicemails that he had left her the few times he tried to call her. Now that he was able to talk to her, those messages just seemed embarrassing to him.

"So, who is this Alistair?" She pulled back from his hug. "And why is he always looking at you?"

"Shouldn't we be getting back to your guard dog?"

"Shouldn't you not be changing the subject?" She stuck her tongue out at him. "And he's not a guard dog!"

"You told him that we weren't blood related, didn't you?"

"My parents blurted it out when he was talking to them," she sighed. "He hates being lied to."

"Oh, great," Nick gave a nervous chuckle. "So, he hates me now."

"Oh, he'll get over it." She waved it off. "But I'm not going to get over the fact that you won't tell me more about this Alistair guy."

He was going to have to tell her eventually. He had wanted to tell her so many times. But when he was finally able to, the words kind of got stuck in his throat. Katy had always been supportive of everyone, and was always there for him, just like he was always there for her. But there was always that tiny bit of fear that filled him whenever he thought about telling anyone.

"He's our new warrior!" he told her. "I think he's a pretty good one too."

"He's more than just a warrior, and you know it." Her eyes turned to slits. "You're hiding something from me."

"You always knew how to make things awkward, you know that?"

"Tell me already!" Katy bounced on the bed. It made Nick happy just to see her again. "It can't be that bad!"

"He was a rogue," he said. Katy's light brown eyes grew wide and her mouth turned into a circle. "He wasn't the bad ones that always attacked us though! He's been traveling from all the way in Alaska down to here."

"But Max would never let a rogue into the pack!" Katy said. "He hated them more than anything!"

"Well, it was kind of hard not to when he saved Charlie's life."

"What?!"

"Ah, yes," he sighed. "The infamous 'what' of Katy. I missed that 'what.'"

"Oh, shut up!" She smacked his arm playfully. "What happened?!"

Nick wound up telling her the story about Alistair coming to ask Max for acceptance into the pack, along with the rest of the group that were with him. He was trying to keep it short as the ones in the dining room were probably wondering what was taking so long. But there was only so much you can shorten of a story, especially when he had to talk to her about some of the things that Alistair did on his adventures, like the zoo.

"And then I found out he was my mate. But Max and Charlie had this HUGE fight, because Charlie didn't think that Max was treating Alistair fair. So, he stayed in his-!"

"Wait!" Katy stopped him. "You found out he was what?!"

He was kind of hoping that she wouldn't have been able to hear him say that. But it was funny seeing her reaction to it at least.

"My mate." He shrank as he said it again. His voice had gotten quieter as well. It felt weird telling it to someone. The only other person he told it to was Max, and that was because he was starting to lose his mind at not being able to see him.

"Aww!" she squealed, giving him another hug that was much tighter than before. "You two are going to be the most adorable couple ever!"

"How are we going to be adorable?" He could see Alistair maybe, with how much he acted like a plush sometimes. But not him. He wasn't cute.

"Where's your mark?" She ignored his question entirely and started moving his shirt to show off his shoulder. "I can smell his scent all over you, but I don't see a mark."

"We haven't exactly done that yet." Nick moved her hand away from his shoulder.

"Wait." Her voice got quieter now. Her face fell with her tone. "You mean...?"

"Yeah." He nodded.

"But I thought that your mate was supposed to help with that... problem."

"I mean, it kind of did." He hated just how tense the room had gotten now. He wanted to go back to just laughing with her again, or listening to the new gossip that he knew she would have. "But it wasn't enough to actually make a difference."

"Did you tell him yet?" Katy had known about his problem ever since he found out about it himself. He had tried to keep it a secret from her, but she knew when he wasn't feeling right and pressed it out of him. He was glad to have her around back then, because those were tough times for him.

"Yeah." He remembered back to that afternoon that he wound up crying in Alistair's arms.

"What did he say?"

"He told me that he would wait," he told her. He was looking down at his hands now. They were resting on his lap, folded into each other. "I just don't know if he's going to want to wait as long as it might take."

"You don't think he would try and force it, do you?" Her eyes grew fearful for a second. Nick just laughed at the thought.

"There's no way." He shook his head. "That man's as soft as a teddy bear."

"Aww!" Her face immediately brightened as she squealed again. "That's so adorable!"

"Oh, he's as corny as a bad Romantic Comedy too," he laughed. "You wouldn't imagine."

"I'm so glad you found him," she smiled. "Now neither of us will be alone."

"Neither of us?" He raised an eyebrow. "Did you seriously think at one point that I was going to find my mate before you?"

"Maybe." Now it was her turn to look down at her hands. "I wasn't sure if I was ever going to find my mate until Owen showed up."

"Katy." He got her to look up at him. "I'm the broken man here. It's not like I had plenty of women flocking to come and see me."

"That reminds me!" She gasped. "You're gay!"

"Yeah," he laughed. "I guess this means that I am."

"This is great," she said. "Now we can talk about boys together."

"No."

"Why not?" She pouted.

"Because I'm not a sixteen-year-old girl." He shook his head. "Who calls it 'talking about boys' at our age?"

"Oh, shut up!" She smacked his arm again. "I didn't know how else to say it!"

"I'd name off a few, but I don't want to give you any ideas."

There was a few minutes of silence where they just stared off into the room. It was nice to have her company, even if they weren't talking. He missed just being around her.

"We're going to have to go back in there," Katy sighed. "Aren't we?"

"Of course," Nick smirked at her. "The cougar has to check up on her cub."

"Stop it!" She hit him again.

"Ow!" He rubbed his arm, laughing. "That one hurt!"

"Good!" She got up from the bed, motioning him to do the same.

They slowly walked back to the dining room, hoping that nothing bad happened while they were gone. With how angry Owen seemed, Nick wasn't too sure.

CHAPTER 33:

A Blessing from the Stars

"Just because your omegas aren't allowed to talk to alphas like that doesn't mean that ours can't," Max said. Ever since Nick and Katy left, Owen had been arguing with him.

Charlie didn't like this. Owen had just been appointed to take on the role of Alpha of the Blood Moon Pack. He should be treating every pack that he goes to visit with respect. Instead, he complains that Nick was trying to flirt with his mate and should be punished.

And Alistair looked like he was going to explode at any moment.

"I thought you of all people would understand where I was coming from," Owen frowned at Max. "Considering how you act whenever Ian's around."

Oh no. This wasn't going to end well.

"Ian had personally insulted me," Max's eyes turned to slits when he looked at the new Alpha. Charlie could feel him tense up next to him. "And told me that my mate didn't belong to me. Nick, however, hasn't done a single thing other than give his best friend a hug and catch up with her."

"Ian told you that your mate didn't belong to you?" Owen's dark eyes went wide in shock. Charlie sighed internally. At least now he knew that Owen had a bit of understanding in him. Although he doubted the man would ever say that he was wrong.

"Yes," Max answered. His hold on Charlie's hand got tighter. "He apologized for it, and I forgave him. But that is why I may act a different way around him."

"He still lied to me," Owen's eyes were set ablaze again.

"They really are like siblings, though," Charlie told him. His input probably wasn't wanted right then, but he was really trying to simmer this fight down. He had gotten enough excitement for one day. "You can ask anyone here and they'll tell you that the two never had any intimate feelings for each other."

Alistair had been looking down at his plate the entire time. It reminded him of when he first saw him. He couldn't tell if he was afraid or angry. But he would not eat any more, and that worried him.

Owen was going to say something else when the doors to the dining room opened and Nick and Katy walked in. Both of them looked so happy to talk to each other again. Katy looked ten times better than the tired woman that he had seen at the beginning of the day. They were both laughing at a joke that Nick had made.

"Oh yeah!" Nick said. "Alan found his mate, too!"

"What?!" Katy's eyes went huge. Charlie had missed her dramatic reactions. "I missed everything!"

He was really hoping that Katy's mate wouldn't do anything to disturb this great moment. But the man couldn't just let a good thing be. He growled at Nick the second that the chef brushed passed her when getting to her seat.

"Don't touch her!" His voice was menacing, and made everyone on edge. Nick seemed to shy away. Charlie didn't like seeing him scared. The omega was usually never scared of anyone.

"He was just moving past me!" Katy defended Nick. She gave him wicked eyes. "Don't be rude!"

Out of all the people that could have been Owen's mate, he was starting to see why Katy was the one the Moon Goddess picked. She had a sass to her that could tame anyone. It definitely worked for Owen. He looked away from her, grumbling about something that Charlie couldn't make out.

"I think we know who wears the pants in this relationship," Max mind linked with him. Charlie had to keep from laughing throughout the awkward silence.

"I told you guys she was going to go off on him sooner or later," Nick popped in. His eyes looked like they held the same humor that they felt.

"So, if she writes a book, is it going to be called 'How to Tame your Werewolf' or 'How to Tame your Alpha'?" Charlie asked. Max almost choked on the water that he was drinking at that one. He coughed to cover it up.

"I'm going to have to ask her that the next time I get the chance," Nick said. He looked much calmer now that Owen wasn't glaring at him. He sat next to Alistair who still had his head down.

"So, Alistair," Katy looked to the albino. "I heard you traveled a lot."

"Yes," he answered. He didn't look up to meet her eye. Charlie had a feeling that Owen had scared him more than anything. His voice had a hint of anger in them, and he kept on glancing over to Nick more than before.

"Hey, what's wrong with Alistair?" Nick asked. He was trying to come off as nonchalant when he leaned back in his seat, but Charlie saw the concern in his eyes.

"Owen was angry that you hugged Katy," Charlie told him. *"I think he's upset because he wanted to defend you."*

"Is that why he won't look at Katy?"

"I think so."

"Damn, I just got him to stop doing that."

Nick started picking up the conversation. It was amazing how well he could calm everyone down. He got Alistair to look up at least, but he still wouldn't meet Katy in the eyes. Charlie had no idea what his past Alpha might have done to him, but he had a feeling that it was going to be a hard thing to overcome for him.

He was just glad that he was able to keep this visit a secret from Ian and Lenny. They would have been too curious about Alistair and there would have been nothing but problems. Charlie didn't think that Ian would have appreciated the argument that Max and Owen had gotten into either.

They talked for a long time, as they all caught each other up on their own lives. It had only been two months since Katy had been away, but so much had happened.

Max was eager to have Charlie show off the ring that he gave him. Charlie had never been that open with his sexuality, so it seemed a little strange showing it off. He wasn't exactly sure about how Owen reacted. The man seemed to be hiding a scowl. But Katy was super happy to hear the news. She hugged him, which, thankfully didn't invoke another growl from her mate. He wasn't quite sure how Max would react to that.

And he didn't really want a fight. It had been too long of a day for that. He just wanted it to end off on a happy note.

"You're inviting me, right?" Katy asked.

"Of course!" Charlie couldn't help but chuckle. "Whenever we actually get around to planning it, that is."

He wasn't sure when they were going to have time for a wedding at the moment. They had been so caught up in their duties, and the rogues were still an issue. Charlie also really did want that honeymoon that Max was talking about. Even if it was just in their suite in the mansion, it would be nice to have a break to enjoy with just him. They hadn't had something like that in a while.

"I've got some of it planned," Max smiled. Charlie gave him a surprised look. "The date is going to be the main issue."

They didn't talk much after that. It was sad to see Katy leave by the end of the night. But she truly looked exhausted, and Owen wasn't exactly the party person at the moment. They said their goodbyes and watched her leave in the black car that they had driven up there.

Just like they had done when she first left for the Blood Moon Pack.

Charlie looked over at Nick. He was happy to see that the man was smiling this time, instead of looking lost and sad when she had first left. Alistair was right beside him.

"Owen's going to be a problem," Max pulled him in closer. "I can feel it."

"Katy will whip him into shape," Nick said. "She's worse than my mom when she's angry."

"I don't think I've seen your mom angry," Charlie said.

"You don't want to," Nick laughed. "That woman could scare Liam if she wanted to."

"That's a fun thought." Max laughed with him.

The air outside was cooler now that the sun wasn't out. The breeze was nice after all the rain that had happened that day, and the sky had cleared up almost completely, showing off the beautiful stars scattered all over.

"We should go for a walk," Charlie said. He had been sitting around for too long for his body to not be antsy. There was no way he was going to be able to sleep unless he found some way to get out the restlessness that he was feeling. That, and the tension from that dinner was enough to make him want to run at that point.

"Sounds good to me," Max said. "You guys want to come with?"

"Sure!" Nick said. Alistair had been looking up at the sky the majority of their discussion. But he nodded his answer quickly. It seemed as though they were all a bit antsy after than dinner.

There was a small little hiking trail that was right by the manor. It was the first trail that Max and him went on when Charlie was brought to the manor. As much as that was a horrifying experience, he liked this path. It was beautiful no matter what time of day it was.

"Alistair?" Charlie looked over to him. Him and Nick were walking behind him and Max. It seemed like the man had somehow convinced Nick to hold hands. Charlie smiled. It was nice seeing them together.

"Yes?"

"Are you okay?" he asked. "You got really quiet."

"I was just trying to show respect." The albino smiled.

"But you didn't have to not look at Katy, you know," he told him. "Owen isn't the type to get mad if you look at her."

"I think he's just mad at me," Nick said.

"He's mad at our pack in general," Max told them.

"Why?"

"The Blood Moon Pack has been the most antisocial out of the three of us. They always stayed in their own territory; in their own little bubble. That's why it makes sense that they don't have internet or phone lines," he explained. "It took my dad forever to get Alpha William to actually like us. Now it seems like we get to deal with the same thing with Owen."

"Like I said," Nick waved it off. "Katy will straighten him out. If they're destined for each other, then she's not going to tolerate that kind of stuff for too long."

"I hope you're right, Nick." Max sighed. "I really do."

"So, what about you, Charlie?" Nick changed the subject. "You didn't exactly seem like yourself when you walked inside."

"It was just a long day." He sighed.

"I think having a day off might be good for us," Max told him. He was grateful for his mate's suggestion.

"Hey, we could always go and do something together," Nick said. "Maybe get your mind off some things?"

Charlie loved how great a friend Nick was. He didn't have to tell him exactly what was wrong. The man just knew when he was upset and offered to help.

"Did you really worry about me that much when we were gone?" He smiled.

"You just…" Nick stopped walking and furrowed his eyebrows. "Hey, wait a second." He turned to Alistair. "You never told me what you meant by that."

"Meant by what?" Alistair looked confused as well. It was funny seeing the two confused together, but now Charlie was too.

"By the ones that the stars bless," Nick said.

"I meant just that." He shrugged his shoulders. "Children of the stars should always be protected."

"Children of the stars?" Charlie asked. He felt like he just popped into the middle of a conversation. What were they talking about?

"Yes." He looked at Charlie with the same confused expression. "You don't know?"

"Know about what?" Max asked this time. Now they were all confused.

"You said that about Charlie," Nick said. "What do you mean?"

"He's a Star Child," Alistair answered.

"A Star Child?"

"You don't know what a Star Child is?" His bright red eyes sparkled in the moonlight. "How did you think you were able to send that message to everyone the night that the rogues came?"

Charlie's heart started racing a bit. He never knew why he could do something like that. It was something that not even Button or Adelle could explain. Every person he ever talked to about it had never heard of someone sending out thoughts like for everyone to hear.

And Alistair knew?

"What is a Star Child?" Max asked this time. He seemed to want as much information about this as Charlie did. He always just assumed that he would never get the answer to why he was able to do that. That they were just freak accidents that happened when he got really scared.

"A Star Child is one that is blessed by a star," Alistair explained. "The stars bless those who they know will bring lots of joy to the world. It doesn't matter what race, species, or gender you are. The stars do not judge. They are the brothers and sisters to the moon."

"Can they all do what Charlie can do?" Max questioned again.

"No," Alistair shook his head. His smile was warm as he spoke, as if this brought back a nice memory. "Much like all the stars are different, so are the abilities that they bless the children with. That's why Star Children cannot give their children their gifts. For it was only them who were blessed."

"Why didn't you tell us this all sooner, Alistair?"

"I thought you knew." He looked confused at the question. "The whole pack is protective of him, just as they should be."

"Why should they be protective of me?" Charlie asked him this time. This was all making his head spin. He had never heard of Star Children before.

"There's a reason why they are called Star Children," Alistair answered. He looked up to the night sky yet again. "They are like the stars in the night sky. As much as they are bright, and shine, darkness surrounds them." Then his ruby red eyes met with his. "Because of the darkness, most don't survive through their childhood."

A shiver ran down his spine at hearing that. All the memories of his childhood were flooding back to him. Max pulled him into a hug to comfort him.

"What happens to them?" He pressed on with the questions. "How old do they usually survive?"

"I don't know exactly," Alistair shook his head. He seemed worried about how upset he was getting about this, but Charlie pushed him to continue. He needed to know about this. "It depends on the individual. As much as they will bring good to them, they also attract darkness. When they are children, it is up to their protectors to help them. Once they are adults, though, they are destined to bring light to the unknown, and will bring their protectors to greatness."

"But I didn't have protectors," he told him. He was holding onto Max for dear life at this point. "I didn't really have anyone during my childhood."

"You didn't have anyone?" the albino asked.

Charlie slowly told him the story of what had happened to him. He hadn't even told Nick about it in detail. It still hurt to talk about, especially when he had gotten so scared when they had drove to Sun City. But the wind was calm, and there weren't many people there. They wound up sitting on the ground on the trail, since they were no longer walking. Alistair listened intently to everything. He was a good person to talk to.

"Well, now I know why you didn't want to tell the whole story to everyone," Nick said. "That's horrible."

"Yeah." He sighed. Max had pulled him into his lap at that point. His hold was comforting. "It didn't help going to Sun City today either."

"You truly are strong," Alistair told him. "Even though you had to get people to help you, it's not often that a Star Child can fend for themselves as children. There are too many horrible things that can happen."

"It might have helped that he was living in a pack territory," Max said. "That may have protected him from any supernatural dangers."

"Their blood is known to be sweet for vampires," Alistair said. Charlie had to hold back a shudder. "If anything, you protected him from being a victim of that."

"Jeez, this all sounds terrible," Nick shook his head. "How do you know that Charlie is one, though? What if the thoughts that he sent out were just a weird way that his werewolf gene was trying to come out?"

"Their scents are always sweet," Alistair said. "It is said that they have an attracting aura about them, that works for good and bad."

Charlie thought back to the drug dealer. Was that the bad that he had attracted? There were a lot of people that treated him horribly throughout his life. But he thought that was just how life worked out sometimes.

"How do you know all of this?" Max asked him. "Where did you learn about Star Children?"

"My old pack had one," he answered. His face always fell whenever he spoke of his old pack.

"Really? Who?"

"My mother."

CHAPTER 34:

When the Sky Danced

Her blue eyes were dull, along with the blond hair that stuck to her heated face. He wished to take the pain away from her, but there was nothing he could do. There was never anything he could do.

"Be like the Traveler, Alistair." She grabbed ahold of his cheek. Her small hands seemed more fragile than they used to. She was now like glass to him. But her smile was still as beautiful as the moon on a crystal-clear night. "Follow the wind and the moon, for they will guide you to happiness."

"You are my happiness," he told her. He had to stay quiet, for the Alpha was right outside of the small shed that they called home. He didn't want him seeing the tears coming down his cheeks. "I can't go on without you."

"Alistair." She rubbed her thumb across his cheek, just as she had done plenty of times before. "No matter what anyone tells you, you are beautiful. You are strong. I've never been so happy than when I was with you, raising you to become the amazing young man that you are today." Her voice was so weak, it pained him to hear it. "When the time comes, run. I need you to keep running, until you get far away from here. Your true home is where the moon and wind guide you. It won't be an easy journey. It will be long, and riddled with challenges. But, if you follow the moon's guidance, and listen to the wind *that she sends your way, you will find a happiness that you have never known before. And you will know the true power of love."*

"I know the power of love." He held the hand that was on his face gently. It was soft and cold. The blizzard had not let up in some time where they were. "I know it just by being your son."

"It's the most powerful thing in the world," she told him. "But I need you to hold on for me, Ali. I may not be able to help you or talk to you like this, but I will always be with you."

"I love you," he told her.

"I love you too, Ali." She smiled weakly at him. It didn't take much longer after that when he saw the life come out of her eyes. Her hand was now limp in his. And her spirit was no longer with them.

"What's going on?" the Alpha said. He had to keep his head down around him. He was merely a servant to him, whether or not he battled to protect them. "Is she alright?"

"She has left to be with the Moon Goddess," he informed. His voice was quiet, to try and hide the emotion that filled it. "I need to bury her."

"We don't have time," the Alpha said. His words were yet another dagger in his heart. He did not know how he was going to survive without her to keep him going, but he would try and keep his mother's wishes.

He knew better than to argue. Even when it felt as though a part of him had died in that room. They should at least let him try and give her a proper burial. But she was an omega. And the Alpha didn't have time to do such things with omegas.

His body was heavy as he walked out of that room. He would not look back at the stiff body that was in his mother's bed. It was just a cold reminder of how alone he was now. Instead, he followed the Alpha out of the shed.

The sky cleared somehow. The blizzard had broken. There was nothing but the chilly breeze that he had grown to love in his short life. The wind was the only thing that made him look up, as it beckoned him to. It wasn't until then that he saw just how beautiful the night sky was.

The Aurora Borealis was what their pack was named after. His mom would always tell him that if the wolves had done well to listen to the Moon Goddess, their souls would dance in the beautiful lights when they passed away. This time, the Aurora Borealis was brighter than he had ever seen it. The different colors danced across the sky in celebration of the new wolf that had come to join them.

That was when he had found out that he was never truly alone. He never had been, even in all the silence that he had dealt with in his travels. He listened to his mother's words of wisdom with everything he did. For the Aurora Borealis pointed him in the direction he needed to go.

Alistair opened his eyes to go back to the present. The memory had come back to him so vividly that he had to close his eyes and let it pass. He learned that the more he tried to fight the memories, the more they tried to come out and hurt him.

"Your mother was a Star Child?" Charlie asked. His bright green eyes were wide with curiosity. He was surprised that no one knew about Star Children. He had learned about them his whole childhood. His mother was a great teacher.

"Yes," he answered. "She was one of the oldest. They said that she survived for so long because of them. But, without her guidance in the pack, we would have gotten in much worse situations."

"What was she like?" He was still curled into his mate after telling them the story of his own childhood. It was horrible hearing what he had to go through. He supposed that the Moon Goddess had been keeping an eye on him as well.

"She was clairvoyant," he told them. They were all sitting on the forest floor as the moon shined brightly down on them. "Unlike your telepathy. She would have visions of what was to come. Sometimes it was as soon as an hour from now, other times it was months away."

"So, Star Children aren't just telepathic then?" Max asked. He was so different from the Alpha that he had growing up. Alistair was grateful for that.

"Their blessings depend on which star they were blessed with," he explained. "It's never anything too extreme, like what some witches can do, though. Star Children are simply meant to brighten up the world."

"So, she was able to look into the future?" Charlie asked.

"Yes," he answered. "She was a wise woman. She told me that she had seen the Moon Goddess herself. She passed along all of the knowledge that she had to me when I was growing up."

He remembered all the studying that she had him do. The Alpha hadn't wanted him to go to school, not even the one that the pack had due to them traveling all the time. They told him that his looks were scary for the other children around his age. His mother seemed really upset that the Alpha would not allow him to have an education. So, she would get books and pencils and teach him herself. Along with that, she taught him all the things that she had learned throughout her life.

He enjoyed her stories the best. She had many stories that she would make up for him when he had gotten bored throughout the day. They were full of adventure and always had a good ending. But there was always a message that she had taught in each and every one of them.

"I'm sorry, Alistair." Charlie's face had turned back into sadness as he spoke again. "You must really miss her."

"I do." He smiled at him. "But she is always with me, no matter where I go. I will always have her memory to keep her alive."

It wasn't until he felt a small squeeze of his hand that he remembered that Nick was there as well. Those hazel eyes looked so worried about him. He wished he could hold him like Max and Charlie were holding each other. He wanted to be close to him again.

"How did she die?"

"She got sick. She had never been the healthiest. They hadn't been able to get her to a hospital, as there were no doctors for miles and miles and they didn't want to travel through the blizzard."

"You didn't have any doctors in your pack?" Max asked.

"No." He shook his head. "Even if we did, finding supplies was too difficult."

"That's just an excuse," Max told him. His purple eyes of royalty showed a hint of anger in them, but it wasn't towards Alistair, "It was your old Alpha's responsibility to that pack to make sure that you all had every-thing that you needed. He could have gotten supplies."

"The place I am from wasn't that easy to survive in," he told him. "Blizzards plagued us as well as many beasts who were searching for food themselves."

"But you were a traveling pack," Max frowned. "If it was too difficult to live there, then your Alpha should have moved the pack somewhere that had better food."

"What he's trying to say, Alistair," Charlie cut into the conversation. "Is that the only one at fault for your old pack struggling is the leader. Every pack needs a good leader to watch over them all. But, most importantly, it wasn't your fault that any of that happened to you."

Those green eyes of his held an understanding that was different from what he had seen in anyone else. From hearing his story, he knew that the man had gone through quite a lot at an early age. But he didn't expect anyone to tell him something like that. He had always been told that everything was his fault, much to his mother's anger. The reason why they lost battles was because of him, or the reason why they had to slow down. He had worked so hard to push himself just because of it.

"I believe I understand now why the Moon wished to make you Luna," he smiled at him. The wind always shifted when Charlie was around.

It always seemed to shine on him as well. The Moon Goddess was proud of this man, just as she was proud of the Alpha.

"Come on." The blond shook his head and started to stand. "I think it's time to head back inside."

He didn't know how long they had been out there talking, but he was glad that they had gone on this walk. They all agreed with Charlie and started walking back to the manor. Nick had been quiet for most of the discussion. He looked like he was exhausted with all that had happened that night. Alistair wanted to curl up with him and get some sleep himself. He was sure that he would have another busy day ahead of him tomorrow.

"Alistair," Max mind linked with him. They were walking back in silence. Alistair enjoyed the cool breeze that the summer storm had brought.

"Yes?"

"This pack will never treat you like the Borealis Pack did." He glanced at him from the side. His face was serious. *"Nor will I. I know that I was harsh on you when you first came in. I'm sorry for doing that to you. But I will never treat you as anything other than family."*

"You didn't even treat me that badly when you brought me here." Alistair looked at him in curiosity. *"Any Alpha in your situation would have just killed me. I trust you because you didn't. You treated me with respect when no one else did."*

"Just know that it won't happen again. You're in my pack now, and we all protect each other."

"Thank you."

He didn't think that he was treated poorly at all when he was brought here. The reason why he was so cautious with everything was because he wasn't sure what would have upset the Alpha. The Alpha of the Borealis Pack was temperamental. He would always get mad at him, even if he hadn't been doing anything. He would always yell orders at him or hit him. Alistair had no choice but to let it happen.

It was quiet in the manor. All the maids had done their duties or were just finishing up, and there wasn't that much traffic in the hallways. Alistair and Nick said goodbye to the Alpha and Luna. Then Nick started pulling him to his room. He wasn't sure how the man was feeling, as his own feelings were too strong to pick up on his mate's. He couldn't wait until he could mark him. Then he would be able to feel his love's emotions no matter what. He loved the idea of being that close to Nick.

As soon as the door closed, the man threw his arms around him.

"I'm sorry." He sounded so sad when he talked.

"What are you sorry about?" Alistair wrapped his arms around the man and moved them to the bed nearby. It was such a small room, but it reminded him of the cabin, and that only had good memories with it.

"Your mom." His face was buried into the side of his neck. As much as he said that Alistair was the cuddly one, Nick loved to cling onto him when they were alone. "Charlie's past. Everything. That all sounds horrible."

"You didn't have anything to do with it." Alistair rubbed his back. They were now curled up on the bed with the blanket around them. Nick liked having a blanket over him, even if he was sweating in his sleep. He had told him that it just felt comfortable to him. "You have nothing to be sorry about."

"I didn't even know what to say to all of that." He shook his head. "And, trust me, that's pretty rare for me."

"You listened," he comforted his mate. "Many times, that's all you can ask for."

They laid in silence for a while, just enjoying each other's embrace. The way that Nick always relaxed when he was in his arms was the best feeling he had ever felt. And his scent was intoxicating this close.

"My mom almost died." Nick broke through the silence. His voice was small. "She almost died when she was pregnant with me."

He sounded so scared when he said it. Alistair never wanted Nick to be scared. He wanted to protect him. But it was difficult to protect someone from themselves.

"How?" He asked him. He pulled his mate closer to him, hoping to comfort him at least through their bond. "Do you want to talk about it?"

"She got hurt from some rogues," he said. "I used to wake up some nights when I was a kid to her night terrors. She was haunted by it for a long time."

"I'm sorry." He nuzzled into a crook of Nick's neck. "Your mother's a good woman. No one should ever have to go through that."

"My whole families been afraid of her dying ever since. You should see my dad whenever she so much as drops something."

"I would be doing the same thing. I wouldn't want anything happening to you either."

"But your mom was the one who actually died." He shook his head. "I'm sorry, I don't know why I turned this into something about me."

"I want to know everything about you, Nick." He lifted the chef's face up to meet his. "This is the best way to get to know each other. It's not just about me, or you. It's about the both of us."

"I wish I could have met your mom." Nick gave him a small smile. "If she was anything like you, I'm sure everyone would love her."

"I would have loved to bring her here." He smiled and looked out the window. "But she's never far."

"What do you mean?" Nick looked out the window with him.

"The Borealis Pack was named after the Aurora Borealis," he started. "It guided us to success and strength, and was our connection to the moon that shined brightly on us. When I was little, my mother told me that the best of the Moon Goddess' children are brought there when they pass. They are what guides us to our fate."

"What does it look like?"

"Absolutely beautiful." He could practically see it as he looked at the night sky. He had stopped being able to see it early on in his journeys, but it was something he never forgot. "It's beyond words."

"I wish I could see it sometime," Nick sighed. He could tell that the man was getting sleepier as he talked.

"The night my mother passed, there was a huge blizzard that had been beating down on us for many days and nights. I was the only one there as her spirit left her body. As much as I was crushed by her death, I walked outside to find that the sky had cleared."

"The blizzard was gone?"

"The Alpha was shocked. He walked in wondering what had happened. He had witnessed the storm stop and clear in a matter of seconds."

"That's strange."

"It was." He rested his cheek on his mate's head. He loved that he was able to hold him close like this. "And, when I looked up, I saw her."

"You saw your mom?"

"Yeah," he told him. "I saw her dancing in the light of the Aurora Borealis. Her turmoil was finally over."

"Did you really see her?" His voice was playfully suspicious. Alistair smiled at him. He knew that it meant he was starting to feel better.

"Well, you can believe what you want," he chuckled. "The last thing she ever told me was that I was going to find happiness beyond anything I had ever felt."

"Did she say that because she loved you or did she actually see into your future?"

"I don't know." He shrugged. "But she was right. I have found happiness beyond even my wildest imagination."

He didn't need to lift Nick's head up this time. Those hazel eyes looked straight into his, showing nothing but love. He never wanted them to look away from his.

"Did you get your romance from your mom?" he asked. The same playful tone was in his voice as he said it, but Alistair knew that he enjoyed all of the compliments that he showered him with.

"Probably." Alistair smiled again. He was always so happy around Nick. The man could never upset him, even if he couldn't hold him when they were around others. "That doesn't mean that it isn't true."

There weren't any lights on in the room. The Moon and the stars were the only thing that helped them see. But Alistair didn't need sight when he felt his mate's lips on his. His hand automatically moved up to tangle itself in his hair. They both held onto each other as if their lives depended on it.

"Alistair?" Nick's voice was breathy as they broke the kiss.

"Hmm?" He moved to start kissing his jaw. He would never stop loving this man.

"Will you move in with me?"

"In here?"

"Well, we could probably get a bigger suite if you want," he said. "I just don't want to be without you."

"I don't have many things," Alistair said. "I could just move in here, if you'd like."

"You basically already live here," Nick chuckled.

"I like this little room of yours." He continued to give him light kisses on his jaw. "But you should really get some sleep for now. You have to get up early for work."

"You aren't exactly helping me fall asleep."

"You started it," he teased.

They talked for a little while longer. But it didn't take long before Nick started yawning. Alistair pulled the blanked further over them both and allowed Nick to shift into a comfortable position.

He could truly say that he had never had such great sleep than he did with Nick. He always waited until after the man fell asleep before he would let himself drift off. But it never took long.

He never wanted it to end.

CHAPTER 35:

Work Out Therapy

Sometimes you just needed something to punch. Something to let all the tension out after everything was said and done. As much as it was good to have people to talk to about issues or to ask for advice, sometimes there was just no advice to be had and no amount of venting that could help.

Trust him, he had dealt with that enough when he was in high school. If he would have known all of the troubles that lied ahead for him back then, he was sure that he wouldn't have been so worried about all those little issues that plagued his mind when he was younger.

But at least it helped him find an outlet for his frustration. Training helped clear his mind, as it took all the tension that had built up away. And warriors didn't just train as wolves. They had to be fit in their human form too. They had to know how to fight in both forms, and well. Because there was always a chance that something happened, and nothing was impossible when it came to battle.

The indoor part of the training ground was a large gym full of every amount of workout equipment imaginable. The rest of the pack were allowed to use it if they wanted to, of course, but the warriors always took priority over others when it came to working out. It was what they got paid for after all.

That reminded him. Isabelle was still working on getting Alistair on the payroll. She seemed curious about the man. Max didn't know until recently that she had a sister that was albino. Tyler had told him that she didn't like talking about it, because it had left her depressed for a long while after that.

He just wished that he had known sooner. She might have known more about albino werewolves than what they had known at the time. Right now, though, she was dead set on trying to help him in any way that she could.

It was a good thing Tyler knew that Alistair was mated. As controlled as he seemed to be, the Beta could get jealous rather easily. So could Isabelle. They were perfect for each other in that sense, but he would rather not have to break up a dog fight if Tyler got too possessive.

They already had enough things to worry about.

That only made him want to punch this bag even more. His favorite workout was boxing, even if it was by himself. Either that, or running and working on increasing his speed. When he was younger, he had challenged himself to be faster than his father. He used to train with him quite a lot.

"There he is!" He heard someone say behind him. He didn't want to focus on whose voice that was, or why they were saying that. He simply wanted to sort out his thoughts while punching this bag and watching it spin around.

It wasn't that he was angry. He was just frustrated. There was so much to do, that they were struggling to do because of all the politics involved. As much as he liked Leonard and Ian, sometimes he wished that they didn't have neighbor packs just so they could have some more freedom to do as they pleased. These meetings were getting ridiculous.

"Max!"

"What?" He didn't stop his punching. It was his day off, and Charlie was still working. He loved having his mate around, but there were times when he was glad that he had some time to himself. He needed to clear his head. It's not like he wanted days away from him. But everyone needed their alone time, and he was glad that Charlie agreed with him on that.

"Have you really been here all day?" Sam asked. He had walked to the other side of the room just so he could face him. Max was faced opposite of the door.

"What time is it?"

"Two." The blond looked at him with a quizzical expression. "And we've been wondering where you've been since about three hours ago."

We? Oh, this was going to be great.

"Here he is, Tyler!" He heard Ed come in. "He's been in the training room the whole time."

"You guys were looking for me for three hours and you didn't think to look in here?" he asked. With how much sweat he had, he was surprised that they couldn't easily just sniff him out.

"We weren't exactly looking for you," Ed said. "Sam was just starting to worry about you."

"You were the one who was talking like you hadn't seen him in years!" Sam argued with him. "And we've only been actively looking for you for about twenty minutes."

"Maybe you all need more training then," he smirked. He had stopped his workout as his friends all came into the huge gym. It was empty today, surprisingly. Max enjoyed working out alone most of the time. Although training was done more with pack members.

"Oh no," Tyler came in. "He's on the punching bag again. This only means one thing."

"I just needed to clear my head."

"Alright," Ed sat down on one of the benches that were around. "I think it's time we have another guys talk."

"Why?"

"Because you've been nothing but a giant ball of stress ever since you came from that meeting the other day," Tyler said. He had an eyebrow raised. "And you still haven't told us everything that happened."

Max sighed and sat down on one of the benches himself. They had all been caught up in their own lives and work that they didn't have too much time to talk anymore. Max didn't get bothered by it. He had Charlie to talk to and he knew that his friends would always be there. But there were some times when he just couldn't sort out his thoughts. Even when he was working out, his mind was a mess of information and memories. He couldn't get them organized.

"I'm still trying to process it all," he told them. His hands ran through his hair, like they always did when he was stressed. Charlie could only help him with it when he was there with him. As soon as he left, all of it came flooding back.

"Ah," Sam said. "So, this is senior year all over again."

"I wish it was." Max laughed. "All those problems seem like such a small thing compared to now."

"Even finding your mate?" Ed elbowed him. "You seemed pretty worried about that for a long time."

"Last year seems like it happened centuries ago." Max shook his head. "Now, instead of getting my mate to want me back, I have to figure out how to convince him that he doesn't have to prove himself anymore."

"Isabelle has been telling me that he seems to be in that mindset," Tyler said. "Especially when he locked himself up in his office for three days."

"Don't remind me of that." He still felt guilty that he had made Charlie feel that way. When the mental barrier was finally brought down, he realized just how much he had hurt his mate through his own words.

Charlie told him everything the morning after. Including how he felt like he had to prove himself to Max as well as the pack.

He never wanted to make him think such a thing.

"Okay," Ed leaned back into the bench, putting his arms over his head. "So, this is about Charlie."

"Partially," he answered. "So much happened within one day."

"Now you know how I feel," Sam joked. "I can't wait until you guys start adopting. Who knows? Maybe you'll start greying by 27."

"I have my mother's hair." He glared at him. "Not my dad's, thank you very much."

"So, what happened?" Tyler pushed.

"I don't even know where to start."

"Start with Charlie," Ed said. "I was kind of wondering why he's been a little more quiet than usual lately."

"I barely know where to start with Charlie." He shook his head again. "The beginning of the day he almost had an anxiety attack again. And the end of the day we find out that he may or may not be a Star Child."

"Anxiety attack?" Ed looked worried.

"Star Child?" Tyler's eyebrows furrowed at the term.

"You see." Max chuckled at them. "This is only the start of my problems."

He started to tell them all that happened with Charlie. He could tell that he wasn't happy with going to Sun City in the first place. But he wanted to appear strong for everyone. Max should have told him no; that he would be fine going by himself to that meeting. But Charlie always had a way with his words, and he swore the man could talk his way out of anything.

It was easy to see that Charlie wasn't feeling well when they got to the city. As soon as his heart rate went up, Max pulled to the side. He wasn't going to wait until it got up too high. They weren't anywhere near the pack house and he did not want to take him to any other doctor. He saw the trauma in those emerald eyes as he slowly came back to reality. When he told him what had happened the day after, Max was beyond furious.

Just what that man had said to his mate when he was nothing but a child was enough for him to want to have his head on a dinner plate, and throw it in a volcano.

He got better when they got to the Cooper's, although he could still feel the nerves that he had. He somehow pulled through all the questioning that Mr. and Mrs. Cooper had, along with the meeting in general. They seemed a bit skeptical of him being a Luna, and looked at Max with a bit of a questioning gaze, but they didn't say anything otherwise. They were just happy to see him again. Max was glad that Charlie was able to relax a bit more around them.

Then there was the whole ordeal with Owen when Katy and him came over. Nick and her were so happy to see each other. They were acting like school kids all over again. Both of them were talking at once to try and catch each other up on what had happened over the past two months. But they never looked like they were flirting with each other in any way. They always acted like siblings.

Of course, Owen didn't see things that way. He had a feeling that Owen was going to have a hard time with his mate if he was going to get jealous of every man that she talked to. She was a hug person, who loved her friends and family. And by seeing Nick's reaction to the man when he barked at him to not touch her was enough to piss even Max off.

They just brushed past each other. Only their arms touched. And he was going to scream at him for that?

"The amount of disrespect that man has when he visits is beyond annoying," Sam frowned. "You won't believe what he told Heather the first time he came to visit."

"I'm kind of with Nick on this one," Ed said. "Katy will straighten him out. That's what omega women do best."

"If he disrespects one more person in this manor, I'm banning him from coming here." It infuriated him that the man would even think of doing things like that at someone else's house. If he did those things as a guest, Max couldn't imagine what he was doing at his own home. "He can come to go to meetings if absolutely necessary, but he's not staying over and he's not going to be waited on hand and foot."

"He's a daddy's boy," Tyler said. "He most likely learned to act like this from him."

Max continued the story about when they left, and them all going for a walk to clear their minds. He could tell that Charlie was antsy after all the tension that Owen had brought when they were eating. He hardly ate anything because of it, which worried Max.

The Star Child thing was a mess in and of itself. He needed to tell all of them to shut up a couple of times before he finished that story. He had gotten Dr. Adelle to look into the term for him while he was enjoying his first day off with Charlie. She found a myth about them, matching up to the stories that Alistair had told, although it wasn't in as great of detail. They were thought of to be extinct due to all the dark forces that had started to wipe them out millennia ago.

"So, that fully explains the telepathy," Sam said. "Even when he wasn't in a pack." They all were starting to look like Max felt at this point. This was a lot to take in.

"Do you think that's why the rogues have been trying to come more often?" Tyler asked.

"No," Max shook his head. "I was thinking about that, but Charlie has been in our territory long before they started getting really dangerous. And he was in Gila, which is the main point that they get in through."

"Oh yeah," Ed said. "How goes trying to convince the others to push their borders up a bit?"

Max groaned and buried his face into his hands.

"Welcome to my next problem, boys," he said.

"You weren't able to convince them?" Tyler said. "I thought they all liked the idea of gaining more land."

"Not when it could hurt the Harvest Moon Pack's humans," he said. "They're still working on building up the defense of their cities before thinking about advancing."

"So, we've basically been the only ones preparing for this kind of thing?" Sam asked. "Even though it was bound to happen sooner or later?"

"Basically."

"What about the Blood Moon Pack?" Tyler asked. "They say just how thirsty for blood they are through their name alone."

"They're waiting until Katy and Owen are more comfortable in their positions before they start to attack."

It all seemed like plausible reasons to hold off on attacking these vermin. But Max had been waiting too long. His pack had been waiting too long. And the rogues thought that they were the weakest just because they didn't have the greatest population.

It didn't help that his father hadn't done anything to them until the very end of his reign. He decided to just chase them out at first, and only attack when they did. Max was the one who started killing them. But, every time he killed a whole group of them, it seemed as if they multiplied.

They weren't werewolves, they were rats. And Max was desperately looking for the nest that he needed to destroy.

"Okay, I lied," Sam sighed. Now they were all sitting down. "This is much more difficult than raising kids."

"That's comforting," Max smiled at the man. "If it was worse than I don't know how I'd survive eighteen years of it."

That was another thing he was thinking about. He had still been planning a few projects regarding the wedding. He was thinking about trying to plan it for the anniversary that him and Charlie officially started dating, which was in December. But with all of these setbacks, he wasn't sure if he was going to be able to.

There were a few other things that he was able to do at least. Herb was helping him with one of those things. He was excited to see the finishing product of that.

"We can't even push past Gila a little?" Tyler brought him back to his present problems. "We need to secure that area or they're just going to keep coming through there."

"That's what we've all been wanting to do," Max said. He could even feel all the warrior's getting antsy about it. With the last attack being the most brutal one, and Alistair getting so close to death because of it, they needed to secure that weak spot.

"The rogues have been getting stronger with each minute that we wait for something to happen," Tyler frowned. "There has to be a way that we can expand a little past Gila without Harvest or Blood getting pissed."

"We could say that it was a way to defend our cities," Ed said. "We've been getting hit the most with the rogue attacks. And I doubt that the other packs will even notice if we just push five more miles. That forest is huge."

"My dad would be killing us all now for even thinking about this," Max said. "If they get pissed about us expanding our borders too soon then it could start a war."

"But Max, think about it," Ed had a sparkle in his eyes. "This is the perfect time to do it! We've got Ian and Leonard that love Charlie too much to cause any harm (plus they're always trying to be peaceful first before anything else) and now with the Blood Moon Pack having connections with us through Katy. It takes both the Alpha and Luna to declare official war. Katy isn't going to want to do that, even if Owen is dumb enough to try."

"For once, he's got a point," Sam said. "There's enough strong connections with the packs that we shouldn't have to worry about war as much as we have in the past."

Actually, Ed was right. The main reason why they had been so worried about war was because of the Blood Moon Pack. They had gotten into plenty of wars with them before. The Harvest Moon Pack had always been peaceful, even before the Crescent Moon Pack was.

And now they finally had someone from their pack who was mated to them. And it was to the Alpha.

If that wasn't a sign from the Moon Goddess that they had the green light, he didn't know what was.

"Okay," he said. "I'll bring this up to the rest of the council first. But we can only push a little farther. I'm not going to push our luck."

"It's going to be difficult getting your dad to agree on this," Tyler sighed.

"Don't worry about my father, or Liam for that matter," he said. They had seen just how much damage the rogues could have done to the pack just by what had happened to Alistair. They may be wary of this plan, but he could convince them. "The only thing I'm worried about is Alistair."

"Why?" Ed asked.

"Because I need him for the push," he said. "And he still hasn't fully gotten down the warrior link." He had been needing more Frontline Attackers for a long time now. And Alistair had trained well over the short time that they had worked to get him out of the mindset that he had before. But no one had ever trained him for the warrior link. And that was one of the most important things when they battled.

"I think it might be worth the risk," Ed said. "He's fought well with the warriors even when he didn't have the mind link. And we're only pushing a tiny bit. This might be a good test for him."

"There's also the fact that he knows that area more than any of us," Tyler mentioned. "He was in that area before coming to our territory. And he's keen on watching his surroundings."

"We'll have to see," he said. They didn't stay in the gym for long after that. There were way more things to do now. And as much as there was a weight lifted from his shoulders after finally coming to this conclusion, there was also a hint of worry.

This was going to be one of the riskiest things he would do as the Alpha. He hoped that it wouldn't blow up in his face.

CHAPTER 36:

The Push

"I'm not going to be that far," Alistair told him. He loved the way his mate held him when they were alone. "And it shouldn't take that long either."

"It's going to take the whole day!" Nick complained. "Do you realize how worried I'm going to be the whole day?"

"I'll come back," he promised. "We have the wind on our side."

"I don't want to lose you, Alistair." Nick sounded so sad when he said that. He could tell that he was thinking about the last fight that he was in. But he had grown and learned since that fight. And, most importantly, he wasn't going to be alone.

"You are never going to lose me." He kissed him gently on his lips. "As long as I have you, I will always come back home."

Nick was his pull, after all. He wasn't going to ever leave him. Even if he wound up getting kidnapped and brought halfway across the planet, Alistair would find him. There was no way that he would ever stray from him.

The warriors had all been called for this. It was more than just a training day. It was their first test to see how easy it would be to push for more territory. And the Alpha had made sure to set up as many precautions with it as possible. There were a set group of warriors that were coming with the Alpha to push the territory borders. The rest were on guard for the entire day, just in case the rogues saw this as a chance to try and attack from a different point.

Nick had walked him to the area that they were all leaving from. Many of the warriors were walking with their worried mates and families. He could tell that Madeline's mate was worried for her as well. She had an excited look on her face though. He was glad that he wasn't the only one who was ready to finally do something other than train.

He hugged Nick one more time, hoping that it wouldn't be enough to make others suspicious. Nick still hadn't wanted to tell anyone about them yet, and he wasn't going to push him to. He just wanted to hold him one last time. Thankfully the man didn't fight with him on it. Alistair could feel the worry radiating off him.

"I'll be back, Bakshir." He mind linked with him. He could feel the man smile against his shirt.

It was dawn when they all departed for their endeavor. It had been a while since Alistair had ran like this. He hadn't needed to since he came to the pack. It was nice to feel the cool morning wind comb through his fur. It was probably going to be a hot day again, but he had the shade of the trees to help him.

The Alpha had personally asked him if he would be in the party that pushed the territory lines. He told him that he didn't have to if he didn't feel like he was ready. But Alistair knew that the man had wanted him to go. He appreciated that he asked him rather than ordering, but he was happy to go along with him. And he was excited to fight alongside the pack. He had grown to like these warriors that he had trained with.

The only thing that he was worried about was the warrior link that they had been trying to teach him. That was the one thing that he couldn't seem to grasp onto. Madeline had told him that he needed to leave it up to nature to solve. He was hoping that this might be just the thing to help him with it.

He had a good feeling about this, though. As much as everyone else seemed worried, the wind gave him comfort. And the moon was shining the night before, as she spread her good blessings onto their pack.

Summer was always a bright season, for both the sun and the moon. The trees were a vibrant green as he ran through them. They showed their strength through their size alone. But the warriors were different from the trees. They varied sizes. Some were large, like the Alpha, while others were small, like Ray and Desmond. Each and every one of them had their own strengths and weaknesses. And Alistair had been able to witness all of them as they each trained him.

It was so different from how he was trained before. Instead of giving orders and yelling if he did them wrong, they taught through action. They were right next to him, teaching him what he had done wrong and showing him the correct way to attack. He had no idea how simple training could be.

It took him a while to stop trying to shield other warriors from blows. That was the main issue that they saw in him. As much as it was a good thing to protect the pack, they told him that warriors shouldn't be shielded that way. When there were enemies around, and one was lunging at a warrior, the best course of action was to attack the lunging wolf, not shield the warrior. That way no one has bad wounds other than the enemy.

The only ones who act as shields sometimes are the defense, and that's only in the case that they aren't able to attack the wolf first. However, since he was going to simply be a Frontline Attacker, he was strictly told to not defend. That was not his job.

The former Alpha, Max's father, was the one left in charge of the pack while they were gone for the day. It was interesting that there were so many former alphas of this pack that were still alive. In his old pack, the only time there would be a new leader was if the old one had died. It had happened more often than not.

The Beta, Tyler, was in charge of the defense of the borders while they were gone. He was accompanied by the Delta as they balanced their responsibilities between each other. The team that was going to push the borders had the Alpha and the Gamma. It was a strange balance in leadership that made sense even though it didn't seem to at first.

The ones in the front of the group were the Frontline Defenders. They were there just in case one of the rogues decided to try and attack them. The way that they ran was so that there were defenders all around the group. The Attackers were in the middle, with enough room to jump out if need be. There were also the trackers that stayed out in front, just in case they caught onto an unfamiliar scent.

But the one at the very front was the Alpha. He lead them to the borders of the territory, like a general leading his soldiers to battle. The red in his fur shimmered in the few rays of sun that made it through the groups of leaves that shaded the forest.

It wasn't until they left the territory that he felt it. The pull that he had from Nick had gotten stronger with how close they had gotten, it threatened to force him back over the territory lines with every second he walked away from it. He had to focus though. He would be back.

Looking around, he could tell that the rest of the warriors could feel it as well. Without the Alpha leading them to their destination, they would be in too much pain being this far away from their family and friends. The Alpha was what gave them drive to continue on with their mission.

He opened the mind link, but no one was talking. It was all feelings that they were going through. He wanted to connect with them, but he had a feeling that it would only distract him from their mission, so he decided that now was not the time to try such things.

They were told that they were only going to push the borders five more miles. It would give them more defense so that they could protect the small city better and keep the rogues from getting far into their territory.

The trees on this side were familiar to him, though. He remembered not many months ago when he first heard the trees through the wind. They told him that there was a fight for peace. That was why he trusted the packs around the area. A fight for peace didn't mean with the rogues that plagued them. Alistair soon found out that it was a peace for the packs.

Even though the Alpha for the Blood Moon Pack had seemed hostile, he could tell that the man did not want a war. He didn't know what had happened between these three packs, but they all had one wish that they all shared: a wish for peace and prosperity, without bloodshed.

Alpha Max had put him and Madeline in charge of helping them get through the uncharted territory without getting hurt. Madeline was best with her nose to the ground. Alistair used his ears to listen to the wind. Together, they worked to slowly weave through the trees that they had only known for a short time.

Everyone was silent at the time. They were tense, waiting for something to happen. There was peace for the majority of the journey. Half the day had passed as they charted through the territory and started to mark it as theirs.

Then there was a shift in the wind. And a figure that Alistair could barely catch with his eyes.

"Rogues," was all he had to say through the mind link, and everyone was on the alert. He knew that there were plenty of the warriors that had better eyesight than him, because it didn't take long for one of them to attack.

Alistair didn't stay in that one spot for long. There was something that he smelt that caught his attention. And it wasn't something that was good.

"Alpha."

"What?"

"I smell the scent of another alpha," he told him. He had already started running after it. He had learned through training that if he spotted an enemy the best thing to do was run after them to be the first to attack. The other warriors would be there to back him up when they caught up with him.

But he didn't like this. An alpha rogue was worse than any other. They were far more brutal too. If they didn't kill him now, then they were going to be dealing with more issues from him in the future. And he didn't like the feeling he was getting from him.

The scent was disgusting. The rogue had a metal smell to him that stuck in his nose as if it was an attack all in and of itself. He used it to lock onto his target. He wasn't going to let him go. His instincts were telling him not to.

He could feel Alpha Max catching up with him. He was faster than Alistair, and it seemed as if he caught onto the scent shortly after he told him of it.

A scream of a woman pierced through the forest. It almost stopped Alistair in his tracks. He immediately wanted to help her. But he was on a mission. He needed to find this alpha before anything else.

"I'm going to find out where that came from," Max told him. *"You keep following that alpha. Hurt him as best as you can, but run if you are losing the battle. I don't want you to get injured."*

He followed the order, grateful that someone else was willing to try and find the source of the screaming as well. But he wasn't sure if he was going to catch up to this rogue. This stranger was fast, possibly faster than Alistair. It angered him when he thought about losing the rogue.

His instincts kicked in, pumping his legs as the wind told him that this wolf was dangerous. He didn't like that it was so close to their territory either. He followed him left and right, every movement that the grey wolf made, Alistair matched it.

It lead him to an opening in that forest, one that was in the territory that they were trying to mark as theirs. It was an opening that Alistair had only seen once. But it seemed as though people had moved there.

And then he saw her.

Bloody and battered, the woman screamed again as wolves dragged her with a chain wrapped around her neck. Max was already hot on their tail.

And Alistair was still hot on the strange alpha's tail. He thought that he had gotten too distracted. But he used this time to jump on the grey wolf. He scratched him all across his back before the wolf threw him off.

There were too many rogues there at the moment. Their fury was almost visible. Their eyes only showed darkness.

Alistair thought back to the last fight that he was in. There were far more of them now than there were in that fight. For a second, he thought that he was alone again. He thought he was simply just a traveler trying to save an innocent human again. And he feared that he wasn't going to be able to make it out this time.

"Alistair," Max linked with him. *"Stay with me!"*

His head snapped over to where his Alpha was. While Alistair was being cornered by all the rogues that were in the clearing, Max was fighting off as many as he could just a little bit further. He could feel that the other warriors were on their way.

He couldn't fight them all. He would surely die if he even attempted to snap at them. Instead, he slowly backed away, letting them think that they were cornering. He needed to buy time.

It wasn't long before one lunged at him. He prepared his body for the pain, and was surprised when he wasn't feeling it. Ed had caught the wolf in the air, starting the battle that they were waiting for.

There weren't too many warriors that had gone out on this adventure. Max had only let the best of them come. Even though the rogues outnumbered them, it didn't take long before most of the enemy was wiped out. Alistair aided in the attack as soon as Ed had made the first move. All he needed was to make sure that the others were here.

It didn't last long. Most battles don't when it came to wolf fights. When they were found to be victorious, they all silently celebrated their accomplishment. Alistair liked that he could feel their pride. He was slowly getting used to the warrior link through battle alone. It was through that link that he thought to buy some time before the rest came. They worked as a team, rather than the individual warriors.

"Stay still," he heard Max say. He looked to find him in his human form, tearing the chains off the woman that he had heard earlier. The chains made the metallic sounds of freedom easily when he broke them apart.

From the smell of it, the chains must have been made of silver. Her skin looked as if it had been burnt from under them.

"I'm going to take you somewhere to get help, okay?" The Alpha looked concerned for the woman. She truly looked as if she had been beat and tortured to near death. It made him shiver just looking at her.

"No!" she cried. She clutched Max's arm and looked at him with desperate eyes. "Forget me. Please, if you have a heart, save my child!"

"Your child?" he asked. Alistair hadn't smelt a child the whole day.

"Please!" she begged, her voice coarse as she coughed. Tears were running down her cheek. "His name is Eric. He has two different colored eyes. Please, save him. They have him! He's only five."

That shook all of them to the core. From the look of this woman, they could only imagine what these people would do to a small child. Alistair's visions of his past threatened to come out. He fought against them this time. He did not have time to dwell in his past right now.

"We need to get you cared for," Max picked the woman up. "What's your name?"

It was too late to even figure out her name. Her breathing became raged and her eyes wide with fear. He could hear her heartbeat going too fast for her to survive. Before Max could even start running, the woman lied dead in his arms.

There was some silence, as the man put her down. She had been covered in her own blood, with slashes all over her body. It was a gruesome sight.

"These were the same one's that Herb, Jackie and I barely got away from," Madeline spoke. They were all circled around the Alpha as he looked at the limp body. "I can tell through their scent alone."

"These rogues have been here a long time," Max told them. "They have plagued us for a long time. It seems like we weren't the only ones that they had hurt."

"What should we do?" Ed asked.

There was some silence which Max looked like he was thinking deeply about it. His purple eyes were filled with rage, but something held that rage in. He had controlled his emotions in the brief quiet that the forest had.

"Bury her," he told them. "We can't follow after them right now. Not when we haven't secured our borders. We'll find her son when we start attacking them more."

He didn't like the idea of waiting to fulfill the dead woman's wish, but he understood why they had to. They would risk their pack by venturing further into the territory. Above all else, they had to keep their pack safe. Without them, they were nothing.

They listened to his orders and quickly finished up their duties. There was just one more spot to mark before the territory would be theirs. Max and them were the ones to finish it, as Madeline and Ray dug a hole so that they could give the woman a proper burial.

He had never felt this feeling before. As soon as the last part was marked, and there were no longer enemies in the land, he could feel it expand. The mind link that they shared as warriors soon connected with the rest of the pack. He could hear the sighs of relief as the rest of the pack had been waiting for them to come home. It was the most amazing feeling that he had ever experienced.

The ones that were with Tyler and Sam were ordered to guard the new territory. Some of them were dismissed. The Alpha's party was ordered to get to the infirmary, so that they could get any wounds checked on.

"Alistair!" He heard Nick's voice in his head. It was only mid-afternoon when they all were sent back to the infirmary. *"Are you okay?"*

"I'm fine." He was happy to hear his beautiful voice in his mind again. It made him want to run towards the pack house faster. *"I told you I'd be back."*

"How'd it go?" He sounded so excited. *"You have to tell me everything!"*

"I have to go to the infirmary first."

"What?!"

"Just a check up, Bakshir." He chuckled as he changed into his human form. They went to the training room first, so that they could change. Thankfully, none of them had gotten hurt too bad. Alistair's wounds had already started healing.

"Alistair," Max called him while they were changing. "What did that alpha wolf look like?"

"He was a grey one," he answered immediately. "I was able to sink my claws into his back, but that was just about it."

"Alright." He combed through his hair with his hand. Then he turned to the rest of the warriors that had come back. "Good job, warriors. We safely secured one of the most key lands to defending our territory. Head to the infirmary and then take the next three days off."

He made sure to shower before heading back to the infirmary. It had been a day of many scents. Some that he didn't wish for anyone else to pick up on.

He could still see that woman when he closed his eyes. He prayed to the heavens that she would be with them, in peace. And that they would find her child. He only hoped that they found the boy before they hurt him.

CHAPTER 37:

Musicals and...

"Okay, so." Nick brought some popcorn out. "We're having a musical night."

"Musical?" Alistair looked at him quizzically. "Those are movies where they sing, right?"

"Yeah!" He sat next to him on his sofa. His little apartment was the perfect size for him and had all that he needed in one room. His bed was in the corner, right next to the window that he had learned to love staring out of. But, when you walked into his room, the first thing that people saw was the little living room set up that he had made. It was perfect for movie nights. "I'm guessing you've never seen any of them, so I've brought out the best of the best."

"Sounds exciting." The albino smiled at him. It didn't take too long before he felt his arm wrap around his shoulders. "Did your father do any of them?"

"I mean, he did some plays of them." He shrugged. "But he was never in a movie. It wasn't his style."

"That's a shame," Alistair pulled him closer. "It would have been interesting to hear how movies like these are made."

It had only been a day since he had come back from the territory push that Max had done. Nick had heard the pack having mixed feelings about it. Knowing Max, though, he had taken everything into consideration. It just didn't help that he had wanted Alistair to come with him outside the territory. It was nerve wracking enough with Max unable to be in the pack link during that day. Without Alistair, Nick had felt lost and bored all over again.

He had done his best to pass time with Charlie, though. He was just as worried about Max as Nick was about Alistair. When they came back, it was the most relieving thing he had ever felt. Charlie jumped into Max's arms as soon as he saw him. Nick just ran into the infirmary. Alistair had told him that he was ordered to let the doctor check up on him.

He told him that there had been a battle. It scared him that there had been that many rogues so close to their territory. They were just outside of the borders by Gila City. And that alone terrified Nick. If it weren't for Max pushing to gain that territory, they would have just kept coming.

"Oh, there's a Behind the Scenes section to most of these." He held up the DVDs of all of the musicals they were going to watch. "Katy and I have watched these all so much we could almost rehearse every line."

"You and Katy used to watch them all?" Alistair had always seemed curious about Katy whenever he asked. He wasn't quite sure why, but it made him a bit uneasy. After what Owen had done just by him talking to her, he wasn't sure if Alistair was going to be angry with Katy now that he knew how close they were.

He snuggled into the man. He didn't want to worry about him being possessive of him right then. He just wanted to enjoy the day off that they both shared. He was going to be on the patrol after his break, and Nick wasn't entirely sure if he was going to be able to see him as much as he got to now.

"Yeah." He pressed play on the movie. "My father was a big fan of musicals as well. A lot of our family movie nights involved musicals. If we complained he would make us practice one of the dances that they were doing in them."

"That's a strange punishment," Alistair chuckled. Nick loved to hear him laugh. It was such a low one that it vibrated through his whole being. Everything about the man made Nick want to be as close as possible to him. And, when they were alone like this, it felt like absolute heaven.

"My family was full of them." Nick smiled. "You should see how Barry and George punish their kids."

It didn't take long to realize just how easy it was for Alistair to get lost in the TV. He had saved up for a nice one to mount up in his room. Him and Katy watched movies enough that the greater size was definitely worth it. Alistair seemed to act like a kid when he saw the pictures on the screen. Nick would have thought that he was completely gone if it weren't for how tightly he still held onto him.

Some time through the first movie, they had laid down on the couch, watching it. He rested his head on the man's arm while his other one had been wrapped around his waist. It was one of the most relaxing things that the man could do. And Nick always needed time to relax with all the tension that the pack was building up. The man had buried his nose into his hair, of course. Alistair always wanted something to do with his hair. Nick still couldn't get over it.

Oh, and he loved popcorn. Nick was already excited for showing him other seasoned popcorn, or kettle corn for that matter. It was fun showing him new foods.

"What's your favorite song from this one?" Alistair asked, still holding him. The credits were rolling, but he was too comfortable to move away just yet.

"Singing in the Rain," he said. "I love the free feeling that it has to it."

"Do you like singing in the rain?"

"No," Nick laughed. "I'm afraid I'm not the most confident when it comes to singing." He wasn't that bad at it. It was another thing that his parents taught him when he was younger. He just didn't think that he had a really unique singing voice.

"Would you sing for me?"

"Maybe." He smirked before getting up. "The next one is Katy's favorite: Mama Mia."

"I'm guessing it has a lot of love songs?"

"Yeah, why?" He suddenly started to worry a bit. Was he dragging Alistair into something he didn't want to do that night? Would he have rather gone to sleep? "Do you not like that kind of stuff?"

"Nick, I think you of all people should know that I love things like that." He chuckled. "I just thought it seemed to fit her from what you told me."

"Alistair." He paused before putting it into the DVD player. "I'm not forcing you to watch these movies, am I?"

"No." He shook his head. "I liked the last movie."

"We could always do something else if you want to." As much as he had wanted someone to watch these all with again, he didn't want to watch them with someone who didn't want to.

"I want to watch these with you." Alistair smiled at him. "I've never gotten to have a night like this."

Nick shook his head. He shouldn't have doubted that he wanted to do this with him. The man was a teddy bear, of course he'd want some reason to curl up with him for the rest of the night. He put in the movie and went back to the couch. As soon as he did, he was snuggled up with Alistair. The man knew exactly how to move his arms to where he could fall right into them without even trying.

He didn't know why he was feeling this way right now. He should be happy that he has someone to watch all of these movies with; someone that he could spend all his days with. But, for some reason, he felt sad. It wasn't as bad as he felt before he met Alistair. It didn't come out every day anymore. But today it seemed to.

"Nick," Alistair whispered in his ear. "Are you okay?"

He wasn't sure whether he liked how well this man could read him, or whether it annoyed him to no end. He didn't know whether he wanted to talk about this. He was honestly hoping that the movies would help him get in a better mood, or that being close to Alistair would. He was going to have both of his days off with him this time. He should be happy that he got so lucky work wise.

"No." He rubbed his face. He hadn't been okay all day, if he was honest with himself. It was just one of those days where you wake up and you feel down. It didn't help that he was dreaming about Katy. They used to always be able to bring each other out of days like these. Whether it be through teasing, or just hanging out and watching movies, they would make the day great by the end of it.

"Do you want to talk about it?" Alistair was rubbing his torso. Nick's back was pressed up against him as they both laid down on the couch in front of the TV. He had saved up a year or so back for some comfortable furniture for his apartment. He was proud of himself for it. His apartment was the hang out spot of the century, as long as there weren't too many people in it.

He remembered when Katy had to talk him out of getting a disco ball for his place. She had to give him a lecture on just how useless it was and that his room wasn't even big enough for him to enjoy it. If he got annoyed of her, he would bring up the disco ball just to mess with her. She looked hilarious when she was annoyed at him.

"No," he said. "I'll be fine." He was kind of hoping that he would feel better after watching these movies. It worked before. But now all they seemed to do was bring up memories of the best friend that he couldn't even talk to anymore.

What place doesn't have cell service nowadays?!

"Nick," Alistair's voice interrupted his thoughts again. "I don't think you're going to be fine."

Great. This was reminding him of Katy too. She never let things like this go. If he was upset, he had to tell her. It helped him a lot with his issues in his childhood, just like it helped her when he pushed for her to tell him what was wrong.

"Don't worry about me." He squirmed in his mates hold. The man only held onto him tighter. "I'm just in a whiny mood."

His mother used to say that all the time to him. It was partially true. He was a kid after all. And kids were always a bit dramatic when it came to the little things. But it didn't mean that it didn't hurt him when she said it.

Yeah. He was one of those kids.

"I don't think you're whining when you say you are." Alistair nuzzled into his neck. "You can talk to me about anything, Nick. I want to be there for you."

He sighed. He couldn't stay annoyed at Alistair. It was like trying to stay annoyed with a giant plush. Everything he did just seemed to comfort him.

"I just miss Katy," he caved. "I haven't been able to talk to her since that dinner."

They still had so much to catch up on. He knew that she was dying to know more about Alistair. And he wanted to know just how that pack was treating her. They had gone from talking every hour of every day to not hearing a word from each other. It was too fast for his liking.

"Her mate seems possessive of her," Alistair said. "But at least you know that she's okay now."

"What if he changes her?" he asked, letting all his doubts come out. "What if the next time I see her, she's going to be just as pompous as him?

I always say that Katy will straighten him out or help him see that omegas are more than just servants, but..."

"But you don't know," Alistair finished for him. "And that's what your worried about?"

"That and the fact that I may not get to talk to her again."

"The Moon Goddess picks the mates for everyone for a reason," he told him. "She doesn't give them a mate that won't help them grow and be stronger. But that doesn't mean that their whole personality will change."

"What do you think about Owen?"

"He's young and stubborn," Alistair answered him. "But it seems as though he's willing to try and change a bit for Katy. I could tell just by how he listened to her when she yelled at him for snapping at you. I doubt that him getting service in his manor was his idea either."

"It's so ridiculous that they didn't have that." He shook his head in disbelief. "That means they couldn't even go on the supernatural databases to look up any information they didn't have."

"They're a more traditional pack, from what I'm guessing." Alistair nuzzled into his neck again. "But they're willing to change. That's a good sign."

"I know." He sighed. "I just miss her."

"I know," Alistair said. His low voice could barely be heard through all the hair that he had insisted Nick let out of its ponytail. "I'm sorry, Nick. I'm sure she's just as sad about not hearing from you as well."

"I'm sure her mate absolutely loves that." He rolled his eyes. He was trying to think nicely of the Alpha, but he didn't really like getting yelled at for doing absolutely nothing wrong.

"Maybe the Moon Goddess will help him work on his jealousy then," he said. Nick didn't know how, but his words were helping him. He didn't think anyone other than Katy could make him feel better when he was in these moods. He just got grumpy about everything, especially if people tried to figure out what was wrong with him. But Alistair just calmly talking to him was soothing.

"Are you jealous of Katy and I?" he asked. It was another thing he had been worried about since he had seen just how angry Katy's mate had gotten. Was he crazy for having a friend who wasn't the same gender as him? Was it not normal to be that close to someone without being intimate with them?

"No," Alistair told him. "I have no reason to be."

"Why?" he asked. He really just wanted to know what was going on in Alistair's head right then. The movie played in front of them both, but Nick didn't remember a single thing of it. He had been so lost in his thoughts and then in the discussion with him.

"Well, I think about it this way." The man gently turned him around on the couch so that he could face him. His eyes had a sparkle to them. "Have you ever held her like this?" He hugged him tightly.

"No," he answered. He was enjoying the man's embrace and the playfulness in his tone.

"Have you ever kissed her?"

"No."

"Then what do I have to worry about?" He smiled at him. His red eyes showed nothing but love for him. It was something that Nick had never seen before. "That's why I don't mind you talking about her, and I'll never force you not to talk to someone. I love you."

Nick didn't know what to say. Somehow, Alistair had managed to take all of his insecurities away. He had slowly chipped away at every one that he ever had, and replaced it with happiness.

He kissed him hard. Having Alistair as a mate was more than he could ever ask for. And he hadn't even asked at all. The man just kind of popped up when he was least expecting it, and dove right into his heart.

The kiss didn't stop. Neither of them wanted it to. They both just melted into each other, creating a heat that was almost foreign in him. The deeper the kiss went, the more Nick moved to be closer to him. His arms were around his neck, and his legs were tangling into his mates. He didn't know what was compelling him to do all of this, but he couldn't stop it.

There was a low growl that came from Alistair's chest. He was pressed so tightly against him that he felt the rumble in his chest before he heard it. He loved it. The sound only made him want to make him do it again.

Alistair moved to be on top of him on the couch. He was being buried in nothing but bliss at the moment. The man's hands were slipping under his shirt to rub at his sides again. The spark from them were making all of his senses heighten. Every part of him was begging for more.

It wasn't until Alistair met his waist with his own that he finally realized what was going on. It shocked him to the point of finally breaking that kiss that they were sharing.

"Alistair," he gasped. His brain was only partly working at the moment as his body was slowly taking control of his being.

"Do you want me to stop?" the man asked. He had froze above him, showing fear in his eyes. Nick didn't want to see that. He wanted to see the dark irises of his expand, like he knew that his was doing right now.

The lack of friction anywhere on his body was driving him mad. Alistair was going to move away, but he hooked his legs around the man's waist to try and bring him closer.

"No," he answered. He shamelessly worked his hips to create the friction that his body desperately needed. "I need you."

That was all Alistair needed. His body slammed into his, pressing down on him. Nick had no idea that anything could ever feel this good. But it wasn't enough. For once in his life, he needed more than just friction.

"Alistair," he moaned. With the kiss being broken again, the man had decided to move his attention to Nick's neck. Which was only sending more waves of pleasure through him.

"What do you need, Nick?" he asked. The hot breath on his neck along with his low voice were sending shivers all through him.

"More," he moaned again. He had never felt this needy about this before. "Please."

He was glad that the walls of this manor were all thick. With how loud he was, there was no way they wouldn't have already woken someone up.

Alistair obliged quickly. Within a few seconds he was being picked up and brought to the bed. When they collapsed on it, the man quickly worked to slip off all of their clothes. As soon as he took off his shirt, Nick's hands went to move across his chest. Those red eyes were now almost completely dark. He could see the lust in them, and he was sure that he matched it.

Alistair's hands had traveled lower than they had before. They teased him with how slow they were going, but, as soon as they got there, they worked fast. They massaged him and held onto him as tightly as possible. He was desperate to bring back the friction that they had when they were on the couch, but those hands held him still.

"Stay still for just a second longer," Alistair whispered in his ear. "I don't want you to get hurt."

"You would never hurt me," he said back. His voice was very breathy and not consistent at all, but it was audible at least.

"Exactly." He kissed just below his ear. The second seemed like an eternity. He was close to begging him at this point.

Then he felt those hands work their way inside him, something slick on them. Another gasp escaped him as the man brought him more and more waves of pleasure. He could tell that Alistair was just as wanting as he was. His scent alone said it all. It was a warm scent that he had no idea how to describe other than aromatic ecstasy.

It was turning him into a mess.

He tried to push his hips into them more before they left him. He was surprised that he was still like this right now. Any other time he was even a little aroused, it would take a few minutes to take care of it and that would be that. This time he was getting sent deeper into his desire.

Alistair still had ahold of his hips that he was desperate to move. He quickly moved them ever so slightly, before he leaned his own down to Nick's. It was easy to tell that it wasn't his fingers entering him this time.

It wasn't comfortable at first. Alistair slowly pushed into him, giving light kisses everywhere his lips were able to go. He couldn't say he didn't like it, though. His mate had a way of making everything feel good. His hand had actually moved to the thing that had been dying for friction ever since they got onto the bed.

And then he hit one spot that had Nick seeing stars.

He had no idea that something could ever feel so good. His mouth had a mind of its own as it moaned at every single movement the man made. Nick's hands were digging into Alistair's back, trying to cling to him, cling to this moment, for dear life. The longer this went on, the faster Alistair went. It sent wave after wave of mind-numbing pleasure that he had no clue his body could even handle.

He was so close. He hadn't been this close for this long in his entire life. Both of them were in sync with each other. It was a foreign dance that he hadn't realized that he knew the moves to until now.

Alistair had been kissing his neck the whole time, trying to find the perfect spot. It wasn't hard to tell when he found it, because he latched onto it and wouldn't stop attacking it. They were so close to each other, that it wasn't difficult for Nick to find a spot on the man's neck either. The man gave another growl when he found it. The animalistic nature in him was what Nick loved the most at the moment.

Nick was the first to make his mark on Alistair's pale skin. Alistair plunged deep into him before biting down on Nick's.

The release was simultaneous, leaving him breathless. He licked the bite that he made on Alistair's skin to close it, barely having much energy at all. Alistair did the same and then moved off from him. Even though they were half asleep at this point, Alistair still managed to pull him into his arms.

"I love you," he said. He curled up to the man's chest with the little energy he had left.

"I love you too, Nick," Alistair kissed the top of his head. It was the last thing he remembered before drifting off into a deep sleep.

CHAPTER 38:

Once in a Blue Moon

He felt different when he woke up. Alistair didn't quite know why. It seemed like a normal morning. The sun was just waking up from its slumber, acting as a gentle reminder for everyone else. But he didn't want to open his eyes this time. Normally he would listen to the sun's calls, at least to make sure of his surroundings. But there was something stopping him this time. A feeling that he hadn't felt in his entire life.

Peace.

It filled his entire being, allowing him to simply enjoy the moment. He didn't know why it had come so randomly, but it did. And he was glad that he could enjoy the bliss that he was in.

"Alistair." A gentle voice brought him out of the nothingness that his mind had gone into. He felt hands glide along his back. It only made him hold the man tighter.

His memory was slowly returning to him. He didn't want it to, though. At least, not right then. He wanted to enjoy this blissful heaven just a little bit longer. But those hands were coaxing him to wake up. They gently traveled up and down his back. Then to his hair. It was almost as intoxicating as the smells that he was starting to notice.

"How the hell do you wake up when you need to go to work?" Nick asked. His voice was quiet, bringing him back to that relaxing bliss that he was in before. Alistair had nuzzled into the crook of his neck while he was asleep.

"I don't need to go to work today," Alistair smiled. His voice was a bit groggy, but he was awake now. And, remembering everything that had happened the night before, he was glad that he was awake.

"You have the weirdest way of waking up." Nick shook his head. "How do you feel all of that before you even open your eyes?"

"What do you mean?" He looked at him curiously now.

"I mean you have the strongest sense of feeling when you first wake up." Nick's hazel eyes were beautiful in the sunlight. "Is that normal?"

"When I'm in a deep sleep," he answered. He almost forgot that they could sense their feelings after they marked each other. He was still really happy that they finally were able to mate. He could sense that Nick was happy as well. "You haven't woken up like that before?"

"Not really." He shook his head. Neither made a move to leave each other's arms. "Feeling that from you felt like being put in a trance."

"A trance?" He cocked his head a bit. He knew how much Nick liked to see him do that. "What kind of trance?"

"The good kind." Nick laughed. "It felt like I was on a cloud or something."

Alistair just hummed a reply. He was enjoying the mark that he made on the man's neck. It showed right where the shoulder met. It was lighter than the rest of his skin, but it wasn't too obvious. He noticed that the more he nuzzled into it, the more Nick would react to it. He could easily pick up that Nick was enjoying the attention he was giving it.

Being able to feel what his mate felt was amazing. He could sense when he was feeling down or nervous before, but this was much better. It was like being able to look underwater, rather than just from the surface.

Both of their emotions reacted to the other, like two different waves crashing into themselves. Nick would react to what Alistair was feeling, and then he would do the same. It was a conversation on a whole different plane.

"You're such a teddy bear," Nick said. They were still holding onto each other, enjoying the moment.

"I don't have a cute nickname to call you," Alistair said.

"That's because I'm not the cute one."

"Yes, you are."

"No, I'm not."

"Yes, Bakshir." He kissed his mark lightly. "You are."

The man gasped and leaned into him immediately. There was something about marks like these that always made them more sensitive in that area than before. It made Alistair remember everything clearly. He started kissing the mark more, inciting more noises from his mate. He loved every sound that came out of him.

"Wait," Nick said. His voice was weak at that point. Alistair stopped as soon as he heard it, though, just as he had done before. He could sense a bit of fear coming from the man. But it wasn't aimed at Alistair. He couldn't quite pinpoint it.

"What's wrong?" he asked. He looked up again to see those hazel eyes. All of those insecurities of his were now out in the open, and Alistair was on a mission to destroy all of them.

"W-well," Nick stuttered a bit. There was a little bit of color on his cheeks. Those hazel eyes were now darting in every different direction that wasn't his. "I j-just-!"

"Nick." He lifted himself to be hovering over his mate. He held his face to have those beautiful eyes focus on his own. That fear that he had sensed before was growing now and he didn't know why. "Don't be afraid."

"I'm not afraid of you, Alistair." Nick sighed and leaned into his hand. "I'm just…not sure how to say this."

"What are you afraid of?" he asked.

"I-I don't know," Nick went to move to a different position, but he wouldn't let him. He tightened his hold on him just a little bit. If they didn't figure this out now, he was sure that it would come up in the future.

"No matter what you say," he told him. "I will never stop loving you, Bakshir."

He could feel the happiness that his mate had from him saying that. He was sure that the man could sense all the love that he had for him at that moment as well. He never wanted him to be afraid to tell him something.

"I don't know if we'll be able to do what we did last night all the time," Nick said. He looked embarrassed to talk about it. Alistair didn't want him to ever be embarrassed. "There's a slight chance where finding your mate can cure this, and I'm not sure if it will. Then there's the fact that if it does cure it, I still might not be as…active with it as someone like you."

"You're talking about me wanting to have sex with you?"

"Yeah." He let out a nervous chuckle.

And he said he wasn't cute.

"I don't care about how often we have sex." He started kissing right below his ear. The way the man reacted to his kisses were the most amazing to him. "I can wait until the next blue moon if we need to."

"Even after you mated with me?" Nick sounded shocked at that.

"Of course." He kept kissing him. He wanted to wipe all of the man's worries away. "Just because I lived in the wild most of my life doesn't mean that I'm lustful."

"You're acting like it," Nick teased. Alistair just smiled as he kept peppering kisses all along the man's neck.

"You are too," he said back to him. It was Nick who was leaning into every kiss. His whole body was lifting to try and meet his. He had still been hovering above him. And Nick's actions were tempting, to say the least. "Are you sure that it's not cured?"

"Positive," Nick groaned. Alistair could feel the frustration that was now forming inside him.

"How?" he asked. "Talk to me about it. I want to understand."

"It's the most annoying thing ever." He shook his head. "Because every part of me wants you right now, and wants this. Every part except for the most important part."

"Ah." He was wondering why he could barely smell his arousal. If he could smell that, he would have lost himself to the man already. It was demanding, and easily took control of all of his thoughts.

But he could still smell a little hint of it. And it wasn't just from the night before. It was a fresh scent, and it made him all the more curious about this problem of his.

"Can I try something?" Alistair asked. His hands had been enjoying feeling his mate's naked body all over again. Even if they didn't take it any further than this, he would be happy. There was nothing else in the world that he would ever want than just having Nick in his arms.

"What are you going to try?" Nick asked. He seemed curious, but cautious at the same time.

"Nothing too extreme," he told him. "I won't do anything that'll hurt you, if that's what you're worried about. I just want to try something."

"O-okay," he stuttered.

Alistair hadn't heard him stutter before. As much as it was cute, he wasn't sure if he liked him talking like that. He only seemed to do that when he was really scared or nervous about something. Alistair never wanted him to be scared or nervous around him. He would protect him from everything and everyone with his life if he had to.

He met his lips with his own before anything. He wanted Nick to relax a little. He wanted him to be comfortable with this. Nick was the complete opposite of how he was last night. Instead of clinging and begging, he was awkward about almost every movement. It was like he wasn't sure of his own instincts that were trying to take over.

He broke the kiss and started traveling to his jaw. His hands moved along his sides, massaging everywhere they went. He could feel Nick melt into his arms as he continued. It was easy to see that he was enjoying the attention at least.

Then he moved his hands to his inner thighs. He didn't get a chance to explore that smooth skin before. Nick moaned just a little when he teased him. And that smell got just a little stronger.

Alistair trailed kissed down his neck until he got to the spot he marked him. He was always drawn to that mark now. When he kissed it, Nick gasped again and weaved his hands into his hair. He loved it all. Every sound that he made; every way he moved. He loved everything about his mate.

His hands slowly moved up along his thighs. He could sense the worry that Nick was feeling about his actions. He wished he could just kiss them away. Right before he got to the point he wanted to, he stopped.

"You can tell me to stop at any time, you know," he said. "I won't get upset by it."

"No, I-!" He was stuttering again. Only this time, he seemed to be flustered in a different way.

"You what?" Alistair asked.

"I don't want you to stop," he admitted. His voice was small when he said it. He sounded so vulnerable.

Alistair left no more room for talk. He moved back up to his lips and kissed him passionately. His hand went to his penis simultaneously. It moved a little at his touch, but was still mostly limp. He could feel Nick's frustration. He was about to cry again. Alistair didn't want that.

"Shh," he soothed him. "No matter what, Bakshir, I love you."

Nick seemed to calm down a little at that. He wasn't sure if this was going to work. But, even if it didn't, he still wanted him to enjoy it.

He started to massage him, slowly moving his hand up and down. It took a little while, but his plan was slowly working. Soon Nick was moaning into each kiss. His slim hips were moving up to meet with his hand with every thrust.

The smell of Nick's arousal was enough to drive him mad. He used the lube that he had the night before and put some on his free hand. Nick's body was just as needy as before with all the coaxing he gave it. And he was caving into the way that Nick was moving under him.

"Alistair!" he moaned his name. His legs were going around his hips. They were strong compared to the rest of his body. They hooked onto him and would not let go.

He couldn't say it didn't drive him wild.

He worked his fingers into him quickly. Thoughts weren't quite forming in his mind. They were replaced with everything that his senses were picking up about his mate. Every touch; every sound that he made. The taste of his mouth when he claimed it as his. A part of him never wanted this to end. He wanted to forever live in this moment, just to be able to see Nick like this more. He was beautiful.

But time never stopped for anyone, and they both had needs. He took out his fingers and moved his hips in the best position. He entered him slowly, just as he did before.

He was going to keep going slow, so as to not hurt him. But then Nick did something unexpected. He leaned into him and kissed the mark that he had left on Alistair's neck.

"Mine," Nick said, his body urging him to move faster. He was but a slave for him after that. It sent wave after wave of lust that he had never had to go through. His once controlled movements were now faster and wilder.

A part of him worried that he was hurting his mate, but the man proved him wrong when he moaned like he did, and pushed his hips against him. It only made him go faster, and deeper. The deeper he went, the louder his mate became. It was an intoxicating dance that he was easily becoming addicted to.

With one last thrust, he finished deep inside him. Nick finished at the same time, laying limp under him after it.

"I didn't think it could ever feel that good," Nick said, his voice light and breathy.

"Me either." He smiled. He laid down next to him and pulled him close to his chest. Nick clung to him immediately.

"I don't know how you did that." The man shook his head, still trying to catch his breath.

"I could smell your arousal a little when you were first telling me to wait." He kissed the top of his head. His black hair was tangled, but still as soft as ever.

"Really?"

"Yes," he told him, "That's why I wanted to try something."

"You're the only person I've ever really been this open with about this stuff," Nick said. He moved up to where his head was just below Alistair's chin.

"I want you to be open with me about everything," he told him.

"I'll try," he sighed. It was nice seeing him so relaxed. He had been so tense the past few days.

They laid there for a little bit longer before he picked Nick up and got out of the bed with him.

"Where are we going?" Nick laughed at his spontaneity.

"To the shower." He walked swiftly across the small room. "I need to perfect getting all the conditioner out of your hair."

"That." Nick laughed harder. "Is an impossible mission."

"Nothing is impossible," he told him.

"I still don't know why you're so obsessed with my hair."

"It's beautiful," he answered. "I've never seen such beautiful hair."

"You're so weird."

He enjoyed pampering Nick like this. Having him in his arms was therapeutic all in of itself. The man brought him the peace that he had been looking for his whole life. Not even his mother could give him peace. She could only tell him vaguely what he needed to do in order to achieve the peace he had so desperately wanted.

"Alistair?" Nick brought him back to the present.

"What?"

"What are you thinking about?"

"You." He smiled. He couldn't stop smiling at the man.

"Do you always have to say things like that?" Nick chuckled and hid his face as the shower hit his back.

"You're blushing." He coaxed his lover's head to come back up, "Aren't you?"

"No."

"Liar," he teased. It was fun seeing Nick like this. When he was around anyone else, he was the out-going chef that loved to tell stories. This side of him was reserved strictly for Alistair. And he was enjoying the softer side of him.

"I'll answer that truthfully if you're able to get all the conditioner out," Nick teased back.

"I'll take that challenge."

CHAPTER 39:

Trouble in Paradise

"You've got some kind of voodoo magic." Nick ran his hands through his hair. "This is the second time you've been able to do this."

"It's not as difficult as you think." Alistair smiled. It was only three days into their vacation, and Nick was enjoying the alone time that he was able to have with his mate.

"Did you forget the part that not even a firehose could get all of the conditioner out of my hair?!" he asked. He couldn't believe the man could even get all of it out the first time, let alone do it again. "Not even my mom was able to get all of the conditioner out when I was just a kid!"

"Does this mean you're going to let me wash your hair more often?" Alistair wrapped around him in the bed. He couldn't get enough of being in his arms.

"This means that you're going to be the only one washing it now." He was still patting his head to see if there were any spots with conditioner. The man had done what a firehose couldn't.

They had been having a lazy vacation for the most part. Nick didn't exactly want to walk around the manor at the moment. He didn't want to deal with everyone's reaction to him finally being mated. There was going to be so many questions. And, as much as he was a socialite, he didn't want to have to explain this over and over again.

Some things were just better left without an intricate explanation.

Of course, he knew that most of the pack were told about him. He was a chef, which meant that Aldi would have had to been told that he was going on his vacation. Nick had decided to talk to Max directly instead when he asked for the time off, just because he really didn't want to hear what Aldi was going to say.

But, once Aldi knows, the kitchen knows.

And once the kitchen knows, the pack knows.

He was just hoping that he could enjoy the week before facing everyone. It was already embarrassing in general that it took so long to find his mate. And the few that knew of his condition were going to be wondering if it had been magically cured because of Alistair. They were going to ask so many questions.

Truth be told, he was pretty sure that he had been cured, just in a strange way. He wasn't as lustful as he had been the first day. And he was sure that he wasn't going to be able to do all of that with Alistair all the time. But the man really did know how to bring it out of him. And, when he did, it was like burning in a volcano.

But he was never, ever, going to tell anyone that. Not even Katy. And he knew that she was going to be wanting as much information about it as possible. She loved hearing about stuff like this when talking to the maids. Nick would always walk away when she started asking those questions. He hated hearing them talk like that.

"What are you thinking about?" Alistair started kissing his shoulders. Everything he did sent an electric current through him. It was a great distraction from all of the things that he wasn't looking forward to doing when he got back.

"All the questions that people are going to ask when we get off our vacation." He sighed.

"We still have a long time until then."

"You're the one who always talked about the bigger picture."

"Exactly." He continued to scatter kisses all over his shoulders and neck. Nick was enjoying all the pampering that Alistair was giving him. "And, in the near future, you won't even have to worry about something like this. It'll be a thing of the past before you know it."

"And so will this vacation." He sighed again. He didn't know why he was thinking about all of this. They were still in the beginning of their days off and he was already thinking about it ending. He had done that a lot as a kid when he was in school. The vacations just always seemed to move by faster than any other time.

"So, it's best to enjoy it while it lasts," Alistair held him tightly as he said that.

"You're turning me sappy, you know that?" Nick smiled. Alistair was the only one that he could talk so freely to about anything. Even with Katy he had his limits. Alistair just found his way through all the doors that he had kept shut, and took away all the fears and worries he had.

"I think you were always sappy." The man chuckled. "You just didn't let that part of you out."

"So, it's my fault that you made me sappy?" he teased. He loved joking around with him. It made everything more fun. While these vacations for new couples were mainly just to be bed-ridden and talking about each other, Nick and Alistair's had some fun times where they just kicked back or went out.

They had gone out in the middle of the night to have fun. It was the best way to not have to talk to most of the pack members, and Alistair's skin hated the sunlight anyway. They would either walk around on some of the hiking trails or run as wolves along the forest. Alistair really seemed to love playing with him in his wolf form. As much as it was annoying because the wolf kept nipping at his tail, he loved just how happy Alistair was with just a little bit of playing.

When he asked him why he kept going for his tail, he just said that it was too fluffy not to. Nick was going to tell him to stop, but the white wolf looked too cute when it was playful.

"Yes." Alistair laughed again. The way he laughed felt like a vibration through his whole being. "All your fault."

Nick actually really enjoyed their late-night adventures. Working in the morning shift, he never was able to stay up too late. This vacation reminded him of the days when he was a kid and he would stay up really late on the nights that he had no school.

Recently, they had started sneaking into the kitchen at night. Nick really wanted to cook for him, so they started coming when it was closed and he would use one of the work stations. So far, he still hadn't found a dish that Alistair didn't love.

"Maybe I just love your cooking," he had told him. Nick swore he said these things just to try and make him blush. It was hard to hide it when Alistair picked up on his emotions so easily.

Herb and Jackie had somehow sensed that they were in the kitchen that night, because they popped in there. Jackie had gotten a pregnancy craving and was too afraid to ask someone where to get it. So, Herb had brought her to the kitchen. Nick couldn't be mad at the couple. They didn't ask too many questions, and they mainly just talked about how their mate bond was like.

"You guys are still the weirdest mates in the history of werewolves," Herb had told him. He, of course, was scarfing down some more food. The man was always talking and shoveling food into his mouth. "I mean, that was the calmest way I've seen mates when they find each other."

"They aren't weird, Herb!" Jackie smacked his arm. "Not every couple acts that way when they first see each other!"

"Oh, come on, Jackie!" He argued back. "Even Madeline ran to her mate when she finally saw him! And that woman has never showed any romantic interest in anyone. You can trust me on that."

"Wait," Nick stopped them. "Is that what you two were bickering about that morning?"

That was when Nick had found out exactly how early the couple had known about him and Alistair being mates. He was glad that the couple were understanding and didn't tell anyone else.

"We figured that it was best to just wait until you guys announced it," Jackie told him. "We just didn't think it was going to take this long until you did."

"I would have actually won that bet with Madeline," Herb chuckled. "I almost made a bet with her that Alistair was going to take his time."

Nick was glad that they treated this so normally. Because the kitchen workers were going to act like this was some sort of reality TV show and start asking him about everything.

He was glad that Herb and Jackie were in their pack now. They really seemed to fit in well. Herb had already made some friends with some of the other builders in the pack. And there were so many women that were expecting that Jackie made friends easily. There were even some women her age that were pregnant.

It happened more times than people thought.

They actually planned a spicy curry night before they left. Nick was excited about that. Just because this was supposed to be a vacation with your mate didn't mean that he couldn't hang out with others as well. Alistair seemed to love the idea anyway. And he was still wanting to take up the spicy challenge.

He was a goner.

But, right now, they were planning on relaxing in their room and watching more of the movies that Nick had brought out. Alistair was enjoying holding him and moving him from the bed to the couch. He felt like he was being lazy, but the man wouldn't let him get out of his grasp.

He didn't think he could be this happy, if he could be honest with himself. When he was with Alistair, it just seemed like he could do anything or say anything without worrying about what others would think. They could go from a serious talk one minute to joking the next. And he seemed to understand Nick in a way that no one else did.

And he could get all of the conditioner out of his hair.

"Are you still trying to see if there's any more in your hair?" Alistair chuckled. He nuzzled into the damp hair, right where his neck was.

"I don't believe this is real," Nick joked. "Are you sure you didn't use magic or something?"

"I'm positive." He kissed his neck. He had wrapped them up in a blanket on the couch. They were supposed to be watching a movie, but Alistair was distracting him from pressing play.

"Alistair." He smiled as the man continued kissing down his neck, stopping only when he got to Nick's mark. "We just took a shower."

"I won't do anything," Alistair promised. "I'm just enjoying the moment."

A knock on the door interrupted whatever moment they were going to have. Nick would have used his nose to see if he could recognize the scent, but all he could seem to pick up on was Alistair's at the moment.

"I'll see who it is," Alistair said. "You stay here."

He watched as the man untangled himself from him and got some shorts. He was too comfortable to argue with him, so he just stayed in the blanket.

That was, until the door got opened.

"Hello." He heard Alistair say.

"Why are you here? Where's Bakshir?"

Oh shit.

"Mom?!" He sat up from the couch and looked over it. "What are you doing here?"

Alistair moved to the side as both his parents walked in. His mother was the one that scared him the most. She had completely changed from the sweet old lady with a thick accent to the angry Indian mother that he had grown up with.

"Why is he in your room?" She spoke in Hindi. She loved doing it when she didn't want anyone hearing what she was saying.

"Isn't it obvious?" he asked, speaking Hindi as well. It was common for their family quarrels to be in that language. It didn't exactly make him like the language, unfortunately.

"Why does he smell like you, Bakshir?" Her eyes were cold as she spoke. "Are you even wearing anything under that blanket?!"

"I wasn't expecting visitors," he told her. His voice got a little smaller as he spoke this time. "This was my vacation to be with my mate." It was still strange to say it. And she was the last person he wanted to tell, if he was being honest. Nick was hoping that he could tell the rest of his family first so that they might be able to support him a little more when he did face her.

"He is not your mate, Bakshir!" she yelled at him. "You are supposed to be my gift! You are supposed to be mated to a beautiful woman so that you can grow a family of your own! You are-!"

"Stop!" he yelled at her. It was the first time in his life that he had raised his voice at his own mother. He just couldn't take another lecture from her. Not about this; not about Alistair.

"Don't raise your voice at me!" They were still yelling at each other in Hindi. At this point he wouldn't be surprised if the whole manor could hear them.

"Can't you be happy for me?!" He looked at both of his parents. His father was silently letting his mom yell at him. "Why does it always have to be me that has to do better?! Why do I have to be the one that goes on to dance on Broadway? Why do I have to marry someone who I can have kids with, even though I haven't even been able to get turned on until now?!"

"Bakshir, that's not what I meant!"

"Yes, it is! Neither of you could ever be happy that I wanted to stay here to follow my dreams of cooking. You wanted me to be the one to make a difference in the world! What's so wrong about staying here? Why can't you just be happy that I'm finally happy?!"

Tears were already starting to fall. This was supposed to be a good day; a good week. He just wanted to enjoy something. But, if there's one thing that anyone should know about families, big or small, it was that they weren't perfect. And his family was showing that at the worst time.

"Because the Moon gave you to me for a reason, Bakshir," she told him. "She made you strong so that you will listen to her when she calls and do as she says."

"And what makes you think that she doesn't want me right here?" he asked. "Why does this always have to be me leaving and going on some crazy adventure? Do you really want me to leave that badly?!"

"Of course, I don't, Bakshir!" she told him. "But the Moon Goddess does not want you to be mated with him." She pointed to Alistair. The poor man looked so confused as he tried to figure out what they were all saying.

"No, mom." He sighed. "*You* don't want me to be mated to him."

"Come on, Myra." His father gently grabbed his mom's shoulders. He seemed a little more understanding about the situation. Although he was sure that it was because of Nick's oldest brother. "Let's leave this be for now and talk about this later."

"There's nothing left to talk about," his mother huffed. She stormed out of his room, her hair quickly falling out of her bun with all the shaking she had done. His father looked at him apologetically before following her back out of the door.

They always had to be hard on him. For some reason, even though he was the baby of the family, his parents always thought that he was going to be the star that they had been trying to make. As much as he loved dancing and telling stories, he never wanted to do it as a living. He loved to cook. Aldi had seen his interest in it as soon as he was put on kitchen duties when he was just a boy. As soon as he started learning how to make his favorite foods and watch as people enjoyed it, he quickly found just how much he loved doing it.

They hated that he wanted to be a chef. It wasn't like they thought poorly of Aldi, they just wanted more from Nick. At first, he thought he owed it to them to try and do what they wanted him to. But he couldn't live a lie. He would have been ten times more miserable than when Katy left.

"Nick," Alistair sat on the couch behind him, wrapping his arms around his waist. "What were they telling you?"

"That I could do better." He sniffed. "In life in general."

"Is this why you wanted to wait to announce us being mates?" He was holding Nick so close he was about to break down on the man's chest.

Nick just nodded. He couldn't stop the tears that were still streaming down his face. He buried his face into Alistair's chest and let it all out. Alistair didn't ask him any more questions. He just laid there with him and rubbed his back.

He should call Fred, his oldest brother. He was the only other one of his siblings that had turned out to be gay. He wondered how he got back on their mom's good side. He wasn't even born at that time, but he heard from his siblings that it didn't really go that well. He wished that he could ask what happened so that he could get out of this mess. He didn't want his own mom to be angry with him over something he couldn't even control.

"Families are always complicated." He sniffled. The tears were slowly drying up. "There's always something that threatens to tear them apart."

"They both still love you, Nick," Alistair told him. His low voice was soothing. "If it helps, I don't think they're going to be mad at you forever."

"I hope not." He shook his head. "I don't know if my mom's ever going to talk to me ever again." That's what really hurt him. He could take all the nagging about how he could do better with his life, but he wasn't going to be able to handle not talking to them.

"It'll turn out alright," Alistair soothed him. Nick clung tightly onto him as he slowly started to calm down. "I think she was more shocked than anything."

"I'm sorry, Alistair." He rubbed some tears out of his eyes. "I shouldn't have kept it a secret from everyone for so long. I should have just told my family slowly. That way, it would have never come to this."

"You don't have to be sorry." Alistair moved his hand away from his face and replaced it with his own. He lifted his face so that their gazes would lock together. Those ruby eyes were as gentle as ever. "I wasn't in a rush for you to announce it, just like I wasn't in a rush to mark you. It never bothered me that you wanted it to be a secret."

How did he wind up getting a mate like Alistair?

"What did I do to deserve someone as good as you?" Nick smiled at him. The man never failed to make him feel better, even after his mother decided to burst in and cause a scene.

"I ask the moon that question about you every day," Alistair smiled back at him. "You truly are the love of my life."

CHAPTER 40:

Totem City

"Are you sure you can't come with?" Charlie asked. They were both getting ready for the day. "I'm sure Wynona would love to talk to you again."

"She only invited the other Luna's," Max told him. He didn't quite look too happy about this plan himself. "If I went then Owen would throw a fit about not being able to go."

"Can Nick come?" He really just wanted someone else to come with. Max had gotten Ed to come just as a guard, but he really just needed someone to help him calm down when he was heading out. And Ed wasn't exactly the person to do that.

"I'll see if Aldi's okay with it." Max kissed his cheek while adjusting his tie. He had a bunch of paperwork and other duties ahead of him that day.

This was the first time he was going to leave the territory without Max with him. Wynona had started calling him ever since they met. She was really nice, and he actually found himself enjoying her phone calls. He was able to give her some pointers for paperwork as well. It wasn't much. He just told her how their pack had organized it all. Other than that, though, they both talked about many different things. She loved talking about her baby, and Charlie loved hearing about him. There was a whole point during that day in Sun City where he had simply held the boy in his arms. He was so adorable. He just fell asleep as soon as Charlie had put him up to his chest.

When they got on the conversation of Katy one time, she suggested that they all have a get together one day, just the Luna's. Since the Harvest Moon Pack was in the middle of the three pack's territories, it was decided that it would be on Wynona's side of town. Charlie was just happy that he was able to convince her to not choose Sun City for the event.

Instead, they picked Totem City. It was an old city well known for its good food and expensive shopping stores. He was sure that Katy would love the idea. He was definitely excited to see her again. It would still be a while until they got service over at her house.

Nick wound up being able to go. Max had apparently told Aldi that Nick was to 'accompany the Luna for the day'. The way that Nick repeated it was hilarious, and Charlie was already happy that he could bring the man along.

He didn't seem that different now that he was mated. He looked a little more tense around everyone though. Charlie had heard that his mom wasn't exactly happy with his mating. Charlie didn't get it, though. Why wouldn't you just be happy that Nick was happy? The chef really did look happier, especially when he was with Alistair. They both shined brighter with each other around. It was adorable to see.

He wasn't sure how the man was going to be when they left the territory, though. They were all going to be completely cut off from the rest of the pack as soon as they left. Of course, they had the Alpha's permission to go, so they weren't going to be broken off from the pack, as would usually happen when you got out of the territory lines. But the three of them, Ed, Charlie, and Nick, wouldn't be able to mind link with the rest of them.

"So," Ed started up the car. He was going to be the driver for all of this, of course. "Who's all ready to go to Totem?"

"Let's get going." Charlie chuckled. He kissed Max one more time before leaving. It seemed like Alistair was giving Nick a quick goodbye as well. They were just going to be gone for a day, but it felt like it was going to take months until they were going to get home.

Ed blew Emily a kiss before he started driving off. A part of him was jealous that their relationship was so relaxed as it was. They were okay with being away from each other, even if it meant completely off the territory. Charlie could already feel the anxiety kicking in.

It was just one day. He could handle one day. And they were mainly just going to be shopping and eating and talking. The day should fly by. It was just the roads that wouldn't.

"Hey Nick," Ed said. It had been quiet in the car for a little bit. "I forgot to congratulate you, by the way."

"I don't need any congratulating." Nick rolled his eyes dramatically. "And you knew before everyone else, anyway."

"Oh man!" Those golden eyes looked back at them through the rear-view mirror. "That was so difficult to keep a secret! Do you know how many times a day I talk to Clara?"

"I'm glad you did." He leaned back in the seat. "My mom just about had a heart attack when she found out."

"Oh, that reminds me!" Charlie looked at him. "Were you able to get ahold of Fred?"

Nick had told him about what had happened with his mom during his vacation. The woman wasn't talking to him right now, and it really seemed to be bothering him. He told Charlie that his oldest brother, Fred, had dealt with coming out to his mom before and had a similar experience.

At least that was the one thing that he didn't have to deal with in his childhood.

"Yeah." Nick sighed. "He said that there was a whole year that she didn't talk to him after he left with his mate. But that could have been because of him being so far away."

"She'll get over it," Ed said. "If she got over it with Fred, she'll get over it with you."

"I know that," he told him. "I'm just worried about the 'when' part."

"I could always talk to Fred's pack and see if they'd be willing to bring him down to visit," Charlie suggested. "Maybe he could talk to her a little."

"It would be really fun if all of my brothers and sisters could come home to visit," Nick said. "We really are a blast at parties when we're all together."

"Don't make that wish too loud, Nick," Ed joked. "Knowing Charlie, he might actually try and do it."

"If it would help him out in any way," Charlie answered. He felt horrible that Nick had finally found someone who made him happy, and his mom was giving him the silent treatment for it. Alistair really seemed to take care of him. Why couldn't she see how happy Nick was with him? Especially after how depressed he looked when Katy had first left.

"Don't worry about it," Nick shook his head. "Our family reunion isn't for another two years, and that's all that we could ever really plan as far as getting everyone to come together. They all have their own lives and jobs to deal with."

"Then maybe I'll just get them all on a group call or something." He smiled at the thought.

"If you do that then we won't be able to hear anything." Nick laughed. "They'd all be talking over each other."

"Do you think they all know by now?" Ed asked him.

"Probably," Nick said. "My mom probably called them all up screaming about how I'm gay."

"That's not right." Charlie frowned. He really wished he could figure out some way to help him. Nick was one of the closest friends he had.

"It's not like they're going to start hating me." Nick gave him a small smile. "I'll be alright, Apple. Don't worry about me."

He was going to argue more, but Nick really didn't look like he wanted to talk about it. This outing wasn't supposed to wind anyone up, anyway. Wynona had actually planned it so that they could all get away from some of the stresses and just have fun. She had even gotten Lenny to watch over their baby, which actually made Charlie sad. He would have loved to carry that adorable baby everywhere with him. He was such a calm baby too. He just fell asleep whenever he was being held.

Ed was great at distracting the both of them of the fact that they were off from Crescent Moon territory. The car ride didn't seem so long with him around. Nick actually told a few stories himself. It didn't take long before they were already in the city.

It was beautiful. The buildings were adorned with flowers every-where, and all the stores were connected together, to make it look like one long walkway.

"The stores here are super expensive," Nick warned. "I've been here with Katy once to try and find a party dress for her. Let's just say they were way over our budget."

"Don't worry about budgets," Ed said. He smirked as he held up a black card. "One of the perks of driving you guys is that I get to enjoy the perks of Max's black card."

"His black card?" Charlie looked at him with a curious expression. Why would Max give him that? That was a card that they only used if they needed to. And they didn't need to get a bunch of things for this get together.

"Yup!" He was almost jumping in his seat. "One of my strict orders is to make sure you both get to enjoy yourselves as much as possible."

"Oh, I don't really need anything," Charlie told him. He got his clothes from Leah and Sam. That was enough for him to be happy with. He didn't want to take things that he didn't need from the pack. And, as much as Max had been born into wealth, that money also went to the pack if they truly needed it. It was a credit card, but also a security fund for if they needed something to fall back on.

"Oh, this is going to be fun!" Nick was looking just as excited as Ed. And Charlie was slowly starting to realize that he was outnumbered in his decision. "Apple, you gotta have some fun with this thing."

He just shook his head and got out of the car. He wasn't there to shop. He was there to see Wynona and Katy. They planned to meet up at a small café to start their day off. He was worried that they had gotten there a little too early when he heard a familiar squeal.

"Nick!"

"Katy!"

They both ran towards each other and hugged, although Nick seemed a bit more cautious about hugging her for too long. Charlie saw that he wasn't the only one who had brought someone with him. There was another warrior that had been with Katy from the Blood Moon Pack. She was stone-faced and emotionless as she watched Katy's every movement.

"It's nice to finally see you again, Charlie." Wynona came up to him. She was a hugging person as well. It seemed that all three of them had that trait in common. He caught up with her as they walked back to the table to order their breakfast. Katy and Nick were catching up, of course.

"You got marked!" Katy squealed again. Charlie was having a blast overhearing them.

"Yeah," Nick told her. "It's kind of something that mates do, Katy."

"Does that mean that you're feeling better now?" she asked. "In that department?"

"Why do you always have to ask the most embarrassing questions?"

"Because you get embarrassed about this stuff too easily!" she argued back. "And it's a legitimate question!"

"I think I'm beginning to understand what you mean by them being like siblings," Wynona told Charlie. She seemed to be having fun watching the two friends catch up as well. "They remind me of my sister and I talking about our husbands."

"I told you," Charlie chuckled. "But I'll admit that I did ask them if they were a couple when I first met them."

Wynona was a breath of fresh air when it came to the Cooper family. They were always bubbly and talkative to the point where they would bring up anything and everything about whatever person or thing they were talking about. Wynona was simply happy with talking about anything. Charlie was surprised with how many times she had called him for advice on certain papers.

"You have no idea how much Ian has been bugging me to have him call you instead," Wynona told him.

"I'm pretty sure he'd get too distracted to finish his work." Charlie laughed. Ian was always looking for an excuse to not do work, especially when it involved paperwork.

"Well, I finally got him to stop after I told him that I was going to tell Ben just how annoying he was being," she said. "He shut up really quickly after that."

"I'll bet," he said. Ian and Ben were a good couple. Ben always knew how to reign Ian back in when he needed it. And, besides all the hugs and closeness that him and Charlie shared, Ian still did really love Ben. He could see it in his eyes.

"You know, Charlie." Wynona smiled at him. "I'm so glad I got to meet you. With all the drama that goes on in that household, and how serious the other packs are, you and Katy are the complete opposite."

"I don't know." Ed popped into the conversation. He made his voice slightly louder. "I'm pretty sure Katy is dramatic!"

"I am not!" Katy yelled back to them. Nick was snickering right beside her.

"Hey, that reminds me," Nick said. "Did you tell Owen about your little crush on Max when we were in high school?"

"I DID NOT HAVE A CRUSH ON HIM!!!!" She smacked his arm. Her mane like hair was flying around her face.

They all enjoyed the laughter that came. The morning had gone by fast as they hopped from store to store. Ed decided to act like Max when they were there, and would buy anything that Charlie seemed to show even a slight interest in.

"I'm on strict orders to spoil you." Ed winked at him. "You know Max wouldn't have it any other way."

"Oh!" Wynona grabbed his attention. "I didn't get to see your ring, by the way! Now I get to congratulate you in person."

"It's not that big of a deal," Charlie said. He wasn't used to getting this kind of attention from people. "We still haven't figured out a date yet."

"I'm invited too, right?" Katy asked. Both her and Wynona were looking at the ring that was on his hand.

"Of course, you are." Charlie chuckled. "You and Nick were some of the first friends I had in the pack."

"This is going to be so much fun!" Katy squealed. "I love weddings so much!"

"Maybe I'll get you to help me plan for it then," he told her. "There's so many things to think about for it."

"I could help!" Wynona looked at him with excitement in her blue eyes. "You already helped me enough with all the paperwork that we do. I would love a chance to return the favor."

"Only if you want to," he said. He didn't want to push her into doing it. "I still haven't thought about what color theme to go with. And that's one of the first things to figure out."

"Why not green and purple?" Katy said.

"Jeez!" Nick shook his head. "And here I thought I had a bad sense of style when it came to parties."

"Gold and silver?" Wynona shot out.

"Too Christmassy," Katy said. Charlie just sat back and enjoyed watching his friends get themselves in the same rut that he had run into when planning this."

"White and Black?" Nick asked.

"That screams dinner party." Katy rolled her eyes at him. "And that's too traditional for Charlie and Max. Knowing Max, he's going to want to go all out with everything for Charlie. It's not going to be traditional."

They continued like this for the rest of the morning. As much as he was already homesick, Charlie was enjoying the time they spent here with them. It really was nice to get away from all of the stress that his life had been the past few months. So many things were going on at the moment that it seemed like time was flying. It was already in the middle of summer.

Then Wynona stopped talking for a minute or two. It only took a second to look at her dilated eyes and see that she was mind linking with someone. After that second, she sighed and looked at them with sad eyes.

"I'm sorry," she said. "I may have to cut this short."

"Why?" Charlie asked her. "Is something wrong?"

"Nothing too crazy," she told him. "Something just came up with the pack and they need me there to help deal with it."

"Ah." He nodded his head. "I know that feeling."

"That happens so much in the Blood Moon Pack," Katy said. "I swear, the first week of being Luna I didn't get any rest."

"I'm so sorry guys," Wynona said. "I had tried to make sure that everything was going to be perfect for the pack while I was gone, but something came up."

"Don't worry about it," Charlie told her. "I'm sure Alpha Owen will be happy to have his Luna back home early anyway. I know Max will be happy."

"You and Max are so adorable," Katy said.

"Here," Wynona said. "Why don't I drive with you guys to the border? The least I can do is escort you out of our territory."

"How are you going to get a ride back?" Katy asked. "And which car are you going to go into?"

"I can just take a taxi back." There was a sparkle in the woman's eyes. "Don't you worry about that. And I think I may take your car, since Charlie's ride seems a little full."

"We could both go to highway 27 and say goodbye there," Ed suggested. "There's a fork at exit 53 that splits off in both directions."

"Sounds like a great plan." Wynona was practically jumping at this point. Charlie was glad to see her so happy.

They got into their vehicles and started driving. He was a little disappointed that it was going to be leaving so soon. But he was excited to see Max's reaction when he got home. He was probably worried sick about him, even though he had been texting him all morning. He even got a picture of all of them and sent it to him. They were all wearing some funny hats.

He was going to text him to tell him that they were coming home early, but that would ruin the surprise of it. Instead, he watched as Katy and Wynona's car drove in front of them. Nick seemed happier now that they had gotten out. He was glad that his friend wasn't as stressed as he had been.

It didn't take long until they got to exit 53. Katy's car had flashed its lights at theirs to signal that they were pulling over to say goodbye. He was almost about to take off his seatbelt, them merging onto the exit.

But before either of them could stop, Ed swerved the car. Charlie didn't know what was going on at that point, but he knew that it wasn't good. There was a flurry of crashing and loud sounds that were coming from every direction. The whole car shook and he heard some familiar voices as well as stranger's.

Something grabbed him and started pulling. As much as he was afraid, he couldn't call for help this time. The thing that had grabbed him put something over his mouth. His eyes were too droopy for the panic to keep them up.

They closed and left him in a deep sleep.

CHAPTER 41:

Invisible Mask

Nick didn't know where he was. He woke up in a dark room, that felt like hard wood on the ground and walls. He could barely make out anything, but he knew that something was wrong. He tried to recollect his memories.

They were having a shopping day with Wynona. She was a nice woman, but he was happier to be able to see Katy again. She was complaining about all of the work that she had to do and the things that she was trying to change in the pack. He was worried about her body guard overhearing them and thinking badly of her, but she had said that her bodyguard was trained to never tell a soul what she was saying or doing during her outings. It was interesting to hear that the Blood Moon Pack had such a thing.

Then Wynona had to cut it short. He hated that. As much as he missed Alistair, he wanted to talk to Katy more. They still had so much catching up to do. And she told him that there were some setbacks to getting the service in her new house. All of it was frustrating. But Nick decided that it was best to just be happy that he had even a little bit of time with her. And Owen wasn't there to get jealous of their friendship either.

It was nice that Wynona wanted to see them out of her territory. Charlie didn't quite know everything about pack politics, or he would have known that her doing that was a sign of great respect and trust. She's a Luna after all. It meant that they all trusted each other with one of the most important members of the pack.

It was probably why Owen and Max agreed to it. They wanted to show that they wanted peace between their packs. And what better way than to have their Lunas hang out with each other?

But something happened when they were leaving the territory. Ed noticed it first and tried to swerve out of the way. Nick remembered watching him shift into his wolf form right in front of him. The highway was empty, surprisingly. They had beaten the lunch rush by the looks of it.

When he finally realized that they were under a rogue attack, he didn't even have time to change. He wasn't that great of a fighter, but that didn't mean he wasn't going to try. Before he could, though, they had grabbed him. And no amount of thrashing in the world could get them to lessen their iron grip on his limbs.

He must have passed out somewhere during his struggle. They must have given him something. His head felt cloudy and heavy.

Nick looked down. His eyes had finally adjusted to the darkness. There wasn't a window in the room that he was in, so he couldn't tell whether it was day or night. But he could see the silver shackles that were around his ankles and wrists.

No wonder he felt weak. Silver was a werewolf's worst enemy. That and wolfsbane. Shackles like these were meant to keep a werewolf from shifting into their wolf form. His had chains attached to them. He looked behind him to see that they were chained to the wall. He lifted his heavy hands up to his throat to feel that there was another band of it around it as well.

Panic surged through him. He wanted to call for help, but he knew that it would only cause more problems for him. They weren't in the pack's territory, which meant that he couldn't mind link with anyone. He was all alone.

The sound of shuffling almost made him jump. He turned towards the sound to see a shadow of a person. A person who looked like they were shackled as well. A groan came from them, sounding a little recognizable.

"Katy?" His voice was weak from the silver around his neck. It was thick and fit around his neck like a choker.

"Nick?!" Her shrill voice filled the room. At first, he was glad to hear a voice that he recognized. But that happiness was quickly turned into more panic.

That meant that Katy was now trapped here too.

"Katy?" Another familiar voice filled the silent room. "Nick?"

"Charlie!" Nick immediately tried to walk towards the sound, but it was too far away. "Are you okay?"

"I think so," his gentle voice answered. "Where are we?"

Now wasn't that a good question. He wondered that himself. Before they could say anything else, though, light came into the room. A door had opened, the light barely seeping in. Against the light was a shadow of a man gazing in on them.

And he smelt like metal.

"Glad to see that you're all awake," the man said. His voice felt like razor blades going down his back. He had never been this afraid of a simple voice before.

A small light came on from a single light bulb in the middle of the room. Nick looked around to see that all of his friends were shackled up just like he was. Wynona was waking up just then to the light. Her long black hair was matted and dirtied.

"Who are you?" Charlie asked. Nick was surprised that he was the first to speak. Those green orbs looked absolutely terrified of the man.

Nick was terrified of the man too. But his reason was completely different from Charlie's.

"I don't think that matters right now, darling," the man said. His turquoise eyes were now solely on the blond. He was only wearing black pants with no shirt on. Scars adorned his muscular frame, showing to them that he had been in plenty of battles before. It was difficult for werewolves to get scars like that unless they got hurt in the same place over and over again. Martha, one of the pack warriors, had plenty of scars from her continuous fighting. The freshest one on the stranger, though, was a long, deep scratch on the man's back.

He smelt like an alpha. That was the main thing that terrified Nick. Alpha rogues were the most dangerous of foes. They fought ruthlessly, and sometimes liked to form their own kind of rogue pack.

But right now, he was more focused on Charlie. His smell was only getting stronger with how terrified he was. And the alpha seemed to be absolutely infatuated with it.

"So, you're the new Luna around here." He lifted the man's chin up to look at him. Nick saw the other hand start to wander down to his sides. "I've been wondering why the Alpha of the Crescent Moon Pack was trying to hide something so delicious in his territory."

"S-stop," Charlie said. The stranger had already put his hands under his shirt.

"You're not in the right place to make demands right now, Luna." The man chuckled. He sounded like a lion teasing its prey that it had trapped. "I wonder how your mate would feel after I'm done with you."

Nick knew where this was going to go. There was only one thing that rogues did with Lunas if they caught them. He knew that Charlie, nor the rest of the ones chained here, weren't going to be able to fight him off. Especially not in these shackles. And he wasn't going to just stop with Charlie. He knew that for sure.

Max had promised Charlie that he would never let anything like this happen to him. After Nick had heard what the blond had gone through in his past, he knew that he couldn't let Max break that promise, even if it wasn't his fault at all.

"I know who you are," Nick said. He made sure his voice was as loud and clear as could be. He knew he couldn't help any of them physically, but there was something else he could do. This was for all the Lunas that were there. Without them, their packs would fall into another rut.

The man stopped his taunting and turned to face Nick. He looked like the exact replica of the person that Nick had only seen drawings of. Minus the scar on his face.

"Who am I, little omega?" He looked down at him, sneering, yet curious.

"You're a Darius," Nick faked confidence by keeping his head held high. "Aren't you?"

"And just how do you know of the Darius family?" He stalked towards him. Nick could see the flashes of anger in those rich blue eyes. He knew that not backing down to an alpha would piss them off. That's what he needed.

"Because Gene Darius was the weakest alpha I've ever heard," Nick smirked. He must have really been good at hiding his fear. Because it was so great that it was almost crippling. But he had to overcome this. If he sacrificed himself for all the Lunas, then he would have an honorable death. And there were just some people worth dying for.

He fell to the ground quickly as pain seared his face. The man had back handed him so quickly that he couldn't even tell until he was on the ground.

"Why do you speak of my father that way?" he growled. He sounded like a demon that was this close to eating his soul.

"Because." He laughed through the pain. He knew that his laughter would only make the man more pissed off. "He couldn't even kill my mother."

Everyone but Katy was looking at him with nothing but confusion on their faces. Katy's expression was one of recognition and fear. She knew exactly what Nick was talking about. She had been close enough to his family to hear this story in detail many times before.

"What are you talking about?!" The alpha's holler was loud enough to shake the entire room. Nick still hid his fear with his invisible mask.

That's what his father had taught him. The thing that you always needed to learn when dancing for Broadway and doing plays was called the invisible mask. You put it on, and you're an entirely different person. It doesn't matter what you're feeling at the moment. You only show the feelings of the character that you need to act out.

He'd have to thank his father the next time he saw him for teaching him that trick. If he was going to see him again, that was. He wished Alistair was somewhere close by. He would save them. So would Max.

"Gene Darius had taken an omega woman during one of his attacks on the Crescent Moon Pack," Nick explained. "This woman just so happened to be pregnant. Gene could have killed her at any time. But he decided to torture her by trying to make her miscarry the baby that had already grown big in her belly. He shackled her in a room like this one and tortured her. It took a week for the pack to find her. But," He smiled at him again. "When they did find her, and the alpha tore off Gene's head, they found that the infant was still alive inside the omega. I'm living proof that your father was too weak to kill an infant."

That was why he was such a sickly child. It was a miracle that he was even born after his mom had gone through all of that torment. He remembered waking up to his mother's screams. She had gotten so many night terrors from that one week of torture.

She had drawn Gene Darius. She had done it so that she could burn it to try and rid herself of the memory. But no matter how upset she was, she just couldn't do it. Every time she looked at that painting, she would cry and lock herself up in her room.

The only reason that Nick had seen it was because of one of those times she had tried to burn it. She ran into her room again and left it on the table. When Nick asked his father, he just told him that he was a very bad man that mom hated to look at. It took a long while until he was finally told the story.

He was the pack's miracle child. A gift from the Moon Goddess.

Pain shot through his leg as he fell to the ground yet again. The smell of metal was filling the room. He had done a great job at getting the alpha good and angry with him.

"My father wasn't weak." The alpha spat at him, pulling him up by his shirt. "You know, for an omega, you have quite a way of speaking to those above you. You're Alpha must be weak himself if he allows his omegas to talk like that to him."

He was thrown into the wall so hard that he saw stars. He had prepared himself for the stranger to grab him again, but he didn't. When his vision returned, he saw that he had gone to a cabinet that was in the room.

"It looks like someone needs to teach you that lesson, though," his voice sent a chill down his spine. "You know. I wasn't too happy when my men brought you with them. After all, what would I want with some dumb omega? But," The cabinet slid closed. "Now that I know what you are, I'm glad that they did."

Nick smelt it before he saw it. It left him more terrified than before. And he didn't think his fear could get any greater.

Wolfsbane. He had it on a whip. It was made into a purple solution, and half of the whip was soaked in it.

That was what his mother had gone through. Her tormentor had whipped her and beat her. He barely gave her anything to eat and would love to find ways to scare her so that she might lose the baby through her fears alone.

He really wished he had been able to talk to her one last time. He wanted to at least let her know that he loved her. He didn't care what she thought of him at the moment, he just didn't want to die knowing that their last talk was a fight.

He should have just held off on mating with Alistair a little while longer. Then he would have at least gotten into this situation with the peace of mind that his mom still loved him. He wanted to hear that one more time.

Maybe if he just thought about all the times that he would wake up crying in his room. His mom was always right there, not even a second after hearing him. She would pull him into her lap and start singing lullabies that her own mother had sung to her.

When he stopped crying, she would kiss him on the top of his head and tell him how much she loved him. No matter what was going on in his life, he had always had his mother to turn to. She would always be there if he needed to cry or just to get a hug.

He remembered the first time he had seen her cry after one of her nightmares. She was on the couch, in the darkness. He was just a kid then, but he went up to her and crawled onto her lap. He sang those same lullabies to her that she sang to him that night. The smile that was on her face was a memory that he would always cherish.

"You are a gift to this world, Bakshir." She held him tightly. "Don't ever let anyone tell you otherwise."

Now he was going to be reliving her nightmares. Their story had circled back to the very beginning. Only, this time, he was lucky enough that his mom wasn't there to watch the agony that he was about to be in.

"Maybe your Luna can learn how to best train you omegas," Darius brought his attention back to the present. He was wearing black gloves while the whip glided through them and onto the floor. It was like a poisonous snake getting ready to attack. "All of you are nothing but worthless heaps of fur, anyway. No one's going to care if you don't come back to your pack."

He was wrong about that. All of the people of the pack cared about each other. Even if some of them had a disagreement. That was why Max had wanted to make sure that no one died from unnatural causes during his reign. He was going to protect all of them, just as his father had done before him.

He had instilled that into Max from an early age: to protect everyone in the pack. Max had felt it so strongly that he even protected everyone in school from bullies. He was like their big brother.

He prayed to the Moon Goddess that he would come soon. But he didn't even know where they were. All he had was his faith. In a pack, faith in the Alpha was the greatest thing you could have.

The whip cracked and tore at his skin. He wanted to hold in his pain. He didn't want to let him hear his agony. But he couldn't stop that. His invisible mask held no match for the burning that was entering his body. He screamed with every slash that tore his skin.

Max had promised to keep the pack safe. But the most important were the Lunas. Without them, their packs would fall into despair. He didn't dare look at any of the faces of his friends as the man whipped him. He knew that they were probably terrified. But he was doing it for them. He would rather die than watch the man do those things to them.

He just hoped Max came before it was too late.

CHAPTER 42:

Silence isn't Golden

"Martha." He brought her to attention right when she walked in. "Did you find anything?"

He had a strange group of people in his meeting room that morning. Martha and Madeline had been on duty to patrol the new area for the past few nights and he wanted to see if they could pick up on anything strange. So far, they hadn't found anything of the alpha rogue that Alistair had spotted when they were first claiming the territory.

"There were some infrastructures from where they were possibly living in," she answered. "But they hadn't been living there for long. It seemed like they were always on the move."

"It sounds like a traveling pack," his dad said. Him and Liam were in the meeting room as well. He needed their advice about this situation. "If they're rogues, that would explain why they've been such a problem for us over the years."

"It would also explain why we haven't already wiped them out yet," Liam said. "Rogues don't keep coming like they have been the past few years. Especially not in groups of ten."

"Madeline." He looked at her. She had proven to be a good tracker, but he needed her for something else at the moment. "You said that you got attacked by rogues before you came here, right?"

"Yeah," she frowned. "It was them. Although, we didn't stick around long enough to see them do something as horrible as what they did to that woman."

"That reminds me." Dr. Button put down a small folder. "I think I may have your mystery woman."

"Give us the briefing, Dr. Button." Liam sighed. "We don't have time to be passing down the folder for everyone to read."

Max was starting to realize just how Liam was as an Alpha during his reign. He liked to see the man more when he was actually willing to work with him rather than against him. Charlie seemed to bring that out of him.

Charlie. He still missed him. He couldn't say no to letting him go to see Wynona. As much as it was dangerous to be going away from pack territory right now, doing this might help their relations with the Blood Moon Pack, since Katy was going as well.

But there was something in his gut that was telling him to make him stay. He didn't want to seem controlling over his mate. And he didn't want to start a fight that could end up like before. But he couldn't shake the feeling that something was going to go wrong.

That's why he told Ed to give him hourly updates. As much as this meeting was important, so was Charlie's safety. Ed was one of the best warriors that he had, as much as he didn't come off as it. And he knew that Katy would be having someone from the Blood Moon Pack come with her to protect her as well.

"Lisa Herring," Dr. Button started. "She was the Luna of the Goldshield Pack. Mated to Jeremiah Herring, who was murdered by a rogue attack."

"A rogue attack?" Max asked. "How far is this pack from here?" He still had that promise that he gave to her before she died. Even if he wasn't an Alpha who had to keep promises, he couldn't disrespect a dying woman's wishes. And a kid shouldn't have to go through whatever those rogues might be doing to him.

"I've heard of the Goldshield Pack," Madeline spoke up. "They were neighbors to the Citrus Valley Pack. They were small, but relatively strong. They all either got killed or disappeared after a huge rogue attack, though. None of them have come back to try and reclaim their territory."

This was another alarm that set Max off. If these rogues were able to destroy a whole pack, even if it was small, then that means they were going to try and do the same with theirs.

He needed to call Leonard and try to get ahold of Owen. They needed to know what they were up against.

"What did the rogues do when you first met them around this area?" Max asked. He needed as much detail as he could. He was planning on racking Alistair's brain soon too.

"They told us to either join them or die," Madeline said. Her voice had gotten a little less confident when she answered. "Obviously, we didn't want to be a part of a rogue pack, so we tried to out maneuver them. One of them were able to get a good scratch at me, though. That's where that wound came from."

"Was one of them an alpha?"

"No." She shook her head. "Not any that we saw."

"He's probably using his underlings to pick up recruits," Liam said. "Considering how many have died by our hands, I'd say he probably needs them."

"That means," Tyler spoke up for the first time. Max would have had him go with Charlie, but he needed his Beta with him for this meeting. "That if we didn't start killing them once they crossed our borders when we did, they would have tried to destroy us already."

Tyler had a point. When Max thought about it, it seemed like the ones that were just running through or that they chased out were scouting the area. It would explain why they were able to get as close to the pack house as they had.

"I'm bringing Alistair in," Max said. "He was the only one who got a good look at that wolf." He hadn't even been able to get a good idea of the scent of that beast. It was strange, and there were so many other smells that the forest had around him that he couldn't focus on it. But Alistair had seemed to have his eyes locked on him. He would have followed the beast all the way to the middle of the uncharted territory if Max had let him. But he didn't want the man to get hurt, and he had other matters to deal with.

It didn't take long for the albino to come through the meeting doors. He had been in training that morning, so he wasn't far away.

"Tell us about the alpha rogue," Max said as soon as the man sat down.

"He was dark grey," Alistair started. "I didn't make out the eyes, as I was behind him the whole time. But he had scars all over him."

Alistair had given them a better description than he could have asked for, but it would have been better if he had seen the rogue as a human. It would have been easier to find in the database.

Scars meant that he had battled plenty before and had survived them all. It made Max all the more concerned about the stranger's strength.

"The most interesting thing about him, though," Alistair continued. "Was his scent."

"What did he smell like?" his dad asked him.

"He smelt like metal," Alistair shook his head at the thought. "I had it stuck in my nose for some time after that. It was strong."

Metal? He had never heard of someone having a metal scent to them. There were welders who had the smell of metal on them, but it was never a scent.

"If it was a metal smell," Martha said. "Then Madeline and I may have found something after all."

"What do you mean?"

"There was a smell of some sort of metal all around that new area," Martha answered him. "It didn't seem natural, but I didn't want to speak my concerns until I knew for sure what they were."

"Martha." Max ran his hands through his hair. "Do me a favor and never do that again. I want to know everything, even if you aren't sure about it."

"Understood, sir." She bowed her head quickly. "My apologies."

"He's trying to mark territory," Liam said. "That's not a good sign."

"None of this is a good sign." Max sighed. "We need to tell the other packs about this information. If they're trying to claim territory, then they'll be trying to push the other packs back as well."

"Do you really think they're the same rogues that attacked the Goldshield Pack?" Madeline asked. Her golden eyes had a hint of fear in them.

"Yes," Max said. "And we all need to launch our attack on them as soon as possible."

He needed to tell Charlie this. After this little outing, he was going to have to tell him that he couldn't leave the pack house until this was over. If they were going to be at war with these rogues, he couldn't have Charlie be anywhere that was life threatening. He was the strength of the pack as much as Max was.

But first he needed to call Leonard. He needed to tell him what was going on. This was something that couldn't be held back anymore, and they all knew it.

It was a good thing that the meeting room had a phone in it. After Max dismissed Alistair, Madeline, and Martha, he dialed up Leonard's number. The man surprisingly picked it up quickly.

"Max!" he said. "How're you doing?"

"Not good," he said. "I found out some more information about these rogues that I think both you and Owen are going to need to hear."

"Is it immediate?"

"Yes," Max told him. "They're starting to form a rogue pack."

That was serious enough for Leonard to listen to him.

"Well," He sighed. "I'm in the middle of a pack issue right now. But I'll try to see if I can send someone over to get Owen. I mean, I could get Katy to give him the message. She should be heading back to her pack right now."

"She's heading home already?" Another spike of panic surged through him. "Is she not feeling well?"

"Ed didn't tell you?" Leonard sounded a bit confused over the phone. "Wynona has to help me deal with something, so we had to cut this outing a bit short."

Oh, he was going to kill Ed.

Come to think of it, he hadn't gotten any texts from Charlie for a while either. He had been texting him that whole morning.

"Are they still in your territory right now?" Max asked.

"Yeah," Leonard said. "Wynona's riding with them to the border, I'll tell her to have them call you as soon as they can. She's-!"

He heard the phone drop on the other end and a groan of pain.

"Leonard!" Max stood up at this point. He wasn't sure what was happening on the other side of the receiver, but he didn't like it.

He heard some shuffling as another person walked into the room that he was talking in. Everything sounded garbled. But he was able to make out Ian's voice.

"Lenny! What's wrong?"

"Wynona," he heard the Alpha say.

"What about Wynona?"

"She left the territory," Leonard told his brother. Max could hear the pain in his voice. If a Luna left the pack territory without permission, it left the Alpha in pain. If it was intentional, then it could sever their bond.

"Leonard!" Max hollered. He needed to act fast. Because if Wynona left the territory, then that meant that Charlie and Katy did too. "Pick up the phone, dammit!"

He must have heard him that time, because he heard him ask Ian to pick it up and give it to him.

"I'm sorry Max, I-!"

"There's no time for apologies," Max cut him off. "Where were they going?"

"Highway 27," he said. "Exit 53."

"I'll be there," he said before hanging up. He didn't have to make any orders to the ones who were still in the meeting hall. They all knew what was going to happen. Tyler immediately followed him out. Max decided to try and call Charlie's cellphone, but it didn't even ring. Ed's rang but didn't pick up. Nick's was the same as Ed's. And now he had to figure out where they were.

What if they were hurt?

"Madeline." He got her attention. She had still been on the third floor, just in case he needed to ask her more questions. Alistair was too. But he didn't need Alistair at the moment. "You're going to be coming with me."

"What's going on?" Madeline asked. She picked up on the sense of urgency easily and quickly followed them down the stairs.

"I need your tracking skills," he told her. Other than Martha, she was the best tracker they had. But Martha was too slow for how quick he needed to be. "This is going to be a long run."

He already sent an order to Sam. He needed his best warriors right then. And the best were his council. Madeline stopped asking questions about it and just followed them as they got out of the manor.

"Max!" Emily stopped him in his tracks. She looked absolutely terrified as she ran up to him. "Something's wrong with Ed!"

That only made his fear rise. Because if something was wrong with Ed, then something bad happened.

"What did you feel from him?" he asked. If there was one thing that a mate bond could do that a pack bond couldn't, it was the ability to sense each other's feelings.

"He got hurt," Emily said. Tears were in her eyes, and she looked close to breaking down. "I couldn't pick up much, though. I just know that he needs help."

"We'll get him back," Sam assured her.

They didn't have much time. As soon as they got outside, they shifted, shredding the clothes that were on their backs. Max used the run to give Madeline and Sam a quick explanation of what had happened.

Their pack wasn't connected to the Blood Moon territory. They were separated by the uncharted territory that Max had been wanting to claim for so long. But they were connected to the Harvest Moon's territory. Traveling there was easy when they were wolves. They ran through the forest quickly. When they got to their neighbor pack's territory, he found out that Leonard had asked some of his warriors to escort them.

They quickly followed them to the highway. Luckily, through Leonard's friends in the city, the exit was completely closed off. He immediately picked up on Ed's scent and bolted towards it.

There were two people on stretchers, when he got closer. One was a woman who had the scent of the Blood Moon Pack on her. The other was Ed.

Leonard had been the first to get there. He tossed Max and his party some clothes that they could change into. It only took Max a second to shift and get the pants on before he ran towards Ed.

"Ed!" He held onto the man's arm. He was being bandaged at the moment. It looked like he had gotten mauled. "What happened? Are you alright?"

"I'm sorry, Max." Those golden eyes never looked so sad then at that moment. He didn't seem like he could focus that well, either. "I couldn't protect them."

"Tell me what happened, Ed," he begged the man. "Where are they?"

"Rogues," the woman on the other stretcher replied. Max looked over to see that she was having to gasp for air. Her ribs were broken and blood was all over her. "They came."

"What did they do?" Leonard asked.

"Attacked." The woman gasped for air again. "Took the Lunas."

"I'm sorry, Alpha," one of the EMT's interrupted them. "But these two need to get immediate medical attention."

"Go," Leonard ordered. He looked at Max with lost eyes. He could see that the Alpha had no idea what to do. And he couldn't blame him. Without their Lunas, they were lost.

But Max wasn't going to lose Charlie that easily. He was going to find him if it was the last thing he did.

"Sam." He looked to his Delta. "I need you to run to the Blood Moon Pack and tell them what happened. Owen needs to know what happened to his mate."

"Do you want me to tell them about the alpha rogue?"

"Alpha rogue?" Leonard asked. His face showed surprise as well as terror. "You didn't tell me that there was an alpha among them!"

"I was planning on telling you during that phone call," Max said. "We just found out this information recently. His scent smells like metal."

"Hey Alpha," Madeline spoke up for the first time since they got there. She had been looking around the cars that Charlie and Katy were in. They both looked like they had fallen off a cliff with how many dents that were in them. "I hate to interrupt, but I found something."

All of them walked over to her. The wreck had blood all over it. It was a horrendous sight. But Madeline didn't bring them over there to show them the cars. She picked up two things and showed them to him.

One was a ring that Max had recognized immediately. It was the ring that he had proposed to Charlie with. All of the garnets and diamonds were still in it and, other than it being dirty, it was in perfect condition.

It took all of his strength not to keel over at that very moment. The fear and panic were trying to paralyze him. He had promised Charlie that he would never let anything bad happen to him. This was his mistake. This was his fault. He shouldn't have let Charlie go. It was too dangerous. There were too many risks.

This was all his fault.

A hand clasped onto his shoulder. He looked to see Tyler's brown eyes meeting his gaze. He must have known that he was panicking, because his eyes showed the strength that Max needed to see. The Alpha wasn't an Alpha without his pack, just like a pack wasn't truly a pack without an Alpha. They all came together to help each other out when it came to things like this.

"What's this?" Leonard asked, pointing at the other item that she held. It was a clump of grey fur that looked to be a bit bloody.

"It must be the attacker's fur," Madeline said. "Smell it."

Max took it and did as she said. The metal smell that Alistair was talking about was strong. It hit his nose like knives to meat.

"The alpha," Max said. He tore the clump in half and handed one of them to Leonard. "Have your warrior's smell this. This is the scent that we all need to follow."

"You think we can find them?" Leonard asked him. He looked just as terrified as Max felt. But he had to hide it. Now was not the time for him to run in fear.

"I know we can find them." He grasped onto the man's upper arm and met his gaze. "And we're going to find them by the end of the day."

He didn't know what that alpha was going to do to all the ones that he captured. All he knew was that he wasn't going to let this hellhound do anything to any of them. He was going to save them.

Or he was going to die trying.

CHAPTER 43:

A Telepathic Call

The screams still echoed long after they were over. They echoed in his head, haunting him with the terror that it was caused by.

He should have stopped him. He should have gotten the man's attention and brought it back to himself. But he didn't like the way that man touched him, or the things he said. It all reminded him of the man who was friends with his parents. They both had the same sickly-sweet tone to their voice. The kind that he knew had poison in it.

"Nick?" Katy was the first to break the silence. The man had left the room, probably bored with his torture. He turned off the light, leaving them in the same pitch black that Charlie couldn't see through before. "Nick, please say something."

"I'm okay, Katy," Nick's voice sounded weak as it came through the darkness. "I'll be okay."

"He whipped you until you were unconscious, Nick!" Katy's voice was a stage whisper as she talked to him. None of them wanted the man to come back. And they were pretty sure that he wouldn't appreciate yelling. "How are you going to be okay?"

"I can last." Nick was breathing heavy as he talked. Charlie knew that he was in a lot of pain. He knew that from the screams that he heard. He never thought he'd have to witness someone being tortured right in front of him.

"You shouldn't have done that, Nick," Charlie said through the shadows. "You shouldn't have made him that mad."

"It was the only way to keep him off from you, Apple," Nick said. He could hear the worry in his voice. "And I'll be damned if I let him hurt a Luna."

"I don't want you to die, Nick," he said. It was getting more and more difficult to talk. After that man was done trying to kiss everywhere on his neck, he had put a thick silver ring around it. It was cold and made it to where he could barely move his head around.

And he was allergic to silver. He could feel his wrists and ankles swell from it. Since it was around his neck too, it wouldn't take long for him to stop being able to breathe.

But he had to fight through it all. He had to last a little while longer, until he could find a way out. He needed to save them, before they all wound up under that very same whip.

"Charlie." Nick's voice came from the depths of the darkness. "Max promised you that he would protect you. That wasn't just a promise that he made, but that the pack made. I'm not going to let him hurt you for as long as I can help it."

"Max also promised to the pack that he would protect all of them," Charlie told him. "No one wants you to die Nick."

"I'll survive," Nick said. His panting was getting worse. "If my mom was able to last these tortures for a whole week, I can last."

He had no idea that his mother had been tortured like that. He didn't even know how Nick knew that the man was this Gene Darius' son. He wanted to ask, but his throat was hurting too much. He needed to preserve his voice for when he really needed it.

"Did that really happen to your mom?" Wynona spoke. It was the first time since they had gotten there. She didn't sound like she was doing too good either.

"Yeah," Nick answered. "My oldest brother was only seventeen at the time. Him and my dad were absolutely terrified the entire week that they were trying to look for her. And, even then, it took so long for her to recover that Dr. Button wasn't sure she would ever be able to walk again."

Charlie shuddered at that. The fact that his mom could survive a week's worth of torture was a miracle if it was anything like what he had just witnessed. But he wasn't sure if Nick could survive a week. He wasn't even sure if he could survive the week himself. He wasn't allergic to silver to the extent where he needed to bring an EPI pen with him all the time. But he could die if he was exposed to it for too long. Especially if it was around his neck. And this kind was strong.

"I'm sorry, everyone," Wynona broke the silence again. "I shouldn't have planned this. This is all my fault."

"No one could have planned for this to happen," Charlie said. He didn't want the woman to feel bad just for trying to plan a day of fun for all of them. "If Max had even thought that there was going to be an issue, he would have never let Nick and I go."

That reminded him. Where was Ed? He didn't remember seeing him after he swerved the car. He prayed that the man was alright. His mind was still hazy when he tried to recall what had happened before they were all brought here.

The door opened again, making them all jump. Even with the little bit of light that the room past theirs brought, it was still enough to blind them.

He really didn't want it to be that man again. Hadn't he gotten enough entertainment? What was wrong with people like this? Why would anyone want to do this? It didn't make sense to him. None of this did.

But the silhouette in the doorway was much smaller than before. When he flipped the switch to turn on the light in the room, they were all blinded for a few seconds. It was only after Charlie's eyes adjusted that he saw a small boy holding a tray in his hands.

The boy was cute. His black hair was curled and frizzy. The most prominent thing about the boy were his eyes. They were both different colors. One was a light blue, while the other was a dark brown. It was more common in animals than in humans, if he remembered correctly.

The poor boy looked thin. He had nothing but rags on. When he focused on him, Charlie noticed that there were cuts and bruises all over his tiny body. And it didn't look like it was from rough housing.

He walked in and closed the door behind him. Those unique eyes showed nothing but fear as he looked around at them. He must not have been used to seeing something like this. Charlie immediately felt bad.

"Hi." He sat down when he talked to the boy. "I'm Charlie, what's your name?"

"Why do you wanna know?" the boy asked. His childish voice echoed a little in the bare room.

"You don't have to tell me if you don't want to." Charlie shrugged. He was trying to make his voice as friendly as possible. As much as it pained his throat to do so, he wanted to calm this boy down. "I just wanted to know who to thank for the food."

The boy looked down at the small tray, as if he had forgotten that he had it in his hands. He slowly walked over to him and handed him a piece of fruit that was on it. Charlie made sure that his movements weren't too quick or too slow. The boy probably thought he was going to grab him or something.

"Thank you." He smiled at him. The boy gave a little smile back. He was adorable when he smiled.

The boy then went around the room, handing the rest of them fruit from the tray. Wynona and Katy tried their best to be as friendly as possible, but they were in pain from the shackles that were weighing them down.

Nick was the one that the boy really seemed scared to go by. Charlie didn't blame him. It wasn't that Nick looked dangerous. He was just so badly beaten. Blood was all over him, soaking the clothes that he had on, which were nothing but rags at this point. His shiny black hair was now caked in blood as well, and his face had nothing but cuts and bruises on them.

"He won't hurt you," Charlie told the boy. "He's just a little too weak to lift up his hands all the way to where you are."

"It's okay, Little One," Nick gave the boy a small smile. How he was able to smile through all of the pain he must be in astonished Charlie to no end. "You don't have to give me anything, I'll be alright."

Don't give him anything? Nick was the one that needed food the most at the moment. His cuts were healing, but not at the rate that they normally would. He knew that the silver shackles must have something to do with it. But his body needed something.

"How are you still alive?" The boy asked him. He looked astonished. "No one has ever lasted that long under Alpha Damir's whip."

"That's because I'm a Moore," Nick answered. He sounded so proud when he said it. "And an omega is a lot stronger than you may think."

"A Moore?" the boy asked.

"That's my family name," Nick explained. "We're a big family. We've all been through a lot."

"Mom used to say that omegas were strong," the boy told them.

"Well, my mom was an omega." Nick chuckled. "And I'd say that she was pretty strong."

"Where is your mom?" Charlie asked. Those small eyes were looking at his again. But, when he asked that, he could see the tears forming in them. There was nothing but pain in them.

"He killed her," he said. It was unsettling hearing an innocent voice like his say something so horrible.

"I'm so sorry." Charlie could feel himself tearing up at hearing that. He could feel the child's pain just by looking at those two different eyes. He wished he could comfort him. He wanted to hug him at least. But the shackles would probably hurt him. For there was no way that the boy was human, not in the place they were right then.

He needed to find a way to get them all out of there. He needed to save this boy now too. There was no way he could leave him behind.

"I'm Eric." The boy broke through the silence.

"It's nice to meet you, Eric." Charlie smiled at him. He was glad that the boy looked much less stressed than when he first came in. Those eyes were getting less afraid the more they spoke to him, and Charlie was glad of that.

The boy handed Nick the piece of fruit and watched as they all ate theirs. Charlie was grateful for the juice that slid down his throat. It didn't help much, but it was cool enough to feel good going down. He was still hungry, but he wasn't going to complain about that at the moment. At least he had gotten some kind of food.

"That's all they would let me give you," Eric said. He looked down as if he was disappointed with himself.

"That's okay," Katy spoke this time. "Anything is good right now. Thank you."

He seemed so serious for such a small boy. But, from what they just found out about his mom, Charlie imagined that he had to go through quite a lot.

Eric was closest to Charlie when the door opened again. That small face looked terrified once more and he scattered to hide behind Charlie's back. He instinctively put an arm behind him to wrap around the boy.

"Where is he?" the stranger spoke. His blue eyes looked demonic as he talked. They scanned the small room that they were in, until those eyes landed on Charlie again. There was something that changed about that face of his. He looked hungry when he met his gaze. Charlie really didn't like being looked at like that.

He held onto Eric tighter. At that moment, he didn't care about what happened to him. He just wanted to keep the boy safe. He didn't know what the man was going to do to him, but he didn't want any harm coming to this innocent little boy.

Damir walked over to him. He tried to stand up, but he was too slow with all the heavy shackles that were weighing him down. The man yanked him up by the chain that was attached to the one around his neck. He gasped for air as the man trapped him in his arms.

"And just what do you think you're doing?" His hot breath burned his ear. And his hands were quickly roaming around his back.

He wished he could say something; anything. He needed to protect Eric. But all he could do was gasp for air. He wanted to squirm away from the man. He could feel just how aroused he was getting with how tightly he was pressed against him. It was disgusting. He wanted to vomit.

"Leave him alone!" Eric shouted. Fear shot through him as he was immediately dropped from Damir's hold. There was a smack as he saw the boy fly across the room and hit the floor.

"Get out of here you little rat!" Damir yelled at him. The boy's face was puffy and red. And there were tears falling from his beautiful eyes. Eric looked like he desperately wanted to help, but didn't know how. Charlie wished he could tell him that he didn't have to try and help them. He was just a boy, and there wasn't much that boys could do in situations like this. He just didn't want him to get hurt anymore.

Eric ran out after that, thankfully. He didn't want the boy to go through more abuse. Nor did he want him to see the abuse that was about to happen.

"Why were you hiding him?" Damir looked at him. His turquoise eyes looked like they had been lit on fire. "Did your Luna instinct kick in? Did you think that you could try and protect him?"

No. But he still did want to try. Because that boy didn't deserve to get hurt.

"You're going to get punished for that, Luna," Damir's voice was right by his ear again. And Charlie couldn't help but shudder as he feared what was going to happen to him.

Chuckles interrupted the man's speech. He looked over to see Nick watching their kidnapper with nothing but hatred in his eyes.

"He gets punished?" Nick spat at him. "You still haven't been able to kill an omega, Damir. What makes you think you could punish a Luna?"

Damir seemed shocked that Nick knew his name now. His attention was now completely off from Charlie once again.

He couldn't handle this. He couldn't handle watching his friend get tortured anymore. The screams were enough to break his heart into a thousand pieces.

But there wasn't anything he could do. If he got the attention of Damir now, then he would know that Charlie was trying to get him away from Nick. Then he'd only hurt Nick more because of it.

There had to be something he could do. Some way of getting out of here. But they were all too weak to try and get out of these shackles. And Charlie could feel his strength leave him with every second that they stayed on.

He wished he could call for Max. They needed the pack to come and save them. They needed their family. But if Charlie tried to call for him through his own telepathic abilities, he might not just be heard by him.

Every time he had done it, it had been heard by all the wolves that were in the nearby area.

He had to try something, though. If he focused on just Max, then maybe it would work. It was a risky move. If the rogues around here heard it, they might do more than just torture them. But he had to try something. Anything to make this end. He would take the fall if it failed.

He closed his eyes and tried his hardest to block out the screams of agony from Nick. He thought about Max. All the memories that he had with him. It was not even a year since he met the man, yet he was already willing to marry and spend the rest of his life with him. It might be foolish, but Charlie didn't really care. He would stay with him through the thick and thin.

All other sounds were nothing but white noise now. All he could hear was Max's voice. All he could see was that handsome face that he woke up to every day. All he could feel were those arms around him and that chest that he always fell asleep on at the end of the day. Every feeling; smell; sight; sound; taste. He could remember it all now like it was happening at that very moment.

"*Max,*" he called out. He kept the memory of him strong in his mind. He willed this to work. "*Max, can you hear me?*"

"*Charlie?!*" He heard him! He actually heard him! Charlie almost lost his concentration, he was so relieved to hear his mate's voice again. "*Charlie, where are you?*"

"*I don't know,*" he answered him. "*We got attacked at the borders of the Harvest Moon territory. The rogues took us somewhere.*"

"*Who all is with you?*"

"*Katy, Wynona, and Nick. We all woke up in this wooden room with shackles on.*"

"*Is everyone okay?*"

"*No.*" He was starting to lose concentration. His thoughts were being brought back to the present. He had to focus on Max's voice, though. He had to get him to come and help them. "*Nick's getting tortured, Max. And the rest of us aren't doing well. The shackles are made of silver.*"

"*Charlie, I need you to give me every detail of the place you're in.*"

It was going to be difficult to describe it all. But maybe he could show him. Charlie kept his mate's voice in his head as he brought back the memory of the room. He showed him what it looked like when they first got in. He didn't know how he was doing it. But, somehow, he knew that Max was seeing it from where he was. The only thing that he didn't show him was his memories of Nick getting whipped. That would make him lose his concentration.

He could sense that Max was confused at how he was able to do this. To be honest, Charlie didn't quite know himself. He just willed it to work enough, and it did. His body was weak right now, but his mind was stronger than his body. It always had been.

The last thing he showed him was Damir's face. The man had a handsome face that was turned ugly through the way he expressed it. All the ways that he looked at him made him seem more like a beast than anything else. He could feel Max's anger as he shared the fearful feelings with him.

"*I'll find you, Apple,*" Max told him. "*I promise I'll find you all. And, when I do, I'm never letting you out of my sight.*"

"*Please hurry, Max,*" he begged. The pain from his wrists, ankles, and throat were starting to get worse. "*I don't know how much longer any of us can last.*"

CHAPTER 44:

Follow the Pull

"That doesn't even make sense!" Leonard yelled through the phone.

"It doesn't have to!" Max hollered right back. "At least, not right now." He didn't have time to explain to the man what they had learned about Charlie. All he had time for was to tell Leonard so that he could keep him up to date.

"And you're sure that it was Charlie?"

"Yes," he said. He knew his lovers voice from anywhere, especially if it was as clear as the one that came to his mind. "I'm positive."

They had been looking for four hours now. Max had to go back to the manor to update his father, since he hadn't brought his phone on the run. And he had been sending wave after wave of search parties into that uncharted territory. The less he found, the broader the search became. He had started it from the Harvest Moons territory and branched it out there. It didn't take long for the warriors of the Blood Moon Pack to join them in the search.

This alpha made the greatest mistake of his life. He must have had a giant ego if he thought he could capture three Lunas and survive. Max was going to tear the beast limb from limb. He would have his heart as a trophy by the end of the night.

That image of the rogue that Charlie showed him was as clear as can be in his mind. He kept that image. He needed to know exactly what this man looked like in both of his forms.

He couldn't believe that he had heard Charlie either. The conversation that he had was like a mind link, but much more private. It was like talking in a quiet room. Everything that Charlie said was clear. It was like he was right next to him. He didn't know how his mate had been able to do it, but it was so good to hear his voice again.

The image of the room that they were in looked like a cabin. There were plenty of them in those woods. But Max knew that it must be one that was abandoned. It had to be deep in that forest.

He remembered feeling the fear that Charlie had when he talked to him. It was especially prominent when he showed him that rogue's face. It made him angry enough to chew bricks.

"It's the only thing we have to go on, Leonard." Max broke the silence that the phone call had gotten. "Neither of us have time to argue about whether it was real or not. And the abandoned cabins seem like the best place for rogues to hang out at."

"You got a point," Leonard said. "I'll tell my warriors to start looking."

They hung up quickly after, neither having time for goodbyes. They were both trying to stay working so that they didn't let the panic settle in again.

"Button." Max opened the mind link. *"How's Ed?"* They had brought him to the manor after three hours of being at the Harvest Moon Pack's hospital. They had one that was special for werewolves, just in case they needed immediate medical attention.

Just in case something like this happened.

"He's stable," Button answered him. *"Just getting some rest right now. When he wakes up, he should be fine."*

"Thank you."

They had needed to bring him here most importantly because of Emily. Mates needed each other, especially when one was hurt. Ed needed to feel that his mate was near, so that he could heal better. And there was no way that Max was going to let her go to that hospital outside of the territory.

He had already made that mistake once that day.

He was really waiting on Tyler and Sam to get their things in order. They were going with him on the next search party. He told Madeline to prepare herself again as well. He needed her nose for this.

She had done a great job at finding a scent for them to try and follow. The only annoying thing was that the scent was practically everywhere at this point. This alpha had been trying to claim land for his fake pack for a long time now.

When Max had claimed that territory by Gila, he was sure that the rogues were pissed off at that. Their attacks had slowed down and gotten weaker as Max strengthened his defense on that extra land.

Now he just needed to find where they had the Lunas.

"Alpha," Alistair's low voice came into his thoughts. Max knew that he would have to talk to the man eventually. His mate was another who was lost at the moment. But there were so many things that he was worried about himself, that he was hoping he could hold this conversation off a little longer.

"Come in, Alistair," Max said out loud. He caught onto the man's unique scent quickly. He knew that the albino was by the door. When he came in, he could see that his face was pained. He knew exactly what he was going through.

"Nick," he said. There were plenty of chairs in Max's office, but he chose to stand instead. "Nick's getting hurt."

He remembered Charlie telling him that. He said that Nick was getting tortured. He didn't know why. What would that rogue want with him? But he knew that he couldn't let Nick die. He couldn't let anyone die. They were all crucial members to their packs. Each and every one of them a gift to their packs in their own unique way.

Nick especially was.

"I'm going with a search party in just a few minutes." He tried to comfort the man to no avail. "And I have a hunch of where they are. We'll find them."

"I can help." Those red eyes looked at him with a sense of seriousness to them that Max hadn't seen before.

"I need you here." He shook his head. If Alistair got hurt while Nick was hurt then they could both die. And that was something that Max wasn't willing to risk. "We don't know if those rogues are going to try and come into our territory."

"I can find Nick," Alistair told him. "Please let me go with you."

"Alistair." He combed his hair with his hand. "If something happened to you while we were saving them then I wouldn't be able to forgive myself."

"I know how to better fight now," he told him. "Let me prove myself to you."

"How do you expect to find Nick?"

"He's the reason why I am here right now," Alistair answered. "If not for him, I would have been much further south than this pack."

"What do you mean?" Max furrowed his eyebrows. There were so many things that this man seemed to know that he didn't. But he didn't have time to discuss something like this at the moment. He needed to get this search going.

"It's easier to show you than explain," Alistair told him. His eyes looked glossy with tears as they so desperately tried to convince him. "Please."

The last member of his search party mind linked with him to tell him that they were ready. He had to make a decision about this now. As much as Alistair was an amazing warrior, it was still really easy for him to get hurt. He needed his best men to handle the many enemies that they were going to face.

But something was telling him to believe in those wide eyes that bored into his. Something in his gut told him that this might be the wild card he needed to actually be able to find them.

"You better be ready now," Max told him. "Everyone else is outside."

"I'm ready," he smiled.

This was going to be a true test of how well Alistair had gotten at his new battle position. They were going to have to fight, and it could very well be a big one.

They walked quickly to the front doors of the manor. Out front was Tyler, Sam, and Madeline. When Madeline saw Alistair, she looked happy. He hoped that the two could work well together. They trained together pretty well.

"He's coming too." Max quickly updated the rest of his party. No one said a word. They just nodded and got ready to shift at his command. Tyler, and Sam had both trained with him since they were all kids. They knew when it came to situations like these to not question him. They could ask questions when this was all said and done.

They all shifted and started running. The warrior link quickly became the dominant one in everyone's mind so that they could use it in battle. The only one who still couldn't get accustomed to it was Alistair. That was another reason why he didn't think he was ready for something as dangerous as this.

He could tell that the white wolf was trying. The way he let out breath so quickly showed that he was getting frustrated by it. But he could feel something coming from the man. Max reached out with his mind to try and help him connect it. It was like two arms trying desperately to grab onto each other. Then, after a second, it worked just a little bit. There was a little hint of a connection with the warrior link. He was feeling something from him. It felt strange.

Like a pull.

As soon as Max realized that, his mind became one with Alistair's, along with everyone else's. It was an epiphany that needed to be had to find the missing puzzle piece. But the strangest thing wasn't how Alistair had finally connected to the warrior link. It was what he was feeling at the moment.

Through Alistair, he could sense his surroundings in a way that he never had before. Ever leaf or blade of grass had his attention. When they left the territory, it was the same thing. The wind whistled past them as they ran faster. It spoke in whispers, but only Alistair seemed to know what it meant.

The others were just as shocked as Max was to finally see what was going on in the albino's head. Max let him take lead and pulled back just a little bit. Alistair was being pulled by some unknown force, and he urged them all to follow it. They ran with him deeper into the woods as Max tried his hardest to figure out what that pull was.

Every sense except for his eyes were heightened. Max learned that Alistair paid close attention to the sounds that came from the woods. Every bird in the tree was caught by his ears. His nose picked up a scent that Max recognized after a while of them running.

That rogue. He must have been there recently. That metal smell was fresh, but not immediate. The pull was getting stronger as well, and Max couldn't help but feel a rush of energy as they got closer. The sun was just setting and he still had a promise to keep.

Then he caught onto Charlie's scent. Relief washed over him. He was worried that he was never going to get to smell that scent again, or see those beautiful green eyes. Max took lead and followed it in the same direction that the pull was bringing them to. It gave him a new energy that he hadn't had before.

They wasted no time trying to be sneaky. Max didn't want any chances of them escaping with their hostages. He was going to get them out of there alive.

The clearing that they were brought to was small. It didn't look like there were that many guards. Knowing them, Max could easily assume that the remainder of their pack was dealing with the search parties from all the packs surrounding them.

He hoped they all died.

Max told them to attack as soon as he saw them. They had surprise on their side, because the werewolves that were outside had no clue that they were there until it was too late. They quickly tore into the wolves that were outside. Even though they had the advantage of surprise, it didn't ensure their success in this battle. The cabin that was in the middle of the clearing opened and poured out a second wave of them, all attacking immediately. While it could have overwhelmed them, Max knew that it wouldn't. Not with how his warriors were trained for battle. While this was going on, though, he had a sneaking suspicion about this fight. Their leader wasn't anywhere to be found.

He went around the back of the cabin to see that someone was trying to sneak out. A snarl came from his muzzle as he looked at the alpha dead in the eyes. He hatred was so strong that he thirsted for his blood.

The rogue had ahold of something: a small lump that he couldn't make out. When the man saw Max, he dropped it and started shifting. The grey wolf started to run away from the scene as the rest of his followers were getting mauled in the front of the building. It was the coward's way out, and it only enraged him more. Max was going to follow him and sink his teeth into his back, but Tyler stopped him.

"Max, you're going to need to see this."

"We need to get that rogue."

"Charlie and the rest are really hurt," Tyler told him. *"And there's a kid here who's scared out of his mind."*

He stopped once he heard him say Charlie. As much as he wanted to kill this alpha, he needed to get Charlie and all of them to safety.

He shifted and ran into the cabin. It was worn out and looked like it had been abandoned years ago, but it was lived in. There were clothing and pots and pans scattered all along the floor. Max followed Charlie's scent until he got to a thick door. Tyler had broken it open, and he could tell that Alistair was already in there.

"Charlie!" Max ran over to his mate. All of them had been chained up to the walls with what looked to be silver shackles. He used his strength to break the shackles that was around his neck. Charlie seemed like he was having a hard time breathing. And, when he took the silver off him, he saw why. His neck was red and horribly swollen.

"I'm allergic to silver. It makes my skin get puffy."

He told him that all the way back in Christmas. But he had no idea just how bad the allergic reaction might be. He quickly started breaking the rest of the shackles that were on his wrists and ankles, seeing the same thing with them. Charlie clung to him as soon as he was free from the torture.

"Get," he wheezed. "Nick."

He looked around the room to see that Tyler and Sam were breaking the others out of their prisons. Wynona was too weak to walk and Katy was just crying the entire time.

But Nick was the worst out of all of them. He didn't recognize the man that Alistair cradled in his arms. There was so much blood caked onto him, and his face was bloody and bruised from multiple beatings.

"What did he do to him?" Max asked. He wasn't exactly sure who he was asking, as he wasn't sure if any of them could talk at the moment. All he knew was that he couldn't let his friend die like that. He would do anything to keep Nick alive. He promised them all that he would protect them. That's what Alphas did.

"He distracted the rogue from Charlie," Wynona said. She seemed the calmest out of all of them, but her blue eyes still looked traumatized. "He whipped him and beat him."

Katy was just holding onto Sam sobbing her eyes out. After what he saw of Nick, Max didn't exactly blame her. He had to get them all to a doctor.

They were closest to his pack, surprisingly. Which meant that he was going to have to take care of telling the other two Alphas that he had found their mates.

"Alistair. Sam." He got their attention. "You two are the fastest. I need you to run all of them to Dr. Button."

He was going to have to trust that they would bring Charlie home safely. Owen and Leonard were probably going insane trying to find them. And Max wouldn't have even gotten this far if not for Alistair's pull that he had been feeling. He would have to thank the man for that later.

Both of them nodded, and they all proceeded to carry them outside. Max had found some blankets. They would work for what he was going to need them for.

He told Alistair and Sam to shift. When they did, he wrapped the ones he had saved up in the blankets and tied it to each wolf. Sam carried Wynona and Katy, while Alistair carried Nick and Charlie. He knew that Alistair was faster, so he put the ones who needed the most immediate help with him.

"Don't worry about staying together," he told them. "Just get back to the pack as fast as you can. Give my father an update after you bring them to Dr. Button."

They both nodded their heads and started running.

"There's one more thing," Tyler said as they watched the two wolves run.

"What's that?"

"There's still a child in there," Tyler told him. "He's hiding under one of the beds."

He completely forgot about the child. Now that he remembered, he could have sworn that the rogue alpha had been holding something that resembled a kid. It had a scent to it, at least.

They both walked back inside the cabin and looked around. It didn't take long before he saw two tiny eyes looking at him from across the room. They were unlike anything he had ever seen before. One was ice blue while the other was a dark brown. They looked at him curiously, but fearfully at the same time.

"Are you Eric?" Max asked. He remembered that woman who died in his arms. She had told him that her son had two different colored eyes. And he had also promised that he would find him.

The boy seemed surprised when he said that.

"H-how do you know my name?" he asked. He looked so scared. It broke his heart.

"I met your mom," he told him. "She asked me to come and save you." He was trying to come off as friendly as he could, but he was sure that the blood of those other wolves that was caked onto his skin wasn't helping him.

"My mom's dead." The boy shook his head. Tears were falling down his face. When Max's eyes adjusted to the darkness that consumed the cabin, he was able to see what the boy looked like a little more.

He was beaten too. His face was swollen from more than just tears and his lip was scabbed from being busted open. This only added to his anger towards this rogue. Who beats a child like this? What had he ever done to deserve this?

"I know she is, Eric." Max knelt down to meet his level. "She died in my arms. Before she passed, she told me to find you though. I want to bring you somewhere away from all of this. Somewhere that will be safe."

"Is that where you're bringing Charlie?" Eric asked. He looked like he wanted to trust him at least. It was a good sign. Max was surprised that he knew Charlie's name, but glad at the same time.

"Yes," he told him. "Him and Nick are going to my doctor right now."

The boy thought about it for a second. He looked worried still, and afraid. Max was worried about what he'd do if Eric said no. He couldn't just leave him here. He needed medical attention too. It looked like he hadn't eaten anything in days.

"Okay," he agreed. Max let out a sigh of relief as he said it.

"Tyler," he told his Beta. "I need you and Madeline to bring him home. I'll be going to the other Alphas to tell them where their mates are."

"It's dangerous to travel here alone," Tyler argued. Those brown eyes of his showed worry. A fear that his Alpha might get hurt during his journey.

"I'm faster than anything out there," Max assured him. "It'll only take me another half hour and I'll be back home. Make sure to tell my father this too."

Tyler still looked worried, but he agreed. They went outside and he changed into his wolf form so that Max could put Eric on his back. He put a blanket over him just in case he couldn't hold onto the wolf tight enough. Eric trusted him enough to let him do what he needed to.

He waited until both wolves were out of sight until he started his own journey. His legs moved faster than they had ever before. He prayed to the Moon Goddess that all of them would be alright. It took six hours to find them. It was a record for their pack. But they had all still been hurt pretty bad, especially Nick. And Charlie was having a hard time breathing.

"Please let them all be okay."

CHAPTER 45:

Praying for A Miracle

Alistair ran faster than he had ever thought he could. He had always challenged himself to push past his limits when he trained, but this was much different from training. This had people's lives at stake.

He had felt the pain that Nick was feeling through their bond. It hurt to feel the agony that his mate had. He could feel the terror that Nick felt too. But he hadn't known just how bad it was until he saw him chained up. He barely looked human with all of that blood on him. He was barely recognizable, yet Alistair knew that it was his mate that he was looking at. He knew from the second that he looked at him that it was the very Nick who would always smile and laugh with him.

And now he was racing against time to try and save his life.

He could feel his heartbeat get fainter. He wished he could do something other than run. He wished this could all be over with.

He could hear Charlie's breathing getting worse as well. The two of them were the worst off out of the group that got kidnapped. He wasn't going to let either of them die if he could help it.

He didn't know how far Sam was from him, but he didn't dare try and look behind. All he could do was hope that Sam would be able to make it without getting attacked. There weren't any rogues that he could sense around the area, though. He was sure that the other search parties had already taken care of them.

When he got back to the Crescent Moon territory, the pack started to go crazy. There were so many people trying to mind link with him at once that he could barely keep up with any of it. He blocked it out and kept his eyes set for the manor, where Dr. Button was. He had to follow orders.

"*Dr. Button,*" he sent a message through the mind link to him. He was the only one that he would talk to until Charlie and Nick were under his care. "*I have Charlie and Nick. Both are in really bad conditions.*"

"*I already have rooms ready for them,*" the doctor replied immediately.

"*Thank you. Sam should be bringing Katy and Wynona. Both of them need medical attention as well.*"

"*Noted.*"

The other warriors were running with him to the manor at this point. They weren't trying to bother him. It was a means to help him, if anything. They made sure that no one was in his way as he ran. When he got to the manor, they shifted so that they could carry Charlie and Nick off from his back and race him to Dr. Button.

"What happened?" Max's father asked as soon as he shifted to his human form. He was the active Alpha of the pack at the moment. Which seemed to work well for them.

"Alpha Max told us to bring them here," he told him. He could feel Sam crossing the borders into their territory as he entered the mind link. "Sam has the Lunas from the other packs. We were closer to our territory than anyone else's."

"How did you find them?" Alpha Leo looked astonished. "That forest is huge."

"Nick," Alistair answered him. "I felt his pull."

The man was going to ask more questions, but Sam came to the same spot, escorted by more warriors. Wynona and Katy were still conscious at least. Charlie had lost consciousness sometime when he was running and Nick hadn't woken up since he first found him.

"Max wanted me to tell you that he's going to be telling the other Alphas their mates are with us," Sam told the Alpha. "That alpha rogue was the one who kidnapped them."

"Did you kill him?"

"No," Sam answered immediately. "Max had to let him go in order to save all of them."

Alistair wished he never let the wolf go when he first saw him. The pain from his mate being tortured was turning into rage. He remembered feeling the rage that Alpha Max had when they were fighting off those wolves at the cabin. He had wanted to kill that rogue so badly. Alistair didn't blame him. He wanted that rogue dead too. He wanted to make that man pay for what he did to Nick.

"Alistair," Alpha Leo caught his attention. "Get some clothes on. Nick's going to need you with him if he's got any chance to survive."

He followed those orders as fast as he could. The panic of possibly losing his mate was starting to settle in. He had fought it off the entire time that he had been missing, but there was only so much that he could control of his emotions.

He couldn't lose Nick. The man was the only one who had loved him other than his mother. He had finally mated with him. Everything was going well at the start of that day.

Alistair was actually excited for Nick to come home. He had spent the time that he was gone talking to his mother. He knew just how much she meant to him. The fact that she wasn't talking to him wasn't good. Alistair knew just how hurt Nick was by it. That's why he was glad that he had gotten to go and see Katy again. He knew that she could cheer him up. He was hoping that they could work together to make him happy. She could work on making him happy during the outing, while he could make him happy when he came home.

He had convinced Nick's mom to talk to him. She didn't seem like she wanted to keep this silent treatment going anyway. And when Alistair had told her that he wanted to do nothing but protect him, she seemed to calm down a little more. Nick's brothers had decided to visit during that time and they had a long talk about it. Barry and George were better at getting through to her than Alistair was.

They were all planning on meeting in Nick's room when he was on his way back. They were going to make it a surprise, so that Nick wouldn't be sad that Katy was gone again. Barry had seemed surprised when he found that Alistair wasn't jealous of Nick and Katy's closeness. He didn't quite understand why he would be jealous. There was a reason why people talked to more than one for the rest of their lives. Even strangers can have a closeness to them that's different from lovers.

Alistair wasn't going to be upset that Nick was happy to see his friend. He was always happy every time he got to see Madeline or Herb and Jackie. It didn't mean that he was going to ruin his relationship over a friendship.

He had gained their respect for that. Even Nick's father was moved by what he had said. Alistair had worked hard all that morning to gain the respect of Nick's family.

And now it was all for nothing. Now, he had to worry about losing Nick. He didn't know what he had done to deserve this, but it was enough to bring him to the point of breaking down.

He got to the infirmary just as Dr. Button had started sowing Nick's wounds up. The first thing that he smelt when he had picked his mate up in the cabin was the wolfsbane. It had gotten deep in the cuts that were all over his torso. He wasn't sure if it was enough to kill him. That was one thing that he was worried about.

Button didn't acknowledge him. He was too focused on his task. He had Nick hooked up to two different I.V's and was using some kind of medicine to clean the wounds. The wolfsbane oozed out of Nick. Alistair couldn't do anything but watch in absolute horror. The purple liquid was enough to fill a sink.

He sat down next to the bed that his mate was laying on, gently caressing the man's forehead. He looked so bad. But Alistair needed him to live. He closed his eyes and began to pray that he would make it out of this alive. Nick was his gift from the Moon Goddess. The one good thing that had happened to him ever since his mother died.

He was so focused on his prayer that he barely noticed that Tyler and Madeline had come back. He could normally feel it through the mind link. But his mind was too focused on what he was trying to manifest.

"I've got another patient for you, Button," Tyler's voice surprised him. He jumped up to see that the man was carrying a child in his arms. The poor thing looked like he had been beat as well.

"Bring him to a room." The doctor did not look up from what he was doing. "I already have Rudy working on Katy and Wynona. Charlie has been stabilized. He's resting now."

Alistair was glad to hear that. He wanted to ask the doctor more, but he didn't want him to lose his concentration. His ice blue eyes were focused solely on Nick. It was as if he was trying to will him to live as he continued to work on him.

"Nick's mom is outside the room," Tyler mentioned. "Should I tell her to wait?"

"I don't want her seeing him until I have him stabilized." Button looked more frustrated the more the man talked to him. Alistair understood. He was trying to save a life, not get interrupted.

Alistair wanted to help, but he didn't know what he could do. He watched as the doctor reached for certain tools. He would try and help him by handing him the tools, but that might be getting in the way of his work than anything else.

Instead, he started grabbing the extra rags that the doctor had. He used them to clean up the blood and wolfsbane that was still coming out of Nick. When Button noticed what he was doing, he didn't stop him. Alistair carefully worked around the doctor so that he wouldn't disturb what he was doing.

"Thank you," Dr. Button told him.

"I'm just trying to help," he replied.

"I'll take it," Button said. "Help me turn him onto his stomach."

Alistair listened and they gently turned him to show his back where most of the slashes were. Most of them had scabbed, the wolfsbane keeping them from healing all the way. Dr. Button wasted no time telling him where the extra rags were stored. He had already used all the ones that he had on his tray. He grabbed some more material that Button had around the room and brought it to him as well.

"He's really a tough one," Button said. They were wrapping him in gauze for the time being. All the other wounds had been sown up and Nick's heartrate was going back to normal. "He must get it from his mother."

"Is he going to be okay?"

"He's stabilized right now," he told him, wiping some sweat off from his brow. "But that wolfsbane did a number on him. He might be sleeping for a while."

He looked back at his mate. Nick had gauze all over him at this point. The silver had done a number on his neck, wrists, and ankles. All while the wolfsbane had tore up his torso and back. Even his forehead was wrapped up because of a gash that he had.

And all Alistair could do now was pray again.

"He'll make it, Alistair." Dr. Button put a hand on his shoulder. "I'm going to make sure of it."

He saw determination in the man's eyes. It seemed more than just a doctor's want to keep someone alive. There was a story in that gaze he had; a story that he couldn't ask about right then. Alistair wasn't sure if he wanted to, anyway. He was too worried about what would happen to Nick now.

"Thank you." He patted the hand that was on his shoulder. It was nighttime now. Normally at this time everyone would be asleep. But the pack was wired and stressed as they waited news about their Luna and Alpha.

"Alistair." He heard Max's voice before he felt him enter the territory. The pack seemed to all sigh in relief at having their Alpha back. *"How's Nick?"*

"His heart rate is back to normal," he answered. *"Dr. Button said that Charlie was stabilized as well."*

"Good, I'll be there soon."

Dr. Button had gone to check on his other patients for a few minutes. He heard him talking to Nick's mom right outside of the door. He told her just what he had told him. They agreed to not go in the room for the night and let him rest. After a few minutes, Button came back with Max hot on his tail.

"He was going through an allergic reaction," Button said. "It was simple to take care of with an EPI pen."

"And there's nothing else wrong with him?"

"No," the doctor answered. "He's just sleeping, just like the rest of them are."

"And Nick?"

"Nick was the worst out of all of them," Button told him. Max nodded at Alistair when he came in. "It seemed like the whip that the rogue was using was caked in wolfsbane. I had to clean a bunch of it out of him, and there could be more."

That was the first time that Alistair had ever seen an Alpha look scared. As soon as wolfsbane was mentioned, Max looked terrified. He shared Alistair's fear of losing him.

"He's on the strongest antibiotics right now," the doctor continued. "His heart rate being normal is a good sign. But the infection might leave him in a coma."

"A coma?" Alistair interrupted the conversation. Button didn't tell him this. What if Nick never woke up?

"I'm going to try my best to make sure he doesn't slip into one," Button told him. "But that head injury was a bad one as well. He's not in good shape."

Max sat next to him on the small chairs that were by the bed. His hand ran through his hair in the same fashion that Alistair had learned he always did when he was stressed. There was nothing they could do for Nick, not even the Alpha. All they could do was hope for a miracle.

"You're going to have to prepare yourself," Max told Button. "Leonard and Owen are on their way right now."

"Wynona and Katy should wake up soon," Button said. "Wynona should be able to walk again within a day or two. As far as Katy, I think she's more traumatized by whatever they did to Nick than anything else. Her body should heal fine. I'm just not sure about her mind."

"I'm not sure about any of our minds if Nick doesn't make it out of this," Max said. "I'll give them the news when they come in. You get some rest."

"I'm not going to rest until I know that they're all going to be okay," Button said. There was the same determination in his eyes that he had before.

"You need rest, Button," Max frowned.

"I've had plenty of rest the past few months."

"Why are you so strong headed about this?" Max looked annoyed with the doctor. Button was the only one that Alistair had ever witnessed argue with the Alpha like this. "I said I'd watch over everything tonight."

"I didn't go through all that work to save Myra and Nick when she was pregnant with him just to have the man die on my table," Button said. His tone was cold, even if it wasn't raised at all.

"What do you mean?" Alistair asked, too curious to ignore his words anymore. "You've had to save Nick before?"

"Myra was tortured in almost this same way when she was pregnant with Nick," Button's face grew soft. "It was a miracle that she had survived as long as she did. I worked around the clock tending to her and the child she was pregnant with at the time: Nick. They both fought tooth and nail to survive all the wolfsbane that she had gotten in her system."

That was why she said that Nick was her gift. Alistair couldn't imagine a pregnant woman having to go through such torture. She must have truly been blessed by the moon when she married Nick's father. He remembered when Nick told him that story.

"That was why Nick had so many health problems growing up," Max told him. "He was lucky that the wolfsbane hadn't done too much damage when he was just an infant."

"Exactly," Button said. "That's why I'm not resting until I know that he's okay."

"Fine," Max said. "But make sure you take care of yourself too, Button."

Max left to prepare for the other Alphas coming, leaving just Alistair and the doctor in the room again. Button sighed and sat down in one of the chairs this time. He had been standing the entire night.

"I should insist that guest beds be put in these rooms." He leaned his head against the wall.

"Guest beds?" Alistair asked.

"Well, it's more like a small pull-out bed." His mouth curved to a small smile. "Some hospitals have them in the rooms if you wish to spend the night with the patient."

"Maybe some couches would be better," Alistair said. "They're more comfortable than these chairs, and take up less space."

"That's a good idea." Button looked at him. "You know, I'm glad you're here with us, Alistair. This pack needs someone like you."

"Someone like me?"

"Calm and rational," he explained. "Those are qualities you don't see in people that much. You'd do well in the medical field."

"I just want to make sure that Nick is okay." He shook his head. He liked the conversation that the doctor was trying to have with him, but he was too worried about his mate.

"He will be," the doctor said. "He's a Moore."

CHAPTER 46:

Trauma

He woke up in a dimly lit room. His mind was too foggy to really think about where he was, but it was somewhere that he recognized.

"Max?" he called. For some reason, his mind was telling him to reach out to him. There was a part of him that was trying to say something urgent, but he didn't know what.

"Charlie!" Max's voice appeared in his mind almost immediately. *"You're awake!"*

He was going to say something else, but then he forgot. His mind was so tired from something that he could not recall at the moment. It was slowly trying to pull him back to sleep, but he fought it off. He needed to be awake right now. He needed Max.

The door opened and a pair of strong arms went around him. He sighed in relief as he clung onto his lover.

"I missed you so much," he told him.

"I'm so sorry, baby." Max held him tighter. He loved when he held him like this. "I'm so sorry. I should have never let you go to Totem City."

Totem City?

Charlie stiffened in Max's hold as the rest of his mind woke up in a split second. The shopping spree; the car wreck; the room; the chains.

The whip.

"Nick!" He fought against his lovers hold. "Where's Nick?" Max was holding him tightly as he struggled. He didn't know why he wasn't letting him free. He had to go see Nick. He had to make sure that he was alright. But, instead, he was trapped in Max's arms as they rubbed his back.

"He's okay, Charlie," Max soothed. "Everyone's okay."

He calmed down a little at that. He looked around again to see that he was in one of the infirmary rooms back at the manor. It was still dark out when he saw through the window, but the sky was lightening oh so slowly. He knew it must have been early morning.

He just couldn't process what had happened before he got there. Everything was flying through his mind, coming back to his memory with all their horrors. He wanted to break down and cry. Just to lay limp in his arms again. But that wouldn't help anyone at the moment. Charlie wasn't even sure if it would help him.

"What about the child?" he asked him. "Did you save the kid that was there with us?" He still couldn't get the image of the man smacking him across the room out of his head. Everything about that man made Charlie's stomach queasy.

"Yes," Max assured. "We don't know how he got beat up so bad, but he's doing okay under Button's care."

"He hit him," Charlie told him. "He hit him for trying to defend me."

Max's hold on him just got tighter as he said that. He knew that he was angry. But he was too worn out to feel anything other than an urgency to do something. His emotions were making him wired.

"Charlie!" Katy ran into the room. She hugged him with Max. It would have been funny to get a group hug like this if it weren't for the circumstances. "You're awake!"

"I'm okay." He gave her a little smile. "I'm just a little tired right now."

Owen was immediately in the room. He seemed more possessive of her, if it were possible. Charlie didn't blame him this time. He was probably worried sick about her when he found out that she had been kidnapped.

Lenny was the next to come in. Dr. Button had chosen to put him in one of the larger rooms in the infirmary. Charlie was glad. If he had gotten one of the smaller rooms than it would have gotten squished fast with all the people walking in.

"How's Wynona?" Charlie looked at Lenny. The man looked like he had just gone through the most stressful event of his life. He must have not gotten any sleep.

"She's recovering well," Lenny told him. "But she won't be able to walk for a few days."

"I'm so sorry, Lenny," Charlie shook his head. "If I would have called Max before we started leaving, we could have prevented this."

"Don't beat yourself up over it, Charlie," Lenny said. "No one would have expected a rogue trying to kidnap three Lunas at once."

Well, it wasn't like they were completely alone. Katy and Charlie had brought members of their packs to act as guards.

That reminded him.

"Where's Ed?" He looked at Max. He had no clue where anyone was or what happened during the time he was chained up in that room.

"He's fine," Max told him. He was still holding him, bringing a comfort to Charlie that he didn't know his mate could do at the time. "I can see if he'll come down, if you want."

"Actually." He moved away from him again. "There's someone else I need to talk to."

"Right now, you should be getting more rest," Dr. Button entered the room. "And you as well, Katy." He looked stressed and tired, much like the rest of the people that were in the room.

"I can't." Charlie shook his head. "Not until I speak to Nick's mom." This was something that was too important to wait on. And he was sure that he wouldn't be able to sleep without this anyway.

"Why Myra?" Button asked. His tired face looked curious.

"It's important," he said. He looked into Max's purple eyes. They looked so worried about him. But he wasn't the one who everyone needed to worry about. He'd be fine. "Please, Max?"

"Alright," Max said. He slowly put him back onto the bed and moved his arms away. "I'll see if she's awake."

Charlie would have simply mind linked with her, but he was too tired to make his brain work like that. He was surprised he had called for Max right when he woke up. He looked at Katy to see that she knew exactly what this was going to be about. He wasn't sure if she wanted to stay, but he wasn't going to try and push her out of his room.

"What are you going to talk to her about?" Owen asked this time. His dark maroon eyes showed a gentleness to them. He had failed at trying to hide the pain of almost losing his mate. Charlie wasn't going to point it out to him. It was good to show emotions, and pointing it out might make the man try to hide them again.

"It's something that I want you all to be here for," Charlie told him. "It's just better if it was explained this way."

Even Max was curious when he heard him say that. It wasn't very often that Charlie wanted the other Alphas to be in a discussion with them unless it was about something beyond their pack alone. The territory meetings were enough for Charlie not to want to talk to them for a short time afterwards. It was exhausting.

Soon enough, the small Indian woman came through the door. Charlie was glad to see that Nick's dad was right next to her. He might need both of their inputs.

"You called for me?" Her thick accent showed, even when she spoke lowly. The other Alphas being there seemed to be making her more stressed out. As much as Charlie never liked to stress people out, he needed answers.

"Myra," he started. "Did you know someone named Gene Darius?"

She froze at that name. Her shoulders tensed up and her entire being showed fear. He hated to see her like this. And he knew that Nick wouldn't be too happy with him making his mother upset like this, but this was important.

"Yes," she answered. Her voice sounded pained. "Why do you ask?"

"Nick had told the rogue that captured us that he knew who he was," Charlie explained. "He egged the rogue on by telling him a story about how Gene Darius tried to kill his mom and failed."

Nick had egged the man on so that he wouldn't do anything to the rest of them. For some reason, he seemed really interested in Charlie, which still sent shivers down his spine whenever he thought about it. He could still feel those cold hands rubbing his back and sides. He got off on Charlie's fear.

"Gene Darius was the one who tortured me while I was pregnant with Nick." She looked at him with horror. "You're saying he told the rogue this story?"

"He used it to make him angry at him," Charlie explained. Katy was choking up in the corner of the room. He looked into her eyes to see that she was reliving the same things that he was at the moment. "The rogue said that Gene Darius was his father. Nick used himself as a sacrifice to try and save us all."

Everyone in the room was quiet at that. He could hear Myra's quiet sobs as she stood there. All the other Alphas just looked around at each other.

"Hold on," Myra spoke through her tears. "I'll be back. I need to get something."

They let her and her husband leave. The click of the door shutting was the last bit of noise before silence took over. Katy had buried her face into

Owen who was holding her. Charlie wanted to crawl back into Max's arms, but he needed to finish this little meeting that he had started.

"Didn't your father kill Gene, Max?" Lenny looked at him.

"If I remember right," Max said. "If he had known that he had a son he probably would have tried to kill him too."

They would have to bring Mr. Locke in to try and learn more about the Darius family. But, before he could even think to mention it, Myra and her husband came back. Myra was holding a piece of paper that looked like it had been folded and crinkled many times over. Tears were still falling down her face as her husband tried to comfort her as well as he could.

"I had drawn him," she explained. "The year that I was recovering. I had heard that it would be a good way to get all the bad thoughts out of my head."

She slowly turned the paper around to show the drawing she made.

It was him. Minus a few extra scars that the man in the picture had, along with some extra age lines, it looked just like Damir. As soon as he saw the picture, he shivered. Everything that Damir had done flashed into his head with a matter of seconds.

Max was quick to try and hold him again, but Charlie grabbed his arm to tell him that he was okay. He couldn't be weak right now.

"That's what he looks like," he told the Alpha's. "Only he doesn't have a scar going down his eye, and he's younger."

"Myra, did you ever show this picture to Nick?" Button asked her. He looked worried about her.

"He accidentally found it one night," her husband answered for her. He looked just as disturbed as all of them. "I had to tell him the story before he went to try and show it to someone else, or got too curious about it and asked Myra."

"What did he do to him?" Myra looked into Charlie's eyes with nothing but pain.

"You should have seen him, Myra," Katy finally spoke. Her eyes were puffy and her smile wasn't as bright, but she was smiling nonetheless. "He was the bravest out of all of us. He laughed right in his face. It was like he was a completely different person when he talked to him."

"The Invisible Mask," Nick's father said. "I taught him how to do that a long time ago. I didn't expect him to use it for a situation like that, though."

"What's the Invisible Mask?" Lenny asked.

"It was an acting technique," he explained. "When you needed to act a difficult character out, just imagine putting on an invisible mask. Then, when you have that mask on, the characters thoughts become your own."

"I never thought Nick would be the one to laugh in an Alpha's face," Button said.

"Is he going to be alright?" Charlie asked the doctor. Nick was one of his closest friends. As much as he was all of theirs' hero, he didn't want to lose him. Not for this.

"The antibiotics are working well to fight off the infection," Button said. "He's showing progress for recovering. But I won't know for sure until he wakes up."

"Make his room and Wynona's room a top priority for the Nurses," Max said. He looked to Owen after that. "You're going to have Katy stay with you, right?"

"Right," Owen answered, pulling Katy closer. She just leaned into him. It looked like she didn't have that much strength in her. Charlie had heard that it was a side effect of the silver that they were all exposed to. Her neck showed just a hint of a red mark on them, which was a great sign that she would heal soon. But all of this was probably making her so exhausted.

"Myra." Max looked over to Nick's mom next. "Would you mind if we made copies of that picture?"

"You can take it." She sniffed. "I've held onto it long enough."

Max handed it to Button and told him to keep ahold of it for now. They all started to leave after that. There were still their wives to see to, and much to do afterwards. When the room cleared, Charlie sat up on the bed.

"We need to tell your father about this," he told Max.

"Nope." Max picked him up. "We can do that tomorrow. You need rest."

"I can stay up long enough to tell him what happened," he argued. He was already melting into those familiar arms. "We need as much information as we can get."

"What we need to do is get you a nice bath and a good night's rest." He kissed his head. "Button, he's okay to leave the infirmary, right?"

"Of course," the doctor answered. "Get some rest."

"But-!" He tried to argue more, but Max was already walking them to their suite. It seemed like it had been an eternity since he had been in there.

"You did enough, Apple," Max told him.

"What about Nick?" he asked. He felt so guilty. "I didn't do anything to stop him from getting hurt. I have to help him in some way."

"He would have done something much worse to you if you tried to stop him," Max lead them to the bathroom and turned on the water.

Charlie couldn't stop the full body shudders this time. Just the thought of the man terrified him. He could still feel every touch that he gave him. When he first came in that room to greet them, he had taken off the silver on his neck to kiss it. Charlie was sure that he was going to bite the mark that Max had made on him too if Nick hadn't distracted him.

"Apple." Max's voice brought him back to the bathroom that they were in. "What did he do to you?"

"Nothing." He shook his head. "All he did was touch me."

"Why do I smell his scent all over your neck then?" he asked. His hand went to Charlie's neck to gently caress it. It felt so much better with Max's hand there.

"He kissed me," he admitted. He grabbed onto Max's hand for some kind of comfort. "Just on my neck, though."

"Charlie." Max took ahold of his chin and moved it to meet his eyes. "Please, tell me what he did to you."

"It's not bad." He shook his head again. "Nick was the one who got it the worst."

"Just because Nick had it the worst doesn't mean that what you went through wasn't bad." Max's purple eyes looked worriedly at him. "You don't have to try and be strong all the time, Charlie."

That's when he lost control. Charlie sobbed into Max's chest as the man held him. Max didn't say anything. All he did was rub his back. They sat on the floor of the bathroom at this point. He supposed that Max didn't want to try and take off his clothes for the bath when he was like this.

Charlie slowly told Max everything that had happened. He started from the moment that they left the house at the beginning. And he didn't end until he passed out on Alistair's back. Every detail that he remembered from that horrible room he told to Max. He didn't know why he could remember everything so vividly, but it terrified him. When he told him about the way Damir touched him and kissed him, Max held him tighter. He liked being in his hold at that moment. He didn't want him to ever let him go. Not after what he just went through.

He also told him about what the man did to Nick. Every scream echoed in his head again and again. He could never forget them. He told him what Nick had said to them before his second beating. He talked about the promise that Max had made to Charlie.

"I tried to tell him that you made a promise to him as well," he said between sobs. "But he wouldn't listen. He just kept saying that we were the most important people in the pack."

"He's always been the type of person who did everything for his friends," Max told him. "That's why he did it."

"But now he might not make it." Charlie let out another sob. Max's soothing hand on his back barely did anything when he talked like this.

"We can't think like that," Max said. "The medicine is working. He's getting better. We just need to wait until he wakes up."

Max was right. He couldn't keep thinking like that. He needed to think about Nick getting better instead of worse. It was hard to train a brain to do that. But he was sure he could try.

After he stopped crying, Max changed him out of his clothes and brought him to the bath. He laid limp in his arms as he washed away all the touches that the rogue had given. He washed him with such a gentleness that it felt almost like it was healing him in a way. He leaned into him, his body too worn out to want to make an effort to move at all. The bath was comforting. He had good memories with Max in this bathroom. Like the time when he had massaged him when Max was really stressed. He liked that day.

"Charlie." Max carried him out of the bath and was starting to dry them off.

"Hmm?"

"I'm never letting you go anywhere for a long, long time."

"I'm okay with that." He huffed a laugh. He would be okay with being glued to the man's side for the rest of his life after what he just went through.

"Oh, there's one more thing," Max walked them over to their bed.

"What?"

Instead of giving him an answer, Max slipped something onto his finger. He moved his hands up to see his wedding ring. He had been so worried that he'd never see it again.

"I still plan on marrying you," Max smiled at him. "Charlie Locke."

CHAPTER 47:

He heard voices, but he couldn't make out what they were saying. His body was having its own battle with trying to wake up. The abyss that he had been in was trying to pull him back. It had a numbness to it that had been comforting for a while. But now there was something that was making him feel again. Something made him try and crawl out of that hole. He didn't quite know why. But once he got out, he realized that there wasn't a way for him to get back.

He wished he could go back. At least he didn't have to feel this irritation when he was in that abyss. It was an itch that he couldn't ignore. He soon became stuck in the middle of the abyss and the need to deal with that itch. This was worse than being stuck with just one. He kept getting pulled from one to the other. It was like he was stuck at sea, forced to follow the currents that dragged him back and forth.

That itch was getting worse, though. As much as he wanted to ignore it, he couldn't. Now it was turning to pain. He started to force himself up to it. It was hard to move, but he was too bothered by the feeling to just let it go.

His eyes darted open and his body was electrified. He didn't know where he was, or what had happened. All he knew was that he needed to itch this. He couldn't even see anything. His eyes wouldn't focus. His mind felt like it was melting. But all he could focus on was this itch.

His body sat up on its own as his hands tried to dig into the cause of his anguish. But there was something else that he had to get past. He couldn't itch it.

"Nick." A low voice went right by his ear. He found comfort in that voice. A warm body slid behind him, making him realize just how cold he was. His whole body shivered at that thought, leaning into any warmth it could find.

He wanted to say something. He wanted to tell him what was wrong. But he couldn't. The only thing his mouth could do was help him breathe at the moment. For some reason it was hard to catch his breath. Gentle hands grabbed his and forced them down, away from the itch. He tried to fight against it, but the low voice came to soothe him again.

"It's okay, Bakshir," it told him. He was kissing his shoulders lightly as he said it. Nick wanted to like it, but now the body was too hot. His brain felt like it was boiling and he just didn't know what to do.

"*Max,*" he called out. "*Help.*"

He didn't know why he called out that name. It was just a name that gave him comfort. It made him feel safe when he called it. There was another name that did the same thing, but he couldn't remember it at the time.

A door opened, and a hand was quickly placed on his forehead. His eyes still couldn't focus on anything, but he could tell that there were more people that had come in.

He struggled against the person holding him. He needed to get rid of this itch. It was to the point where the pain was unbearable.

"He keeps on trying to itch something," the low voice said. It didn't seem like he was talking to him. "And he's getting hot flashes."

"He has a fever," a familiar voice said. It wasn't Max, though. He would know if it was. "I'm checking right now how bad it is. As far as the itch, we can check it out when we change the bandages on him. We need to get this fever down first."

"Doctor." A female voice came out. "He's got a fever of 104°F."

"Get an ice bath ready," the doctor said. His tone was urgent, even though it was quiet. "Do it fast."

"How bad is that?" the low voice asked.

"Bad," the doctor answered. Nick felt a prick in his arm. "If we don't get the fever down as quickly as possible, a fever that high is life threatening."

He didn't know what any of this meant. All he knew was that he couldn't struggle against the strong arms that held him for long. He wished he could just tell them something. His chest was now hurting him, along with all the other pain that he had.

"It's ready," the female voice said.

"Good," the doctor replied. "Help me move him there."

To where? He had no idea. But he struggled against their hold. As soon as he was away from the warm body, he was cold again. It was torture going through something like this. His body didn't know what to do other than try and fight off the ones that were carrying him off somewhere.

If he thought he was cold then, he had no idea how frigid he could be once they dunked him in water. The water was as cold as the Antarctic. His first instinct was to get out, but they held him in, pouring some of it onto his forehead.

It didn't take long for his eyes to finally be able to finally focus. He was in a bathroom at the manor. He knew that much just from the design that the walls had on it. They were the same as most of the bathrooms on the first floor. It took a lot of weight off his shoulders just to see something familiar like that pattern on the wall.

"Alistair." He smiled at the man on top of him. He had been holding him down while one of the nurses were pouring water on him.

"Shh," he soothed him. "It's alright."

"His fever's going down," the nurse said. He liked her. She was one of those nurses who had been training with Dr. Button since she was sixteen. She was hoping to be one of the next pack doctors, but she needed to go to a lot of schooling for that.

"My chest," Nick said. There was something on it that was irritating him. But Alistair had been keeping his arms away from it. "It hurts."

"Take off the gauze, Alistair," Button said. He was relieved to see the doctor. It was only after Alistair followed the doctor's orders that the cold started to settle in again. He wanted to cling to the man, but he still pushed him down into the cold, assuring him that he would be alright.

"What's going on with Nick?" He heard Max's voice before he saw him come in. The man looked like he had just woken up.

"He had a fever," Button explained. "Thankfully, it went down."

"Max!" He smiled through the pain. It felt so good to see the man again. He felt like he had something urgent to tell him, but he couldn't remember anything at the moment.

"Nick!" He raced to his side. "I'm so glad you're awake."

He was going to say something else, but something stopped him. He got another wave of irritation on his chest as Alistair finished taking off the gauze. He wanted to itch it. It was worse than a bug bite, and he was sure that it was much bigger.

"Button." He heard Max say. "What are those?"

"Cysts," Button replied. "They need to be drained."

"Cysts?" He looked down to see three huge bumps on his torso. The biggest was a purple one right by his collar bone. That was the one that had been itching the most at the time. The cold water was helping to numb them at least, but it was still enough to drive him insane.

Button came back quickly and told the nurse to drain the tub. He turned on the shower head next. Alistair had decided to focus on holding his arms that he was still trying desperately to move.

"This is going to hurt a little, Nick," Button warned.

"Just do it!" he yelled. It was getting too much. Now that the fever was gone, it was the center of attention.

He felt the doctor cut through the bump with a scalpel. It hurt at first, but it immediately relived him of the urge to itch that spot.

"What's coming out of it?" Max asked.

"Wolfsbane," Button answered. "I was worried that I hadn't gotten it completely out." He proceeded to cut into the other two that were on his front. Nick wanted to look down at it, but Alistair was keeping his head up. He nuzzled and kissed him while holding him.

The water that went down him was warm. It felt nice compared to the iciness that he had just been under. But as soon as the ones on his chest were taken care of, he started to notice more.

"My back," Nick said. Alistair wasn't exactly hurting him when he held him from behind, but he could still feel the slight discomfort in some areas.

Wait. When did Alistair get behind him? Everything was happening quickly, yet slowly at the same time. He was glad that his eyes could focus at least. When Button was done with the front side of him, he got him to sit up more to see his back.

"Holy shit," Max said.

"What?" Nick asked. "Can someone tell me what's going on please?!" He didn't like how Max reacted to that. It scared him. What was on his back?

"It's okay, Nick," Button assured him. "There's some cysts on your back as well. I'm just going to do what I was doing with the others."

The nurse worked to bandage the sores that were on his chest while he felt the doctor cut open his back. Alistair had moved again, but he knew he was still there. He just couldn't focus too much on the man at the moment. He was too busy trying not to scream as he felt the burning going down his back.

"It's burning him," Alistair said. He was grateful that Alistair could talk for him at that point. If it weren't for their mate bond, he wasn't sure how he'd be able to tell Button everything that was going on.

It took a little while longer until he was wrapped up in gauze again and carried out of the tub. Alistair must have taken the bath with him, with how soaked he was. He was the one who carried him back to the bed that he was in.

"I'm going to have to hook you back up to one of the I.V's Nick," the doctor told him. "Thankfully, you don't need the I.V. of blood anymore. But you need to have as much of those antibiotics as possible."

"I know the routine." Nick gave him a small smile, still trying to catch his breath. This reminded him a little of when he was a kid under Button's care. He practically lived in this infirmary at one point. "I'm just happy that those things are gone."

"They aren't gone just yet," the doctor told him. "It'll take a while for them to fully heal. They might need to be drained a few more times."

Nick groaned at that. He didn't want to feel that again. It was the most frustrating feeling of his life.

"Nick?" Max came up to the side of his bed. "Do you feel a little better now?"

"Yeah." He nodded. "How long have I been out?"

"About two days," Max looked so worried when he watched him. "We weren't sure if you were going to wake up."

"You can actually thank the cysts for that." Nick chuckled a little. "If it weren't for them irritating me to no end, I wouldn't have woken up." He still remembered that abyss. It scared him with how void of everything it had. He couldn't remember anything in that void, or feel anything for that matter.

"Is that why you mind linked with me?"

He did what now? He didn't even remember doing that. His brain was still a little bit foggy. When he thought about it some more, though, he vaguely recalled needing to tell him something important. There was something in his mind that was dying to get to the surface.

Then it hit him like a ton of bricks. All the memories that had come from that one day. He could remember every sight; every smell. He could remember the sound of every slash that the whip made. And the pain that it caused.

"Charlie!" He looked to the Alpha. "Is Charlie okay?"

"He's doing fine," Max said. "Everyone made it out of there alive and recovered pretty quickly. Everyone but you."

"The alpha," he shook his head. He didn't want to see the man's face when he closed his eyes, but it happened. It was as if he was standing right in front of him. "He's the son of Darius."

"We know, Nick," Max said. "Charlie told us everything, okay? Don't worry about all of that right now, just focus on getting better." Those purple eyes that Nick had seen his whole life looked so worried for him. He wished that he could say there was nothing to worry about, but this was a new kind of pain than the kind he had dealt with in the past. And he was too weak to try and face it alone.

"And Ed?" he asked.

"Right here." Ed walked in right on cue. He looked a little worn out, but overall, he seemed like he was in good shape. "Good to see you, Nick."

He was so relieved to see Ed again. He was relieved to see all of them again. There was a time when he didn't think he'd ever see anyone again. That was the scariest moment of his life.

"Bakshir!" His mom came running into the room, his dad was right behind her. They both hugged him, although his mom wasn't as gentle as his dad had been with him. He had missed her, though. He missed them both so much. He really didn't want to leave the world after they had gotten into a fight.

"Mom." He tried to hug her as tightly as possible. "I missed you so much."

"I'm so sorry, Bakshir." She was crying at this point. She was going to make him cry if she kept it up. "I'm sorry I didn't talk to you before. I'm sorry that I pushed you too much. I love you so much, Bakshir."

"I love you too." He smiled. That's what he really wanted to tell her.

They talked a bit after that. Nick kept smiling throughout the conversation. He didn't want to show them all the fear that he had been hiding since the beginning of all of this. He didn't want to ruin a happy moment.

George and Barry came in to say hello. Charlie came to, just so that he could immediately hug him right when he saw him. He was so glad that they found them all before that sick man had tried to do anything else to Charlie, or any of the other Lunas for that matter.

"How did you find us, by the way?" Nick asked.

"That was a mixture of two things," Max said. "The first was because of Charlie. He sent me a message telepathically to help me find you. That's how we were able to figure out that it was one of the abandoned sheds."

"You were able to send a message that far?" Nick asked Charlie. His green eyes looked tired, but happy. They sparkled when he looked at him. "Is it about the whole Star Child thing?"

"I think so," Charlie said. "I had to focus really hard to do it, though. And it made me so tired afterwards."

"That's a pretty great gift for a Luna to have," Nick smiled at him again. It was so nice seeing him healthy. "But what was the other way you found us?"

"That was actually due to Alistair," Max answered. They all looked over to the man who had been patiently staying still while people visited him. "If it weren't for this pull that he had, it would have taken a lot longer to find all of you."

"A pull?" He looked at Alistair. "What do you mean, pull?"

"That's actually something that I've been meaning to ask you myself," Max looked at the albino.

"The pull is what I felt when I was running over to this pack," Alistair answered. "I didn't know what it was that was pulling me until I met Nick. He was the one who brought me here."

Nick looked at him with surprise. A mate bond was usually never that strong before they even met. The fact that Alistair had been able to use it to bring Max to that cabin was miraculous all in of itself.

"That's a rare kind of bond," Button chimed in. "One that proves useful in many situations."

"What kind of bond is it?" Max asked.

"It's one that we used to call a Fate Bond," the doctor said. "A bond that was fated to be."

The room was a little silent after that. Nick just looked at Alistair. The man was still a mystery to him, and there was still so much that he felt like he needed to learn about him. But those ruby eyes held nothing but love for him, and he couldn't help but share his feelings.

"But I thought all bonds were fated," Barry said. "Why is this one specifically called that?"

"A Fate Bond is one in which the beings lived far away from each other, with a slim chance of ever crossing each other's paths," Button explained. "It was said that when the Moon mated couples like that, she would pull them together through fate alone so that they could be together."

This was just confusing, but he let it continue on without him. Being in the hospital bed surrounded by everyone talking reminded him of his childhood, for both good and bad reasons. For now, he'd just remember all the fun times that he would have with his family all huddled into one tiny infirmary room. The laughter from George as they told an old joke was just like those times. They really hadn't changed a bit since then.

It was moments like these that were truly worth living for.

CHAPTER 48:

Possessive

There were so many people that had gone into that little room that day. After Nick woke up early that morning, it seemed like the whole pack was trying to talk to him. Alistair was happy that his mate had finally woken up. Nick's smile as he talked to everyone lit up the room.

But Alistair felt something from Nick. It was a sense of needing to hide something. Like he didn't want to show how he was truly feeling. It made him uneasy. He didn't want Nick to have to hide his emotions. Not when he had just survived something as horrible as he did. But he knew that the man truly did want to see all these people.

Even Charlie had popped in. He hugged Nick for a long time when he saw that he was awake. Alistair knew that the Luna felt guilty about what had happened. He could see it in those emerald eyes. But Nick just smiled at him and told him how happy he was that he was alright. They talked for a little bit before Max came in to grab him. Alistair could only imagine how much the Alpha hated not having his Luna by his side after what had happened.

Luna Wynona came in to visit as well. She told him that she had never seen someone as brave as Nick. She said that she would have to find some way to repay him for what he had done, but Nick just brushed it off and said that anyone would do what he did. Alistair didn't believe that. His travels showed him otherwise. Kindness was always scarce, as well as brave acts like the one that Nick did.

Other than the Lunas, the rest of the pack talked about normal things that were going on, probably to try and help Nick from thinking about the event. Alistair was happy that there were so many caring people in this pack. They'd normally mind link with Alistair to ask him certain questions, just in case it might hurt Nick. He was sure that Dr. Button had told everyone to be careful with what they talk about with the chef. This was his first day of being awake, after all.

"I was wondering when we were going to see the badass again," Herb came in with Jackie and Madeline. Alistair smiled at the sight of his friends. It had seemed like such a long time since he had seen them.

Madeline had gone with them when they found all of them. He was sure that she was just as terrified to see Nick as he was in that horrible room.

Those two days of waiting for him to wake up had been the most tortuous thing Alistair had ever gone through. It was worse than seeing his mother die. At least he knew that there was no saving her. She was meant to pass when she did. But Nick wasn't that way. He still fought to stay alive, just as he had fought to protect the Lunas.

"I wouldn't call myself that." Nick smiled at Herb. They all took turns hugging him. "I'm pretty sure I wouldn't be in this hospital bed if I was the true badass."

"Are you kidding me?" Herb raised an eyebrow at him. "Not only can you make curry spicy enough to make the devil cry, you actually laughed in an enemy alpha's face! How more badass can you get?"

Alistair laughed to himself. He remembered the spicy food challenge that they all did together. It was one of the nights that Nick and Alistair had off for their vacation. Herb even invited Madeline and Alan. They were surprised to see that Alan could handle all the heat that Nick had cooked into that curry.

Alistair, however, was just good at keeping a straight face. His whole body burned for a long time after eating that bowl. Madeline had bolted towards one of the fridges to chug a gallon of milk. The whole night was a blast. It helped Nick forget about what had happened earlier that week with his mother. It took Alistair a while to make him happy after that.

He wished they were back in that week. Alistair wanted to do nothing but hold Nick in his arms and keep him in that bed in their room for days on end. It would just be nice to wrap his arms around him like he used to.

"If you think that curry was bad." Nick gave a weak laugh. "You're going to have fun trying my mother's curry."

"Oh, please no," Madeline said. "That curry was so spicy, there's no way that it could get any hotter."

"I did warn you guys." He put a finger up in the air. "That you wouldn't be able to handle the spices of India."

"I'm still in shock that Alan could finish it." Herb shook his head in disbelief. "He did not strike me as the kind of man who could handle heat."

"He seemed more like a chocolates guy to me," Jackie said.

"That's because of Clara, one of my sisters," Nick said. "Apparently he had the biggest crush on her in school. He went to eat with her and my parents one time and my mom made her famous curry. We were all shocked to see how much he loved it."

"He had a crush on one of your sisters?" Madeline asked. She looked a little upset when she heard that.

"He's been trying to find his mate for a long time, Madeline," Nick told her. "I wouldn't worry about it, honestly. Clara's always been in her own little world, away from everyone else. I'm surprised her mate can put up with her most of the time."

"I wasn't worried about it." Madeline rolled her eyes. "I was just asking."

"You didn't look like you were just asking," Alistair said.

"I can't be curious about my own mate?" She gave him a playful smirk.

"Ah." Herb chuckled. "That must be the possessiveness showing. I was wondering when it would come out."

"Possessiveness?" Madeline gave him an annoyed look. "I am not possessive of Alan!"

"Mates are always possessive," Herb argued. "It's our instinct to want someone all to ourselves. It's a part of the instinct to protect your mate. You just have to make sure it doesn't overpower you."

"Oh Herb." Jackie shook her head this time. "Not every mated couple are the same."

"No, but they all have the same characteristics with them."

"I'm not possessive of Alan," Madeline huffed. She seemed really upset about this. "Why is it that I ask one question and it gets turned into me being possessive?"

"Just because you're possessive doesn't mean that everyone else is, Herb," Jackie said. The way they were talking reminded him of the argument about mates first seeing each other.

"If you really don't think I'm telling the truth" Herb put up a hand. "Then give me one example of a mated couple that isn't jealous of each other."

"He's got a good point." Nick chuckled a little bit.

"What about Charlie and Max?" Jackie asked. "They seem like they're the perfect couple."

"When Charlie first came in and learned about Max's first relationship, you could see his face fall," Nick answered. His hazel eyes sparkled as he relived the memory he spoke of. "And Max was about to punch Ian through a wall when he saw how he acted around him."

"Why does that guy act that way towards Charlie anyway?" Madeline asked this time. "He shouldn't be acting that way towards Charlie, especially since he's already mated."

"I think it's his scent," Alistair said. "Sometimes people can get obsessed with the scent like his."

"That's still really weird," Herb said. "It's probably only making his mate more possessive of him."

"Benny's put a tight leash on him." Nick laughed some more. "He's got him under control. I'm just grateful he didn't point any of that jealousy towards Charlie. That would not go down well."

"What about the doctor and his wife?" Madeline asked. "They don't seem possessive of each other."

"That's just because they had to keep their relationship a secret for so long," Nick explained. "Dr. Adelle showed her possessive nature towards him plenty of times when they were younger."

"I bet you all the ladies wanted him." Herb chuckled.

"They had to keep their relationship a secret?" Jackie asked.

"It was before the pack allowed mated couples where the females were stronger than the males," Nick explained. "We've gone through quite a lot to get this pack to the place it is today."

"That sounds horrible." The woman shook her head. "I can't imagine how much it would hurt to have to keep something like that a secret just because of a silly rule like that."

"What kind of wolf is she?" Herb asked.

"She's a beta," Nick told him.

"A beta woman and an omega man." Herb leaned back in his seat. "Now that's an interesting combo."

They talked a little bit more about different topics. Alistair liked how well Nick relaxed around the three friends of his. With all of the people that came in, it seemed like he was trying to put on a show. But when it was just them, he was a little calmer. There was still that hint of fear that Alistair picked up from him, but it wasn't as bad as it had been.

They had to leave when lunch came out. Dr. Button wanted to make sure that Nick actually got some rest now that he was finally awake. Nick was going to argue with him about it, but Alistair held his mate's hand and told him that it might be best if he did. Those hazel eyes calmed when he said it.

Alistair had been dying to be alone with him the whole day. It wasn't that he wanted the man all to himself, he just wanted to talk to him. He wanted to see what was going on in his mate's mind, so that he might help to rid Nick of the fear that he had.

But he wasn't going to ask him that while they were eating. He didn't want Nick to be upset and not eat. Instead, he tried to make him smile the best he could and kept the conversation going. It always helped Nick when he had something to talk about. He could see that he was getting tired, though. He wished he could hold him in his arms and carry him back to their room. He'd care for him hand and foot until he recovered.

"Okay, Teddy Bear," Nick said. "What's on your mind?"

"You," he answered. Every time Nick called him that he wanted to hold him again. If it weren't for the I.V. that was in his arm he would have.

"What about me?"

"How happy I am that you're awake," he told him. Being able to sense his mate's happiness when he told him that was enough for all the pain and worry of the past two days to be worth it.

"I'm glad I'm awake too." Nick sighed. He had finished his food. They had given him a big portion, but he only ate half of it. "Thanks for telling Button about the sores."

"I was just trying to help in any way that I could," he said. He had known right when Nick woke up. He was sleeping right on the small chair beside his bed. Nick had woken up in a frenzy, trying to scratch the bandages that had kept the wounds protected.

"You do a good job at helping." Nick held Alistair's hand. He couldn't help but press the slender hand to his lips. It was the only intimacy he could have with Nick at the moment.

"Nick." He broke through the short silence. "Can I ask you a question?"

"What is it?"

"Why are you afraid right now?" he asked. "Do you want to talk about it?" He wanted to know what that man had done to him. He wanted Nick to open up to him about that so that he could try and wipe that fear away.

"Honestly." Nick sighed. His whole figure seemed to fall at hearing his question. Alistair almost felt guilty for asking him it, but he knew that Nick had been hiding this for the majority of the morning. "Right now, I'm just afraid to fall asleep."

That was not an answer that he was expecting. He wasn't expecting that Nick would have that fear. He was too worried that the man would be traumatized by what had happened that day that he was lost.

"Are you afraid of the nightmares?" he asked him. "Or are you afraid of not being able to wake back up?"

"Both." He shook his dark hair. It looked messy and tangled after all the sleeping he had already done. "I just wish this didn't happen."

"I do too," Alistair told him. He rubbed on the hand that he held. "I'll never let anything like that happen to you again."

"I love you." Nick smiled at him. "You're one of the only ones that I can really talk to about this stuff. Other than Katy, of course."

"That reminds me." Alistair smiled back at him. "Her and Owen haven't left yet. I can see if Katy wants to visit before you take your nap."

"That would be great!" The sparkle came back to those lovely eyes. "I could probably use something to calm my nerves before bed anyway."

He really wished he could just slip into that bed with him. He would make sure that he didn't have nightmares. His mother always said that mates could fight off things that you couldn't. He would try and fight off those nightmares if he could. But he had to wait until he could finally bring him home.

Instead, he would help him have some happiness. That's all he wanted Nick to feel after all that had happened. Alistair mind linked with Max and asked if he could invite Katy to the room so that Nick could see her. He was surprised that she hadn't come earlier, with how worried she had been. But something told him that she was still battling her own trauma from what she had witnessed. He felt bad when he saw her look so horrified every day she visited Nick.

It didn't take long before a small knock on the door came. Nick was the one who said come in this time, which only seemed to make the door open faster.

"Nick!" Katy ran up to him. She looked like she had been crying for hours and her hair was wilder than Alistair had seen before. "I'm so glad you're awake!"

"Katy!" Nick immediately opened his arms out to get a hug from her. "You're okay!"

"Of course, I am!" Katy said. "You were the one who got the worst of it." She looked like she was going to cry again, but Nick just pet her head. When Alistair watched them, they both looked like siblings trying to comfort each other. He had seen close siblings before on his journeys. They both had caring eyes when they saw each other.

"He was a wimp." Nick smiled. "He couldn't see past his own ego."

"Nick!" Katy's dramatic voice filled the room. "You almost died!"

"But I didn't," he assured her. "I woke up today and I got to see you with possibly the worst bed head you've gotten yet."

"Hey!" She pouted and moved one of her hands to her head. "You're lucky you're under Button's care so I can't smack you right now!"

Nick just laughed at that. They both looked like they had gone back in time to when they were kids. Alistair found that it was fun to watch them talk. He had talked to Katy a few times when she was visiting Nick. She seemed like a fun person to talk to. She was like Nick in the sense that she had plenty of stories to tell. But she was far more dramatic about her story telling.

"Oh, congratulations, by the way," Katy smirked at him. Her brown eyes looked playful for once.

"For what?" Nick looked confused. Alistair had to suppress a chuckle. He knew where this was going.

"For officially getting mated," she said. "I didn't really get to congratulate you when we were together last." Then she crossed her arms. "And I'm still mad that you didn't want to talk about it that much when we were shopping together!"

"What?" Nick laughed. "Did you want me to yell it out to the shopping square?"

"Awwww!!!" She squealed. "That would have been so cute! I could have taken a video of it and sent it to Alistair."

"I'm not that into doing stuff like that," Nick shook his head. "I'd much rather just keep things as normal as possible in public."

"Nick, we're werewolves though," Katy argued. "We're not normal. And people do stuff like that all the time. They propose in public too, you know!"

"Worst thing you could ever do." Nick shook his head. "If the person says 'no' in public then you're left embarrassed beyond belief and left with a broken heart."

"It's romantic!"

Alistair had a feeling that these two argued with each other like this normally. He wished that he could watch them talk like this more often. It was nice to see someone else being able to calm Nick down.

The happy moment was disrupted with a growl that came from the direction of the door. Alistair didn't know what it was at first, but he growled in response. His instincts to protect his mate were stronger than his will to wait and see who it was that he growled back at. Alistair had been taught to never growl. But he wasn't going to let anyone hurt his mate.

Owen was standing by the door. He looked angrily at his mate who was still being held by Nick. But when Alistair growled at him, he seemed to snap out of it. Those dark red eyes snapped over to him instead. At first, they were confused. Then something clicked and he seemed to understand.

Alistair was expecting a fight right then. Even if this Alpha had realized that Nick was his mate and he was just trying to protect him, he was still threatening an Alpha. And that was terms for death where he came from. But he would do anything for Nick. Nick was his to protect and love.

The Alpha didn't do that. He just seemed shocked. Alistair didn't have time to try and figure out all of what the young man was feeling at that moment. It only took a few seconds for Katy to get out of Nick's hold and smack him.

"Stop it!" Katy screamed at him. "I can't hug the one person I've known since I was a kid?! The one person who saved me when we were trapped with that rogue?!"

"Katy, I-!"

"Enough excuses!" she yelled over him. Her eyes were flames at the moment, and her hair was just as alive as her. "The fact that you've been jealous of so many people that I talk to shows more about you than it does about them. You don't give me anything Owen! You wouldn't even let me go to the city to make a phone call because I 'needed protection'! You and the pack expect so many things out of me, and I can't even get a little bit of freedom?!"

"But Katy-!"

"Don't 'But Katy' me!" She interrupted him again. "I'm done trying to do everything for you without anything reciprocated." Then she threw something small at him. "I'm done!"

Alistair had never seen someone yell at an Alpha like that. He could tell that Katy was strong, but he never knew how much fight she had in her until that moment. She ran out of the room as Alpha Owen just looked at the thing that she had thrown at him. Alistair was standing by Nick, on instinct to protect. His eyes were bad, but he could still see the item shine in the Alpha's hand. That shine usually only meant one thing.

It was a ring.

CHAPTER 49:

Elderly Advice

She couldn't believe this! After all that she had gone through just to try and learn what it took to be Luna. After all the sacrifices she made to be with him. After all the arguments that she had ended, even though she knew she was right, just because she didn't want to go to bed angry.

After getting kidnapped and surviving that horrible shed.

And he was going to get jealous of Nick again?! How many times had she told him and argued with him that Nick was like a brother to her? His responses were all the same:

"That doesn't prove how he feels."

"How do you know? He's lied before!"

"Are you sure that you and him haven't done anything when you were teenagers?"

The last one was what made her give him the silent treatment for the rest of the day. It made her so mad when he said that. She was sure that people could see steam coming out of her ears. Most of them left her alone that day.

Owen apologized each time that he made her upset. She knew that he loved her. She could sense it in him through their bond. But he was so stubborn that she just couldn't get through to him unless she screamed.

Katy sat down on the ground and sighed. She had gone to one spot behind the manor that no one usually went to. It was right by the gym, but still hidden enough to where the warriors couldn't spot her. Not that they would be in the gym right now anyway. It was night time at this point, and she had been expertly avoiding Owen for the whole afternoon.

He made Nick jump when he growled. Katy had hardly ever seen Nick scared. And she most certainly didn't ever want him to be scared because of her. But she looked at him and saw that he had been taken back to that room where that rogue had growled at him. She could see it in his eyes.

It only pissed her off even more.

She could handle a lot when it came to people. And she had definitely worked on her patience a lot when she mated with Owen. But this crossed the line. She wasn't going to have him be afraid of her mate anymore. Nick was her best friend; *is* her best friend. And she wasn't going to be told to not talk to him or hug him.

Tears ran down her cheeks. She was always told how much of a crybaby she was. Everyone in school used to bully her for it. Nick was the only one who ever seemed to be okay with it when they were little. He always tried to make her smile, even if she was just being dramatic about it. He was her comfort when she had none.

They helped each other with their issues as kids. She had to help him with all of his insecurities too. His wolf was a big hurdle to get over. Even though it didn't look too different from everyone else's, it was still different enough to get the other kids in the pack to make fun of him.

Her, Ray, Desmond, and Max all had to work to convince him that he wasn't some weird monster. When they were kids, they all would convince him to run with them and they would play in the rain as wolves and do all sorts of things.

She missed those days. As much as she still had her own problems, they weren't as bad as this. She wasn't as stressed as this. Owen was good at bringing her peace, but it was only when he stopped trying to tell her everything she needed to do. She knew what to do. Of course, she needed some help, but she wasn't some naïve girl who had been too sheltered to know anything about the real world.

At least Nick had found a mate that was understanding of him. The more she had talked to Alistair, the more she realized why the two were meant to be together. They were both calm, but troubled. They both gave great advice and always wanted to help make people feel better. And he was an albino, while Nick had his health problem.

They were perfectly imperfect.

And Alistair didn't seem to be jealous of her and Nick either. Max told her that Alistair invited her to go see Nick that day. She had been crying in her room the entire morning, or else she probably would have known that he was awake. Owen had to go do talk to Alpha Leonard about something, so she had gone alone to visit him.

Alistair didn't seem alarmed at all that she was hugging Nick. He just seemed happy that they were happy. It felt so relieving to have someone just immediately understand them. They seemed like the perfect couple.

The moon shined brightly that night, as if to mock her. She watched it shine down on her in the clear starry sky.

"Why do I get to have the tough one?!" she asked the moon. She hadn't realized just how dry her throat was until then. She hadn't really eaten or drank water that whole day. "What did I do to deserve someone who won't even listen to me?"

"Katy?" She jumped at the sound. For a second, she thought that the moon was actually talking to her. But when she looked to her right, she saw Martha standing by the corner.

"Hi Martha," she sighed. She had talked to Martha plenty of times when she was a kid. Martha was the oldest members of the Crescent Moon Pack, and had gone through at least three generations of Alphas through the pack. She was also Aldi's aunt, which was how Katy found her passion to cook.

Martha would always be the one to find her and Nick when they wandered off too far. She also helped her with a lot of her problems as a kid. They had a lot of late-night discussions under these stars.

"It's been a while since you've been in this spot." Martha sat down next to her. She was such a short, bulky woman. It was baffling to think that there wasn't an ounce of fat on her. All of it was muscles in some way.

"It's been a while since I've been here in general," she said. "I missed this place."

"We've all missed you too, honey." Martha smiled. "Especially Nick."

"At least Nick has Alistair." She sighed again. She looked up at the stars and watched them twinkle.

"So, you came to this spot to yell at the moon about your mate?" Martha asked. There was a hint of humor in her voice.

"It's not fair!" She pouted. "This isn't even about Nick and his mate. Why do I get to be mated with someone who's younger than me and more stubborn than me? Why do I get to deal with someone who won't even listen to a thing I say? Who brings me to a pack that fights against everything that I try and do to change it?" She had really been trying to give the omegas of the Blood Moon Pack more freedom. They really still had a hierarchy system. She didn't believe it until she noticed that the only omegas around were servants.

"Change isn't easy to accept," Martha told her. "That's just how life is. If you want to change something, it could take years before it happens. And, I'm afraid the Blood Moon Pack is one that has tried to stick to tradition as much as possible."

"Some of their traditions aren't good though." She frowned. "And, no matter how hard I try and get them to see that, they don't want to believe me."

"It takes time to make a big change," the burly woman said. "Sometimes it's the little things that count."

"I just wish I were back to living here." She sank her face down to her hands. "I just want to be a cook again."

"There's a reason why alphas and omegas are paired together more often than not," Martha told her. "Do you want to know why?"

"Why?"

"Because it creates balance," she explained. "When you have the strong and weak together, it helps better shape an understanding of the pack. The omega has seen what it's like to be at the bottom of the pack, and the Alpha knows what the strong are like. They are mated to each other to help create balance in their pack. So that members are treated equally."

"But the Crescent Moon Pack hasn't had an omega Luna since I can remember," she said. Charlie only partly counted as one, since he only has a small percentage of werewolf in him.

"That's because we've had to go through many rough times," Martha said. She smiled and looked up at the stars. "But each Luna in this pack always had a level head on their shoulders and a heart of gold."

It was crazy to think that Martha had seen so many Alphas and Lunas in her life. She was even older than Liam, and had seen more than enough of what the pack had gone through. The kids would always love circling around her when she was done training just to hear the many battle stories that she had. Or the stories about the pack history. She knew so much about their home.

"I don't think I can do this," Katy said. "I can get the paperwork down. I can deal with some of the people not agreeing with what I have to say. But I can't handle a mate that won't even try to understand me."

"That's what Laura said when she first came to this pack." Martha chuckled.

"What?!" she looked at Martha in shock. "Luna Laura and Alpha Leo are, like, the perfect couple though!"

"They weren't always," Martha said. "Leo was a lot like Max when he was younger, only he didn't have a mother to reign him in when he needed to."

"What do you mean he was like Max?"

"He was rowdy, stubborn, and full of endless energy with a need to put it towards something," she explained. "When he had first became Alpha, his mission was to deal with the rogues too. He had wanted to expand our territory, in hopes that we would be able to grow in population."

"But Alpha Leo has always been against that." Katy knitted her eyebrows together. "At least, that's what I thought."

"There was an issue with trying to push for territory back then," she continued her story. "Our warriors were much slimmer than they are now, and weaker due to the civil war that had plagued the pack during Liam's reign. Leo couldn't see the damage that he was doing to the pack by pushing them to gain territory. All it was doing was killing more pack members and making more enemies. Laura saw this, but she struggled to get through to him."

"What happened then?" she asked. Martha always had a way about her where she got people invested in her stories. "How did Alpha Leo see that it was bad?"

"Laura and him had an argument about it. They had been arguing for the better half of the year since they gained their titles. But this particular day was after a bloody battle in which we had been on the losing side of. Laura was so fed up with Leo's stubborn ways that she ran from the manor. She ran and ran and ran. Leo didn't know what to do other than follow her. He was afraid that she would get hurt by the rogues that could still be around. That or that she would leave him forever.'

"She ran all the way to the edge of the territory, where that bloody battle had taken place. When they got there, she shifted into her human form and told him to look at the scene. The warriors hadn't been buried yet at that point, as we were too worried that more rogues would come attack us while we were trying to honor our dead.'

"Leo looked at the dead warriors and all the bloodshed that was on the forest ground. He looked up to his mate. She told him that it was his fault that they died. That they needed to protect the pack in order for it to grow, not continue attacking."

Wow. Katy hadn't heard that story before. She couldn't believe that it had even happened. Alpha Leo was always protective of the pack. He always told the warriors to defend rather than attack. He taught them to be peaceful yet cautious.

"So, I'm going to have to make Owen chase me to a battle scene to get him to actually understand me?" Katy asked.

"The Moon Goddess picked you as his mate for a reason." Martha's dull eyes looked at hers. "And if he truly wants to keep you, I'm sure he'll give in."

"This sucks." She pouted again. It helped to hear that story, though. At least she knew that she wasn't alone when it came to being mated to stubborn Alphas.

"Just enjoy what you do have, dear." Martha patted her back. "It could be much worse."

"How much worse can it get?!" She groaned. Her frustration was all coming back to her. "I can't even get him to see that some of the omegas in the pack have the potential to help them by getting jobs outside of the manor! Career's help the pack grow money wise as well as with knowledge."

"He'll see what you mean." Martha chuckled. "Like I said: it could be much worse."

"How?"

"Well." The old woman's face fell a little bit. "You could have been rejected."

A whole new wave of pain struck her being. The thought of Owen rejecting her almost made her want to cry. She had only heard rumors of what that can do to a person. Most of the time it caused the werewolf to commit suicide.

"I forgot about that." Katy's voice became small as she spoke. "I can't imagine what that's like."

"It's not too bad," Martha said, her dull brown eyes looked pained. "If you can get over the initial pain of it."

"Have you met someone who was rejected?"

"Yes." She nodded. Now it was her turn to look at the stars. The moonlight sparkled in her short grey hair. "I was rejected by my mate when I was young."

"What?!" Katy looked at the elder. The idea of someone who got rejected by their mate living as long as Martha did was baffling. "What do you mean you got rejected?! When?! How?!"

"It was a long, long time ago." Martha shook her head. "I was only eighteen. The one I was mated to, I found after a battle." She looked back to Katy with a small smile. "He was actually a warrior in the Blood Moon Pack."

"Really?" She wondered if she knew him. If she did, she was going to give the man a piece of her mind when she got back. Martha was the grandma of the pack. She knew everyone, gave them advice from time to time. She protected them.

"He's long since passed away, dear," Martha answered the question before she could answer it. "I felt him pass thirty years ago."

"But why would he reject you?!" Katy asked. Martha was the toughest woman she had ever met. Surely her mate would have been proud of her for her strength.

"It was a different time," Martha said. "You see, I met him on our last battle during a war against the Blood Moon Pack. Tensions were still high, even when peace was declared between our two of us. We both knew that if we were to officially mate, we would have to deal with much backlash from both of our packs."

"There was also the fact that I was a delta woman who was a warrior. During the time when I was young, there were no such thing as those. Only beta and alpha women could become warriors. The rest needed to stay safe and be the child bearers of the pack in order to help it grow."

"That's the dumbest thing I've ever heard!" Katy huffed.

"It wasn't just our pack that did this." Martha smiled at her. "Most packs had this social rule to keep the population up. But the Luna at the time favored me and taught me how to fight. She convinced her mate to let me fight alongside the warriors. It took a while, but eventually they started to like me fighting with them."

"But your mate didn't like it?"

"No," she answered. "He didn't like the fact that I was a warrior, and that I wasn't willing to give up that lifestyle if we mated officially. He wanted a normal mate to have a family with. I wanted to work alongside and grow with him."

"So, he rejected you?"

"Yes." Martha sighed. "It was the most excruciating pain of my life."

"I'm so sorry, Martha." Katy hugged her. "That's so horrible!

"It's okay, dear." Martha hugged her back. She always had such strong hugs. It made Katy feel safe every time she hugged her. "That was a long time ago. I haven't seen him since then, but I have forgiven him."

"He doesn't deserve to be forgiven!" she yelled into the woman's shirt.

"Oh, but everyone deserves at least one chance at being forgiven." Martha pet her hair. "I think you should forgive your mate at least one more time."

She groaned when she heard that. Of course, this was going to wind up coming back to her.

"I don't want to talk to him," she muttered.

"Even if he's standing behind you with chocolate covered cherries?"

Katy stopped hugging Martha and looked behind her to see Owen standing there. He looked like he had been stressed out all day. He had a container of chocolate covered cherries in one hand, and a bouquet of roses in the other.

"I'll leave you two to talk." Martha got up. She gave a respectful nod towards Owen before she walked off towards the manor.

Katy stayed on the ground, looking up at him. Those dark red eyes had softened a lot since she first met him, but it didn't change her mind about what she felt. She had seen those eyes look fierce whenever she was around any of her friends. He wanted her all to himself, and it wasn't going to work.

When Owen saw that she wasn't going to stand up, his face fell a little more. He actually looked upset, and not in an angry way.

"I apologized to Nick," he told her. "It wasn't right of me to act like that towards him. Not after what he had done to make sure you weren't hurt."

That made her feel a little better. At least he was apologizing to people now. Knowing Nick, he already forgave him. Nick was always that way, if you really meant your apology, that was. He was good at figuring out if people were just trying to mess with him or not.

"Was he the one who gave you the idea for the chocolate covered cherries?" Katy asked.

"Chocolate covered cherries, a bouquet of flowers, and as many musicals as I can find." Owen smiled a little at her. "He also told me that I shouldn't bother trying to find one that you hadn't watched before."

Katy couldn't help but giggle a bit at that. Her and Nick had been on a mission to watch every musical known to man. They even had ones in languages they didn't even know. It was a fun game they had of trying to figure out what the people were saying.

"You can't be jealous of everyone who knew me before you met me, you know," she said. "Because that's a lot of people, and I'm not going to throw them out of my life."

"I know." He sighed. "I'm sorry, Katy. I don't know why I did that."

"You apologized to Alistair too, right?" Her eyes became slits.

"Yes."

"And Max?"

"Yes," he answered. "The only one I haven't apologized to is you."

"Did you spend the whole rest of the day apologizing?!"

"Kinda." He put his hand on the back of his head. He looked so cute when he did that. She loved when he put down his serious act. "Katy. I know I'm not the perfect person, and there's been a lot of things that I've done wrong while being your mate, but I can't lose you." Those eyes met hers with such pain in them. He set down the bouquet and the cherries and got onto his knees. "Please, don't leave me Katy. We'll work through everything, I promise. I just can't live without you."

Katy hugged him. "I'm not going to leave you Owen. I was just frustrated that you weren't listening to me."

"I'll listen, I promise." He held her tightly. "I love you."

"I love you too." She smiled.

"Am I going to have to propose to you again?" Owen asked as they started walking back towards the manor.

"Yes," she said. "And it's going to have to be in public. And I want Nick there."

Owen chuckled as he lead her back to their room.

"Anything for you."

A buzzing came from one of her pockets. She still kept her phone with her, even when she didn't have service. It was mainly out of habit. Now that they were here, though, all of her messages could come through. She fished her phone out of her pocket and looked to see a text message.

Nick: I told you that you'd be able to whip him into shape ☺.

"Nick!!!!!" Her scream echoed in the manor as they walked in. And all she could hear afterwards was laughter coming from the direction of the infirmary.

CHAPTER 50:

A Restless Night

Charlie walked aimlessly around the manor. It was night, so not much was going on. He just couldn't sleep. It didn't help that Max had gone to escort the visitors out of their territory. Lenny and Wynona were the first to say goodbye. He was going to miss having Wynona around. Even after all they had gone through the past week, she was always so sweet about everything.

He was shocked when Owen apologized to him. He looked guilty for how rude he was being. Charlie later found out that there had been a fight between Katy and him the day before. As much as Owen was annoying some times, he didn't wish for him and Katy to separate. Thankfully they were able to get past it. Katy looked happier that day, and they had gone to visit Nick as often as possible.

Owen just seemed to be someone who had to grow up fast in life. He was like Charlie in that sense, but they went about dealing with it in different ways. Where Charlie just worked and tried his best to avoid conflicts, Owen stayed just as busy and got more serious. Hopefully Katy could help him relax a little bit more.

For now, though, Charlie was just alone to his thoughts in the dark manor. It was late at night and most of the pack had gone to bed a long time ago. It was a little unnerving having Max outside of the territory again, but the rest of the pack was assured that he would be back by morning, if not sooner. He went with the best warriors they had, minus Alistair, of course.

With Max gone, Charlie had the whole pack keeping an eye on him. With what had happened that day in the Harvest Moon territory, none of them wanted him to get hurt again. He understood their concern, but he had never had to worry about getting hurt when he was in the pack house.

Sam had been the one who had been following him most of the day. He couldn't go with Max due to his children, so he offered to keep an eye on him until he came back. Charlie was glad for a chance to talk to Sam again, he was always fun to talk to when you got on the topic of his kids. But it wasn't long before he got tired and headed for bed.

Charlie had told him that he was going to get some sleep as well. He wasn't lying, he really tried to sleep. But that big bed felt so cold and empty without Max to hold him.

He thought about visiting Nick, but he was sure that he was asleep by now. Alistair was doing a great job making sure that Nick did everything the doctor needed him to do. It was adorable to see how easy he could convince the cook to listen to the doctor. Alistair was so calm with everything when it came to Nick.

He was there more than Nick's mom. As much as that woman visited her son and brought him food, Alistair was the one that basically lived there. He would not leave Nick's side for anything. He was happy that Nick had someone like him, too. Nick was always so nice with everyone, he deserved someone who was as caring as Alistair.

Charlie sighed and sat down in one of the living rooms. He was probably going to be up all night at this point, so he might as well think of something to do. Maybe he could make some pies to occupy the time. That always seemed to calm him down.

He walked over to the hallway that the kitchen was in. He had known this hallway all too much when he first came to this manor. It held a lot of fun memories. He still remembered the nook in the walls that Max pulled him in and tried to kiss him. Button had ruined that when he started calling from the halls, but it was still a great memory.

All of that seemed like such a long time ago. Back then he had to worry about having enough money for rent and enough food to stay alive. Now he had a whole bunch of people to try and keep protected and happy.

And now they had many more rogues to deal with.

A scurry of something caught his attention. Charlie didn't know what it was at first. The lights weren't turned on so that he wouldn't disturb anyone. He was simply wandering through the halls to the moonlight that was shining through the windows. It was beautiful.

"Is anyone there?" Charlie asked. He knew that it was something, but he didn't know what. He was too far away from the light switch to turn that on at the moment.

More shuffling noises came from one of the closets in the hall. He walked up to it. Hopefully it wasn't new mates. He remembered the first time he witnessed a mated couple in a closet. That was not a fun experience.

Thankfully that wasn't what he saw when he opened the small door this time. Instead, there were two small eyes that popped open to meet him.

"Eric?" Charlie recognized those eyes immediately. He was the only boy that he had seen with two different colored ones. "What are you doing in here?"

"I don't know." The boy shrugged. He made no move to leave the tiny closet though. Charlie was a bit worried about that. The poor boy looked scared again.

They had been working on trying to get him to talk to them more. He had almost healed completely from the physical wounds that horrible man gave him, but they had no idea the severity of the mental wounds. He had lost both of his parents to that rogue, and had probably seen a lot of horrible things.

Charlie visited him a lot, actually. The boy opened up to him about some things. They found that he wasn't as shy around him, which made him happy. He wanted Eric to feel welcomed here. This was where he was safe. They would protect him.

"Did you have another nightmare?" Charlie asked. He let out his hand in hopes that the boy would take it.

"Maybe." His voice was so small, it only made that closet look tinier. But he took Charlie's hand and let him take him out of the closet.

Another thing that Dr. Button had found about the boy was how underweight he was. Charlie could see it. For a five-year-old, he looked more like a toddler. His black hair bounced with every step he made. It looked much calmer now that he had been able to clean himself.

"It's okay," Charlie comforted him. He slowly lead him back to the infirmary room that he was staying in. "I get nightmares too."

"You do?"

"Of course." He smiled at him. "Just because you get older doesn't mean that there aren't things that scare you."

"I know that," Eric said. He was looking down at his feet. The poor boy looked so troubled.

"You want to know what I do when I have nightmares?"

"What?"

"I find someone who wants to have fun," he told him. "After I'm calm enough, I usually try to talk about it. That way it doesn't stay in the back of my mind."

"I don't want to talk about it," Eric shook his head. His little hand squeezed Charlie's just a little bit.

"That's okay." He held his hand just a little tighter. "You don't have to. It doesn't always work, anyway. It depends on the person."

They got to the room that he was in. But before he could try and tuck the boy in, he shied away from the bed.

"I don't like this room," he told him. He looked at Charlie with pleading eyes.

"Why not?" He knelt down to be at his level and wiped away some loose strands from the boy's head. From what he had heard, Charlie was the only one that Eric would even talk to like this. It was sad that he didn't feel comfortable with anyone else. He talked a little more to Max, but he still would barely talk about what had happened.

"It's too empty," Eric said. He was still trying to look down at the ground. "I feel all alone when I'm in here."

Charlie knew how that felt. When he was stuck in the infirmary at night, and he couldn't fall asleep, he felt the same way. This manor was so big, and always bustling with people, but there was something about the infirmary that made it seem like it was completely empty. It was as if it was a separate building to the manor all together.

"Let's go find a better place for you to sleep then," he told him. Eric had healed enough to be put in an actual room anyway. They were just trying to figure out where he should go. It was difficult trying to figure out who wanted to take care of the adorable kid. They would have to get through all of the poor boy's mental barriers that he had seemed to put up. But he could find a better spot for him to sleep for that night at least. He'd figure out the rest tomorrow.

Charlie went to stand up and lead him out of there, when Eric jumped on him and hugged him. He couldn't help but hug the boy back. He was really sweet when he opened up, even if it was just a little bit. He wished he could hold the little thing forever.

"Can I sleep with you?" he could barely hear him when he asked. His face was buried in his shoulder. "I don't wanna be alone."

"Alright." He kissed the back of his head. "Let me carry you then." He wasn't sure if Eric could handle going up the stairs yet. He was still weak due to the lack of food that he had been given. They were basically starving him.

Eric nodded and wrapped his arms around his neck. He was as light as a feather when Charlie picked him up. He liked how the boy felt in his arms, though. The way that he clung to him reminded him of all the dreams that he would have of making his own family. He had always wanted to adopt when he had the money. He had dreamed of having a big family with someone he loved. That included having a bunch of kids.

He wasn't sure if that's what Max wanted. At least, not at the moment. Max had been too focused on trying to get these rogues out of the way. He told Charlie that he wanted to make sure that the pack was safe before he brought a new child into it. Charlie understood. They were both working hard to get rid of these rogues as well. And they hadn't even married yet.

But having Eric in his arms brought back those dreams. Just having someone as small as Eric made him wish that he could take care of him. He was proud that he had gotten him to open up to him a little more. And he knew that the boy liked Max too. After all, he wouldn't have listened to Max when he was in that cabin if he didn't trust him at least a little bit.

He just wasn't sure how Max felt about all of this. At the moment, he was too busy just trying to keep Charlie by his side. They had all been affected by that kidnapping. And Max was helping him get through all of what he had experienced in that cabin, along with seeing what that man had done to Nick.

It still made him flinch whenever he thought of Damir hitting Eric across the room. It reminded him of when his own parents had hurt him as a child. Only he was a lot older that Eric was when his parents started hurting him.

"Okay." He opened the door to his room. "Welcome to my suite."

"It's so big," Eric looked around. He was happy to see the boy's eyes were wide with wonder.

"Yeah." Charlie chuckled. He set him down to look around. Eric went and opened every door that he had. It looked like a part of his real self was coming out when he wondered through the suite.

"You have a balcony!" Eric said. Charlie followed his voice to find that he was looking in awe at the clear glass doors that the stars shined through.

"That's my favorite part too," Charlie said. "It's nice waking up to the sunshine in the morning."

"My dad and mom had one in their room too," Eric said. His voice went back to being really quiet at that moment. And his two different colored eyes looked lost in a memory. "We would go out there every night to look at the stars."

"Do you want to go out there?" Charlie asked. It hurt him to see how sad the boy looked. He wished he could make him feel better in some way.

"No." He shook his head. He turned back and hugged Charlie again. "I don't want to remember them right now."

"That's okay." He picked him up. "It's okay to feel what you feel, Eric."

"It is?"

"Of course." He rubbed the boy's back. "Sometimes it's best not to think about all of those things. Sometimes it's best to try and enjoy the good things that are happening today."

"Like you?"

"If I make you feel good." Charlie smiled. Eric was such a sweetheart. The more he talked to him the more he seemed to fall for the little cherub.

He brought Eric to his and Max's bed and wrapped the blanket around them both. The small child quickly curled into him, clinging to his torso.

"Goodnight, Eric." He kissed the top of his head.

"Night," the boy mumbled. It didn't take long before he was passed out under the covers. Charlie just smiled and continued to hold him. The feeling of having someone to hold again was comforting. He still missed Max, but the sound of Eric breathing peacefully and the warmth did have a lulling effect on him.

He didn't know that he had fallen asleep until he heard the door to his suite open, and arms wrap around him from behind.

"What's going on, Apple?" Max whispered in his ear. He must have felt that he was holding Eric. The boy was still asleep, curled into him.

"How was the trip?" He stalled. He wasn't sure whether Max was going to be upset or not that he had brought Eric to their room without even asking.

"There weren't any rogues, thankfully." Max sighed. He buried his face into his shoulder and pulled him closer. It felt so peaceful having both Max and Eric cuddled up to him at the same time. "Now why are you sleeping with Eric?"

"Shh!" He smiled a bit. "You're going to wake him up."

"Why are you trying to avoid the question, Apple?" He mind linked with him. It woke him up a little more.

"Because I don't know if your mad at me or not," he answered truthfully. He was too tired to try and direct the conversation in any other way. Especially not in his head.

"Why would I be mad at you?"

"I brought him up here without asking." He held onto Eric a little tighter.

"I'm not mad at you for bringing a child to our room." Max chuckled quietly. His hands rubbed Charlie's sides comfortingly. He didn't realize how much he missed his touch until just then. He found himself leaning into the man more. *"I'm just wondering why, baby. That's all."*

"He was scared," Charlie answered him. "And he asked if he could sleep with me."

"We need to figure out who's going to be taking care of him soon." Max kissed his shoulder. "He really doesn't like the infirmary."

He wanted to ask if they could take care of him, but something stopped him. He was worried about Max telling him that the time wasn't right.

"Maybe for now we could put him in a room close to ours?" he asked. Finding a middle man in the situation was better than just asking upfront. And Max seemed exhausted from his run that night. "He's only really opened up to us. Maybe if we put him somewhere close, he might feel more comfortable and start talking to more people."

"That's not a bad idea." Max agreed. It made Charlie happy that he was willing to work with him on that at least.

The sun had come up just a little by then. Charlie was glad that he had gotten some sleep at least. He knew that Max would be trying to stay up the rest of the day so that he could get himself back on their normal sleeping schedule. Charlie would probably be doing the same.

Max shifted in the bed and gently moved Charlie to where he was on his back. Eric had clung to him so much that he went with him when he moved. He was now on his stomach, sleeping deeply.

"He's so cute," Max said. Charlie looked up to find the red head smiling at Eric. "It would be hard not to find someone who didn't want him."

"Yeah." He looked down. Eric was slowly starting to wake up from the sunshine that was coming through the balcony.

"Morning, Eric." Charlie smiled at him. The boy just nuzzled up to his chin and groaned.

"Quite the sleepy one we have here," Max said. Eric looked a little scared hearing Max's voice, but when he looked to see the man smiling at him, he quickly calmed down.

"When did you get back?" Eric yawned. Now he was sitting up a bit on Charlie. He was so clingy, it was adorable. "I thought you went on a run or something."

"Something like that," Max said. "I got back an hour or two ago. I'm glad to see you kept watch of Charlie for me."

"He found me, though," Eric said. It was so cute watching him react to all the things that Max was saying. He was still shy towards them, but it was much less than when he was around anyone else. "I just couldn't fall asleep."

"I couldn't either," Charlie laughed. "So, I guess you did help me too."

"I did?" The way he smiled was enough to make his day. He was still trying to rub the sleep out of his eyes when he looked at them.

"You're going to have to keep an eye on him more often," Max ruffled his hair. "Especially when I'm gone."

"Okay." He nodded.

"Come on." Charlie laughed. "Let's go get some breakfast. Are you hungry, Eric?"

"A little," he answered. He fell back down on Charlie and let him carry him out of the bed. "I'm still sleepy."

"Alright then, sleepy." Charlie held him tightly. "Let's get some food and then you can go back to sleep."

"Okay," he mumbled.

Max chuckled. They both walked out of their suite and towards the dining room. Max had a hand on his back to keep him close to him. Charlie couldn't help but just enjoy the moment. This was something that he had always wanted. Someone he could love for the rest of his life and someone he could help give a good life to.

Now he just had to slowly plot his plan to get Max to fall for the little boy.

CHAPTER 51:

Family Reunion

"Alistair," Nick laughed. "You know I can walk now, right?"

"No, you can't." Alistair nuzzled into his neck.

"I still don't know how you convinced Button to let me go back to my room." Nick shook his head a bit. He was still really sore and couldn't move around too much. From what Dr. Button had told him, he was still fighting off the infection, but his body was definitely winning the battle.

It helped that Aldi made sure to make him the best foods for it. He had leafy greens, yogurt, fruits, the works. Nick had to somehow convince his mom to stop bringing her food over. She always brought too much when she gave someone food. He didn't exactly want it all to go bad.

Then again, he could probably just invite Herb and Jackie over for a leftover night. The lumberjack always had a huge appetite. And Jackie was eating for four with the triplets growing fast in her stomach.

"I promised him that I would take care of you," Alistair answered his question. He laid them both down on the bed and curled up with him. "And that's exactly what I intend on doing."

"Okay Teddy Bear." Nick laughed again. It really did feel good to be back in his room. The infirmary got so stuffy and boring. At least in his room he could be comfortable and watch movies if he got bored.

The first night he finally came back to his room he was so relieved. He didn't know just how nice it would feel to be back in his comfy little apartment. Alistair absolutely loved it too. They could finally fall asleep together in the same bed, rather than the hospital bed and the chair next to it. It had been a few days of being back in his room and he wasn't complaining at all.

Now he was getting treated like royalty basically. If there was something he wanted, Alistair would go get it for him. Of course, he didn't want the man to do everything for him. He just did. He really wished that he could convince him to at least let him walk. But every time he mentioned it, Alistair would just tell him that he was worried about his wounds opening back up.

That had happened after the first day. With the cysts, they had to keep them open so that all the puss would drain out. It was the most uncomfortable few days of his life. He was glad that Alistair was there to comfort him at least a little.

Alistair taught himself how to change his bandages too, which probably helped in convincing Button to let him go to his room. Nick was shocked when he found that out. He was so gentle with everything that he had barely noticed his bandages were even off. He'd usually change them every day after bathing him.

Needless to say, Nick was getting pampered. And he couldn't help but enjoy it from Alistair.

"Well, I can tell that you're feeling better." Alistair moved Nick's hands away from his hair. "You're still checking for conditioner, aren't you?"

"There hasn't been one time that you've missed a spot, and that's suspicious." Nick joked. It was really relaxing having Alistair wash and brush his hair. His mom always made it hurt, which was why he never let anyone touch his hair in the first place. But Alistair's touch was always gentle, even when his hair was in tangles.

Alistair just chuckled and kept sending light kisses all over his neck. It was still sore from the silver, but it felt better than his stomach and his back at the moment. Alistair held the firm belief that kisses made everything better. Nick would be lying if he said that his mate's plan wasn't entirely working.

He was so sappy and romantic in such a quiet way. When Nick thought about romance, he thought about all the things that Katy talked about: flowers; public display of affection; pouring out your heart in the most grandiose ways; candle lit dinners on a starry night. While that candle lit dinner sounded like fun, the rest just wasn't for him. He didn't like showing that stuff in public. It wasn't that he was insecure about it, that was a whole other story. He just didn't want to show something so intimate to complete strangers.

Alistair showed him that romance depended on the person. And he was a sucker for all the romantic acts that Alistair did. Instead of kissing in front of people, their romance was simply the connection they shared when they talked to all of their friends. They didn't have to hold each other to show that they were together. And Nick wasn't the type of person to want to announce that stuff to the world anyway.

For some reason, Alistair taking care of him seemed really romantic. It was so comforting to know that he had someone to help him while he was healing. Someone who wasn't going to leave him to himself at all. After what had happened just a little over a week ago, Nick really didn't want to be alone to his thoughts. The more he thought about those memories, the more they started to consume him.

"Nick." Alistair's voice came as a soothing distraction from his mind. His hands pulled him closer just a little more. "It's okay. You're safe."

He hadn't even known he was starting to freak himself out. Those memories liked to pop up out of the blue and haunt him. The first few nights of being in the infirmary, he wound up bawling into Alistair. He was so terrified of even closing his eyes. He'd kept thinking that he would see that horrible face again. He didn't want to be trapped in that nightmare ever again.

"I'm okay," he told him. He took comfort in the caresses that Alistair always gave. He was his cure for this. Just like all of his insecurities, Alistair had slowly been able to wipe away most of the fears that tried to consume him.

He would never be able to thank the Goddess enough that he had Alistair. He couldn't believe that someone like him even existed in the world. He would have never believed that there was someone so calm and loving until he met Alistair. The gentle giant had a way of slipping into everyone's heart. Even Liam liked him, which was saying something.

Nick found out sometime in that infirmary that Alistair had been keeping himself busy that day that he was out with the Lunas. Barry told him that the day he was out, Alistair had spent his down time talking things over with his mom. He couldn't believe that he would even try to go up to her when she was still really mad, let alone try to convince her to talk to him.

He had apparently gotten her to listen, too. It took them forever to convince his mom to accept Fred for who he was. But with Alistair, it only took a day.

"It must have been because he talked to her in person," George told him. "When Barry and I came to visit, Dad told us that he had been there all day."

"Oh, it was the most adorable thing ever!" Barry gave him a playful look. "He talked about how he just wanted to protect you; how he loved you; how he knew that if mom didn't talk to you, he was sure that your heart would break."

"Okay, you can stop now." Nick had to look away. His family absolutely loved embarrassing him.

"I should have known he was going to be sappy," Clara said. She had come to visit him in that infirmary a lot too. "Knowing Nick, he was going to have to be."

"Shut it, Paint Brain," Nick said. Clara was the only one in the family who inherited his mom's skill for drawing. She had actually sold quite a few paintings. But, because of it, she always seemed to be aloof and to herself. There was always some idea floating in her brain that she was trying to shape and perfect before she got it on canvas.

It was nice getting to tease her again. They all came at least twice a day to visit him. His parents came at least six times, though. He wound up getting to see all of his nieces and nephews a thousand times over. They all varied in ages. But all of them were dying to see their cool uncle again.

Alistair seemed to fair well with them all. They asked about a million questions about his adventures and how he looked. He just smiled and answered them all. It was easy to see that he loved kids.

He couldn't wait until their next family reunion. It was going to be fun having Alistair meet the rest of his siblings and their kids. He was going to have to warn him about them ahead of time. A lot of them were rowdy.

The kids too.

"I have a surprise for you, Bakshir," Alistair said. He must have known that his thoughts were flooding his mind too much for him to try and get any sleep. Button had been telling him to basically sleep like a cat throughout the day. The medicine helped with that for the most part. He had been so tired lately. But today he felt more awake than he had before. He didn't know whether it was a good thing or a bad thing just yet.

"What is it?"

"A surprise," Alistair answered him. Nick frowned at him, knowing that he was going to be put in a loop of never getting an answer. Alistair just kissed the frown away and chuckled. "You're so cute."

"I'm not the cute one," Nick argued. He would have this argument until the end of time. He was not cute. Alistair was the teddy bear.

"Yes, you are." Alistair's smile reached his eyes when he looked at him. "And so is your wolf."

"Does the surprise have anything to do with my wolf, then?"

"No." Alistair shook his head and slowly slipped out of the bed. "I just think your wolf is cute."

"Wait." He grabbed his hand. "Where are you going?"

"Nowhere far, Bakshir." Alistair leaned over him and kissed him again. Nick hated that he was being clingy at the moment, but he was so scared of being alone. "We both need to be wearing something for this surprise, though."

"Oh." Now he felt dumb for holding onto him. It was strange not having Alistair's arms around him when he had practically been living in them for the past three days.

He didn't take long, though. He came back wearing some shorts and a blue shirt. His arms came around Nick again and quickly moved the blanket off of him.

"Wait!" Nick tried to stop him. "I can put my own clothes on!"

"Can I please dress you, then?" Alistair was by his ear when he asked. He was lovingly placing kisses all over his jaw.

"Fine." Nick sighed. He couldn't help but cave into him. It wasn't like he had much energy to keep fighting a pointless battle. "But you have to give me a hint as to what this surprise is."

"Deal." The man seemed way too happy to be agreeing to this. "It has something to do with your family."

"Are they coming here to visit?"

"Yes."

"Really?!" He looked at him. "That was my surprise?" Exactly how many times has his family visited him in a day? He swore his apartment had never been as filled with people. And Clara hadn't even been in his room until then.

"Trust me, Bakshir." Alistair kissed him again. "You're going to love it."

He didn't quite know what was going to be any different than the usual visits he had with his family, but he didn't ask anything further. This was something that he was just going to have to see for himself.

He decided to put his hair up in a braid. As much as Alistair loved it when it was down, he needed it away from his face. And braids didn't hurt your head when you laid down on them.

"When are they coming?"

"Right now." Right as Alistair said that there was a knock on the door. He didn't bother trying to find the scent of who was behind it. He knew that it was his family at this point. He was starting to wonder whether this was really a surprise or not when Alistair opened the door.

Boy, was he wrong.

"Fred!" He smiled when he saw his eldest brother. The man was now in his late thirties and was looking more and more like their father every day.

"Nick!" He ran up to him and gave him a hug. "I'm so glad you're okay!"

Fred wasn't the only one who came through that door. His small apartment was soon bustling as all of his siblings came into the room along with his parents.

Did he say all?

Because he meant all. All eleven of them came up to him and hugged him. They were all talking at once and trying to catch up on lost time.

Nick looked at Alistair in disbelief.

"How did you get everyone here?" he asked him. They normally don't all come together like this unless it's for their reunions. Nick was sure that all of their kids probably came with them as well.

Heather was probably having a heart attack with all the rooms she was going to have to get ready for all of them.

"He didn't," Charlie came into the room. "I may have made a few calls, though."

"It was mom, too," Fred said. "Do you really think we wouldn't come down here after hearing that you almost died?"

"Well, no." He shook his head. "I just can't believe that you're all here and it's not a reunion."

"This doesn't count as one, by the way!" Sophia, the third oldest in their family, said. "I've already gotten the plane tickets for two years from now and I do not want to be on hold for two hours to try and get them refunded!"

"What?" Barry teased. "You could find a new drink mix to sell at your bar in that time!"

"There's a reason I call that drink an 'On Hold, Please Wait'," Sophia laughed.

"I still have yet to try that one," Nick told her.

"Oh, that reminds me!" She gasped. "I wasn't able to be here for your 21st!"

"It's okay." He put his palms out in front of him as a means of surrender. "I'm not ready to be blacked-out drunk anyway."

"You know I wouldn't let you get that bad!" Sophia teased. "Maybe I should bring you over to my place and we can celebrate a late 21st when this is all said and done."

"I'm sure Alex would love to see that." He laughed. The Beta of the pack that she had moved to was a blast at parties. They were a fun bunch.

"I don't think Max is going to let anyone go anywhere for a while after this." George shook his head. "Maybe we should do it for his 22nd instead."

There were so many of them in that little room of his. He almost forgot what it was like having his family over like this. Right now, there was just a bunch of catching up that they were all doing. But there were usually a bunch of dancing and partying that went on when they were all together. That's just how their family was.

This was just a different circumstance.

"I'm sorry." He overheard Charlie say to one of his sisters. "I'm afraid I forgot your name."

"That's okay," Nick hollered above the noise of everyone else. "We forget each other's names all the time!"

Laughter erupted in the room. He missed the fun atmosphere that always surrounded his family. They were always such a blast to be around.

"Roll call!" his dad yelled out. He had trained them so well that they all knew what to do when he said something specific or did something with his hands. That was how they were able to do so many surprise dances at parties and in public. Those were so much fun.

"Roll call?" Charlie looked over to his dad with amused curiosity.

"We all made a little rhyme together when we were all kids," Nick explained. "Instead of us just telling our names over and over, we made up an earworm so that it would be harder to forget."

"Why don't you do it this time, Nick?" Fred asked. "Since you're the only one that has to sit down."

He had wanted to stand, but Alistair gently kept him down. He probably didn't want him to strain himself too much. Nick didn't mind, honestly. He was happy that he could at least sit up when he talked to people rather than having to lay down all the time like he did in the infirmary.

"You see, Charlie." He put a finger up in the air and gave him a playful look. "The Moore Family Roll Call goes a little like this:

Alex and Myra started this all,

With a marriage by a moonlit waterfall.

Then came Fred,

Who had a big head,

And Josephine the Princess,

Or, at least, that's how she liked to dress.

Sophia the Barista,

Who found her love through her charisma.

Noreen and Kat,

Twins that love to bat.

Barry was the middle child,

Surprisingly, he was very mild.

Clara the bookworm,

Who never got any work done.

Charlette the dancer,

The professional, at least.

George, the brain,

That's what the parents say.

Willow's like a pillow,

She lays around too much.

Hailey, the fighter,

Who's started out as a biter."

He paused for a second. He had been pointing to everyone that he had mentioned. They had done this routine so much they could all do it off the top of their head. Charlie and Alistair looked like they were enjoying it at least. But there was one last verse that this little poem had that he still had to say.

"The last was Nick,

The boy who was always sick."

Everyone was a little quiet at that. It kind of struck a little too close to home at the moment. He could see just how worried they all were about him. They didn't need to be. He was going to be fine, just like he always had been. But his family always worried. They had started worrying as soon as his mom had gotten kidnapped when she was pregnant with him.

"We really need to update this little roll call," Sophia said. She hugged Nick gently.

"It was made when we were all kids," Nick said. "We all could have said much worse about each other."

He swore he could spend the whole day with all of them here with him. It was so nice that they were all here. They all seemed to like Alistair too, which he was glad of. Most of the time they just told old stories of when they were kids. But, when their mom left, Fred sat next to him and pulled him into another hug.

"Nick, can I ask you something?"

"What is it?"

"Are you positive that the rogue that took you was a Darius?" He looked serious now. Everyone else had hushed down to hear his answer as well. Nick was the only one who wasn't around for when their mom got kidnapped, although Hailey was still really young as well. It affected all of them when they were growing up. And that man had been the cause of a lot of strife with their family for a long time after he had died.

Nick sighed and looked down. It hurt to think back to that day. He didn't even know how much time had passed. It all seemed like it was just one big blur.

"Yes," he said. "He looked just like him."

"How do you know for sure, though?" Hailey asked. "It could have just been his doppelganger."

"Because I told him the story," he explained. "I told him that Gene Darius was weak. For he couldn't even kill a pregnant omega."

"You said that?!" Fred looked shocked at him. "Why would you tell him that when you were tied up already with no way of escaping?"

"Because." He took in a deep breath. "I knew that he would be just like his father: too weak to even kill an omega."

He had definitely called the man's bluff too.

CHAPTER 52

The Safest Place

"Leo!" Fred hugged the old Alpha. Charlie had been seeing him walking around the manor more than the rest that had come. They were a fun bunch, even if they couldn't stay around for too long.

"Fred!" Mr. Locke hugged him back. His eyes sparkled at seeing the man. "How've you been? I haven't heard from you in forever."

"Oh, you know how it goes." Fred rolled his eyes. His were hazel, just like Nick's. Charlie was glad that he had helped him get the rest of the siblings. "The kids are going through more schooling; works a mess; and Bill's thinking about adopting more."

"You guys adopt?" Charlie asked. He had known that Fred was gay when he had first heard about him. Nick and him had been really close, even with their huge age gap. He didn't know they adopted, though.

"Oh yeah!" Fred told him. "We have to make sure they're werewolves too, of course, just because of them being raised with the pack. But we've adopted about five kids so far. They're so much fun to help raise."

He could tell how Nick and him got along so easily after just a few minutes of talking to him. Fred was the type who always talked and talked and talked. He was a story teller too, much like everyone in that family. But he told his stories differently than Nick. It was fun to see all the similarities as well as the differences in all of the siblings.

"You're going to have to show Charlie and Max the ropes, now," Mr. Locke said. He had a playful sparkle in his eyes. "They're going to be adopting sometime soon."

"After all this rogue business is said and done," Max said. He looked a bit grumpy when he said it. Charlie knew that he wanted to deal with these rogues first, but it still made his heart sink when he heard him say that.

That's what was keeping them from marrying too. Everything was put on hold for these rogues. He hated it. As much as he knew that these rogues needed to be taken care of, and they were dangerous, it made Charlie wonder if they would ever rid themselves of them.

This pack had been dealing with rogues since the dawn of time. Even if they did get rid of this Damir, there was always going to be more that sprung up. And if Max didn't want to do anything until he thought the pack was completely safe, then Charlie might be waiting a long time.

"I wouldn't wait until then," Fred said. It seemed like he was picking up on Charlie's emotions better than Max was at the moment. "Rogues have been a problem for every pack since the beginning of existence."

"I know that." Max sighed. "But these ones are only here because of that territory that was left unclaimed for thousands of years. And those rogues are dangerous."

"But that shouldn't mean that you put your life on hold." Fred frowned. "Life is full of danger, Max. And this pack house is the safest, by far, compared to any other pack I've visited."

"We'll see what happens when we get there." Charlie put a hand on Max's arm. He didn't want to have this argument right then. "We haven't even gotten married yet."

"What?!" Fred's eyes got wide for a second. "Do you guys have a date at least?"

"Just sent the invitations," Max smiled. It was nice to see him smile again. He had been so stressed lately. "We're looking at December 6th."

"A December wedding?" He looked at Charlie. "You must be so excited! Hopefully it won't be snowing, though. I know that you guys are probably going to be doing it outside anyway."

"Well, it's good to finally have something planned." Charlie smiled at Max. "I still have quite a lot to try and figure out, though."

"If you want, I know a guy," Fred suggested. "He's a great wedding planner. It might be the perfect thing so that you don't have to do all the work."

"I was thinking about getting some friends to help, actually," he told him. He already had Wynona giving him ideas for it every day. And Katy had finally gotten service at her pack house. They had already started doing conference calls during their working hours just to talk while doing something.

"Well." The man dug into his pocket to pull out his wallet. "I'm going to give you his card, just in case. He really is a great wedding planner. Or, if anything, you could call him and get some pointers for certain things you might need."

"Fred." Mr. Locke got the man's attention. "You're doing it again."

"What?" He looked at the man, completely innocent. "All I'm doing is recommending him someone."

"And acting like you're on commission at the same time." Mr. Locke laughed. "Do you forget how many weddings happen in this very manor every year?"

"Okay, fine!" Fred pouted a bit. "Take all the fun out of everything, just like you've always done."

It was fun seeing Mr. Locke talking like this to someone. He had no idea him and Fred were friends. They had an age difference, but it didn't seem to affect their friendship at all. They both talked like they had known each other since they were kids.

Charlie's mind drifted as the conversation went on without him. He had been thinking about adopting for a while now. But he had wanted to wait until he was secure enough to take care of a child. Him and Max had enough money to handle a kid, but they were still both completely knew to their careers. And Max was hell bound on trying to take care of these rogues before their marriage.

But he really wanted to adopt Eric. The boy had gone through so much already, and he was happy with them. He had even started to cling onto Max every once in a while. Charlie couldn't help but carry the boy around with him when he was working. He had gotten some kid books for him to draw on so that he could try and teach him some things. They hadn't quite figured out whether he was staying here or not yet, so they had decided against enrolling him in school.

Charlie didn't really think the poor boy was ready for school just yet anyway. He was still extremely shy when it came to talking to others. The only other two that Charlie had gotten him to talk to was Alistair and Nick. Eric actually smiled at Nick when he saw him.

"You were right," he had told Nick. "He couldn't kill you!"

Nick told him plenty of stories about their pack and his family in general when Charlie brought him to visit. It was nice to see him in his room rather than in the infirmary. Eric had grown to dislike it after being stuck in there for so long.

The way the boy always lit up whenever he saw Charlie or Max made his heart melt. He wished he could tell if Max liked the boy as well, but he really didn't know. So, he figured that he would just help the boy learn as much as he could and get him to talk to more people.

Max's arm had gone around his waist to pull him closer to him. It snapped him back to the conversation that they were all talking about.

"No," Fred shook his head. "He's still in trouble for trying to have a food fight with his sister in the school cafeteria."

"I remember hearing your mom yell at you for doing the same thing," Mr. Locke laughed. "I swear the whole manor shook with how loud she was."

"Oh, mom was always overdramatizing everything." Fred waved the thought off. "Especially with us boys. She always thought she had to be harsher on us. Nick was the only one of us that was treated like an absolute baby."

"Nope." Max shook his head. "She's yelled at him plenty of times too."

"Ah, yes," Mr. Locke said. "Max would know. When they were teenagers, Max was the main reason why Nick got in trouble so much."

"It wasn't my idea to sneak into the pantry." Max smiled. "Not the first time, at least."

"Pfft!" Fred almost burst into laughter. "She yelled at him for sneaking into the pantry?!"

"Not just for sneaking in there." Mr. Locke clarified. "They ate at least half of the supplies we had in there."

"There was no way we ate half." Max rolled his eyes. "Aldi just overexaggerated because he was mad."

"Charlie?" A small voice interrupted the conversation. Charlie looked to see Eric standing in the doorway. He looked scared again. He knew that the poor boy must have had another nightmare.

"Hey, Eric!" He moved away from Max's hold to go up to the boy. "What's wrong?"

"I had a nightmare." He rubbed his eyes.

"Who's this little guy?" Fred asked. Charlie looked behind him to see that Fred had gone into his own parenting mode. He had knelt down to the ground to make himself seem less scary for Eric.

Wait. Charlie should have thought of that! That could work to help him be comfortable with other people when he first meets them.

"This is Eric," Max explained. "He's the one we found when we saved Charlie and all of them."

"Hi, Eric!" Fred waved over to him. "I'm Fred!"

Eric seemed a little warry of him at first. But he waved back. He walked closer to Charlie and held his hand. Charlie couldn't help but smile at him.

"He's a little shy when it comes to new people," Charlie told him.

"Oh, that's okay." Fred assured him. "Most kids in his situation are."

"You look like Nick," Eric said.

"Well, I shouldn't be surprised that you know Nick." Fred chuckled a bit. "I'm his brother, actually."

"Really?"

"Yeah. I want to say I'm his best big brother, but Barry and George might come in and argue with me if I say that."

The boy giggled at that. Charlie was shocked to see just how easily the man had made him comfortable with being around them all. He still held Charlie's hand, but he seemed more willing to talk than before.

Fred had motioned for Eric to come closer to him. For some unbeknownst reason, he listened. He took his small hand out of Charlie's and went up to him.

Was he doing something wrong with trying to help Eric? Maybe he wasn't cut out to be a parent like he thought he was. If Fred had been able to so easily get this boy to calm down, then how was he going to be able to match up to that?

"Where's your home, Eric?" Fred asked.

It looked like he didn't know what to say, so he just pointed at Charlie.

"You live here, then?" Fred asked again. Eric just nodded his response. "This is a nice place. Do you like it here?"

"I don't like the cold room," Eric told him.

"The cold room?"

"He means the infirmary," Charlie told him. "He had to go there to get taken care of when we first found him."

"Ah," he said before looking back to Eric. "That's okay, no one really wants to be there. We just go to get better and leave when we're healthy."

"Nick got to leave when he wasn't healthy," Eric said.

"Well, that's because sometimes the best place to heal is in your home." Fred ruffled the boy's hair a bit. "Home is where you're the most comfortable, after all."

Eric nodded again and looked back to Charlie. He looked a little nervous, but Charlie nodded at him that he would be okay. This is the most he had seen him talk.

"So, do you like the rest of the place?"

"Yeah." He smiled a little. His smiles were always so adorable. "I like the office."

"We've been going there to get some work done in the mornings," Charlie explained.

"That's what I did with Max all the time." Mr. Locke smiled. "It was the best way to keep an eye on the rascal without dumping him on someone else to watch."

"I wasn't too bad as a child." Max rolled his eyes. He seemed to be watching Eric as well.

"You weren't the one having to parent," Mr. Locke said. "You just don't remember all the times you would throw a tantrum if I so much as left the room."

Charlie laughed at that. It was good to know that Max had been clingy since he was a child. That definitely explained a lot about him now.

"Do you like being with Charlie and Max, Eric?" Fred asked. He had a certain shimmer in his eyes that showed Charlie that he had some sort of plan. When he looked at him, the man gave him a slight wink.

"Yeah," Eric said. "They make me feel safe."

He could feel Max tense. He was holding Charlie close to him again as Fred had asked him that. Charlie wasn't entirely sure how Max had felt about what Eric had said, but he had to fix this situation, and fast.

"I should probably bring him to bed," Charlie said. "It's way past bed time." He could already see the poor boy yawning. Eric gladly let Charlie pick him up.

"It was nice meeting you, Eric." Fred waved. Eric waved a little back at him before Charlie walked him out of the room. He was already starting to fall asleep on his shoulder. He loved the feeling of someone falling asleep in his arms. Usually, Max would always wait until he was asleep before he let himself drift off.

"Can I sleep with you and Max again tonight?" Eric asked.

"Sure." Charlie held him tighter. He quickly walked up the stairs to him and Max's suite. It was never that long of a walk. At least, it never seemed that far. The manor was still huge. And Max was planning on building an extension on the manor to have more rooms for the growing pack. But his room was always the easiest to find.

When he got into the suite, he laid Eric on their bed and tucked him in.

"You get some rest." He kissed his forehead. "I'll be back in just a little bit."

He still had to go and say goodnight to Fred and Mr. Locke. He wasn't sure if he was really up for more talking. He was too troubled at the moment to keep up a good conversation. There was just so much to think about and try to figure out. Luckily Eric just nodded and curled into the bed. It was adorable how he always tried to put himself into a little ball when he slept.

Before he could even get out of the door, Max came in. Their bedroom was closed off to the rest of their suite, so he just closed the door to it before he faced Max.

He had a feeling that this wasn't going to be good.

"Charlie, I need to talk to you."

"Okay," he said cautiously. They both sat down at the dining table that they had. "Is this about Eric?"

"Yeah." Max rubbed his face. "I think it would be best to see if Fred would like to adopt him."

Charlie's heart broke at those words. He was hoping that he could hold off on thinking about someone adopting him at least until all of the issues with the rogues were over. He shouldn't have stayed to talk to Fred. Now there would be no chance of him even seeing the little boy.

"Why?" he felt compelled to ask. He hated making things more difficult for Max, but a part of him didn't want to let this go.

"Charlie." Max grabbed his hands and started to rub them. His eyes looked just as sad as he felt at the moment. "I know you want him. I want him too. But I don't know if this is the safest place for him right now."

"What do you mean?" He had to hold back tears. It was good to know that Max wanted the boy too. But he was still willing to let him go?

"As soon as Nick's health is good enough for him to be without his mate," Max started. "I'm going to be setting off with the warriors into that forest. Leonard and Owen are gathering their warriors for the same thing. They're waiting on me to make the first move."

"When is this going to be?" Charlie's heart started to pound for a whole new reason now. "Why didn't you tell me about this?"

"Because you've been healing from what that damn rogue has done to you," Max said. "And I didn't want to put any pressure on you after what you went through."

"So, this is going to happen as soon as Alistair is ready, then?" Charlie asked. "When is that going to be? How long are you guys going to be in that forest?"

"Button said that Nick should be healthy enough in a week," Max answered. "With all these armies going into the uncharted territory, I'm thinking it that it should only take a week for us to fully expand our territory and get rid of the rogues that are scattered in that area."

"How many people know about this?" He needed to know just how much he had been kept out of the loop.

"Not many," Max said. "Only the council knows at the moment. But, when we go into that forest, there's a chance that some of those rogues will come into our territory again and try to come for the manor."

"So, you do want him," Charlie clarified. "You're just worried that he could get hurt?"

"Yeah," Max kissed Charlie's hands. "The pack that Fred's in has had experience with orphans before, especially troubled ones. They don't have any wars going on and very little enemies at the moment."

It made him feel a little better that Max was still trying to look out for the little boy. Charlie understood where he was coming from. With all that bloodshed that could happen, it probably wouldn't be a good idea to have him around to see all of that. It might hurt the boy more by bringing him back to the point where he had been traumatized.

"Okay," Charlie agreed. His heart was breaking into little tiny pieces as he was saying this, but he wanted to keep Eric safe too. "Let's go talk to Fred then."

"No!" Eric came running out from the bedroom. Charlie barely had any time to look in that direction before the boy jumped into his arms. "I don't wanna go!" He burst into tears. "Please don't make me! I want to stay here, with you!"

Charlie held him close to him and tried to calm him down. He was sure that he had fallen asleep by the time he had tucked him in. It made him feel even worse that he had heard all of what they were talking about.

"Eric." Charlie moved his hand up and down the small boy's back. "It's okay, I promise. We just want to protect you."

"But you can protect me here!" Eric argued. "Why do I have to go somewhere else?"

"Eric." Max got his attention this time. "There's a lot of enemies that we're trying to get rid of right now. It might not be the safest to be with us."

"Then I'll help fight!" Eric said. He looked so confident in himself as he said it. "I can protect people too! I protected Charlie before!"

"But you got hurt while you did that, Eric." Charlie held him closer. "We don't want you to get hurt."

Eric burst into tears again after he said that. He buried his face into Charlie's shirt and held onto him as tightly as a little boy like him could.

"Please let me stay!" he begged. "I love you."

Charlie looked at Max. Those purple eyes looked just as pained as before. He could tell that he was fighting an inner battle with himself.

"Remember when you told me to stop thinking about the 'What if's'?" Charlie mind linked with him.

"Vaguely, why?"

"I think, maybe, we should stop thinking about all the things that could happen, and focus on what we want."

"It's a little more difficult when there's a little boy's life at stake, Apple." Max ran a hand through his hair.

"What do you want, Max?" Charlie looked at him intensely. *"Forget about everything else for a second, and tell me what you want."*

"I want to start a family with you, Charlie." Max sighed. It looked as if a ton of weight just came off his shoulders as he admitted that. *"I want to marry you and have a family with you. I want to adopt Eric. But-!"*

"There is no 'But's." Charlie smiled at him. *"Let's just make it happen. We can't keep waiting for life to get better before we start trying to live it."*

"And what if something happens?" Max looked at him with another worried expression. *"How's he going to react when I'm gone for a week or longer?"*

"We'll work through all the problems that life throws at us together." Charlie grabbed his hand. "I can take care of him while you're gone. We'll figure out the rest when you get back."

Max looked at him for a second or two longer. Eric was slowing down in his cries. It seemed like Charlie comforting him was helping at least a little.

"Okay, Eric." Max knelt down to get to his level. "We'll take care of you."

"You will?" Eric looked out from Charlie's shirt, still sniffling a little.

"We will." Max smiled at him. "But I need you to do one thing for me."

"Anything." Eric nodded.

"I need you to take care of Charlie while I'm gone." Max looked at Charlie as he said that. "I'm going on a trip for a week, and I need someone who's brave enough to protect him while I'm not here." He started wiping off some of the tears that had fallen from Eric's cheeks. "Can you do that for me?"

Eric smiled and nodded. Without a second thought, he moved his hold from Charlie to Max. The look on Max's face as the boy held onto him was absolutely beautiful. He hugged Eric back, smiling like a proud father would.

"Alright." Max picked him up as he stood. "How about we all get some sleep now?"

Charlie smiled as they all walked back into their bedroom. After all the stress that they had gone through that day, with all the Moore's coming to visit, along with this talk with Eric, he was sure that they all needed a good night's rest.

He was just glad that he could go to bed happy, with both the people that he loved cuddled against him.

CHAPTER 53:

The Ceremony

"It's going to be okay, Bakshir." Alistair held him in his arms. "I won't be far."

"You guys are going to be going through that giant forest." Nick held him tightly. "You're crazy if you think that's not far!"

"It isn't when I compare it to how far from here I was when I first felt your pull." He nuzzled into his neck. He had enjoyed being able to help Nick heal from those wounds that he had. The Alpha of his old pack would never let him do something like that when his mother became ill. He always said that there were more important things to be done. Or he would tell him that they didn't have time.

The fact that Alpha Max had completely put this on hold until Nick was healthy enough told Alistair that he truly was a good leader. He wanted to make sure that everyone was going to be okay before setting out on this mission. Alistair was grateful for that.

"I'm still going to miss you." Nick sighed. "I know Max said it was a good idea that Fred and all of them leave before you guys go, but now I'm not going to have anyone to talk to."

It was fun to meet all of his siblings. Alistair always wanted siblings of his own. He had wanted someone to play with when he was young, but no one was ever allowed to play with him. Their parents would just look at him in disgust. Nick's family all seemed to like him. They loved telling jokes and embarrassing Nick. It was funny to see his mate blush so much at everything they said. He was sure that he was the only one who saw it, though. That dark skin could hide it so easily.

"I heard that Katy got reception at the Blood Moon house finally," Alistair told him. "And I'm sure that Charlie is going to need some company."

"I guess." Nick clung to him. "But what if you get hurt?"

"I didn't get hurt the last times I traveled in that forest," Alistair assured him. "I'm not going to get hurt, Bakshir. There's too much to live for."

Nick groaned and buried himself in Alistair's shirt. It only made him hold the man tighter. A part of him was sad that he had to go. He wanted to keep Nick in his arms forever. He already longed for the days that they could lay around in their room and just enjoy each other.

But there was another part of him that he had been trying to keep at bay since he had saved Nick from that cabin. It was a fury that was getting more difficult to contain every day. He needed to get revenge for all the things that this Damir did to Nick. He needed revenge for his Luna, and the other two Lunas that had gotten captured.

He needed to watch this man bleed to death in front of him, with eyes of fear.

One day that Nick was asleep, he had mind linked with Max on advice to keep this strong emotion at bay. It was strange to go directly to the Alpha, but he didn't know who else to ask at the time. Max told him that he had that very same rage every time he saw Nick in those bandages, and every time he thought about how bad Charlie had been. It was good to know that he wasn't alone with his feelings about this situation.

That's when Max had told him about this plan. He had told him that when Nick was healthy enough to be away from him, that they would start their push into the uncharted territory, and start expanding their land. They were going to begin by cutting the rogues off from the one part of the forest that they could use to escape. Then they would keep marking territory until they cornered them.

It helped him control his emotions better after hearing that. The knowledge that the Alpha had a plan to eliminate their problem made him feel much better, along with the rest of the warriors when they were told. They all seemed eager to get this done.

"Come on, Bakshir." Alistair rubbed his mates back. "I need to get going."

"There's no way to get out of this, is there?" Nick sighed, loosening his hold on him. It almost hurt to take himself out of his mate's arms. He still wished that he could hold him forever.

"It's only a week." He kissed him on the cheek before he got up to change. "We don't have much more of them, anyway."

Nick got changed with him after that. They walked to the training room in silence. That was where all the warriors were meeting before they went on their run. Just outside of the training room was where the Alpha would lead all of them past the territory lines.

"Aunt Martha!" They looked to see Aldi following the elder warrior to the room as well. "You can't be doing this! You're 91!"

"And next year, I'll be 92." Martha chuckled. "You worry too much for me, Aldi. Did you forget how many wars I've fought in?"

"Did *you* forget that you're the oldest member in the pack?!" It was the first time he had ever seen the chef look so angry. "What if you die out there?"

"Then I will have a warrior's death," Martha told him. "I'm not going to retire when there's dangerous rogues as close as our doorstep, Aldi."

"I'm not saying retire," Aldi said. "I'm just saying that I don't want you to die!"

"I won't," she assured him. "I've been in battles like these and come out of them alive countless times, Aldi. I can do it again."

They weren't the only ones that were arguing with worried family members. The closer they got to the training room, the more arguing they heard from the warriors. Many of them were mated couples that showed lines of worry on their faces. Ray and Desmond's mates were both on the verge of tears as they were saying their goodbyes.

Ed and his mate, Emily, were having a heavy moment as well. Ever since Ed had come back beaten by those rouges, his mate has been staying by his side. They all understood why she would want him to stay. A part of Alistair wanted him to stay as well. He worried that the man might still need time to heal.

But he also knew that Ed felt guilty for not being able to protect Nick and Charlie. He had come to Alistair when Nick was still in the infirmary to apologize. He didn't know why he should apologize to him. Ed had done everything he could to fight off those rogues. His golden eyes had looked dull for once.

"Don't let your guilt eat you," Alistair told him. "There wasn't anything you could have done to prevent that."

He heard that Ed had almost died in that fight. If it weren't for Alpha Leonard and Max finding him on time, he could have very well lost his life. That's what Ed was prepared to do to save Charlie and Nick. That was nothing to be ashamed of.

When he told him all of that, he was glad to see the spark come back to those eyes. Ed seemed a little happier, even though they were all worried about Nick at the time.

"All I know is that I'm going to get a good bite out of at least one of them," Ed had said. "And, when I do, I'm going to make sure that they pay for what they did."

That's how all the warriors felt at the moment. All of them were outraged at what had happened to their pack members; to their Luna. All of them were itching for something to do; some way of getting revenge.

Now was their time to prove themselves and show the rogues just how powerful they were.

"Look." Alan came up from behind them with Madeline by his side. "All I'm saying is that you could just tell them that you *think* it, and no one would bat an eye!"

"I'm not going to say that I *think* I might be pregnant to get out of this, Alan." Madeline rolled her eyes. "We need every single one of these warriors to get rid of these guys for good."

Nick laughed at what they had said.

"Hey, Nick!" Alan put his attention towards him. "Long time, no see!"

"You visited me plenty of times, Alan." Nick chuckled again. "It's good to see you again, though."

"It's been a while since I've seen you up and moving around, though." Alan smiled at him. He seemed a lot happier now that he was mated. Alistair was glad. "Does this mean that you're going to be coming back to the kitchen soon? We've all been missing how quickly you could cook those pancakes."

"I hope so." Nick held onto Alistair's hand tighter than he did before. "Or else I'm going to be way too bored for the entire week."

"Yeah…" Alan's face turned into one of worry.

"Good to see that the Teddy Bear's come out to play," Madeline joked. She looked excited as she talked to him. "You ready for the run of a lifetime?"

"I've been running my whole life," Alistair told her. "I can handle running for a week."

"Good." Alan butted into their conversation. "Because you better protect her out there."

"You have my word." He smiled at him.

"Oh please!" Madeline rolled her eyes. "I don't need any protecting."

Before they could even begin to start bickering, they heard some noises coming from the door to the training room. They walked inside to see just about the entire pack in the room. It made it look much smaller than before. They poured out into the backyard as well.

"There they are!" Barry yelled. Him and George were standing together in the crowd. Alistair smiled. They were probably waiting for Nick to come out so that they could be there for him when he left.

"You guys here for the ceremony too?" Nick asked as they ran up to him. Alistair had already had to get used to the hugging nature that the family had. They hugged everyone they could when they greeted them. It made sense that Nick was as cuddly as he was after meeting his family.

"Of course!" George said. "Do you think we wouldn't be here to see Alistair off?"

"Me?" He furrowed his eyebrows at that. He thought they were just there for Nick.

"Yeah, you!" Barry clasped his hand onto Alistair's arm. "You thought that we wouldn't?"

"No one's come to see me off before." Alistair shook his head. "Other than Nick, that is."

"Come on, Alistair." George smiled at him. "You're a Moore now. You're family."

Family? He didn't know how he was feeling at hearing that. He had always wanted a family. But he thought that it wasn't possible after his mother died. Nick was the first person he had ever gotten really close with after her.

Nick squeezed his hand to snap him out of his shock. He looked at his mate to see that he was smiling at him as well.

"Thank you." He turned back to George and Barry. "That's truly the best gift you could give me."

"I don't know if I'd say that yet." Barry laughed. "There's some mandatory skills you have to learn in this family, like dancing."

"They aren't mandatory." George rolled his eyes at his brother. "I thought you were going to tell him about babysitting or something."

"Oh, the kids love him!" Barry waved off. "As long as he's willing to let them climb all over him, he'll be fine with that."

He really did like this family. They all had a way with words that could calm anyone down. He thought that he would be happy with simply having Nick for the rest of his life. And he would be. But belonging to a family is something that he hadn't felt in a long, long time. It was a feeling that he had almost forgotten.

They talked a little more after that. Herb and Jackie were there as well. Jackie was already in tears as she ran up to them. Madeline tried her best to calm the poor woman down, but she seemed just as worried as everyone else for them.

There was still plenty of time before they left. The warriors came more and more with each minute that passed. But Alistair soon got distracted and his mind drifted to the trees that he would soon be running through.

The wind had shifted. It seemed calm, but there was electricity in the air. He could feel the tension that the forest had to it. It called to him.

"Hey, Alistair?" Madeline snapped him out of his thoughts. "You okay there?"

"Yes." He smiled at her. "Just thinking."

"About what?" Nick asked. He hadn't left his side the entire time they left the room.

"The wind," he answered. He looked back to the forest. It was evening at the moment. They weren't planning on going until night had come, so that they might be blessed by the Moon for their travels. It was going to be a full moon that night as well, which meant the Moon Goddess would guide them to victory.

"What about the wind?" Madeline asked. "Is it saying anything this time?"

Alistair smiled when he remembered the first time he met her. He had listened to the forest to hear what it had to say about the people in the land. A fight for peace was the first thing that he heard from it. After that, though, he hadn't heard much. It was peaceful in the trees of their territory.

"It's calling us to go," Alistair told her.

"What does that mean?" Barry asked. They had all stopped talking at that point and were focused on what he was saying.

"It means that the forest is giving us her blessing on our endeavor," Alistair answered. He didn't want to tell them about the tension in the wind, or what it meant. He was sure that it would only worry them more. He would make sure to tell the warriors when he got a chance, though.

"*What are you hiding this time?*" Madeline's voice popped in his head. He glanced at her to see those golden eyes giving him a suspicious look. She had always been able to tell when there was something he was keeping from everyone. Nick wasn't feeling well enough to pick up on it, but Madeline was like a mother hen checking up on her chicks.

"*There's tension in the air,*" he told her. "*It's the reason why the forest is calling us.*"

"*Tension? What does that mean for us, then?*"

"Fighting," he answered. *"When the wind is tense around a forest, it's telling you that there is danger. Right now, I believe that it is calling us to help with that danger."*

"So, that means that the rogues are still out there, then," Madeline said. *"They haven't escaped yet."*

"I don't think they're planning on leaving their part of the forest any time soon."

"They will when we're done with them," Madeline promised.

They went back to talking about normal things. Alistair tried to keep Nick from getting too nervous about him leaving. He was tempted to try and buy a bear for him, just because of the nickname that he was given. But he hadn't been able to leave the packhouse to try and buy one. He had been too busy staying as close as possible to Nick during the time that he was healing.

The sun settled into the horizon slowly. It was one of those summer days that seemed to last forever. But, when it ended, and the sun went down, that was when the ceremony began.

The council came out to the balcony that was connected to the training room. Ed, Tyler, Sam, and Alpha Max were all out there, creating a hush in the crowd. The next to come out were the old council, the fathers of the council now. Alpha Leo was going to take charge of the pack while Alpha Max was gone with them. His council would be the ones in charge of the smaller things that needed to get taken care of while their children were away.

Charlie stood beside Max. He seemed a little worried for his mate, but there was also a look of determination in his eyes. He held a level of confidence that not most noticed until they really looked at him. It was a good trait for a Luna to have, as it helped the rest of the pack be put to ease.

The full moon shined brightly on all of them as Max looked from the balcony. He wore his necklace that showed the symbol of Alpha of the pack.

"Warriors." His voice boomed through the entire yard. "Line up."

He hugged Nick one last time before he went to the designated spot. They all stood there in front of the balcony, as the Alpha looked down to them. He took the necklace and lifted the symbol above his head. The entire house was silent. No one said a word as he turned around to face Alpha Leo.

Alistair felt something again. The electricity in the air was growing, as well as the wind that was starting to pick up. He couldn't figure out what it was trying to tell him this time. The more he focused on it, the more confusing it seemed to get.

"To declare war on our enemies," Alpha Leo started to speak. "The ones who have tormented us for far too long, the Alpha's knife is needed. An Alpha with his knife sheathed to his symbol shows that he is willing to fight to kill in both forms, and has the skills to do so." Something shiny was brought to the air. It took a while until Alistair could focus his eyes on it. It was a hunting knife that shined in the moonlight, looking as sharp as can be.

Alistair didn't know the meaning of the Alpha's knife before. His old Alpha had a knife attached to his symbol all the time, no matter what the circumstance was. He just assumed it was so that there wasn't a chance of forgetting it somewhere.

He didn't know that it meant war.

"As Alpha of the Crescent Moon Pack," Max started to speak now. "I accept the knife, and declare war on our enemies." He took the knife that his father held and turned back to the rest of the pack. He put both the knife and the symbol in the air above him and sheathed it in the moonlight. "We will not lose to this scum, nor will they harm any of our pack; our family any longer. We will fight, and we will win!"

The pack cheered as he said that. He sounded like a general, but there was something in his voice that gave hope to the pack. It took the worry that everyone was showing at the beginning of the ceremony away at least a little.

He felt it again. The wind picked up more. This time, it was more ferocious than before. Alistair focused on it more to try to hear what it was trying to say.

Then he heard it.

War.

The forest was declaring war with them. And it didn't feel like they were alone in this endeavor either. The wind connected them to the other two packs that night. The other two Alphas must also be declaring war on the rogues.

Max hugged Charlie, who was wearing his Luna symbol that night. Then he nodded to the men of his council. It only took a second for them to jump over the balcony. They all landed on their feet, and Max started the walk towards the forest. As soon as he did, his council did, then the rest of the warriors.

After they had gotten a safe distance from the crowd, the Alpha shifted. His clothes tore off as fur erupted all over his body. The only thing that didn't tear off was the necklace with the symbol on it. The knife was still sheathed in a pocket behind the symbol. It was meant for the Alpha to wear in both forms.

The rest of them followed his example.

"*I love you, Bakshi.,*" He mind linked with Nick one last time. "*I'll see you soon, I promise.*"

"*I love you too, Alistair. Please, be safe.*"

"*I will,*" he assured him.

Without a glance back, the warriors started their run.

CHAPTER 54:

The Orion Forest

"I don't know whether I should've done it, though," Max had told his father.

"What are you afraid of?"

He had to pause before he answered that. Not because he needed to think about it, but because he needed to prepare himself to say it.

"What if I die when we're out there in that forest?" He spoke low when he asked his father. He was the Alpha. And if anyone heard any word of him fearing death, then the whole pack would go crazy. "I already know that Charlie would be devastated if that happened, but Eric already lost his parents. He lost everyone that he had known in the short time he's been alive."

"That's a reasonable thing to worry about." His dad put a hand on his shoulders. "You dying would also put the entire pack in disarray too, you know."

"And wouldn't that just make things worse for the boy?"

"I think." The man sighed and leaned back in his chair. They were talking in Max's office, the one that used to belong to his father. "I think that there's only one solution to this."

"What?"

"Don't die." The brunette grinned. "You have a lot to live for, Max. If anything, this should be more of a reason to want to finish your mission and come home."

"I don't think it's as simple as 'Don't die.'" He frowned. His dad used to be the best at giving him advice. Now he was questioning it.

"Warriors always need a reason to come back home." His father just shrugged. "That's why most of them are mated."

"So, that's all you've got for me?" Max looked at his father incredulously. "Don't die?"

"Yup," His father stood up. His purple eyes had the same twinkle that it always had in it after Max became Alpha. He looked so proud of him. He was glad. "Don't die."

That was the last piece of advice he had gotten from him before this. It was the last thing they talked about before the ceremony.

Max truly did love Eric. The boy was easy to fall for, and it just seemed to feel right when he came to them every time he had a nightmare. He was never too far from Charlie, which Max thought was funny. Charlie had started to bring the boy everywhere with him since that night that Max had been escorting the other Alphas out. He looked so happy when he was holding him, too.

When he first saw him sleeping with Eric in his arms, it was a moment that he wished he could take a picture of and hold onto forever. The one thing that Max had always wanted to do was start a family. He had wanted that before he had even found Charlie.

But was right then really the best time for it? He was still chasing a deadline that he had made for himself to marry him. He was still trying to deal with this problem with the rogues.

The rogues.

Oh, how he wanted to tear their throats out. Damir would pay for what he had done, he would make sure of it. No matter how many dangers that lurked in these trees, he would have Damir's head, along with the rest of his followers.

The first thing they had planned to do was cut the forest off from any other uncharted territory. Up north was just a bunch of cities with very little forests or reasons to claim them as a part of their territory. There was a small line of trees that most rogues would run through to get to the forest they were in now.

That was their escape route. And that was the first thing they intended to block off.

It was going to be Max and Owen's job to do. They ran and marked the entirety of their side, until they met in the middle. They would not claim the territory yet, though. Claiming a territory while your enemies were still in it was too dangerous.

They got there the first night, with the full moon still bright in the sky. It wasn't the first time that Max had seen Owen's wolf. His wolf was dark grey with a darker design on his back. He wasn't fully black like Max's father was when he was in wolf form. But he could be mistaken for a black wolf in the darkness. He blended into the shadows well.

It was, however, the first time he had seen him with his Alpha symbol around his neck. It resembled a blood moon, just what their pack was named after. It was a giant circle that glimmered a dark red when the moonlight hit it. His knife was sheathed behind the circle, visible only when he ran.

Leonard's was similar to it. He had seen that necklace plenty of times on his visits to his pack. It was circular, just like Owen's. It wasn't red, though. Instead, it was a yellow-orange color, to resemble the harvest moon. He didn't see the Alpha yet, but he was sure that he would be wearing his knife as well.

Max's Alpha necklace was different from the others. The Crescent Moon Pack had no circle as the Alpha's symbol. Instead, Max's necklace resembled that of a crescent moon by just having a sliver of white shimmering metal.

The pack had always been proud of their symbol. The edges were made to be sharp, so as to show that they weren't to be messed with, no matter how small they seemed.

Of course, it made Max's knife all the more noticeable. Where Owen and Leonard's symbols hid their knives, Max's symbol showed it right down the middle of the crescent moon. It made it known when they were going to fight.

The first night had been meeting with Owen and his warriors. Since he had the most out of the three of them, they agreed that he leave his to guard the forest exit. Max left some of his warriors there as well. He left Sam behind to lead the few that he had brought. Sam was always the best at defense. He would have left Martha there, but he needed her for something else.

The greatest thing about having an old warrior like her on his side, was that she had the most experience in this forest. She had fought the most battles out of all of them combined. And she was the only one who knew a lot about the history of the Orion Forest.

Alistair was another person he was glad to have come along. Now that he had finally gotten used to the warrior link, it was useful being able to sense his awareness to certain things.

Like a strange building up ahead.

This forest had been littered with cabins, houses, and old fishing sheds. People had tried to live there, but since it wasn't protected by any of the packs, the rogues and other supernatural dangers must have scared them off.

"*But there's something different about this one.*" Alistair's voice came clear through his head.

"*He might be onto something, Alpha,*" Madeline told him. "*It smells awfully different around here.*"

"*Do you smell metal?*"

"*I don't quite know what it is,*" she answered. "*It smells like something burnt, though. I'd have to get closer to get a better idea of it.*"

He ran closer to their paths to try and get an idea of what they were smelling. Sure enough, it smelt like something that was burnt. But it had to have been a long time ago. That smell was so faint, it was barely noticeable.

They had almost gotten to the center of the forest, where all the Alphas would meet to tell each other what they had found and to decide where to go from there. It only took half a day to run there. Max would be happy when they could claim all of this territory for the pack. All the extra room would be perfect for the growing numbers.

"*Follow the smell,*" he ordered. "*I'll follow you. The rest of you keep to the plan unless I say otherwise.*"

None of them had to say anything in response to him. He knew that they had gotten his orders.

Him and Madeline followed the scent. Alistair fell behind them a bit, as his nose wasn't the best. His ears were the one sense that they needed him for. That and his sharp teeth. They had come across plenty of rogues that morning that had fell victim to Alistair's fangs. Max was proud of him.

Madeline was right about the smell being something that had been burnt. When they found the source, they saw it to be a burnt building of some sort. The clearing was huge, along with the debris from the wood of the house. The foundation was still there, which proved that it must have been made well. It took up most of the clearing with how massive it was. Most of it was covered with grass and other plants that the forest had. There were still some pieces of wood that stood up from it. It looked old, and burnt, yet it still stood tall.

"*People lived here,*" Alistair said. "*A long time ago.*"

"*That's not too hard to figure out,*" Madeline said. "*The main question is: who? And what happened to them?*"

"*Search the area,*" Max ordered. "*Maybe we'll find some answers after we look around some.*"

There wasn't much there. He didn't know when this had burnt down, but it must have been a long, long time ago. The forest had absorbed it within its plant-like embrace. Rubbish and wood were buried in the dirt and the leaves that had fallen from the trees.

There was still one wall standing, out of everything that had fallen. It was a small one, but there was something on it. When Max went over to it, he saw a faded drawing that was carved on it. It looked like a male figure, but he couldn't quite figure it out.

"It looks like a constellation," Alistair said. He had come over to see this wall as well.

"Why would there be a constellation drawn on here?"

"Maybe someone saw it in the sky and wanted to draw it." Alistair shook his fur. Nick had to brush him again before his travels so that he wouldn't shed more of his winter coat all over the forest. *"You never know with how old it is."*

"There's something unique about this," Max told him. *"Why else would they put it on a wall, of all places?"*

"They could've looked up to him," Alistair mentioned. He looked at the drawing with warm eyes, as if he was remembering a good memory. *"My mother had told me a story about this one. She called it 'The Hunter'. She told me that it was one of the few constellations that could be seen all around the world."*

"The Hunter?"

"Alpha." Madeline interrupted the discussion, her voice sounding urgent. *"You may want to see this."*

Max followed her scent across the field. Her curly brown fur was easy to find on the flat terrain. The dirt caked onto her paws showed that she had been digging. He looked behind her to see a large area that had been dug out.

That's when he understood why her tone was so urgent.

"*Martha.*" He called out to his oldest warrior. "*Has there ever been any packs that lived here before?*"

"*About a thousand years ago, yes,*" she answered immediately. "*Did you find something?*"

"*I need you over here,*" he told her. "*Tyler, go to the other Alphas and tell them to follow you here as well. This place isn't too off from the center of the forest.*"

"*Will do.*"

He knew it would take a while for both of them to complete their new missions, but he believed it was necessary.

After all, when you find two graves that have an alpha and luna symbol on it, it becomes important.

"*They must have not had that much time to bury them,*" Madeline said. "*It didn't take too long of digging until I saw the casket.*"

"*Once we're done here, we need to bury it again,*" Max told her. "*We've already disrespected the dead by digging them up.*"

"*The Alpha symbol on that casket.*" Alistair pointed out. "*It looks just like the constellation that was drawn onto that wall.*"

He went a little closer to see that he was right. The Alpha's symbol was circular like Owen's and Leonard's. Only it was a dark blue, like the night sky. In the middle of it was that same marking that he had first seen on the wall.

The Hunter.

Leonard and Owen were the first ones to get there. When they did, they seemed just as alarmed as he was. They had lived in a part of this forest their whole lives, and none of them had ever known that there was another pack.

"*One of my warriors, Martha, might know something about this,*" Max told them. "*She's fought in this forest before.*"

"*I wonder why they would pick this symbol,*" Leonard said. "*Why would you pick a constellation as your symbol for a pack?*"

Before they could think any more on the idea, the old battle-axe wolf came out of the trees. Max always thought it was fun to watch people's reaction when they first met her. It's not usual to see a wolf like her. Her scars typically scared people, but her mannerisms did the exact opposite.

It was best talked about in their human forms at this point. It was either that, or Max would have to play the messenger and repeat everything that Martha said to them.

"Well." Leonard looked at him with a quizzical expression. "This is definitely the most interesting thing that we've found."

"All I've found is empty cabins and rogues," Owen said.

"The rogues are hitting my area hard already." Leonard frowned. "I think they believe we're the weakest."

"We can help you with that," Max assured him. "But, right now, we have to figure this out."

"The Orion Pack," Martha all but whispered to herself. Max turned to see the old woman looking at the old caskets in wonder. "Adelle would have loved to see this."

"The what pack?" Owen asked.

"The Orion Pack," Martha spoke again. "It fell way before even I was thought of."

"How do you know of it?" Max asked her.

"It used to be a story that was told to children when I was growing up," Martha answered. "Adelle was quite fond of it when I told it to her. She's been dying to try and find more information on them since I spoke of it."

"So, this was an old pack?" Leonard asked. "Not one that was recent, that these rogues just took?"

"They died about a thousand years ago," Martha told him. "They are what the forest is named after."

"What's the story?" Alistair spoke this time. "If I can ask."

"They were a pack of nobility," Martha said. "They were The Orion; The Hunters. But, also the protectors." She looked at the wall that had the constellation on it. It was midday when they had found the wide clearing, so it was easier to see things from afar. "Much like the man that the constellation was named after, they both fought off their enemies as well as protected the ones that were in their forest. It's rumored that they are the sole reason why the humans of the area were so willing to make peace with our packs. The Orion Pack protected everyone, no matter the race or gender. They lived with equality and peace."

She paused and it seemed like her dull eyes were lost in a memory. Max knew that she had plenty of stories in her. Old warriors always have the best of stories to listen to. But he had never heard of this one.

"What happened to them?" Alistair asked. His red eyes seemed just as lost by the story as she was.

"The last thing they protected their forest from," Martha answered. "Vampires."

"Vampires?" Leonard furrowed his eyebrows. "But there hasn't been vampires anywhere near here for almost as long as our packs have been around."

"That's why." Martha smiled. "There was a war between the Orion Pack and the vampires. It took years and years of war and bloodshed. They almost had them, but they failed in being able to kill off the leader. The Alpha's last words before he died were to curse the race to never be able to step foot on these lands for three thousand years."

"And it worked?" Owen looked at her in shock. "I don't think someone can just speak a curse and it'll magically happen."

"You can believe what you want," Martha said. "It's been a story that's passed down from generation to generation, so it might not be completely truthful. You should ask your elders and see if they remember hearing any stories of them. Either way, though, this proves that they were definitely alive."

Max looked at the caskets once more. If this pack had truthfully done all this for the forest, then they should be honored at least. No matter what they did, it was always sad to hear about a pack dying. Max wondered just how different his, Owen's and Leonard's packs would be if they were still around.

"When we claim this land," Max spoke. "We should build this house back up."

"Why?" Leonard asked. "What would you do with a house this far out into the woods?"

"It'll be a meeting house," Max turned to them. "A place where we can all meet in the middle to discuss important matters between our packs."

"Sounds safer than traveling to each other's pack houses all the time," Owen said. He looked like he was already agreeing with this. "It would definitely be secluded enough for us to not have to worry much about spies of any sort."

"I guess that makes sense," Leonard said. "If anything, it would be a great gesture of peace between all three of our packs."

Max liked that idea. The last thing any of them wanted was another war on their hands. Especially after these rogues were dealt with.

"Then it's settled." Max nodded. "When we claim our lands, we'll build this and make it our meeting house."

"I can't believe you're already thinking about after this is over." Leonard smiled and shook his head. "We still have a long way to go."

"We're just being the exterminators," Max joked. "Now that this is over, let's kill some vermin."

CHAPTER 55:

Worry

"So, what do I have to write again?" Katy asked.

"Do you see the second part that's written in bold?" Charlie explained. They were on a three-way conference call with Wynona at the moment.

"Yeah."

"Right there is where you put all the information that's on the top of the other paper that you have."

"You talk like this is the easiest thing in the world." Wynona chuckled. "It still takes me a good hour just to fill out one of these papers."

"Ugh!" Katy groaned. "Apple, can I hire you to do all of this?"

"I don't think Owen would be happy with you handing out important pack information." Charlie chuckled. He had been enjoying their calls for the past few days. With all the warriors gone, or patrolling for the week, the pack seemed to be tense and worried. Charlie didn't blame them. He was worried too. But he wasn't going to let that stop him from doing his work or enjoying himself.

"How did you learn all of this in two weeks?!" Katy asked. "I've been here for months and I still haven't figured all of this out!"

"It helps when you were basically raised in a charter school for lawyers," Charlie said. "I had to do stuff like this for homework all the time."

"That sounds like a nightmare," Wynona said. "I don't know why in the world someone would voluntarily go to a school like that."

"Well, I didn't wind up going to Harvard," Charlie told her. "But I'm glad I went. I learned a lot of things that I needed outside of school there. One of my teachers even taught me how to do my taxes."

"You see," Wynona said. "That's something I wish they'd teach in normal schools in general. Do you know how complicated it can be to do taxes when you own your own business?"

Another groan came from Katy's side of the line. "Don't remind me of taxes. I'm not ready for next year!"

"Taxes are easy when you get the hang of it." Charlie laughed again. "My teacher taught me them outside of class though. I asked him for help when I realized that I needed to do them after getting emancipated."

"You poor child." Wynona laughed a little. "I wish that someone adopted you instead. That really sounds like a horrible way of living for someone that young."

"I wasn't exactly in the best mindset," Charlie told her. "I really just wanted to get out of that city. No offense to you, Sun City really is beautiful. It just…"

"Has bad memories," Wynona finished for him. "I understand. I just wish Max found you sooner."

"Me too." Charlie smiled. He remembered when he first saw him in that restaurant. He couldn't believe how much those eyes made him freeze. He had to make sure he wasn't drooling the whole time Max was there. It was funny thinking back to that day and comparing it to now. He could still feel those arms around him pulling him into a hug.

Max had been clinging to him the whole week until the ceremony. He wouldn't do anything else unless it was with him. They had a lot of fun moments with Eric that way. It was easy to see that Max had fallen for him. Eric had even started to talk more around him. He loved to hear any action stories that Max would tell him.

Charlie sighed at his desk.

He really missed him.

"You know," Katy said. "It would have been interesting having you in high school with all of us. I'm sure Max would absolutely love you for your baking skills alone."

"He's just like his father when it comes to sweets." Wynona laughed. "I remember meeting his dad for the first time. He wanted us all to go out to eat, and the first thing he decides to pick is a small bakery that we had in the town."

"Max doesn't have that much of a sweet tooth." Charlie rolled his eyes. That was a funny thought, thinking about Mr. Locke like that. He had known the man loved sweets the first day he met him. He was the easiest customer to please as soon as he offered them all free dessert for their wait on the food.

"That's because he has you," Katy told him. "Did I mention that you two are adorable together?"

"About a thousand times." He laughed. These two always seemed to know how to make him laugh. But all of it was just reminding him that Max was far away from home and it would still be a while before he came back.

He didn't know what was going on in that forest. It had been a few days and they hadn't heard any news. He liked to think that no news was good news, but that didn't seem to be the case with this situation. The warriors told him that they would be told if the Alpha needed them. And that would only be under dire circumstances. So, he could find relief in that. The warrior link was different from the pack link. It connected all the warriors together, even the ones that had been sent outside of pack grounds.

He just really missed Max. He worried about what would happen in that forest. He kept on flashing back to that room that he was chained up in, and that face that looked at him with a predatory gaze. Would Max be able to find him? Would he be able to kill him? What if Damir wound up hurting him? Or hurting one of the warriors?

There were so many scenarios of what could go wrong. They were hard to get out of his head, but he tried his best to push it down. Luckily, everyone in the pack was trying to be there for each other at the moment. Even Aldi seemed nervous about this mission that the warriors were on. And he had always been calm about everything.

He felt a tug on his pants that distracted him from his thoughts for the moment. Colorful eyes looked at him with a worried expression. Eric had been staying by his side the whole time Max was gone. It was adorable that he wanted to help out the best that he could. But Charlie didn't want to burden the boy. He was just a kid. Children were supposed to be enjoying themselves, not trying to take care of others.

He had been planning play dates with Isabelle and Leah's children. The both of them had been dealing with quite a handful with their husbands away. Charlie just let Isabelle have the week off for the meantime. He needed more work to keep him busy anyway.

There was also the youngest cousin that Max had. Charlie hadn't met him until that day that he was trying to remember the names of all of the children of the pack. While Scott was an early teen, he had a younger brother named Reginald who was the runt of the family. He was adorable, and shy. Him and Eric fit each other so easily.

He was glad to see that the boy had been opening up more to kids his age. They were all still pretty young, but he managed to make friends with some of them, just as he had with Reginald. Reggie was the only one that Eric played with that was the same age as him. The only issue was whenever Charlie left the room. Eric would immediately leave to go and find him. He worried that the boy was getting too clingy. But everything was so tense right now, that he figured it was best that he didn't try to push the poor boy to do anything he didn't want to do right then.

"Are you okay?" Eric asked. The call had still been going as Wynona and Katy started talking about random things that were going on in their lives. Charlie had simply gotten lost in thought during the time.

"Of course, I am, sweety." He picked him up. They were still working on getting him to a normal weight. He was still as light as a feather and that worried him. "I'll always be okay."

Eric didn't say anything. He just hugged him. His hugs were oddly comforting for a five-year-old. The poor boy was probably just as worried about Max as he was. He remembered when Max told Charlie about the boy's mother, and when they found her. There was no way of saving her, and her husband, the Alpha of the Goldshield Pack, had already died in the rogue attack. It was heartbreaking to hear.

If that was what Damir did to that pack, Charlie didn't want to know what would have become of him, Wynona, and Katy if they had stayed in that room for any longer. Or Eric for that matter. Charlie held the boy tighter to his chest when he remembered that man smacking him. Eric was the sweetest child he had ever met. It hurt to think that anyone would want to do that to something so sweet.

"Oh, Charlie!" Wynona's voice came through the speaker. "I just heard the news that you and Max are adopting!"

"What?!" Katy shrieked. Charlie wondered if it was too late to invite Nick over to the office. He could hear his laughter in his head right then. "No one told me this!"

"We kind of just decided last week," he answered. "Sorry for not telling you sooner. It's just been some crazy times lately."

"Don't we all know." Wynona chuckled a bit. "So, who is it?"

"Eric." Charlie looked down at the boy in his lap. "Do you wanna say 'hi' to my friends?"

"Eric?" Katy said. "Is that the boy that we found in the forest?"

"Yeah," Charlie answered. "He's been staying with Max and I since he was able to leave the infirmary."

"Hi Eric!" Katy's smile could be heard over the phone. "I'm Katy! I don't know if you remember me, but you were the one who gave me a fruit."

"I remember," Eric said. He looked at the phone with a shy smile on his face. "Hi."

They had a blast talking to him while Charlie finished up the rest of his paperwork. He had decided it best to just stay busy during the week. So, he had taken on more responsibilities. He decided to let Isabelle off for the week so that she could take care of her kids, which meant that he had to file everything himself. But he had also decided to take on the workload of all the paperwork that the council usually did. That way no one would be behind when they came back so they wouldn't have to worry about all of the work they had to do after just coming from a fight.

He would say that he was doing a good job at it. The only role he wasn't filling at the moment was the Alpha role. Mr. Locke was doing a decent job at taking care of that. He told Charlie when he asked that he didn't need any help and to just keep doing what he was doing. He left it at that. Mr. Locke looked like he enjoyed being back in that office. He was still pretty young to retire so early. But, whenever Charlie asked, the man would wave it off and tell him that his greatest achievement was having Max take on his role.

It was really heart-warming to see just how proud he was of his son. Charlie was so happy to be a part of this family. They had always been so kind to him.

For now, though, he just had to finish up all the paperwork. He figured that it would take a whole week to finish up all the extra paperwork he had given himself. He didn't work that hard all of last week just so he would have more to do for this one. Eric would always color or play with some toys that he got him while he was working. He came to Charlie when he was tired and ready for a nap, though. Whenever Charlie would try to bring him to the small couch he had in the office, the boy would wake up and try and curl into his lap again.

"Come on." Charlie kissed his head. "I think it's time to go to bed."

They both said their goodnights to the girls and hung up the phone. Charlie had made sure that he walked around the pack house every now and then throughout the day. But he mainly stayed in his office to try and keep busy. He had, of course, made some pies for Mr. Locke, as a way of thanking him for all the work that he was doing.

Of course, whenever he tried making pies for one person, he wound up needing to make some for everyone else. That had been a fun day to say the least.

At the moment his mind was worn out from all the papers he had to write and file. He wished he could fall asleep faster. The bed felt ten times colder when Max wasn't there to wrap him in his arms. Even if Eric was curled up on his chest, Max still found a way to pull Charlie close to him.

It had been the most blissful moment he had ever had.

"Can I sleep with you again?" Eric asked. He had been asking every night since Max had left.

"Sure." Charlie smiled at him. "Do you wanna go to the balcony to look at the stars tonight, or do you just want to go to bed?"

"I wanna see the stars," Eric said. It had become one of their routines that they had started that week. Eric loved looking at the night sky. Usually, Charlie would wind up telling him a story until he fell asleep on that balcony. The calm of the night seemed so strange considering the war that the forest held at the moment.

Charlie walked him into his suite and through the French doors to the balcony. He hadn't had the chance to use it too much until Eric came along. He mainly just liked the light that came through it in the morning. It was nice to enjoy it with someone, rather than just having it all to himself.

The night sky was as clear as could be, with the moon shining down on them as brightly as ever. Nick had told him that Alistair felt something from this forest before they left. He told him that the forest was on their side. Charlie just hoped that it was true. He didn't know what he would do if Max didn't come back after this.

"My dad used to bring me to his balcony." Eric broke the silence. His voice seemed so small at the moment. "We used to watch the stars move and make up stories about them."

"Really?" Charlie asked him. Eric hadn't ever talked about his father until then. "What was your father like?"

"He was brave, and strong," Eric answered. "He had eyes like me, too. He told me that it meant good luck to have eyes like mine."

"That's interesting." Charlie looked at his eyes again. They really were unique. It wasn't every day you met someone with a brown eye and a blue eye. "I heard something about dogs that have the same eyes as you."

"Really?" Eric snuggled back into Charlie's torso. They were sitting on one of the benches that were there. "What did you hear?"

"Well." He pulled him in closer. It was nice having him there to simply hold. "Dogs have different colored eyes all the time, especially huskies. It's said that their eyes are different colors so that one can see on earth and the other sees on heaven."

"Really?" Eric looked at him in shock.

"Well, that's the story at least." Charlie smiled at him. "You'll have to learn to speak to dogs to truly find out."

"I wish I could see into heaven." The boy looked to the sky again. "I wonder if they're up there."

"They're definitely up there." Charlie rubbed the poor boys back. It was obvious that he still missed his parents so much. "I think the Moon Goddess has a special place for them too."

"Where?"

"I don't know," he told him. "Maybe she put them in the sky, so they could always watch over you."

"I miss them." He sniffled. Tears streamed down his face as he buried himself in Charlie's shirt again. He held him tighter and let the boy cry. It was the first time he had cried about this in front of him.

"I know, sweety." Charlie kissed his head. "You know it's okay to feel this way, right?"

"But I'm supposed to be strong." Eric wept. "I'm not supposed to cry."

"Eric." He lifted the boy's face to look at him better. "Everyone cries. Even the bravest and the strongest cry. It's not something that makes you weak."

"Does Max cry?"

"Even Max cries." He rubbed that small face with his thumb. He had seen Max cry a few times. He mainly showed his pain silently. He'd always hold Charlie for comfort if he really needed it. Charlie always knew when he was upset because he wouldn't say anything. He'd just hold him and sigh into his shoulder.

"Do you cry?"

"I cry a lot more than Max does." Charlie chuckled a bit. "That's actually how we wound up together."

"You got together through crying?"

"Kind of," he said. "He comforted me when I really wasn't okay. I wasn't doing the greatest back then. But sometimes you need to cry. And sometimes you need someone to help you so that you can be stronger."

"You really think so?"

"I know so." He hugged him again.

It didn't take long before Eric tired himself out. He always seemed to calm down when Charlie had him in his lap. It made him happy having him around. He didn't think that he could still be happy with Max not around. That's why he had decided to keep himself busy. He wouldn't have stayed up all night doing paperwork if not for Eric needing to stay on a sleeping schedule. There was no way he could fall asleep in the office. Charlie wouldn't want him to sleep there anyway.

He was having fun spoiling the boy.

It had been so peaceful with Eric in his arms. And the moonlight was acting as a lulling effect on him. He was so focused on watching the forest, rather than the sky, though. He wished he could see Max coming through those trees. He was still so worried about him.

Charlie hadn't known that he had fallen asleep until he had felt someone picking him up.

"Mr. Locke?" He rubbed his eyes. One of his arms were still around Eric. "What are you doing?"

"Bringing you inside." Mr. Locke told him. "Max would kill me if I didn't make sure you took care of yourself."

"Eric wouldn't fall asleep without going to see the stars."

"And you wouldn't fall asleep without Eric." Mr. Locke brought him back inside and laid him on his bed.

"You should have just woke me up," Charlie said. "You didn't have to carry me to bed." It was probably so late. And he had probably already stayed up this late just doing all the paperwork that Max usually did.

"If I did that, then I wouldn't really be a good father-in-law, would I?" He smiled at him. "You need to get a good night's sleep for once, Charlie." He took off his shoes and pulled the blanket over him and Eric.

"Mr. Locke?" Charlie got the man's attention before he could walk out of the room.

"Hmm?"

"Do you think Max is going to be okay?"

"Of course." Mr. Locke went back to give him a quick hug. "He's trained his whole life for this moment."

"But what if something happens?" He asked him. "What if he gets hurt? Or someone else gets hurt?"

"We have two other packs on our side," he told him. "And rogues whose numbers are already dwindling due to our attacks on them before. There's a lot more going for us than against us."

"But that Alpha…" He still couldn't get the image of that man out of his mind.

"Is going to have to face three others," Mr. Locke assured. "Who are all piping mad at the fact that their Lunas were kidnapped and hurt."

Charlie sighed. He didn't know why he decided to speak of all of his worries then. He just felt comfortable with Mr. Locke. He had always acted like a father to him. A father that he had never had before.

"I'm sorry," he said. "I'm just worried."

"I know you are." The man hugged him again. "It's okay to be, Charlie. Just know that there's nothing Max cares about more in the world right now than you and Eric. He'll come home."

He left the room at that. Charlie didn't know why, but he felt better after saying all of that. He had been holding all his worries about this war from the rest of the pack. He wanted to stay strong for them. Just like Eric was trying to be strong for him, he guessed. With Eric still curled up asleep on his chest, he let himself relax into the soft pillow that his head now rested on.

He would have to worry about Max coming home another time.

CHAPTER 56:

Trials

They had been doing nothing but searching and fighting for half of the week at that point. They rested when they could, but most of their energy was spent on tracking down the rogues that had infested the Orion Forest.

Max had no idea how many there would be in those thick trees. He thought that they wiped most of them out when he started killing off the ones who went into Crescent Moon's territory. But it seemed like Damir had been building up his army for a long time. Everywhere they turned, there was more and more that they would find. Usually, it was in the abandoned cabins that were scattered around the forest. Almost every one of them had at least some rogues in there.

It made sense, at the same time, as to how quickly this rogue was able to build up his army. Rogues were always easy to find, as they had nowhere else to go other than uncharted territory. And it was in a wolf's instinct to listen to an alpha, no matter if they were the leader of a pack or not.

Knowing what he had found out about Madeline's encounter with them, they probably threatened plenty of them to join their pack as well. It was a common strategy for rogue packs. They were brutal and did not follow rules that the official packs abided by. Because of this, they were usually more ruthless than others.

He wasn't going to show any of these vermin mercy. Max was still on a hunt for the nest; the center of all the chaos that were these rogues. Damir had been all over that forest, and he knew that the alpha wasn't gone. He just seemed too good at hiding at the moment. His minions tried to do all the work for him.

Max's warriors were small in numbers, but they were the only ones who had all lasted throughout these battles. Many of Leonard's warriors were wounded due to surprise rogue attacks when he was attempting to meet Max and Owen in the center on the first day. Luckily none of them had died that day. Most of them had actually come back to join the fight.

Owen's warriors were extremely skilled when it came to fighting. He enjoyed battling next to the man himself. They both seemed to work well as a team. But the Blood Moon Pack had not prepared themselves as much as the Crescent Moon Pack had. They had been training for this day all their lives.

As far as he knew, only two werewolves in the three packs had died from attacks. Max's were the only ones that had been able to keep every member of his party. But the Blood Moon Pack had trained their warriors to fight to the death if necessary. They showed aggression in their fighting strategies. Max had tried to mix strategies so that he could keep the enemies guessing. Their main skill was defense. That's how they were able to defend their territory this entire time. Working with the Blood Moon Pack made it perfect, as they were able to balance each other out as far as defending and attacking. Owen had much more frontline attackers than Max did.

Leonard's warriors were well rounded in both. They were skilled in using their surroundings to help them in battles. Max remembered training with Leonard when he was young. It was when his father was trying to mend relations with the three packs. Max was shocked to see Leonard use so much of his environment to help him in their mock fights. It had given him a greater understanding of how the Harvest Moon Pack had gotten so big, though. They were adaptable, ever changing with the times.

Their downfall was that they were too tame. They had let their human side take over their beast too much. The best thing to have was a balance. That way, both sides of your soul could benefit. The human side allowed for you to think more critically, and to empathize with others. The beast side helped when it came to survival and fighting.

These were all the things that Max thought about when he had any time to think. He wouldn't think about home at the time. That would prove to be too much of a distraction. He needed to stay focused on finding Damir. His hatred for the rogue was at the surface of his mind and heart. It gave him the fuel to keep going, even when he didn't remember the last time he had slept.

The next cabin they went to was sturdier than the others. It must have been expensive when it was first built. He could tell by the shine that the wood had on it. It stood tall; proud that it had survived the test of time.

Damir's scent was everywhere around it.

"*Surround.*" He gave out the order. The last time he had given that order was almost a year ago at that point. And that was for a completely different reason.

Ed was with him that day too. Only, he was in a much better mood back then. Ever since what had happened with the Lunas, the man had the same amount of hatred in his heart that Max did. He hoped that he didn't let it consume him, but for now he needed that hatred for this war.

The black wolf slunk around to the back side of the cabin, ready for if any of them decided to try to escape the back way. His golden eyes shined with a will to prove himself. Ed never needed to prove himself to Max, not even after what had happened. It wasn't Ed's fault that those rogues had flooded into that highway and outnumbered him so greatly. Max was just grateful that the man didn't die.

Max would have to talk to him about all of this when the week was through. He was still sure that they would be able to claim their territories within the week. They had already cut through the rogue numbers greatly. And with Owen's warriors blocking off the means of entering or escaping the forest, there were no means of gaining new recruits during the time.

Martha had been in his party this time. Even with Madeline around, Martha was still his best tracker. He was sure that Bella would become a great tracker when she got older, but there was no way he was bringing a minor to war with him. Bella had already gone through enough with rogues.

"There's more here," Martha told him. "But none of them are Damir. The scent isn't strong enough."

"He must have ran again." Ed almost growled in his position. The hatred looked like it was oozing off his fangs. "The coward."

"Let's take care of the ones here and keep moving," Max told them. "We may be on the hunt for the leader, but I'm not going to leave his followers alone to cause more mayhem."

"How many are in there?" Ray asked. He was another member that was fighting with him at the moment. Max had sent Tyler and Alistair in a group together so that they could try and go through all the cabins that they saw.

"There's too many old smells," Martha said. "I don't know if I can give a proper answer to that."

They were close to Leonard's territory at the moment. Max called out for the Alpha to see if any of his warriors were around. He wasn't going to risk going into this battle blind. That cabin was huge and there could be too many of them for his small group to deal with at the time.

"Ian's group is the closest," Leonard told him. "I'll send him your way."

"Thank you."

As much as Ian and him had their differences, Max still liked the man. Ian was more feral than his brother, and it helped when it came to battle. He had helped quite a lot when it came to fighting the rogues on their side.

"Wait!" The sound of a man came from the house. "Don't attack! Please, don't attack!" A scrawny man came out in nothing but rags. Dirt caked onto his face as his eyes widened with fear. He came out of the cabin with his hands up in the air in surrender.

Max told everyone to stop in their attack. He wanted to see what this man was going to say. He made sure to send some more people to the back of the cabin, though. He wasn't going to let anyone escape.

When the man saw that they weren't going to attack, he looked a little more relieved. His muggy brown eyes immediately fell on Max, out of all the other wolves that were there. Max didn't like how he knew that he was the leader of the group already. Ian was an Alpha as well, even if he didn't lead a whole pack. But this man new exactly who was the most powerful.

Strike one.

"We don't want any harm," the man said. It was obvious that he was a werewolf from his scent alone. But it also didn't help that he talked to them so freely. That was a clear sign that the man knew exactly who he was talking to. "We've been prisoners of Alpha Damir. Please, let us be. We mean you no harm."

"*Silver shackles are scattered all over this cabin,*" Ian told him. "*If this was one of Damir's main hideouts, then it's likely that these could be his prisoners.*"

"*He would have tried to take them with him,*" Max said. "*He even tried to take the boy with him when I found all the Lunas. He didn't stop carrying him out until he saw me and had no choice but to run.*"

"*He could easily be getting desperate.*"

"*Damir has always been desperate,*" Max said. The man who was claiming to be a prisoner was scrawny, but he didn't look as badly beat as the ones that he had seen half buried in dirt throughout the forest.

Madeline had told him that most of them looked like warriors from the Goldshield Pack. She had fought with them plenty times before. He had to let her rest so that she could overcome the trauma of seeing them dead on the forest floor.

"Please." The man begged. His hands were still up as a means of peace. "We don't want any harm."

"What pack were you from?" Max called out to the man's mind. He wasn't going to change into his human form to talk to him. He hadn't been in his human form since the first meeting with the Alphas.

"I-I was from the Goldshield Pack," the man answered. It seemed like he wasn't used to the mind link. He put his head down, seeming afraid. All Max could think about was the fact that he couldn't see the stranger's eyes.

Strike two.

"What was your Alpha's name?" he asked him.

"You mean Eric's father?" the man asked. "I haven't even seen that boy in weeks. Please, if you find him, you have to save him! My old Luna died trying to protect him."

"You didn't answer my question." Max growled at him. The man flinched at the sound. But his head was still down. It could be to show submission. Max would give him the benefit of the doubt on that. But he wasn't going to trust someone just because they knew Eric's name. "What was your Alpha's name?"

"Herring," the man answered.

"His full name." Max demanded. The fact that this man was prolonging this wasn't helping him believe the stranger's story. When you're in a pack, you always know the full name of the one who's leading. They're the most important person in a pack. They're the person that you take your orders from.

"James," the scrawny man said. "James Herring."

Strike three.

"Wrong answer," Max said. He launched his attack on the cabin right after he said that. As the Alpha of a pack, it's important to know about every member, especially new ones that were joining. That was why he had been so hesitant on letting Alistair in his pack in the beginning of all of this.

Even before he had found Eric, he knew who his father was. He knew who the leader of the Goldshield Pack was. Jeremiah Herring was easy to find in the databases. He was an honorable man who cared for his small family, and tried his hardest to give them everything they needed to grow. When Max had looked at the folder that Button had made, when he finally had time to, he could tell that the man was in his prime for leading. He had even helped his relations with the surrounding packs so that there would be peace amongst them.

He had wanted to know everything he could about Eric at that point. The boy looked just like his father. It was a shame that his pack was destroyed.

Max wasn't going to let anyone degrade that pack anymore, especially not by using it as a means of escaping.

He was right to have asked Leonard to send Ian's group over. There were tons of them in that cabin. They flooded out through the doors and even windows.

"Get the ones who are running!" Max ordered. *"They're trying to run to Damir."*

He knew that he couldn't simply follow them. They would lead them right into a trap if he tried that. But he wasn't going to have anyone act as a messenger for the wretched beast.

The scrawny man had turned into a wolf fast. He was a decent fighter, which only proved Max's suspicions, but he was no match for Max. It didn't take long before he had the wolf pinned down to the ground.

"Where's Damir?" He growled at him. His fangs were out and barred at the small wolf's neck.

"I don't know!"

"LIAR!" he barked at him. The wolf underneath him whined at the sound of his voice in his head. *"Do you think that the Alpha that was able to find my Luna and Omega within six hours is stupid enough to believe you?!"*

He bit down on the wolf's back, making him howl in pain. He wasn't going to kill him yet. He was going to get his answer.

"ANSWER ME, GAMMA!" He made his voice as loud as can be in the enemy wolf's head. He sunk his teeth deeper into his back, making him yelp. He struggled a little to get out of his hold, but stopped when Max clamped further into him.

"East!" the wolf finally cried out. *"He's in a cabin in the east! Just follow the river! You can't miss it. Now, please let me go!"*

"And have you warn him that we're coming?" He growled lowly at the wolf. *"You're only reward is going to be a faster death!"*

Before he could say anything more, Max bit into his neck. With a quick clamp of his jaws, he felt the bone break in his mouth. The wolf lied limp on the ground after only a few seconds.

"I don't get it." Ian finally came over to him. The rest of the wolves that had come out of the house had been easy to find and kill with Ian's group assisting them. *"How did you know the Alpha's name, and he didn't?"*

"Because I do my research on every new member that comes into my pack," Max told him. *"And all this wolf had been thinking was that Herring was an Alpha that needed to be killed. He didn't have to focus on the man's name."*

"Smart move," Ian complimented. *"I'm sure your dad would be proud of you right now."*

He didn't want to think of his dad at the moment. That would only lead him down the path of homesickness that he had been trying to bury the entire journey. He missed his family; he missed his parents; he missed all the people in that pack house; he missed Charlie; he missed Eric.

As much as he was trying to convince himself that he didn't want the boy, he couldn't deny that Eric had crept into his heart. He had a need to protect the boy ever since he saw him in that cabin, and heard that Damir beat him. Learning about the pack that he had been born into, and the parents that had raised him for only five short years, only made him want to protect the boy more. As far as they knew, Eric was the sole survivor of the Goldshield Pack.

All because of Damir.

"Alpha!" He heard Ray call to him. *"We need you over here."*

"What happened?"

"Martha!" Ray's tone was urgent and worried. *"She got hurt badly!"*

Max ran over there as fast as he could. Martha was one of the most important members in their pack. Not only was she the oldest and had the most knowledge of their history, but she had been the one who had trained all of the warriors in the pack. Each and every one of them had trained under her. Even the alphas.

He couldn't let anything happen to her.

It only took a second for him to get over to where Ray was. Even Ed was there at that point. They were all circled around the old wolf until Max came. Blood was seeping out of her rough fur and her body lay on the ground, too tired to keep moving.

"Martha." Max used his nose to move her head a bit.

"I'm alright Alpha," Martha answered. She could barely lift her head to look up at him. Max was just happy that she was conscious.

"What happened to her?"

"She jumped in to take a hit when I was still fighting," Ray told him. *"One of them was trying to sneak up on me from behind."*

"*I don't think she can stand,*" Ed said.

"*Max,*" Martha's voice came into his mind. She sounded weak and small. It was the only time he had ever heard her that way. "*I need to tell you something.*"

"*What is it?*"

"*It has been an honor watching you grow into the leader you are today,*" she started. Her breathing was getting heavier. "*I'm proud to have finally lived long enough to see my pack at its peak. It's been amazing watching this pack of ours grow into the beauty that it is today.*" Her dull brown eyes sparkled ever so slightly when she looked at him. "*I'm glad that I can leave this pack with the peace of knowing that it is in the hands of a great leader; one that will bring them nothing but happiness.*"

"*Martha.*" Max nudged her a little bit. "*You aren't dying on me. We still haven't finished bringing peace to our pack. There's still so much left to do.*"

"*A warrior's death is an honorable one.*"

"*Not when I can still save you.*" Max called for Ian and asked for him to bring one of his medics over there. They were already on the way. "*Think about your family, Martha. Think about the kids that always look up to you to tell them stories of the old times. They still need you. I still need you.*"

It broke his heart to hear what Martha had said. He couldn't have her give up. Martha had lived through four generations of Alphas, and trained three of them. She was as much of the foundation of the Crescent Moon Pack as the rest of them.

"*If the Moon Goddess wills it,*" Martha said. "*Then I will survive. I've survived much worse circumstances.*"

He wasn't going to have anyone die. Not on his watch. He urged Ian to tell his medic to come faster. Even Ian understood the urgency. He had trained a little under Martha as well. It was funny to see his reaction at getting beat by her the first time. He had a lot of ego to come down from when he was a child.

The medic came and stitched her up. Martha had been blessed with the ability to heal from her wounds quickly. With a shot of adrenaline, her cuts closed and she was given enough energy to stand.

"Go home and rest, Martha," Max ordered. He left no room for arguing in his tone. *"Ed and Ray will escort you."*

She nodded. She knew when an Alpha gave an order to not argue against it. Max was grateful of that.

After watching them disappear through the trees, Max ordered Alistair and Tyler to come over to where he was. After that, he looked to Ian.

"Call in your best warriors. Have Owen do the same," he told him. *"It's time to finish this once and for all."*

CHAPTER 57:

The Old Battle Axe

"So, the guy was trying to trick Max?" Nick asked her.

"Yes," Martha smiled. She had been in the infirmary since she had gotten home that morning. Button threatened to tie her down if she didn't stay put. "I'm surprised that the rogue even tried something like that with Max. Considering all the rogues we had killed in the past few days, it would have been smarter to just stay in the cabin and lock all of them in there."

"Was Alistair with them?" Nick asked her. They had all been wondering what was going on in that forest the whole week. They hadn't really gotten much information out of the warriors on patrol at the moment either. They told them that Max had been too focused on finding Damir to give them many updates, but if it was urgent then they would be notified.

"No, dear," Martha shook her head. "He was with Tyler last I heard. They were following a trail of footprints in hopes of finding and killing more rogues."

"How did Max know that the man was lying to him?" Charlie asked. Nick almost forgot that the Luna was there for a second. He had been so focused on trying to find out about Alistair. He hoped he was okay.

"The man said that he was from the Goldshield Pack," she said. "So, Max asked him for the name of his Alpha."

"How does Max know the name of the Alpha of the Goldshield Pack?" Nick asked. That seemed a little strange for him to know. "He could have said any name and Max wouldn't have known."

"The Alpha of the Goldshield Pack was Eric's father," Charlie explained. His face looked a bit pained as he said it, and Nick immediately felt bad for asking. "Max found that out through Button the day that we were with Wynona."

Nick hated thinking back to that day. It was supposed to have good memories with it. It had been a lot of fun buying things with that black card, and teasing Katy about her mate. But then it had to forever get tainted by Damir.

That name still made him want to shiver whenever he thought of it. Those cuts from the whips had left scars all over his front and back due to the wolfsbane on them. Nick hated that they did. Now he would forever remember that moment whenever he saw them.

Alistair had done a great job at making them feel like they were nothing but beauty marks on him. That whole two weeks that they just hung out in their apartment was nothing but bliss for him. All of his nightmares were a thing of the past and every time he had any new insecurity about something, Alistair easily swiped it away with a loving look.

Now he could barely get any sleep and all of those negative thoughts were fighting to come out. He was glad that his family was still there for him. He had decided to live with Barry and his wife in the meantime. His apartment reminded him too much of Alistair now. And the pain from not having him around was enough to cripple him.

He didn't know how Charlie was able to do it. Nick's relationship with Alistair was nothing compared to Charlie and Max. Those two always clung to each other, especially after all that had happened with Charlie. Max always had an arm around him after that. They were inseparable.

With Max gone, he was sure that Charlie wasn't getting enough sleep. He worried about him. Charlie was the type of person who would let himself go if he were too stressed. He was just glad that they decided to adopt Eric before Max decided to leave. Nick heard from Fred just how much Charlie had fallen for the little guy. Once he was finally healed enough to walk around a bit, Nick started to see it himself. The man glowed when he was carrying Eric around.

Come to think of it, it did make sense that Eric was an alpha. He had the same clinginess that Max had, especially to Charlie. And he always talked about needing to protect or be strong, even though he was just a boy. Nick chuckled to himself when Charlie told him that the other day. It reminded him too much of Max when they were all kids. Max always wanted to protect everyone. When he couldn't, he would be so upset.

He remembered one time he couldn't protect Katy from detention when they were in elementary school. As a kid, detention was considered your worst nightmare. At least, that's what Katy had made it out to be. Max was so worried that she was going to get hurt with all of the whining she was doing about it.

He threw an absolute fit when they got home. Nick remembered hearing his wails all throughout the house. Max's mom had to spend the whole rest of the day calming him down before she could tell him that they didn't actually hurt children in detention.

Katy got quite a talking to after that.

"So, he didn't know the Alpha's name?" Charlie asked Martha.

"He was close," she told him. "He said James instead of Jeremiah."

"Jeremiah is a name that you really don't see that much nowadays," Nick said. "I'm surprised he forgot it."

"I'm glad he did," Charlie said. "Or else there might have been more than just you coming back to recover."

He was glad that Eric wasn't there. Charlie had somehow convinced the boy to wait with Isabelle and her kids. He had been so clingy to Charlie that Nick was surprised he had been able to convince him to even go to the opposite side of the room.

"I wouldn't worry so much about Max." Martha smiled at him again. Her old eyes shined with pride. "He's been doing great out there."

"Do you know if they found any clues about where that alpha rogue is?" Charlie asked. Nick was sure that he didn't want to speak his name. That man still had an effect on the both of them.

"I think Max was trying to get an answer out of the one who tried to trick him," she answered. "I'm not sure whether he was successful or not, though. There was too much fighting going on."

The room had been packed before they got there. Everyone was wondering if the grandmother of the pack was going to be okay or not. Button seemed beyond stressed when Ed and Ray brought her back in the first place. They didn't have much time to explain before they headed back out. Nick had been fast enough to get them some food at least. The two of them scarfed it down before they went back out.

At least he could help out a little. Right now, he felt kind of useless. He was glad that he was back to working in the kitchen, though. At least that kept him occupied.

Aldi had been so worried about Martha when she first came in, he practically flew to the infirmary to check up on her. When he was sure that she was alright, they could all hear the head chef yelling at her for going with the warriors in the first place. Nick felt bad that he was yelling at such an old woman who was still recovering, but then he heard Martha laugh.

They were such a weird family.

Alpha Leo had come in to see her right after Aldi. He had also been a bit out of the loop. From what Martha said, though, it seems as if everything had been going according to plan.

Everything except her getting hurt.

"I wish you could see him, Leo," she had told the Alpha. "You would be so proud of him."

Martha really did speak like a grandma when she talked about everyone in the pack. She always looked out for everyone and gave them advice when they needed it. That's what made her an important member to the pack. That and she was the Battle Axe. She was the only one who could take a bite or two and still rip the throat off from her enemy.

Button had been the most worried about the infection that had been trapped in her cuts at the moment. Rogue wolves didn't exactly have the cleanest teeth. They usually ate whatever they could in the woods. Which made their teeth filthy.

But the crazy old woman had already been fighting off the infection with just a few hours of rest. She was 91 and still had the metabolism of a young warrior.

It reminded him of Alistair. He had a pretty good metabolism, even if he did bruise and burn easily. If he could have gotten tough skin like Martha had, then he would definitely be a force to be reckoned with.

"Alright," Button came in with a clipboard in his hands. "That's enough questioning, and enough story-telling."

"Uh oh!" Nick elbowed Charlie a little bit. "Looks like the fun police are here to take us away."

Martha laughed at that. Nick loved making her laugh the most out of anyone in the pack. Most of the time she would have such a serious face on her that it would seem so crazy whenever she did. She had the laugh of a heavy drinker at a pub. It was always loud and obnoxious. But it had a way of bringing you to a good place. For Nick, it would always remind him of music, dancing, and telling stories until their throats were too hoarse to talk. Martha loved telling her stories as much as Nick and his family loved telling theirs.

The only thing he couldn't ever seem to do was surprise her. That woman had lived so long that he swore she had seen everything and heard everything.

"I really did miss you, Nick," Martha said. She patted his hand that he had left on the railing. "You always know how to make everyone feel better."

He really didn't know what to say to that. He always thought he was bad at comforting people. He kinda just joked around in hopes that he could get them to laugh and feel better.

"Sleeping would also make you feel better," Button said. He always had a parental tone to him when it came to things like this.

"You always say that." Nick smiled at him. "I swear, that's your catch-phrase or something."

Another thing about Martha's laugh? Completely contagious. As soon as she started laughing again, so was Charlie. He swore even Button was smiling a bit. Although it seemed like he was hiding it by rolling his eyes dramatically.

It was good to know that she was okay at least. When he first felt her come back to the territory, they all thought the worst. She had been the main person that the entire pack was worried about when the warriors left.

Sure. She had been in plenty of battles. She had fought in wars and outlived all the warriors that had ever doubted her when she first joined their ranks.

But she was 91.

Ninety.

One.

Werewolves generally had a longer lifespan than humans, but to have a warrior that could still fight at the age of 91 was remarkable in and of itself.

Wait. Werewolves live longer than humans.

Did that mean that Charlie was going to die before him?!

Shit. He had to stop thinking about all of these horrible thoughts. Even when he was having a good time enjoying a good moment, his mind would venture off into the darkness of all of his worries.

What would Charlie look like old?

He had a feeling that the man was still going to look young no matter what. He had that face about him.

"Nick." Charlie snapped him out of his thoughts. "Are you okay?" They were just walking out of the infirmary. Button had finally been able to shoo them away so that Martha could get some sleep.

"Yeah." Nick shook his head a bit. "I'm fine, Apple. I'm more worried about you, honestly."

"It's just a few more days." Charlie sighed and rubbed his eyes. "Then this will all be over with and we'll all be celebrating a victory of a lifetime."

He liked that Charlie thought that way. There were so many things that could go wrong in that forest. But the fact that Martha was the only one who had gotten wounded badly enough to come home early was a good sign that they were doing pretty good out there.

"How goes getting all that paperwork done?" Nick asked him. Charlie had taken the role of doing all the paperwork except for the Alpha's. Max's dad would die before putting more work on Charlie's belt. Nick heard that the old Luna had already come over to Charlie's office to help him with some of it. When he tried to argue with her, she just told him that she had nothing better to do.

"Oh, it's so nice being a grandmother finally," she told Nick. She had been going around the pack trying to lighten up everyone's mood now that they were all worried and stressed. "If Max wasn't going to agree to adopt him, I would have smacked him all the way to the other side of the country."

The kitchen got a laugh out of that. Aldi just about keeled over and died right there with how much he was laughing. Nick remembered the first time she had told Max that she would. She was so angry with his antics that her voice sounded like the fire that her hair had practically turned into.

What were his antics, you might ask?

It was in the kitchen again. Max could never get enough of messing around in that kitchen, especially with Aldi. It was really funny, his pranks, when they were all kids. But, after his mom told him that with her 'Flames from Hell' voice, he stopped even going into the kitchen for a while.

And whenever he made Aldi even the slightest bit angry, the chef would bring that up and see Max's face get pale.

"I'm actually getting a lot done with Mrs. Locke around to help," Charlie told him. "At this rate, I might have all the paperwork for the month done."

"I can imagine the look on Sam's face now when he hears that." Nick smiled. Sam was the main person who dealt with paperwork other than the Alpha and Luna. He was just the best person at it, so he took on some of the lesser stuff. He also did things for his business. But Nick doubted that Leah would let Charlie help her with that.

As much as they all loved that Charlie was trying to take a load off their shoulders, Nick was sure they were all just as worried as he was about the Luna.

"I'm looking forward to the looks on all of their faces when they come back." Charlie smiled with him. "Maybe I'll actually get Tyler to look shocked for once."

"I'll make sure to get the camera ready," he joked. He walked with him to Isabelle's room, where she was taking care of Eric and her two kids. Her and Tyler had the best behaved children, Nick was shocked. There were always at least some kids that actually acted well, but most of them were troublemakers.

That's what made kids, kids.

"Charlie!" Eric ran straight into Charlie's arms. And, just like that, all of those stresses that Nick had seen on the Luna's face just about disappeared.

"Hi, honey." Charlie kissed the side of his head. "How was your play time?"

"I missed you." The small voice said.

Katy would be having a heart attack with all the adorableness that was going on. All Nick could do was smile and wish that he had a camera to record this. Max was definitely missing out on some great stuff.

"You're supposed to be having fun, Eric." Charlie chuckled. "Thanks for watching him for me, Isabelle."

"No problem." The woman smiled. Nick was too busy making funny faces at her kids and making them laugh to focus on her too much. "He's a sweetheart."

The kids were trying not to laugh too loud, which was hilarious to Nick. Children were the easiest to entertain, which is why he was always the favorite uncle to all of his nieces and nephews.

They said goodbye to Isabelle and her kids and it was now just the three of them. Nick wasn't sure what to do. He was thinking about just doing an extra shift at work or something just to keep his mind busy. But he also wanted to see if Charlie wanted to do something. He was worried that the man was going to just stay in his room the rest of the day.

"You want to come outside with us, Nick?" Charlie asked. "I think we both could use some fresh air."

"Sounds like a good idea," he said. "But the door to the bottom floor is that way." He used his thumb to point to the direction behind him.

"We're not going to the bottom floor."

"We're not?" Now he was confused. He followed Charlie anyways. He needed a good distraction, even if this was a weird one.

"Nope," Charlie said. "I don't think I ever showed you the rest of my suite actually."

"I mean, there hasn't really been a reason to," Nick told him. "But I thought we were going outside."

"You'll see." He opened the door to the suite. Nick had seen rooms like this before, but this one definitely topped all of the other ones. He knew that the Alpha and Luna always get the best room, but he didn't exactly know how good it got until he saw this one.

When Charlie and Max had shown him the first room, he was in absolute awe. That had been a while ago, though, before they had really been able to decorate it. Now that it was all done up, it looked ten times better.

The front room was a little dining room that had doors all around it connecting it to different bedrooms and bathrooms.

Why they need more than one bedroom or bathroom was a question that he had for a long while. Now he understood, though. Max had probably been planning on adopting kids with Charlie long before he even started thinking about moving into a suite like this.

"Come on." Charlie beckoned him to the bedroom. It was just as elegant, with light colors to brighten up the place. Charlie was headed for the glass doors that were on the side of the room.

"You have a balcony?" Nick asked. Out of all the things that he knew about Charlie and that he talked to him about, Nick had no clue about this.

"It's Eric and I's favorite spot." Charlie chuckled. He opened the door and motioned for Nick to follow him outside. "We mainly come out here at night, though, to see the stars."

He could imagine. The view from that balcony topped any other spot in the manor. It looked out to the forest perfectly, the sky clear and sunny as it shined down on them. It felt so amazing having the sun warm his skin again. There was a gentle breeze that made it perfect for enjoying the great outdoors.

"This is a pretty good spot." Nick sat down on one of the benches that were there. "It would be great if you could see it, Eric."

The boy had stayed hidden in Charlie's shirt the whole time they were walking. Nick guessed that he was still scared of him after seeing him all bloodied in that room. There was one time he visited him and looked happy to see him. But Nick wasn't sure whether the boy was still traumatized from that alpha rogue.

"He does this whenever he's away from me for too long." Charlie chuckled. "Come on, Eric. Don't you remember Nick?"

"Hi," Eric said through Charlie's shirt. His voice was muffled. It made Nick laugh just hearing it.

Nick put his hands over his mouth and said "Hi," right back to him. It sounded just as muffled. When Eric looked up at him, confused as to what he just did, Nick made a funny face to make him laugh.

"Do you like the balcony?" Eric asked. Nick had successfully gotten him to giggle enough to come out of the hiding spot in Charlie's arms.

"Of course!" he said. "One thing that you should know about your uncle: I love the outdoors."

"Uncle?" The boy looked confused. Charlie looked a bit confused himself at what Nick had said.

"Well, not by blood of course," Nick told him. "But you're a part of our family now. So, I get to be you're cool Uncle Nick, okay?"

Eric smiled the brightest smile at that.

"I never had an uncle."

"Well, now you do," Nick said. It was so cute seeing this little boy come out of his shell little by little. "I mean, you have two dads now, so you're going to have to have an uncle."

"What am I going to call my dads then?" Eric asked. His two different colored eyes and black hair made him look like an adorable puppy confused about a new thing that it had found behind the couch.

"You can just call us by our names," Charlie answered. "You don't have to make it complicated."

"No, no." Nick shook his head. "That's not right. Kids shouldn't call their parents by their names."

"What are you thinking then?" Charlie gave him a curious smile. Nick was glad that he was enjoying this as much as he was.

"Hmm…" Nick put a hand under his chin dramatically. "Well, how about Charlie's your Dad, and Max is your Papa? That or Charlie could be your Daddy and Max just your Dad."

"I really don't think this is necessary." Charlie shook his head. "It might just get confusing."

"Daddy!" Eric hugged Charlie again. Nick almost died at seeing Charlie's reaction at hearing Eric say that. He looked like he was going to cry out of joy.

"Glad to know that's settled." Nick smiled.

They enjoyed the rest of the afternoon talking about everything they could under the cool breeze and the warm sun.

Nick would have to tell Max about this. He truly was missing out on some amazing moments.

"Thank you," Charlie said. Eric had fallen asleep after an hour of them being out there. The boy was still healing from all of his wounds and it was making him sleepy. "I didn't think I'd be so happy hearing him say that."

"Don't thank me yet." Nick chuckled. "Max is going to kill me once he hears that I took a moment like this from him."

"There'll be better moments." Charlie smiled.

"Like what?"

"When he calls Max Dad or Papa," he told him. "I'm going to make sure I'm there to see that reaction."

"Like I said." Nick winked at him. "I'll make sure to bring the camera."

CHAPTER 58:

Alpha's

He could smell him. Damir's scent was everywhere in these woods, but it had never been as strong as it was right then. He must have thought that the river would have taken the scent away, washing it off his body like some sort of baptism. It didn't work when he had a scent like that, though. Alphas could never hide their scent. It was strong so as to show others their authority.

Max lead his strongest warriors down the river. Owen and Leonard would be there soon. That wolf that he forced to tell him Damir's location could have easily been bluffing just to try and save himself. But Max didn't have time to try and call his bluff, and that wolf had already pissed him off to no end.

He didn't have Martha's nose. And Madeline was all the way on the other side of the forest, so he was going to have to rely solely on his. When he was younger, he was trained in almost all the fighting positions. As a leader, he needed to know how to fight as best he could. He was taught to track first, as it was the easiest to teach someone as young as him at the time. He had started his training as early as five years old. Even when he couldn't shift, he was taught it through watching others.

The cabin was small. It almost blended in with the shadows. Max had been watching it all day just to see if anyone would come out. Leonard and Owen had been slow to coming due to more rogues that were in both of their areas. It wasn't that Max needed them to launch his attack. He just knew that they wanted their revenge as well.

And he wanted to watch this cabin. He wanted to see if he would come out and show his face. It was obvious now that he was in there. The worst thing was how the cabin was decorated, if he could call it that. Bones and skulls were scattered all around the grounds of the cabin. They were a mixture of wolf and deer bones. All of them lay without any form of meat on them.

He was wondering why the deer population had been going down throughout the years. These leaches had been causing that as well. Max could tell that the wolf bones were merely just void of meat due to how they died. Some looked like they had been burnt to death, others killed through wolfsbane or silver.

The smell of it all was enough to make someone vomit. It was a mixture of death, rotting wood, and the metal scent of Damir. If he couldn't tell that this wasn't going to be an easy battle, he could now. This rogue had tricks up his sleeve.

That was okay, though. So did Max.

"He's in that shed right there?" Owen creeped up to him. His wolf easily blended in with the night. Max had been watching the cabin all day, patient to see if he could find anything new about it. He had found the buildings weak spots as well as all the exits. This included windows, as these rogues liked to use those to surprise them.

"Yeah," Max told him. *"He hasn't left the entire day. I don't think he even knows we're here."*

"The idiot is getting cocky," Owen said. He almost growled at the thought. Max knew the man had a big ego when he kidnapped not one, but

three Lunas at once. Even if they are your enemies, it's not smart unless you want all three packs to go after you at once.

They were proving that right then.

Max saw a hint of caramel eyes from across the cabin. Leonard had come finally with his warriors. At first, Max had told them that it was a priority and that they should come right at that moment. But, when he had gotten to the cabin, he realized that it would be best to wait until night to launch an attack. The moon was still bright enough to give them light, and it would aide them in their surprise attack if they were under its watchful guidance.

So instead, they all agreed to take out as many rogues that were wandering around as possible. That way Damir wouldn't have that many of them to lead. Max had lost count of how many they had killed in the forest. He had counted fifty before he decided that he couldn't focus on that anymore. And that was only what his pack had killed. Most of the rogues had left the area that was close to his territory. It seemed as if they had finally gotten the message after almost a year of slaughtering them every time they had come into the territory.

Max had five warriors with him to help him fight: Tyler, Sam, Ed, Alistair, and Desmond. They were the most skilled for this final battle that they were going to have. He only wished he could have had Martha with him, but there was no way he was going to risk her getting hurt again. Not after hearing her talk like she was ready to die.

Since Max had been there all day, and was the one to find this spot, he was going to be the first to launch the attack. After looking at everyone to be sure that they were ready, he crept over to the back entrance. His coat may not have been black, but he could mold in with the shadows easily. He positioned Alistair by the front of the cabin. Knowing Damir, he was going to try and run again. And Alistair was one of his fastest. The rest were surrounding the cabin in a circulatory fashion. When Leonard and Owen saw Max doing this, they mimicked him, adding extra men to each area surrounding it.

His attack was silent until he slammed into one of the doors. He knew he needed to get in there without changing into his human form. Since he could smell the wood rotting from a mile away, he figured it would be easiest to just try and knock it down.

He was right.

The door came down with a giant thud, taking a part of the wall with it. Everyone who was in there was immediately alerted to him. Two of them stayed to try to fight him off while the rest of them tried to get out of the cabin through the windows and the front door.

It was like shining a flashlight on a bunch of cockroaches. They all scrambled to escape without realizing that they were running straight into the jaws of their enemies. He could hear the fighting outside. Screams filled the night as bones broke and growls turned into ferocious snaps of teeth.

But these roaches weren't the one that he was looking for. Now that he had found the nest, he was looking for the king.

Max killed off the first two that were trying to hold him off easily and ran towards one of the rooms of the cabin. He broke down the door just like the last one. He could smell Damir in the room. But, as soon as the door slammed to the ground, he saw nothing. No one was in there.

What trick was he trying to pull now?

Max followed the scent and went around the room. He was sure that Damir was there. He had even heard moving in the room earlier. There was no way that no one was there the entire time.

The scent was lower to the ground than before. He pulled back a small rug that was on the floor to find a latch.

Great. This coward was an escape artist.

"Alpha!" Alistair got his attention. He showed him another small latch outside just by the river. It had been left open. Through the warrior

link, he could tell that Alistair had been able to lock onto his scent as well. He knew where he was going.

"Tyler!" he ordered. *"You and Alistair follow that scent! Don't let him escape at all costs!"*

"Yes, sir." Tyler's voice sounded like a soldier in his mind.

Max bolted out of the cabin and towards the direction of that alpha. He didn't have time to tell the others about Damir's escape. They would find him when their battle was over with. And he knew he could trust the rest of his warriors with them. They needed them as much as Max did at the moment.

It was easy to lock onto the metal scent as soon as he jumped over the river. Connecting to Alistair and Tyler's link showed him that they had gotten closer to the rogue than he thought they would. Tyler could see him running in front of him. Alistair, who's eyes were bad at night, could hear the rogues labored breathing as he ran from them.

Max darted through the trees as if he had ran in them his whole life. He felt like he had with how many times he had gone through these areas in search for this beast. He had almost caught up to them when he saw Alistair jump for the rogues hide. If it weren't for his great vision, he would have missed the split second that the white wolf sunk his teeth in the man and got thrown off him. The rogue had bitten Alistair in the front leg and then thrown him into one of the thick trees.

"Tyler, hold back!" Max told him. Alistair hadn't gotten up and he wasn't going to have his Beta go through the same thing. *"Try to take care of Alistair. Leave this one to me!"*

Tyler followed his order and ran towards the white wolf. He was still awake, which was a good thing. Max didn't know how badly he had gotten hurt, though.

He had gotten to the point where he was right behind Tyler before he changed directions. He had used Tyler's large frame to hide behind and perform a sneak attack on the rogue. He was slower than before now that he had a huge gash on his hide. It was the second wound that he had gotten from Alistair, funnily enough. Max was sure that Damir was pissed about that.

Max was going to pounce on him when the wolf changed quickly into his human form. His much smaller frame caused Max to jump over him. He swerved around to face him and lunged towards him again.

"What's the matter, Alpha of the Crescent Moon Pack?" Damir taunted. He dodged another one of his lunges. "Are you upset that I had so much fun with your Luna? Is that what this is about?"

A growl escaped from his throat. He couldn't let his words get to him, not when he had finally found him. This was just a distraction so Damir could buy some time.

He couldn't get him with his wolf form, though. Every lunge was evaded as Damir used his smaller size to his advantage. He must have done this a million times.

"He sure was a good snack, you know." His feral smile went all the way to his turquoise eyes. "Especially when he was scared. A part of me wishes you had been there."

Max changed into his human form. He was going to have to do this the old-fashioned way. It had been almost a week since he had been in his human form, and he didn't have time to get reacquainted with it. His eyes were locked on the man who had caused his pack so much strife for years.

"This ends here, Damir," Max said. He pulled out the hunting knife that was connected to his Alpha symbol. "Don't think you can run from me. I know how to find a coward."

"I have one of those too, you know." Damir's smile got bigger. He pointed out a necklace that he had been wearing. It was in the shape of a shield. In the light, it shimmered with gold. "These things are so easy to come by, you know. All you have to do is kill some fool who is stupid enough that he can grow such a tiny pack. I think yours will also be great for my collection."

Another growl came from his chest. He knew right when he saw the symbol that it was from the Goldshield Pack. Damir disgraced them by wearing it like a trophy for everyone to see.

"I'm not going to die from a coward!" Max spoke. He lunged at him again with his knife out and ready. It was immediately met with the blade that Damir took out of the stolen alpha symbol he had gotten. They fought blade to blade for what seemed like an eternity. Every attack blocked by both sides.

Then, with a flick of the wrist, Damir had disarmed him. Max worked just as quickly to disarm the rogue while he was distracted by his accomplishment. They fought hand in hand now, wrestling each other in the bright light of the moon. All the hatred that Max had towards him was brought out. All of the fear that he felt from Charlie. All of the pain that this man had caused his family and friends. All of the times he had told himself he was going to kill this man the second that he saw him.

He wasn't going to go against that promise.

One of them were going to slip up eventually. It just so happened that it was Max who missed Damir's fist the first time. Damir grabbed Max's arm and slammed it against a rock, hearing a bone break. Then he swung him across the forest until he hit a tree.

He was winded for a few seconds. As he tried to get his bearings, Damir ran straight to where he was and grabbed him by the neck. He lifted him up against that same tree again.

"And they said that you were the best?!" Damir laughed. "I'll have to say, you were a challenge at first. But you are nothing compared to the Alphas I've slayed."

He struggled against the man's hold, but the lack of oxygen was only making him weaker. Damir was using both of his hands to wrap around his neck. He was trying to suffocate him as quickly as possible.

Max's life flashed before his eyes at that moment. He saw himself growing up with his parents. When he had first met Nick and Katy when they were just kids. He remembered the first time he saw Charlie, and all the problems that he had to deal with.

He remembered just before coming to this forest, and seeing Charlie holding Eric. He looked like an angel with how much he glowed when he held the child. Max never thought that Charlie could look more beautiful. He remembered during that week, when Eric first crawled onto his lap and hugged him. He had been so harsh on the boy without meaning to. He had promised himself that he would make it up to him.

He could see himself growing old with Charlie. They would watch as the pack grew and families got bigger and bigger. He saw himself holding Charlie in his old age with all the children they wound up adopting. All the joy of finding love and growing a family would be passed down to them.

"That's all you've got for me?" he asked his father. *"Out of everything I just told you, your only advice is 'Don't die'?"*

"You have a lot to live for, Max." His father's eyes still had a twinkle to them. He always looked at him with so much pride now that he was the Alpha. "And a lot of life left to live. Let that be the thing that pushes you in your moment of weakness. It's always family that brings warrior's home."

"Don't start celebrating yet," Max said through the vice grips that were still around his throat. Those turquoise eyes were wide with a surprise that he could even speak after all the pressure that he had put on his neck. Max wasn't going to lose all that he had fought for just from this weak filth of a man. He used his legs to knee the man in the groin. The man's grip weakened enough for Max to tear his hands off from him.

The next thing he did was grab his own arm. With a loud crack, he snapped the bone back into place. His werewolf abilities would heal it in a matter of minutes. And the pain was nothing compared his throat that was burning for air.

Max didn't waste any time, though. He punched Damir in the face. While he was down, he stomped on the man's legs. The cracking of bones had never sounded so good as it did right at that moment. Max was blood-thirsty as he grabbed the arms that Damir was using to block his face and began to break them too.

"Do you really think I would go down that easily?!" Max yelled at him. Before the man could even think to answer, he grabbed him by the neck and pinned him to the tree that he had tried to kill him on. "You, Damir, are nothing but a coward who preys on the weak, just like your father before you!"

The man was trying to say something, but Max put his thumb right where his windpipe was to block off all air flow.

"Do you know that it was my father before me who killed yours?" Max snarled at him. "You underestimated me and my pack, Damir. That was your first mistake. And it was your most lethal one."

"Max!"

He turned to see that Ed was right there, along with Leonard and Owen. Ed must have brought them here. He could see the hatred on all of their faces. He could see the same bloodlust that he had in all of their eyes.

Ed held up Max's hunting knife. The sign that an Alpha was at war. It shimmered in the moonlight.

"Thank you," Max grabbed it. He looked to Leonard and Owen. "Pull out yours, both of you. I will give this kill to all of us, as a means of victory and peace for all our packs."

Leonard had looked like he wanted to say something. But they didn't have time. Damir was still squirming under Max's grip. His eyes were wider than they had been before now that he was finally realizing he had met his demise.

They both took out their knives. Max was the first to stab the rogue. He plunged his knife deep into his chest. When he knew that he wouldn't be able to escape, Max threw Damir onto the ground so that the other Alphas could get their revenge. Leonard was next. He stabbed the rogue through the stomach to watch all the black bile come out. Owen stabbed him through the eye. The other turquoise eye stayed wide with fear as the soul that was in this body left.

Max was breathing heavily. All that he could do was look at the lifeless body that had caused him all this pain. He almost took away two of the most important things to him, and one of them he hadn't even met until he had found Charlie in that cabin.

"It's finally over," Ed said. Max looked up at him to see that his golden eyes were bright again. He was glad. It had been far too long since he had seen him look that happy. But, after a few minutes of Max not replying to him and still breathing heavily, Ed looked a bit concerned. "You okay Max?"

"I'm fine." Max shook his head. "Fucker tried to choke me to death."

"Let me call one of my medics over," Leonard said. "He can take a look at it."

"Send him over to Alistair," he told him. He knew that he would be fine after just a few more minutes. His healing rate was faster than anyone else in the pack. "He got hurt pretty bad trying to slow the bastard down."

"My people are already on that, actually," Owen said. "When we were trying to look for you, Ed helped us track you down. We found Alistair and Tyler fighting off some more rogues as well. My medics were the closest."

"Thank you." Max smiled at him.

"You would have done the same for me," Owen smiled back. "It's been an honor fighting with you."

"Are there anymore rogues?" he asked. Just because they killed the leader didn't mean that there weren't still stragglers around the forest.

"Probably one or two here and there," Leonard said. "I'm sure that we'll find them while marking our territories, though. I wouldn't be too worried about them."

"Max!" Tyler showed up. "There you are! What happened?" His brown eyes looked especially concerned when he saw Max's neck.

"Don't worry about it." Max waved it off. His breathing had been slowly getting back to normal. "Damir's dead."

Tyler looked down at the dead body. They hadn't taken their knives out of him yet. All of them were shocked that it was finally all over.

Leaning down, Tyler removed the Goldshield necklace off from the rogue's body.

"That must be where this came from." He held out the knife that Damir had pulled out in the beginning of the fight. Tyler quickly sheathed it.

"I can't believe he wiped out an entire pack," Leonard said.

"There's still one member left, actually," Max told him. He gestured for Tyler to hand the necklace to him. "I hope we're all in agreement to return this to that last member."

"The kid?" Owen asked.

"Eric," Max nodded. "This belonged to his father."

Now that he had dealt with getting justice for his pack, he was proud to have gotten justice for Eric and the pack that had raised him.

Their strife was finally over.

CHAPTER 59:

Coming Home

"They'll be here any minute, honey," Charlie told Eric. The entire pack had come outside to greet the warriors coming home. Charlie hadn't known they had won until he felt the territory expand and he could finally hear Max's voice in his head again. The whole pack was celebrating by setting tables up and having as much food as possible.

"*How much longer?*" he asked Max.

"*Just a few more minutes, Apple.*" Max's voice came crystal clear in his thoughts. Charlie missed him so much.

"He's probably got quite a story to tell," Mr. Locke said. Him and Mrs. Locke were standing right next to him. "I can only imagine what had happened in that forest."

"I'm just happy that it's finally over now." Mrs. Locke sighed. "Now we have the territory that everyone's been wanting for so long, and rogues won't be coming around as much as they were before."

"How long have you guys been trying to gain that territory?" Charlie asked.

"Don't worry about that." Mr. Locke waved it off. He looked a bit nervous when the topic got brought up. His wife was giving him the stink eye as well. "The point is that it's finally over, and it's not going to cause anyone strife anymore."

"Where's Uncle Nick?" Eric asked. Mrs. Locke had been holding him at the moment. Eric liked his new grandmother. He told Charlie that she reminds him of Max. It was easy to see that Eric had missed him, even though him and Max had barely gotten to really be with each other.

They were pretty happy when Eric started calling them grandpa and grandma. The boy hadn't been with them for that long at all, and Charlie and Max had only just decided to adopt him, but there was something about what Nick had told him that just seemed to make Eric happy with considering them family already.

"Right here!" Nick popped up out of nowhere. He immediately started poking Eric a bit to tickle him. "Miss me?"

Charlie wasn't sure if Nick was going to ever adopt, but he would make a great dad. He really seemed to do well with kids. For now, though, it seemed like he was simply happy with being the cool uncle and babysitter.

"Oh good!" Mrs. Locke said. "You got the camera!"

"Didn't think anyone wanted to miss out on some great moments," Nick handed the camera to her. Knowing Nick, he was probably going to run for Alistair the moment he saw him. As much as he had tried to hide it, it was easy to see that his friend missed him. Mr. and Mrs. Locke could take care of the picture taking anyway. They had told Charlie and Nick that it's what grandparents did best anyway.

"That and spoil their grandchildren," Mrs. Locke had said. "But I'm sure he's going to get spoiled by you and Max a bunch as well."

Charlie was already spoiling him. He couldn't help it. Eric looked so adorable when Charlie got something for him. He was still so small from the months of abuse that he had gone through. He learned from Button that most werewolf children have the same healing rate as a normal human. Sometimes it's just a little better than average, and they usually don't get as sick as most kids, but they still heal from wounds at a human rate.

Eric had to get put on the same diet that Charlie was on when he first came to the manor. It was funny just how much everything seemed to be coming in a circle. Aldi was having a blast feeding the kid too. Charlie brought Eric to the kitchen earlier that week when he wanted to make pies and Aldi just fell for him immediately.

"I just hope he doesn't wind up a troublemaker like Max was when he was a teenager," Aldi said. "If that happens again, then I might actually retire."

He couldn't imagine Eric being a bad child, but, then again, he couldn't really imagine Max being a troublemaker either. He was just going to have to deal with that when he got there.

"Here they come!" Someone said from the front of the crowd. Knowing that Eric was safe with Mrs. Locke, Charlie tried his best to squeeze through the hoard of people and get to the front.

They all looked amazing running back like they were. All the warriors were now off duty and running home to be with their family and friends after a week of little to no sleep. Charlie couldn't focus on that many of them. He was too happy to see the big red wolf that was leading all the others back home.

He didn't care if Max needed to change or put some clothes on first, he ran up to him anyway. The wolf shifted into a man quickly and wrapped him in his arms. The first thing that Max did was kiss him as passionately as he could. He didn't know how long they were in that embrace, but he never wanted it to end.

"I missed you so much." He told him when they broke their kiss. Max never took his arms off from him, and he loved it. It felt like he belonged in them, especially at that moment.

"I missed you too, Apple." Max started kissing his jaw and neck. They hadn't been this intimate since Max had left. And it had definitely had an effect on them.

"Wait," Charlie stopped him for a second. "What happened to your neck?" It looked red with finger marks on it. He lightly brushed his fingers on it.

"That." He picked him up. "Is a long story. One I intend to tell later."

"Is it going to heal?" he asked. It worried him that Max had gotten such a bad wound. "Dr. Button's going to go crazy once he sees it."

"It'll heal up in no time, Apple," Max said. He started walking towards one of the sheds for some clothes. "For now, let's just celebrate that this is all over."

Charlie let it go for the meantime. He would ask Max when they went to bed that night. He was sure that the man was exhausted from all the fighting that he did. And he could tell that he hadn't gotten that much sleep due to the tired expression that he wore. But the happiness of finally taking care of those rogues outshined the tired lines on his face.

"Alistair!" He heard Nick yell. He turned to watch Nick practically jump on his mate. Alistair looked just as tired as Max did. All of the warriors did. But he smiled so brightly when he had Nick in his arms. Charlie couldn't hear much of what they were saying, as most of it was sweet mumblings to each other. But he was happy to see them together again.

There were so many people greeting their loved ones. Emily was crying in Ed's arms, just as she had done when he was leaving. She had told Charlie that she changed her mind about waiting to have a family. She didn't want to put her career over her marriage.

Alan had run to Madeline and swung her around. Charlie smiled at the squeal that filled the air when Madeline was shocked. Ray and Desmond both ran to their wives instead of the other way around.

Sam was greeted by his wife and all of his kids. They all looked so happy to see him, they were absolutely giddy. Tyler was still holding his wife along with his two children. They spoke quietly, but Charlie was glad to see happy faces on them.

"This is always the best part." Max put his arms around him again. He was behind him as they both watched everyone greet each other. "Seeing everyone so happy when they get home."

"It's a lot better than when you guys leave." Charlie leaned into him. All of his worries melted away as soon as Max was holding him. "This week's been horrible."

Max hummed his answer as his hands slipped under Charlie's shirt. He slid him onto his lap and started planting kisses all over his shoulders and neck.

"Max." Charlie laughed. "Stop it."

"Why?" He could practically see him smiling just by his tone alone.

"Because you stink." He squirmed a little. "And you still have to greet everyone else who misses you."

"Do I really stink that bad?"

"You haven't showered in a week!" Charlie giggled as the man kept him hostage. "What did you think was going to happen?"

"I don't know." He kissed his shoulder again. "You might make good perfume, though."

"A shower makes the best perfume," he argued. Slowly, he got out of his grasp. It was hard to stay even a little away from him at the moment. Right now, all he wanted to do was be in those arms.

They walked back to the manor where everyone was greeting the warriors. They hugged and praised Max when they passed them. Even Liam looked proud of him, which was something that Charlie had been wishing to get his grandfather to be for a very long time.

"What's this?" Button asked. Charlie snickered as the doctor immediately noticed the mark on Max's neck. He couldn't say that Charlie didn't warn him.

"Later, Button," Max told him. "Please?"

"As long as later still means today." Button folded his arms. He seemed happy to see him, no matter what he was saying.

"You're going to need to check up on all the warriors," Max said. "Especially Alistair."

"What happened to Alistair?"

"Got the rogue by his hide and got thrown into a tree," Max said. "The Blood Moon Pack helped him out with their medics, but he still might need a check-up."

"Let him and Nick have their moment," Charlie said. "Nick's been worried sick about him the whole week."

"So has everyone else," Dr. Button said. "When Martha came home, that only made everyone's worry greater."

"How is Martha, by the way?" Max asked, he looked really worried when they mentioned her name.

"She's doing fine," Button answered. "It didn't take her too long to heal up, thankfully."

"Good." Max sighed. He could feel the tension leave his shoulders right when he heard that.

Mr. and Mrs. Locke were the next to finally reach them. Eric was still with them, thankfully. Charlie took him into his arms as the two took turns hugging their son.

"So, you got him?" Mr. Locke said.

Max answered that question by taking the knife that was on his necklace off and unsheathing it in front of all of them. The hunting knife was shimmering with red. He only showed it for a second, though, so that Eric wouldn't have a chance to see it.

That and it probably smelt absolutely horrible.

"The war is over." Max handed the sheathed knife to his father. "Though short lived, it will never be forgotten."

More cheering came when he said that. Charlie hadn't known that everyone was watching them until that moment. Now they were all laughing and dancing. One of the technicians had set up speakers and had gotten some music to play. It was soft at first but now the party seemed to be in full swing.

"Papa!" Eric reached out from Charlie's hold.

"What?" Max looked around, confused. When he saw Eric, he smiled, but his overall expression was still confused. Charlie couldn't help but hide a chuckle. "What did you say?"

"Papa!" Eric said again. He looked so happy to see Max after a week of him being gone. "Uncle Nick said I could call you Papa!"

Charlie would never forget just how Max looked when it all clicked in his head. It was a mixture of surprise and absolute joy. He wondered if that's how he looked when Eric first called him 'Daddy'.

Click

"I got it!" Mrs. Locke shouted. They all looked over to see her smiling with the camera in her hand. "This one is definitely going in your album."

"I don't understand." Max shook his head and looked at Charlie. "Did you guys plan this?"

"Well." Nick popped up out of nowhere again. "Him doing it to Charlie was too spontaneous, so we figured we'd make sure to get a picture of your reaction."

"Nick, you're going to have to see this!" Mrs. Locke said. "I think this is the best picture I've taken of Max yet!"

"What does he call Charlie?" Max asked. He looked a little disappointed. "What else did I miss while I was gone?"

"Nothing else, really," Mr. Locke said. "We just got everything planned out for all the warriors to not have to worry about the rest of their responsibilities for a while."

"He did what?!" They heard Tyler's voice before they saw him. He was staring at Isabelle with an exasperated look. "That takes me at least a week to finish one page!"

Click.

"I got this one!" Leah said through the crowd. She was holding a camera too. Charlie couldn't help but laugh at the silliness of this all. It had such an innocent happiness to it that it purified him.

"I want to say this was Nick's planning," Charlie told Max.

"How many surprise pictures did he plan on taking?" Max started looking around for cameras.

"I think just those two," he told him.

"He already got a bunch of me." Alistair came up to them. He was smiling as he watched Nick run over to Leah to see the picture.

Ed immediately jumped on the bandwagon and grabbed a camera off someone.

"At this point, we're going to wind up with a collage," Mrs. Locke said. "This was probably the best idea that we could have come up with for today."

Max chuckled a bit and looked back at him. "I'm just sad they didn't get a picture of your reaction. I would have loved to see it."

"Nick was saying that you were going to kill him for taking that moment away from you." Charlie leaned his head against the man's shoulder. Max had picked Eric up somewhere during the camera chaos. Charlie patted the boys head as he hugged Max as tight as a small boy like him could.

"That reminds me." Max nudged Eric a little in his arms. "Eric, I have something for you."

"Really?" His eyes went wide with excitement as soon as Max said that.

"Yup." He set the boy down and started to kneel down to his level. "There's something I found that belongs to you."

They all watched as Max pulled something out of a small bag. Charlie didn't even know that he had been carrying it around. He was so focused on simply seeing Max alive and well.

What he pulled out of it was more shocking, though. It was an Alpha necklace, but not to their pack. The symbol was a shield made of gold.

"It might need a little bit of polishing," Max told him. "But this was your fathers, before he died. I know he'd want you to have it."

He didn't know how the little boy was going to react to this. It was difficult getting him to open up about his parents at all. Charlie could comfort him a little, but he knew that it was something that only time could truly heal.

Eric was quiet for a second or two. He looked at the symbol in awe. It looked like there were a thousand memories flooding his mind through those different colored eyes.

Then he hugged Max and started crying. It was the most crying that Charlie had ever seen out of the boy. Max just rubbed his back and shushed him.

"It's okay, Eric," Max told him. "Do you know what this means?"

"What?" He continued to sob.

"It means that they're at peace now," Max told the boy. "And that they'll always be with you."

Eric's crying slowed down a little bit, but he could still see the pain in his eyes as he pulled away from Max.

"You need to promise me that you'll take care of this, and keep this safe, okay?" Max asked him. Eric clutched the necklace to his chest and nodded. "This is your legacy. This is where you came from. You'll always be a part of the Crescent Moon Pack now, but don't ever forget where you came from."

"I won't," Eric said. He stood up a little straighter after that. He looked confident, for once. It was nice to see in the boy. "Thank you."

"No problem." Max ruffled his hair a bit.

"Here." Charlie offered Eric his hand. "Why don't we all find a good place for this in your room?"

"Okay," Eric took his hand. Max and him began walking to their suite.

"Where did you even find that?" Charlie asked Max.

"Damir had it. He used it during our fight."

"Isn't that a sign of disrespect?"

"It is. Damir didn't exactly care about those kinds of things."

They stayed in their room for a little bit that day, just to relax from all the stresses that the week had brought. Charlie hadn't known just how much he had worried about Damir until now. He felt like a weight was lifted off his shoulders. A weight that he didn't know he had put there.

"You're sure he's dead?"

"Positive." Max pulled him closer to him. *"No one's ever going to hurt you again, Apple. You or Nick, for that matter."*

Charlie leaned into him again. There was so much peace that those words gave to him. He truly believed that there wouldn't be anyone like Damir again. Not after what Max and all of them had done to destroy them.

They had actually done it.

They had brought this pack to the golden age.

CHAPTER 60:

Scars

"I'm fine, Nick," Alistair smiled. They had been resting in their room for the majority of the day. Everyone was planning on a week-long celebration to have for their pack, but all the warriors were much too exhausted to deal with something like that at the moment. So, the day after they returned was a rest day.

Alistair wasn't entirely sure if he wanted to participate too much in this celebration. He loved how happy the pack had been, but he had missed Nick too much to want to be away from him even if it means just a little bit. He knew the man didn't like being held in public, and he wasn't going to push him to, but he didn't want to stop holding him after all that had happened.

"You sure you don't need anything?" Nick asked. He had been as hyper as ever the past couple of days. Alistair could feel the absolute joy that he felt at seeing him come back. He was happy to be home too. It was extremely relieving knowing that Damir was dead as well. He had wanted to be one of the reasons the man had died, but he supposed he had helped at least.

It was Ed who had found him. Tyler had been busy fighting off rogues that were trying to run in Max's direction. Ed had sniffed him out when he was helping Alpha Owen and Alpha Leonard find Max. Alpha Owen immediately sent for one of his medics to come and patch him up. Other than a couple of broken bones that needed to be snapped back into place, he had come out of that fight in good shape.

"All I need is you, Bakshir." Alistair pulled him in close. Nick had been trying to do everything for him lately. It was nice and relaxing when it was something like helping him bathe the night before. But now all Alistair wanted to do was rest with his mate in his arms.

"Are you sure you're not hungry at least?" Nick asked. "I'm sure I could make something for you. Or I could have Aldi make something."

"Isn't the kitchen closed for a week?" he asked him. From what he had heard, Alpha Max had given most of the workers the week off to be with their families. They had been doing little catering events. Alistair overheard the Alpha and Luna talking about getting a bakery to cater for one of the days. It was a bakery of a friend of theirs that they hadn't talked to in a while. As soon as Charlie started talking about the baker's pies, everyone started shaking their heads.

"We'll never convince him," Nick had told him.

"Convince him of what?"

"That his pies are ten times better than Ryan's," Nick had stage whispered. "He's looked up to Ryan since we first met him. None of his cooking will ever beat that chef, I swear."

It was fun learning a little more about everyone. They all talked about their stories of the past and good memories that they had. They talked a lot about Max when he was younger and Charlie when they had first met him. It saddened Alistair that Charlie had thought so lowly of himself. The man truly was gifted. Sam and Tyler were shocked to hear that he had managed to get all of their paperwork done for the month in the short week that they were gone.

It was good to know that he had gotten help from the past Luna. She seemed nice, although she was a bit dramatic at times. It truly made the mood all the more lighter when she started going on about different things her son had done to cause trouble when he was younger. She reminded him a lot of Katy in a way. She wasn't as dramatic as her, but her expressions were entertaining to say the least. It was easy to see why she was chosen to be Luna before Charlie. She always had a motherly nature to her that seemed to make everyone less stressed.

"You're right." Nick sighed into him, bringing him back to the present. So much had happened in such a short time that it was hard to process everything. Alistair was still in shock that Damir was dead. "I forgot."

"I'm not hungry right now anyway," he told him.

"But Dr. Button said that you needed to make sure that you rested and ate a lot," Nick told him. All the warriors had to go to the doctor's office the night before to make sure they were all still healthy. Alistair's wounds had healed for the most part, but it would take another day or two for it to heal completely.

"Then we'll order something," he suggested. "Why are you wanting to move around so much, Bakshir?"

"I don't know." Nick sighed again. When they were close, Nick had his arms wrapped around him as tight as could be. Alistair could tell that he wasn't used to him not being around after the weeks of his recovery. Alistair wasn't entirely used to it either. He hadn't gotten much sleep throughout that week, but he was sure that if he did, he would be dreaming of his mate. "I just want to make you as comfortable as possible now that you're finally back and my mom used to always...oh no."

"What?" He moved Nick away a bit to see his face. It was shocked, and Alistair didn't know why. All he knew was that something was wrong. He didn't like it.

"I'm turning into my mother!" Nick cried out dramatically. Alistair couldn't help but laugh at the silly statement.

"I don't think you're anything like your mother, Nick," he assured his mate. "If anything, I'd say you're much more like your father."

"Why do you say that?"

"Because he's calm about most things," Alistair explained. "Except for his mate."

"Great." Nick buried his face into Alistair's chest again. "So, I'm just like my father."

"You are your own person." He pulled him tighter into his hold. "Just because you might have some of the same traits as your parents doesn't mean you're exactly like them."

"I know," his mate huffed. "I don't know why I'm being like this. I'm sorry. I just…"

"You just what?" he coaxed.

"I just missed you," Nick's voice shrank when he said that. He could hear the pain that he had in those words. "It was only a week, but it's been the most stressful and worrisome week of my life. I couldn't even calm myself down by talking to Katy. Nothing worked. And then I was scared that you were going to get hurt out there, and you did."

"Bakshir." Alistair stopped him from rambling on further. "I wasn't going to die out there. Not when I had you to come home to."

"You have no idea how worried everyone was when Martha came home," he told him. "Everyone was thinking that more of you guys were going to come back home wounded or something."

"That's what the medics were for." He rubbed Nick's back. "I'd say that the other packs helped us a lot simply through those medics."

"We really need to try and get more doctors for our pack." Nick snuggled back into him. "Then we wouldn't have to rely on other packs to help us heal our warriors."

"Knowing Max, he's probably going to try working on that next." He buried his face in his lover's hair. Just having Nick's scent around him was heavenly at the moment. "But, right now, we don't have to worry about any of that."

"Then why do I still feel like a mess?"

"You can't forget what you've gone through, Nick." His hands automatically started to move to the man's sides. "It's been a really rough month for all of us, and for you especially."

"I think I just missed you."

"I missed you too." He smiled.

"Are you sure there's nothing I can get for you?" He asked again. All Alistair did was chuckle at how caring his mate was trying to be.

"The only thing I want." He turned them around on the bed so that Nick was underneath him. "Is you, Bakshir. I said it once, and I'll say it a thousand more times."

He kissed him before he could say anything to him. He was too tired to truly enjoy his mate when he came home the night before. But now, all the time they had spent apart had built up his passion for him. His hands moved underneath the shirt that Nick was wearing. He almost forgot how soft the man's skin was. It was almost as addicting as those legs going around his waist.

He wanted to take this slow, though. He wanted to savor the moment. He stopped kissing him to try and pull Nick's shirt off from him when his hands were suddenly grabbed.

"Wait!" Nick's voice was breathy as he spoke. Those hazel eyes showed fear in them.

"What's wrong?" He moved one of his hands to hold his lovers face. He thought he already dealt with all of Nick's fears about this. He knew he wasn't forcing this on him either. The smell of his mate's arousal had already clouded his mind.

"Nothing." Nick shook his head and pulled down his shirt. "Forget about it."

He tried to pull Alistair into another kiss, but he stopped him.

"Why don't you want your shirt off?" He leaned close to his ear, planting kisses all around it. His hand had moved underneath the thin fabric again.

"That's not why I stopped you." Nick leaned into his touch.

"Why are you lying?" He could feel that his mate was troubled by something. He just couldn't figure out what at the moment. "Please talk to me."

"I just…" Nick sighed and tried to move out of Alistair's hold. "I'm sorry, this is supposed to be a good moment, and I'm just ruining it."

"You never ruin anything, Bakshir." He nuzzled against him. He knew that it always comforted him when he was this close to him. "Please, tell me what's wrong. I want to help."

"You can't help," Nick said. "I just feel…"

"Feel what?"

"Ugly," the man finally said. He grabbed the hand of Alistair's that was rubbing his torso to make him stop. "I feel like you aren't going to like me now that the bandages are off."

Alistair really did wish he were the one to kill that man. He caused so much strife in less than a day. He hoped he burned for all eternity. But his anger towards a dead man wasn't going to help him at the moment. He knew that it was best to let that go. No matter whether you hated them or not, it was best to let the dead rest.

"Nick." He forced those eyes to look at him. They were soft and insecure, just like the first time he had tried to be intimate with him. "You forget that I was here to change those bandages of yours. I was with you when you first woke up and the doctor had to drain those cysts that were all over you. I was the one who carried you out of that cabin and ran you home that night. Throughout all of that, I never once thought anything about you other than how much I love you."

Tears started coming down Nick's face as he wrapped his arms around him again. Alistair made sure to wipe every tear away. He might not be able to change what had happened to his mate, but he could help him heal from it. That would be the true way that he could get revenge on that rogue. For you give people power if they're in your mind, even the dead.

Nick kissed him hard. He couldn't help but match his passion. He wove his fingers through the man's soft hair and deepened it. His hands slowly started to move Nick's shirt up again. He wasn't going to try and take it off this time. He had a better idea.

"Stay like this, Bakshir." He rubbed the man's sides. "Please?"

His eyes showed him discomfort, but he nodded at him. Alistair then moved the blanket off from their top half and lowered himself just a little bit.

The wolfsbane had created scars. They were thin and purple, but they weren't as bad as the scars that he had seen before. They blended in well with his tanned skin. Even though it came from a horrible event, Alistair didn't love Nick any less because of it. He was beautiful to him, no matter what.

He started near his waist, kissing every scar that was on his stomach and chest. It wasn't long before he felt the man moving his body up to meet his lips. His hands were still caressing his lover's sides, slowly slipping the shirt up off him with every gentle stroke. He traveled all the way up to his collar bone, where one of his worst wounds were. It pained him to think how close that wound had been to his heart.

The shirt slipped off Nick. He didn't seem like he was thinking at the moment. He was distracted by the lips that Alistair used to make all of those memories disappear. Alistair kissed the mark that he made on Nick once he had gotten all the way up.

"Turn around, Bakshir," he whispered into his ear. His mate obeyed without a word. He could tell just how good this was making him feel. He wanted to make sure that Nick never thought about this man again. He knew that it might take a while, but he had always prided himself on his patience. And he was pretty sure he could do this for the rest of his life.

Nick moaned as Alistair kissed the mark on his neck again. His thin frame tried to push into him more and more with each kiss. He continued to kiss every scar that had been on his back. The greatest one was a slash from a whip that went all across it. Alistair made sure to take his time with that one.

He enjoyed being able to see Nick this way. He loved being able to calm him down or excite him.

He took the time to slip off the shorts that Nick was wearing. It was starting to get colder out and Nick had told him that he got used to wearing clothes to bed when he had stayed the week over at his brothers. Alistair was glad that he had someone to watch over him while he was gone.

"Alistair!" Nick moaned as he put his fingers inside him and started massaging. His lips had traveled to his shoulders at that point. He was losing control the more noises he was getting out of his mate. This wasn't the thing that he missed the most when he was away from home, but it was on the list. He missed the intimacy that him and Nick had when they were alone.

"You're beautiful." He kissed behind his ear.

He wished he could stay in this moment. Every time he was with Nick, he wanted to pause time just to try and remember everything that he could. The slender man underneath him was intoxicating. Being able to sense how his mate felt only seemed to fuel Alistair's own desire.

He took his fingers out and moved his hip to enter him. They both quickly began their own dance off passion. Nick met his hips eagerly, making him go deeper with every thrust. His face was now buried in the pillow, muffling all the moans that he was giving. All it really did was make Alistair want to be closer to him. He kissed Nick's neck, trying to get more sounds out of him. He loved hearing him like this.

His hand moved to his penis, stroking it to help him finish. With all that had gone on within such a short time, they both needed this.

With one hard thrust, he finished inside him. Nick climaxed almost simultaneously, giving a loud moan. He had missed those noises. He had missed a lot about Nick when he was gone. He didn't realize just how much he had missed his mate until that moment.

"You're such a teddy bear," Nick chuckled as Alistair wrapped his arms around him again. He turned the man around and started nuzzling into his neck just like before.

"If I was then maybe you'd be okay with me holding you outside of our room," he said.

"I'm not against you holding me in front of people, Alistair." Nick's hand weaved into his hair. He was enjoying the sparks that came from it.

"I thought you didn't like doing things like that in public."

"Holding someone is different from making out in front of everyone," Nick explained. "My sister, Charlette was the absolute worst when she found her mate."

"You didn't want to do things like that because of your sister?" Alistair couldn't help but chuckle a bit at that. He wished he had siblings to be embarrassed by.

"Trust me when I say that it was the closest thing to porn that I had seen at the time," Nick groaned. "And I was, like, thirteen."

"So, it wasn't just making out?"

"No, it still isn't. Whenever they come over, they can't keep their hands off each other. The only time is when they're dancing. My mom's yelled at her about it so many times."

"She was the professional dancer, right?"

"Yup." Nick smiled. "You remembered from the rhyme, huh?"

"She was nice to talk to."

"You are not good at avoiding the question." Nick laughed. Alistair was happy that he had successfully gotten Nick back to being calm again. They both sank deeper into the bed with every second, enjoying the bliss of finally being in each other's arms again.

"I'm glad that you said I could hold you in public," Alistair said. "Now maybe I will go to that celebration."

"You weren't going to go?!"

"I missed holding you too much." He kissed him again. He couldn't get enough of Nick. He fell in love with him again and again with every touch and taste. It reminded him of the first time that he had woken up with Nick in his arms.

"My families going to be pulling us apart to talk to you, you know."

"Are you trying to convince me back into staying home?"

"No!" Nick giggled. "I'm just warning you."

"Then I'll bring you with me everywhere they pull me."

They talked like that a little more. Of course, Alistair would go if Nick wanted to. He was sure that it wouldn't be that bad honestly. It would be nice to see Nick dance again. He was a good dancer.

"Hey, Alistair?" Nick said after a while of them lazing around.

"Hmm?"

"I love you." His arms went around his neck as he pulled him tighter to him.

"I love you too, Nick." Alistair smiled. "Please don't think you're ugly."

"I don't know." His mate gave him a playful look. "It was kind of fun having you change my mind."

"You're far from ugly, Bakshir." He kissed him again. "I'll say it as many times as you want me to."

CHAPTER 61:

The Pack's Rejoice

"Dexter, did you even make sure that there was a spare tire in here?" Owen asked.

"Hey, dude." Dexter put his hands up. "How am I supposed to remember everything when you're giving me a thousand orders at once?"

"That's where you listen, or ask me again!"

"You were the one who was yelling at me to get all the luggage, BEFORE I even stepped outside to check!"

Katy sighed.

Boys will always be boys.

"Will both of you just stop?" She got out of the car. They were so close to getting to the Crescent Pack territory it wasn't funny, and they, of course, get a flat right before they get there. "I bet you don't even know how to change a tire."

"Of course, I do!" Both of them said at the exact same time. Katy just laughed. Their friendship reminded her of Ray and Desmond. They fought with each other, but always wound up laughing at the end of the day.

They were a lot tamer when they both found their mates.

Was that just a guy werewolf thing? Now that she thought about it, she hadn't really met a guy who wasn't that way before they found their mate.

Nick didn't count.

Neither did Alistair.

Katy batted Owen's hand out of the way and started taking things out of the trunk.

"The extra tires are usually in a hidden compartment," she explained. "In case you *men* forgot."

Of course, they probably didn't know that. Owen was treated like he was some kind of prince when he was growing up, which explained the attitude quite a lot.

She was so glad that was over. Ever since that night she yelled at him about scaring Nick, he really had been listening to her. Of course, nothing was perfect on the first try, and they had fought a little bit. But he was getting better at trying to see her side of things. And that was all she really wanted.

Trying to get a prince to see something that he didn't want to see was the most frustrating thing imaginable.

"I was trying to get to that compartment, but he wouldn't let me take anything out!" Dexter complained. He was only seventeen, so she guessed he had an excuse for why he was acting like this.

"Stop whining already!" Katy told him. "Just help me take the damn thing out!"

Thankfully, they listened to that. The tires for off roading were always heavy. They had to be so that they wouldn't get flat with every twig or spine they came across. Katy and Nick had gone off roading a lot. But Nick was stronger than her, so he would always be the one to pick up the tire and then they would both work to get the bolts out and change it.

"Do you actually know how to change a tire?" Dexter asked. He placed the tire against the car right next to the one that was flat.

"Do you know how many tires I've had to change just from driving to school and back?" she told him. "It always took forever to use the main road in the morning, and we always woke up late, so we would just take one of the Jeeps through the woods."

"That's badass," the brunette said. His smile sparkled in the sunrays that were shining down on them.

"No." She bopped him on the nose. "It's something that everyone should know how to do, whether they're a woman or not."

Owen chuckled a bit when she bopped his friend on the nose. The two were only a year apart but they were so different from each other. Dexter acted like he was at least two years younger, except when he wasn't training.

She had missed so many of them during the week that they were gone.

"I'm so glad your brother's my second." Owen shook his head and helped lift the car up. They didn't have a part to help lift up the car, so he just used his strength. "You wouldn't be able to remember anything I told you."

"First of all." Dexter helped her lift the flat tire off from the hinge. "I helped you with so much strategizing in that forest just a few days ago. Secondly." He then helped hold the other tire while she but the nuts in place. "I'm glad I'm not you're second too. That way I can still talk to you like a friend rather than 'The Boss.'"

"I'm still your boss, dumbass." Owen smiled.

"Yeah, but you're not," He changed his voice to mock his brother, "'The Boss.'"

"Please tell me he doesn't actually say that when I'm not there."

"Oh, all the time!" Dexter laughed. "It's the one thing I give him shit for."

Katy just shook her head. She loved hearing the two of them when they weren't bickering over something dumb. They were good friends. Dexter was actually one of the first people who had listened to some of her points on certain subjects. He wasn't a part of the council, but it felt nice having someone agree with her at that time.

Apparently, he was more open minded due to something with his family, but she could never find the right time to ask him about it.

"Okay." She wiped the dirt off her hands and stood up. "Let's pack everything back in and get on the road again."

"That was faster than half of our chauffeur's!" Dexter looked at her in shock. "How many times did you have to do this?"

"It helps when you have help." Katy chuckled. "Max's dad was actually the one who taught Nick and I how to change out a tire quick."

"Really?" Owen raised an eyebrow. "I wouldn't think that the Alpha of a pack would have time for stuff like that."

"There's always time if you make time." She bopped him on the nose next, causing Dexter to laugh. Owen just caught her hand and kissed it. "Awww! You're so cute!"

"Ewwww!" Dexter said. "That was supposed to be funny, not the beginnings to a romance novel!"

"Shut up before I make you run back home!" Owen growled at him a bit. She was shocked when she first heard Owen growl at his friends, until she realized that it was more of a playful thing rather than a threat.

Owen growled a lot.

She was still working on that with him.

They got back in the car and continued their journey to the Crescent Moon Pack house. Since her pack and their pack had finally gotten connected borders, it made traveling much easier now that there wasn't that much of a threat of rogues. She heard from Charlie that Max was already planning on making a road through the forest to the different pack houses. It was mainly going to be from Blood Moon to theirs since that was the only way they could get there without traveling through the Harvest Moon Pack first.

"You're going to let me hug everyone when we get there, right?"

"Do you really have to hug everyone?" Owen asked. She knew that was one of the things that Owen was trying to work on, but it still annoyed her a bit when he asked questions like that.

"Owen, wouldn't you be glad that everyone that you grew up with was still okay after all of that?!"

"I guess you have a point." He smiled at her. He was so handsome when he smiled.

The rest of the drive was nice. Fall was starting to come, and the cool breeze showed it. She couldn't believe just how fast the year had flown. It was amazing that they had been able to do so much, and had gone through so much.

On second thought, it wasn't so amazing what they had gone through.

BUT! It was all over now and everyone was okay. She was mainly happy about that.

Owen started talking to them about this old pack house that was smack dab in the middle of the forest. To honor the pack that had originally had that forest as their territory, they were going to rebuild the house and turn it into a meeting house for the packs. She had no idea how they could come up with such a great idea, but she was excited to see all these changes that were going to take place.

While Owen was gone on his mission, she had actually convinced the council to allow some of the lower pack members to have some more freedom in their careers. They had desperately needed some more people to help pick up the slack that the warrior's absence had created. Builders and electricians of the pack were trained as warriors just in case of a war breaking out. Since they had all been sent out into the forest, they were kind of in a crisis.

And Katy had found the perfect omega to challenge their views.

His dad was a builder and his uncle was an electrician. While he wasn't the best at it, he actually helped quite a lot while they were all away.

1 point Katy.

0 points Council.

"So, Max actually adopted that little boy?" Owen asked. She had totally spaced during the entire conversation that him and Dexter were having.

"Yeah!" Katy replied. "I've only seen him once, but I hear him over the phone all the time. Nick had this crazy plan to convince the boy to call Charlie 'Daddy' and apparently it worked! I'm so sad I wasn't there! Do you know how adorable that would have been?!"

"I hear he's got two different colored eyes," Dexter said.

"Yeah!" she told him. "Which only makes him more adorable! You guys have to see him!"

"Oh no." Dexter gave a sly smile towards Owen. "Better watch out, buddy. I think they're going to give her baby fever."

Oh please!" She slapped his shoulder. He was in the driver's seat. "I have enough kids to deal with in this pack. I'm looking at one right now!"

Before either of them could say anything more, she saw the bright lights of the pack house coming through the trees. It was still daylight, but the trees were so thick that it was easy for the days to look dull in the fall.

And there was one person in particular that she saw right out front of the manor.

"Nick!" She ran out of the car towards her friend.

"Katy!" They both hugged each other as soon as she reached him. It was so good to see him again. The last time she had seen him, he was still bed ridden and all bandaged up. Now he looked like his normal self again.

"You ready to teach your Alpha how to dance tonight?" He gave her a playful look.

"What do you mean?"

"What do you mean, what do I mean?" Nick laughed. "He's going to have to know how to dance if he's coming to Charlie and Max's wedding."

Oh no.

She totally forgot about that.

Nick could probably see that she had completely spaced out about the event through her face alone.

"I know how to dance." Owen walked up to them both.

"You may know how to dance the slow ones." Nick put a finger in the air. "But, if you're going to be partying with Katy, and probably the rest of my family, you're going to have to know a lot more."

"Wait!" Katy was practically bouncing at this point. "Are you saying that your whole family is coming?!"

"I think." Nick shrugged. "There's always some sort of complication with someone. But they all said that they were going to try and come."

After what had happened to Nick, they better all come. She was sad when she heard that they had all came to visit Nick right after she had left for home. She was looking forward to seeing them all again. They really were a blast at parties.

"Wait, I don't get it." Dexter came up after parking the car. "Are you two related or something?"

Did she mention that she loved this man child?

"Something like that," Owen answered. He didn't look that uncomfortable around Nick anymore, which she was glad of. "Come on, let's get inside."

He guided her to the front of the group as they walked up to those big doors. She was already suspicious before she heard Nick and Owen whispering about something.

"Did you bring everything?" Nick asked.

"Yup," Owen whispered back.

What were these two planning?

Wait!

"You two are actually talking to each other?!" She turned around to look at them.

"I mean." Nick shrugged again. "He did apologize."

She was going to ask more questions when the big doors to her childhood home opened up and more familiar faces appeared.

"Max!" She ran up and hugged him. "How's your neck?" She had heard from Owen that Damir had tried to choke him to death. He was breathing pretty hard for a while after that.

"All healed up," Max assured her. "How are you?"

"Well," she started. "Apparently, I'm the only one out of the three that knows how to fix a flat; Nick and Owen are actually talking; Oh, and this is Dexter!" She pointed at the kid that was staying close to Owen and Nick.

"I've met him before," Max told her. Dexter was walking up to them after he heard his name. "Nice to meet you as a human, though."

"I'd say the same for you." Dexter smiled at him. "You guys had one hell of a battle strategy. Those were some good fights."

"We've been trying to get those rogues out of here since the dawn of time." Max sighed. "I'm still shocked that it's over."

"Hey Katy!" Nick called from where he and Owen were standing. "I forgot to ask, you did put on water proof makeup, right?"

"Why?" She slitted her eyes at him when he walked up to her.

"Because you're going to be doing a lot of crying with all the adorableness that's around." He smiled at her.

"I am not!"

"Are too."

"Am not!"

"Hey, Katy!" Charlie's voice came from the open doors. They hadn't even made it inside yet. "It's good to see you again."

Her heart almost stopped. There Charlie was, holding the most adorable child in is arms. Both of them were adorable. She knew from the moment that she met him that he was going to make an adorable dad.

Or was it mom?

Oh, who cares! He was as bright as rays of sunshine when he had that cute little ball in his arms.

"Awwwww!" She squealed. "You guys look so cute together!"

She did tear up when she saw them, dammit all. She was a big cry-baby when it came to cute stuff. But she was smart enough to know that this stuff was going to happen. She had put on water proof make up. She just wasn't going to tell Nick that.

"You want to say hi to everyone, Eric?" Charlie asked the tiny ball of a child that was in his arms. She had only heard the boy over the phone. Other than when they were all trapped, of course.

She'd rather not think about that.

"Hi Eric!" She went over to the little guy. "Remember me? We talked a lot over the phone."

"Katy?" He peeked up from Charlie's shirt. He was so shy!

"Yup!" She nodded. "It's nice to see you again."

He was easy to open up to her at least. She could tell that Dexter was giving Owen a smirk from behind her, but she wasn't going to focus on that right now. She was too happy to see this adorable baby that she had only heard about.

"Well, it looks like we're going to be out here for a while," Max said. She was going to ask why when another car pulled up. Out came the Harvest Moon Pack in all their glory.

"Wynona!" Katy ran over to her. She couldn't hug her, because she had her baby with her. But it was so good to see her again. She had actually been there a lot for her through the beginning of her being a Luna. Wynona had been from the Blood Moon Pack, so she knew a little bit more about how it worked than Katy.

"It's good to finally see you all again!" Wynona said. She gave Leonard the baby to hold while she went to hug her and Charlie. They had talked over the phone so much the past couple weeks it felt like they had known each other since forever.

Eric seemed to remember Wynona by her voice too. She was glad, honestly, that the boy didn't remember them much from when they first met. He looked so happy in Charlie's arms. Max looked happy just watching them.

It was all so cute.

Her heart was going to explode.

"You sure you don't need to put on that water proof make up?" Nick's voice came up from behind her. She immediately turned around and smacked his arm.

"I'm not going to cry!"

"I'm sorry we're late," Wynona said. "There were so many setbacks, you wouldn't believe!"

"Oh, don't worry about it!" Charlie told her. "This is meant to be a celebration! There's no need to stress over being here on time."

They finally went inside to see that the party was in full swing. Dancing, music, food. They had it all.

Oh, and pies!

"Hey, Charlie." She got the blonds attention. "Did you find out if Eric like's pie?"

"Yup!" Charlie told her. "His favorite is apple."

They all laughed at that. Even though Eric wasn't their son by blood, he did seem to have a lot of their characteristics. He definitely had a lot of things in common with Max. And the way he clung to the people he was comfortable with reminded her of Charlie.

It was all so cute.

"When are we going to have pie, Daddy?" Eric looked up at Charlie.

"Awwww!" Her heart was going to implode with all this adorableness!

"We're going to have to hear a lot of that," Dexter asked Nick behind her. "Aren't we?"

"Oh, yeah," Nick told him. "She's a sucker for romance and babies."

She turned around to stick her tongue out at Nick. As much as she always thought that Dexter and Owen acted like kids when they were together, she couldn't help but be childish with Nick. They always acted like this around each other.

"That is pretty cute." Wynona chuckled. "Congratulations, Max. I'm glad that you decided to adopt the little guy."

"Me too," Max told her. He looked at Charlie and Eric with nothing but pure joy in his eyes. She didn't think she had seen him so happy before.

It was utter chaos after that. Everyone was getting separated from each other, trying to find another person. People were talking, Nick was trying to teach Owen some dances, which was hilarious to see. Alistair had finally found them. She was wondering where he was. Even with this crazy party, his whole aura was calm. And everywhere he went, he brought that calmness with him.

He was an interesting person to say the least.

She also finally got to meet the other new members to the Crescent Moon Pack. They had joined just after she had left. She absolutely fell in love with Jackie. The omega was so kind and innocent. And she had the longest brown hair, Katy was so jealous of it.

She was big and pregnant then, but still as happy as can be. When she told Katy that it was going to be triplets, she almost spat out her drink! Triplets were so rare to have! And she was so tiny! Knowing Dr. Button, though, she was going to come out of that healthy with healthy babies.

Her husband, Herb, was absolutely hilarious. He reminded her of a lumberjack for some reason. She didn't quite know why until the man started laughing at one of Nick's jokes. That man's laughs could shake the whole forest!

Madeline, which was Alan's mate, was the last of the new members that she met. She had a motherly feel to her, although she hadn't had any kids. Her and Alistair seemed to be great friends. It was fun to see Alistair joke around and tease with someone. He was such a strong, silent type. His stories were crazy, though! Dexter was automatically magnetized to him as soon as he heard that the man had fought a werebear.

But there was someone else that she had been dying to see for a week now. Knowing that person, though, there was one place that they'd be for sure at a party like this.

"Martha!" She squealed and ran up to the woman. She was by the bar area, with a pint of beer in her hand. She didn't drink much, but when it came to a party, she loved to stay around the bar and tell old stories. Her laugh rivaled Herb's. Which, interestingly enough, was how they became friends.

"Katy!" The old woman held her tightly. "It's good to see you again!"

"You're okay!" She actually started crying in her arms. She heard from Nick that she had returned early from the mission and she was wounded. She was so worried, even when he told her that she had healed up. She wished the old bat had a phone. But that was just something that she didn't want to learn.

"Of course, I am!" Martha pet her head. It brought her back to all the times when she was little and the woman comforted her. "They can't kill this battle axe off that easy."

"But you got hurt!" she started, tears still flooding down her eyes. "And then Dr. Button was worried, and Aldi was worried, and-and!"

"Shh, dear," she cooed. "I'm alright. Don't worry."

They talked a little after that. Aldi had come to hang out with her. She was shocked to hear that Max had given everyone the week off to celebrate the homecoming of the warriors. She was sure that the cleanup for all of this was going to be crazy. But it was good to see Aldi and his aunt again.

That reminded her.

"Owen, you have to come here." She mind linked with him. *"You need to say sorry to Aldi."* She had almost forgot that he had yelled at him before they even mated. She was so mad at him, and she hadn't even met him yet.

"I promise I will," Owen said. *"But I need you to come here first."*

"What?! Why?"

"I need to talk to you."

Oh great. This only meant good things. Someone probably told him about the one time she gave Max that compliment in high school. She swore no one ever shut up about that.

Sighing, she told Martha and Aldi that she would be back and headed over to find Owen. Hopefully, this could still be a good day. Ever since Owen had come back, they had nothing but good days. She was so happy, but also worried that it wouldn't last that long. They had gone through so much already, and there was still so much to do and take care of.

She followed his scent until she was in the middle of the dance floor. He must have been learning more dance moves with Nick. But she couldn't see him.

"Owen?" She looked all around. There were so many people dancing and it was so crowded that she could barely make heads or tails of anything.

"Right here."

She turned around to see him knelt down right in front of her. The dance floor cleared without anyone saying anything and a spotlight shined on them.

What was going on?

"Katy," Owen started. "I know I haven't been the perfect mate, and it's been a rough time throughout the little while that we've been together. But I truly don't think I could ever live without you. You are the one thing that grounds me, and my true love. Katy," He pulled out a box from his pocket and opened it to show a ring. "Will you marry me?"

Now she really was going to cry. This was the most romantic thing she could ever imagine.

"Yes!" She squealed her answer. She knew he was going to ask her again at some point, but she didn't know when. That was the fun of it. And she was glad that she had asked him to do something like this.

Owen put the ring on her finger and stood up to kiss her.

"And cut!"

She turned to see Nick with a camera on the other side of the room. Then she looked back to Owen with shock. The realization of everything was hitting her.

"You planned this with Nick?!"

"Of course." He smiled at her. "How else would I be able to find the best scene, and the perfect place to do it?"

The tears came again as she hugged Owen. As much as they had all their rocky parts, she hadn't stayed with him just because she had to. She stayed with him for the moments like these.

In sickness and in health.

For better or for worse.

She wouldn't have it any other way.

CHAPTER 62:

December Sixth

A knocking came from the door, tearing his attention away from his hair. It always knew the best days to not work with him. The red flames went every which way, and he was too worried that if he put too much gel in it that it would look even more ridiculous.

Great, he was going to have to call his mom to come in and help him. He couldn't exactly see Charlie at the moment. That was against the rules when it came to this sort of thing.

"Come in!" he said. He really hoped that it was Tyler or Ed. He needed them to help calm his nerves down.

Instead, Max looked through the mirror to see that Liam had walked in. Shocked, he turned to see the man.

"That hair isn't going to comb down, you know," Liam said. There was a small smile on his face. It was strange to see the man smile. Max hadn't really seen him smile since he was a kid.

"I'm just going to have to get mom up here." Max sighed. "She's the only person, other than Charlie, who knows how to get this monster to actually look right."

"I remember when you were a kid, just how many times you'd run away from her when she was trying to brush your hair." His purple eyes lightened a bit as he relived a memory. "It's funny to think that she's one of the only people that you trust with it now."

"Why did you come in here?" Max looked at him confused. "Are you saying you want to help try and fix my hair?"

"No!" Liam shook his head dramatically. "That was the one thing that I was the worst at, even with my own."

Huh. Well, he knew where he inherited that trait from now.

"I just wanted to say something," Liam continued. "Before you head out to your big day."

Max tensed. He wasn't sure just how this conversation was going to go. He knew that the man hadn't liked some of his choices in life. And he really didn't want to get into an argument today.

Today was supposed to be a good day.

"What is it?" He was too curious not to ask anyway. He felt like he was gambling with how this conversation could go. There was a 50/50 chance of it going for better or for worse, and he didn't like those chances. Maybe he should have just held off on this conversation for another day.

"It's nothing bad." Liam put a hand up. He seemed to immediately know what Max was thinking. "I just wanted to congratulate you."

"You wanted to what?" His eyes went wide. Was he seriously hearing this right?

Liam. The man who always argued against him on everything involving politics. The man who had hated that he had been mated to a human man. The man who had almost pushed Charlie out of his life with his own words.

And he was congratulating him?

"I think I was a little too harsh on you last year," Liam admitted. "You may have had an untraditional way of solving a problem, but you've proved to be an amazing leader. You were able to keep to your word about getting rid of the rogues within a year, and, by doing so, you achieved the one thing that not even my father had during his reign."

"That wasn't just me." Max shook his head. "If it weren't for the other packs assisting us in that forest, we wouldn't have been able to cover as much ground in such a short time."

"Yes," Liam said. "But it took a lot of convincing from both you and Charlie to get them to finally help. Your father might have helped create peace with the packs, but it was you who cemented that peace. You accomplished that, and even had time to plan your own wedding." The old man smiled as he put a hand on his shoulder. "I'm proud of you."

That hit him more than anything else that the man had ever said. He was the person who always made Max challenge himself to do better. He hadn't known just how badly he had been wanting to hear those words until now.

"Thanks, Grandpa." Max smiled back at him. He had stopped himself from hugging the man, those old memories of being a child and laughing and playing with him all coming back to him. He had missed that side of the man. It had been a long time since he had seen it.

"I couldn't have asked for a better grandson." His grandpa hugged him. It didn't last long before he pulled away and looked at him again, though. "Alright, we're going to have enough sappy things when you're at the altar. I'll let you get back to getting ready."

He didn't say anything to that. He just nodded and watched as the man left. That was probably the best gift he could have given him. With all the support that his father had given him, Liam was the opposite of that. It had frustrated him to no end. But now he was left standing in the middle of the room with nothing but fuzzy feelings.

"Earth to Max?" Ed's voice snapped him out of his thoughts. "You're going to be late, man!"

"Sorry." He shook his head to get him back to the present.

"Okay, I just saw Liam come from here." Tyler walked in. "What did he say? I swear if he tried to yell at you on the day of your wedding, I'm going to punch him."

"Damn, Tyler!" Ed laughed. "You're acting like it's your wedding we're talking about!"

"It wasn't anything bad." Max smiled. "He came to congratulate me. That's all."

"Your grandfather?" Tyler's eyebrows raised in shock. "The grumpiest man in the universe. He congratulated you on the wedding that he didn't even want to happen in the first place?"

"Yeah." Max chuckled a bit. "Weird, huh?"

"You know, with everything that happened this year," Ed said. "That was one thing I wasn't expecting. Looks like all your wishes are coming true, Maxipad!"

"What is this, a Throwback Thursday or something?" Max rolled his eyes. He hadn't been called that in a year! It brought back some fun memories. The Max from a year ago would have never expected to have gone through this much in such a short time. It felt so strange to think that time had flown that quickly.

"Hey, I had to!" Ed grinned. "It's your wedding day man! Which means that we get to tease you until you run off to your honeymoon."

It was good to have the old Ed back. It had only been a few months since that incident with the rogues and the war that they had on them, but it felt like an eternity. There was still so much to do, but he was rather enjoying the thought of his honeymoon. He had that all planned out too.

"That reminds me." He looked to Tyler. "Did you hear word from Herb?"

"Just came back from his way, actually," Tyler said. "He says that everything's good to go on his side."

"Good." He turned back to the mirror. "I want everything to be perfect."

"I don't know who's the greatest perfectionist." Ed laughed. "You or Charlie. I heard from Wynona that it's been hell just trying to get him to stay in his room at the moment."

He almost forgot that Wynona was visiting them. They had a lot of people that had come to see this party. Max had personally flown all of Nick's family too. They were the best party people and he knew that Charlie would love to see all of them again.

The annoying thing was it seemed like they multiplied like rabbits. Those plane tickets had been pretty costly because of it.

"Papa!" Eric came running through the already open door. Max leaned down to pick him up. Whenever he called him that, he couldn't help but have a smile on his face. He was happy that the boy had finally gotten to the point where he was completely healthy. The day that Button had said that he had finally got to his healthy weight was one of the best of his life. Now the boy was as energetic as ever. Although he still loved to jump into people's arms.

"You're supposed to be getting ready, Eric." Max feigned a serious voice.

"But I am ready!" Eric just giggled. He seemed just as excited as they were about this event.

"Where are your shoes?" he grabbed his feet and started tickling them. "I can't have a barefoot ring bearer."

"They're right here." His mom came in with some small black shoes. "I got distracted talking to someone and this little one decided to try and run away from me."

"I wanted to see Papa!" Eric giggled again. Max was still tickling his feet.

"Mom." He looked at her with pleading eyes.

"Don't say another word." She set her purse down on the dresser that was in the room and started pulling things out of it. "I had a feeling that your hair would start acting up today. You wouldn't believe how annoying my hair was on my wedding day."

"Like mother, like son," Ed joked.

"Here." He handed Eric off to him. "Now you have to hold him."

"Aww!" Ed immediately started cooing over the child. "You're such a lady killer."

Tyler face palmed at that while Max just laughed.

"I can't wait until you finally get kids," Max told him.

"Actually." Tyler looked to Ed. "With Max having officially adopted Eric, paperwork and all, that means that you're the only one of us that doesn't have kids yet."

"Oh, I don't think it's going to be that long." Ed winked at them. "Maybe, in about nine months, I will."

Max almost forgot that his mom was there. She yanked the comb through his hair while he was trying to stand up.

"Emily's pregnant?!"

"You guys finally decided to do it?!" Tyler furrowed his eyebrows. "I thought you were waiting until Emily was done with law school?"

"We were going to wait." Ed had the biggest smile on his face. "But, after everything that had gone on this year, Emily kinda thought it would be best to take a break for a while and focus on something else instead."

"Like having a family?"

"Yup!" Ed was beaming at this point. "I was going to wait until after the wedding to tell you guys though. I didn't really want to take away from the happiness of that."

"That's great, Ed!" Max smiled at his friend. "I don't care about you telling me on my wedding day. I'm just glad that you're finally going to be a dad." He knew that Ed had been dreaming of that for a while. When they had grown up, they all wanted to grow families. It was one of the many things they had in common with each other. Tyler and Sam were just the first ones to do so.

"Thanks," he said. "I'm really glad too."

"Oh, there was no way Emily was going to be going anywhere on her schooling trips after what happened with you, Ed," his mother said, pulling Max down in the chair so she could continue her work. "That week you were gone, she had been crying the whole time."

"A lot of the people here were having a rough time," Max said. Charlie had practically clung to him for a month after he came back from that war. He had worn himself out with all that paperwork that he had done, and Max could feel all the worry that had built up. Even Eric was worried about him when he was gone.

There was no greater joy than coming home to those you loved and that loved you.

"Congratulations." Tyler put a hand on Ed's shoulder.

"Hey, today isn't about me." Ed shook his head. "We can celebrate that stuff later, when Max finally comes back from his month-long honeymoon."

Ah, he was looking forward to that. Of course, he would still be in the pack territory, just in case they needed him for an emergency, but he was going to be cut off from them for the most part.

"Sam's going to go crazy." Max shook his head. "Have you told him yet?"

"Are you kidding me?" Ed said. "He has more of a chance of hearing from Leah, through Emily, than me with how much running around he's been doing."

"He's got a point there," Tyler said. "Sam's always busy."

"Oh, that man needs to start taking the time to hang out with you guys more." His mom butted into the conversation. She had almost finished with Max's hair thankfully. "He's going to burn himself out if he spends all his time with his wife and kids."

"That's just how Sam is," Max told her. "He's an obsessed family man."

"I bet you Leah's going to want to have even more kids after this." Ed laughed. "Her and her sister still have that competition going about it."

"Sam's going to start balding at an early age." Tyler laughed with him. "I can feel it."

"Okay." His mom lifted the comb out of his hair and took a step back. "I think I did pretty good on this one."

Max turned to look in the mirror. His hair was surprisingly slicked back, just how he wanted it.

"What do you think?" his mom asked.

"It's perfect!" He hugged her. "Thank you."

"Oh, you don't have to thank me." She patted his back. He missed his mother's hugs. "That's what mothers are for. You just go out there and enjoy yourself. This is your day sweety. Enjoy it."

CHAPTER 63:

Church Bells

"I do," Charlie said. It was amazing to be in that moment. He felt like the rest of that morning had just drifted by, like the few clouds that were in the sky.

It had finally happened. They were finally getting married, after one crazy year full of struggles, frustrations, and very few fights. They had finally gotten to this point.

And he couldn't be happier.

Charlie had planned a lot of the wedding during the many times that he was in his office. While Max had started the planning in the beginning, Charlie was the one who went all out and figured out all the extra details.

With the help of Wynona and Katy, of course. Wynona was just as well organized as he was, which helped with planning for things like this. They all decided that it was best to simply keep it traditional, since they didn't want to stress people out about any different colors they wanted to have. The whole point was just to finally wed, anyway.

Max was the one who said that Charlie should wear a white suit. He hadn't really thought about it until then, but he didn't hate the idea. They planned the location to be a clearing in the forest, just a mile or so away from the pack house. That way it would be easier for all of Charlie's guests to come, since they were all human themselves.

Ryan seemed a little shocked that he was already getting married. It did seem like things were moving fast. But it had been a fast year. Pearl seemed to simply be happy to see him again. He apologized for how long it had been since he had seen them, but they brushed it off.

"I don't think I've seen you this happy." Pearl hugged him. "Besides, I love weddings! Maybe you could hook me up with one of the hotties that your fiancé hangs out with, too!"

He failed to tell her that they were all happily married. She had been too busy at the time to really be able to talk to him too much. Ryan had loved the thought of catering for him, though. Wedding cakes were one of his specialties.

They were more shocked to see Eric in his arms when he went to see them. It really did seem like he had moved too quickly in life. But, when he told him that he had been in a horrible situation, they seemed to understand a little more. And Eric seemed to love Ryan's cooking, so the chef couldn't help but like the boy.

"He reminds me of you, Charlie," Ryan had told him. "He's got that same charm to him."

He was happy to hear that. Eric had really grown a lot in just the little while that they had him. And it wasn't just his weight. He had a blast running around the pack house and playing with all the other kids that were there. Him and Max's little cousin, Reggie, had become best friends at that point. It made him happy to see that he had finally come out of his shell.

But the happiest moment had to be the one he was in right then.

"You may now kiss the groom," the officiant said. Max wasted no time. He grabbed him and swooped him down low, kissing him with all the passion that he had. All Charlie could do was return that passion. His joy was beyond words. Max had given him all that he had ever wanted in life.

Love, family, and a home.

Now he had everything.

He hadn't known that someone had let the doves out until after they finally ended their kiss. Max brought him back up to see all the birds in the sky. That was Wynona's idea. She had really wanted to do something big for that. Everyone cheered, some cried, and there was nothing but happiness all around.

They had kept the decorations a nature theme, to match the forest around them. Fairy lights were put in place to keep the massive seating area, and stage lit up when it got darker, and the small fences that guided people to the event had all kinds of beautiful flowers on them.

Everyone was congratulating them the moment they walked towards their seats. Katy was crying into Owen, which brought a smile to his face. Ian hugged and congratulated him. He looked really happy for him. He was glad that they had been able to keep their friendship with all that had happened.

Of course, the greatest part of the wedding had to be the party that came with it. Max had flown all of the Moore's in. Charlie had no idea how many children they had. It was insane just how many of them there were. They were a blast to hang out with.

"I'm so glad you convinced Max to adopt him," Fred whispered to him. Charlie looked over to see Max with Eric in his lap, tickling him. "I knew he was going to regret it if he didn't."

"I don't think I would have been able to live with myself," Charlie told him. It was so cute seeing Max with Eric. He really was a great father.

"It seems like he chose you guys, anyway," Fred's mate said. He was a nice man. Charlie was glad that he finally got to meet him. "You both make great parents for the boy."

"Thanks." Charlie's smile got bigger. He couldn't remember a time when he had smiled this much.

"Okay." Fred set his drink down. "Now for phase 2."

"Phase 2?" He looked at him, confused.

"I'll get the baby," his mate said. They both had a serious look on their faces.

"Wait, what?!" Charlie didn't know what they were talking about. But, before he could try and get an answer out of them, his chair was lifted up. "Hey!"

He looked down to see Barry and Hailey both carrying him above their heads. It was a little frightening to be up this high, and a little more frightening to see someone as small as Hailey helping to carry him.

She was the fighter, right? She definitely didn't look like one. She had a small frame with long black hair that was up in a braid. She looked a lot like Nick, only her skin was pale, like her father.

Then he looked across from him to see that they were doing the same to Max. He frantically looked for Eric to find that he was safe with Fred's husband. The man was already on his way to Mrs. Locke, who was laughing and reaching her arms out to hold him.

Phew.

Now that the panic from that was all gone, he could try and figure out what this deranged family was trying to do. He saw Nick in the front of the dancefloor, trying to get the whole crowd to clap. He looked to Max to see that he was laughing at the antics.

"Remember when I told you they liked to do surprise dances?" Max mind linked with him.

"Are they going to dance with us in the air?!" Charlie really didn't like that idea. He was already feeling sick to his stomach.

"I don't think they have the strength to keep me up in the air for that long, Apple," Max assured him. *"Just enjoy it for now. You're going to love this."*

When they finally set him down, he felt better. The music had changed from calm to upbeat and all the siblings, with some of their mates, had started dancing around them. They really were amazing dancers. It was as if they were their own choreography team. Nick had even started tap dancing a bit during a part of the song. It was really cool that he knew how to do that. It seemed like a lost art.

When they were finally done, and the song was over, everyone cheered.

"Congratulations, Apple!" Nick stuck his hand out to pull him out of his chair. "I'm so glad that you came to us when you did."

Charlie hugged him as soon as he got up. Nick had really become his closest friend in the short year that they had known each other. It warmed his heart to hear that from him.

"I'm glad I met you all too," Charlie told him. "You're the best friend I've ever had."

"I feel like I should apologize," Fred said as he walked up to him.

"You scared the living crap out of me!" Charlie frowned. He wasn't really upset. But it didn't help that he had been so worried about where Eric was.

"You should have taken Eric away first." Nick chuckled a bit. "Sorry we scared you, Apple."

"I was more afraid of where Eric had gone." Charlie shook his head. He couldn't be mad at them. "When your husband said that he would get the baby, it didn't exactly help!"

"He's an asshole sometimes." Fred laughed. "You'll have to forgive him. We were trying to surprise you in a good way."

He still had fun, and the dance was amazing, but he rushed to get Eric back from his grandmother as soon as he could get off stage.

The party went in full swing after that. He could barely spend time with Max. Everyone was pulling him in different directions, to talk or dance. He wouldn't complain, though. He was going to be able to be with him for a month after all of this.

"I never knew that Nick's family went all out," Madeline said. She had told Charlie that she had been trying to avoid meeting them simply because she really didn't want to dance. "Nick is so much calmer than the rest of them."

"It's the men who are the calmest, surprisingly," Alistair told her. "His sisters are full of energy."

"Thankfully they haven't seen me yet," Herb said. "There's no way I'm dancing."

"But dancing is fun!" Jackie pouted. "You get to hold each other close, or just go all out and have fun! And you can dance with anyone!"

"Jackie," Madeline gave her a motherly look. "Please don't try to dance tonight. You just had your babies."

That was a crazy day. There were so many people who were waiting by those infirmary doors that the kitchen workers could barely make it through their doors to deliver food. That was all the way in October, though. And her three babies were as beautiful as their mother. Charlie swore that the whole pack cooed over the girls for the rest of the month.

"But I was thinking about just doing a slow dance," she said. "I never really had the chance to dance at a party like this before."

"The Citrus Valley Pack never let you dance?" Charlie asked.

"They never let the omegas do anything really," Jackie told him.

Herb sighed and stood up.

"I'm absolutely horrible at it." He offered her his hand. "I'm warning you now."

Jackie didn't even seem like she heard his warning. She just jumped into his arms and hugged him. Then they were racing through the crowd to the dancefloor.

"She's going to be the death of him." Madeline smiled at the two. "I've seen that man try to dance. The poor bloke will do anything for that woman."

"I could see if Nick could help him a little right now," Alistair said. "If I can figure out where he went."

"You can't find him?" Madeline smirked at her friend. "I thought you just had to follow that pull of yours?"

"It's a little difficult when he's running around everywhere." Alistair's eyes darted around the area. "His scent is everywhere too."

"Why don't you just mind link with him?" Charlie asked.

"Because I know he'll be coming back soon." Alistair smiled. Before he could even try to ask anymore questions, he heard laughter coming from the crowd.

"Alistair!" Nick ran towards him, laughing hard. "Alistair, you have to help me!" He jumped behind the albino, clinging to his back. His eyes shined with mischief.

"Do it!" Charlotte was running towards him.

"You'll never make me!" Nick yelled from over Alistair's shoulder. Alistair had one of his arms reached out behind him to hold him protectively in place, even though he was confused.

"Come on, Nick!" his sister whined. "You only have one life to live!"

"Yeah!" Noreen, one of the twins of the family, yelled. She caught up to them all. "Just do it once! We'll never ask you again!"

"What's this about?" Max came over. Nick and his sisters had caused a big enough scene with all of their childish yells. Tyler, Ed and Sam were right behind him. Charlie was sure that they were having fun catching up on everything.

"I'm not going to twerk!" Nick ignored Max.

"We know you could do it, Nick!" Kat, the other twin, yelled over the crowd. "You have the ass for it!"

"Shut up!"

"Eww!" Katy ran over to them. "Are you trying to convince him to twerk again?"

"Either him or you." Charlette smirked at her.

Charlie really wasn't sure whether this was a funny moment, or an embarrassing one. But, then again, Nick did seem to be laughing in Alistair's shoulder.

"No!" Katy screamed.

"What's a twerk?" Alistair asked. Charlie really had to stop himself from laughing at that question. Ed didn't hold back, though. He started laughing so hard he looked like he was going to fall on the floor.

"You don't want to know." Max patted him on the shoulder.

"It's something that I'm not going to ever do!" Nick shouted over Alistair's shoulder again.

"Come on, Nick," Charlotte egged. "Aren't you supposed to be the best dancer in the family?"

"I will step down from that title if it means I have to twerk." Nick put a finger in the air. He was so dramatic when his family was around. It was funny. "I'd much rather be the best cook of the family."

"Oh, leave him alone, Charlotte!" Sophia said. She looked to be one of the older siblings. She had been behind the bar the entire party, making everyone drinks until just now. "You can't make someone do what they don't want to do."

Charlie was glad, at the moment, that he never had any sisters. He couldn't imagine being in Nick's shoes right then. The level of embarrassment would have been far too much for him.

"But I rarely get to see him!" Charlotte complained and looked over to Nick. "You gotta do something at least!"

"I. am not. Twerking!"

"Then kiss!" Kat finally got to where they were.

"Kiss?" Nick looked at her in confusion. "This isn't my wedding!"

"Aww!" Katy chimed in. "That would be so cute!"

"Does this happen a lot when Nick's sisters come over?" Charlie mind linked with Max. The man had wrapped an arm around his waist as soon as he came over there.

"Let's just say there's a reason the kids are all in a separate area right now."

He was going to have to remember this for the next time they came over.

"It's just one kiss," Noreen said, rolling her eyes. "It's not like we're asking you to be like Charlotte with her husband."

"We aren't that bad!" Charlotte argued.

"Yeah," Noreen looked at her with a straight face. "You are."

"No," Charlotte mocked her sister's tone dramatically, "We're no-!"

"You're straying from the point!" Kat yelled at them, then she turned back to Nick. "Just kiss him already!"

While Charlie couldn't say that he particularly liked the pushy nature of these siblings, they were pretty fun to watch. Max made no move to try and stop this, so he assumed that this wasn't going to wind up a disaster.

Before Nick could argue against it any longer, Alistair pulled him out from behind him and their lips met. Charlie was surprised that the man would do something like this in front of a crowd, but it was nice to see them both happy. Nick leaned into the kiss easily.

The sisters were all cheering at that point, which only got the attention of the rest of his siblings. They were all flooding over to them by the time Alistair and Nick had finally broken the kiss. His hazel eyes sparkled as he looked at Alistair.

It was cute.

"Hey, Alistair, buddy." Ed elbowed the albino when it was all said and done. "Do yourself a favor, and never ask that question when you're anywhere near Charlotte."

"Why?" He looked confused, but amused at the man's advice.

"Because you are not going to like her answer to that." Ed cracked up again.

Charlie just shook his head at it all. There were always the crazy ones in every family. He supposed that Nick was just the crazy one for being the only sane one out of all of them.

The rest of the party flew by, with a mixture of eating, dancing and talking. Everyone had stories to tell, and reasons to run around the area. He was glad that he had decided to go with the largest clearing in the forest to have this wedding. There were so many people there, he had almost lost count of invitations that he had sent out.

"I'm going to miss you." Eric hugged him. It was getting dark out, which meant that the party was coming to an end.

"We're just going to be gone for one week, honey." He held him tightly. "Then you can come with us."

That was the last-minute plan that they had to make. They didn't exactly want Eric to be with his grandparents for the whole month of their honeymoon. Eric was still going through some trauma, and was still really clingy towards them because of it. But Charlie knew that he would be okay with a week of them being gone, at least. Nick had told them that him and Alistair could help with keeping him distracted anyway. He was already planning on convincing Aldi to let him sit in the kitchen with him while he cooked. Charlie knew that the boy was going to enjoy that.

"But I'm going to miss you for that week," Eric argued.

"I know, sweety." He rubbed his back. "But I promise you that you're going to have fun no matter what. The week's going to fly by."

"Okay," he said.

"*I have a feeling he's going to be clingy to you for a while, Apple,*" Max said.

"*I'm sure he'll get over it when he gets older.*" Charlie leaned into him. Partying like this all day was really tiring.

"*Knowing you, you're going to baby him even when he's an adult.*"

"*I don't want to think that far ahead yet.*" Charlie frowned. Time seemed to fly by as it was. He didn't want to think about Eric being grown up already.

He handed the little boy off to Mrs. Locke and was rushed into one of the Jeeps. Everyone was cheering and throwing confetti as they left. It truly was amazing.

It had really been all that he had ever dreamed off.

CHAPTER 64:

Babies

"Georgia." Nick whined at his niece. "I thought I was your favorite uncle!"

"You are!" The little girl giggled.

"Good nieces don't pull on their favorite uncle's hair!" It was definitely a mistake letting her mess with his hair. He was just trying to find a way to keep the girl from getting bored.

"I can't believe you let anyone touch your hair that wasn't Alistair," Katy said over the phone. She seemed to be getting a kick out of his turmoil.

"I'm already regretting it." He sighed. "Eric's the easiest kid to keep entertained. But my sister's kids? I have to find a thousand Boredom Busters for them!"

"Boredom Busters?"

"One of their papers from their schools says: 10 Boredom Busters for the Winter Break!" he explained. His nieces and nephews weren't on their winter break at the moment, but they were getting close to it. Georgia's school had a little newspaper that the kids could bring home to their parents.

"That's the most ridiculous term I've ever heard!" Katy laughed. "How did they come up with that?"

"I don't know." Nick laughed with her. "But it's now my go-to saying for when I'm talking to them. They absolutely hate it."

"How much longer are they going to be there?" she asked. Nick knew that Katy absolutely loved his siblings. Her and Hailey were pretty close when they were growing up. She practically toppled her over when she saw her. It was a good thing that Hailey was as fit as a body builder. She threw a lot of people off with her small frame.

"Two more days," Nick said. "And today, I get to do all the babysitting while they have their date nights and look around the cities."

"You're such a good brother." She giggled.

"I just don't have a life," Nick told her. He wasn't babysitting all of his nieces and nephews. That would be like trying to take care of an entire daycare center of kids. At the moment, he was just watching five of them. Three of them were climbing all over Alistair at the moment, which was pretty funny to see. Alistair really didn't seem to mind their antics, which Nick was glad of. He absolutely hated when the twerps would try that on him.

"So, Charlie and Max are going to be taking Eric to their secret hideaway after this week?"

"That's the plan," Nick told her. "I'm sure that they already miss him just as much as he misses them. That boy's so spoiled."

"He's too cute not to be!"

"You were cute when you were a baby," Nick said. "That doesn't mean that your parents should have spoiled you. Look what that did to you."

"Hey!" she yelled. "I'm not that bad, am I?"

"No." Nick laughed. "I'm just messing with you, Katy. Why are you so jumpy lately?"

"Oh, yeah..." She trailed off over the phone. "I've been meaning to tell you that, actually."

"Tell me what?"

"I may or may not be pregnant?" She ended it off like someone would a question. Her voice getting higher at the end.

"Owen knocked you up already?!" Nick laughed. "What happened to you already having enough children to deal with?"

"I don't know!" Katy whined. He always loved how dramatic she was about everything. It was the most entertaining thing. "It just kind of happened!"

"Do I have to repeat the sex ed talk that your mom had with you?" he teased.

"No!!" She drawled the word out like the world was about to end. "That was the most embarrassing thing in my life!"

"You guys aren't even married yet. How are you going to find a wedding dress?"

"I don't know!" Katy whined again. "I just wasn't thinking and I was so happy about the war being over, and Owen coming back, and everyone being okay, and then things have actually been going pretty good over here, and Owen proposed, and-!"

"Katy, breathe!" Nick stopped her. The woman rambled on way too much when she was stressed. "It's going to be alright! There's plenty of dresses for pregnant women. I was just messing with you!"

"I don't want to wear a pregnancy dress though!"

"Then you should have worn a condom."

"I bet you don't."

"We're not talking about me," he told her. "Besides, werewolves can't get STD's. Unless its crabs."

"Eww! That's so gross!"

"You're the one who brought it up."

"Ugh!" He heard a noise that sounded like she flopped onto her bed. "You're so annoying sometimes."

"Love you too." He smiled. Then his hair was yanked again. "Ow! Georgia!"

"Sorry, Uncle Nick!" The girl giggled again.

"Here." He heard a low voice from behind him. "You braid it like this."

He immediately relaxed into those hands as they combed through his hair. All the pain from Georgia pulling it just seemed to go away when Alistair started working on it.

"Ooooh!" Georgia said from behind him. "Like this?"

"Exactly," Alistair said.

Nick loved moments like these. Alistair was the only one who could truly help calm these kids down. He let them get out their energy, but he wouldn't let them take it far enough to where it would hurt someone or break something. He was the best babysitter.

And he was adorable around kids.

"Well," Nick talked through the phone again. "You can join the club of all the other women who got pregnant after the war. Our pack's going through a crazy baby boom at the moment."

"Really?" Katy got excited. She loved gossip, especially when it involved stuff like this. "Who?"

"Well, Emily, for one. That's the biggest one."

"Emily got pregnant?!"

"Yup! She decided to start raising a family after Ed almost died by those rogues."

"I don't blame her." Katy sighed. "That was the worst day of my life."

"You could say that again."

"Well, who else is pregnant?"

"Madeline, Alan's mate. Isabelle's pregnant again too. Then there's Daphne, the dishwasher." He started naming off what seemed like a thousand more. "I'm sure they're going to all plan a baby shower as one huge event."

"Imagine if they did it around Easter!" Katy said. "That would be so cute."

"Don't you have to wait until your, like, eight months pregnant before you have it?"

"I don't know! Who cares! It's not like you have to follow rules like those!"

"Jeez, Kate." Nick sighed. "I can't believe that it's already almost Christmas again."

"I know!" Katy sighed with him. "It seems like only yesterday when we had last Christmas with Charlie. Back then we were all just happy to make him happy."

"Yeah..." He stared off into space. "I can't believe it's already been a year."

"I can't believe all that stuff happened in a year."

"Me either." It really did shock him. So much stuff had happened: people finding their mates; the Alpha and Luna getting into a fight; Katy leaving to another pack; kidnapping; wars. It was all so crazy to think that it could all happen in a year.

"Wait." Katy snapped him out of his thoughts. "We're still going to see Charlie and Max for Christmas, right?"

"Yeah." He chuckled. "Max's parents would be furious if they didn't stop by to spend Christmas with all of us. It's not like they're going to be out of the territory. And they already have a ton of presents for Eric lined up under the tree."

"So, we have someone new to spoil this year?"

"We have a ton of people to spoil," Nick told her. "There's still Madeline, Jackie and Herb. I'm thinking of getting Herb a fancy shaving kit. His beard turns crazy really fast."

"Aww, you stole my idea!"

"I call dibs!" Nick shouted. "There's also Alistair too."

"He's in the room, isn't he?"

"Yup." That was why he hadn't mentioned him before. He knew that Alistair had too good of ears and too great of a curiosity to not listen in on them. "It's going to be a fun Christmas."

"I'm going to have to plan a day with Owen to just go Christmas shopping," Katy said. "That's been one thing that I've been procrastinating the past couple months."

"Better do it soon, before all the stores sell out."

"Maybe I'll do it tomorrow," Katy yawned. "There's always so much to do."

"Yeah, that comes with being a Luna," Nick said. "Anyway, I gotta get all these twerps to bed. It seems like Alistair did a decent job at wearing them down."

They said their goodbyes and hung up. Nick was going to stand up and get the kids when he noticed that the room was now empty.

Shit.

"They're all asleep," Alistair told him. A wave of relief went over him right as he heard his voice. "I put them to bed right before you hung up the phone."

"You're the best." He fell into Alistair's hold. Then he noticed something weird with his hair right when it moved a bit.

"Did you guys French braid my hair?"

"It was Georgia's idea." Alistair chuckled. The man easily picked him up and carried him to bed. They were spending the night in Barry's suite, because he had enough space for all the kids. The one thing he loved about the place was that he had the comfiest beds.

They laid there for a while, just relaxing in the moonlight. It was nice to just enjoy his arms again. After all the running around that he had been doing with his family, he was glad to be taking things slow at the moment.

"I think the moons happy with us," Alistair said. He looked down to see the man lost in the moonlight that was shining down on them. The moon had been bright since the summer, strangely enough. It was uncommon, but no one was complaining.

"What does it tell you this time?" He pet his head.

"It doesn't tell me anything, the wind does."

"And what does the wind tell you?"

"Peace." Alistair sighed. He seemed so relaxed as he lay on top of him. "Peace and happiness for many years to come."

Nick liked the thought of that. It really did seem like the golden ages of their pack at the moment. There were always rough patches, but he was sure that they would be able to get through it. They had already been through so much as it was.

He couldn't speak for everyone, but he knew that he was happy. He never knew what joy was until he had met Alistair. He had taught him what true love and happiness was, even before they officially mated.

Before they dozed off, Nick thanked the Moon Goddess. He knew now that he was going to have a good life, one with nothing but joy and love. He wanted nothing more than to be here in this moment, with the love of his life, and the knowledge that all his friends and family were safe and loved as well.

It was going to be a great forever.

CHAPTER 65:

Honeymoon

"Max." Charlie smiled as he woke up. "Eric's going to wake up soon."

"Maybe he'll sleep in for once." Max continued to kiss his neck. That was how they had woken up every day in this little cottage.

Charlie still couldn't believe that Max remembered talking about building a cottage for their honeymoon. He had said it at the beginning of the year. And, with all that had happened after him saying that, it seemed way too easy to forget.

He was shocked when they drove up to it. Max had told him to leave the honeymoon plans to him and was adamant about not telling him a single thing the entire time they were planning the wedding. Charlie had no idea that he had been doing this in the background until Herb finally talked to them about it.

Herb was the one who had driven them away from the wedding, surprisingly. He thought it was going to be Tyler or Ed. He had no idea that Max had been getting Herb's help to build this little cottage.

"Ever since he was welcomed into the pack," Max had told him.

"It's really the best idea for a honeymoon." Herb smiled. "It's got plumbing, electric, foods all stocked up. The only thing it doesn't have is reception for phone calls."

"That'll be fine," Charlie said. "I'm sure we could just mind link with everyone if we really need something. And we're only going to be without Eric for a week."

It was a fun week, and they had barely left the massive king-sized bed during the entirety of it. But it was amazing picking Eric up and seeing his face light up when he saw them. His grandparents had kept him pretty happy for the week that they were apart. And Nick had a blast with him as well.

It wasn't normal to bring your children with on your honeymoon, but Charlie loved that they did. They played family in that tiny cottage. And, as much as he enjoyed the time that he spent with Max, and all the fun they had when they were alone, he loved all the time that they spent with Eric too.

"I doubt he's going to sleep in." Charlie chuckled.

"Maybe," Max mumbled against his skin. His hands had already started wandering down his body. "If we wish really hard."

"Max." He couldn't help but lean into him. "If we keep this up then he's going to walk in here."

"I hate it when your right." He sighed.

Charlie chuckled again and kissed him. Then he held the man's face and smiled. "We have all the time in the world right now. Let's just enjoy it as much as we can."

Max smiled with him, his purple eyes sparkling with happiness. Charlie had never seen him so happy. It was as if, at that moment, nothing else mattered other than the joy that they both shared.

"Daddy! Papa!" Eric's voice interrupted their moment as he slowly opened the door. "Are you awake?"

"Of course, we are!" Max sat up. They had both decided to wear something while they were sleeping, just in case Eric wanted to sleep with them. They usually just had pajama pants on or something like that. They were just as easy to slip out of as they were to put on.

Eric had finally stopped sleeping with them every night after the first month. Charlie was glad that he was becoming more confident in himself at nighttime, but he still missed him curling into him. There were still times when he would come in because of a nightmare. And the first couple of nights that he had spent in the cottage with them the boy slept with them. He had missed them. But, for the most part, he slept in his little room. Herb had made it last minute with barely enough time to spare.

"Good morning, honey!" Charlie smiled as the boy jumped onto the bed. Since Charlie was still laying down, he was the first one that Eric hugged. "Did you sleep well?"

"Yeah." His voice still sounded groggy as he said it. "I'm hungry, Daddy."

"Okay." He kissed his head. "Let's go get some food."

"You look so beautiful with Eric in your arms." Max mind linked with him. He looked at him to see that he was smiling still. *"You know that?"*

"I could say the same for you," he replied. Charlie was still in awe sometimes when he saw Max doing anything with Eric. A part of him couldn't believe that any of this was even real. A year ago, he didn't think that any of his dreams would actually come true. He was depressed and simply working to stay alive, and staying alive just to see if he could do it.

"Can we have pancakes again?" Eric asked. Nick must have spoiled him in the kitchen of the pack house. He told them that he took him to the kitchen while he was working plenty of times so that he could get him to try a bunch of foods. Pancakes seemed to be his favorite.

"Sure." Charlie sat him down on one of the chairs by the dining table. The cottage was packed with just about everything you could think of food wise. Everything except the perishables, as a lot of them wouldn't be able to last the month that they were going to be staying there.

"You excited for school in January, Eric?' Max asked. He sat right next to Eric as Charlie started cooking. He was just using pancake mix this time around. With the extra time that he had to wait before flipping them, he put some bacon and eggs on the stove as well. Although Charlie still didn't have the greatest appetite in the morning, Max and Eric certainly did.

"I don't know," the little voice said. "School sounds scary."

"It's not scary," Max assured him. Since Eric had gotten out of his shell a little more, they figured it would be best for him to start school. That way he didn't get left behind in his classes. "A lot of your friends are going to be in your class."

"Ana's not going to be in them, though," Eric pouted. "She's going to be a grade above me."

"You can still see her at school, though," Max said. "There's always recess and lunch that you can talk to her. And Reggie's going to be in your class, too!"

Charlie was glad that Eric and Ana became friends. He remembered the first time he met the girl. She was the one who called him a human, before he even knew that everyone in that room was a werewolf. She had just the right amount of talkative energy to her to get Eric more out of his shell. And Reggie was just a tiny ball of energy once you got him comfortable. They all three made a fun little party around the manor.

"I think he should be more excited for Christmas," Charlie said while placing plates of food down.

"Grandma and Grandpa said that they have a bunch of surprises for me!" Eric's eyes went wide with excitement. "And Alistair said that it was going to snow!"

"I didn't know that he could predict the weather." Max raised an eyebrow. "You sure he didn't say that he just thought it was going to snow?"

"Nick said that whenever Alistair looks at the forest and gets lost in thought, he's right," Eric told him matter-of-factly. "And he looked at the forest and said that it was going to snow on Christmas!"

"I hope so." Charlie chuckled. "You really like Alistair, don't you?"

"He's funny." Eric laughed. "He let me ride his wolf too!"

"Sounds like someone was having a blast while we were gone." Max laughed with them both.

"I still missed you." Eric looked down at his food. It seemed like he was feeling guilty for having so much fun.

"It's good that you had fun while we were gone, Eric." Charlie kissed the top of his head before sitting down to eat. "We aren't going to be upset at you for it."

"I know," he said. There were still some issues that they had to help him get past. Charlie wasn't sure when the boy was going to open up to them about everything that happened, but he wasn't going to push him. He was fine with simply making him smile.

"You ready to go shopping?" Max changed the subject. While the first week they barely got out of their bedroom, after they brought Eric there, they had a blast bringing him to as many places they could think of. The mall, the movies, a bunch of different restaurants. It was great to see those little eyes fill up with wonder every time he saw a new place.

"Yeah!" Eric cheered and hopped off his seat. "We still have to get presents for Daddy!"

"Don't worry about me," Charlie told him. "I got everything I've ever wanted right here."

"What is it?" Eric furrowed his eyebrows a little. He looked so cute.

"Well." Charlie knelt down to look at him. "All I ever wanted was a family. And I'm glad to say that I finally found one."

"But Daddy!" Eric whined. "There has to be something you want!"

"Don't worry about it." Max picked him up and whispered into his ear. "We'll get something that he'll love."

They all went to get ready after that. Charlie was the first to get dressed. He looked out of the tiny cottage windows to the beautiful trees around. This place looked like it had just come straight out of a fairy tale. Colorful flowers were everywhere around the outside of the house. They were winter flowers, too, which allowed them to withstand the cold temperatures of the winter.

"You ready, Apple?" Max hugged him from behind. He rested his chin on his shoulder and looked out the window with him.

"Yeah," he answered.

"What are you thinking about?" He sighed into him. If there was anything that this honeymoon had helped them with, it was to relax a little more.

"Just how quickly my life turned around." Charlie held onto his husband's arm.

"It's really been a crazy year," Max said. His voice sounded dreamy as he talked. "I set way too many goals for myself in the beginning of the year."

"And we still managed to do all of it." He shook his head. "I can't believe it."

"Honestly." Max kissed his shoulder. "Me either."

"You know." Charlie leaned into him. "I don't think I ever got to truly thank you."

"For what?"

"For giving me everything that I could have ever wanted." He felt like his heart was going to burst as he was saying that. "I never thought I was ever going to be this happy, or that it was possible to be this happy."

"I should be thanking you." Max hugged him tighter. "Not the other way around, Apple."

"Why?"

"Because I couldn't find peace until I met you," he explained. "All I was before I met you was a ball of restlessness, with an eagerness to make something happen. I wouldn't have been able to do all of these things that I had set out to do without you. And I never would have realized how much I wanted Eric without you, either. You're my sunshine, Apple."

That sent a whole new wave of memories through him. He remembered running in the cold winter rain, just after Christmas. It was when he had gotten fired for almost getting an anxiety attack in the kitchen. He didn't think he was worthy of anyone or anything that night. So, he just ran. He ran and ran until his legs wouldn't take him any farther.

And Max had caught up to him, in that pouring rain.

"All you've ever done is give me light and peace." He lifted his chin up. *"You're my sunshine, Charlie. I can't live without you."*

Tears were falling down his face for a whole new reason now. He could finally look at that memory and know that he wasn't the same person that just ran away from his problems. He was loved.

"Charlie?" Max turned him around and put a hand on his face. He looked worried. "What's wrong?"

"Nothing." He smiled through his tears and hugged him. "Absolutely nothing. I just love you so much."

"I love you too, baby." Max held him tightly in his arms.

"Daddy! Papa!" Eric's voice filled the tiny cottage. "Are we going yet?"

Charlie laughed and wiped the rest of the tears away. "We should get going before he starts trying to run through the forest again."

"Come on, then." Max helped him stand. "Let's go live our happily ever after."

Charlie smiled at the thought. This really was a happily ever after, wasn't it? Sure, life was always going to have its ups and downs, and troubles were always going to be there when you least expected it. But, as long as they had each other, he was sure they could make it through anything.

Life was going to be great. Now all they had to do was enjoy it.

Far Away from Home

"Eric!" his Pop hollered. "You better be ready in five minutes!"

"You already said that!" he yelled back.

"I mean it this time!" He could hear the frustration in his voice. "We're going to be late!"

"Will you both stop yelling across the manor?" His dad mind linked with them.

"Pop started it."

"Well, I'm ending it," his dad said. *"Now stop arguing and come down for breakfast."*

"Is Uncle Nick cooking?"

"When is he not?"

With the promise of food, Eric got out of bed and threw some clothes on. He bolted downstairs as fast as he could.

It wasn't like he didn't have any other reason to get out of bed that morning. He was excited for more than just food. This was the day that he would actually get to go to one of the important Alpha meetings that his dad always went to. He was nineteen, but he had been holding off until now for some reason.

It annoyed him beyond belief. Usually, you become the Alpha right when you turn eighteen. But, for some reason, he had to wait until he found his mate or something. He didn't really think that he needed a Luna. He could do all the paperwork for both jobs. He had helped his dad enough with that stuff. He was always over working himself.

Which was another reason why he just wanted to lead already.

There was also Reggie, his cousin. He was away right then, or else he would have come with them. They were both potential candidates for being the next Alpha of the pack, but Reggie hadn't found his mate yet either. Dad and Pop would always stop whenever an argument about that came up. It didn't matter right now. His parents were still wishing to keep working and leading no matter what.

"Hey Eric," Ana got his attention before he went to the kitchen. She was one of his childhood friends from when he first came to the pack. "Did you remember it?"

"Remember what?" He looked at her with furrowed eyebrows.

"Oh, I don't know…" Her brown hair moved from side to side as she dramatically rolled her eyes. "Only the one thing that you've been wanting to take with you to these meetings since forever."

"Oh yeah!" He bolted back to his room. "Thanks freak!"

"You're welcome, brat!" She yelled from down the halls.

He couldn't help but laugh. Even though Ana had found her mate already, they still found time to hang out. Thankfully her mate didn't mind that they were friends. A few of his other friends had told him that it was common for mates to get jealous of others a lot.

That's what had happened to Aunt Katy.

Man, that was a funny story for Uncle Nick to share. Aunt Katy looked so annoyed with him after that! They were so funny when they got together.

When he got back to his room, he opened his closet and started rummaging through it. He was sure that he left it there. It had to be. He hardly ever touched the thing.

Aha!

He picked up a black case that was in the farthest nook of his closet. Even though none of the maids came into his room to clean it, he still didn't want anything to happen to the case.

It held one of the most important things in his life.

He sat on the bed and slowly opened the case. In it was a necklace of a golden shield, shining in all of its glory. He made sure to polish it at least once a year, even though he never wore it. It was only for special events, and was deemed disrespectful towards everyone if worn otherwise.

Eric took it out of its case and held it for a while. All it took was seeing his reflection in that shimmering gold for him to get lost in a sea of memories.

His blood parents had always let him look at this. His father used to tell him great stories about the necklace and how important it was to their pack. His mother had a necklace that was similar to that one, but he wasn't ever able to find it.

His mother…

He hated remembering her. It wasn't because she was a bad mom. She actually was the opposite. She had tried to protect him the night that the rogues had attacked their home. Even after they both witnessed his father getting slaughtered, she still tried to fight them off tooth and nail. Not just for herself, but for him.

He didn't like remembering her because all that would fill his mind were images of her being tortured by that man.

"Eric, I thought I told you-!" His Pop cut his words short as soon as he walked in the room. Eric didn't look up. He could just tell that he had come in. He had forgotten to shut his door in his rush to grab the necklace. Now, it was like he had forgotten why he needed to rush.

He was still in a sea of memories. He was so young when all that happened, but he remembered everything about it vividly. Even the smell of blood and wolfsbane as his mother screamed in pain.

He also remembered seeing his Dad and Uncle Nick there. It was horrible seeing Uncle Nick like that. He looked just like his mother had before they dragged her out by the chain wrapped around her throat…

"Eric." His Pop put a hand on his shoulder. "You want to talk about it?"

He finally looked away from the necklace and to his Pop. He still looked young for someone who was close to being in his forties. Eric was sure that it was due to the thick red hair that he had. He always thought it made him look fearless and strong. But maybe that was because he always thought that Pop was that way.

He had always felt safe with him, no matter how many times the past tried to get to him. Him and Dad, for that matter. His dad always knew how to make him feel better after he got a nightmare or if he was simply not having a good day.

"No." Eric shook his head. "It's all the same stuff we talked about before, anyway. I was just going to ask if I could bring it to the meeting."

"Fine." The Alpha smiled. "But you can't be showing it off. It'll be disrespectful towards the other Alphas there."

"Who all is going to be there?" he asked. He was getting more and more curious about this meeting that they were going to have.

"Alpha Owen and Alpha Leonard," Pop said. "And their wives."

"Does this mean I get to see Aunt Katy again?"

"Yes." Pop chuckled. "Now come on! Let's get something to eat before your Uncle Nick says it's too late for food."

Uncle Nick was the head chef of the morning crew. And, as much as Eric loved to sleep in, he never wanted to miss out on breakfast or lunch. The man could make some amazing food. Even when Eric wasn't sure what he wanted to eat that day, he would always come up with something new for him to try.

Whenever he did that, though, Uncle Alistair wasn't too far away. He loved to try new foods that the chef made. Eric had a lot of fun times with them in the kitchen.

"Nope!" He heard Nick say. They had just walked in. "Sorry, we're all out of food." He gave them a playful look.

"Aww!" Eric couldn't help but fall for his uncle's trap. "Uncle Nick! There's always food!"

"Not for the tardy!" Nick feigned a serious look.

"Please?"

"Why is it that you're always the last person up out of all of your siblings?" Nick shook his head. "You know my food tastes better when its fresh off the stove, right? Not just in the fridge for you to microwave?"

"Spare us the talk, Nick," Pop said. "I'm running late cus of the boy as it is."

"I'm not a boy anymore."

"Trust me." Nick smiled at him. "If you're anything like your Pop, then you're definitely still a boy at age nineteen."

"Well, it's a good thing I'm nothing like him, then." He smirked at the chef and crossed his arms.

"You can't say that after you two were screaming down the stairs at each other." His dad huffed as he walked through the kitchen doors, his blond hair bouncing as he hurried over to get something out of the pantry. He was holding Eric's youngest sister, Sasha. They had just adopted her two years ago. She had only been a year old at that point, but she had no family and no parents that would claim her as theirs.

"Max and his mom used to do that all the time." Nick laughed. "Sorry, buddy. You may not be related by blood, but you're definitely your father's child."

"Sorry, Apple." His Pop hugged the blond.

"I already have to deal with making sure the kids are going to have someone to take care of them for the day." His green eyes shimmered with a mild annoyance. "And you can't even walk upstairs to make sure that he's out of bed?"

Eric left them to their bickering and grabbed a plate of food. They would always do this when they were stressed out. It always lead to Pop being all lovey dovey on him and apologizing a thousand times. He didn't like to watch them do all of that. It just got gross after a while.

"So." Ana sat next to him in the dining room. "Did you convince Alpha Max to bring it along?"

"Yup!" He puffed up his chest proudly. "Now I get to see the Orion Meeting House. And you don't!"

"Like I would want to!" She stuck her tongue out at him. "It all sounds boring anyway. Like, sure, you get to see one of the cool buildings that Alpha Max built around the forest. But all you get to do is sit and listen to a bunch of old farts arguing for a whole day!"

"But it's so much cooler than that!" Eric told her. "Because you get to find out what's going on with the other packs and help out with other problems!"

"Still sounds like a bunch of old farts arguing." She rolled her eyes.

"But all you do is garden!" he yelled at her. "That's, like, ten times more boring than listening to people argue!"

"Hey!" She pointed her fork at him. "I help grow the food that winds up on your plate, remember that."

"What are you gonna do?" He smirked. "Poison me?"

"Please!" she teased. "You wouldn't be worth it!"

They talked like this all the time whenever they shared a meal together. He loved messing with her about her gardening. He respected her for it, though. He remembered helping them pluck weeds one time.

Man, that was a workout.

"Eric! We're leaving!" Pop yelled. Eric ran from the table to the front door just in time to see his dad slapping his pop on the arm.

"What were we just talking about?" he asked.

"How much I love you?" Pop smiled at him. His dad rolled his eyes and shook his head. There was a smile on his face though. He tried to hide it when Pop grabbed his chin and forced him to look at him.

Were mates always suckers for each other?

"Come on!" Eric interrupted their stare down. "I thought we had to go already!"

His Pop just sighed and stepped away from his husband. "You know, Eric. I miss when you were just a boy. At least when you interrupted us then, I could think about how adorable you were."

Oh no.

"Aww!" Dad's face lit up and he looked to him. "You were the cutest thing when we first got you!" He walked over to him and hugged him. "I miss when you would come into the room and curl up with us at night. You grew up too fast."

"Dad." He hugged him back. He couldn't help it. He liked his dad's hugs. They were always soft and sweet. "This is nice and all, but I thought we were going to be late?"

"Knowing Katy and Owen's luck with flat tires," Pop said. "We proba- bly aren't going to be the only ones."

"Besides." His dad smiled at him. "I don't get to hug you and baby you like this anymore."

He did remember all the times that he would go into their room at night and curl up with them. Most of the time it wasn't because he had a nightmare. Most of the time he just liked his dad's arms around him, holding him tight.

But he was never, ever, going to say that out loud.

They finally got to one of the Jeeps and started driving off. Eric was going to ask to drive when Pop opened the back door for him. Anyone else would think that the red head was trying to be nice to his son. Eric knew that it was actually used as an answer to the question that he seemed to be able to read on his face.

How was it so easy for the man to know what he was going to say?

At least when he did it for Dad, he didn't spend ten minutes making out with him this time. That was so annoying to watch.

Okay, maybe it wasn't ten minutes, but it felt like hours.

"So, what's this meeting about?" Eric was practically bouncing in his seat. They were already a few miles away from home at that point, heading down the dirt road that Eric had always heard lead straight to the Orion Meeting House. He always wanted to sneak over there just to see what it looked like, but Pop found him every time he tried.

"Well, since we have some time before we get there," Pop said. He had one hand on the steering wheel and the other holding Dad's. "There are some rogues that are requesting sanctuary."

"Really?!" His jaw dropped at that. They hadn't had a rogue request membership since he was sixteen. "Who is it? How many are there?"

"A woman beta named Janet is the leader of them," he answered. "From what I've heard, there are roughly ten in total."

"Do they have any children with them?" Dad asked. His light green eyes looked worried.

"I don't know yet." Pop frowned. "We decided that it would be best to bring everyone there so that all of our questions would get answered without having to repeat them over and over."

"Wait." Eric leaned closer to the driver's seat, peering into the front of the car from the middle. "I thought that rogue requests just involved one pack, though. Why are we all going?"

"Because they asked sanctuary from any of us," Pop said. "They said that they would be grateful to whoever took them in."

"I guess it's better than going from pack to pack," Dad said. His blond hair was getting blown back by the wind. "It's going to be winter in a couple of months, too, which could also be why they're getting a little more desperate."

"This is going to be so cool!"

"You better at least act like the son of an Alpha," Pop warned. "This is a serious matter, Eric."

"I'm just getting it all out now," Eric said.

Their conversation turned into a mesh of different things after that. They talked a little bit about their pack, and how they were going to have to build another extension to the manor with how quickly they were still growing. Pop always loved the idea of building new things in the forest. Usually, they were small sheds that could be used as safe houses if need be. Eric didn't understand why he bothered with building all of them. After they claimed these woods, there hadn't been any serious attack on their pack.

The Orion Meeting House was built at the center of the forest, so that all the packs could meet up and still be in their territory. It was split, even in the house, which part belonged to which pack. They were still allowed to walk through the whole house, but it would be considered outside of territory lines if you went to certain parts.

It was confusing.

Eric loved confusing. It was the perfect thing to work his mind on through the long drive that it took to get there. He wished they could just run there as wolves. It would be so much faster. But Dad didn't exactly have a wolf to shift into. He was a human. So, on they drove.

Getting there was the best part, though. It was lit up with lanterns. The whole place worked through generators. It would have been too difficult to try and get electricity and plumbing this far through the forest. It wasn't a tall building, it only had one level to it, but it was huge and beautiful. Everything about it blended with the trees and brush around. On the doors to enter the building, there was the constellation of Orion: The Hunter. He loved hearing his Pop tell him the story of this ancient pack. It sounded so mysterious.

Aunt Katy and her mate pulled up right as they did. Alpha Leonard and his Luna were waiting by the entrance for them all. They were the ones that the rogues had first gone to with their request. It was interesting that they didn't just accept them to their pack already. The Harvest Moon Pack was the kindest out of the three.

"Eric!"

"Aunt Katy!" He hugged her as she ran up to him. She was always fun to be around. Although Uncle Nick said that she used to be ten times more dramatic.

"I'm so glad I get to see you again!" She squeezed him. Then she went over to his parents and hugged them as well. "You guys are trying to teach him the ropes then, huh?"

"Well, we don't exactly want to retire yet," Dad said. "But it's always good to get some practice in anyway."

He still thought that his Dad worked too hard. The man would still forget to eat from time to time. Eric remembered all the times he would come home from school and ask his dad if he had eaten. He would give him a shy smile and tell him 'not yet'.

Once he told Uncle Nick this, him and Pop have been on his case about it ever since.

"This is an interesting case," Leonard said.

"What's the issue?" Pop asked.

"Well, there's ten of them," he started, taking a deep breath to relieve his own tension. "And they've been on the road for a very long time."

"Were you able to find anything on the database?" Alpha Owen asked. His dark red eyes showed caution as soon as he heard what Leonard had said.

"Not yet," he told him. "I'm still working on it though. That's why I wanted to have the meeting with all of you. If we turn them down, then they will try asking you both afterwards."

They had all walked inside at this point. The door opened to a humongous room with a giant table in the middle of it. On each wall held a map of each of the pack's territory. It was a circular room, one that had other rooms connected all around it. Those were rooms to sleep in or change if need be.

Like he said, Pop was obsessed with safe houses.

"Are they here yet?" Pop asked. It was always so interesting seeing him go from his usual way of talking to moments like then. He was always so stern and serious when things like this happened. He bet that Alpha Leonard had no clue just how much of a goofball Pop could be.

"We brought the leader," Leonard said. "The others we're keeping in our territory under surveillance."

"Alright." Alpha Owen sat down in his chair. "Let's get this started."

They all sat down after him. The chairs had been moved to where they all faced one direction. He sat next to his parents, of course.

When they were all ready, Leonard motioned for one of his pack members to bring the rogue in. The first thing that Eric noticed about her was how young she was. She looked to be about his age. She had blonde hair that was in a messy braid and dark blue eyes. It looked like Leonard had at least let her use some decent clothes. Knowing how rogues usually were, they probably didn't have anything but rags.

Why did she look so familiar to him? He could have sworn that he had seen her somewhere. Her scent alone made him focus on her more. It was a smell that reminded him of wildflowers. Wildflowers that he swore he remembered too.

"What's your name?" Pop was the first to ask. The woman looked at him straight in his eyes with an unwavering gaze. No matter how hard Eric stared at her, she would not look at him.

"Janet Briggs." Her voice was soft, yet stern.

"How many members of your party are there?" Alpha Owen asked.

"Including myself, there are eleven of us," she answered quickly.

"Are any of them children?" Dad asked this time. His tone was a lot softer than Pops or Owen's.

"Some teenagers." She nodded. She had been shifting her gaze to the eyes of everyone that she had been asked a question to. At first, Eric thought it was strange. But it seemed to calm the Alphas down when she did that. That's when he realized that it was so that she could show them that she wasn't lying.

This woman was smart, he could say that at least.

"How young are they?" Leonard asked this time.

"The youngest are my sisters," she answered truthfully. "They're sixteen."

"How long has your group been rogues, Janet?" Aunt Katy asked this time.

Janet. Whenever he heard that name there was something in him that started stirring. It was like an old memory that had disappeared a long time ago.

She took her time answering this question. It was obvious that she was nervous as to what their reactions would be. With a deep breath, she looked to Aunt Katy.

"Fourteen years, and six months," she answered.

Fourteen years?! Not even Uncle Alistair had been a rogue for that long! All the Alphas guards were up as soon as she said that. Fourteen years was no laughing matter when it came to rogues. It meant that they knew how to fight, and they could very well be brutal.

But Janet didn't look brutal. She looked strong, like she had been through a lot. She didn't look cruel in any way. If anything, she looked like any leader of a pack would. Her shoulders were held high, her back was straight. She stood tall, and proud.

"How have you survived fourteen years?" Wynona, the Luna of the Harvest Moon Pack, asked. "Especially with children?"

"We were..." She paused and let out a deep sigh. "Before you make any assumptions of me and the people I call family, I beg you all to please listen to my story all the way through." Her head then tilted down, her eyes mesmerized to the floor boards. "We were a part of a small pack before all of this. One with a good Alpha and Luna. We were on our way to growing our families and making our pack stronger. But," She swallowed hard. "We got attacked by rogues ourselves. They killed all our leaders and their children. My father was the only one of our small council that was able to get away with me and my sisters. He died just a couple of years ago. There were twenty of us at the beginning of our journey."

"Hold on." Pop leaned into the table, his gaze intense. "What was the name of the pack that you were a part of?"

Eric couldn't get over the pain that was in those eyes held when she told her story. A part of him wanted to go over there and comfort her in some way.

"*Don't cry, Eric.*" *The little girl came up to him.* "*The Alpha will always protect us, no matter what happens.*"

"*But that was scary!*" *He wailed.* "*How can Dad protect us against ghosts?*"

"*Because your dad can do anything with that shiny shield around his neck!*" *Her blue eyes sparkled as she comforted him.* "*He's invincible!*"

"Jane?" Eric didn't even know that he had said that out loud. But the whole room was now looking at him. Including Janet.

He remembered those blue eyes. Janet was the daughter of the Beta of his old pack. They were friends back then. He protected her from bullies, while she comforted him whenever he got scared. But, right then, they sent sparks through him. He wanted to hold her gaze for as long as possible.

"Eric?" She looked at him in fear. She looked like she had seen a ghost. "You're...?"

"Wait," Leonard said. "You're all from the Goldshield Pack?"

"I-uh." She looked all around the room, almost speechless. If this weren't that serious of a situation, he would have thought it was cute. "Yes. We were from the Goldshield Pack. Until a group of rogues attacked." She then looked to Eric again. "But we thought they killed you."

"They almost did." He gave her a small smile. He really wanted to run up and hug her. But he didn't know how the rest of them would feel about that.

"I thought that the Goldshield Pack had all been wiped out?" Owen said. He still looked suspicious.

Really?

"I have proof," she told him, rummaging through her things. "There was something that we were able to salvage from our old pack. We brought it with us to give us luck."

What she pulled out made his heart stop for a second.

It was his mom's necklace. Her Luna necklace. It was made of gold, just like his father's.

Eric took out the necklace of his fathers. He had left the knife at home, as that was only for war times. But the rest of it shined in all of its glory. He slowly set it on the table.

"I think that about settles it." Pop leaned back in his seat. Eric looked at him really quick to see that him and Dad were smiling at each other. He had no idea what it meant.

"I think it does too," Dad said. His green eyes had a sparkle to them. "Janet Briggs, with the last remaining members of the Goldshield Pack, we welcome you to the Crescent Moon Pack."

"W-what?" She was already shocked at seeing Eric, now she was more surprised. "You do?"

"Of course." Dad smiled at her. "We've already had one member in our pack for a very long time. I think the rest of the remaining members will be a fine addition to our pack."

"I," she stammered. "I don't know what to say. Thank you."

There was a lot more talking after that. Most of it was about the minors that were in her group, and whether anyone had gotten their education. But Eric tuned it all out. He simply focused on those eyes that kept darting in his direction every now and then. Every time their gazes met, there were sparks.

He could tell that she was his, because he was hers the moment that their eyes met.

It looked like he wasn't going to have to wait for his mate as long as Pop had after all…